Books by Daniel Peters

Border Crossings

The Luck of Huemac: A Novel About the Aztecs

Tikal: A Novel About the Maya

TIKAL

TIKAL

A Novel About the Maya

DANIEL PETERS

Random House New York

Library of Congress Cataloging in Publication Data
Peters, Daniel.
Tikal: a novel about the Maya.
I. Mayas—Fiction. I. Title.
PS3566.E7548T54 1983   813'.54   83-3273
ISBN 0-394-53278-3

Manufactured in the United States of America
Typography and binding design by J. K. Lambert
2 4 6 8 9 7 5 3
First Edition

This book is dedicated to the memory of
Mark Schorer, C. Hugh Holman,
and Dennis Puleston

Foreword

THE CLASSIC PERIOD of the lowland Maya dates roughly from A.D. 300 to 850. It was characterized by several distinctive traits: the use of the corbeled arch in the construction of monumental architecture, the periodic erection of stone monuments (stelae), and the development of hieroglyphic writing. During this period, the Maya raised great cities in the jungles of the Peten (the northernmost portion of present-day Guatemala) and surrounding portions of Mexico, Belize, and Honduras. They also refined their complex of calendrical and astronomical systems, practiced various forms of intensive agriculture, and built enormous temples and tombs for the members of their ruling elite.

The erection of stelae reached its peak throughout the lowland area in A.D. 790 (9.18.0.0.0 by the Tun Count) and tapered off rapidly thereafter. Over the course of the next hundred years, the greatest of the cities—Tikal, Copan, Yaxchilan, Piedras Negras—were abandoned one by one, for reasons that still remain a mystery to us. Archaeologists have formulated a variety of theories to account for this collapse: warfare or revolt, epidemic disease, ecological disaster, extreme climatic change. No one theory, however, appears to offer an adequate explanation in itself. At Tikal, for instance, there is little evidence of warfare, and no epidemic would cause the 90 percent decline in population that apparently occurred at the site between A.D. 790 and 830. The depletion of the environment has long seemed a tempting possibility, but it is a difficult proposition to prove, given the passage of over a thousand years, in an area that receives an enormous amount of rain.

As George Kubler has said, "Mesoamerican studies often impress readers as a Sahara of guesses, where travelers crazed with a thirst for certainty suffer various mirages." This novel, despite its air of authority, should be regarded as another of these mirages, though hopefully one worth following to its end. Our knowledge of what *really* happened to the Classic Maya will probably always be incomplete, given the limited nature of the evidence left to us. Only a handful of Mayan codices (books made of leather or bark paper) survived the Spanish Conquest, and these Post-Classic productions bear an uncertain relationship to the beliefs and practices of the Classic Period. The rest of our evidence consists of painted polychrome pottery, the contents of tombs, and the imagery and glyphs the Maya carved so beautifully in stone, stucco, bone, and wood (as well as one magnificent set of wall murals). Inasmuch as our knowledge of these people has been largely reconstructed from such materials, this novel is truly a work of *science* fiction. The author is indebted to the many archaeologists and scholars who have labored to make the world of the ancient Maya comprehensible, though he assumes, as well, full responsibility for the fictional use and/or abuse of their findings and speculations.

A Note on the Mayan Dating

The ancient Maya were astronomers and timekeepers of a high order, maintaining a long and detailed record of the movements of the sun, moon, and stars. Their calendrical systems were based on this astronomical knowledge and were designed to permit the broadest range of calculations, so that earthly time could be brought into precise conjunction with the movements of the heavens. Time was thus imbued with religious significance, and discrete segments of time were thought to possess a distinct and recognizable potential. The potential of a given period (favorable, unfavorable, or ambiguous) was believed to reoccur with the turning of the calendar, so that the Mayan priest could examine past periods in order to determine the possible nature of a period to come. Thus, the future was regarded not as a blank slate upon which the activities of men could be recorded but as the continuation of a series of known influences with which men had to contend.

Since this novel has been structured according to the Mayan Long Count, some preliminary definitions of the time periods are in order:

> Month: A period of 20 days
> Tun: A period of 360 days, or nearly 1 year
> Hotun: A period of 5 tuns, or nearly 5 years
> Katun: A period of 20 tuns, or nearly 20 years
> Cycle: A period of 20 katuns, or nearly 400 years

The dry season at Tikal begins in January or February, with the hottest and driest weather occurring from March to May. The rainy season begins in late May or June, with the heaviest rains occurring from July to September. The harvest of most crops probably took place in November or December.

The action of this novel takes place during the last five tuns of Katun 11 Ahau, or approximately A.D. 785–90. The reader interested in decoding and following the Long Count—so crucial to the ordering of the Mayan world—should consult the appendix on calendrics at the back of the book.

Acknowledgments

The author wishes to express his deep gratitude:

To the following Mayanists: Teobert Maler, Alfred Tozzer, Sylvanus Morley, Tatiana Proskouriakoff, J. Eric Thompson, Gordon Willey, William R. Coe, Christopher Jones, David Kelley, George Kubler, Peter Harrison, Dennis Puleston, Marshall Becker, Peter Furst, Frederick Wiseman, Jeremy Sabloff, Ralph Roys, William Rathje, T. Patrick Culbert, Anthony Aveni, F. B. Smithe, and A.F.C. Wallace;

To my correspondents: Joshua Rosenthal, Lawrence Feldman, Peter Mathews, and John Justeson;

To Clemency Coggins, who generously shared her knowledge of Tikal's art and history in letters and conversations; and to William and Anita Haviland, who took me into their home and shared their experiences of the Tikal Project;

To Mylinda Woodward and the other helpful people on the staff of the University of New Hampshire Library;

To my intrepid readers: Susan Lescher, Tony Backes, and Gary and Judy Lindberg;

To my in-house inspirations: David Gregory, Blackburn Peters, and Peter Lindberg;

To Annette, who climbed every temple with me;

To the spirits of the ancestors, whose presence is deep, and abiding.

CONTENTS

THE PEOPLE

The Jaguar Paw Clan

Akbal Balam (Ahk-bal Bah-lam), Night Jaguar; youngest son of Pacal Balam and Ik Caan, and brother of Kanan Naab and Kinich Kakmoo; father of Nicte (2); painter and master of craftsmen.

Bacab (Bah-cob), Around the Earth; Living Ancestor and guardian of the young Stormy Sky (circa A.D. 425).

Balam Xoc (Bah-lam Shock), Jaguar Shark; brother of Box Ek and Cab Coh; father of Chac Balam, Pacal Balam, and Pom Ix; grandfather of Akbal, Kanan Naab, and Kinich Kakmoo; supervisor of building projects and Living Ancestor of the clan.

Bolon Oc (Bo-lon Ock), Nine Oc; son of Pacal Balam and his second wife, Ixchel; half brother of Akbal, Kanan Naab, and Kinich Kakmoo.

Box Ek (Bosh Eck), Shell Star; older sister of Balam Xoc and Cab Coh; married to Kan Mac of Ektun; great-aunt of Akbal, Kanan Naab, and Kinich Kakmoo.

Cab Coh (Cab Coh), Honey Puma; younger brother of Box Ek and Balam Xoc; father of Nohoch Ich and grandfather of Chac Mut; master of craftsmen.

Chac Balam (Chac Bah-lam), Red or Great Jaguar; eldest son of Balam Xoc and Nicte (1); died early in Katun 11 Ahau.

Chac Mut (Chac Moot), Red or Great Bird; youngest son of Nohoch Ich and Haleu; assistant to Pacal Balam, royal steward, and clan steward.

Chibil (Chee-beel), Eclipse; adopted member of the clan; healer and one of the Close Ones.

Coba (Co-ba), Chachalaca; daughter of Kinich Kakmoo and May.

Haleu (Hay-lew), Agouti; wife of Nohoch Ich and mother of Chac Mut.

Hok (Hock); adopted member of the clan from Quirigua; one of the Close Ones and clan witness.

Ik Caan (Ick Kahn), Wind Sky; Sky Clan woman and wife of Pacal Balam; mother of Akbal, Kanan Naab, and Kinich Kakmoo; died early in Katun 11 Ahau.

Ixchel (Ish-chel), Moon; from Nohmul; the second wife of Pacal Balam; mother of Bolon Oc.

Kal Cuc (Kal Cuck), Moon Squirrel; boy attached to the Jaguar Paw House; assistant to Akbal and adopted member of the clan.

Kanan Naab (Ka-nan Nahb), Precious Water Lily; daughter of Pacal Balam and Ik Caan and younger sister of Akbal and Kinich Kakmoo; one of the Close Ones; married to Yaxal Can.

Kan Balam Moo (Kan Bah-lam Moo), Precious Jaguar Macaw; daughter of

Jaguar Paw (d. A.D. 376); married to Curl Snout of the Cauac Shield people; mother of Stormy Sky.

Kinich Kakmoo (Kee-neech Kak-moo), Sun-Eye Fire Macaw; eldest son of Pacal Balam and Ik Caan and older brother of Akbal and Kanan Naab; father of Coba; warrior and nacom (warchief) of Tikal; clan nacom.

May (May), Deer; wife of Kinich Kakmoo and mother of Coba.

Nicte (Neeck-ti), Plumeria Flower (1); wife of Balam Xoc and mother of Chac Balam, Pacal Balam, and Pom Ix; died early in Katun 11 Ahau.

Nicte (Neeck-ti), Plumeria Flower (2); daughter of Akbal and Zac Kuk.

Nohoch Ich (No-hoch Eech), Great Eye; son of Cab Coh and Pek; father of Chac Mut; Tun Count priest; head of the clan council and one of the Close Ones.

Opna (Op-na), Parrot House; former priest from Copan; one of the Close Ones and an adopted member of the clan.

Pacal Balam (Pa-col Bah-lam), Shield Jaguar; youngest son of Balam Xoc and Nicte (1); father of Akbal, Kanan Naab, and Kinich Kakmoo (by Ik Caan), and of Bolon Oc (by Ixchel); head of the clan council, royal steward, and chief steward of crops.

Pek (Peck), Dog; wife of Cab Coh; mother of Nohoch Ich.

Pom Ix (Pom Ish), Copal Jaguar; eldest daughter of Balam Xoc and Nicte (1); sister of Pacal Balam and Chac Balam; married to a man from Uaxactun.

Stormy Sky (name derived from glyphic inscriptions); son of Curl Snout and Kan Balam Moo; probable ruler of Tikal (A.D. 426–57).

Tzec Balam (T'seck Bah-lam), Skull Jaguar; high priest of the clan.

The Sky Clan

Ah Kin Cuy (Ah Kin Kwa), The Priest Owl; member of the Order of Katun Priests; high priest of Tikal.

Ain Caan (Ayn Kahn), Crocodile Sky; son and heir of the Ruler Caan Ac; nacom and leader of campaign against the Macaws.

Caan Ac (Kahn Ock), Sky Boar; son of Cauac Caan and grandson of Cacao Moon; father of Ain Caan; probable ruler of Tikal (A.D. 769–?).

Cacao Moon (name from glyphic inscriptions); father of Cauac Caan; probable ruler of Tikal (A.D. 681–733).

Cauac Caan (Ka-wock Kahn), Rain Sky (name from glyphic inscriptions); son of Cacao Moon and father of Caan Ac; probable ruler of Tikal (A.D. 733–69).

Curl Snout (name from glyphic inscriptions); leader of the Cauac Shield People, of mixed Kaminaljuyu/Teotihuacano parentage; father of Stormy Sky; usurper and probable ruler of Tikal (A.D. 382–425).

Kuch Caan (Kuch Kahn), Turkey Sky; nephew of Caan Ac; Tikal diplomat.

Lady Twelve Macaw (name from glyphic inscriptions); mother of Cacao Moon.

Stormy Sky (name from glyphic inscriptions); son of Curl Snout and Kan Balam Moo; probable ruler of Tikal (A.D. 426–57).

The Serpent Clan

Hapay Can (Ha-pay Con), Sucking Snake; high priest of the clan.
Yaxal Can (Ya-shal Con), Greenish Snake; clan priest and Tun Count priest; married to Kanan Naab; adopted member of the Jaguar Paw Clan.

The People of Ektun

Ah Kin Tzab (Ah Kin T'sob), The Priest Rattlesnake; high priest of Ektun.
Batz Mac (Bots Mock), Howler Monkey Turtleshell; father of Chan Mac and Zac Kuk.
Chan Mac (Chon Mock), Maize Turtleshell; son of Batz Mac and Muan Kal; father of two daughters; brother of Zac Kuk; diplomat and adopted member of the Jaguar Paw Clan.
Chuen (Chewn), Spider Monkey; pet monkey of Zac Kuk.
Kan Mac (Kon Mock), Yellow or Precious Turtleshell; husband of Box Ek.
Kutz (Kuts), Turkey; from Palenque; wife of Chan Mac.
Muan Kal (Mwan Kal), Screech-Owl Moon; Moon Clan woman and wife of Batz Mac; mother of Chan Mac and Zac Kuk.
Zac Kuk (Sock Cook), White Quetzal; daughter of Batz Mac and Muan Kal; younger sister of Chan Mac; married to Akbal Balam; mother of Nicte (2).
Zotz Mac (Sots Mock), Bat Turtleshell; ruler of Ektun.

The People of Yaxchilan

Bird Jaguar (name from glyphic inscriptions); probable ruler of Yaxchilan (A.D. 752–69).
Keken Ahau (Ke-ken A-how), Boar Lord; warrior and nacom.
Shield Jaguar the Elder (name from glyphic inscriptions); probable ruler of Yaxchilan (A.D. 707–42).
Shield Jaguar the Younger (name from glyphic inscriptions); probable ruler of Yaxchilan (A.D. 769–?).

Others

Cauac Shield People (Ka-wock Shield People): warrior/merchants of mixed Kaminaljuyu/Teotihuacano parentage; usurpers at Tikal (A.D. 382).
Macaws (Ma-kaws): inhabitants of present-day Tabasco; possibly Chontal; featured prominently in the glyphs of Yaxchilan.
Putun (Poo-toon): intruders from the west in the Terminal Classic (A.D. 800–900); possibly Chontal or Itza.
Szinca (Sin-ka): non-Mayan-speaking tribes of the Motagua River Valley, in the vicinity of Quirigua.
Zuyhua (Soy-wa): the highland Mexicans of Teotihuacan; influential at Tikal, circa A.D. 380–430.

THE PLACES

Acantun (A-can-toon) (Dos Pilas): Classic Mayan site between the Chixoy and Pasion rivers, in the present-day Department of the Peten, Guatemala; possible home of Cacao Moon before his accession at Tikal.

Altun Ha (Al-toon Ha): Classic Mayan site near the coast of present-day Belize.

Bonampak (Bo-nom-pok): Classic Mayan site west of the Usumacinta River, in the present-day state of Chiapas, Mexico; notable for its painted wall murals.

Chetumal (Che-too-mol): Classic Mayan site on the Caribbean coast of present-day state of Yucatan, Mexico.

Copan (Ko-pon): Southernmost Classic Mayan site, on the western border of present-day Honduras.

Ektun (Ek-toon) (Piedras Negras): Classic Mayan site on the eastern bank of the Usumacinta River, in the present-day Department of the Peten, Guatemala.

Holmul (Hol-mool): Classic Mayan site to the east of Tikal, in the present-day Department of the Peten, Guatemala.

Kaminaljuyu (Ka-mi-nal-who-yoo): Early Classic highland Mayan site, just outside of present-day Guatemala City; notable for the strong influence of the Mexicans of Teotihuacan.

Lacanha (La-kan-ha): Classic Mayan site west of the Usumacinta River, in the present-day state of Chiapas, Mexico.

Nakum (Na-koom): Classic Mayan site to the east of Tikal, in the present-day Department of the Peten, Guatemala.

Nohmul (No-mool): Classic Mayan site between the New and Hondo rivers, in the northern portion of present-day Belize.

Palenque (Pa-len-kay): Classic Mayan site to the west of the Peten, in the present-day state of Chiapas, Mexico; notable for its fine stone and stucco sculptures.

Quirigua (Kee-ree-gwa): Classic Mayan site in the Motagua River Valley, near the eastern border of present-day Guatemala.

Tikal (Tee-kol): Largest of the Classic Mayan sites in the present-day Department of the Peten, Guatemala.

Uaxactun (Wa-shock-toon): Classic Mayan site to the north of Tikal, in the present-day Department of the Peten, Guatemala.

Yaxche (Yash-chey) (Seibal): Classic Mayan site on the Pasion River, in the present-day Department of the Peten, Guatemala; notable for a strong foreign intrusion (possibly Putun or Itza) in the Terminal Classic (A.D. 800–900).

Yaxchilan (Yash-chee-lon): Classic Mayan site on the western bank of the Usumacinta River, in the present-day state of Chiapas, Mexico.

Yaxha (Yash-ha): Classic Mayan site south of Tikal on Lake Yaxha, in the present-day Department of the Peten, Guatemala.

TIKAL

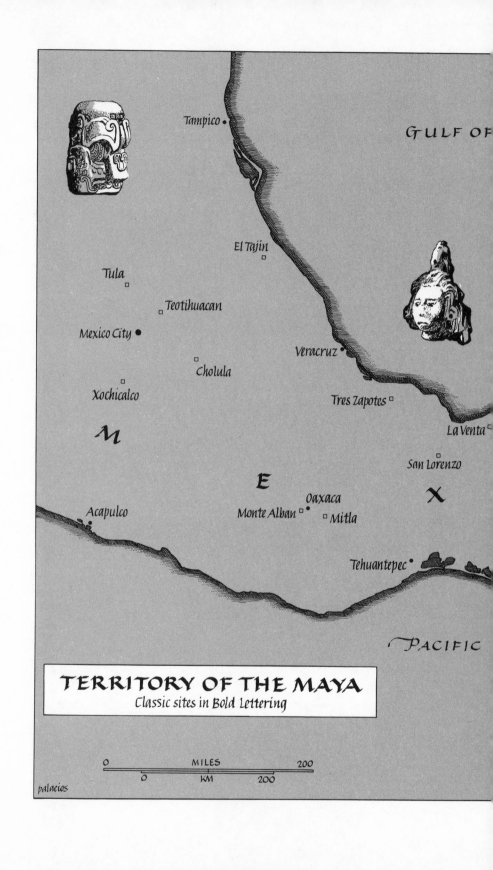

Tampico •

GULF OF

El Tajín ▫

Tula ▫

Teotihuacan ▫

Mexico City •

Cholula ▫

Xochicalco ▫

Veracruz •

Tres Zapotes ▫

La Venta ▫

M

San Lorenzo ▫

E

Acapulco •

Oaxaca •
Monte Alban ▫   ▫ Mitla

X

Tehuantepec •

PACIFIC

TERRITORY OF THE MAYA
Classic sites in Bold Lettering

O ⊢———————⊣ 200
  MILES
O ⊢———————⊣ 200
  KM

palacios

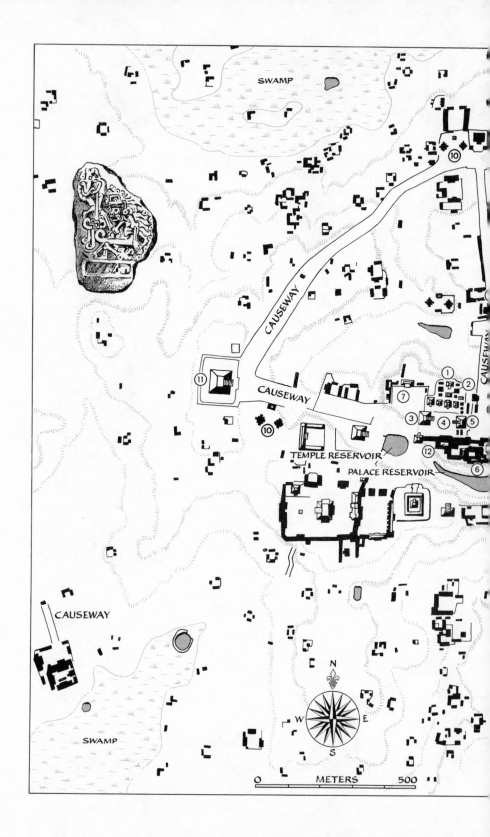

SWAMP

CAUSEWAY

CAUSEWAY

⑩

⑪

CAUSEWAY

⑩

⑦

①
②

③
④
⑤

TEMPLE RESERVOIR

⑫

⑥

PALACE RESERVOIR

CAUSEWAY

SWAMP

N
W   E
S

0   METERS   500

TIKAL

1. Clan Temples
2. Shrine of the Jaguar Protector
3. Temple of Twelve Macaw
4. Plaza of the Ancestors
5. Temple of Cacao Moon
6. Ruler's Palace
7. West Plaza
8. East Plaza
9. Market Place
10. Katun Enclosures
11. Temple of Cauac Caan
12. Clan Houses
13. Jaguar Paw Clan House
14. Temple of the Inscriptions

SWAMP

HIDDEN RESERVOIR

CAUSEWAY

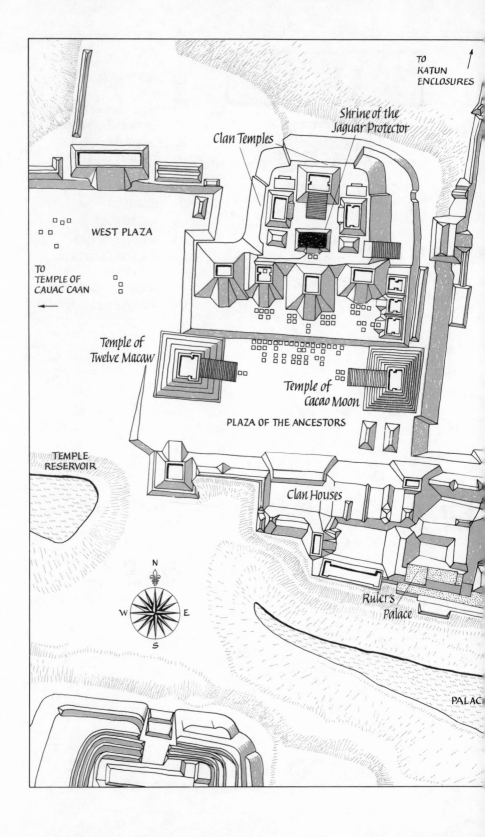

TO
KATUN
ENCLOSURES

Shrine of the
Jaguar Protector

Clan Temples

WEST PLAZA

TO
TEMPLE OF
CAUAC CAAN

Temple of
Twelve Macaw

Temple of
Cacao Moon

PLAZA OF THE ANCESTORS

TEMPLE
RESERVOIR

Clan Houses

N

W   E

S

Ruler's
Palace

PALAC

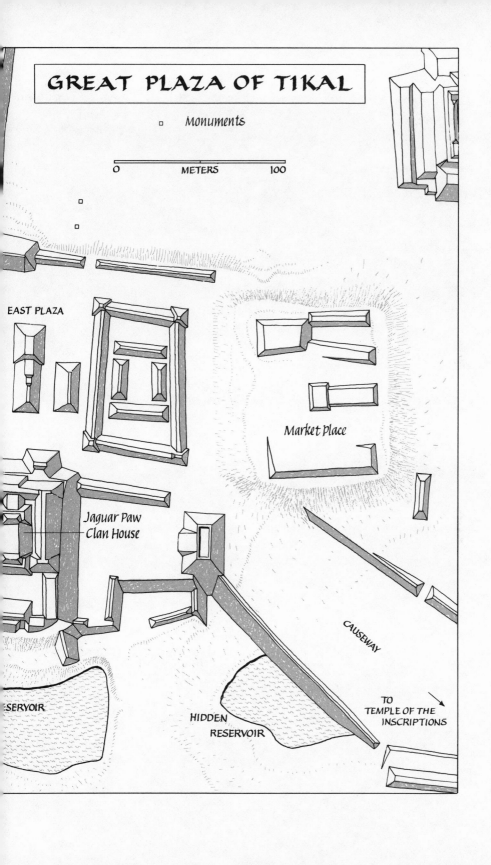

GREAT PLAZA OF TIKAL

▫ Monuments

0   METERS   100

EAST PLAZA

Market Place

Jaguar Paw
Clan House

CAUSEWAY

RESERVOIR

HIDDEN
RESERVOIR

TO
TEMPLE OF THE
INSCRIPTIONS

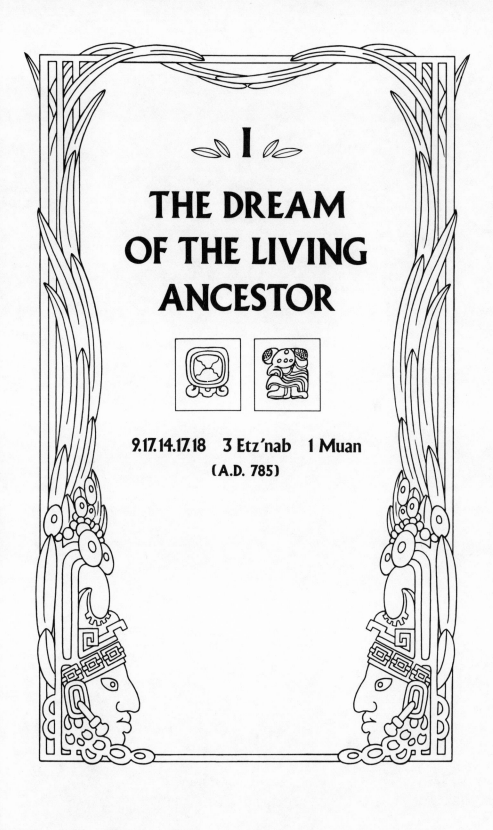

I

THE DREAM OF THE LIVING ANCESTOR

9.17.14.17.18   3 Etz'nab   1 Muan
(A.D. 785)

THE STILL green waters of the alkalche glittered brightly in the sunlight, producing a glare as intense and powerful as the shrilling of the locusts in the distant trees. Pacal Balam squinted as he stared eastward over the vast swamp, which was dotted with mudflats and islands of low jungle in those places where the waters had receded over the course of the dry season. Closer in toward the bank where Pacal stood, the alkalche had been divided into long, even channels by means of raised earthen ridges that had been built up out of the mud and faced with limestone marl. Lines of naked men with sweatbands around their tufted heads stooped in the thigh-deep water of the channels, dredging baskets of muck from the bottom. They handed the baskets up to other men, who dumped the thick mud over the top of the ridges and spread it evenly with wooden hoes. Surrounded by clouds of gnats, the men moved very slowly, stopping frequently to wipe the sweat from their faces and glance upward at the sun. There was no one to hurry them, for their supervisors were standing in a group around Pacal, who was observing the workers from the shade of a tall grove of feather palms.

"Tell them to stop now, and rest until the sun is lower," he said at last, and the supervisors immediately dispersed and spread out along the shore, blowing on wooden whistles and waving their men in. The workmen abandoned their hoes and baskets atop the ridges and sloshed toward the bank, their faces and bodies spattered with mud and algae. Those who passed near the place where Pacal stood bowed briefly in deference to the royal steward, before heading for the thatched houses that lined the shore of the alkalche in dense clusters.

Pacal also dismissed the scribes and messengers who had been attending him, telling them to return when they had eaten and rested. He kept his assistant, Chac Mut, with him, gesturing for the young man to sit beside him in the shade. Chac Mut collapsed upon the ground with a grateful sigh, slumping backward against the trunk of a palm.

"Sit up straight," Pacal told him sharply. "You have reason to be weary, but you must have the discipline not to show it. You are not some common workman, but the representative of the ruler."

"I am sorry, Uncle," Chac Mut murmured, reluctantly pushing himself away from the tree. The patterned cloth wrapped around his long head was dark with sweat, and an insect-bitten lump swelled on his cheek. He was nineteen years old, the son of Pacal's cousin, Nohoch Ich. Since neither of Pacal's own sons had been drawn to their father's occupation, Chac Mut had asked for the opportunity to train as a steward, unaware that it would entail this much physical discomfort. Already that day they had walked to the southern boundary of Tikal to inspect the maize fields and then had come an equal distance east to the alkalche.

"Forget your hunger, as well," Pacal went on in an unsparing tone. "We will eat soon enough, and better than any of these men. While we are among them, let them see only your dedication and fortitude. You will not impress them with your fatigue."

"Now," Pacal said abruptly, waving off further apologies, "tell me what you see here."

Chac Mut glanced hastily at the long rows of ridged fields, abandoned now in the heat of the midday sun. Some of the ridges were obviously in a bad state of repair, their facing stones sunken and their sides beginning to erode. Others, while solid, were overgrown with weeds and cluttered with the dried vines and broken stalks of last season's crops. A single row of stunted, nearly leafless cacao trees testified bleakly to an experiment that had failed.

"Much work remains to be done," he ventured judiciously. "Much more, it seems, than was true of the maize fields."

"Would you recommend, then, that we shift some men from there to here?"

Chac Mut hesitated, sensing a trap behind his master's question. He squinted up at the sky, then out over the swamp.

"Perhaps. The onset of the rains is very close," he added shrewdly. "The dredging of the channels will be more difficult once the alkalche is flooded again."

"Indeed it will," Pacal agreed. "But the planting of the maize must accompany the onset of the rains. The manioc and macal we grow here will not be planted for two more months. So, even though our task will be more difficult, we will have more time to do it, and perhaps more men." Pacal paused to let this information sink in. "I did not ask the question to shame you, only to impress upon you how much you have to learn. A good steward has to be an expert in everything he oversees. He must understand the business of farming as well as one who was born to it, even if his hands never touch a digging stick."

"I will remember," Chac Mut promised, grimacing at the effort of all he had to store in his head. Pacal smiled in recognition.

"Do not be discouraged, my son. Such breadth of knowledge does not come easily to anyone. Your father is a learned man, but his knowledge is confined to those matters that properly belong to the priesthood. You will know more of *his* business than he will ever know of yours."

Chac Mut appeared mollified, and Pacal decided to allow him to absorb the lesson in peace. He turned his attention away from the young man, looking off to his left, where the ground was slightly higher and the remaining water had collected in a few low, stagnant pools. A shoulder-high forest of thorny bushes and stunted logwood trees filled the swamp bed, and weaving through this jungle was a narrow path that led across the alkalche from east to west. As Pacal watched, a lone individual came into view, stepping carefully from hummock to hummock and pausing frequently to search out the best way to proceed. The man wore only a loincloth, and his body had been painted with black paint, the sign of fasting. He carried a tasseled incense bag over one shoulder, but was otherwise empty-handed.

"There are many holy men this year," Chac Mut observed mildly, staring in the same direction. The solitary, blackened figure was now halfway across the alkalche, and the marks of ritual bloodletting could clearly be seen on his shins and forearms.

"*Too* many," Pacal said emphatically. "They will crowd out the other pilgrims at the ceremonies."

Chac Mut stared at him blankly, openmouthed with surprise. Pacal pursed his lips and then sighed, as if reconciled to an explanation he had hoped to put off.

"As the son of a priest," he said evenly, "you have been taught to respect the holder of a vow, whatever his rank or clan. That is proper, and certainly you must behave correctly in their presence. But that does not mean you should be naïve about their meaning or unmindful of the cost of their devotion."

Frowning involuntarily, Chac Mut wet his lips several times before speaking.

"I do not wish to be naïve, Uncle. But I fail to understand what their devotion can cost us."

"In two days' time, the completion of the hotun will be celebrated, and all of the clans will perform their ancestral rites at the clan temples. The ceremonies themselves are quite costly, and the honored guests and the delegations from other cities will have to be feasted and provided with gifts when it is over. We recover some of this cost in offerings and some in trade, though not nearly as much as we expend." Pacal gestured brusquely toward the pilgrim. "But men such as this one bring only themselves as offerings, and they do not visit the marketplace when the ceremonies are over."

"But is not their devotion as valuable to us as their trade?"

"I cannot judge the value of their devotion," Pacal said curtly. "I leave that to men like your father, or my own. My concerns are for the things of *this* world, and as the steward, I cannot be pleased that so many have given themselves to vows rather than to work. More than their devotion, they demonstrate their fearfulness and their lack of faith in the ruler's ability to provide for their needs.

"*Think,* Chac Mut," he continued, raising a hand to forestall the young man's protest, "consider *why* so many have taken vows at this time. Surely, you are more aware than most of how poor the crops have been for the past two seasons."

"The rains were unkind . . ."

"As they have been many times in the past," Pacal finished for him. "But this is Katun Eleven Ahau, is it not? And was the prophecy of this katun not filled with signs of danger and hardship? Were we not told that the spirit of this katun, Buluc Ahau, would be harsh and unforgiving, and that our crops would die in the fields?"

"Indeed," Chac Mut murmured.

"So, you see, it does not matter that fifteen tuns of this katun will soon be completed, and in safety. It does not matter that only five tuns will have to pass before we can escape the threat of Buluc Ahau. The people are still watchful and anxious, and quick to lose trust in their leaders. That is why so many of them have taken vows of their own instead of attending to their normal tasks. And that is also why *we* are out here in this heat instead of back at the palace, where we belong. Despite the shortage of men, we must see that everything possible is done to insure the success of this season's planting. We must convince these black men that it is safe for them to go back to their homes and their work and to put their trust once more in the ruler and his servants. Without that trust, Tikal cannot maintain its greatness, and *all* of the people will suffer."

Chac Mut nodded gravely, too impressed to speak. Pacal had not raised his voice, but there had been no mistaking his passion. It was an emotion Pacal seldom displayed, and one he had always taught Chac Mut to suppress. He seemed to recognize this with a slight, self-deprecating smile.

"I have broken my own first rule: Have many thoughts, but speak few of them. It was time, though, that you understood the urgency of the situation."

"I am grateful that you have confided in me, Uncle," Chac Mut said hoarsely. "It is a great responsibility that we bear."

"Yes," Pacal agreed. The pilgrim had disappeared from view, down the trail that led to the center of Tikal. But another dark figure could just be seen at the far edge of the alkalche, searching for the beginning of the path across. Pacal gestured abruptly to his assistant and stood up.

"Come. There will be no work on the day of the ceremonies, and the rains could begin at any time. Let us see to our men."

Chac Mut jumped up and came to Pacal's side as he headed for the houses along the shore. They both felt the pressure of the sun upon their backs as they came out into the open, and the stagnant, gaseous odor of the swamp seemed to billow up from beneath their feet.

"The supervisors will not want to move," Chac Mut predicted as they approached the first house. Pacal simply shrugged.

"They never do. But at least we can begin the arguments without delay . . ."

9.17.15.0.0   5 Ahau   3 Muan
The Hotun-End

BALAM XOC, the Living Ancestor of the Jaguar Paw Clan, had begun his fasting twenty days prior to the end of the hotun. He had abstained completely from meat, salt, and chilies, eating only fruit and a little maize gruel every day. He had spent his time in relative seclusion, studying the ancestral books and conferring with the clan priests as they prepared for the hotun ceremony. He saw no women during this period, and none were permitted to look upon him.

Four days before the ceremony, he entered his confinement within the Shrine of the Jaguar Protector, the guardian spirit of his clan. Here he would remain in solitude, sequestered with the spirits of his ancestors, whose bones were buried deep beneath the pyramid platform on which the shrine stood. Their power and the purity of his own spirit would have to sustain him for the duration of his confinement, for he was permitted no food and only one gourd of water.

This ceremony would mark Balam Xoc's tenth tun as the Living Ancestor, and he settled himself within the darkened chamber with the confidence of one familiar with the rigors of his task. He was in the sixty-fifth year of his life, but he carried his age lightly, and he knew the strength that lay in patience. Laying out his ritual implements on the mats around him, he crumbled a handful of sticky white copal into the slowly smoking incense burner and murmured a prayer to the ancestors, asking that they accept the gift of his vigil.

Time passed in silence, marked only by the presence or absence of the dim glow of light admitted by the ventilator holes high up in the corners of the vaulted chamber. Balam Xoc chanted and prayed in the darkness, calling upon the ancestors to visit and enliven him with their presence. He became weary and felt the weakness of his hunger grow upon him, even as the pangs of hunger itself diminished and left him empty. Then he fell into a dream.

He was in a watery place, perhaps a swamp. Thick rushes with bulbous heads rose out of a vaporous mist, and water lilies floated alongside the canoe in which he sat. Fearing crocodiles, he pulled his hands in close to his body, causing the canoe to rock gently from side to side. He sensed that there were boatmen in the bow and stern, but they were obscured by the mist, and the canoe did not move.

Then he heard the echo of voices, and a small wave slapped against the left side of the canoe. He peered out into the mist as the voices grew louder and nearer, and suddenly the bow of another canoe thrust into view, passing him only a short distance away. The paddler in front wore an ornate headdress and had the shape of a man, but his eyes were large and yellow, with tiny black pupils, and a thin, reptilian tongue licked out of his mouth as he dug into the water with his paddle. He glanced sideways at Balam Xoc and seemed to sneer, showing a single curved fang against the redness of his gums.

There were three passengers in the canoe, two women and one man, sitting one behind the other. Even with the mist scudding across his vision, Balam Xoc recognized them instantly. They were his wife, Nicte; his daughter-in-law, Ik Caan; and his eldest son, Chac Balam. He knew then that he was in the Underworld, for all three had died long ago, in the early tuns of Katun 11 Ahau.

They stayed within his view for only a moment, just long enough for fragments of their conversation to drift to his ears, surrounded by watery echoes:

"He thinks he is holy, but he merely hides from trouble . . ."

"He hides from his grief . . ."

"He cannot see the sorrows of his people, he will not act to save them . . ."

The suddenness of their departure left him stunned, and then a crushing sense of shame descended upon him as he realized that his loved ones had been talking about *him*. He began to shake, rocking the canoe so violently that it abruptly overturned, pitching him headlong into the depths of the water . . .

He awoke upon his back, blinking upward at the darkness overhead. He lay where he was, recalling the dream and the shame that it had caused him, a shame that was still a gnawing pain within his heart. The pain swelled at the memory of his wife's face, and suddenly he was weeping uncontrollably, his body racked with spasms of long-suppressed grief. He writhed helplessly on the floor, confused and embarrassed by the emotions surging through him. This was no place for weeping and indulging his sorrow, but he could not stop the sobs that burst from his throat or the tears that streamed from his eyes. He wept for the loved ones who had been taken from him so unexpectedly, and for the loneliness that had been his life for so long.

When the attack had finally passed, he barely had the strength left to raise himself into a sitting position. Fumbling for his incense bag, he added more copal to the burner, seeing a reassuring redness flare up behind the eyes and mouth of the jaguar mask affixed to the side of the cylindrical vessel. *I have dishonored myself before the ancestors,* he thought, and tried to recollect the proper prayer of expiation. But his thoughts were too disordered, and the words eluded his grasp. It took all of the power of his will simply to remain sitting up, and the fear that he would begin weeping again kept his lips shut tight upon the prayers he could remember.

He fell in and out of consciousness, losing all track of time and all control over the thoughts that entered his mind. A dim murmuring came from the corners of the room, and unseen wings fluttered by overhead, a breathy sound that echoed beneath the high, vaulted ceiling. Demonic faces leered at him out of the darkness, causing his body to jerk backward in terror, movements that made his aged joints throb with pain. Never had a confinement affected him so grievously, and he wondered if he were dying. As the Living Ancestor, he had prepared himself thoroughly for the journey he would one day take through the nine levels of the Underworld, but in his present state, the prospect made him tremble with helpless fear. *He thinks he is holy, but he merely hides from trouble . . .*

Memories blended with dreams, forming a dense web of images from which he could not extricate himself. Scenes from his own past mingled with ancient ceremonies he had never witnessed, except as pictures and glyphs painted in the sacred books; strangers rushed up to greet him and were transformed into his sons and daughters, or into people whose names he had long ago forgotten. Their greetings woke the shame he had experienced in his dream, making him feel that he had failed them somehow, that he had been unwilling to act on their behalf. He remembered the people who had come to him when he sat as the Living Ancestor in the clan house, humble people who would spill out their misfortunes to him and then bow in leaving, grateful for his blessing and the promise of his prayers. *He cannot see the sorrows of his people* came to him again and again, striking like a knife at what remained of his pride and self-esteem.

Then he came out of it briefly, gasping for breath but lucid. He felt empty and fragile, his mind bruised and exhausted from too much thought. But his confusion was gone, and the meaning of his dream was at last clear to him, so clear that it seemed he had always known it. Certainly, he had been grief-stricken when Nicte and Chac Balam had died within months of each other, shortly after the katun began. And Ik Caan, the wife of his second son, Pacal, had been the one who had taken over his household and given him comfort and company in his mourning. When *she* died in childbirth, he had been inconsolable, too wounded himself to be any comfort to Pacal or his children. Soon after Ik Caan's burial, he had undertaken his initiation as the Living Ancestor, turning his back upon the world that had caused him so much grief.

Hiding, Balam Xoc thought bitterly. Throughout the period of his delirium, he had been nagged by the anxious thought that he would not have the strength to perform the ceremony for which he had entered this confinement. Now it did not seem to matter. Of what use were the prayers of one so blind? He had seen his people change during the ten tuns of his service, yet he had refused to acknowledge their suffering, just as he had hidden from his own. They had come to him with tales of husbands who abused their wives, of children who sickened and died without a struggle, of sons who were abandoning the clan and moving away from Tikal. He had heard them from a distance, immune to the reality of their pain, and content to render his blessing upon their mere survival.

Yet even as he castigated himself, Balam Xoc did not know how he might have acted to save the people of his clan. He had no revenues to dispense and no power to alter the material circumstances of their lives. These things were no longer vested in the Living Ancestor, though they once had been. Now he held only an honorary seat on the clan council and was not expected to attend their meetings. His role was to be an example and an inspiration, and to concentrate his energies on the correct performance of the ancestral rites.

Balam Xoc felt his confusion returning. He no longer admired the example he had been, but he could not conceive of how else he might have inspired his people. He did not know the source of their discontent; he could not point to a certain enemy. And if, as they thought, it was the katun that oppressed him, could he do more to lift their burden than was already being done by the ruler and his priests? He was only one man, a weak old man who possessed little of the holiness he claimed, and thus little right to be an inspiration to anyone.

Despair drained off the last of his strength, and he sank wearily onto his side. He could barely remember the vigor and confidence with which he had entered this confinement; they seemed to belong to another man. *Perhaps I am going to die now,* he thought, and felt the darkness close in around him. Something brushed against his leg, and a cool hand seemed to stroke his forehead. Balam Xoc recognized the presence of the ancestors and tried to rally himself to act, for one last time, on behalf of his people. He called out once, but his voice broke into a thousand whispers that were quickly absorbed by the silence that yawned around him. Blackness filled his head, and he gave himself up to death . . .

Then the vision came, possessing him completely, and he slipped downward, weightless, into a world of shifting, indecipherable images. Spirit voices murmured reassuringly, telling him to have courage, telling him to listen and see. Shapes materialized out of the colors that surrounded him: Dancing figures and fantastic birds, their plumage whirling; a spotted yellow jaguar crouching beneath the arched blue body of a two-headed serpent; grotesque faces that stared at him hungrily with glowing red eyes . . .

The redness spread, then receded, until he could see that the color was painted upon the walls that surrounded him. To his surprise, he found that he was standing upright, wearing the heavy, elaborate costume of the Jaguar Protector. Yet he could not feel its weight. Uncertain whether he was awake or dreaming, he moved automatically toward the open, sunlit doorway, experiencing no sense of the effort of his limbs. Trailed by priests whose faces he could not see, he walked out of the shrine and descended the short flight of stairs to the terrace below. Here he took his customary place, standing atop a round stone pedestal, his costumed figure clearly outlined against the smooth shaft of stone that rose behind him, the monument that would stand in his memory when he had gone to join the ancestors. The monument bore no trace of paint or carving, and its yellowish-white surface had been rubbed to a dull gleam.

From the height of his pedestal, Balam Xoc looked down over the people of his clan, who were assembled in even rows, completely filling the small plaza before him. He was aware for the first time of the beating of a drum, and of the voices of the priests, singing in a chorus around him. All was in order, and by habit he began to raise the staff he held in his right hand, the signal for the ceremony to commence.

But a sudden wave of movement in the crowd stayed his arm and made him peer out at them more closely, his eyes shaded by the enormous jaguar headdress he wore. He saw then that the people were not watching him at all, but had their faces turned toward the sky, their mouths open in expressions that mingled expectation and dread. Balam Xoc also threw his head back to gaze upward, but the headdress confined him utterly, and he could not see past the wicker frame that supported the upper jaw and head of the Jaguar Protector. Angry at being ignored for something he could not even see, he tried again to raise his staff, but there was no strength in his arm; he could not lift it. Nor could he cry out to attract their attention. He gathered his breath to shout, but when he opened his mouth, the only words that escaped were those of the ceremony, a melodious invocation that caused not a single head to turn in his direction.

What do they see in the sky? he wondered furiously. He could see the faces of his son Pacal and his brother Cab Coh, of his nephew Nohoch Ich and the other priests, of the full-lineage members and the common people. All wore the same abject expression, as if waiting for some unknown threat to materialize above them. All stood transfixed, as helpless to move as he was himself. A scream of frustration formed like a knot in Balam Xoc's throat, but it could not burst free, and he felt himself strangling upon it, descending into blackness . . .

Then the costume was gone from around him, and he could see. Turning his eyes upward, he saw a sky filled with dark, turbulent clouds, promising a terrible storm. Yet as he watched, the clouds seemed to open outward into an enormous, billowing canopy, which began, gently, to descend toward the earth. As the air thickened and grew darker, Balam Xoc looked back to his people, expecting them to flee while there was still time. But they had not moved, and their expressions had not changed, as if they did not perceive the threat pressing down on them from above. He loosed the scream in his throat, but it was too late, and the sound of his terror was lost in a sudden rush of air. The people before him never moved, and then they were swallowed up by a grey, roiling mass that hid them completely from Balam Xoc's sight.

We are lost, he thought, and wept tears that burned his eyes with bitterness and regret. He looked downward at himself and saw that he was naked, his body coated with the black paint of fasting. He saw, as well, the old woman who crouched at the base of the pedestal, her black-robed body bent double beneath the load upon her back. The tumpline stretched taut around her forehead prevented her from raising her white-haired head to look upon him, but her thin, reedy voice came clearly to his ears:

"Once the katun had no face," she cried mournfully. *"Once we did not teach our children to fear the future."*

Turning away from him, she crept off into the clouds, but before she disappeared, he saw that the burden she carried upon her straining back was the mask of Buluc Ahau, the ruler of Katun 11 Ahau. The blunt, heavy-lidded face glowered at him briefly and was gone. A cold, sucking wind suddenly swirled up around Balam Xoc, a wind so cold that it seared his lungs and caused the paint to crack and fall away from his skin. He cried out in anguish, and then the clouds closed in around him, and he saw no more.

HE AWOKE to a darkness without shape or shadow, the dizzying blackness of the tomb. A vague whirring filled his ears, and his heart fluttered wildly as he raised himself into a sitting position, gripping his knees for support, waiting for the commotion inside his chest and head to quiet. Only very gradually did his senses return. He first made out the dull, reddish glow emanating from the eyes and mouth of the jaguar mask that hung in the air before him. Then he perceived the sliver of a reflection caught upon the surface of his water bowl, and the gleaming shapes of his bone implements on the mat beside him. He extended an unsteady hand toward the jaguar mask and felt the heat of the coals still burning within the incense vessel, and he knew then that he had returned. He and his people had not perished; they had not all been swallowed by the sky.

He slumped back against the wall behind him, too numb to feel the exhaustion in his muscles, yet aware of a distinct coldness that seemed to surround him where he sat. It seemed, in fact, to be coming *from* him. He ran a hand over his thigh and felt the paint break beneath his fingers and come off in dry, dusty patches. *I have captured the wind in my heart,* he thought dazedly; *I have brought a piece of my vision back with me.*

Strangely invigorating, the coldness spread throughout his body, bringing order and clarity to his thoughts. He could not dwell on the details of his vision, though, for he was too affected by the simple yet awesome fact that he was still alive. In his own mind, he was certain that he had died, and that his certainty was not a product of delirium. He could not merely have recovered, for he had given up his hold on life, and from that there was no recovery. He had surrendered his spirit to the ancestors, yet they had thrust him back into the world of the living. They had transformed him and had sent him back to complete his task upon the earth.

And they have shown me the way, Balam Xoc thought; *they have revealed the true enemy of my people.* It was not the katun that oppressed them, but their own fear of the katun's potential. And it was the ruler, Caan Ac, who had inspired that fear with his prophecy and then had profited from it, increasing the power of his own clan, the Sky Clan, at the expense of all the other Tikal clans. Balam Xoc had been a member of the ruler's council; he remembered only too well how Caan Ac had used the threat of the future to extort additional levies of warriors and workmen from the clans, and to make them surrender their daughters for marriage alliances with the cities of the west. It did not matter if his belief in the katun prophecy and his desire to avert its potential were genuine. He still had not hesitated to use them for his own advantage.

More even than the ruler, though, the katun prophecy itself was the enemy. *Once the katun had no face,* the old woman in the vision had said, and Balam Xoc, for whom the events recorded in the books of the ancestors were a second memory, had no doubt as to her meaning. He knew that there had indeed been a time in Tikal's long history, over four hundred tuns in the past, when the rites of the katun and its attendant prophecy had been unknown here. It was the Cauac Shield people—the foreigners who would later found the Sky Clan —who had first brought katun worship to Tikal and had forced its acceptance upon the other clans. This had not been accomplished without resistance, however, and had led finally to the clan wars that had nearly destroyed Tikal in the last Katun II Ahau.

Balam Xoc paused, daunted by where his thoughts had led him. Was that to be his task, then—to revive the clan wars? His own clan, the Jaguar Paw, no longer had the power of either numbers or wealth. They had only their ancient blood and the prestige of the sacred rites held by their families since Tikal's earliest beginnings. These might not be enough to protect him were he to challenge the dominance of the Sky Clan and question the legitimacy of *their* rites. His own son was one of the ruler's stewards, and many of the other clan leaders drew their livelihood from the royal revenues. They would be slow to side with him in a dispute with the ruler, and their reluctance would be shared by the clan priests, who would not wish to upset the delicate balance of ritual power that characterized the religious life of the city. He would be alone in this battle, sustained only by the power and truth of his vision.

It will be enough, he decided abruptly, and felt the coldness coalesce into a hard knot of determination, a force of purpose such as he had never felt in all of his sixty-five years, not even in the ambitious days of his youth. His pride and his grief were gone, and he could never again be daunted by the fear of death. He had only to act upon the truth shown to him by the ancestors, a truth other men could not see, or did not wish to. There could be no duty more sacred and compelling than this, and none more fitting for one who claimed the title of the Living Ancestor. *I will not forget what I was shown,* Balam Xoc vowed silently. *Let them think me mad, let them raise their hands against me and clamor for my removal. Still, I will remember, and act as I must. Whatever the cost, I will make my people turn their faces to me once again.*

He had been aware for some time of the muted reverberation of a drum, and now he heard the murmur of voices from the next room. *It is time for the ceremony,* he thought, and took a few sips from his water bowl to loosen his tongue and throat. Then he rose slowly to his feet, stamping gingerly upon the stone floor to restore the circulation in his legs. He felt the sudden touch of air against his skin as more of the black paint fell away from his body, a last reminder of his vision and his vow.

The priests of his clan were standing in a group just inside the next room, and they jumped back in surprise when Balam Xoc pushed through the heavy cloth curtain and appeared before them, blinking painfully at the light streaming in through the single entrance to the outside. The high priest, Tzec Balam, greeted him with a bow, appearing visibly relieved, as if he had been debating the necessity of coming in to rouse him. Gesturing the other priests out of the way, he signaled to the costumers to begin dressing Balam Xoc for the ceremony. Two apprentice priests stepped forward with wet cloths in their hands, but Balam Xoc held up a hand to stay them from washing his blackened body.

"Use dry cloths," he commanded hoarsely. "The sign of my fasting leaves of its own accord."

The sound of his voice produced a moment of shocked immobility in the room, the eyes of the apprentices roaming anxiously at this unexpected violation of the silence. Even the stern Tzec Balam appeared perplexed. Balam Xoc's nephew, Nohoch Ich, was the first to recover himself, coming forward with a dry towel in his hands. The stiff shell of black paint that surrounded Balam Xoc's naked body shattered and came away in large pieces at the first touch of the cloth, drawing an involuntary gasp of amazement from those watching. His own face shiny with perspiration, Nohoch Ich stepped back with wide eyes, leaving his cloth to one of the apprentices, who proceeded to rub Balam Xoc's aged, sagging body clean of its fasting paint.

The tension in the chamber had heightened perceptibly, but Balam Xoc felt it no more than he did the heat, which had everyone around him sweating profusely. He stood impassively while the apprentices wrapped a richly embroidered cloth around his loins and straightened the long apron that hung down in front. Next came leggings of jaguar skin, secured to his waist with leather thongs and bound at the bottom with anklets studded with flat pieces of smoky-green jade. Then the apprentices stepped aside and the costumers brought forward the costume of the Jaguar Protector: a large, hollow, wicker frame covered with jaguar skin, surmounted by an enormous jaguar head with its painted jaws agape.

Balam Xoc stooped as the entire frame was lowered over his head and its padded weight brought down upon his shoulders, his head emerging into the snugly fitted socket beneath the jaguar's upper jaw. Hands steadied the frame from the outside while other hands groped beneath the covering to tighten the straps that tied it to his body. Aware of the smell of the men's bodies and tense whistling of their breathing, Balam Xoc carefully thrust his arms into the jaguar-skin sleeves sewn into the sides of the covering, shifting his shoulders to balance the weight of the overarching frame. When he was comfortable, he held out his wrists for the tight-fitting jade cuffs and allowed the costumers to tie the heavy jade belt around his waist, beneath the swollen torso of the costume.

A painted effigy head of the first Jaguar Paw was attached to the belt, and then he was led over to the waist-high bench that ran the length of one of the side walls of the room. Two men stood upon the bench, holding the crested feather headdress and the plumed train of blue-green quetzal feathers that would be attached to the back of the frame. Balam Xoc held himself rigid against the tugging of their fingers upon the lacings behind him, feeling the additional weight of the headdress descend upon him little by little as it was lashed into place. He could feel, as well, the force that Tzec Balam and Nohoch Ich were exerting upon the costumers to complete their work both quickly and efficiently, without any of the fumbling that might mar the ceremoniousness of the occasion.

That is how I have been, Balam Xoc realized, *stiffly concerned with my ritual duties, to the exclusion of all else.* He glanced directly at Nohoch Ich, who hastily averted his eyes, out of respect for the Living Ancestor. Balam Xoc studied him coolly, noting the lordliness of his nephew's features: the drooping eyelids and slightly crossed eyes, the full lips and small chin, the long, pendulous nose. His broad, shaven head sloped back abruptly just above his eyebrows, into the elongated shape given to his forehead in earliest childhood, when his mother had pressed upon the still-soft flesh with hollowed boards, imparting the appearance of nobility with a gentle but concerted insistence.

Many tuns before, Balam Xoc had seen his wife perform this same act upon each of their children, just as it had been performed upon him by his own mother. He knew that his own features mirrored those of Nohoch Ich, except for the lines drawn by age. Yet now, as the costumers made their final adjustments behind him, he saw his nephew's face as a mask and his nobility as a disguise, a pose as rigid and conventionalized as those of the figures carved upon the stone monuments. Nor could he locate any of the feelings he had always held for this man, whom he had helped to raise and whose heart he knew as well as that of his own son. There was only the coldness, and the knowledge that he must shatter the mask and change his nephew as deeply as he himself had been changed. He acted now as the Living Ancestor, not as uncle or father, not as a man who shared the emotions of other men. He must change them *all.*

Having secured the headdress and attached a fresh white water lily to the ear of the jaguar head, the costumers released him, and Balam Xoc stepped forward unassisted to receive his ceremonial implements from the priests. He was given a painted wooden staff tied in the middle with a streamer of red cloth, which he took in his right hand, and a three-pronged "jaguar paw"— a sculpted piece of wood painted dark red and hollowed in the center for a handhold—in his left.

The priests all stepped back and bowed, humbled in the presence of the living incarnation of the Jaguar Protector, the ancestral god of the Jaguar Paw Clan and the patron of the sacred precinct of Tikal. Balam Xoc knew that he could speak now without shocking them, and that his words would be especially treasured by those who would hear them. And while he had no desire to warn them of the plans forming in his mind—plans that would touch them all—he knew that he should not lose the opportunity to make them think.

"For ten tuns, I have performed the rites of the Living Ancestor," he said solemnly, looking at each of them in turn. "I have rehearsed the journey of the Night Sun Jaguar through the nine levels of the Underworld, enacting his transformation and ascent to his dwelling place in the sky. I have prepared myself well for the death and transformation that will one day be mine, when I go to join the ancestors above.

"I will perform these rites again today," he continued, then paused for their full attention. "But I will also dance today for the living. I will dance to renew their strength and courage and to lighten the burden they carry in Katun Eleven Ahau. Announce this to the people."

The faces in the room reflected a wide range of responses, though foremost among them was wonder at this departure from custom. The high priest squinted narrowly at Balam Xoc, then silently dispatched Nohoch Ich to deliver the message. The drumming outside slackened momentarily, then started up again, swelled by a rumbling murmur of approval. Rapping once with his staff upon the stone floor, Balam Xoc brought the group within the chamber back to attention. Then, his eyes straight ahead, as if seeing none of them, he began to walk toward the open doorway, into the sound of drumming coming from the plaza below.

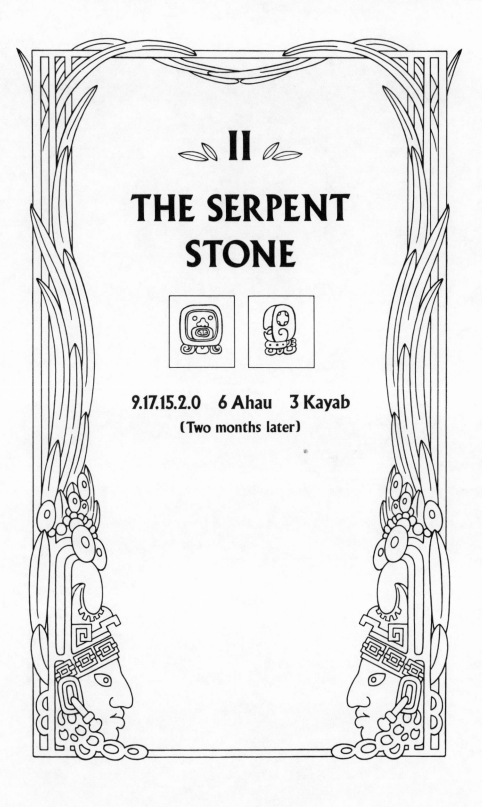

II
THE SERPENT STONE

9.17.15.2.0   6 Ahau   3 Kayab
(Two months later)

C AB COH left the Jaguar Paw Clan House with uncharacteristic haste, proceeding across the plaza to the east at a pace that paid no regard to either his age or the intensity of the morning sun. Only when he had reached the foot of the trail that led north to his house did he remember himself, and immediately felt dizzy and short of breath. He wandered into the shade of the breadnut trees that stood beside the trail and rested for a moment, leaning against the side of one of the tall trees.

I am too old to be ordered about like this, he thought wearily. *It is not the kind of treatment I deserve from my own brother.* He realized now that it would have been wiser and easier to have sent a messenger, but he had not stopped to think upon leaving the chamber of the Living Ancestor. Balam Xoc's parting words had left him too rattled to think, as they had no doubt been intended to do. They still echoed tauntingly in Cab Coh's head:

"If you need to consult the clan council to know what is proper, by all means do so. I summoned you because I know that you will be the one to carry out the order in the end. Is your own authority not sufficient, Cab Coh?"

Telling himself to be calm, Cab Coh left the sheltering trees and resumed his journey. He was comforted in some measure by the thought that none of the others in the chamber could have interpreted Balam Xoc's tone in quite the same way that he had himself. They had not grown up in Balam Xoc's footsteps, the younger brother who was constantly mocked and presented with challenges to his natural timidity. Cab Coh could not remember the last time that Balam Xoc had used that condescending tone with him, though it might have been as long as fifty years ago. *Our hair is white and our step slow,* he marveled ruefully, *and still he would push me against my will.*

The trail rose sharply, and Cab Coh again felt the heat as he climbed to the top of a narrow ridge that ran between the clusters of houses on both sides. Outside of the ceremonial center of Tikal, the terrain was rough and uncertain, broken by numerous ravines and extensive areas of low, seasonal marshland. The dwellings of the various families occupied every bit of ground dry enough to build upon, the thatched-roof houses clustered tightly around interior plazas, each group surrounded in turn by groves of valuable trees and the family garden plots. Since the rains had come on schedule, and plentifully, the gardens Cab Coh passed were powdered with the fresh green of new shoots, and women and children labored on their knees, pulling weeds and heaping up earth around the tender stalks.

Soon the houses had thinned out and the trail passed through a long stretch of open swamp, awash again after the recent rains. Bright birds flitted among the reeds and rushes, lighting briefly among the branches of half-submerged logwood trees. In the distance, well away from the trail, a grey heron stood poised upon one slender leg, its long-beaked head cocked delicately to one side, eyeing an unseen prey. Cab Coh listened gratefully to the songs and whistles of the birds, recapturing some of his equanimity as he drew closer to the houses of his family. He would forgive his brother in time, he knew, and perhaps the crops would be so good this season that the cost of Balam Xoc's demand would not prove to be a lingering problem for the clan. *He danced to lighten our burden,* Cab Coh reasoned, *and perhaps he has done so.*

Then he had passed the houses of the nearest neighbors and could see those of his own family through the trees ahead. Rising above all the others was the great yaxche, the First Tree, which stood at the far eastern end of the cluster of houses. Hanging in its branches—or so it seemed to Cab Coh's dimming eyes—was the dark red roof comb of the family shrine, a squat, heavy structure that overlooked the upper plaza from atop a high platform. There were two plazas separating the houses, the first considerably lower and slightly to the south of the one behind. At the western end of this lower plaza was the collection of adjoining buildings known as the craft house, for here was where the artisans under Cab Coh's direction did their work for the benefit of the clan.

Cab Coh entered the long main building at its northern end, nodding to those who greeted him in passing. The walls of the building were made of poles covered with mud and plaster rather than of stone, and there were several broad doorways on both the east and west sides, making the single large room seem inordinately light and airy. Men of all ages sat or squatted upon the reed mats scattered around on the floor, their hands busy with the delicate tasks of incising, polishing, and painting. Cab Coh saw immediately that Akbal was not in his usual place, but he paused to examine the large, open bowl that had been left to dry upon a piece of oiled cloth.

The background color of the bowl was a deep reddish orange, and its rim had been painted a vivid shade of red. Rings of tiny black beads rose concentrically from the bottom, forming a lower border for the black and white feathers that decorated the low, flaring inner walls. Cab Coh pursed his lips in admiration. Even without polishing, the colors were rich and vibrant, and the precision of the lines had not been blurred by overcoating. Only a hand as sure as Akbal's would dare to apply the paint so thickly on the first stroke, he reflected, conscious, as always, of how little he had to teach his young kinsman, at least in terms of technique.

His satisfaction with the workmanship of the bowl made him feel a little less embarrassed at having to ask the other men where Akbal had gone, though the older men did not conceal their amusement at the question. Akbal had been working here since he was a small boy and was known to all of them, but it was only a matter of days since the young man had finally decided to accept the role of Cab Coh's assistant and successor. Now the assistant was gone, and the master did not know where to find him. It seemed only too predictable, knowing both Akbal and Cab Coh as they did.

But none of them could enlighten him as to the young man's whereabouts, so Cab Coh walked outside and went down to the other end of the building, where the women had their workroom. Peering in under the overhanging thatch, he saw Kanan Naab, Akbal's sister, sitting with her work spread out around her in the broad swath of light pouring in through the open doorway. She was instructing two younger girls—distant clan cousins—in the painstaking task of stamping designs upon a length of cotton cloth, showing them how to steady their wrists before applying the dye-stained pottery stamp. When Cab Coh's shadow fell over her, she looked up and saw him beckoning to her, and came outside to join him, gathering her long skirt around her.

"How may I help you, Grandfather?" she asked politely, as Cab Coh inclined his long, cloth-wrapped head in greeting.

"I must find your brother Akbal, my daughter. Do you know where he might have gone?"

"I have not seen him since earlier this morning. Perhaps he is in his room," Kanan Naab suggested. "Or perhaps he has gone to visit the stone carvers again."

"Stone carvers!" Cab Coh exploded, having finally found the subject upon which he could vent all of his annoyance. "I have indulged that boy for far too long. What kind of assistant will he make if I cannot ever find him? Stone carvers!"

Kanan Naab caught her breath and drew back from him, astonished and alarmed by his outburst. She had never heard him complain so vehemently about anything, and especially not about Akbal.

"I am sure that he would not have gone if he had known that he was needed," she ventured in her brother's defense, and Cab Coh hastily composed himself, realizing the impression he was making. It was not often that he had to remind himself of Kanan Naab's sensitive nature, since he was not usually a man who acted in startling ways.

"No, he did not know of this, my daughter," he said gently. "No one knew. Balam Xoc only decided this morning that the ancestral books needed to be repaired or replaced. I had no more warning than anyone else."

As quickly as it had come, Kanan Naab's apprehension seemed to vanish at the mention of Balam Xoc's name. Clasping her hands in front of her breasts, she looked up at Cab Coh with an interest as complete as it was sudden.

"Does the request of the Living Ancestor displease you in some way, Grandfather?" she asked, in an incongruously solemn voice. Cab Coh gave her a searching look, hearing a reverence behind the question that was, in itself, a judgment upon the answer. *She, too, has been touched,* he thought, remembering the expressions on the faces of the pilgrims who had crowded into the clan house after the Hotun Ceremony.

"Only in the way that he made it," he said carefully. "He has never made such a demand upon me in all his time as the Living Ancestor, and he was not gentle. He would not wait to consult the clan council."

"Is it a large task?"

"Very large. He has singled out the oldest of the books, the ones that will be most difficult to copy. That is why I need Akbal: He is the most talented of our painters, and he is not so set in his ways that he would be thrown off by glyphs he has never seen before. But . . ."

Cab Coh trailed off abruptly, unwilling to admit to her that he had more important things for Akbal to do. He, too, had seen Balam Xoc dance for the people, and he had been moved and uplifted by the experience. He had even taken pride in the number of pilgrims who had flocked to see his brother afterward. But he had not been as profoundly affected as they had appeared to be, or as the girl in front of him so obviously was. The discrepancy made him feel nervous and apologetic, and he looked for a way to end the conversation gracefully.

It was enough for Kanan Naab, though, that he had hesitated. Lowering her eyes, she placed an arm across her chest and bowed in deference.

"I will tell Akbal that he is needed, if I see him," she promised, and bowed again before turning back into the craft house. Cab Coh nodded belatedly and stood for a moment after she was gone, pondering the awkwardness of their exchange. *What has my brother done,* he wondered, *to make us suddenly so unsure with one another, and with ourselves? Is this how he intends to lighten our burden?* Cab Coh could make no sense of it, and he turned away to search elsewhere for Akbal, thinking again that he was too old to be ordered about so roughly.

THE BIRD lighted on a low branch and hopped in a quick circle, eyeing his surroundings warily. Then he ducked his head under a wing and began to groom himself, separating the reddish-brown feathers with a thin, sharply curved beak, his long, forked tail feathers swaying rhythmically for balance. The tail feathers were a brilliant greenish blue, with black tips that stood out against the glossy green of the undergrowth.

Crouched below, the boy slowly brought the wooden blowpipe to his lips, curling his tongue around the clay pellet in his mouth as he took aim. The bird stopped his preening and danced higher on the limb, glancing back over his shoulder with a bright brown eye. The boy waited patiently, elbows braced beneath the blowpipe, not moving as mosquitoes settled upon his bare back and bit through the skin. The bird presented himself in profile and again began to preen, and the boy noiselessly sucked in his cheeks, offering a brief, silent prayer to the spirit of the bird whose feathers he was about to take . . .

But suddenly a great thrashing noise erupted on the other side of the wall of foliage, and the bird vanished before the boy could shoot. The boy pulled in the blowpipe and prepared to run, his mind conjuring images of large beasts. But although the thrashing continued, it came no closer. A human sound, perhaps someone chopping vines for rope. Removing the clay pellet from his mouth, the boy cast a disgusted glance at the branch where the bird had been and went to investigate the noise. He threaded his way expertly through the dense foliage, keeping an eye out for snakes and using his blowpipe to clear spiderwebs and thorny vines from his path.

He heard the man's heavy breathing before he saw him: a tall, somewhat slender man who was standing with his back to the boy, grunting as he hacked away at the undergrowth with a stone ax. It was extremely hot this far down into the ravine, and the man's reddish-brown skin was glistening with sweat. The ax he was wielding, the boy noticed, had a narrow, pointed head of the kind used by stone workers, and was not at all appropriate to this sort of work. Still, the man had cleared all the saplings and high growth in a rough circle around the place where he stood, chopping at a low, brush-covered mound. Even as he recognized the mound, the boy thought he saw a slithering movement among the leaves piled close beside the man's feet, and he cried out instinctively:

"Behind you—a snake!"

The man's body jerked spasmodically, and he released the ax in midswing, letting the handle bounce off his shoulder as he whirled and jumped in the boy's direction, hopping from one foot to the other as his startled eyes searched the ground for danger. But there appeared to be no snake, and the boy saw for the first time who it was he had disturbed. It was Akbal Balam, the one known as the Painter, the youngest son of Lord Pacal Balam. The boy bowed hastily and spread his hands in apology, gesturing toward the mound the man had been clearing.

"There is a large serpent—a yellow jaw—who has his burrow somewhere near the stone. I thought I saw him among the leaves."

The man kneaded his bruised shoulder and gazed at the boy intently, though without recognition. The boy bowed again in embarrassment.

"I am Kal Cuc, my lord," he explained timidly. "I live with my grandmother, who is a cook in your father's house."

The man continued to stare down at him, his liquid black eyes narrowing slightly, as if he were memorizing the boy's features. Kal Cuc shifted his feet and slapped at a mosquito, made shy by the intensity of the man's attention. He had heard his grandmother and the other women talking about this Akbal Balam, who had returned to his father's house only a few days before, after completing his education in the clan house. They, too, had noticed his staring, but they had found it amusing, the source of jokes about the yearnings of young men, jokes that Kal Cuc did not fully understand.

"So you also know about the stone," Akbal said at last, in a voice that forgave the boy for startling him. Kal Cuc nodded affirmatively.

"It has always been here, as long as *I* have been hunting in this ravine."

"How long is that?" Akbal asked, bending to retrieve his ax from where it had fallen.

"Almost four years," Kal Cuc said, counting quickly in his head. "Ever since my parents died and I came to live in the Jaguar Paw House."

Wiping dirt from the handle of the ax, Akbal appraised him more broadly, his eyes lingering on the blowpipe in the boy's hand and the short flint knife at his waist.

"And what do you hunt?"

"Birds and rabbits and lizards, and the snakes that are not dangerous," Kal Cuc said, shedding his diffidence at the memory of his own skills. "I sell the feathers and skins to the costume makers," he added proudly, "and my grandmother and I eat the meat."

"Yes, the meat," Akbal agreed in a bemused tone, as if he found the idea mysterious. "I have never hunted anything," he confessed with a small shrug. "But when I was a boy—younger than you—I used to play in this ravine with my older brother, Kinich Kakmoo. He would stand upon the stone and pretend that he was the ruler addressing his captives."

"I have always stayed away from it," Kal Cuc said uneasily. "Because of the yellow jaw."

"I was not thinking of snakes," Akbal said quietly, approaching the mound with his ax in hand. "Only of *this* . . ."

Hooking the pointed tip of his ax into the tangle of vines and brush that covered the mound, he tugged until the entire leafy mass came loose in a shower of reddish earth, exposing the dirty yellow surface of the stone that lay below. Kal Cuc came forward to stand beside him, staring first at the jagged, vaguely rectangular shape of the stone and then up at the man, who wore the rapt smile of someone who had just uncovered a treasure. The boy squinted at him quizzically.

"It is an old piece of stone," he suggested tentatively, wondering if there was something he had failed to see.

"Yes," Akbal agreed absently, measuring the half-buried slab with his eyes. "But look at the *size* of it. I would never be allowed a piece of new stone this large. Not for myself. Not to carve."

"To carve?" Kal Cuc echoed blankly, then remembered himself and quickly looked away, as if he had not spoken. It was not his place to question the wishes of a son of the house, however strange they might seem. He darted a glance at Akbal and saw with relief that the man was no longer paying any attention to him. He had heard that Akbal had recently completed his eighteenth year, the age of manhood, but somehow he did not seem that old to Kal Cuc, who was himself ten. A grown man who had never hunted, who stared rudely at people and smiled at stones? Surely, this was a strange kind of man.

"I will need men to help me raise it," Akbal said abruptly, glancing from the stone to the path he had cut in descending into the ravine. "Perhaps as many as six, if we are to get it all the way to the top."

"The men are all away," Kal Cuc blurted impulsively. "They have been called to help with the planting."

"Of course," Akbal conceded, after a moment's pause. He looked at the boy with renewed respect. "In the meantime, though, perhaps *you* would be my helper, Kal Cuc. I will need a path cleared down to this place."

"It is my duty to serve the members of the house," the boy said loyally, though he was truly reluctant to involve himself with this peculiar man.

"I will find a way to repay you and those you get to help," Akbal offered, causing Kal Cuc to shake his head stubbornly, flushing with shame at the thought that he had allowed his reluctance to show so plainly.

"It is my duty," he repeated emphatically. Akbal hefted his ax and took a last look at the stone.

"I must return to my duties. But I will be back very soon," he added softly, and started back up the side of the ravine, leaving Kal Cuc behind to wonder if the words had been addressed to him or to the stone.

IN THE two months since his father had danced at the Hotun Ceremony, Pacal Balam had received numerous urgent messages from the high priest, Tzec Balam, asking Pacal, as the head of the Jaguar Paw Clan Council, to summon a meeting of the full council. The most recent requests had been phrased as warnings and had included the information that Balam Xoc had undertaken an examination of the clan accounts.

But Pacal had been far too busy with the planting to pay any attention to the affairs of the clan. The last few days before the coming of the rains had been a frantic race against time, as the last of the breadnuts were harvested and stored in the underground chultunes, and the fallowed maize fields were cut and burned in preparation for planting. Then the rain clouds had rolled in from the east, answering the ruler's prayers and filling the reservoirs from which the people drew their drinking water. Just as timely—and as important, in Pacal's view—had been the return of the merchants who had gone to trade with the western cities. Not only were they welcome for the goods they carried, but the many porters who had accompanied them were put to immediate use in the digging of the fields and the planting of seed. The maize, beans, and squash planted in the outlying fields had all benefited fully from the rains, and in the days since, the raised fields in the alkalches had been shored up and sown with the cotton and root crops that grew so well in the damp, loose soil.

It was now the month of Kayab, and they had entered the period of hot, clear weather that always occurred just after the rainy season had begun and before the Sun reached his time of standing still. The sunlight and dry air were beneficial to the young crops, which could not survive if the soil were too wet, as it had been the season before. But too long a period of dryness would wither the new growth and leave it stunted, a prospect that made this a time of tense and anxious waiting, a time for praying that the rains would return before it was too late.

Pacal chose instead to turn his attention to matters over which he had some control, and he decided that it was time to respond to Tzec Balam's request and deal with the sudden activism of Balam Xoc. Before the council meeting was to begin, he met privately with the high priest in the latter's room, which was off the north courtyard of the Jaguar Paw Clan House. He was surprised to find the normally impassive priest in a state of open agitation.

"I cannot treat this matter as lightly as you seem to," Tzec Balam said sharply. "I *saw* the paint fall away from his body. And I have seen the excitement he has aroused in our people, especially among the poorer members of the clan."

"It does not seem to have harmed us, however," Pacal pointed out calmly. "Many of the pilgrims have sent back offerings that more than made up for the cost of their visit. You must pardon me for thinking of the practical aspects, Tzec Balam, but it is my first duty as the head of the clan council."

"And what are the duties of the Living Ancestor?" the priest inquired. "Is there any limit to them? The books he has been studying go back hundreds of tuns. The powers and prerogatives of the Living Ancestor were very different in the time of our most distant forebears."

"But what prerogatives has he usurped," Pacal asked, "beyond ordering the repainting of the books? I grant you, his behavior has been unusual. But he was once the head of the clan council himself, so he is not unaware of the limits on our revenues and manpower. He can be made to listen to reason."

Tzec Balam crossed his arms on his chest and regarded Pacal with austere skepticism, as if lifting himself above the level of this debate.

"Perhaps not unaware. Perhaps only indifferent," he suggested in a cool voice. "Then it does not concern you that he has been studying the clan accounts as well?"

"The records are open to anyone who can read them. I have no misgivings about the scrupulousness with which they have been kept. No doubt my father has been examining them in order to prove to the council that the cost of renewing the books can be absorbed by the clan. And it can be. I consider it but a small price to pay for the service he has done us. The people have a great need for reassurance, and he has spoken to that need more eloquently than have the elders or the priests."

"More eloquently than the ruler himself, perhaps," Tzec Balam retorted stiffly. "I will leave Balam Xoc to you, then, since you claim to understand him so well. I had thought that I did, but I am no longer so sure. He has spoken only vaguely of what he experienced in confinement, and he has not chosen to present it to us for our interpretation. Indeed, he has shown no inclination to explain himself at all."

"Perhaps he will begin today," Pacal suggested easily, but the priest merely grunted and turned on his heel, leading the way toward the council chamber.

THE COUNCIL chamber was on the second floor of the clan house, its two doors opening onto a gallery that faced west, overlooking the extensive complex of buildings that belonged to the other clans. The vaulted room was longer than it was wide, and its floor space was further limited by the raised stone bench that lined the walls on all sides. The members of the council seated themselves cross-legged upon the bench, taking the places allotted to them by rank and custom. As their head, Pacal sat in the center of the line against the back wall, facing the blank expanse of wall that separated the two doorways, which provided the room's only light. The High Priest Tzec Balam sat in the honored position, to Pacal's right, and beside him were his two eldest sons, one also a priest and the other a leader of the clan warriors. To Pacal's immediate left was his uncle Cab Coh, the head of the clan artisans, who was flanked in turn by his son, the Tun Count priest, Nohoch Ich. The heads of the other major families—six in all—were ranged on either side of these, while the representatives from the outlying districts of Tikal occupied the less prestigious seats along the side and front walls. A pair of scribes sat at the foot of the bench in front of Pacal, with their paper and paints laid out before them.

Pacal had offered his father a seat on the bench beside him, but Balam Xoc had chosen instead to sit directly opposite his son, in the space between the doorways. He was wearing the jade necklace and the spotted cloth headwrap of the Living Ancestor, and though he was sitting in the place usually reserved for those who had come to petition the council, he displayed none of the ingratiating earnestness of the typical petitioner. He greeted those who approached him with politeness, but he did not engage any of them in conversation, and his impassive face showed no response to their compliments concerning his dancing. He sat with his eyes fixed upon the floor in front of him as Tzec Balam solemnly offered a prayer consecrating the purposes of this meeting.

"Let us begin," Pacal said when the priest had finished. He looked across at his father. "Do you wish to address the council, Grandfather?" he asked, using the term that all within the clan applied to the Living Ancestor. Balam Xoc nodded and glanced around the chamber, gesturing with his hands to hold the attention of the men at the far ends of the bench.

"Fifteen tuns of Katun Eleven Ahau have passed," he said slowly, "yet surely no one has forgotten the dire prophecy with which the katun began. All of us within this chamber were present when the Katun Enclosure was dedicated and the sacred maize was cast to foretell the future. All of us heard the ominous words of the ruler and felt the cold shadow that Buluc Ahau cast over our lives."

Balam Xoc paused and looked from left to right, the only animate creature in a group grown still as stones. He allowed his gaze to come to rest upon Tzec Balam, and he continued staring at the priest as he resumed his recitation:

"Some few of us also attended the ruler's council afterward. Caan Ac was new to the throne then and had not yet won the full respect of the clans. His father and grandfather, Cauac Caan and Cacao Moon, had been forceful leaders, and they had both lived long lives. They had expanded Tikal in every direction, and they had built Katun Enclosures and great temples dedicated to the spirits of their ancestors. They had spent freely from Caan Ac's inheritance and had exhausted much of the resources and goodwill of the clans as well. We were not a pliant body during the first tuns of Caan Ac's rule.

"But after hearing the katun prophecy, we felt we had no choice but to accede to his wishes. Only he and the katun priests, with their offerings and their penance, could allay the threat and bring the rains for our crops. In return for his performance of the katun rites, he had the right to demand much of us. So we gave our consent to all the measures Caan Ac proposed for the protection of our city. We agreed to concessions we knew would create hardships for the people of our clans, and we did so without argument or negotiation. I myself gave my youngest daughter in marriage to the royal house of Quiriguá, though it pained me greatly to send her so far from her home. I believed—as we all did—that we would suffer a disaster of incalculable proportions if we did not make the sacrifices demanded by the ruler."

Balam Xoc paused again, drawing a solemn nod of recognition from Tzec Balam and silent gestures of agreement from the older members of the council. He went on in the same, even tone, as if speaking of matters upon which all agreed.

"We were grateful, then, when the days became months and the months tuns, and still no disaster had descended upon us. The hardships of the people, though they seemed to grow greater with each tun, could not compare with the fearful things we had been led to imagine. We bore our troubles without complaint, believing that we had been spared from something far worse. Thus, we were blind to what our lives had become, and we did not notice the poverty into which we had fallen."

Every head in the room came up at this last statement, though none more quickly than that of Pacal. He stared at his father in disbelief, his jaw muscles rigid with the effort of containing his objections. The other men stirred uneasily in their seats, glancing sideways at their fellows without meeting one another's eyes.

"I must accuse myself of this same neglect," Balam Xoc said, "for no one can speak honestly of our condition without admitting his complicity in bringing it about. I listened to the tales of suffering my people brought to me, but I did not let myself hear them. Nor did I speak out on their behalf, for negligence encourages silence, and makes it seem a tradition. I danced upon the stone as a sign that I had broken with this tradition, and I call upon you today to do the same."

The tension that had been building in the chamber as Balam Xoc spoke erupted in a wave of murmuring and muted exclamations, a sound composed equally of bewilderment, approbation, and dissent. Pacal raised his hand for quiet but was ignored for several moments, as all attention continued to focus on the implacable figure of Balam Xoc. Then it was again silent.

"You must explain this 'poverty' that you perceive, Grandfather," Pacal said in a dry voice, making no effort to conceal his skepticism. The men along the bench craned forward expectantly, some already shaking their heads in unconscious disagreement.

"I have no reason to doubt what the people have been telling me for many tuns," Balam Xoc replied calmly. "And I have heard even more in the time since I danced for them. This has led me to examine the records of the clan, and I have discovered many curious things there. I found that the clan lists no longer resemble the documents I remember from the time I served upon this council. There are many more blackened spaces among the names of the living, and it is no longer only the old who are numbered among the dead or departed. Perhaps the total is no smaller, but there has been a movement, and there are fewer of those allied with our clan who find their prosperity close to the center of Tikal. I have been told that this is due to the fact that certain occupations have become closed to all but the members of the Sky Clan. Is this not why your eldest son, Nohoch Ich, went to Holmul to find work as an architect?"

Surprised at being singled out, the priest could only nod mutely. Then Balam Xoc turned back to face Pacal.

"Or perhaps it is because those who *have* maintained their ties to the clan have not benefited from their loyalty," he suggested mildly. "Perhaps they see too little return for their long days of labor."

"Our books are open to everyone," Pacal responded stiffly, "and any man may come to this council for an accounting if he has a complaint."

"I counted for myself," Balam Xoc told him. "And I count in the simple way of our ancestors: I do not give numbers and value to things that do not exist. I consider promises worthless until they are fulfilled."

"Of course," Pacal agreed easily, warming to the kind of argument with which he was most familiar. "But I do not know the promises to which you refer. Surely, you cannot expect the merchants to carry our goods to Copan or Yaxchilan and return with our payment in a single day?"

Balam Xoc gave him such a cold, unblinking look that Pacal involuntarily dropped his eyes.

"I am not speaking of days. We hold promises that go back months, some even more than a tun. And all bear the glyph of the Sky Clan. Perhaps the council wishes to believe that the promise of the ruler has value regardless of fulfillment. I do not."

Too astonished to speak, Pacal glanced around at the other men, whose faces reflected a bemusement bordering on fascination. The men at the far ends of the room seemed particularly entranced. Only Tzec Balam met Pacal's eyes, and his sardonic expression repudiated Pacal's shock at this attack upon the ruler's integrity.

"But the word of the ruler is the word of Tikal," Pacal finally managed. "Surely you cannot doubt his ability to supply what he has promised?"

"Is the ruler more powerful than his prophecy?" Balam Xoc demanded in return. "Or is his prophecy only the power he holds over us? When the troubles descended upon us in the last Katun Eleven Ahau, many of the Sky Clan families abandoned their homes here and went to the west, to Yaxche, Ektun, and Yaxchilan. They left us to endure a life of hardship under rulers even more foreign than they."

"Foreign?" Pacal echoed foolishly, but his father seemed not to hear him.

"Five tuns remain to this katun. We will see its completion in ruin if we do not act to change our ways. We must accept no more promises in payment for our wares and our labor. Let the ruler pay us in men for the things he must have. Let him release some of those he has levied for his work crews if he has no other means of payment. That way, at least, we might be able to provide our people with what they need."

"But this is impossible," Pacal cried, spreading his hands wide in an appeal for common sense. "The crops must still be cultivated and brought to harvest, and the construction of the Katun Enclosure is several months behind schedule. The ruler is desperate for workmen as it is. We cannot ask him to release those already in his service!"

"Perhaps *you* cannot, Pacal Balam," Balam Xoc said, using the name as he might that of a stranger. "But surely the families of our clan would not find it impossible to put their men to good use. The reservoirs that belong to us have long been in need of repair and do not hold the water they used to. The thatch on many of the houses is old and infested with vermin, and it no longer keeps out the rain and cold. These matters must be attended to before more of our children sicken and die. And our people have their own crops to tend, crops that can be watered by hand if the rains do not come as the ruler promises. If *again,* they do not come as he promised."

In the uproar that followed, many voices clamored to be heard, and some even began to argue with one another when they could not attract Pacal's notice. Tzec Balam finally clapped his hands sharply, reminding the men of their manners and bringing the room back to order.

"As the head of this council," Pacal said when it was quiet, his voice hissing through his teeth, "I am aware of the problems confronting our people, and

I have discussed them thoroughly with everyone in this room. No one has shown any displeasure with the way our affairs have been conducted, though all have had the opportunity. Yet if anyone now feels that I have failed in the performance of my duties, let him call for my removal as your head."

Lifting his chin, Pacal gazed boldly up and down the line of men, displaying no fear of finding an adversary in their ranks. Even Nohoch Ich, his cousin and frequent rival within the council, gave back no hint of a challenge.

"I am calling for it myself," Balam Xoc interjected curtly. "Your position with the ruler has made it impossible for you to serve our people with any effectiveness. You would allow the Sky Clan to absorb us little by little, until we had no fate left to call our own. As the Living Ancestor, I cannot countenance such a thing. I am putting forward the name of Nohoch Ich as your replacement."

Pacal sat stunned, his eyes blinking furiously at the effort to control his emotions. He did not even notice that Nohoch Ich was in a similar state of shock, or that Tzec Balam was gesturing violently for the chance to speak on his behalf. Never in his life had his father rebuked him so publicly, and he could not even begin to frame a response or a denial.

"You need not count heads," he said hoarsely. "I would not oppose the wishes of the Living Ancestor, even in this . . ."

Uncrossing his legs, he lowered himself off of the bench and went to stand before his father. Grasping his left shoulder with his right hand as a sign of deference, he bowed beneath the unrelenting eyes of Balam Xoc, who showed nothing that would indicate he was affected by his son's pain. Then Pacal turned and walked out of the chamber, surrounded by the humming silence of his humiliation.

GATHERED at the edge of the lower plaza of the Jaguar Paw House, six men wearing only loincloths and headbands squatted silently in the shade of the breadnut trees, drawing designs in the dirt while a seventh, younger man spoke to them. They eyed the nearby coils of rope and the stack of cedar poles with weary resignation, appearing not to listen as Akbal Balam earnestly explained the task he had for them. They had already reconciled themselves to doing this work, since it had been authorized by Cab Coh and came at the request of a son of the house, so explanations did not matter to them. They wondered why Akbal did not know this and why he simply did not tell them what to do, as his father or his brother Kinich Kakmoo would have done without wasting either time or breath. If some stone was to be moved, they would move it. What did they care about where it was or why he wanted it?

They were relieved when Akbal finally finished talking and gestured toward the rope and the other tools. Then he slung a broad-headed ax over his shoulder and led them away from the plaza, back through the trees in the direction of the ravine.

"The Painter," one of the men muttered softly, though with more bemusement than scorn. Since none of them were artisans, they had had little contact with Akbal, and knew him by reputation only. They knew that his extraordinary skill with a brush had revealed itself while he was only a boy and that he had worked alongside the older artists on projects of great importance. It was said that he had already brought many valuable commissions to the clan and that he had turned down the chance to join the artists attached to the court of the ruler in order to become Cab Coh's assistant. This apparent lack of ambition had not increased his stature in the workmen's eyes, and they did not hurry to keep up as they followed him through the grove of fruit trees that grew up to the lip of the ravine.

When they arrived at the top of the steep declivity, though, they found that Akbal had already had a wide path cleared through the dense, thorny undergrowth that filled the ravine. They glanced at one another and shrugged approvingly; perhaps the Painter knew his business, after all. It grew perceptibly warmer as they went down the path, for there was no sheltering canopy of trees over the ravine, which would gradually fill with water over the course of the rainy season. Already, there was standing water in the bottom of the gorge, and no shortage of mosquitoes to torment the sweating men.

A small group of boys holding digging sticks and wooden rakes were waiting at the bottom of the path, and they greeted the men excitedly, speaking in nervous whispers and gesturing toward the clearing they had made in the jungle. Then the men could also see the slab of stone sticking up out of the weeds, and the shimmering serpent that lay coiled upon its exposed surface.

The snake had a swollen, lance-shaped head, and its dusky, greyish-green body was crossed with dark bands that faded to a dull yellow at the edges. Though it lay motionless upon the stone, none of the men made a move toward it, and one of them signaled sternly for the boys to stay behind them. It was a yellow jaw, the serpent with fast death in its teeth. Since it was known to be a night hunter, its presence upon the sunlit stone was all the more disturbing and made the men hesitate about simply trying to frighten it off. Ignoring Akbal, they began to argue quietly among themselves over who should climb back up the path for a weapon. As the leader of the boys, Kal Cuc volunteered to go for them, but he was an orphan whose parents they had not known, and they did not wish to give him the honor over one of their own sons. Their voices began to grow louder and more querulous.

Akbal had stood by silently, understanding little of the men's conversation or of the reasons for their hesitation. He saw only a sleeping snake that lay between him and his stone. Suddenly raising the ax over his head, he went forward before anyone could stop him, crossing the clearing in two silent strides, already bringing the ax down as the serpent woke and sluggishly reared its flat, angular head. Dust exploded with a loud bang, and the long, banded body lashed wildly around the stone, causing the men and boys to jump back in a group, holding their breath until they saw that Akbal had not missed. He lifted the dead snake by the end of its tail and tossed it aside, dropping the ax as he bent over the bloodied stone, a hand extended to support himself.

The men stayed back and restrained the boys out of respect, knowing the fear that could come to a man after approaching death so closely. They would not have thought less of Akbal's courage if he were to be sick. But when he straightened up and turned back to them, his handsome face wore a relieved smile.

"It is not much damaged," he announced, gesturing for them to come closer and bring their tools. The men did so reluctantly, casting significant glances at the corpse of the snake, which lay where Akbal had so unceremoniously discarded it. They were waiting for him to acknowledge the spirit he had just taken, to dip his fingers into the blood of the serpent and apologize for having been forced to kill it. Kal Cuc waited as well, until he remembered that Akbal was not familiar with the customs of hunters and therefore could not know what was expected of him. The boy had the momentary urge to explain this to the other men, then just as quickly realized that he did not dare. It would only add to Akbal's embarrassment to have an orphan boy apologize for his bad conduct.

Akbal had begun digging around the stone with his ax, churning up large chunks of reddish earth matted with roots, unaware for several moments that no one had joined him in the work. Only when he paused to wipe the sweat from his eyes did he notice that the men were still hanging back, staring at the dead snake. Resting his ax against the stone, Akbal took a cedar pole out of the hands of the nearest man and lifted the limp sack of coarsely scaled skin off of the ground, showing them the nearly severed head.

"See? It is dead," he said, tossing the corpse toward the edge of the clearing with a flip of the pole. It landed in the weeds with a thump that made the other men flinch, and no one reached out to claim the borrowed pole when Akbal turned to hand it back. He blinked then, and seemed to realize that he had done something wrong. One of the men coughed in the silence, and Kal Cuc licked his lips and kept his eyes averted, not daring to meet the imploring glance Akbal sent his way.

Finally, Akbal turned and walked back to where the snake had landed, and knelt beside it in the weeds. He laid the pole on the ground and bowed his head over it for a few moments, then got up and slowly backed away from the spot. The men said nothing, but they picked up their tools and began digging in a circle around the embedded stone.

When the stone was fully exposed, the men wedged their poles under the slab and pried it from its bed, finding no more snakes but flushing a multitude of scorpions and centipedes, which the boys quickly flattened with their rakes. Then came the arduous task of tying ropes around the stone and dragging it back up the slope, which was too steep and uneven to permit the use of log rollers. The heat forced them to stop frequently to rest, but Akbal was always the first to pick up a rope and begin hauling again, and the men could not stand by idly while he strained his slender body in their place, bloodying his painter's hands on the coarse fiber ropes. He would not allow anyone to quit until the stone had been set upright at the edge of the breadnut trees, its most jagged end buried in the ground and its back buttressed with wooden wedges and supporting poles.

The men collapsed cross-legged on the ground, drinking gratefully from the water gourds one of the serving women had brought out to them and spitting onto their rope-raw hands. Akbal walked slowly around the stone, running his fingers over the rough, pitted surface, which was splotched with scaly green lichens and still marked with the blood of the yellow jaw. It stood chest-high where it had been broken off many years before, one piece of an ancient monument that might once have stood before the clan shrine, or even in the Plaza of the Ancestors. Perhaps it had outlived its usefulness and had been ceremonially "killed" by those who owned it and then dumped into the ravine. Or perhaps a rival clan had broken it in revenge during one of the periods of interclan strife long in the past. It was a plain monument, with no carvings or inscriptions to hint at its origins and history.

"Is it not magnificent?" Akbal asked quietly, still staring at the stone. When no one answered, he turned to look at the seated men, then down at his body, as if realizing his own condition in the sight of their thorn-bloodied, insect-bitten faces.

"I am sorry," he said in a flustered voice. "You have my deepest gratitude. I will see that you are each given two measures of salt and two of maize, and ten cacao beans apiece. And ten beans for each of the boys."

The men rose quickly to their feet, flustered themselves at this unexpected show of generosity. They bowed effusively and murmured their thanks over and over, though none of them got too close to Akbal or the stone. Gradually, they and the boys drifted away, and Kal Cuc appeared from behind a tree, holding the body of the snake, now completely lacking a head, draped over his thin arms. He stood uncertainly for a moment, then walked up to Akbal and deposited the serpent at his feet.

"Would you have me skin it for you, Lord?" he asked timidly, watching Akbal's face as the young man stared down at the flaccid pile of shiny skin, seeming not to recognize it.

"No. It is yours," Akbal said at last. Then he looked closely at the boy, seeing his hesitation.

"Take it, Kal Cuc," he said curtly. "The disrespect surrounding its death was not of your doing. I must bear the blame for that."

Without another word, the boy scooped up the snake and trotted away, leaving a dark red spot upon the bare ground. Akbal stared at the spot, then at his hands, which had begun to swell and burn. His knotted muscles began to ache in unison, and he clawed furiously at the insect bites on his back before he could make himself stop. But he had his stone, and even as the pain made him sink slowly to the ground, he began to imagine what the slab would look like when it was cleaned, and what he would carve upon it when it was.

THE LATE afternoon sunlight came through the open doorway on a sharp, eastward slant, so that Box Ek did not break the light as she stepped upon the threshold and looked into the room. It was empty, though she could hear someone shaking out a mat in the room beyond, where the family members slept. She was about to announce her presence when she noticed the way the light was falling upon the back wall, painting a bright yellow rectangle a few feet to the right of the doorway to the inner room. In the center of the rectangle, as if deliberately framed, was the portrait that Akbal had painted of his late mother, the Lady Ik Caan.

Box Ek shivered and drew her cotton shift closer around her shrunken body, leaning forward with one hand upon the short wooden cane she used for walking. Almost twelve years had passed since Ik Caan had died and Akbal had painted her face upon the plastered wall. Yet the delicate tracings of red paint still stood out clearly, burnished to a deep orange by the rich light pouring into the room. Box Ek realized that Akbal must have painted it at just this time of day, kneeling upon the bench with his back to the door, creating a companion for himself in the last hour before darkness would fall. Or perhaps he had believed, in his six-year-old mind, that he could bring his mother back from the Land of the Dead by drawing the image of her that lived inside of him.

In a way he had, for it was an extraordinary likeness. Even Box Ek, who had not known Ik Caan well, was compelled to recall the vivacity of the woman's presence. Akbal had exaggerated the blunt Sky Clan nose and strong jaw somewhat, but he had perfectly captured the knowing arch of his mother's brow and the lively glint in her teardrop-shaped eye, features that had given Ik Caan her particular power and beauty. Many members of the family still wept upon seeing the portrait, but no one had ever suggested removing it, even after Pacal had remarried.

Memories washed over Box Ek, making her vision blur and her breathing grow shallow. She remembered returning here from Ektun, back to the house that had been her father's, but which now belonged to her brother Balam Xoc. She remembered the heaviness of the grief that had hung over the Jaguar Paw House, and over her brother and her brother's son, Pacal. And forlorn in their midst were the three children, Kinich Kakmoo, Akbal, and Kanan Naab, the latter only three years of age, a child born only days after the beginning of the katun. Box Ek's own children had long since grown, and she had been a widow for over ten years, but she had tried, with an old woman's awkwardness, to fill the emptiness created by their mother's unexpected departure.

Kanan Naab suddenly emerged from the inner room and stopped short, a hand fluttering to her throat in surprise when she noticed Box Ek standing motionless in the doorway. Then she also saw where the light had fallen, and she dropped her hand and lowered her eyes self-consciously. She was in every physical detail a replica of the woman on the wall, except for just those aspects of personality that her brother had rendered with such instinctive cunning. Her lips were pursed tightly, and an unflattering crease had appeared between her downcast eyes, revealing her awareness of the subdued image she presented alongside that of her mother. *A precious jewel,* Box Ek thought sadly, *yet lacking the glitter of the stone from which she was struck.*

"I was remembering my return to Tikal, so many years ago," she said quietly, breaking the shaft of light as she moved to Kanan Naab's side. "I was remembering the child that you were."

Kanan Naab nodded silently and slowly raised her eyes to Box Ek's face, though the older woman barely came up to her shoulder. Box Ek reached up with a withered hand to gently smooth away the worried crease between Kanan Naab's dark eyes.

"I was recalling, as well, the poor substitute I made for your mother. No, do not deny it, my child. I do not doubt the fondness you have for me, or I for you. I have taught you many things, and have helped to make you a woman. But I was too old to give you the kind of attention and caring that only a mother can provide."

"You are very dear to me, Grandmother," Kanan Naab said plaintively, taking the gnarled, misshapen hand into her own. "You have given me more than anyone else."

Box Ek shook her white-haired head with stubborn modesty, but she smiled as she gestured for them to seat themselves on the bench. Kanan Naab took the cane from her and helped the tiny woman climb onto the bench, where she settled herself with her back against the wall and her legs stretched out to one side. Box Ek was sixty-eight years old and had been afflicted with crippling pains in her bones and joints from the middle of her life; she had long ago lost the ability to bend her knees into the proper sitting position.

"You are nearly fifteen now," she began, when Kanan Naab had seated herself cross-legged beside her on the bench. "Soon you will be chosen in marriage. Do not look away from me, Kanan Naab," she said sternly. "This last cold season was very hard on me; I felt the closeness of death in my bones. I cannot wait until you are ready to receive my counsel."

Kanan Naab met her gaze with chastened eyes, her brow again creased.

"I honor your words, Grandmother," she said softly. "But I do not know who would want to choose me for a wife."

"You carry the blood of the Jaguar Paw Clan in your veins," Box Ek scolded, "the blood of the oldest lineage in Tikal. Our daughters are regarded as highly as those of the Sky Clan, perhaps even more so, since there are fewer of us. Your hand *will* be requested, Kanan Naab, do not think otherwise. *Whom* you attract is perhaps the only thing you can affect, since in these times, the young men often desire to meet the woman before an overture is made to her father."

"Was that not always the custom?" Kanan Naab asked. "Had you not met the Lord Kan Mac before you married him?"

"Of course not. The match was made at the request of the Ruler Cauac Caan and was arranged solely by our fathers. I had never been away from Tikal before, much less to a city as distant as Ektun."

"You must have been very frightened," Kanan Naab suggested, encouraging the old woman to talk. Box Ek nodded solemnly and opened her mouth to go on, but then caught herself and stopped, glaring suspiciously at Kanan Naab.

"You are only leading me away again," she said accusingly. "You know all these things, and you have heard the story of my journey to Ektun many times. There, you are smiling! How cruel you are, Kanan Naab, to distract me with my own memories! Especially when you refuse to learn from them, as any well-mannered person would. You are wicked and perverse, and much too clever for your own good."

Embarrassment had darkened Kanan Naab's cheeks, but she could not fully suppress the smile that kept spreading across her face. She lowered her eyes shyly, but could not keep herself from responding to Box Ek's summation of her character.

"Is it not clear, then, why no one would choose such a person for a wife?"

Not deigning to reply, Box Ek cocked her head and studied the young woman's face, as if seeing something she had previously missed. Kanan Naab felt the scrutiny and dropped her smile, becoming nervous again.

"Quite the opposite has become clear to me," Box Ek said finally. "You are very attractive, my daughter, when you allow yourself to smile and show your pleasure. Even though that pleasure comes from teasing an old woman and making light of her advice."

Now Kanan Naab was genuinely embarrassed, and did not raise her eyes from her restlessly kneading hands.

"Yes, I have been wasting my breath," Box Ek concluded with a kind of satisfaction. "I have been belaboring you with advice you understand all too easily, so that you cannot listen to it with seriousness. It does not challenge your cleverness, so it is not important to you. But there are men who like a clever woman," she added shrewdly. "And now you have shown me how they might be led to discover your attractiveness."

"What have I shown you?" Kanan Naab demanded curiously, but Box Ek merely shook her head in denial.

"You do not need to know," the old woman said smugly. "It is only the things you do not understand that truly interest you. Is that not why you go so often to the soothsayers, and why you are always pestering your grandfather and Nohoch Ich with questions about the ceremonies?"

Box Ek let the question hang in the air between them, until it became clear that Kanan Naab was not going to attempt an answer. Box Ek grunted softly, not entirely pleased at having silenced the young woman so thoroughly. She was about to adopt a gentler tone when a great shadow fell over them where they sat, and they looked up to see Kinich Kakmoo standing in the doorway.

"Father has been removed as head of the clan council," he said in a muffled, nearly toneless voice. He came farther into the room, his thick hands clenched into fists that he held away from the sides of his body as if they were weapons. "And the man who has done this," he continued, "is his own father. Your brother, my lady . . ."

"Grandfather," Kanan Naab murmured breathlessly, looking from Box Ek to her brother in confusion. Kinich Kakmoo put a hand on the back of his neck and rotated his massive tufted head, as if to loosen the grip his anger had upon him. He was a man nearly as wide as he was tall, with heavily muscled arms and shoulders and the strongly pronounced features of his mother's line. He displayed his calling in the broad, crooked hump of his nose—broken in battle long ago—and in his sharply filed front teeth, which had inlays of jade and pyrite in the gaps between, in the style favored by the warriors.

"What reasons did Balam Xoc give for this action?" Box Ek asked him, and he shrugged impatiently.

"He has dredged up old debts, and even older resentments against the Sky Clan. He accused Father of serving the ruler at the clan's expense."

"And the council accepted this?"

"Father did not subject himself to the humiliation of a vote. What choice could they make, after hearing him denounced by his own father?" Kinich swayed on his feet, his glittering teeth bared. "At Grandfather's suggestion, the council has elected Nohoch Ich to take his place. What does a priest know of such things?"

The two women did not answer, and Kinich turned in a small circle, giving off anger in taut, muscular waves.

"Where is Akbal?" he demanded when he had turned back to face them. "He should be *here* when Father returns, and not in the house of Cab Coh."

"He is out behind your house with a stone he has found," Box Ek replied. "One of the servants told me so earlier. Go and fetch him, my son. And you," she said to Kanan Naab, "find your stepmother and inform her of this. But gently, Kanan Naab. You know how easily Ixchel may be upset."

"I will try," the young woman promised as she prepared to follow her brother, who had already left the room. "But I do not understand why Grandfather has done this. Why would he tear the clan apart after his dancing had brought us together?"

"I do not know, my daughter," Box Ek admitted sadly. "It was *I* who encouraged him to seek the title of the Living Ancestor, in the days after your mother had died. He needed a purpose to make him forget his grief. I did not know that it would lead to this."

Kanan Naab looked at her solicitously, as if suddenly reminded of the old woman's age and frailty.

"I am sorry that I teased you before, Grandmother. I am unworthy of your kindness."

Box Ek managed a wan smile.

"Unheeding, perhaps," she allowed, "but not unworthy. Go to Ixchel, my daughter. Use your cleverness to persuade her to remain calm, and see that the cooks prepare an especially good dinner. It is always up to the women to keep the family together in times of stress, and we will do what must be done. But I fear that it will not be easy, now that Balam Xoc has created this rift among our men . . ."

III

FAVORS

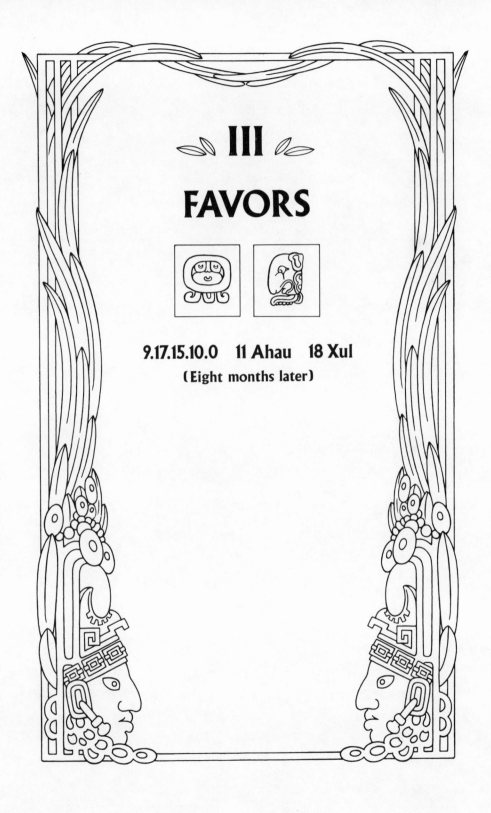

9.17.15.10.0   11 Ahau   18 Xul
(Eight months later)

ACOLD, fitful rain blew over the clustered buildings of the Jaguar Paw House in periodic gusts, spattering noisily upon the thatched roofs and dimpling the surface of the puddles that drained slowly toward the corners of the plazas. Kal Cuc came out of the craft house first, wrapped in a blanket against the chill, and he was followed closely by the hunched figure of Balam Xoc, whose shoulders were covered by a thick fiber cloak. The boy led him out of the lower plaza and past the open-sided cookhouse that stood behind the house belonging to Kinich Kakmoo. The women squatting around the hearth broke off their conversation and bowed their heads to the Living Ancestor, who smiled briefly and extended a hand toward them in benediction. Then he bowed his head against the wind and rain and followed Kal Cuc in under the breadnut trees, his sandaled feet making a crunching sound upon the carpet of old leaves and dried husks. They wound their way through the uneven rows of trees for only a short distance before the crude shelter Akbal had erected for his stone became visible. Balam Xoc stopped and gestured for the boy to go no further.

"Thank you, my son," he said, raising his voice above the thrashing of the leaves overhead. "You may go back now to where it is warm and dry. But remember to bring me the skin of the snake later."

"I will not forget," Kal Cuc promised, then shivered and departed with a grateful bow. Balam Xoc went on toward the shelter, which appeared to lean in his direction, away from the force of the east winds. Akbal had constructed an open-sided frame of poles around his stone, topped by a flat thatched roof just high enough to permit him to stand up straight beneath it. The thatch had been inexpertly layered and had already begun to pucker and leak in places, and the whole structure creaked and swayed flimsily in the wind. Yet Akbal did not seem to notice the wind swirling around his unprotected body or the water dripping upon his head as he worked on the stone, smoothing its pitted surface with fine sand and a stiff cloth.

"So this is the Serpent Stone," Balam Xoc said as he stepped in under the fraying roof. Akbal turned in surprise, his face and arms smudged with yellow dust, the cloth crumpled in one hand. Then he dropped the cloth and bowed deeply to his grandfather, crossing his arms upon his chest in deference.

Balam Xoc walked past him and made a slow circuit of the stone, which had been cleaned of its dirt and lichens but had only been sanded in a few places. He felt Akbal's eyes upon him and sensed the young man's uncertainty. There had been no reconciliation between father and son in the months since Balam Xoc had asked for Pacal's removal as head of the clan council, and only Box Ek moved with ease between the two houses. Akbal had been put in a particularly delicate situation, attached as he was to Cab Coh, whose son was currently doing Balam Xoc's bidding upon the council. *Besides,* Balam Xoc thought, *he is afraid, from what he has heard of me lately, that I will take his stone away from him.* Akbal confirmed this by flinching slightly when Balam Xoc turned back to address him.

"You have washed away the blood of the serpent," he observed quietly. "Have you also cleansed it of the offended spirit of its guardian?"

Akbal flushed darkly and shook his head, hugging himself against the sweat cooling on his body.

"I meant to visit you, Grandfather," he explained, "once I had finished cleaning it. I would not begin to carve it until I had done so."

"I have saved you a visit, then. But you must tell me first why you have this compulsion to become a stone carver. Cab Coh could not explain it to me, except as a youthful indulgence. He does not understand why you would waste your talents on the kind of work done by commoners."

Akbal wet his lips and ran a finger across the dusty surface of the stone, which was streaked by the raindrops that had penetrated the roof.

"It is not easy to explain," he said hesitantly. "I have worked with a brush since I was very small. I have painted on cloth and pottery and the white paper of the books. I have drawn my designs on wood for the carvers, and I have incised them myself onto pieces of jade, obsidian, and bone. Yet most of the jade and obsidian is destined for burials, and I have seen how pots break, and how the books rot in the dampness, and how the borers carve their own designs into old wood. Only time, or other men, can diminish the beauty of that which is carved upon stone."

"Then it is permanence you want," Balam Xoc concluded in a neutral tone. Akbal grimaced in thought, then slowly shook his head.

"I know that such a thing cannot be attained, here upon the earth. But still . . . is it not natural to want the beauty we create to stand after we are gone?"

Balam Xoc gave a short laugh.

"Your father mistakes you, Akbal. He thinks that you have no ambition." The old man turned to examine the stone once more. Then he looked up into Akbal's eyes. "It has been many years since a stone was carved in honor of our clan. You have my permission to do so, but you must approach this task with more respect than you showed toward the serpent."

Akbal nodded earnestly, accepting the reprimand with gratitude and relief. Balam Xoc hardened both his gaze and his voice as he went on:

"Cab Coh has indulged you in this, and you must repay him for his kindness. But it is no indulgence that I extend to you. I will give you this stone, and I will take upon myself the offense you committed against the creature who guarded it. The boy who brought me here still has its skin, and he has promised to bring it to me. He could find no one else who would trade with him for it, once he had explained how he came to have it. I will take it to the priests of the Serpent Clan and see that the appropriate rites are performed."

"I am grateful, Grandfather," Akbal said humbly. "Will you also guide me in deciding what I should carve on this stone?"

"No," Balam Xoc told him flatly. "That is a challenge you must face on your own. You have revealed a lofty ambition to me today, and only you can truly know when and if you have achieved it. If you settle for less, you will have to live with the evidence, and explain it to *your* grandchildren. Remember that, Akbal, and let it give you the patience and respect you will need to succeed."

Placing a hand flat against the stone, Balam Xoc bowed his head and murmured a brief prayer, the words lost to Akbal in the gusting of the wind. Then he turned abruptly and walked away without another word, the fiber cloak flapping against the backs of his legs as he headed back toward the houses. Akbal watched him go, hardly able to believe that his grandfather had actually come out in the rain to see his stone. Not only that, but he had come prepared to purify the stone and give his permission for it to be carved. Akbal felt awed by the honor that had been paid to him. He would not have thought that he was in his grandfather's thoughts at all, given the number of important matters over which Balam Xoc had so recently asserted his control. Of what importance were he and his stone compared with the turmoil Balam Xoc had stirred up within the clan, or with the dispute he had initiated with the ruler himself?

Akbal turned back to the stone, which seemed to glow with a soft yellow light against the dark, rainswept background. Its blank surface seemed suddenly daunting, and made him wonder at the way he had spoken to his grandfather. Had his ambitions truly been as lofty as he had claimed? Or had he simply wanted to try his hand at a new skill, and to work on something that would be *his*—something that would not be carried off by the merchants as soon as it was completed?

These were also his reasons, but he had not raised them with his grandfather. Nor could he any longer feel that the stone was simply his. He had been given a commission, even though it was unlike any he had ever been offered. He was to be both artist and patron, creator and judge. Akbal had not reckoned with such a dual responsibility when he had gone in search of a stone. He had assumed that whatever he finally decided to carve would prove pleasing to those who would see it; he had never had any difficulty in pleasing others before. But now the ultimate judgment would be his own, and the prospect suddenly made him feel very, very young.

He squatted in front of the stone, hooding his eyes against the stinging particles of sand and dust blown up by the wind. The cloth lay where he had discarded it, and he reached for it tentatively, then drew his hand back. Even the simple act of sanding had taken on new significance, since it would bring him that much closer to decisions that now seemed almost too large to be contemplated. Akbal hunched his shoulders against the chilly air and stayed where he was, and did not reach for the cloth again. He began to ponder the meaning of patience and respect, and the nature of the commission his grand-father had given him.

AS THE HARVEST approached, the farmers of Tikal were able to look back upon a season of splendid weather, an almost perfect balance of sun and rain. The maize had grown tall in the fields, the stalks twined around with the climbing vines of the beans, while the broad-leaved squash sprawled and flourished in the rows between. Nor had there been much of a problem with insects, except for a few isolated plots that had become infested with maize borers and had been burned off. The work crews completed their final weeding early in the month of Yaxkin, at which time the ripening ears of maize were bent double to protect them from the misty, late-season rains. With the date set for the harvest less than a month off, even the most pessimistic estimates predicted a yield as large as any on record.

But then the winds from the east, typical at this time of year, began to gust and blow with real force, bending the trees and filling the air with the salty odor of the Great Waters that lay some five days' walk in that direction. The sky turned black, and the wind roared over Tikal for a day and a night, accompanied by torrential rains that caused the reservoirs to overflow and the plazas to run ankle-deep in water. The construction scaffolds at the site of the new Katun Enclosure were blown down, and the houses in exposed areas lost all or part of their roofs. The poorest people saw their huts of poles and mud plaster collapse completely in the downpour and were forced to take refuge in the buildings of their clans.

The devastation extended into the fields, where the maize lay flattened in the mud. And although the fallen ears of green maize were gathered immedi-ately, to salvage whatever was edible, at least half of the crop had been lost. The beans and squash had not been much harmed, and the root crops had survived the lashing the exposed raised fields had received, so there was no reason to fear a famine on account of this storm. But the anticipated surplus of maize, so valuable as a trade item, had disappeared upon the wind.

Pacal was able to assess most of the damage at firsthand, for he had been sent out to inspect the fields before the storm had fully spent itself. Wet and disheveled, he remained in the field for many days afterward, supervising the repair of the ridged fields in the alkalches and trying to save what he could of the cotton crop, which had been particularly hard hit by the ferocious winds. As soon as he had dealt with one problem, he would receive directions to attend to another, usually on the opposite side of the city. Only when all the repairs had been made and the main harvest had been completed was he recalled to the palace and allowed to rest, though his return was not greeted by the ruler with any of the customary displays of gratitude.

Having grown accustomed to such treatment by now, Pacal bore his punish-ment with tight-lipped silence. The ruler had been slow to believe that the

Jaguar Paw Clan would persist in their recalcitrance, refusing to accept Pacal's contention that he could no longer control his own clan council. But once he had perceived that such was indeed the case, he had not hesitated to take his annoyance out on Pacal, demonstrating his displeasure by excluding his steward from important meetings and assigning him duties well below his station. Pacal now walked the halls of the palace like a stranger, conscious of the decisions being made without him, and of all those who had suddenly begun to avoid his company.

The delegation from Yaxchilan came to Tikal in the month of Zac, after the trails to the west had dried sufficiently to permit travel. Caan Ac received them with great ceremony, assembling his entire court to hear the exchange of greetings and the speeches that followed. The primary purpose of the delegation was to extend a formal invitation to the marriage rites of the son and heir of their ruler, Shield Jaguar, and they fulfilled their obligation with the requisite amounts of both boasting and humble entreaty. After Caan Ac had accepted on behalf of his city, he signaled his desire to confer privately with the head of the delegation, and the members of the court began to disperse. Expecting to be dismissed along with the rest, Pacal had already turned away when he heard the ruler call him by name, summoning him to remain behind with the ambassador from Yaxchilan. Though thoroughly surprised by this sudden show of royal favor, Pacal did not fail to notice the proud smile that appeared on the face of his assistant, Chac Mut, and he could feel the envious glances cast in his direction as he made his way to the platform where the ruler waited.

Caan Ac was seated upon a padded throne shaped like a drum, his legs dangling down in front of him, in the foreign manner adopted by his father and grandfather. He had grown portly in recent years, and a roll of brown flesh showed between the gleaming jade pectoral that covered his chest and the waistband of his embroidered loincloth. He gestured for Pacal to sit upon the platform, further surprising the steward by offering him the honored place to the ruler's right. The white-haired ambassador stood facing the throne, his head slightly inclined and his eyes hooded in an attitude of respect.

As soon as the three of them were alone, without even a scribe to record the proceedings, Caan Ac bluntly raised the issue of main concern: the trade negotiations that would be conducted in Yaxchilan once the marriage of Shield Jaguar's son had been properly celebrated. He was especially concerned about the terms of the cacao trade, and Pacal quickly gathered, from the specific nature of his references, that preliminary terms had already been proposed by Shield Jaguar. No doubt Caan Ac and the other stewards had been studying and discussing them for some time, formulating counterproposals of which Pacal had no knowledge. Goaded by a sense of undeserved inadequacy, he listened with all his attention, straining to comprehend the basic outlines of the pact under discussion.

What he heard baffled him at first, the amounts seeming out of proportion with what previous experience told him was reasonable. He waited for more to be offered, growing numb with shock as he realized that he was hearing the full proposal. He stared at the ambassador, unable to believe that he was in earnest. But the old man remained politely insistent and did not flinch in the face of Caan Ac's increasingly pointed questions. Yaxchilan had other sources of cacao now, he explained: some through trade agreements with the tribes to the north and west of their city and some through raids upon their enemies in the same areas. Shield Jaguar had recently seized a cacao orchard that had belonged to the Macaw people, an extensive, heavy-bearing grove planted on ridged fields in the floodplain of the Chikin River. Thus, the ambassador concluded calmly, if Tikal insisted on trading in cacao, they would have to provide more of it and expect less in return—less of the jade and obsidian, the animal pelts and precious feathers, the salt and other valuable commodities that came downriver to Yaxchilan from the highlands. As alternatives, Shield Jaguar preferred to be paid in maize or dried fish, or in the finely worked craft goods for which Tikal was famous: carved wooden bowls and panels, dyed and embroidered cloth, painted pottery, jade jewelry and featherwork crests, and ceremonial items made of shell and bone and stingray spines.

The expression on Caan Ac's round, puffy face remained petulant and dissatisfied as the ambassador finished his recitation, but he did not respond with the immediate gesture of outright refusal that Pacal expected. Instead he began to speak of the composition of the delegation he planned to send to Yaxchilan, raising the names of the lords who *might* be persuaded to honor the wedding of Shield Jaguar's son with their presence. There was also the honor guard of warriors to be considered, as well as the musicians and dancers, the painters and craftsmen, and the priests and learned men who might be sent to mingle with their counterparts in Yaxchilan. The prestige of this delegation was something beyond price or negotiation, Caan Ac contended; it was a matter of his personal regard for his kinsman, Shield Jaguar, and a symbol of the long ties of respect and blood relationship that bound their two cities together.

The ambassador agreed wholeheartedly and revealed that he had been empowered to make certain concessions in anticipation of Caan Ac's generosity. The free exchange of gifts between rulers was of course an ancient and honorable custom, and never to be confused with the bartering that went on between merchants. Therefore, the ambassador would be most pleased to reveal the gifts Shield Jaguar wished to bestow upon his friend in Tikal and to hear in return the nature of the delegation Caan Ac planned to send to Yaxchilan.

Pacal listened with grudging admiration as Caan Ac and the ambassador matched "gifts" with each other, gradually evening out the terms of trade as the Tikal delegation grew in both size and rank. Yet Pacal's concern diminished only slightly, for the cost of outfitting the delegation would be great in itself, and the city would then have to bear the additional expense of having so many of its most important leaders away for a period of months. For all of Caan Ac's cleverness, he would not be able to make up the difference with the kinds of concessions he was coaxing from the ambassador. *It was a mistake to trade so heavily on our prestige,* Pacal thought, *especially when the terms being offered might reasonably be considered an insult.*

But Caan Ac and the ambassador had reached an agreement, and the ruler prepared to dismiss his guest, as if all of their business had been concluded. The old man interrupted him gently, wondering if the great lord had forgotten Shield Jaguar's other request. Caan Ac reacted immediately, swelling with apparent anger. Such a thing was inconceivable, he stated emphatically; the lords of Tikal would never stand for it. He could not believe that Shield Jaguar felt himself deserving of such an extraordinary token of respect.

The ambassador responded with more humility than he had so far shown, acknowledging that the gesture might be misinterpreted by some, but stressing the satisfaction it would bring to Shield Jaguar. His tone indicated a clear willingness—almost an eagerness—to make further concessions, and he left no doubt that this "gift" would be repaid many times over. Still, Caan Ac claimed not to be moved, and dismissed the ambassador without further discussion, saying only that they would talk again before the delegation had completed its stay in Tikal.

A servant entered the chamber after the ambassador had left, but Caan Ac waved him out again and looked sideways at Pacal, resting his forearms on his fleshy thighs.

"So, Pacal," he said with abrupt familiarity, "you see the situation in which we find ourselves. Yaxchilan takes its cacao by force, just as the wind has taken our maize. Nowhere is there an easy bargain for me, not even with some of our own clans."

Pacal bowed his head in resignation, accepting the rebuke his father had earned for him. He wondered if he had been brought here to take the blame for the ruler's current difficulties; if he had been made to listen as punishment. But then Caan Ac went on in a different voice, his tone softened by sympathy.

"I see that you are also in a difficult position, Pacal. Your father insults me almost daily, speaking of my ancestors as 'foreigners' and questioning the validity of the katun rites. And he has persuaded your clan council to deny me the warriors and workmen our city needs, in order to collect old debts. I have been too angry to accept your innocence in this, or to recognize the shame it has caused you."

"I cannot disown my responsibility for the actions of my people," Pacal murmured penitently, "as much as I might regret them."

"Still, the Jaguar Paw is but one clan," the ruler said magnanimously, "and by no means one of the largest. I can afford to allow them to bargain hard with me, and to concede gracefully rather than provoking a confrontation. And Balam Xoc has not won a wide support among the priests and Living Ancestors of the other clans, who have wisely prevented their people from listening to his heresies. He will find no more converts if he is not given a platform from which to spread his ill-considered doctrine."

"I am grateful for your forbearance, my lord," Pacal said, with a sincerity that made his voice quiver. Caan Ac nodded in a fatherly manner, holding up a palm to indicate that no gratitude was necessary.

"As a sign that I bear no ill will toward you or your clan, I am naming your son Kinich Kakmoo as one of the nacoms who will lead the warriors going to Yaxchilan." Caan Ac paused, looking steadily at the man beside him on the platform. "And I want your other son, Akbal, the Painter, to go to Yaxchilan for me as well."

"Akbal?" Pacal repeated in surprise. "Would you have him paint something for you?"

"Not for me. For Shield Jaguar. That was the request I rejected so rudely a few moments before. Shield Jaguar has asked all of his allies and subjects to include an artist of noble rank in the delegations they send to his son's wedding. They are each to paint a burial vase that will be provided to them in Yaxchilan. Each vase will have an inscription, and it will show the artist, as the representative of the ruler who sent him, paying homage to Shield Jaguar."

Pacal discreetly held his tongue, having already heard that Caan Ac intended to fulfill this request, despite his show of anger in front of the ambassador. Yet the anger seemed by far the more appropriate response. The ruler of Tikal owed no homage to Shield Jaguar, and certainly this request was presumptuous, if not actually a kind of taunt.

"I have never heard of such a thing," Pacal said carefully, and Caan Ac's gaze flickered past his face.

"It has been done before, though not since the time of my grandfather. Can you obtain the services of your son?"

"Is this a royal commission, my lord?" Pacal asked, and the Ruler shook his head.

"I must ask this as a personal favor, Pacal. I spoke the truth when I said that the lords of Tikal would not stand for it, and that is why I have not mentioned this particular request to the council. If it is done quietly, they will have to accept my explanations later."

Pacal nodded thoughtfully, seeing the shrewdness that lay behind the choice of Akbal. He was of noble blood but had earned little rank for himself; the importance of the gesture would thereby be diminished, at least in the eyes of the Tikal lords. Yet Akbal's skill with a brush would no doubt keep Shield Jaguar from feeling cheated. Caan Ac might well escape from this with little damage to his prestige, *if* it could be done as quietly as he wished. Pacal frowned involuntarily, thinking of his father.

"My son is the assistant of my uncle, Cab Coh," he explained, "but he is currently engaged in repainting the ancestral books of our clan. I will have to ask my father for his release."

Caan Ac grimaced and scratched his chin, appearing to reconsider the proposal. Then he shrugged and raised his hands, palms up, passing the problem back to Pacal.

"Do what you can, then. You have seen for yourself how important this is to Shield Jaguar, and how much it might do for the terms of our trade. You might remind your father that the Jaguar Paw Clan shares in the fortunes of this city, whether he chooses to trust me or not."

"I will do my best to persuade him," Pacal promised, hearing the note of dismissal in Caan Ac's voice. He bowed once, then bowed again after rising to face the Ruler, who acknowledged his departure with a weary nod. Pacal walked out of the chamber with his head held high, knowing that he had been publicly returned to favor and that he would soon be accepting apologies from those who had so recently snubbed him. Yet he felt keenly disappointed by everything he had heard today, and by the course Caan Ac had chosen to follow. It would have been better to refuse Shield Jaguar's request and look for trade elsewhere, perhaps to the east or south. Pacal would certainly have suggested such a response earlier, had he been present when the preliminary terms were first discussed. Now it was too late, and he could only do his duty as he had promised and hope that his father would not thwart him again.

A NARROW flight of stone steps descended from the upper plaza of the Jaguar Paw House at its southwest corner, terminating in a log bridge that crossed the deep gully separating the upper from the lower plaza. The gully functioned as a drainage ditch during the rainy season, and its sloping sides had been terraced and faced with limestone marl to prevent erosion. Rows of avocado and cherry trees had been planted along the upper terraces, and the levels below were green with ferns and wild ivy, which competed for space between the banks of flowers planted by the women of the clan. The dry bed of the gully had been taken over by thorny berry bushes that flowered beneath a humming cloud of yellow bees.

Halfway down the length of the middle terrace was a low stone bench, set back against the terrace above and shaded by the overhanging branches of the cherry trees, which were thickly furred with pink and white blossoms. The bench had been placed there at the request of the Lady Ik Caan, who had also planted the brilliant red flowers that flanked the bench on both sides. Kanan Naab had come here many times in the years since her mother's death, seeking a quiet place to rest and restore her courage when it began to falter. The bench was the only solid reminder of the mother she had hardly known, the bright, forceful woman who looked out at her from the wall of her father's house.

Today, however, Kanan Naab had come here out of choice rather than need. She was tired, but not with the fatigue of anxiety. She had had no time lately to dwell on her own feelings, because she had been much too busy trying to calm the nerves of others, most notably those of her stepmother, Ixchel. The actions of Balam Xoc had set everyone on edge, and unexpected outbursts of emotion had become an almost daily occurrence. Her father, when he was around at all, was moody and withdrawn, and her brother Kinich Kakmoo could not complete a meal without denouncing his grandfather at least once. Even Akbal appeared tense and preoccupied, no longer the carefree boy of their childhood. It was no mystery why Ixchel, who lived more deeply in the shadow of Ik Caan than even Kanan Naab, should feel lost and helpless in the midst of this family storm.

Kanan Naab seated herself cross-legged on the bench, breathing in the mingled fragrances of the flowers, the cherry blossoms, and the vanilla vines that climbed the boles of the trees. Hummingbirds were everywhere, darting from flower to flower like bright, buzzing jewels, their needlelike beaks probing among the petals as they hovered on blurring wings. Kanan Naab watched their abrupt, bobbing movements with delight, laughing aloud when a tiny green bird hung briefly in the air in front of her, challenging her presence with a belligerent, chipping call. Then it was gone in a flash of iridescent green feathers, blinding her with its shimmering brilliance.

I must be wicked, she thought, *to be so happy at a time like this, when the rest of my family is suffering.* Yet it was true: Whatever lay behind her grandfather's actions, they had had an undeniably beneficial effect upon her. The insecurity he had inspired in the other members of the family had only made her feel more normal in their midst, and had in fact given her a kind of advantage. She was a child of the katun, familiar with insecurity and the fears it generated, and able to respond with compassion to those who were surprised by what they were feeling. This compassion had drawn the others to confide in her and look to her for strength, giving her a sense of personal power that she had never dreamed of possessing.

Though she would not have admitted it to anyone, she felt deeply that this power was a gift from her grandfather. She felt, in fact, that everything that

Balam Xoc had done since the day he danced upon the stone had been somehow aimed at her. She had been in the back of the crowd on that day, pressed in among the other women and unable to see over the men in front. But when Balam Xoc had begun to dance for the people, the black-painted pilgrims in the first row had dropped to their knees in deference, forcing the men behind to do the same. Magically, as if a great hand were clearing the way, the ranks of men obscuring her view sank slowly to the ground. The women, however, could not kneel beside their men, so she was permitted to observe the entire dance.

Kanan Naab was certain that she would never forget the sight of the great Jaguar dancing upon the stone, hopping slowly from one leg to the other, shaking his staff in time with the drumming and clawing the air in front of him with his dark red paw. The painted effigy head danced rhythmically upon his jade belt, and the feathered train swirled about his legs, threatening to trip him up. Yet he did not trip or falter, however close he came to the edge of the pedestal. He turned in a circle, shedding blue-green feathers that floated slowly to the ground as he came around to face the people again. Dancing in place, he had suddenly thrust his staff and the sharp red claws of the jaguar paw into the air over his head, shaking them at the sky and letting out a loud, piercing cry that echoed in answer to itself off the stone walls of the surrounding temples.

"Is that you, Kanan Naab?" a voice asked, and the girl came out of her reverie to see Ixchel coming toward her along the terrace. Lulled by the memory of her grandfather's dance, she smiled up at her stepmother, who stopped in front of the bench, regarding Kanan Naab with concern.

"Are you ill, my child?" Ixchel asked, and Kanan Naab smiled again, touched by the older woman's solicitude, however misplaced it seemed. Only seven years separated them in age, and Ixchel was in fact a year younger than her stepson Kinich Kakmoo, which did not contribute to her authority in a house still ruled by the spirit of Ik Caan. Childless after five years of marriage to Pacal, Ixchel was seldom capable of sustaining a motherly attitude toward her stepchildren, even when they were genuinely ill. On an impulse, Kanan Naab patted the bench beside her.

"Come sit with me, Ixchel," she coaxed. "It is cool here in the shade."

Ixchel cocked her head quizzically, her thin lips moving silently as she hesitated over the offer. She had a long, narrow face that was not unattractive in repose, whenever Ixchel could muster the confidence to let herself relax. Though she was not relaxed at the moment, she did allow herself to accept a seat on the bench next to Kanan Naab.

"Are the flowers not beautiful?" Kanan Naab suggested gently. "And their smell!"

"Yes, it is very nice here," Ixchel agreed, ducking instinctively as a hummingbird buzzed past overhead, nearly touching the plaited coils of her hair. She smiled belatedly, holding herself still as the same bird returned the way it had come.

"They are very busy," Kanan Naab remarked. "Just as we have been. It is good to rest here and replenish ourselves."

Ixchel nodded, tilting her head back to gaze up at the cloud of cherry blossoms that hung over them. Her nostrils flared, drinking in the sweet aroma, and she closed her eyes for a moment, as if to savor the smell more deeply. Yet Kanan Naab could feel the tension beginning to reassert its hold on Ixchel's slender body, and she saw the woman's jaw clench in resistance, her eyelids fluttering as she sought to keep them closed.

"You came to find me," Kanan Naab said quietly. "Is there something you wished to tell me?"

Ixchel's eyes popped open, and she released the breath she had been holding. She looked at Kanan Naab with gratitude and relief, her vulnerability erasing the difference in their ages, so that Kanan Naab suddenly felt like the older woman.

"You seemed so happy," Ixchel said wistfully. "I did not wish to disturb you at first. But the Lady Box Ek sent me to find you. Your father has invited Balam Xoc to dine with us this evening."

"But that is *wonderful* news," Kanan Naab exclaimed. "Perhaps they will finally settle their differences, so there can be peace in the clan again."

"That is my hope as well," Ixchel said without conviction. "But what if they argue instead? I could not stand to have another meal ruined by bad feelings."

"My grandfather would not permit such a thing," Kanan Naab assured her. "And we will make a meal too good to be argued over. Kal Cuc brought in some frogs today. I will have his grandmother prepare a stew with tomatoes and chilies."

"My father has just sent some cacao from our family's groves in Nohmul," Ixchel said suggestively, carried along by Kanan Naab's enthusiasm. "I will sweeten and whip it myself."

"I am sure it will be delicious," Kanan Naab said decisively. "Let us take some of these flowers as well, to brighten the house."

Leaning down, she plucked one of the delicate red flowers, holding it briefly to her nose. Then, detaching the blossom from its stem, she turned impulsively to Ixchel, revealing her intentions by holding the flower up to her own head. Spots of color appeared on Ixchel's high cheekbones, but she happily gave her consent, tilting her head so that Kanan Naab could fix the flower between the coils of black hair above Ixchel's ear. Then Kanan Naab held still while Ixchel returned the favor, and the two of them sat smiling and admiring each other like girls at their first feast.

"You are kind to me, Kanan Naab," Ixchel said softly, her whole face lit by the reddish glow of the flower in her hair. Stricken by a sudden shyness, Kanan Naab lowered her eyes from Ixchel's grateful face. She had only been following the impulses of the moment, and was not prepared for the effect she had had upon her stepmother. They had come too close too quickly.

"We are all in need of kindness," she murmured nervously, unable to meet Ixchel's eyes. To conceal her confusion, she rose and began to gather flowers, and was relieved when Ixchel followed her example without hesitation. *I am still afraid of this power,* she thought, *afraid of the way it makes others look to me for the strength they do not have.*

She bent lower over the flowerbed, choosing only the largest, most perfect blossoms. Tonight she would eat with her grandfather, who did not have fears like hers, and did not shy away from the dependency of the weak. She hoped that Balam Xoc would be as kind as she had claimed on his behalf, and would not spoil Ixchel's dinner. She hoped, with a fast-beating heart, that he would notice her, and perhaps give her a sign, a small gesture, to confirm her belief that he had danced for her.

BALAM XOC held his sister by the arm as they walked the short distance from his house to that of his son, moving at Box Ek's hobbled pace and accompanied by the hollow tapping of her cane upon the pavement. Pacal and his wife met them at the door and exchanged the obligatory greetings before leading them inside, where woven mats had been laid in a circle upon the floor. There were clean cloths at each place, along with wooden bowls of water in which a single red blossom floated. Boughs of pink-and-white cherry blossoms hung suspended from the rafters overhead, and the bowls of fruit that had already been put out were surrounded by wreaths of red flowers and shiny green leaves.

"This is most beautiful, Ixchel," Balam Xoc said warmly. "And you look as radiant as the flower in your hair."

Ixchel beamed with delight and bowed deeply to her father-in-law.

"The flowers were Kanan Naab's idea," she said modestly. "And she has helped me prepare this meal."

"Then you are both to be complimented. Come sit beside me, my daughter," he said to Kanan Naab. "And you, Akbal, on my other side." He looked across at Pacal. "I see that you have not chosen to invite my other grandson."

Pacal hesitated for only a moment, then looked his father directly in the eye.

"I could not trust Kinich to control his temper," he admitted truthfully. "He is still very angry that you have forbidden the warriors of the clan from attending the ball game."

"He is not alone in his anger," Balam Xoc observed mildly, then allowed the subject to drop, turning his attention to the food the servants were bringing in. There was the stew of frogs' legs and tomatoes, still bubbling from the fire, hot yams with honey, maize dough mixed with chilies and greens, and breadnut cakes flavored with vanilla. There were also bowls of avocados, papayas, sapotes, and hearts of palm, and tall gourds of rich cacao whipped to a cool froth.

Pacal had been certain earlier that he had no appetite, but the smells alone filled his mouth with water, and he was soon partaking as enthusiastically as the others. He kept an eye on his father, though, waiting for Balam Xoc's mood to change. He had decided—since he could not defend the merits of Caan Ac's scheme—to be as frank with his father as the discussion demanded. The admission of Kinich Kakmoo's anger had been a test, and Balam Xoc seemed to have responded well. Pacal took a sip of cacao, reminding himself that the meal had only begun, and they were still a long way from the discussion that had made it necessary. But Balam Xoc's apparent geniality gave him reason to be hopeful, and he watched with fascination as the old man conversed with his grandchildren, drawing them out on the doings of their lives.

"There is much that you might learn from the old books," Balam Xoc was saying to Akbal. "Much that might help you decide about your stone."

"I have been working on the paintings of the monuments of the first Jaguar Paw," Akbal said with great seriousness. "They are very different from the monuments that still stand in the city. The ruler wears no feathers."

"You are observant," Balam Xoc praised him. "The wearing of feathers also came to us with the Cauac Shield people. It was a new source of wealth for Tikal, because the speakers of Zuyhua, for whom the Cauac Shield people were traders, treasured the colorful feathers of our birds. They paid us well in a fine green obsidian that has not been seen here in many katuns."

"Who were the speakers of Zuyhua, Grandfather?" Kanan Naab asked impulsively, ignoring a warning gesture from Box Ek. But Balam Xoc answered her quite willingly, as if it did not matter that she was a girl.

"They came from a great city far to the west of here," he explained, "a place whose name we no longer know. They established themselves first among the people of Kaminaljuyu, the city in the highlands to the south of Quirigua. They were worshipers of the rain spirit we call Cauac, and they carried a strange weapon that allowed them to hurl short spears with great force, just as Cauac hurls his lightning bolts in a storm."

"Did they also bring us the Count of the Katuns?" Kanan Naab asked immediately, but Box Ek interrupted impatiently before her brother could respond.

"These are not matters to be discussed in front of women," she contended, glaring at Kanan Naab. "What does this girl know of the Count of the Katuns?"

"Perhaps too much," Balam Xoc suggested cryptically. "She has lived all of her life under the prophecy of *this* katun, has she not? No, my daughter," he said intently, turning back to Kanan Naab, "the Count of the Katuns was brought to Tikal by the Cauac Shield people, who had the blood of both Kaminaljuyu *and* the Zuyhua. They were more like us than the Zuyhua, but they were still foreigners, people who had no ancestors."

Pacal listened to his father's explanation with amazement, realizing that he was speaking of events that had occurred in the previous cycle, over four hundred tuns in the past. So *this* was the basis of Balam Xoc's contention that the Sky Clan were descended from foreigners, Pacal thought incredulously. Yet he also noticed the rapt expressions on the faces of his son and daughter, and he could sense his wife's deep involvement as well. He glanced sideways at Ixchel, finding her lovely in her absorption, yet wondering what a woman from Nohmul cared about the history of Tikal. He recalled, with new misgivings, the ruler's assurance that Balam Xoc would not continue being persuasive.

"Enough history," Box Ek declared. "We should be looking to the future instead of the past. Have you given any thought, my brother, to finding your granddaughter a suitable husband?"

Balam Xoc gazed sympathetically at Kanan Naab, whose round face was dusky with embarrassment. Then he turned back to his sister, adopting a bantering tone:

"Is this a matter of concern to you, Box Ek?"

"We cannot begin too early with this one," the old woman complained gruffly. "She is difficult and perverse, and she thinks she is too clever for most men."

"No doubt she is," Balam Xoc agreed easily. "The blood of great rulers flows in her veins. If she were a man, she would be a priest like her uncle, or an administrator like her father, or perhaps even . . . the Living Ancestor."

He paused to meet Kanan Naab's shining eyes. "Why should she be any less clever than her ancestors?"

"Women have never ruled in Tikal," Box Ek retorted. "They have all had to find husbands instead."

"And so she will. But would you rush to dispose of our treasure? I have acted as I have in order to *preserve* the strength and vitality of the Jaguar Paw Clan," he added in a more serious tone. "This child is our life's blood, however difficult she may be. I would never give my consent to a match that squandered her gifts."

Am I to have no say in my daughter's marriage? Pacal wondered, and almost raised the question in jest. But he had heard that proprietary tone before— during the council meeting—and his father seemed no less certain of his rights in this case. He had silenced Box Ek and had simply overwhelmed Kanan Naab, who was gazing at her grandfather with the adoring eyes of a convert. *And who am I to argue with him,* Pacal thought helplessly, *when I am already in the position of having to beg for the services of my own son?* He remembered the high priest, Tzec Balam, asking him, months ago, to define the limits of the Living Ancestor's power, and he realized now, with a sinking sensation, that within the confines of the clan there were none.

Night had fallen with its customary swiftness, and torches were lit to provide light and keep off the mosquitos that had found their way into the house. Finally, the remnants of the meal were cleared away, and the conversation began to lag. Ixchel was the first to excuse herself, as was proper, and disappeared into the back room, smiling at Balam Xoc's parting compliments. Then Akbal and Kanan Naab received their grandfather's blessing and went out with Box Ek linked between them, Akbal carrying a torch to light their way. Pacal brought out long rolled tubes of mai, the smoking leaf, and ceremonially lit one for his father and one for himself. They smoked in silence for several moments, listening to the singing of the insects and the muted cries of the night birds.

"It was a most enjoyable meal," Balam Xoc said at last, blowing out a ring of smoke that hung briefly in the torchlight. "Perhaps now you will tell me what it is you wish from me."

Pacal blinked at his father's directness and drew on his cigar to collect himself. Everything he had heard tonight had convinced him that there was only one way to approach his father, and that he had to be as truthful as he had originally planned. Still, his stomach tightened with anxiety at the thought of what such honesty could cost him if his father betrayed him again. He glanced at Balam Xoc and saw that he was waiting patiently, his deep-set eyes hidden in shadow. *I have no choice but to trust him,* Pacal thought, and gave up on strategy, experiencing the peculiar, bracing relief of risking himself in plain talk.

He explained first about the proposed delegation to Yaxchilan and its relationship to the terms of trade. Without mentioning amounts, he described the unfavorable nature of the terms as accurately as possible, admitting his own dissatisfaction with the fact that they had been accepted at all. Nor did he make any effort to defend the concessions Caan Ac had made in return, though he presented them to his father in almost compulsive detail. Balam Xoc offered no comments, his attentive presence enough to keep Pacal talking. Soon all of it had been revealed: the appointment of Kinich Kakmoo as a nacom, the request of Shield Jaguar for a painter, Caan Ac's feigned refusal and his shrewd plan to use Akbal. Only the Ruler's remarks concerning Balam Xoc himself —a confidence Pacal did not dare betray—had been left out of the account.

Balam Xoc examined him narrowly in the dim light, then gestured with his cigar, drawing a red line in the air.

"Concerning this burial vase," he said abruptly. "Caan Ac said only that it had been done before? Yet he knows very well for whom it was done, since it was his own grandfather, Cacao Moon. The other cities, including Yaxchilan, sent their painters *here*. How is it that Yaxchilan has gained the stature to demand the return of this favor?"

"Caan Ac will make them pay dearly for the privilege," Pacal pointed out halfheartedly. "But even he cannot justify it. Yaxchilan is only one of the cities with which we trade, yet it is the most important to Caan Ac. He cannot forget that his grandfather came from the west, and that his ancestors helped to found Yaxche, Yaxchilan, and Ektun."

"He is sentimental," Balam Xoc said scornfully. "Did you tell him that there are other cities with which we might trade? Did you remind him of our long ties with Uaxactun, and Chakan, and Nakum?"

"He gave me no opportunity," Pacal confessed. "I was not part of the initial deliberations concerning Yaxchilan's terms."

"Because of me, no doubt," Balam Xoc observed shrewdly, and again gestured with the red-eyed cigar. "Where else will this delegation go?"

"Only to Ektun," Pacal said quickly. "They will leave in two months' time and will return in two, perhaps three months."

"You will have to see that Cab Coh is supplied with a replacement," Balam Xoc told him, and Pacal swelled with hope.

"Then you will release Akbal to me?"

"On whose behalf do you ask this favor?"

"My own," Pacal said hesitantly. "The ruler has asked this of me as a personal favor."

"He has not earned it," Balam Xoc said bluntly. "But of course I will grant your request. You are my son."

"But," Pacal blurted, then trailed off, unwilling to express any of the thoughts flooding through his head. They were all tinged with rancor and repudiation, and an ingratitude he could not afford to show.

"But?" Balam Xoc inquired sardonically. "Akbal is my grandson, as well. It will be good for him to visit Yaxchilan and Ektun. *You* will have to decide whether pleasing the ruler in this instance will be good for our city, or for you."

"Was it for my own good that you denounced me in front of the council?" Pacal demanded angrily, then caught himself and waved his hands apologetically. "Forgive me. It is ungrateful to argue with you . . ."

"I do not want your gratitude," Balam Xoc snapped. "I would *prefer* that you argued with me. Perhaps that is the only way you will learn to argue with Caan Ac. You have told me that you disagreed almost completely with his course of action. Yet openly you disagreed with nothing. How long can you live with your knowledge in silence, Pacal?"

Pacal glared at him combatively, but when he spoke, his voice was low and tightly controlled.

"Caan Ac could crush us if he chose. I am not certain why he has not moved against you already."

"And you would be my protection? Or would you be the hand that moves against me?"

Pacal reared up on his haunches, his face working furiously. Then he lost control of his breathing and began to cough, bending double and clutching at his throat in an effort to calm the spasms in his chest. Balam Xoc pushed a water bowl into his line of vision and waited while Pacal drank. Pacal stared at him reproachfully, blinking back the tears brought on by his coughing.

"I am not accusing you, my son," Balam Xoc said with sudden gentleness. "But I would like your answer. It will prepare us both for the future."

Pacal narrowed his eyes, grudgingly considering the implications of his father's insistence. Balam Xoc watched him expectantly, letting the possibilities of the future take shape in the smoke that hung in the air between them. Pacal sighed forcefully.

"I could never come against you," he said in a hoarse whisper. "You are my father."

Balam Xoc leaned back, gripping his kneecaps for balance. For just an instant—a flicker of the torchlight—he seemed to smile.

"I have not forgotten," he said simply. "See that Akbal is sent to me before he leaves for Yaxchilan. I will prepare him for his task . . ."

∽IV∼

THE TIKAL
PAINTER

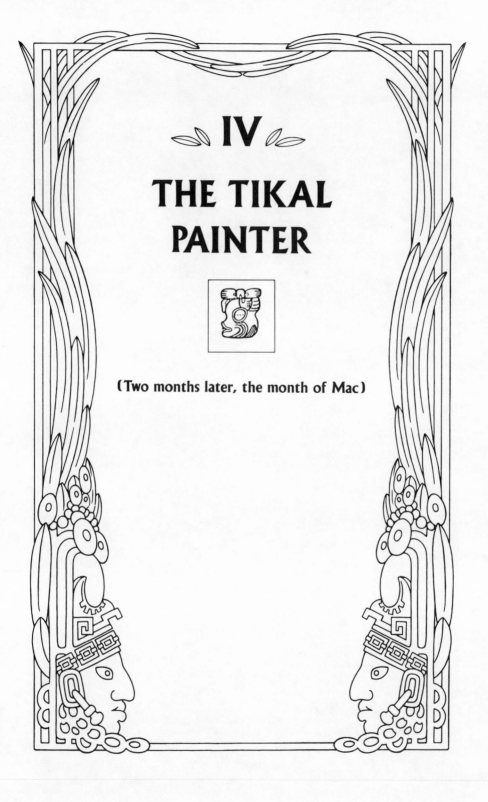

(Two months later, the month of Mac)

AKBAL was awakened by the shock of water dripping onto his face, and he blinked upward at the thin shroud of cotton netting that was tented on sticks above him. A large brown spider was struggling to make its way across the sagging mesh, which was sodden with dew and sank beneath the spider's weight, releasing fat drops of water onto Akbal below. Yawning, Akbal reached up a hand and casually flicked the spider away, causing the netting to bounce and douse him with the rest of its collected dew. Akbal barely noticed the wetness, though, for the blanket around him was completely soaked through and clung to him like a moist second skin. He had stopped thinking about being dry some days ago, when the procession of which he was part had left the last of the open areas and entered fully into the jungle.

The birds and monkeys had not yet awakened, and the only sound was the sporadic dripping of water upon leaves. Yet Akbal could see—in the brief open space over the trail—that the sky was just beginning to turn white, and a sudden excitement made him peel off the blanket and crawl out from beneath the makeshift tent. His breath hung in front of his face in a white cloud as he gathered up his blanket and netting and slung them over a shoulder, reaching into his pack for the pouch containing his washing implements. The other men of his party lay sleeping along both sides of the trail, some huddled beneath crude shelters of sticks and palm leaves, others wrapped in blankets around the cold fires. The sleeping figures lay along the trail in both directions for as far as Akbal could see, though he knew that the main body of the delegation was camped around the bend to the west, where the dignitaries and their wives were comfortably bedded down in the wayside huts maintained by the traveling merchants.

For the past ten days, Akbal had marched at the rear of the column with the craftsmen of low rank, sleeping in the open and eating meals of cold beans and charred meat. He had carried his paper and paints and extra clothing in a pack upon his back, his forehead chaffing and peeling beneath the unfamiliar leather band attached to his tumpline. Yet he had adapted with surprising quickness, and he harbored no resentment at being hidden away in the back of the delegation. The other men had been suspicious of him at first, but they had gradually come to accept the earnestness of his attempts to be one of them, seeing that he did not expect anyone to gather firewood for him or help carry his pack. They had not said much to him, but they had given him a place around the campfire, letting him listen to their songs and stories while the bats fluttered through the darkness overhead.

Giving himself a satisfying stretch, Akbal started back along the trail, feeling the excitement with which he had awakened expand inside of him, bringing a buoyancy to his step. A warrior with a spear stood leaning against a tree where the path to the water hole diverged from the trail, but he had seen Akbal coming and merely nodded in recognition.

"Your brother is ahead," the warrior said. "For your own good, do not come up softly behind him."

Akbal nodded agreeably, then paused in front of the older man, unable to suppress the cause of his excitement.

"We will be in Yaxchilan today," he said enthusiastically, and the sentry laughed at his eagerness.

"By noon, young one. Wash yourself well."

Shrugging at the impossibility of such advice, Akbal climbed the narrow path, immediately aware of the jungle pressing in upon him on both sides. He had never seen vegetation this thick and lush in the vicinity of Tikal, even in the alkalches, and this was the height of the *dry* season. Box Ek had forced a heavy-fiber rain cloak upon him, claiming he would need it in Ektun. And although it had not rained upon him yet, the sheer density of the undergrowth was evidence that it must rain here often. Trees grew around and on top of other trees, roots mingling with branches to form a latticelike wall of foliage, the trunks barely visible beneath the twining tendrils of vines and air plants. Giant ferns and plants with shiny leaves the size of a man filled the lowest story, dripping water onto the enormous yellow mushrooms that grew in their shade. A bluish-grey iguana scuttled off the path at Akbal's approach, making him think of Kal Cuc and of the success the boy would have hunting here.

A broad area had been cleared down to the water hole, which was green and still, with ribbons of white mist floating just above the surface of the water. Kinich Kakmoo squatted at the water's edge, splashing water onto his arms and shoulders, his spear and flint knife on the ground behind him. Akbal coughed to announce himself, causing Kinich to whirl quickly around, scooping up his knife in the same motion. Seeing Akbal, he stuck the knife, blade first, into the mud and stood up with a smile on his broad face, his jade and pyrite inlays shining in the growing light.

Akbal spread his blanket and netting out on the bank to dry and came down to stand beside his brother, who was regarding him with a proprietary air, his hands on his hips. Though he was a whole hand taller, Akbal had none of his brother's muscular girth, which always made him feel frail and weightless in the warrior's presence. And Kinich had the powerful Sky Clan features of their mother, whereas Akbal was the only one of Pacal's children to inherit his father's slender build and long, delicate features. Strangers seldom took them for brothers, and Akbal himself often forgot that his brother was only five years the elder, and not a man from another generation.

"You are up early, Little Brother," Kinich said approvingly, wheezing slightly through the broken hump of his nose. "Perhaps the life of the trail agrees with you better than you had thought."

Akbal ducked his head modestly, impressed by his brother's perceptiveness. Kinich seldom read him so well, though this was the first time Akbal had been with him in his true element.

"I did not sleep well at first," Akbal confessed. "But I have learned to ignore the creatures that move about in the night."

"Do not ignore them too much," Kinich admonished, scanning the perimeter of the water hole with practiced vigilance. "You will wake to find a snake in your lap, or a jaguar about to make you his meal!" Kinich paused and laughed, a wet, snuffling sound that seemed to bubble out of his ruined nose. "Though I have heard that you have no fear of snakes."

"People say many things," Akbal said, ignoring the taunt as he stripped off his loincloth and waded into the water up to his knees. Kinich squatted on the shore, hefting his spear with one hand and watching Akbal with apparent amusement.

"I am glad that you are so brave, Little Brother. You will be appreciated in Yaxchilan."

Akbal was scrubbing his shins and thighs with a foaming piece of soaproot, trying to remove the thick, yellowish grease that had protected him from insects while he slept.

"It will be good to get really clean again," he said, squatting down in the murky water to wash his chest and face. Kinich snorted derisively and scratched himself with one hand, his eyes roaming restlessly along the shore, as if seeking a target for the spear he still held in his other hand. Somewhere in the distance the howler monkeys began their morning racket, a hollow, booming roar that rolled across the treetops, awakening the birds.

"I was told not to ask," Kinich said in a muted tone, no longer teasing, "but perhaps you can give me some kind of hint as to why you were included in this delegation, and why you have not been given the place your blood deserves . . . ?"

"I have a task in Yaxchilan," Akbal replied with equal seriousness. "That is all I can tell you."

"I have not asked, then. But if you have been sent to pay honor to Shield Jaguar, do it well, Little Brother. He is a great ruler, and a captor of men. The leaders of Tikal would do well to emulate him more closely."

Akbal nodded absently, having already heard about Shield Jaguar from his grandfather, and in a much more critical manner. He remembered the charge that Balam Xoc had given him in parting: "You will be going among foreign people, my son, even though you share some of their blood. You must respect their customs and learn from them. But you will also have the opportunity, while in their midst, to discover what it means to be a man of Tikal. You must be aware of yourself, as well as observant, if you are to learn what you will need to carve your stone."

Akbal looked up from the water, realizing that his brother had spoken but he had not heard. Kinich was regarding him with the angry scowl of one not used to being ignored.

"I *said,*" he repeated loudly, "that for all the respect you pay me, I ought to walk away and let the crocodile eat you."

Akbal jerked himself upright and sloshed toward the shore so fast that he fell headlong at his brother's feet. Kinich sat back on his buttocks, snuffling with laughter.

"What crocodile?" Akbal demanded suspiciously, as he picked himself up out of the mud. Still laughing, Kinich pointed off to their right, where the end of a submerged stump poked up out of the marsh grass.

"*That* crocodile," he said emphatically, throwing a stone at the stump, which disappeared in a sudden swirl of green water. Akbal's mouth fell open, and he glared accusingly at his brother, who clapped him roughly on the back.

"I was watching him," Kinich assured him. "And I did not think he was big enough to take a man of your size."

"Why did you not warn me, at least?"

"I was admiring your courage, Little Brother," Kinich said mockingly. "I thought you were trying to impress me with your fearlessness. But come, do not look at me like that or I will start laughing again. Take my root and finish washing yourself."

Akbal gave him a last, sour look before taking the soaproot and returning to the water's edge. This time, however, he paused to scan the whole pond before putting his hands into the water.

"You are learning," Kinich commended him from behind, and Akbal looked back over his shoulder and nodded respectfully, acknowledging the usefulness of the lesson his brother had taught him. Then he began slowly to wash away the rest of the mud and grease on his body, fully aware, for the first time, of the dangers that often lurked just beneath the surface of things.

THE PROCESSION slowed gradually and then came to a halt, with the warriors walking back along the line to see that everyone kept their places. The men in the rear shifted their burdens and swatted restlessly at the flies, wondering how long the delay would be this time. Then word came back that the river had been reached and that the heads of the delegation were boarding canoes for the final leg of the journey. The men around Akbal immediately slipped out of their tumplines and squatted on the ground next to their loads, knowing that there would be no hurry to ferry *them* across to Yaxchilan. Indeed, the porters who were bearing needed gifts were brought past them and led around the bend in the trail, which hid the river from sight. Akbal had also removed his pack and resigned himself to more waiting, but then the warrior who had spoken to him earlier that morning appeared at his side and gestured silently for him to follow. The other men stayed where they were, seeming not to notice as Akbal shouldered his pack and went off with the warrior.

Once around the bend, they emerged into the open, blinking at the harsh glare emanating from a yellowish, overcast sky. The crowd of dignitaries ahead were talking and gesticulating, exchanging bows and greetings with the warriors who stood in paired lines, funneling the delegates onto the stone piers that extended out into the river. The warriors all held long spears with ceremonial obsidian points, and their tall headdresses were bright with parrot feathers and the long white plumes of the egret. Some wore the heads of cougars and ocelots as headdresses, and one particularly ferocious-looking individual stared out from beneath the curving tusks of a wild boar.

But Akbal was particularly struck by their faces, which were uniformly broad and aggressive: Sky Clan faces, though with exceptionally prominent noses and thick, pouting lips. He wanted to stand and stare at them, but the warrior guiding him pulled him away. They skirted the crowd and went down to a smaller wooden pier, where a single warrior awaited them, squatting on the dock with a hand on the canoe floating beside him. He gestured with his other hand for Akbal to take a seat behind the bow paddler, then jumped in lightly behind him, simultaneously shoving off from the pier.

The river was slow-moving and dark green in color, fading to a pale yellow as they drew away from the tall trees on the bank. It had the pungent, earthy odor of the jungle—the smell of pressed and rotting vegetation—along with the distinctive oily aroma of fish. Akbal scanned the water for stumps that might be crocodiles, but saw only some turtles with black-and-yellow-striped backs, sunning themselves on algae-covered rocks. Looking past the paddler in front of him, he squinted at the far shore, seeing several other piers jutting out from a line of low trees. Terraces rose from the piers to the ridge above, where the buildings of the city were stretched out in an unbroken line in both directions. Few were of more than one story, though many bore tall roof combs covered with stucco figures and designs that had been painted in vivid shades of red, green, yellow, and blue. This first ridge obviously extended some distance back from the river, but then the terrain rose sharply and irregularly, and more buildings could be seen along the sides and tops of the hills that overlooked the lower city.

The most impressive edifices were perched on the tops of the highest hills, which were discernible as hills only because of the groves of trees left standing along their steep flanks. Otherwise, with their broadly terraced stairways, they might have been mistaken for the great temple pyramids that dominated Tikal's hill-less horizon. There was one large group of buildings on a flat-topped hill to the north, and a single structure with a magnificent two-story roof comb that stood high above the center of the city, its three doorways facing the river. Slightly to the south and hundreds of feet higher up—on still another hill—three brightly painted temples loomed out of the mist that hung across the tops of the hills like a permanent veil. In an effort to get a look at these, Akbal leaned so far back in the canoe that the warrior behind him finally prodded him in the kidneys to make him straighten up.

Sitting up, he could no longer see past the first line of buildings, for the canoe was drawing close to the shore. But Akbal had seen enough to rekindle his excitement at being in such a foreign place. The flowing water and lofty hills were as strange and exotic as the faces and headdresses of the warriors, and Akbal gripped the taut edges of the pack in his lap, trying not to let the newness of everything confuse and overwhelm him. He had instructions from both his father and his grandfather, and a lesson learned from his brother that very morning, but keeping anything in his head at the moment—beyond the flood of impressions he was receiving—was proving most difficult.

They docked at a small pier to the north of the main docks, where Akbal could see the first members of the Tikal party being greeted by a long procession of dignitaries and warriors from the city. There was no one to greet him, and the warrior quickly led him off the pier and up the stairlike terraces that climbed the embankment to the city above. Akbal hurried to keep up, lugging the pack over one shoulder, since it would have been undignified to put on his tumpline. They skirted the edge of a temple that was painted completely red and entered a long passageway that brought them out onto a plaza. A tall stone monument stood upon a platform in the center of the plaza, flanked by stone crocodiles and surrounded by a number of round stone pedestals. Both the pedestals and the monument were carved and painted in brilliant colors, but Akbal had no time to make out their designs as he followed the warrior across the plaza and into another passageway between the buildings.

Then they were climbing, ascending from one level to the next by means of short flights of stairs, each of which seemed steeper than the last. Akbal was breathing hard by the time they reached the top, where three temples stood in a line upon separate raised platforms. Akbal looked back and saw the plaza with its monument far below, and a second plaza with more monuments farther south. But the warrior had not paused for breath, and he gave Akbal an impatient glance as the latter hastily caught up and followed him up the steps of the last temple in the line.

"You must wash and eat something," the warrior said when they had reached the top platform. "Dress yourself carefully, for you will be given an audience with the Ruler very shortly. You are to bring your paints and other materials."

"I will be honored," Akbal began, but the warrior had already turned away and started back down the steps. Anger flared up in Akbal, and he was tempted to call after the man and upbraid him for his lack of manners. Young as he was, he was used to being treated with more respect than anyone had shown him so far. But he decided to keep his peace, remembering his father's admonitions to be circumspect and avoid attracting attention to himself. He was a man of Tikal, but he had not been sent here to proclaim that fact.

Forgetting his anger, he took his pack and went through the central doorway of the temple, which was spanned by an uncarved stone lintel. The first chamber was long but not deep, and two doorways opened onto another room beyond. There were eight or ten men in this first room, all engaged in various stages of dressing and undressing, their clothing and jewelry laid out upon the benches that lined the walls of the chambers. For a brief moment, Akbal felt all of their eyes fasten upon him, scrutinizing his face and clothing and the dirty pack in his hands. Then they just as quickly went back to what they were doing, not hiding the fact that they were not impressed. They were all considerably older than Akbal, and the fine jewelry and elaborate headwraps that some of them still wore revealed both noble blood and high diplomatic rank. He stood uncertainly in their midst, looking around for an empty bench on which to deposit his pack.

"Here is a place," a man near one of the inner doorways said to him, moving his bundles to make a space on the bench. He was a short man with a round, pleasant face, and was himself younger than most of the other men, perhaps the age of Kinich Kakmoo. He spoke with a broad, drawling accent that seemed slightly familiar to Akbal, though he could not identify its place of origin. Akbal put his pack down and nodded awkwardly to the man, feeling that he should introduce himself yet reluctant to reveal his own place of origin in front of everyone.

"There are towels and water in the next room," the man added smoothly, as if the amenities could wait. "And there is food if you are hungry."

"I am grateful," Akbal murmured, and slipped past him into the next room. Here he washed himself thoroughly, including his long black hair, which he twisted into a fresh topknot on the back of his head. He had no appetite for the many dishes of food that had been laid out, though, and drank only a little cacao to calm the nervousness in his stomach. He was glad, when he returned to his pack, to find that the short man had left his bundles and was talking to another man at the far end of the room. He did not think that he could have escaped an introduction a second time, for his sense of what was proper was much stronger than the circumspection his father had urged upon him.

Bundling up his dirty loincloth, he took out the clothes his father had chosen for him: a dark red loincloth with a long apron in front, embroidered with his birthsign—Akbal—in black; a short red cape that fastened at the throat and covered his shoulders and chest; and a black net headwrap that he secured with slender pieces of bone, forming a stiff black cone around his topknot. He left his sandals in his pack, knowing that he was expected to appear before the ruler barefoot.

The other men were similarly dressed, the distinctions in their rank put aside with their jewelry and other insignia. And all held leather pouches much like the one Akbal removed from his pack and quickly inspected, seeing that all his paints, brushes, and paper were intact. Several warriors had arrived and stood just inside the doorway, and finally they announced that it was time and led the group out of the temple in single file, with Akbal taking a place toward the rear of the line. Again there was the magnificent view of the buildings and plazas below, and the winding green river in the distance. The sky had grown considerably darker, eliminating the glare but putting a moist promise of rain into the air. Akbal pressed his pouch tightly against his ribs to keep out the dampness, thinking of the fiber cloak rolled up in the bottom of his pack.

After descending several levels toward the plaza, they were brought to a long building with a red stucco frieze above its three doorways. The doorways were wide by Tikal standards and were spanned by stone lintels that had been carved in low relief and painted with colors that had lost their luster with time. As he passed beneath the central lintel, Akbal could see—with an ungainly upward glance—that there were two figures carved upon it, surrounded by rows of glyphs. But then he was inside the chamber, and heard the men ahead of him being announced to the man who sat upon a drum-shaped throne against the back wall, beneath a loose canopy of blue cloth.

Akbal did not have to be told that this was Shield Jaguar, the man Kinich had referred to proudly as the Captor of Macaw. He was a stocky man, with a deep chest and thighs so thick and muscular that he was forced to sit with one bare foot dangling over the side of the throne. His face matched the aggressiveness of his posture, with a huge nose that jutted out like the beak of a parrot and thick red lips that hung slightly open, revealing the white points of his filed teeth. Jade earplugs hung almost to his shoulders, and he wore a tall cloth headwrap that was banded with water lilies and topped by a single black-and-white muan feather. An additional spray of long, bluish-green feathers was attached to the back of the headwrap and hung down behind him in a limp arch.

Noticing that the line ahead of him was shortening, Akbal forced himself to listen, and heard the short man who had aided him earlier being introduced as Chan Mac, the representative of the ruler of Ektun. Chan Mac crossed both arms across his chest and bowed from the waist, and Shield Jaguar acknowledged him with a raised palm and a courteous nod, displaying obvious familiarity with the man in front of him. The representatives from Bonampak, Lacanha, and Aguateca were likewise presented, the last two going down on their knees in their desire to show deference to the ruler. Then there was no one between Akbal and the man on the throne.

"Akbal Balam, of the Jaguar Paw Clan," a voice intoned. "Ambassador of Caan Ac, the Sky Clan Ruler of Tikal."

Akbal's heart beat faster as he felt the attention of the room focus upon him, but he did not lose control or forget how he had been told to present himself. Very deliberately, he reached up with his right hand and grasped his left shoulder, and bowed with his other arm hanging at his side. Though no one made a sound, he could feel the reaction to his limited show of deference sweep through the room like an invisible wind. Shield Jaguar straightened up on his throne, his arms folded upon his chest, his black eyes glaring at Akbal from behind the flaring nostrils of his great, hooked nose.

Without intending to, Akbal met the ruler's gaze and held it, seeming to lock eyes with him in a battle of wills. But in his mind, he was drawing the man in front of him, struck by the transformation that had just occurred. The ceremonial stiffness had dropped away, and the real man had emerged in a pose that was dynamic and uncalculated, so much so that Akbal felt a moment's fear of physical violence. *This is the man I must paint,* he thought, noticing as well how young Shield Jaguar was, perhaps only in his late thirties. *Younger than my father,* Akbal reflected, *yet arrogant enough to demand burial goods from the ruler of Tikal;* no wonder Balam Xoc had referred to this request as a taunt.

Then Akbal realized that he was staring, and blinked, having no notion of how long he had done so. He did not think of time, or even of politeness, when he was capturing a subject with his artist's eye. Shield Jaguar was still looking at him, though with less open anger and perhaps even a hint of interest. Akbal decided to bow again, and did so in exactly the same limited manner, as if to underscore the fact that he was acting correctly, in accordance with the wishes of the man he represented.

This time Shield Jaguar raised a hand in acknowledgment, though his eyes followed Akbal as he went to take his place among the other men, some of whom had already taken out paper and were making sketches of the seated ruler. Akbal did not notice the curious glances he drew as he sat down with his pouch, and he did not pay any attention to the introductions that followed his own. He wanted only to get the impressions in his mind down on paper, and he made several quick charcoal sketches of Shield Jaguar's face and body before pausing to prepare his paints and brushes. Some of the other men had set up easels for themselves, but Akbal worked flat on the floor, painting steadily until he had achieved a likeness that satisfied him. Only then did he look back at Shield Jaguar, and only to note the details of his costume. The ruler's face had gone slack with the boredom of sitting still, and he no longer resembled the arrogant warrior who glared at Akbal from the paper before him.

The ruler left shortly after Akbal had finished, and the young man sprinkled fine sand over the stiff painted sheets, waiting patiently for them to dry. Most of the other men were still working hard, and Akbal examined them carefully for the first time, knowing that he would be sequestered with them for several days before their task would be completed. He was immediately struck by the fact that few of them held their brushes as if they knew how to paint. They dabbed uncertainly at the paper, their faces contorted with wishful indecision, as if guessing at the proper stroke to apply. The few drawings Akbal could see were crude and ill-proportioned, less than caricatures.

Then his eyes met those of Chan Mac, and the older man nodded and smiled at him, a quiet, knowing smile that made crinkly slits of his eyes above the round cheeks. It was apparent that Chan Mac was also finished with his drawings, and had observed Akbal's reaction to the clumsy efforts of the other men. Akbal did not know why this man should act so kindly toward him, but he was suddenly very grateful for the recognition, and he did not hesitate to return the nod and the smile. Chan Mac's attention warmed him and made him feel that he was not totally alone in this strange place, this city of warriors. *I do not have to hide myself any longer,* he realized, with a sense of relief that allowed him to feel, for the first time, just how tired and hungry he was, and how much the brief encounter with the Ruler had cost him. Looking back at Chan Mac, he pointed toward his mouth and stomach, and the man smiled again and lifted his chin toward the doorway, indicating that they should leave. Akbal immediately began to pack up his drawings, eager to test the possibility that had presented itself to him so unexpectedly, a possibility that no one had thought to warn him of beforehand: that he might find a friend for himself in Yaxchilan.

A FINE, misty rain was falling when Kinich Kakmoo staggered out of the warrior's lodge and headed toward the place in the trees where the men urinated. He had no trouble finding it in the darkness, for he had visited the spot many times already that night. He did not mind the rain, either. It felt cool against his skin, which was radiating an intense heat of its own, the result of all the balche he had consumed. The warriors of Yaxchilan were great drinkers of the fermented honey-water, and Kinich had matched them gourd for gourd as the boasting grew less restrained and the questioning of reputations more pointed.

He had now reached that state of drunkenness that always preceded the unleashing of his temper, a state in which his feelings were very clear to him, but had not yet overpowered his reason. He put his hand against the smooth, fissured trunk of a palm tree and breathed in the moist air, reflecting on the disappointment that had gradually overtaken him as the evening progressed. He had been filled with exhilaration upon his arrival in Yaxchilan, this city of warriors, where he had expected to be welcomed as a comrade in arms. He had been hearing of Shield Jaguar's exploits for many years, and for just as many years he had yearned to visit his distant kinsmen in the west.

At first, it had seemed that all of his expectations would be fulfilled. As the youngest of the Tikal nacoms, he had been singled out by the most ambitious of Shield Jaguar's captains, men his own age who had no desire to listen to the older warchiefs discuss their past campaigns around the fire. They were eager instead to make the wedding of Shield Jaguar's son the occasion for a joint war party against the Macaws, and they had recognized a likely ally in Kinich. Indeed, Kinich had already spoken to his superior about the possibility of just such a venture, and his enthusiasm had initiated the planning necessary to make it a reality.

He had thought that that alone should have been enough to prove his courage and willingness to fight, and he had entered into the feasting and speech making with an open heart, generous in the respect he displayed toward his new comrades. He had not been prepared for the way in which his generosity was repaid: for the envious questions about how he had obtained his rank, the toasts that were not returned, the snide comments about warriors who had built their reputations on ceremonial duty. It was true that Caan Ac preferred to display his power rather than to wield it, and that Kinich and his fellows had spent more time parading than fighting. But Tikal was four times the size of Yaxchilan and much older, and had long ago extended its dominance over a wide area. Though Kinich would have preferred more action for his own sake, he did not feel that Caan Ac should be belittled for his lack of enemies.

He should not be belittled under any *circumstances,* Kinich thought fiercely, feeling his anger beginning to rise. These people did not have the prestige to criticize the ruler of Tikal; they would *never* have that much prestige, no matter how many villages they conquered. He had a sudden urge to chastise them for their impertinence, and he turned back toward the lodge, his big hands clenched into fists.

But then he stopped short and turned his face up to the rain, letting it cool his anger. A brawl would not teach them the proper respect. It was better to ignore their pettiness and let his actions upon the field of battle speak for themselves. He suddenly remembered what his grandfather had said after persuading the clan not to provide the full quota of warriors to the ruler: "Tikal should not need so many warriors to defend her prestige." Kinich had violently disagreed at the time, but now he perceived a way in which Balam Xoc might have been right. Tikal did *not* need more warriors, if those that served the ruler were sufficiently brave.

They will see this when we go against the Macaws, Kinich vowed in the darkness. The thought that he was actually in agreement with his grandfather, though, left him feeling slightly puzzled, and dissipated the last of his anger. He was not even certain why he had recalled Balam Xoc's words, except, perhaps, that his grandfather's lofty tone seemed the appropriate one to take in regard to these impudent Yaxchilanis. Yet Balam Xoc lost no chance himself to belittle Caan Ac.

Kinich did not have the clarity of mind to resolve the contradiction, which persuaded him that he had had enough to drink for one night. Let them wallow in their envy, he decided contemptuously, bypassing the lodge and heading for his sleeping quarters. He would show them soon enough why the ruler of Tikal had given him the title of nacom, warchief.

"YOU THINK that I seek to flatter you, Akbal," Chan Mac said, "but I only tell you what is true. Your work is well known in the cities along the river, and it is especially prized in *my* city, Ektun. I had thought that you were certainly much older, for I have known of you for many years."

The two men were sitting across from one another in the doorway of the temple where they were lodged. A steady rain beat down on the platform outside, obscuring the view of the distant river and lulling Akbal with its drumming vibration. He felt stuffed with all the fish he had eaten for dinner —*fresh* fish, so wonderfully unlike the dried and salted variety he saw in Tikal —and the added pleasure of Chan Mac's company left him with no desire to move from this place.

"I have been working in the craft house since I was a small boy," he explained modestly. "But I think you claim too high a reputation for me. The merchants fetch good prices here for the pots and bowls I paint, but seldom as good as I can obtain in Tikal."

Chan Mac looked back at him steadily, his round face empty of expression, except for the subtly skeptical curl of his finely shaped lips. Akbal was a collector of faces, and he had already come to recognize the diplomatic way in which Chan Mac expressed his doubts. He straightened up slightly against the door frame, shedding his lassitude.

"We should remember that the Tikal merchants are all members of the Sky Clan," Chan Mac said obliquely. "In any case, there was a fine bowl that I bid on only a few months ago. It had a muan feather design and was said to be your work. I wanted it very much, as a gift for my father, and I was prepared to go as high as thirty pieces of obsidian. But I was forced to withdraw from the bidding when others began to offer jade as well as obsidian."

Akbal hated above all to appear naïve in front of Chan Mac, but he could not conceal the fact that his friend's revelation had jarred him. He opened and closed his mouth rapidly and then lapsed into silence, staring out at the rain.

"I am grateful for this information," he said when he had composed himself, but Chan Mac shook his head dismissively.

"It is only what is true," he repeated, then smoothly changed the subject. "Now you must tell me truly what you think of our companions' work. Would you say it is of acceptable quality?"

Akbal glanced over his shoulder, to be certain that none of the men inside could overhear. Then he looked back at Chan Mac, understanding from the veiled expression on his face—and from the way he had asked the question— that he was being sarcastic.

"I would say . . . that they will make Shield Jaguar forget the way *I* insulted him," Akbal proposed, and was rewarded by Chan Mac's throaty, appreciative laugh, a laugh that always felt like praise.

"They are aware of that possibility. They were chosen for their rank, not their artistic ability. You are the only true painter among us."

"You also know a brush," Akbal said sincerely, but Chan Mac hooded his eyes and shook off the compliment as if it could not possibly apply to him.

"My family still insists that our young men learn all of the noble skills, so I am adequate for this task. But few of these others are, and they are all very nervous."

"I am nervous myself," Akbal confessed. "Though more because of the way Shield Jaguar stared at me."

"Yet you stared back at him without fear," Chan Mac pointed out in an admiring tone. "You gained great stature among those who were there to witness it."

"You cannot be serious!" Akbal said in disbelief. "They have not treated me any differently. They have not even spoken to me."

"They feel that they underestimated you, and were rude. They do not know how they can ask you now to help them."

"Help them?" Akbal repeated blankly. "Why should I help them?"

"Does Tikal have more friends than it needs?" Chan Mac asked in return, a note of exasperation in his voice. "Do *you*, Akbal? No doubt you were told to act with a certain aloofness, but was that not meant primarily for Shield Jaguar?"

"I was told not to draw attention to myself. I did not *mean* to stare back at him. These men have misinterpreted what they saw."

"I do not think so," Chan Mac insisted. "Whatever your intentions, Akbal, you acted today like a man from Tikal. You have authority with these men, if you wish to claim it."

"I do not understand what you are asking of me," Akbal said doubtfully. "I was sent here to paint one vase, not ten."

"Yet your vase will be buried in Shield Jaguar's tomb along with the others. Do you wish to see your gift demeaned? Or would you rather use your talents in a way that brings you honor, and the respect of other men? You cannot paint for them, but you can teach them, Akbal. You have *that* power."

Akbal pursed his lips stubbornly, feeling that he was being manipulated. It was Chan Mac's occupation, after all, to be a diplomat, and there was no reason why that should not extend to the way he treated his friends. Yet he had to admit that Chan Mac's reasoning appealed to him, despite his reluctance to accept the responsibility being thrust upon him. It reminded him somehow of the commission his grandfather had given him.

"I do not know that I have the patience to be a good teacher," he complained halfheartedly, but Chan Mac simply smiled.

"Be an impatient teacher, then. We do not have that much time."

"We will need all of it," Akbal predicted glumly, though he smiled when Chan Mac laughed.

"Think of the alternative. Think of spending the next eight days with these men, and watching their anxiety grow."

"Think of *me* as their teacher," Akbal said sarcastically, and Chan Mac laughed again, his round face swallowing up his eyes.

"They will accept you," he said confidently. "Then will come the hard part: trying to persuade *them* that they are painters."

BEFORE he had left Tikal, Akbal had been permitted—at his grandfather's insistence—to examine the Sky Clan books in which facsimiles of the burial vases of Cacao Moon had been drawn. There were two separate scenes on each vase, bordered at the top and bottom by double black lines and set off from one another by vertical bands of sky symbols. In each scene, a lord sat upon a throne beneath a drapery canopy, and standing or kneeling to his right was an attendant of lesser rank, shown displaying deference to the lord. The attendant was the same in both scenes, but the lords were different, one being the ruler giving the gift and the other being the ruler receiving it.

The first thing Akbal did was to make his own copy of the scenes, using a separate sheet of paper for each scene, one with the attendant standing and one kneeling. He worked solely from memory, using black ink and a turkey-feather brush, which allowed him to paint quickly yet clearly. The attendant was himself, dressed as he had been for his interview with Shield Jaguar, his true height slightly diminished in relation to the men on the thrones. The two lords were Caan Ac and Shield Jaguar, rendered in a rather conventional manner yet still easily recognizable. Measuring with his fingers, Akbal reproduced the scenes in roughly the same scale they would have upon the vases, and he carefully blocked out the glyphs of the inscription that would encircle the rim, though he did not paint in the glyphs themselves. Each man had come with a funerary inscription of his own, drawn for him by the priests of his city and not subject to variation.

When he had finished and put down his brush, Akbal closed his eyes and sat quietly for a few moments before looking at the drawings again. He immediately grunted with dissatisfaction and reached for the sheets, but Chan Mac just as quickly grabbed his wrist. Only then did Akbal notice that the other men were gathered around him in a half circle, watching him work. Some were unconsciously mimicking his brushstrokes in the air as they stared down over his shoulder.

"Leave perfection for later, my friend," Chan Mac suggested, "when we have each made our own copy from this."

Akbal surrendered the sheets with reluctance, knowing that he would be forced to look at them for the next several days and would be regretting every hasty flaw over and over again. But he soon came to accept that providing the men with a model had greatly simplified his task as a teacher. His worst students made themselves apparent immediately, simply by the difficulty they had in getting started. Those with more promise or persistence had at least a place to begin, and would be well occupied with their preliminary drafts until Akbal was free to give them his attention.

Though he tried to confine himself to demonstration, letting his brush speak for him, Akbal found that sooner or later, every man had to form some kind of personal relationship with him. This was not always easy, for while most of the men were apologetic about their deficiencies as painters, a few were compelled to be scornful. Chan Mac stayed close at hand for the first few days, and Akbal learned from him, discovering that proud men needed to be listened to rather than impressed, and that even the most insecure man would resist instruction if he were not granted his self-respect. He also learned, from the way that Chan Mac chose to introduce him, that his mother's Sky Clan blood and his relationship to Box Ek—who had married into the ruling family of Ektun—made a greater impression on these men than did the ancient lineage of his father. They could only trace their own ancestry back some seven or eight katuns, and they seemed unable to conceive of a line that went back to the previous cycle, some eighteen katuns in the past.

As he went from one man to the next, Akbal came to rely less and less on Chan Mac for mediation, and he did not notice when his friend left him to go back to his own copying. By the time he had worked with every man twice, he had reached some definite conclusions concerning which of the men were capable of developing true skill and which could only be taught to copy, stroke for stroke, the master he painted for them. The only major hindrance to their progress was the incredible dampness, for it had continued to rain for the better part of every day, and the infrequent appearances of the sun only added to the steaminess of the atmosphere. The paint smeared and ran, forcing them to use charcoal, which tore holes in paper softened by the humidity. The walls of the vaulted chamber where they worked were beaded with moisture, and a furry, greenish mold grew quickly on anything that was not properly aired, including the garments and skin of the men. The oily smell of the river clung to everything, and even their frequent purifications in the sweathouse could not make them feel clean for long. Since they could not curse, they invented songs to sing in their moments of frustration, songs about rafting in paper boats down rivers of paint, with only brushes for paddles.

On the fifth day a group of priests appeared and asked that someone accompany them to the potters, to select the vases that would be painted. Though all the heads in the chamber turned immediately in his direction, Akbal had the presence of mind to wait for someone else to nominate him, and he was rewarded when several voices called out his name simultaneously. The priests did not conceal their surprise when he rose to follow them, for most had been present during the interview with Shield Jaguar. Akbal took his place in their midst with his head held high, buoyed by the knowledge that he had honestly earned the esteem in which his comrades held him.

Shield Jaguar's potters had prepared a large number of identical vases, light orange cylinders about one foot high and half a foot in diameter. As an aid to the painters, the black borders and the outlines of the vertical bands had already been painted on. Knowing how to converse with potters, Akbal questioned them carefully about the kind of clay and temper that had been used, and he examined each vase closely, rejecting those with rough spots or an imperfectly applied slip. When he had chosen the ten most perfect vessels, he joined the priests and the potters in a prayer for the cessation of the rain, for dry weather would greatly ease the task of the painters.

The rain did not stop until late that night, but Akbal used the intervening time well, giving the men their last instructions and having them participate in the preparation of the paints and brushes they would use. This was done according to a strict ritual that Akbal had learned as a child, but whose purpose he had not fully understood until seeing its effect upon these hastily tutored men. They sweated and frowned over the tedious grinding and mixing, and they resented his stern refusal to permit deviations from the customary routine. But when their neatly trimmed brushes were laid out in a row before them, and they had finally brought the thick clay paints to the proper consistency, their faces reflected the calm readiness that came from having confidence in their materials.

The high priest of Yaxchilan came to their chamber at sunrise, wearing his full vestments and accompanied by attendants who carried ladles of smoking copal incense. He called upon the spirits of Shield Jaguar's illustrious ancestors —the famous Bird Jaguar, and Shield Jaguar the Elder—to watch over the painters and bless their holy task. Then the vases were brought in and set down upon the bench where the day's new light fell most directly. The priest said a prayer over them, and each vase was smoked with incense and sprinkled with pure water that had come from the depths of the earth. With a last blessing upon the men, the priest and his entourage swept out of the chamber, leaving a cloud of greyish smoke hanging in the air beneath the vaulted ceiling.

In the long silence that followed, Akbal had the sudden intuition that this was the moment when all might fail; when the men might be paralyzed by the seriousness of their undertaking and overwhelmed by a renewed sense of their own inadequacy. He clapped his hands loudly, a sound that boomed off the stone walls and made the men nearest him jump in their places.

"*Paint,*" he commanded, waving his hands to distract them from their immobility. "But slowly, slowly. With patience and respect . . ."

He and Chan Mac distributed the vases, carrying some to their places for the men who were too nervous to handle them. Some of the men sat cross-legged on the floor, with their vases raised up on low tables. Others knelt on piles of mats in front of the benches, resting their elbows on the stone surface next to the vase. Akbal restrained himself from going too quickly to the aid of those who hesitated, though he ached to draw the first line for them and spare them the agony of beginning. It was essential, he reminded himself, that the actual painting be entirely *theirs.* There should be no doubt as to the source and authenticity of the gift. When he finally rose to help, he did not take a brush with him, and he kept his hands locked behind his back to prevent himself from picking one up.

Just after midday, Chan Mac took Akbal by the arm and led him away from the man he had been helping, over to the vase that Akbal had reserved for himself.

"You have guided us long enough," Chan Mac told him firmly. "Now look to your own task. Be the artist that you are."

There were murmurs of assent from the other men, and the grey-haired representative from Lacanha—Akbal's slowest student—held up his brush to demonstrate the correctness of his grip.

"See? We are all painters now!"

Akbal nodded encouragingly to the man, then turned all of his attention upon the pale orange vase on the bench before him. He had given no real thought to his own painting since the day of his interview with Shield Jaguar, and the prospect seemed at once utterly familiar and shockingly strange. He sat without moving, dizzied by all the experiences he had undergone since his arrival in Yaxchilan. The young man who had come here *only* to paint had been left behind somewhere. A different person sat here now, one who had commanded others to paint, and had been obeyed. A man of Tikal, perhaps.

"*Paint,*" a voice drawled sardonically, and Akbal smiled to himself, nodding in acknowledgment without turning his head in Chan Mac's direction. He reached into his leather pouch and removed the drawings he had made of Shield Jaguar. They were covered with a light film of greenish mold, but even this could not diminish the power of the images, the fierce, arrogant face that seemed to thrust itself at the viewer. Akbal took a deep breath, remembering the moment in which he had stared back at the ruler, seeing his true spirit emerge. He still did not know what had possessed him to stare, but it no longer seemed an accident, since it had given him exactly what he needed for this task: the ability to capture Shield Jaguar's spirit in paint.

Knowing better than to wipe them off while still damp, Akbal stood the sheets up to dry in the sunlight, which came strongly through the doorways out of a clear sky. Then he began to stir his paints, and thought no more about being a teacher, or an emissary, or a man of Tikal. He was simply the Painter, employing the gifts the spirits had given him, engaged in the task for which he had been born.

THE VASE stood upon the bench where Akbal had left it, its colors gleaming even in the dim, predawn light. Kneeling on the mats, Chan Mac turned the fragile vessel carefully between his hands, marveling at the smooth glossiness of its finish, which had been achieved without rubbing or polishing. The brushwork on the figures was meticulous, capturing every detail of their costumes and gestures, and the tiny, inset glyphs that identified the figures were as clear and decipherable as the larger funerary glyphs around the rim. Chan Mac understood completely why Akbal had considered his model a crude and perfunctory attempt. This was work worthy of any man's tomb.

His admiration for the craftsmanship occupied Chan Mac totally for several moments, but then his political instincts began to reassert themselves, and he turned to an assessment of the complicated political statement the vase made. Though he had done so in subtle ways, Akbal had intentionally altered the formal composition in order to reflect the superiority of Tikal and its ruler. He had painted himself as the attendant in both scenes, but in the scene with Shield Jaguar he had only one arm crossed over his chest in deference, while the figure facing Caan Ac on the other side of the vase had *both* arms crossed. Caan Ac also sat upon a throne covered with spotted jaguar skin, while Shield Jaguar's padded seat was painted with the patterns of cotton cloth. It seemed conceivable to Chan Mac that Akbal had been instructed to make these alterations, just as he had been told to limit his show of deference.

The figures of the rulers themselves, however, seemed to convey a different message. Shield Jaguar, with his arms akimbo and his foot dangling over the side of the throne, appeared almost excessively virile. He seemed about to burst out of his ceremonial garments, as if they were too small to contain the restlessness of his spirit. Caan Ac, in contrast, seemed almost effete. His rounded features were serenely composed, and one hand was gracefully extended with the thumb and forefinger just touching, the ancient gesture denoting the ruler's satisfaction.

As the vase was turned, the two rulers confronted each other, the ambitious warrior of Yaxchilan glaring aggressively at the refined, imperturbable nobility of Tikal. Akbal's intentions in creating the contrast so vividly were less clear to Chan Mac, and made him wonder briefly if his young friend were capable of deliberately slighting his own ruler. He had heard rumors that Caan Ac was receiving opposition from the other Tikal clans, and he himself had informed Akbal that he was being cheated by the merchants of the Sky Clan.

But Chan Mac rejected the possibility as quickly as it had occurred to him. He could not have misread Akbal's character so badly, and indeed, a closer look at the vase confirmed his belief in his friend's innocence. There was a kind of power and self-assurance in Caan Ac's tranquillity that muted the contrast, and rescued him from seeming fatuous. He was unaffected, truly oblivious of Shield Jaguar's aggrandizing posture, as if he were above even the recognition of threat. It was suddenly clear to Chan Mac that Akbal shared the lofty obliviousness of his ruler, and therefore did not see it as weakness. He *experienced* this, Chan Mac decided, remembering Akbal's surprise at hearing that his staring had been interpreted as an act of courage. The vase was simply an honest portrayal of that experience, painted by a man who did not suffer from a need for glorification. To Chan Mac, that kind of honesty was a rare and extraordinary thing, and made him proud of the instinct that had led him to cultivate Akbal's friendship in the first place.

Rising to his feet, Chan Mac stepped around the sleeping men on the floor, seeing that Akbal was not among them. He was not surprised by this, even though Akbal had stayed up long into the night, not resting until all of the vases were completed. He had been exhausted and bleary-eyed at the end, his voice reduced to a mere whisper. Yet he had insisted on going out to look at the stars afterward, and probably would have stayed awake to greet the Sun if Chan Mac had not dragged him in to his blankets. Then of course he had immediately fallen asleep, lying like one of the dead.

Chan Mac found him sitting cross-legged at the edge of the temple platform, watching the sun break over the trees to the east. The river and the city below were still shrouded in sheaths of mist, which curled and dissolved in the air like smoke. Chan Mac quietly sat down beside him, and Akbal turned to him with a face that was pinched and haggard with fatigue, the dark circles under his bloodshot eyes making him look years older.

"It is so good to be finished," he said hoarsely. "I could not sleep any longer, thinking of all the things I have not seen here."

"Once Shield Jaguar sees your vase," Chan Mac assured him, "I am sure that you will be permitted a tour. I must warn you, though, that I am less certain of how your accomplishment will be received in Tikal. Your portrait of Caan Ac might inspire some controversy."

Akbal squinted at him thoughtfully, then shrugged. His voice was a painful rasp.

"Shield Jaguar's request was a provocation, and I was Caan Ac's response. My father should never have thought that I could avoid attracting attention to myself. My grandfather knew that this could not be done quietly."

"Was it your grandfather who instructed you in what to paint?" Chan Mac asked curiously, and Akbal looked back over the city, smiling to himself.

"He spoke to me for a long time, and he saw that I was given access to the drawings of Cacao Moon's vases. But he never gives me instructions; he only suggests."

"You have honored his trust in you, then," Chan Mac concluded admiringly. "You have created an offering commensurate with Tikal's prestige and power. You need not defend it to anyone."

Akbal nodded as if he knew this, glancing up as a yellow-breasted toucan flew past overhead, emitting croaking sounds between rapid beats of its short, black wings. The roar of the howler monkeys reverberated from the hilltops behind them, welcoming the appearance of the sun. Akbal yawned, involuntarily hooding his eyes.

"Perhaps you should try to sleep some more," Chan Mac suggested. "We must present our vases this afternoon, and the wedding of Shield Jaguar's son begins tomorrow. You must eat more as well, my friend. You seem thinner than when you first came here."

Akbal gave a short laugh that seemed to hurt his throat.

"Would you be my mother, then?" he whispered harshly, and Chan Mac smiled at him with unconcealed affection.

"If I must," he said firmly. "When we are through here, I want you to be my guest in Ektun. I want you to meet my parents, and my wife, and my sister, Zac Kuk."

"I would be honored," Akbal assured him. "Perhaps I will have my voice back by then."

"Your exploits here will speak for you, and they will precede you to Ektun. But go and take your rest now, my friend. You have earned it, and Yaxchilan will still be here when you awaken."

"No doubt," Akbal concurred, taking a last look at the sun as he rose to his feet. He inclined his long, elegant head in that direction, bowing toward Tikal.

"Finished," he murmured softly, and started back toward the temple on unsteady legs, surrendering at last to his weariness.

V

ALLIES
AND ADVERSARIES

THE **WAR** party left Yaxchilan while the wedding celebration was still in progress, responding to news that a group of Macaws had been seen in the vicinity of Shield Jaguar's recently captured cacao orchard. There were a hundred warriors in ten canoes, the majority from Yaxchilan, though Tikal had contributed fifteen men from its honor guard, and Bonampak and Yaxche five each. Kinich Kakmoo rode in the lead canoe with four of his best men behind him, and beside him was the Yaxchilani warchief, Keken Ahau, with four of his captains. All of them wore quilted cotton armor and crested battle helmets, and the bottom of the dugout canoe was filled with their shields, spears, and war clubs.

They went downstream—north—along the river, portaging around the dangerous rapids that lay above Yaxchilan. It was the first of several arduous portages they would be forced to make, for many stretches of the river were barely navigable during the dry season, despite the intermittent rains. Often the warriors simply disembarked and made their way along the muddy shore while the paddlers maneuvered the empty canoes past rocks and sandbars, pushing off with their notched paddles.

They passed the city of Ektun, on the eastern bank, but did not deign to stop, since the ruler of Ektun had not seen fit to send any of his warriors on this mission. After four days, the river broadened and deepened, winding sluggishly around bend after bend, so that it seemed they traveled as great a distance sideways as ahead. Kinich sensed that they were getting close to their destination, though, and he decided that it was time he broke his self-imposed silence and learned the nature of his enemy.

"How many of the Macaws will there be?" he asked Keken Ahau, turning only his head in order not to disturb the balance of the canoe. His companion was a wiry man of about thirty, with a harsh, angular face and close-set eyes. His upper lip had been tattooed with black, hairlike lines, a marking that Kinich had learned was a sign of status among the Yaxchilan warriors. In keeping with his name, Boar Lord, Keken Ahau wore the tusked head of a peccary atop his wicker helmet.

"Not more than thirty or forty," the warchief replied, raising his eyebrows slightly at the abruptness of the question. "They seldom send out more than that on a raiding party."

"No more?" Kinich queried. "Is this not their own territory?"

Keken Ahau shook his head curtly, causing the bristles to rise on the boar's head above his own.

"Their territory is somewhere farther north; none of us has ever seen it. The orchard belonged to the city of Budsilha until two years ago, when the Macaws took it in a raid."

"Who defends it now?"

"We left a garrison of twenty men behind after we drove off the Macaws. They should be sufficient to hold off a raiding party until we arrive."

Kinich rubbed his chin and did not comment, though he wondered at Keken Ahau's certainty. If they had never even seen the cities of their enemy, how could they be so sure the Macaws would not return in greater numbers? Kinich had always assumed that the title Captor of Macaw referred to the conquest of at least a city, if not more. Had Shield Jaguar based his reputation on chasing off raiding parties?

"How long have you been fighting against these people?" he asked, and Keken Ahau glanced at him sharply, sensing his skepticism.

"Since the beginning of Shield Jaguar's reign, early in this katun," he snapped. "Is there anything else you would like to know, now that you have chosen to speak to me?"

"Are they fierce fighters?"

"Not as fierce as the men of Yaxchilan," Keken Ahau muttered in an unfriendly tone. "But you will see for yourself soon enough. We are almost there."

Kinich turned back to the river ahead, ignoring the anger he had aroused with his questions. He had carried his own anger for too long, and with too much purpose, to allow himself to be provoked by mere words. He had controlled his temper and kept his silence throughout the time when the burial vases were being displayed and the Tikal lords were reeling with surprise and shock at what their Ruler had done. He had listened to the gloating of the Yaxchilani warriors, who clearly saw Caan Ac's offering as a surrender of prestige, and he had not raised his voice to dispute them. He had not even gone to see the vase his brother had painted. He had simply absorbed every insult, every humiliation and feeling of betrayal, every doubt he could not resolve, letting them feed his anger until it had grown into a quiet, seething rage, a fury that could only find its resolution on the battlefield.

As the canoes rounded the bend, the river suddenly opened out ahead of them, sprawling onto a broad, muddy floodplain. The Yaxchilani warriors in the canoe took up their shields and spears, and Kinich signaled his men to do likewise, feeling a familiar excitement begin to build inside of him. He straightened the helmet on his head, which he had been forced to borrow in Yaxchilan. Since his name meant Sun-Eye Fire Macaw, Kinich had always worn a battle crest of scarlet macaw feathers. But this also happened to be the insignia of the Macaws, and to avoid a possibly fatal confusion, he had procured a helmet topped with the black feathers of the chachalaca. He fully intended, however, to return to Yaxchilan wearing the fiery crest of the enemy.

The canoes turned in toward the east bank and entered a deep channel that had been cut into the floodplain, which in this season was slightly above the level of the river. The rich, alluvial muck was thick with matted marsh grass and gave off a powerful stagnant odor nearly as palpable as the clouds of midges and mosquitoes that hung over the water. The canal was choked with water lilies that wrapped themselves around the paddles and impeded the canoes' progress, allowing the mosquitoes to settle on their human cargo. Kinich saw the snouts of crocodiles poking up out of the shallows, and he clutched his spear in alarm when a striped heron rose screeching from a thicket of reeds.

The tall trees of the jungle appeared to be some distance ahead, but there was a lower and more even line of vegetation that stretched out on both sides of the canal at an earlier point, and Kinich gradually realized that these were the cacao trees. They were planted on long, raised fields perpendicular to the main canal, the fields separated by narrower channels that drained water from the canal. Keken Ahau signaled silently to the paddlers, and the canoes turned into the first of these channels, which was barely deep enough to keep them afloat.

"I do not like this," Keken Ahau said, as they clambered out of the canoe and onto the bank. "There should have been a sentry to greet us. We must spread out and go on foot from here."

Keeping his own men to his left and Keken Ahau to his right, Kinich climbed the bank to the ridge above, concealing himself as best he could behind the slender trunk of a cacao tree. More trees stretched out ahead of him, row behind row, their lower branches hanging about chest-high. Nothing could be seen moving in the open spaces between trees, and the only sounds were the whistles of the birds and the hum of insects. Keken Ahau waved a hand, and the men went forward in a line, descending the bank into the thigh-deep water of the channel and surging across to the next bank.

Still nothing moved. Kinich crouched behind a tree, causing water to drip onto the curled yellow husks of cacao pods that lay underfoot. Then he went forward again, taking the initiative from Keken Ahau, who dropped into the channel with a splash in his effort to keep up. He glared angrily at Kinich when they had reached the next ridge, but Kinich merely bared his glittering teeth in an anticipatory grin. All his senses told him that there was danger ahead, and he tightened the strap that secured his notched wooden war club to his waist, so that he would not lose it in the water.

They found the Yaxchilan sentry on the fourth ridge. There was a short wooden spear, perhaps only two feet long, lodged between his ribs, and his throat had been cut from ear to ear. Flies had already begun to gather on his naked body, which had been totally stripped of clothing and insignia. Kinich knelt beside him to examine the spear, which was slender and very hard. Nor did it appear to have been broken off from a weapon of the normal length. The nature of the wound indicated that the spear had been thrown, but Kinich could not imagine how something so light and short had been thrown with sufficient force to pierce the armor the man must have been wearing.

"What sort of weapon is this?" he said to Keken Ahau, gesturing toward the spear. The Yaxchilani briefly glanced away, in the direction from which the weapon must have come. When he looked back at Kinich, his eyes were hard and unrepentant.

"The Macaws have a weapon that allows them to throw these short spears with great force. It is like a sling, only made of wood. It makes them dangerous at a distance."

Kinich stared at Keken Ahau over the dead body, fighting back the urge to kill him. He had endangered the whole group—but especially Kinich and his men—by withholding this information, and he had violated every code that governed the conduct of allies in battle. Kinich abruptly turned away from him, passing word of this weapon to his own men and advising them to keep their shields up and their bodies low to the ground. Then he turned back to Keken Ahau, who regarded him sullenly.

"You are a fool," Kinich said emphatically. "I understand now why you have been fighting these people for fifteen years and have not beaten them yet."

Without waiting for a reply, Kinich hefted his spear and shield and signaled to his men to follow him, plunging down into the water and across to the next bank. He stayed low to the ground as he climbed to the top of the ridge, his shield extended in front of him. He saw something move out of the corner of his eye and then saw Keken Ahau rush past him, charging up over the ridge with reckless anger. Then something hit the Yaxchilani warchief in the leg, and he lurched sideways into the tree, flailing at the branches as he fell.

Instantly, the air was filled with war cries and flying objects, and Kinich saw one of his own men clutch at his shoulder and slide back down the bank.

"Tend to him!" Kinich bellowed. "And stay down!"

The scarlet headdresses of the enemy were visible between the trees, three ridges away, and beyond them a line of men carrying packs and bundles could be seen moving along the top of another ridge, hurrying in the opposite direction from the main canal. Their escape was being covered by the first line of men, whose arms rose and fell in whipping motions, sending spears flying with the long, painted sticks in their hands. Keeping himself flattened against the bank, Kinich hastily assessed the enemy forces, which numbered at least a hundred, counting the escaping bearers.

Ducking instinctively as a spear crashed into the foliage overhead, Kinich crawled over to where Keken Ahau was being tended by two of his men. The spear had hit him in the fleshy part of the thigh, leaving a deep wound that was steadily pulsing blood, despite the men's efforts to staunch the flow. Kinich put his head down beside that of the wounded man, who was breathing shallowly through his mouth.

"Is there another canal?" he asked loudly, to be heard over the screaming of the warriors. "Besides the one that brought us here?"

"That way," Keken Ahau murmured, gesturing weakly in the direction the Macaw bearers were heading. "Not far . . ."

Kinich pushed himself up and came to his knees behind a tree. He looked down the bank in both directions, seeing that all the men were looking at him, waiting for an order.

"They are escaping!" he shouted. "For Tikal and Yaxchilan, let us bring them down!"

Screaming their war cries, the men went over the ridge in a wave, ducking beneath the branches of the trees and plunging into the water with their spears held high. Kinich waved them down as they came up the next bank and were met by a volley of spears, most of which passed harmlessly over their prostrate bodies.

"Now!" Kinich yelled, and charged forward before the enemy could throw again. He got a clear view of them as he jumped down into the channel, and he saw that some had already broken ranks and were joining the fleeing bearers. Digging for footing in the soft mud, he surged up out of the water and threw himself upon the sloping bank, wriggling forward to see over the ridge. Then he was up again in an instant, bellowing at the Macaws, who were now in full retreat along the tops of the next two ridges.

"Run, you cowards! After them! Cut them down!"

With a running start, Kinich leaped halfway across the channel, going down to his knees in the muck but lurching back up again immediately, using his spear to keep his balance. He went over the ridge and up onto the next one before turning in pursuit of his enemy, who could be seen running ahead, weaving in and out of the cacao trees. One of them suddenly dove sideways off the ridge, struck by a well-thrown Yaxchilani spear, and the pursuing warriors let out a cheer as they ran along the parallel ridges.

Ignoring the branches slapping at his helmet and the burning pain in his lungs, Kinich pushed himself to a full run, his shield and spear held low at his hips, his eyes and anger focused solely on the red-feathered men just ahead. A rear guard of Macaws had stopped to throw spears back at their pursuers and had momentarily halted the advance of the warriors on the other ridges. They saw Kinich coming at them along the ridge where they stood in a tight group, and one of their number stepped out and raised his painted stick over his shoulder.

Kinich also raised his spear, but he knew he needed to get closer to use the heavier weapon, so he dodged sideways, losing his helmet in the branches but not slackening his pace. The Macaw hesitated, then cocked his arm again as Kinich burst back into the open, coming at him in a straight line. But Kinich took only two more strides before hurling the spear with the whole force of his body, sending himself sprawling in the cacao husks as he released. The Macaw released at the same moment but never knew that he missed, as Kinich's spear buried itself in his chest and bore him to the ground.

Stunned by the impact of his fall, Kinich nonetheless managed to raise his head, to see if anyone was coming for him. But the Macaws were all running in the other direction, with Kinich's men splashing across the channels to cut them off. Kinich forced himself to his feet, bending at the waist to draw noisy, sucking drafts of air through his mouth and nose. His knees and face were abraded from the rough-skinned husks, and there was a pain in his shield hand, which had borne the weight of his fall.

But there was still anger to drive him on, and he urged his tired legs into a jog, unstrapping his war club and swinging it to restore the circulation in his limbs. It was not enough to chase these men off; they had to be punished, and deprived of whatever they had stolen. That was how the men of Tikal would have it done. Kinich ran faster, seeing open space between the trees ahead, and the backs of fleeing men.

"Tikal!" he cried, and heard answering calls from behind him and to his left. He was still the closest to the enemy, then, which gave him new energy.

Suddenly the trees ended, and the ridge led down in steps to a long earthen causeway that ended in a wooden dock. Several canoes had already pulled out into the canal and were making for the river, but the pier was still crowded with men frantically trying to pile into the remaining canoes. Halfway down the causeway was another knot of men who seemed to be struggling with one another. Kinich paused until he saw his own men coming through the trees behind him, then let out an ear-piercing shriek that echoed down over the men below. The group on the causeway looked up and abruptly parted, shoving half of their number over the side. Kinich was already moving down the ridge as the men toppled in a line into the water, but he was able to see that their hands were tied to a common line, and he knew that his arrival had saved the last members of the Yaxchilan garrison from capture.

The length of the causeway was littered with discarded bundles and spilled baskets of shiny brown cacao beans, and the Macaw rear guard were diving off the dock to swim after the departing canoes. A few turned to fight, though, and Kinich flung himself on the first man who crossed his path, landing a heavy blow on the man's shield with his war club. The man tripped and went down, and Kinich was over him in an instant, his war club raised to strike. The warrior flinched, then let his own war club fall limply from his hand. Kinich kicked it away and reached down with his shield hand to snatch the brilliantly crested helmet from the man's head.

When he straightened up, he saw that the fighting around him had stopped and that other men were also standing protectively over their prisoners. Some of the warriors had righted a capsized canoe and gone out after the Macaws in the water.

"What about the men who were thrown over the side?" Kinich said to one of the Yaxchilani captains, gesturing back toward the causeway. "They are your own."

"They have been rescued unhurt," the captain replied. "They are most grateful that we arrived in time."

Kinich looked around at the nearest warriors, who were all his own men. Four of them, in addition to himself, had taken captives. He grinned at them proudly.

"Yes, it is good that *we* arrived in time," he said pointedly, drawing smiles from his men. Then he dropped his shield and handed his club to another man, and took the captured helmet in both hands. It was much too small for his huge, tufted head, but he squeezed it down over his ears anyway, his contorted face bulging out behind the narrow face guard. When it was painfully in place, he tossed his head gingerly, making the scarlet crest flash in the sunlight. The men around him broke out in approving cheers, and Kinich snuffled with laughter, knowing that he must look ridiculous but not caring.

"Now I am myself again," he declared, and stood over his captive with his hands on his hips, his feathered head raised proudly toward the sun.

THE TEMPLE of Bolon-ti-ku, the Nine Spirits of the Underworld, stood between two other temples on top of the highest hill in Yaxchilan. Its narrow, steeply vaulted central chamber was flanked by two small lateral chambers, one of which contained stuccoed figurines of the Nine Spirits, seated in a row against the wall. Akbal had been permitted to enter this chamber only once, with all of the temple priests in attendance, and the mysterious, baleful countenances of the Rulers of the Night had disturbed his dreams for several nights afterward. But neither that experience nor the long climb up the hill had deterred him from visiting the temple as often as he could, and he had spent four full afternoons here, drawing sketches of the monuments that stood on the terrace in front and studying the wonderful murals that covered the walls and ceiling of the central chamber. Always, he had ended his time by gazing down over the city below, committing its uneven contours and elevated landmarks to memory.

Today he had come to the temple without his pouch of paints and brushes, simply to take a final look. Straining his eyes in the dim, watery light, he drank in the details of the colorful scenes that surrounded him: scenes of battles and the arraignment of captives; of great public ceremonies and private acts of ritual bloodletting; of sacred dances and the awarding of honors. The figures had been lightly etched into the plaster and painted a basic orange-red, and then their elaborate regalia had been added using the full range of colors, even mixing colors to produce browns and purples for the more somber costumes of the priests. The events portrayed, Akbal had learned, were from the life of Shield Jaguar's predecessor, the great Bird Jaguar. Bird Jaguar's tomb lay buried somewhere beneath the temple floor, and Akbal had never quite been able to reconcile the vivid energy of these murals with the funerary purpose of the building itself. The forbidding spirits in the adjoining chamber seemed to sit starkly in judgment upon all this life, as if to render even its memory illusory.

There was nothing quite like this in Tikal, at least that Akbal had seen, and repeated examinations had not lessened his fascination with the lifelike quality of the scenes. The temple caretaker had explained many of the depicted events to him so that he could place them in time and compare them with ceremonies he had witnessed himself. Not that much about Yaxchilan compared easily with Tikal, but Akbal had been steadily refining the differences as he listened and drew, accumulating a record to help him remember all that he had learned.

Hearing the familiar voice of the caretaker calling to him, he reluctantly turned away from his contemplation of the murals and went to the central doorway, where the squat, elderly man stood pointing down at the river.

"The war party has returned, my son," the old man said, and Akbal nodded without speaking, peering through the steadily falling rain at the line of tiny canoes turning in toward the shore so far below. A piece of the main pier was just visible between two buildings, and though Akbal tried to locate his brother among the figures milling on the dock, it was impossible at this distance to make anyone out.

"Do you know this Kinich Kakmoo," the caretaker asked politely, "the nacom who led our warriors to victory?"

Akbal nodded again, grateful that he was still voiceless and did not have to respond. It was an affliction that had saved him many explanations in the days since his vase was revealed, and it allowed him now to keep his brother's secret, if that was what Kinich wished. Kinich had never come to see the vase, nor had he claimed Akbal as a brother, even after hearing him praised in public by Shield Jaguar. Akbal was hurt and baffled by his brother's attitude, which made no sense in the light of Kinich's professed admiration for the Yaxchilani ruler. He had expected his brother to be proud of the way he had paid honor to Shield Jaguar, just as he was proud of Kinich's recent success. But if Kinich did not wish to have his name associated with that of the Tikal Painter—as Akbal was widely known—then Akbal would not embarrass him by revealing their relationship.

"You will want to greet him," the old man said, holding out Akbal's fiber cloak and palm-leaf hat. He gazed fondly at Akbal as the young man wrapped the cloak around his shoulders and settled the conical hat on his head.

"You will soon be going on to Ektun, then," he said quietly, and shook his white head vigorously when Akbal tried to bow to him. "No, my son. It is *I* who am grateful for the time you have spent here. Few of our own young men come to this temple anymore, except to renew their vows as warriors. It is *only* because Bird Jaguar was a successful warrior that they still revere him. They do not pause to admire the monuments he left behind in his memory, or to study the history that is contained there."

"You have taught me much," Akbal whispered painfully, and the old man put a withered hand up to his mouth, urging him not to speak.

"There is much that is being forgotten in this city," he concluded sadly. "But farewell, Akbal Balam. I hope that you will return to Yaxchilan one day, and come again to my temple."

Stepping out into the rain, Akbal turned back briefly to bow in parting and then walked to the edge of the platform. There were three monuments on the platform just below, and then a short flight of steps that led down to a plastered staircase of gigantic proportions. The staircase was thirty feet wide and descended the hill in ten terraced sections, flanked for its whole length by raised stone pylons. Akbal let his eyes wander downward, past the limestone quarry gleaming wetly between the trees, the thatched houses clinging to the sides of the hills, the tall temples and palaces that stood alone or in groups atop the high ridges, their roof combs thrusting into the darkened sky like painted hands. Below the largest of these—Shield Jaguar's own temple—the buildings of the lower city stretched out in both directions, following the curving green flank of the river toward the hills that bounded the city to the north and south.

As always, Akbal was thrilled by the fact that he could stand in one place and see *all* of Yaxchilan. Even from the tops of Tikal's great funerary temples, which all belonged to the Sky Clan, it would not have been possible to hold the whole of Tikal within one's gaze. Nor would Akbal ever be given the access to Tikal's buildings that he had been permitted here. He knew what most of the buildings below him contained, when they had been built, and by whom. He had drawings of sculptures that few Yaxchilanis had probably ever seen, and a knowledge of the city's history that even fewer—given the loneliness of the caretakers—cared to possess.

He had not intended to see and learn so much when he had asked to see Shield Jaguar's city. He had simply wanted to see some of the stone carvings in order to gather ideas for his own stone. But neither Shield Jaguar nor anyone else had ever asked him *why* he wanted to inspect their temples and monuments, as if his curiosity were a compliment in itself. And though he had not suggested it himself, it had been assumed that he would wish to make drawings, and the ruler had instructed that he be provided with all the paint and paper he required, as well as bearers to transport the completed drawings back to Tikal. After that display of royal favor, there was no priest or caretaker who did not wish to have him visit his sanctuary and to have him sit drawing silently while he expounded upon the rites and ceremonies commemorated in the carvings.

A trickle of water slid down Akbal's back, reminding him that he did not have the time to stand here in the rain admiring the view. It was a long walk to his quarters below, and he would have to begin packing his drawings immediately, since they would go back to Tikal without him. But then his gaze fell upon the monument that stood directly below him, in the center of the next platform, and he could not pull his eyes away.

The rectangular shaft of stone was twelve feet high and three and a half feet wide, and the side facing Akbal had been carved in two different depths of relief before being painted. The upper portion, in shallower relief, was filled with rows of glyphs that surrounded a square niche at the very top. Inside the niche were two small, seated figures, a man and a woman, whom Akbal had been told were Shield Jaguar the Elder and his consort. They wore ornate headdresses and appeared to be conversing animatedly.

Below, in deep, bold relief, was the standing figure of Bird Jaguar, to whom this monument was dedicated. He was wearing full warrior's regalia, with jaguar-skin leggings, jade pectorals, and a tall, feathered headdress. Attached to the front of the headdress was a grotesque mask of Kin, the Sun, behind which the face of Bird Jaguar could be seen in profile. He was holding a serpent-legged Cauac scepter over the heads of three men who knelt to his left, their arms crossed in submission. The Calendar Round date above, 1 Imix 19 Xul, Akbal had learned, referred to a date close to the end of the sixteenth katun, when Bird Jaguar had conquered three neighboring cities and laid claim to the rulership of Yaxchilan.

Akbal marveled at the dynamism of the scene, the sense of confrontation between the figures. Like the murals, it was without its counterpart in Tikal, where the monuments seldom bore the portrait of more than one figure. Some of the oldest Tikal monuments, from the beginning of the cycle, portrayed one bound captive, prone at the ruler's feet. But never as many as three, and never facing the ruler. And never, *ever* had Akbal seen a woman portrayed upon a Tikal monument.

These differences, once so startling to him, had come to seem almost commonplace, for women appeared frequently and prominently on the monuments and lintels of Yaxchilan. So did children, priests, captives, and allies, all portrayed in postures indicating relationship or submission. As Akbal had learned, the era of Yaxchilan's greatness had begun in the middle of the thirteenth katun, with the accession of Shield Jaguar the Elder. But the first Shield Jaguar had been a foreigner and a usurper, and despite his military prowess, he had relied heavily on the bloodlines of his wives to establish the legitimacy of his reign. These marriage alliances were thus as worthy of record as the ruler's conquests, and they were often commemorated on the lintels by graphic scenes of mutual bloodletting, a true "mingling" of bloodlines.

By an act of will, Akbal tore his eyes away from the brightly painted monument and forced himself to go down the steps and walk around the great stone, without pausing to examine the equally familiar carving on the other side. He decided that it was good that he would be going to Ektun soon, for the provocative, bellicose images of Yaxchilan had taken an obsessive hold on him, dominating both his dreams and his waking thoughts. The bloodletting scenes were particularly disturbing to him, seeming an inappropriate subject for public display. He needed to get away from this city of warriors and women if he were to attain any perspective on it.

Perhaps that is why Kinich shuns me, he thought, as he started down the great staircase. *Perhaps he feels that I have given too much of myself to this city and its ruler, and have squandered the respect of Tikal.* Akbal knew that there were others in the Tikal delegation who felt this way, who resented him more for what he had done *after* painting the vase than for the painting itself. As if he had flattered Shield Jaguar too greatly by expressing an interest in his city and making drawings of its monuments; as if it were somehow a disgrace to accept the almost unlimited access he had been given to the most sacred precincts in Yaxchilan.

Akbal clenched his hands beneath the protective cloak, angered by the pettiness, the willful ignorance of such an attitude. None of them could know the scorn he felt for Shield Jaguar the Younger, now that he had seen the few, poor sculptures the ruler had commissioned for himself. Nor could they know that he had spent the least amount of time in the most recent temples and that he had heard many criticisms of the current ruler from the caretakers who tended the monuments of his predecessors. *How can Kinich dare to judge what I have done here,* Akbal wondered, *when he is as ignorant as the rest?* Kinich had not even seen his vase, much less the stacks of drawings, or the gifts— like the rain hat—that Akbal had received from the other painters. Some of the gifts were tokens, as well, of private trade agreements he had tentatively arranged between their clans and his own. *Our* own, Akbal reflected ruefully. Wishing that his brother would give him the opportunity to explain himself, he continued down the staircase in the rain, toward the distant plaza where the warriors and their captives were being assembled for the ruler's review.

TWO NIGHTS later, as he was bundling the last of his drawings, Akbal heard a loud voice from the next room, followed by the typically accommodating response of Chan Mac. Stepping into the open doorway, he saw Kinich at the same moment his brother spoke:

"He is my brother. Has he not told you of me?"

"No," Akbal blurted hoarsely, causing them to turn in his direction. Kinich swayed slightly where he stood, breathing audibly through his nose. His broad face was flushed and sweating, and his upper lip had been marked with rows of tiny black lines that gave him a fiercely disdainful expression. He was wearing new jade earplugs beneath his macaw feather headdress, and he had a gourd of balche in one hand and a bundle of painted sticks in the other. Chan Mac glanced from one brother to the other, blinking in disbelief.

"I did not think you wished to be known as my brother," Akbal rasped, and Kinich grunted, lowering his eyes in acknowledgment.

"I had to listen to the gloating of the Yaxchilanis," he said thickly, "and to the warriors from Yaxche and Copan, whose rulers did not respond to the request for painters. Why had Tikal made this concession? And why was my own brother the one who carried it out? I had no answers for these things. None of the Tikal delegation had any answers."

Akbal regarded him with wary silence, unable to take his eyes off of the black lines on his brother's lip. Kinich swallowed and went on, obviously finding it difficult to explain himself.

"I asked tonight to see the vase you had painted, and Shield Jaguar showed it to me. He also spoke of how you had trained the other painters, though you were the youngest among them. I heard respect in his voice, and gratitude. I have never heard either when he has spoken of Caan Ac."

"I only did what was necessary, and proper," Akbal whispered. "I am a painter, as you are a warrior."

"Indeed," Kinich murmured in a rueful tone. "Shield Jaguar did not mention it to me himself, but others have told me how you stared at him, and would not pay him more deference than he deserved. It helped me to understand what I had seen on the vase, and what Shield Jaguar has chosen not to see."

"I witnessed it myself," Chan Mac interjected quietly. "Your brother brought honor to his city, and his clan, that day."

Kinich turned slowly in Chan Mac's direction, and he blinked several times before remembering his manners and executing a clumsy, belated bow.

"I am Kinich Kakmoo, nacom of Tikal."

"I am Chan Mac of Ektun, and I am well acquainted with your exploits against the Macaws. I was there when you presented your captive to Shield Jaguar. I see," he added, glancing politely at Kinich's upper lip, "that you have also been inducted into the warrior lodge of this city."

Snorting scornfully, Kinich ran a finger under his nose, smearing the black lines with his own sweat.

"I accepted induction," he allowed, "but I would not let them tattoo my skin. They may honor me as an ally, but I do not wish to be seen as one of them."

"No one here will make that mistake," Chan Mac assured him. "I would be honored if you would sit with us, and share the smoking leaf."

"I have brought balche," Kinich replied gratefully, but then looked searchingly at his brother, making it clear that he could not offer more of an apology than he already had. Akbal nodded hesitantly, then turned and went back into his room. He reappeared a few moments later, carrying a tightly rolled sheet of leather. He unrolled this and held it in front of his body, showing them the sketch he had done of Kinich presenting his captive to Shield Jaguar. It had been composed in the confrontational style of the Yaxchilan monuments, with Kinich and the ruler facing each other in profile and Kinich's captive crouching on the ground between them.

"It is only a sketch," Akbal whispered modestly, as the two men approached for a better look. Kinich smiled slightly, pointing a blunt finger at the row of tiny glyphs beside his own figure.

"That is the same Jaguar Paw you painted on the vase," he said knowingly. "And that is a macaw. But what is this glyph that precedes it?"

"That is the captor's glyph," Akbal explained in a ragged voice, and Kinich's smile broadened, making his mouth sparkle in the torchlight. Akbal let him look for another moment, then slowly rolled the sheet back up.

"I will paint it for you when I have returned to Tikal," he promised, tucking the roll neatly under his arm.

"You must have this, then," Kinich said impulsively, holding out the bundled sticks. "It is the weapon used by the Macaw I killed."

"I will fetch drinking bowls for this," Chan Mac offered graciously, relieving Kinich of his gourd. Akbal unwrapped the throwing stick and sharp-tipped spears and turned them over in his hands, listening attentively as Kinich explained how the grooved stick was used to hurl the short, dartlike spears. Akbal's eyes suddenly widened in recognition.

"It is the Zuyhua weapon," he breathed, and Kinich cocked his head quizzically at the unfamiliar name. Akbal shook the bundle impatiently, suddenly exasperated with his voicelessness. But the best he could manage was a harsh croak: "The foreigners . . ."

"Drink some of this first," Chan Mac instructed, returning with a poured bowl of balche. "It will loosen the tightness in your throat."

"Indeed," Kinich agreed, taking the weapon back so that Akbal could accept the bowl. "Drink all of it. You have learned things here that you must share with me. And I have been silent myself for too long."

"I would hear you both," Chan Mac proclaimed, taking the roll from under Akbal's arm so that he could freely lift the bowl to his lips. Akbal did so tentatively, conscious of his brother's eyes upon him. He had never taken part in a balche session, but he knew how the warriors drank down the sweet, intoxicating liquid, by the bowl, without pausing for breath. Closing his eyes, he tipped the bowl higher, feeling the amber honey-water flow smoothly down his throat. He gulped once and felt the heat that was already beginning to spread upward from his stomach. *Perhaps I will be sick later,* he thought, but resolved to drain the bowl anyway, just as he had seen the men do in Tikal.

Tikal

9.17.16.0.5 6 Chicchan 3 Muan

(A.D. 786)

THE COMPLETION of the sixteenth tun of Katun 11 Ahau occurred on the day 1 Ahau, and was observed in Tikal with all the requisite ceremonies, which were not as important or elaborate as the hotun ceremonies of the year before. The Jaguar Paw Clan, however, was besieged by pilgrims, some from as far away as Yaxha and Uaxactun, and the attendance by clan members from within and around Tikal was greater than it had been in years. The elders were forced to turn away many of the people who wished to witness the rites of the

Jaguar Protector, and still the crowd overflowed the limited plaza area in front of the clan temple.

Balam Xoc had announced beforehand that he would again dance for the people, and when he emerged from his confinement, he added yet another variation to the customary proceedings. The crowd was told only that the Living Ancestor intended to dress and perform in the manner of the first ancestors, and they did not know what to think when Balam Xoc appeared in the jaguar costume without the plumed headdress or the shimmering train of quetzal feathers. He seemed almost naked to them as he climbed onto his pedestal and began to reenact the journey of the Night Sun Jaguar. But when he had completed the prescribed rites and the drums had begun to pound in a dance rhythm, the crowd witnessed a transformation that gave sudden meaning to the absence of feathers. Balam Xoc's movements quickly rose to a tempo more suitable for a young man, defying both his age and the unwieldy nature of his costume as he danced in dizzying circles upon the stone, thrusting his painted jaguar paw at the sky. Those who had seen him dance before could barely believe the youthfulness and vigor of *this* dance, and could only conclude that he had freed himself from a great constraint by shedding his feathered regalia.

Five days after the ceremony, Balam Xoc received an official summons to appear that afternoon before Ah Kin Cuy, the high priest of all Tikal. Word of this quickly spread through the Jaguar Paw Clan House, giving rise to ominous rumors and speculations, which were carried along with the news by the messengers who hastened to the houses of the clan members scattered throughout the city. By the time Balam Xoc and Nohoch Ich emerged from the eastern courtyard of the clan house, an anxious crowd of over two hundred people were waiting for them in the plaza outside. Many were pilgrims who had come for the ceremony, but there were also women and children and old men, and even a few priests of low rank. The pilgrims, who had so recently washed off their fasting paint, had again blackened their bodies, taking up a vigil for Balam Xoc's safety. Others in the crowd had blackened their faces with soot in imitation, and some of the women had loosened their hair. They knew that the high priest was the second most powerful man in Tikal, and that he had sent those he considered heretics to the executioner before this.

The heat radiating from the plastered stones of the plaza was stunning, and perspiration streaked the faces of the waiting people. Nohoch seemed totally taken aback by their presence and took an unconscious step toward the doorway from which they had come. But Balam Xoc displayed no hesitation whatsoever as he came down the steps with his arms outspread, raising his palms to prevent the pilgrims from kneeling to him. He walked right into the midst of the crowd, touching the hands that were held out to him and nodding to the murmurs of "Grandfather." In the center of the group he found his granddaughter, Kanan Naab, who stared at him devotedly, her eyes shining out of a blackened face. Ixchel stood beside her, wearing the clean, nervous face of an uncertain chaperone. Balam Xoc reached out a hand and gently touched Kanan Naab's forehead, brushing back the loosened strands of hair. Then he looked around at the crowd and brought his fingers to his own face, streaking his temples with soot.

"I am grateful for your concern, my people," he said, raising his voice above their approving murmurs. "But you have no need to fear for me. The spirits of our ancestors are with me, and will protect me from any harm. It is *they* who have shown me the way I must act, and they will not accept me among them until I have completed my work here, among you."

Balam Xoc paused, and Nohoch came to his side, having finally worked his way through the encircling crowd. Then Balam Xoc gestured toward the Plaza of the Ancestors, which lay behind him, to the north and west, out of sight behind the intervening buildings.

"I must go now and speak with Ah Kin Cuy. I ask you to walk with me that far, in silence and dignity. I trust that you will do nothing to violate the decorum of the sacred precinct."

"This is not wise," Nohoch whispered urgently, but had to follow along when Balam Xoc ignored him. The crowd parted to let the Living Ancestor pass, then fell in behind him and Nohoch as they proceeded out of the plaza, past the last of the Jaguar Paw buildings. Their path skirted the edge of the marketplace and one of the city's ball courts, and the warriors and merchants crossing the adjacent plazas stopped to stare as the long, straggling line of blackened faces moved past in silence. Descending a broad flight of stairs, Balam Xoc led them past the ceremonial ball court that lay in the shadow of Cacao Moon's funerary temple, entering the Plaza of the Ancestors at its southeastern corner. One of the warriors patrolling the precinct moved to intercept them, then thought better of it when he saw the extent of the crowd, and went instead to find a superior.

Admonitions of silence were unnecessary here, and the people spontaneously formed themselves into tighter, more orderly ranks as Balam Xoc continued along the southern edge of the Great Plaza. To the north, across the vast expanse of the plaza, were the rows of ancestral monuments, some painted and some plain, and each accompanied by a round stone pedestal. Beyond and above the monuments, elevated upon an enormous, two-tiered platform, were the clan temples, standing upon high, pyramidal platforms of their own, their brilliantly painted roof combs rising skyward like headdresses. Flanking the plaza to the east and west—the directions of the Sun's rising and descent— were Cacao Moon's great burial temple and that of his mother, the Lady Twelve Macaw.

Since the south was thought of as "below," the long building facing onto the plaza from this direction had nine doorways, one for each of the levels of the Underworld. Stucco masks of the Bolon-ti-ku, the Nine Spirits of the Underworld, hung in a frieze over the doorways, from which the ruler and his priests would issue when reenacting the Sun's emergence from his nightly journey through the Underworld. Balam Xoc stopped at the foot of the wide staircase that led up to this building and turned to face his followers.

"Go back to your homes and work now, my people," he told them. "Go with the confidence that you have given me the strength to return to you. Go in silence and respect, so that nothing might be said against you."

Raising his hand over them in blessing, he turned and went up the stairs, with Nohoch close behind. The platform above was lined with priests who had been eyeing the crowd with disapproval and alarm, but Balam Xoc paid no heed to their glances as he strode past them and entered the central doorway. The narrow, high-ceilinged chamber was crowded with priests, whose presence made the darkened room little cooler than the outside. The high priest sat cross-legged on the bench against the back wall, flanked by his assistants on one side and by Tzec Balam, the high priest of the Jaguar Paw Clan, on the other. Ah Kin Cuy was a man some five years older than Balam Xoc, with a long, imperious face and heavily hooded eyes that gave him a deceptively sleepy appearance. After accepting the greetings of Balam Xoc and Nohoch, he gestured for the two men to sit before him, with the assembled priests closing in around them on all sides.

"I have summoned you here," the high priest said solemnly, "at the request of your kinsman, Tzec Balam. He has lodged an official complaint, protesting your deviation from the clan ceremonies."

Balam Xoc looked over at Tzec Balam without reproach in his eyes or face.

"I thank you, my son," he said quietly, "for providing me with this opportunity to express my views."

"You are here for much more than that, Balam Xoc," Ah Kin Cuy interjected harshly. "You are here to answer for the heresies you have been spreading."

Appearing neither moved nor offended by the accusation, Balam Xoc stared back at the priest for a long moment, allowing the silence in the chamber to deepen and swell, until no one seemed to be breathing.

"I am here because you summoned me," he said in an even voice, "and I obeyed out of courtesy and respect. If you wish to accuse me, do so formally. But do not try my patience with idle threats."

White showed all around the high priest's eyes, but he kept his temper, holding up a hand to silence the angry murmurings of the other priests.

"Defiance is not becoming in men of our age, Balam Xoc," he suggested mildly. "It belongs to the rashness of youth."

Balam Xoc looked at him and sighed audibly, as if his patience were indeed being tried.

"You know my age. Speak to me seriously, Ah Kin Cuy. For what do you desire an answer?"

The high priest leaned forward angrily and pointed a bony finger at the man seated below him.

"You have criticized the Count of the Katuns, and cast doubt upon the validity of the katun prophecy. You have stirred the people of your clan into rebellion against their ruler, and you have preached contempt for the rites that protect us all. Answer for that!"

"I have stirred my people to the memory of their own greatness," Balam Xoc shot back without hesitation. "I have told them to seek their protection in the rites of their true ancestors. I do not consider the katun rites to be among these."

Ah Kin Cuy sat back abruptly, holding up both hands to quiet the other priests, who could not contain their outrage and disbelief. Nohoch Ich raised an unsteady hand to wipe away the sweat that was streaming down his face, but Balam Xoc sat like a stone, oblivious of the storm breaking around him.

"You have a very long memory," the high priest observed drily, once silence had been restored. "Do you not trace your ancestry back to Stormy Sky, the founder of Tikal's greatness?"

"To him, and beyond."

"But you would grant that your clan prospered from its associations with him and his descendants, who later founded the Sky Clan?"

"That is true," Balam Xoc agreed easily, allowing himself to be led by the priest's questions.

"And you are aware that the katun rites were first practiced in Tikal during the reign of Stormy Sky?"

"So the Sky Clan has always claimed," Balam Xoc allowed, then suddenly went on, disrupting the line of questioning: "I have studied the ancient books of my clan, however, and I have found evidence that the practice was initiated by the *father* of Stormy Sky. By the man we know only as Curl Snout, because he was a foreigner, one of the Cauac Shield people from Kaminaljuyu."

Poised on the verge of his next question, Ah Kin Cuy seemed unprepared to be disputed on such a fundamental point, and he was momentarily speechless. The priests around Balam Xoc stirred uneasily, frowning at this denial of common knowledge, yet affected by the conviction with which it had been uttered. The books of the Jaguar Paw Clan were a reliable and highly respected source for all of the priesthood, and Balam Xoc himself had been known as a careful scholar before his recent surge of activism. Would he dare to contradict the high priest on a matter of historical fact if he did not indeed have some evidence to stand behind?

"This evidence will have to be examined," the high priest said finally, expressing his own respect for the sources Balam Xoc had at his disposal. "But in any case, you are resurrecting an ancient argument, one that was resolved long before our grandfathers were born. And in doing so, you only confirm the ancient existence of the katun rites."

"I confirm their *foreignness,*" Balam Xoc stated bluntly. "The mother of Stormy Sky was a Jaguar Paw woman, but it was not with *her* family that this practice began."

"You are speaking of events that occurred at the end of the last cycle," Ah Kin Cuy pointed out in an exasperated tone, "nearly twenty katuns in the past. Can you not admit that in the time since, we have made these rites our own, and have all benefited from them? Can you possibly contend that your clan has not shared fully in the fortunes of this city?"

"And in its misfortunes, as well," Balam Xoc averred. "The Prophecy of the Katun has become a burden my people can no longer bear. It is not *theirs* to bear. I have seen this in a vision given to me by my ancestors."

The men in the room seemed to suck in their breath simultaneously, hollowing the silence that followed Balam Xoc's revelation. Ah Kin Cuy's face tightened perceptibly, and he turned to confer with Tzec Balam in a low voice. No one moved in the chamber while he pondered the priest's reply, regarding Balam Xoc with renewed wariness. He seemed reluctant to allow this conversation to go on, given the unexpected turn it had taken, yet the hushed, awestruck mood exerted a pressure of its own, compelling him to respond.

"You have reported no such vision," he said lamely, frowning even as he spoke, as if regretting his words immediately.

"It is not my obligation to do so," Balam Xoc said forcefully, "until I am certain of the vision's meaning and authenticity. I received that certainty during my last confinement, when the spirit of my ancestor came to me for the second time. It was *she* who inspired me to dance without feathers . . ."

"That is enough!" the high priest exclaimed, too loudly, waving his hand through the air, as if to wipe away Balam Xoc's last statement. "I have heard enough," he added with more control. "Go now. I will summon you again when I have reached my decision."

"As you wish," Balam Xoc replied politely, and rose with Nohoch Ich to bow before the high priest. As the two men turned to leave the chamber, the priests behind them backed out of the way, and several of those near the doorway bowed respectfully to Balam Xoc as he passed. Then he stepped out into the sunlight and started down the stairs, his footsteps echoing softly in the great, enduring silence that hung over the Plaza of the Ancestors.

~VI~

THE FEATHERLESS DANCER

9.17.16.0.8   9 Lamat   6 Muan
(A.D. 786)

T HE CITY of Ektun was set into a pocket in the hills on the eastern side
of the river, which was swift and deep at this point, cutting a narrow
gorge between the high ground on both sides. The docks were at the
southern end of the city, which rose in successive levels in an easterly and then
northwesterly direction, its curving shape determined by the steep, broken
terrain. It reached its greatest elevation at its northern end, where a complex
of temples and palaces topped a hill overlooking the river, some three hundred
feet below.

The Tikal delegation arrived at the docks in the late afternoon, in the midst
of a blowing rain that obscured their view of the city above and made disem-
barking difficult and slippery. They were assisted out of the canoes by servants
holding palm-leaf umbrellas, and then were taken immediately to a long,
thatched-roof building with many doorways, where the ruler and dignitaries
of Ektun were waiting to greet them. After the guests had divested themselves
of their rainwear in the outer gallery, they were led into the adjacent chamber,
which was equally long and spacious and had as many doorways to the outside.
Streamers of red and yellow flowers decorated the walls and hung from the
rafters, and cloth-covered mats had been laid out on the floor to provide
seating.

As he took a seat in the middle ranks of the delegation, next to Chan Mac,
Akbal gazed around him observantly, listening to the tone of the greetings
being exchanged. He had missed the welcoming ceremonies in Yaxchilan, but
he remembered well enough the large number of warriors who had been

assembled at the docks. There seemed to be comparatively few among his current hosts, and none at all—at least none in uniform—among those closest to the Ektun ruler, Zotz Mac. Perhaps this accounted for the relaxed attitude of the Ektun lords, who seemed to find nothing improper in smiling and nodding to those they recognized in the crowd, even though the formal speeches had already begun.

Akbal ran his eyes along the line of men standing behind the canopied throne, fascinated by the sheer diversity of their faces. Some were round and smooth like Chan Mac's, some long and delicate and very like his own, and some had the blunt, aggressive features characteristic of the Yaxchilanis and the Sky Clan. Others—like that of Zotz Mac himself—were less easy to identify, seeming to blend a number of distinctive traits, each tempered and rendered less distinct by the others.

This diversity was consistent with what Chan Mac had told Akbal about the origins of Ektun, and the various peoples who had helped to found its greatness: the early emigrants from Copan and the highlands, the refugees from Tikal and Uaxactun during the last Katun II Ahau, the foreign merchants and warriors whom Akbal's grandfather had identified as the Zuyhua and the Cauac Shield people. All of these had mingled their blood with that of the original Ektun clans, giving rise to the wealth and power that had built this city, and to the clans that ruled it today.

The most prominent of these, Akbal had learned, were the Turtleshell and the Moon clans. The latter was also very important at Yaxchilan, and there had been a time, during the reign of Bird Jaguar, when the Yaxchilani ruler had helped to arrange the accession of a Moon Clan member to the rulership of Ektun. Moreover, this Moon Clan ruler had been the son of a Sky Clan woman from Tikal, a daughter of the great Cacao Moon. The Moon Clan did not hold the throne of Ektun at the present time, but Chan Mac had related this history to Akbal so that he would be aware of his own blood relationship, through his mother, to this powerful clan.

Chan Mac's own mother was a Moon Clan woman, but his father came from the Turtleshell Clan, one of the oldest and largest of the Ektun clans. The current ruler, Zotz Mac, was from a collateral line within this clan, the same family into which Akbal's great-aunt Box Ek had married so many years before. Akbal had been well aware of *these* relatives before he had even met Chan Mac, for Box Ek had made him memorize a series of greetings he was to deliver on her behalf.

For that reason alone, he was grateful that his voice had finally returned, though Chan Mac had also made it clear that he would not allow his friend to hide in Ektun. He had already described many of the people Akbal would meet, and had half-convinced him that they would all be as friendly and admiring as Chan Mac himself. Akbal wanted to believe this, and he constantly reminded himself of how well he had done with the painters in Yaxchilan. But he was still very nervous. The household in which he had been raised had become subdued and reclusive after the death of his mother, and had not been given to entertaining large gatherings. Akbal remembered leaving most of the feasts he had attended in the middle, anyway, to go off somewhere by himself to draw. As a result, the twin arts of conversation and gracious gesture did not come naturally to him, and both times he had worked on commission for the ruler he had found the rarefied atmosphere of the court intimidating and distracting. That was the major reason he had chosen to become Cab Coh's assistant, a decision he had only begun to see as another kind of hiding.

A stirring around him brought him back from his thoughts, to the realization that the speeches were finally concluding. Along with the rest of the group, he rose to bow once more before the ruler. Straightening up, he noticed that darkness had fallen outside, though the rain had not ceased.

"Now we will eat," Chan Mac said enthusiastically. "Now you will understand why I am not thin like you."

"You must be anxious to see your wife and family," Akbal said politely, concealing his own anxiousness. "Will they be at this feast?"

"*Everyone* will be at this feast. We would not miss the chance to honor our brothers from Tikal and their wives."

"Your sister will be there as well?"

"Yes, of course," Chan Mac said, observing Akbal's interest with a knowing smile. "We will have to lure Zac Kuk and my mother away from the Moon Clan feast, but they will be most pleased to meet you. I am sure of it. Only you must not be shy about discussing your ancestry," he added, as if sensing Akbal's need for advice and reassurance. "Especially around my mother and sister, you must not be shy. Let them know *all* of the important families to whom you are related."

Akbal frowned unconsciously.

"They might think I was boasting to make up for my lack of rank," he suggested, but Chan Mac shook his head sternly.

"You established your rank in Yaxchilan. You are the Tikal Painter, the favorite of Shield Jaguar. You would be more impressed with yourself if you knew how rarely he shows his favor to anyone except another warrior."

"Must I also boast of my ancestry, then?" Akbal asked plaintively. "It is not something I am used to."

"You will be, before tonight is through," Chan Mac assured him. "And you will find how pleasurable it can be, because my people are not envious like the Yaxchilanis. But they care deeply about a person's background. *Some,* as you will see, more deeply than others," he added significantly, taking Akbal firmly by the arm and leading him from the greeting hall.

IT WAS not until late in the evening, though, well after the food had been cleared away, that Akbal finally laid eyes on Zac Kuk and her mother, the Lady Muan Kal. Messengers had been sent to them at intervals throughout the meal, and always the word had come back that they would soon be coming over from the Moon Clan feast, which was being held in one of the adjoining buildings. Since Chan Mac's father, Batz Mac, did not seem concerned by the prolonged absence of his wife and daughter, Akbal had decided that there must be nothing unusual about it and had not allowed it to concern him either. There were enough new acquaintances to absorb his attention as it was, since the circle of which he was a part also contained Chan Mac's wife, Kutz, and his three brothers, their wives, two of his grandparents, and a constantly shifting assortment of uncles and cousins.

They had proven as considerate and attentive a group as Chan Mac had promised, sharing their favorite dishes with Akbal and explaining how they had been prepared, joking with one another while they gave their guest time to warm to their company. Akbal took an immediate liking to Batz Mac, who was even shorter and rounder than his son, with a large belly and heavy jowls that shook when he laughed. He personally made all of the introductions, proudly describing Akbal as the Tikal Painter, a designation that invariably drew exclamations of recognition and respect from his listeners. Everyone wanted to hear of his meeting with Shield Jaguar and his impressions of Yaxchilan, and he might never have found the time to eat had Batz Mac not intervened frequently, sparing his guest the pressure of sustained questioning.

Zac Kuk and her mother arrived trailing an entourage that included several servants and two well-dressed young men, both wearing the jewelry and head-wraps of diplomats. From his place next to Batz Mac, Akbal recognized one of the men as a high-ranking member of the Tikal delegation, a nephew of Caan Ac. The man did not see him, however, since his attention—like that of the rest of the entourage—was centered on the small, trim figure of Zac Kuk.

Akbal's first impression of her was one of great vivacity and enthusiasm, conveyed by a dazzling smile and wide, wide brown eyes. But he was also struck by the immaculate simplicity of her attire, which consisted of a blue, ankle-length shift embroidered with a yellow, braidlike pattern along the sleeves and hem. A single strand of tiny jade beads hung around her neck, and her shiny black hair was tightly coiled on both sides of a central part. Her face was a perfect oval, the family roundness offset by high, prominent cheekbones and a small, flat nose that flared slightly at its tip, giving her an aura of perpetual amusement, even when she was not smiling. This aura was accentuated by the thick lashes that framed her eyes, hiding the fold in her eyelids and giving her the appearance of being wide-eyed with surprise and pleasure.

Akbal knew that he was staring, and he knew that he should be paying more attention to the mother, who had scrutinized him closely when they were introduced. Zac Kuk had only given him a passing glance, and did not seem to be aware of his staring now. While her father was introducing the two men behind her to the other members of the circle, she bent to pay her respects to her brothers' wives, touching their hair or garments and smiling to show her admiration. Akbal was tantalized and intrigued by that smile, those wide eyes, the manner that somehow seemed in keeping with the neatness of her attire, despite the apparent spontaneity of her greetings. *She is undeniably beautiful,* he decided, but could a smile so easy truly be sincere? And why had she not smiled at *him*?

"You are from the Jaguar Paw Clan?" a voice asked sharply, and Akbal tore his eyes away from Zac Kuk to look up at her mother. A commanding presence, taller than her daughter, with the same high cheekbones and wide eyes. These eyes, though, were probing, calculating, innately critical.

"Yes, my lady," he said politely. "My father is Pacal Balam, steward to the Ruler Caan Ac."

"And who is your mother?" Muan Kal demanded without hesitation, giving no sign that she was impressed by Pacal's position. Out of the corner of his eye, Akbal saw that the others were all watching him now, but he resisted the urge to sneak a glance in Zac Kuk's direction and kept his eyes on Muan Kal's face.

"My mother has gone to the ancestors, my lady. She was the Lady Ik Caan of the Sky Clan, the niece of our late ruler, Cauac Caan."

Muan Kal pursed her lips thoughtfully, looking from Akbal to her husband, who gave a supportive nod on Akbal's behalf. Before she could ask another question, though, she was distracted by the sudden movement of Zac Kuk, who had turned to whisper something to the men behind her.

"Do not be rude, Zac Kuk," Batz Mac said sternly. "If you have a question concerning our guest, you should ask it aloud."

Zac Kuk smiled at her father and shrugged innocently, apparently unembarrassed by his reprimand.

"I merely wondered if the Jaguar Paw is not the clan of the Featherless Dancer," she said simply, glancing from her father to Akbal, as if it made no difference who answered.

"I do not know whom you mean," Akbal confessed, and Zac Kuk turned once more to the men behind her. It was the diplomat from Tikal who spoke, smiling at Zac Kuk before turning to Akbal, whom he regarded with ill-disguised contempt.

"Perhaps you have not heard the recent news from Tikal," he said disdainfully. "Balam Xoc, the Living Ancestor of the Jaguar Paw Clan, was brought before the high priest on the charge of deviating from the ceremonies. He had refused to wear feathers at the Tun-End Ceremony, claiming they had not been worn by our ancestors."

Several people around the circle laughed in astonishment, then hastily clapped their hands over their mouths when they saw how Akbal's face had paled.

"He is my grandfather," Akbal said tightly, staring back at the diplomat with hard eyes. He felt suddenly exposed, conspicuous among the much shorter men on either side; a "heron among frogs," as Batz Mac had said jokingly, earlier in the evening. Now it seemed not humorous, but painfully accurate.

Chan Mac, who was sitting directly across from Akbal, suddenly turned in his seat and looked up at the diplomat.

"My friend has not heard this news. Nor have I. What was the result of this hearing?"

"I do not know," the man admitted. "That is, the high priest has not yet announced his decision. It is said that Balam Xoc was very defiant, claiming that he had been inspired by a vision."

"So he has not been punished in any way, then?" Chan Mac inquired pointedly. "He has not been reprimanded publicly or removed from his office?"

"He has not been touched," the man conceded in a low voice.

"Then we must assume, must we not," Chan Mac pressed him, "that the explanation he gave for his deviation was acceptable to the high priest? Or at least not deserving of condemnation?"

"I do not know what to assume," the man said sullenly.

"Then you should not have spoken," Chan Mac snapped, and turned away from the man in disgust. He looked across at his father, who was shaking his head, saddened by the uncongenial turn the conversation had taken. Akbal sat stiffly upright beside him, his eyes hooded and his mouth drawn into a taut line, obviously not about to go on explaining his ancestry after the rude treatment he had received. Muan Kal and Zac Kuk were whispering urgently to the Tikal diplomat and his companion, trying to persuade them not to leave in anger.

Then a deep voice rose above the whispers of the women, and Kinich Kakmoo appeared at the head of the circle, accompanied by two older men wearing the distinctive red headwrap of the royal family.

"Where is my friend Chan Mac?" Kinich demanded gruffly. "I have come to meet his wife and family."

There was a moment of stunned silence while the people around the circle stared at the warrior, whose glittering teeth were exposed in a ferocious grin. Chan Mac rose to his feet and bowed gracefully in Kinich's direction, spreading his hands in welcome.

"May I introduce the Nacom Kinich Kakmoo, the man who led the warriors of Tikal and Yaxchilan to victory over the Macaws."

"We are deeply honored," Batz Mac asserted, bowing as far as his belly would allow in a sitting position. The others around the circle did likewise, each bowing a second time as Chan Mac introduced them in turn.

"No doubt you are all familiar with my companions," Kinich said when he had heard every name. He gestured toward the men beside him, then toward Akbal. "Except for you, my brother. Yet these are our father's cousins, the sons of the Lady Box Ek."

As he rose from his place, Akbal had the satisfaction of seeing genuine surprise on Zac Kuk's face, and seeing the Tikal lord look away when she turned in his direction. He went up to the two men and bowed deeply before them. Then he straightened up, raising himself to his full height, his youthful face suffused with the solemn glow of vindication.

"I bring you the humble greetings of your mother, my lords," he said in a firm, clear voice. "And the greetings of her brothers, the Master of Craftsman Cab Coh, and Balam Xoc, the Living Ancestor of the Jaguar Paw Clan."

"You need not be so formal," Kinich remarked, eyeing Akbal curiously. "I have already conveyed the greetings of our family, and told them of their mother's health. They wish to speak to you about a commission."

"Come, sit with us," Batz Mac interrupted, dispatching one of his wife's servants for more balche and cacao and waving to his sons to make room around the circle. When everyone had finally been reseated, the Tikal diplomat and his companion had disappeared, and Zac Kuk and her mother were sitting across the circle next to Chan Mac, listening while Akbal conversed with his relatives. The two men wished to commission a painted bowl to commemorate their mother's seventieth year, which would be completed in the year to come. They seemed to have heard a great deal about Akbal's vase, and not only from Kinich; apparently, the members of the Ektun delegation to Yaxchilan had been talking about it ever since their return. The men also knew of Akbal's other work and spoke flatteringly of its quality, claiming to own several pieces themselves.

"You are too generous in your praise," Akbal murmured, keenly aware of the attention of the women across from him. "I would be most honored to paint this gift for you. But I will not listen to any talk of payment; you must let me make this *my* gift to you."

The men insisted they could not hear of such a thing, citing their greater age and ability to pay, and claiming that Cab Coh—whom they both knew—would feel they had taken advantage of his young kinsman. But Akbal was steadfast.

"I am Cab Coh's assistant and have the authority to accept commissions on my own. Besides, my lords, you must remember that it was to help raise my sister and me that the Lady Box Ek left her family here to return to Tikal. She was your gift to me, once."

The men were too affected by the sentiment to argue the point any longer, and they raised their bowls of balche in an emotional toast, pledging their gratitude and friendship. Before they left to return to their own feast, they also made Akbal promise that he would visit their homes and meet their families during his stay in Ektun.

After they were gone, Akbal took another sip of balche to fortify himself before meeting the inquisitive gaze of Muan Kal. Chan Mac and Zac Kuk had moved a little aside and were having what appeared to be a rather heated conversation, and though Akbal was tempted to try to overhear, he knew he should not let anything distract him from what Muan Kal had to say. He felt he owed it to Chan Mac to make a good impression upon his mother, and the balche had long since broken down the restraints of shyness. He even felt slightly belligerent over the way he had been treated earlier, and he did not attempt to hide this from Muan Kal when he looked across at her and made a brief bow, inviting her to speak.

"You must forgive me, my son," she said quickly, as if she had had the words prepared for some time. "When we were introduced earlier, I did not make the proper connections. I did not understand that you were *the* Tikal Painter."

"Perhaps you had been led to expect someone older," Akbal suggested. "Your son and I were the youngest by far of the emissaries sent to Shield Jaguar."

"Perhaps," Muan Kal allowed. "I have surely heard the highest praise for your skill. You must be offered many commissions."

"I receive my share," Akbal said modestly.

"I am surprised that you have not been asked to join the artists of the royal court," Muan Kal observed shrewdly.

"I *have.* I chose instead to work within my own clan, which allows me the freedom to accept the commissions I find most worthwhile."

"But are not the best commissions those that are offered by the ruler?"

"Often that is true," Akbal admitted. "I am available, though, should the ruler desire my services."

"No doubt he will," Muan Kal said affirmatively, "after the way you performed for him in Yaxchilan. My relatives among the Sky Clan have told me of the deep friendship that exists between Caan Ac and Shield Jaguar."

Akbal looked at her sharply, searching for signs that she was being sarcastic. But she seemed completely sincere, and he understood that at least *some* of the members of the Tikal delegation had discovered an explanation for the concession Caan Ac had made.

"It was my privilege to serve them both," he said simply, hoping to put an end to this line of questioning. He was tired of being examined by this woman, who seemed always to be searching for flaws. And he was tired, as well, of being treated like a suitor when he had come here as her son's guest. The balche had enough of a hold upon him to make him want to say so, and perhaps Muan Kal sensed this, for she chose not to pursue the subject.

Akbal relaxed and reached for his balche bowl, then drew his hand back when he realized that Chan Mac and his sister had finished their conversation and were waiting to speak to him. Zac Kuk wore an expression he had not seen earlier, her lips clamped together petulantly and her eyes narrowed almost to a squint. Spots of high color gathered on her cheekbones, making the rest of her face appear pale.

"My brother has said that I must apologize to you," she murmured in a toneless voice. "It was thoughtless of me to raise an issue that might be embarrassing to you."

Akbal looked back at her, remembering the smiles she had bestowed so easily on others, including the diplomat from Tikal. Now she would not even meet his eyes, and the reluctance of her apology was all too obvious. He felt a strong surge of dislike and had to restrain himself from responding sharply.

"I was embarrassed only because of my ignorance," he replied, in what he thought was an even tone. "But I respect my grandfather's wisdom, and I do not like to hear him belittled. Especially not when he is correct. I have seen for myself, in the ancient books, that our most distant ancestors wore no feathers."

Akbal realized too late that his voice had risen, taking on a tone that was almost scolding. It was what he should have said to the Tikal diplomat earlier, but he had not had the presence of mind. Or the balche to loosen his tongue. Zac Kuk was quivering where she sat, her eyes wide with anger and humiliation. Akbal immediately regretted what he had done, but he did not know how to back down without seeming foolish.

"He cannot accept an apology he has not heard, my sister," Chan Mac prompted sharply, and Zac Kuk's head jerked involuntarily. Tears suddenly appeared at the corners of her eyes, hanging tremulously on the ends of her luxuriant lashes.

"Forgive me," she blurted in a strangled voice, bowing low to hide her face from him. The blood rushed to Akbal's face, and he spread his hands helplessly.

"Yes, please . . . do not . . ."

Her head still bowed, Zac Kuk was whispering furiously with her mother, who finally made an angry gesture of consent.

"You must excuse my daughter," Muan Kal said, as Zac Kuk rose and hurried off with her face still averted, trailed out of the room by two of the servants.

"I did not mean to humiliate her," Akbal said weakly.

"She has too much pride," Muan Kal asserted indignantly. "She can never apologize to *anyone.*"

Akbal stared at the doorway through which Zac Kuk had disappeared, then around at the rest of the circle, who seemed not to have noticed the incident, or were pretending they had not. Catching his brother's eye, Kinich raised his balche bowl in a salute from the other end of the circle. Akbal immediately did likewise, glad for the excuse to drink some more, and to try to wash away the memory of the tears he had caused.

PULLING the curtain roughly aside, Chan Mac let the morning sunlight flow into the bachelor's room, which was at the eastern end of his father's house.

Akbal groaned as the light fell over him and tried feebly to turn onto his other side.

"Arise, Akbal," Chan Mac said cheerfully, "it is late. I have already been to the palace to make my report to the ruler. He is sending someone to see you."

"Water," Akbal whispered, as Chan Mac knelt beside him and put down the tray he was carrying. He offered Akbal a steaming bowl, lowering his voice to a more compassionate level.

"Drink some of this instead; it will calm your stomach and soothe your throat. Water would only make you drunk again."

Akbal sat up groggily and took the bowl, which gave off a sharp, musty odor, the smell of bark and roots. The first taste made him grimace horribly, and Chan Mac laughed.

"It is my wife's preparation, and you will thank her for it if you can find the courage to drink it down. Or did you vomit out all your courage last night?"

"I will never drink balche again," Akbal vowed hoarsely, and forced himself to empty the bowl, shivering with every swallow.

"It made you bold enough last night," Chan Mac observed drily. "My mother was very impressed with your poise in answering her questions. She sometimes has an unnerving effect on young men."

Akbal belched and shrugged, frowning as if the memory hurt his head.

"I did not come here as a suitor, so I did not feel defensive. It is a good thing, too, for I doubt that your sister will ever speak to me again."

"She is not speaking to me today," Chan Mac said easily. "But she will get over it. Come, let me show you where to wash. You have to prepare yourself for Zotz Mac's representative."

Handing him a towel and a piece of soaproot from the tray, he led the way out into the sunlight, which was already hot. The rain had stopped sometime during the night, and the puddles left behind on the plastered terrace gave off wisps of steam in the glaring light. Akbal followed along obediently as Chan Mac left the terrace and passed through a small grove of copal trees. A descending series of V-shaped slashes had been cut into the trunk of each tree, and the thick white gum from which incense was made oozed slowly downward from V to V. The resinous aroma of the gum filled Akbal's nostrils and nearly made him gag, so he was relieved when they came out into the open again, onto a small, rounded bluff overlooking a ravine. In the center of the bluff was a shallow pool, a natural depression in the rocky ground that had been deepened to collect the rainwater. Spike-leaved yucca plants had been planted around the pool to provide a measure of privacy, and the pool itself was lapping over its edges from yesterday's rainfall.

Akbal quickly stripped off his loincloth and lowered himself into the water, lying on his back in order to submerge his entire body. Then a hand came down on the top of his head and pushed him under, and he came up spitting and squawking.

"I thought that would awaken some energy in you," Chan Mac said in a satisfied voice, laughing when Akbal splashed water at him in retaliation. Then he sat beside the pool while Akbal washed, telling his friend about his interview with the ruler.

"Zotz Mac was with the delegation in Yaxchilan," he explained, "so he had seen your vase and heard all about your work with the other painters. I naturally embellished upon your achievements, and he asked me to extend his congratulations, noting that you are related to his own family."

Akbal dunked himself for one last time and stepped out of the pool, reaching for the towel Chan Mac held out to him.

"Why is he sending someone to see me?"

"He had questions I could not answer on your behalf. He was puzzled by all the drawings you made in Yaxchilan. He wanted to know *why* you were so curious about the monuments, and I could not tell him. I do not recall that you have ever told *me.*"

Akbal sat down on the towel, spreading his wet hair over his shoulders to dry in the sunlight.

"I was not asked for a reason in Yaxchilan," he said, showing some reluctance to explain.

"If you do not *wish* to tell me—"

"No! I do," Akbal corrected himself hastily. "But you must tell me if I should reveal this to the representative."

"I would want you to speak honestly to him. Unless you were acting under an order of secrecy . . . ?"

Akbal shook his head in negation.

"I acted on my own," he declared, then paused and searched Chan Mac's face, as if afraid he might find some hint of scorn there. "There is a stone, in Tikal," he said softly. "I hope to carve it someday, in honor of my clan."

"Yourself?" Chan Mac asked incredulously. "You hope to carve it *yourself*?"

"I know it is strange, but . . ."

Chan Mac laid a reassuring hand on Akbal's arm, his eyes slitted in a smile of delight.

"Forgive me, my friend. Just when I think I have taken your measure, you prove to me that you are much larger than I will ever know. Ah, and my mother said to me, 'He seems very generous, but not truly ambitious . . .'"

"Then you do not find it a peculiar ambition?"

"Mysterious, perhaps," Chan Mac allowed. "But there have been stone carvers who attained high rank in Ektun, and not all so long ago. In Palenque, the home of my wife's family, the sculptors were of such importance that they constituted a clan of their own. Besides, I do not doubt your ability to master whatever craft you turn your hand to."

"Should I tell this to the representative, then?"

"By all means. Only do not ask him if he finds it peculiar," Chan Mac advised. "Remember that you are the Tikal Painter, and let him draw his own conclusions. You are not the suitor of *his* favor, either."

Akbal winced at the reference to Zac Kuk and looked away for a moment, as if pursuing a thought he did not wish to share. But then he shrugged, picked up his loincloth, and began to dress himself for the interview.

THE HOUSES of Batz Mac and his sons lay to the east of one of the ceremonial plazas, clustered on a narrow spit of land between a tree-filled ravine and a wider valley carved out by a tributary of the river. Stands of cedar, yaxche, and breadnut trees cast their shade over the long, rectangular buildings surrounding the single courtyard, which was wider at one end than the other. All of the buildings had thin walls and many doorways, and all except the family shrine—which had a flat masonry roof—had steeply pitched, thatched roofs.

The family gardens lay outside the confines of the buildings, but the barrenness of the interior courtyard was relieved by the presence of palms and flowering shrubs planted in large pots, and small trees growing out of earth-filled wooden boxes. One corner of the courtyard had been turned into an artificial grove, and it was here, in the lower branches of a fig tree, that Zac Kuk kept her collection of pet birds. These included a toucan, a pair of scarlet macaws, and several parrots of various sizes and colors. Sitting in the top of the tree, and tied to the trunk by means of a long rope attached to his collar, was a spider monkey.

When Akbal and Chan Mac entered the courtyard at its opposite corner, Zac Kuk was engaged in feeding her birds, attended by two elderly female servants, a small boy holding a basket of fruit, and three smiling young men, one of whom was the diplomat from Tikal. Following Zac Kuk's example, the men were taking turns in offering bits of fruit to the birds, laughing at one another's gingerly approaches to the loudly squawking pets. A pair of domesticated turkeys strutted around the edges of the group, pecking at the feed that was being dropped, and the monkey hung down by his long slender tail, chattering at the people below.

Akbal and Chan Mac stood watching this noisy scene for several moments before one of the young men noticed them and hailed Chan Mac, bowing to him across the courtyard. The second young man did likewise, but the Tikal diplomat pretended not to see them, and Zac Kuk lifted her chin and very deliberately turned her face away, showing them her back.

Chan Mac seemed unaffected by the snub, laughing as he pointed out the monkey to Akbal and told him how Zac Kuk had found it as a baby and had given it the name Chuen. Akbal nodded without hearing a word, his eyes fixed on the back of Zac Kuk's head. He was as much amazed by the pain of her rejection as he was hurt by it; he had *known* she would turn away from him, after all. Yet her face—what he had seen of it—had seemed even more alluring in the full light of day, and her sudden turn had left him stunned and bereft, as if he had been robbed of his sight, or of his reason for seeing. He could not bring himself to focus on anything else; not the birds, not the monkey, not the other men, the *suitors*. He felt weak-kneed and nauseous, and swore to himself that he would never drink balche again.

More people had suddenly appeared out of the doorways of the surrounding buildings, and a boy ran past them without stopping and entered the room belonging to Batz Mac. A few moments later, Batz Mac came out of the room in a state of great agitation, adjusting the apron of his loincloth beneath the swaying girth of his belly as he ambled up to his son. Akbal came out of his daze to see people beginning to line up around him and Chan Mac, and Muan Kal hurrying toward them across the courtyard.

"You did not tell me," Batz Mac said accusingly. "You said a representative of the ruler; you did not say the high priest."

"Ah Kin Tzab?" Chan Mac said in surprise, widening his eyes at Akbal. "I was not told to expect a representative of his rank."

"For whom has he come?" Muan Kal interrupted breathlessly, taking her place next to her husband. Batz Mac ignored her, waving to the latecomers to take their places in the ranks of the household. Then a small, stooped man in a white robe hobbled into the courtyard, accompanied by three solicitous apprentice priests. He was considerably older than Akbal's grandfather, his leathery face creased with deep age lines, his hair white where it showed above his headwrap. He stopped in front of the group and raised his hand in blessing over their bowed heads.

"Greetings, my children," Ah Kin Tzab said, in a dry, slightly abrasive voice that hissed through the empty gaps in his teeth. "You must forgive the unexpected nature of this visit. I asked the ruler to allow *me* to examine your guest."

Akbal hesitated, allowing Batz Mac the privilege of introducing him, then stepped forward to bow to the high priest, who studied him with an interest that seemed friendly.

"I was told that you were very tall, and very young. Yes, and I can see a resemblance to the Lady Box Ek. Come, my son, I must speak with you privately . . ."

Batz Mac immediately jumped out to lead the way, and Akbal fell in a step behind the high priest, trying to match the old man's shuffling gait without appearing to tower over him. As they passed the rows of reverent faces, Akbal realized that no one would turn away from him now, and he lifted his head with a renewed sense of self-importance. But then he saw Zac Kuk just ahead, her eyes lowered respectfully as Ah Kin Tzab drew even with her place in line. There was no guile in her face, and none of the frivolousness that had so offended him the night before. As Akbal's shadow fell over her, she looked up at him with wide, unblinking eyes, and any thought of trying to impress her vanished from his mind. In that brief moment, which seemed to stretch on and on, he put his heart into his eyes and appealed to her to forgive him, to see that he was not a man who wished to hurt or humiliate her.

Then he was past, having seen only her eyes, which had taken in his appeal with only the slightest indication of surprise. He wished immediately that he had shown more expression, perhaps even risked a smile. No one else would have seen it; it would have been for her alone. On the other hand, perhaps she would have found a smile inappropriate, and him arrogant for attempting one under these circumstances. Perhaps he should not have looked at her at all. Unable to gauge the impression he had made, Akbal sighed in frustration, so loudly that both Batz Mac and Ah Kin Tzab looked back at him in surprise.

"This will not be such a trial, my son," the high priest assured him as Batz Mac ushered them into a small, empty room off the courtyard. Ah Kin Tzab gestured to Akbal to seat himself and turned to say a few words to Batz Mac, promising to visit with him after his business here was completed. Batz Mac went away smiling, and the old man sat down across from Akbal, who had managed to regain his composure.

"I feel that I know you very well, Akbal Balam," the high priest said without preliminaries. "I have heard about you from many different people, including some of the Yaxchilani priests. I know your family in Tikal as well. So I truly do not need to examine your character. If you wish, I will show you the monuments under my control, though I do not have the power to give you the freedom you were granted by Shield Jaguar."

Akbal blinked, unprepared for such an easy acceptance.

"I have done nothing to deserve this honor, my father," he said truthfully. "But I am grateful for your trust."

Ah Kin Tzab looked back at him steadily, his thin lips curling into a knowing smile.

"You are wondering why I asked to see you if I did not need to question you. First I must know that I can trust your silence. You must promise me that you will repeat what I say to no one else, except your grandfather."

"You know my grandfather?" Akbal blurted in surprise.

"I met him once, several years ago. But first swear to me, Akbal, because it is of your grandfather that I wish to speak."

"You have my word," Akbal said gravely. "By the blood of my ancestors, I swear I will speak of this to no one but him."

"Good," Ah Kin Tzab said briskly. "I have heard that you defended your grandfather's decision to wear no feathers at the Tun-End Ceremony. You have seen the proof he claims to have for this?"

"I only just heard of his decision," Akbal confessed, "and I cannot speak to how it was reached. But I discovered, when I was repainting the books of our clan, that our ancestors wore no feathers on the monuments of the last cycle. I told this to my grandfather, though he appeared to know already."

"It is no wonder Ah Kin Cuy has not moved against him," the high priest said thoughtfully, rubbing his narrow chin. "Tell me, Akbal: Did you see your grandfather dance at the ceremony before this one?"

"Yes. It was unlike anything I had seen before; it made me proud to carry the blood of the Jaguar Paw."

"Did he seem greatly changed afterward?"

"Yes," Akbal said without hesitation. "We have all been affected by the change in him."

"And is it true, as I have heard, that he has seized control of your clan's affairs, and has used his power to defy the ruler of your city?"

"That is how some would see it," Akbal admitted reluctantly. "He has refused to accept any new promises until old debts have been paid. Even from Caan Ac himself. But he has not done this on his own; he has had the support of our clan council."

"Not of your father, surely," Ah Kin Tzab said shrewdly. "But no matter. One last thing: Do you feel, when you are near him, that he is a holy man? A man with a vision?"

Akbal reflected for a moment, his brow furrowed with the effort of remembering and judging what he had felt. He recalled the way Balam Xoc had spoken to him about his stone and, later, about the Zuyhua and the Cauac Shield people. He had spoken of the future, surely, but also of the past, as if in some way the two were indistinguishable to him. Akbal spread his hands in a gesture of humility.

"I know only what the priests have taught me of such things, my father, and it is not enough for me to judge his holiness. But I feel his influence upon my life as I never did before. Is it not because of him that I am speaking to you?"

The high priest smiled in response, showing the gaps in his teeth.

"Indeed it is. You must tell him that his actions are being watched here with great interest. We are aware of Tikal's recent misfortunes, and of the concessions Caan Ac was forced to make to Shield Jaguar. We do not gloat over these things as some do; we gain no strength from Tikal's weakness. You have been to Yaxchilan, so you understand my meaning."

Akbal nodded cautiously, making sure he memorized every word.

"No doubt you have already learned that the Moon Clan is very powerful, both here and in Yaxchilan," Ah Kin Tzab continued. "They have aspirations toward placing one of their own on the throne of Ektun when next it becomes empty, and their candidate will receive serious consideration. That is as it should be, and I will support the man most fit to be ruler. But this must be *our* decision. We do not require the intervention of Shield Jaguar and Caan Ac, acting on behalf of their Moon Clan relations."

Akbal raised his eyebrows at this revelation, and Ah Kin Tzab shook a finger at him sternly to remind him of his oath.

"I tell you this only for his benefit, so that he will know my interest is not idle curiosity. Tikal's dependency is dangerous to others besides yourselves. I do not wish to see all of our young men wasting their lives in battles with the Macaws."

"I will tell my grandfather," Akbal promised after a respectful pause, and the high priest nodded that he was satisfied.

"I will go now, and tell your hosts of my decision, and of my liking for you. Perhaps Zac Kuk can still be persuaded that you are a worthy suitor."

Akbal's mouth dropped open, and the old man laughed.

"The families of this city are closely related," he explained, "and intensely interested in one another's business. Everyone is aware of the daughters who are available for marriage, for the blood of the wife is as important here as that of the husband. It is a remarkable thing when a suitor reduces one of these women to tears."

"It was not my intention to humiliate her," Akbal protested defensively, but the priest held up a hand and wearily waved away his alibi.

"Nevertheless, it was your deed," Ah Kin Tzab chided him. "And perhaps you should not be so quick to disown it. I am told that Zac Kuk acted badly, and that you were defending your grandfather when you spoke to her so sharply. There are those who think you acted quite correctly."

"But," Akbal blurted, then could not go on, embarrassed by his desperate need to apologize.

"But Zac Kuk is not one of them," the high priest finished for him. "Sometimes correctness is no consolation. But I think that we have not been fair to you, my son. You have been here less than a day and have had no time to consider your intentions. I will suggest to Batz Mac and his son that you be allowed a few days to adjust to Ektun before undertaking any further social obligations. Perhaps you will find a way to resolve this matter if left to yourself."

"You are kind to me, Father," Akbal said gratefully. "There are many things I need to think about."

"You may begin now," Ah Kin Tzab said, struggling to his feet and gesturing to Akbal to stay where he was. "I will send for you when you have rested sufficiently."

Akbal bowed deeply, and the high priest raised a hand over him in blessing.

"May the spirits of your ancestors be with you, Akbal Balam. May they guide you and show you the way that is both correct and manly, the way that will bring honor to their memory . . ."

Tikal

KANAN NAAB was standing with Cab Coh outside the craft house when the bearers from Yaxchilan arrived. There were two of them, broad-backed men with sinewy necks and shoulders. Each had a large, square, leather-wrapped bundle attached to the tumpline around his head, and their legs were spattered with mud from the journey. They approached Cab Coh with weary deference, one of them gesturing to the packs on their backs.

"These belong to the Tikal Painter."

"Who would that be?" Cab Coh demanded, waving a hand at the artisans working in the long building behind him. "I have many painters here."

"He means Akbal, Grandfather," Kanan Naab suggested quietly, and both men nodded in confirmation. Cab Coh frowned and pulled on his ear, as if to chastise himself for not remembering.

"Of course," he murmured, though Kanan Naab knew that the designation meant nothing to him. Once he had reconciled himself to Akbal's absence, he had avoided all further knowledge of what his assistant was doing in Yaxchilan. Pacal's desire for secrecy had given him a convenient excuse for not asking, but he truly did not want to know. Anything to which Balam Xoc had given his blessing was bound to be tinged with controversy, and Cab Coh found it easier to appear old and absentminded than to involve himself in matters that might distress him.

"Perhaps the bundles should be opened," Kanan Naab prompted, as Cab Coh continued to ignore the sweating men. He frowned again, but let go of his ear.

"No, they are Akbal's property," he decided. "If you would, my daughter, show these men to your brother's room. His belongings will be safe there."

Kanan Naab nodded compliantly and led the men across the open area of the lower plaza, toward the bridge and stairs that climbed to the plaza above. Kanan Naab's bench on the middle landing was occupied by a pair of young priests who were staying in her grandfather's house, and they bowed to her cordially as she went up the steep stairs with the bearers close behind. The houses of Nohoch Ich and Cab Coh were to her right as she came into the upper plaza, and there were small groups of men and women waiting outside of both buildings, conversing quietly in the shade of the overhanging thatch. Kanan Naab nodded or waved to those who recognized her, then turned left and headed toward her father's house.

There were people sitting in the doorways of Balam Xoc's house, just to the east, but the house of Pacal appeared deserted, two of its three doorways covered by curtains. Kanan Naab felt a pang of guilt every time she was confronted by this contrast, because although she lived in her father's house, she was not cut off from the rest of the family the way he was. On the contrary, she had become the daughter of the house, and had made herself indispensable to Box Ek and the wives of Cab Coh and Nohoch Ich as they struggled to meet the demands of all the guests and visitors drawn by Balam Xoc. She had been the first to understand the need to expand, and to suggest that additional servants be hired, knowing intuitively that the clan had the means for this. She could *feel* the vitality that Balam Xoc had awakened in his people, and she assumed from this alone that they must be more prosperous, as indeed they were. Unlike the older women, she never doubted the value of this prosperity, or questioned its impact upon their lives, and this freed her to act with the authority and foresight that were needed.

As she skirted the front steps of her father's house, Kanan Naab comforted herself with the thought that its air of abandonment was deceptive. The curtains had been drawn at the request of her stepmother, Ixchel, who was suffering through the early months of her first pregnancy, after years of praying for a child. In time, Kanan Naab hoped, even the house of Pacal would show signs of new life and growth, and would share in the rebirth of the clan.

Akbal had the bachelor's room at the far end of the house, the same room that Kinich Kakmoo had occupied before his marriage. Pulling aside the curtain that covered the single doorway, Kanan Naab instructed the bearers to deposit their loads on the dusty floor, waiting outside while they did so. Then she thanked them and pointed toward the open-sided cookhouse that stood behind her father's house.

"Tell the women that the Lady Kanan Naab has sent you to them. They will see to your hunger and thirst, and give you provisions for your journey back to Yaxchilan."

The two men murmured their thanks and went off, and Kanan Naab let the curtain fall back into place. Then she changed her mind and entered the room, a place forbidden to women when its occupant was present. But Akbal might not return for another month or more, and it seemed irresponsible to store the bundles without examining their condition. And indeed, a cursory examination of the tightly bound packs revealed traces of green mold growing in the seams of the leather wrapping.

Once, Kanan Naab would never have dared to disturb her brother's belongings without seeking someone else's permission. But she had too many other responsibilities now to waste time indulging her misgivings, especially when Cab Coh had dispensed with his by delegating this chore to her. Glancing around the sparsely furnished room, she spied a flint knife among the clutter of drinking bowls and carrying baskets in the corner. The knife was chipped and dulled from use, but it was sufficient to saw through the fiber ropes holding the bundles together. As she had suspected, the interior wrappings were heavily spotted with mold, and there were incipient growths on the wooden binders of the drawings and the pieces of reed matting used to cushion the folded paper screens.

Despite the need to air the drawings before they were ruined, Kanan Naab hesitated before actually opening one of them up, feeling that this would be a serious intrusion into Akbal's affairs. He was a man now, and had gone to Yaxchilan as an emissary of the ruler. Perhaps these drawings were supposed to be kept secret, like the vase Akbal had painted. But there would be nothing left to keep if these were not aired, she told herself finally, and opened the screen to its full length on top of the bundle. What she saw took her breath away, and made her stand back from the drawing. Then she slipped her hands under the stiff, two-foot screen and very slowly carried it into the light from the doorway.

The drawing was so complicated, and so exquisitely detailed, that she could not grasp all of its elements at once, and was forced to examine it a little at a time. A woman wearing a feathered headdress and a long robe decorated with Kan crosses knelt in the righthand corner of the scene, holding a bowl in one hand while extending her other hand gracefully, her gaze fixed upward. Curling up from another bowl in front of the woman was the plated, looping body of a two-headed serpent, whose upper jaws gaped widely, reaching all the way to the single row of glyphs along the upper border. Emerging from the serpent's mouth were the head and shoulders of a man who wore a beaded pectoral and a tall, spotted headdress. He looked down upon the kneeling woman, pointing at her with the short, sharply tipped spear he grasped in his hands.

As soon as the full composition of the scene became clear to her, Kanan Naab realized that what was being depicted was the experience of a vision, the visitation of an ancestor. It could be nothing else, yet it was a *woman* who appeared to be the recipient of the vision. A shiver went through Kanan Naab's body, and she was seized by the sudden conviction that she had been meant to see this drawing. Why else had it been the first to come to hand if not as a message to her, a glimpse of possibility? And had she not heard her grandfather say, only the night before, that he had seen a two-headed serpent before his first vision came to him? Could such things be the result of mere coincidence?

Forgetting her earlier hesitation, she propped the screen up on its edge in the doorway and went back to the bundle. The next drawing in the stack was similar in style to the first and portrayed a standing lord who held a flaming staff over the head of another kneeling woman. The woman was holding one end of a piece of rope up to her lips, the other end coiling into a woven basket in front of her. Only after she had carried the screen over to the doorway and examined it closely in the light did Kanan Naab see that the rope in the woman's hands was studded with sharp thorns. Shuddering, she lifted a hand to her own mouth, feeling the moist, tender flesh of her lips and tongue. She knew that the priests and clan elders sometimes pierced their tongues and earlobes in acts of penance. But this was a woman, and not only that, a woman of high rank. What kind of place had Akbal gone to, she wondered in horror; what kind of people practiced this form of bloodletting, and so openly?

Her certainty that she was meant to see these drawings had vanished, and in its place was a strong desire to flee this room immediately. She wanted to be sitting on her bench, alone, smelling the flowers and allowing her fears to melt away in the quiet. But the priests might still be there, or someone else who would want to know why she was upset. Kanan Naab realized how long it had been since anyone had seen in her face that she was troubled, or asked her to explain why. It had once been a frequent occurrence, a reflex she evoked even in strangers.

This is no way for the granddaughter of Balam Xoc to act, she told herself; *he* did not flee from what was shown to him. Summoning her resolve, she stood the screen up beside the first drawing and went back to unpack the rest. She did so as methodically as possible, opening and setting the drawings down in one motion, so that she would not be able to dwell on what she saw. But as she gradually filled up the floor space immediately around her and had to carry the screens farther before setting them down, she could not avoid the images that leaped out at her eye: the bulbous noses and pouting lips of the lords and ladies; the thick-thighed warriors who exchanged staffs or brandished Cauac scepters at one another; a woman in a beautifully embroidered robe presenting the head of a jaguar to a gesturing lord; a warrior hidden behind a Sun mask, threatening his captives; still another woman with a rope to her lips, flanked by a seated man holding a long, sharpened piece of bone next to his thigh.

By the time the last of the screens had been set out to dry and she had worked her way back to the doorway, she was exhausted. She sat down with her back against the doorframe and breathed deeply, trying to get the odors of mildew and painted lime paper out of her lungs and nostrils. The images of Yaxchilan, however, could not be banished from her mind so easily. She would have to tell her grandfather what she had done, and hope that he would pardon her inquisitiveness, and perhaps explain what she had seen. Even if he reprimanded her, she hoped he would explain. She had to know more about these women with their baskets, and bowls, and thorn-studded ropes. She had to know if visions required the shedding of blood.

"Lady Kanan Naab?" a voice called softly, outside the room. "Are you there?"

Kanan Naab rose wearily to her feet and stepped to the edge of the doorway. She had already recognized the voice as belonging to Yaxal Can, a young priest from the Serpent Clan who had done some service for her grandfather and had then developed an interest in her. Kanan Naab had so far done everything possible to discourage his interest, but at the moment she was glad that he had found her.

"Come in," she said, beckoning to him. "There is something you must see."

Yaxal Can was a short man, only a little taller than Kanan Naab herself, so he was forced to look up at her in the doorway. He bowed respectfully but shook his head at her offer.

"It would not be proper. We are alone here."

Kanan Naab made an exasperated noise and stepped down to stand beside him.

"Then look for yourself. I will wait here."

Yaxal Can vacillated for a moment, looking from her to the room in perplexity. He had already been told by Box Ek, in front of everyone, that Kanan Naab was "difficult" and "perverse," and he was no doubt considering the wisdom of an outright refusal. Kanan Naab drew herself up and gave him her most challenging look, letting him know what such a denial would cost him in her eyes. She was slightly surprised at how much it pleased her when he nodded instead and went into the room without another word.

He remained inside for a long time, and Kanan Naab could see him lifting one screen after another, holding them up to the light so that he could read the rows of tiny glyphs. Kanan Naab became aware of how much time had passed, and how many things required her attention, but she could not leave until she had heard Yaxal Can's opinion. She had to restrain herself from interrupting him when he paused in the doorway to examine the first two drawings she had seen, but she managed to keep her silence until he stepped down beside her.

"They are very well drawn," he commented in a neutral tone. "How did they get here from Yaxchilan?"

"Two bearers brought them today. They were drawn by my brother Akbal. But what do they mean, Yaxal? Where could he have copied them?"

"Come," the young man said curtly. "We must not stand here like this. I will escort you to your father's house."

"Perhaps you believe I should not have seen these things," Kanan Naab suggested, making no attempt to move. "Perhaps you will think it proper to tell me nothing."

"I will tell you nothing under circumstances that might disgrace us both," Yaxal said flatly. "But if you will allow me to escort you from this place, I will tell you whatever I can."

"Do you promise?" Kanan Naab demanded eagerly, but Yaxal had turned and started off, and she had to hurry to catch up, nearly tripping over her long skirt. Yaxal paused to let her regain her breath, his dark eyes softening as he looked at her. He had very clear eyes, she noticed for the first time. Serious eyes.

"Yes, I promise that I will tell you," he said earnestly. "I have vows that I must obey, but I would speak forever of anything else, if it allowed me the pleasure of your company."

Kanan Naab felt the heat rise to her face, and she quickly ducked her head and began walking again. Yaxal smiled to himself as he sprang to accompany her, but he said nothing more, waiting patiently for her curiosity to return.

Ektun

THOUGH HE SLEPT often and deeply during the first day and a half he was alone, Akbal was able to find little rest during the hours he was awake. He could think of nothing but Zac Kuk, and being away from her only heightened his obsession without bringing him any closer to resolving his feelings. She appeared in his dreams, which he could never remember clearly later, but which left him feeling aroused and feverish with longing for a long time afterward. He tried to draw a portrait of the face that hovered constantly on the edge of his consciousness, but a satisfying likeness eluded him completely, and he gave up when he caught himself on the verge of breaking his brushes in frustration.

Finally it became so unbearable that he dressed himself and went to the courtyard, determined to find her and make her forgive him. He had no idea what he was going to say, hoping somehow that desperation would supply him with the right words to make her bend, and accept his apologies, and let him look upon her again. He was ready to be humiliated—to humiliate himself— if that was what it took.

But the courtyard was deserted when he got there. Zac Kuk's birds perched somnolently in the shade of their tree, appearing to have already been well fed. Akbal stood uncertainly for a few moments, feeling foolish and exposed. Then a twig fell at his feet, and he glanced up to see the spider monkey hanging by its tail from a high branch directly above him. But the monkey was paying no attention to him. It had a polished piece of mirror stone cupped in the long fingers of one hand, and it was staring intently at its own reflection. *He* was staring, Akbal realized abruptly, noticing the monkey's erected penis, which hung down behind his legs like a stiff pink pod.

Akbal felt a painful shock of recognition, reminded of how he had been staring at his own reflection in the bathing pool, where he had gone to cool the lingering ardor of his dreams. His scalp prickled with shame, yet he also felt intensely relieved that he had not come upon Zac Kuk in his present state. He fled the courtyard as quickly as he had come, grateful to escape unseen, with what little remained of his dignity.

KINICH FOUND his brother out on the bluff behind Batz Mac's house. Akbal was sitting with his back to the pool, staring down into the ravine below. He took his eyes away for only a moment as Kinich quietly took a seat beside him, then continued his staring. Kinich looked in the same direction, searching for the object of his brother's rapt attention. But there was nothing to be seen except jungle. The lush green banks of vegetation seemed bleached and indistinct in the bright sunlight, leaves and branches blending together behind a wavering film of heat and vapor. Tiny birds flitted in and out of the cloud of foliage without causing a ripple, their brief calls lost in the constant, vibrating trill of the locusts.

"What do you see?" Kinich asked finally, unable to locate anything of significance in the scene.

"Just the shadows and shades of color," Akbal said in a dreamy tone, his gaze still fixed on the ravine. "They form shapes and patterns of their own."

Then he let his shoulders slump and rotated his head on his neck before turning to face Kinich, who was examining him skeptically.

"Forgive me, my brother," Akbal said in a normal voice. "It is a technique that Cab Coh once tried to teach me, a way of looking without trying to see. I was never successful at it, because either I would get impatient or my mind would wander. But I have found it useful, these last days, because I have wanted my thoughts to wander."

"You have," Kinich echoed doubtfully. "And where have they taken you?"

"Many places. Back to Yaxchilan, and the things I learned there. And to Tikal, both the Tikal we know and the one that existed in the time of our ancestors. I have also returned to my childhood, to the time when our mother was still alive."

Kinich grunted, deep in his throat, and briefly looked away.

"What can you remember of that? You were, what—six when she died?"

"Six," Akbal agreed. "But I was remembering a time when I could not have been more than three or four, because Kanan Naab was still an infant. I remember our mother taking the two of us to visit Grandfather, who was always sitting in a darkened room by himself. He was so silent, and so sad, that I was frightened of him at first. But Mother would pretend that nothing was wrong and would give him Kanan Naab to hold, and of course she would start to cry. Then Balam Xoc would have to rock her and sing songs to distract her attention, and soon he would forget about being sad and would play with me, as well."

"Yes, I remember that," Kinich said slowly. "She took me, once, but I was too restless. Grandfather had lost his wife and his eldest son within the same year, and he was sick with grief. Father was afraid that he might follow them to the Underworld, so strong was his sorrow."

"Yet Mother cured him," Akbal said with quiet pride. "Before she was taken herself, only a few years later."

"You do not have to remind me," Kinich said irritably. "Why do you want to dwell on these morbid thoughts?"

"Because I have forgotten them for too long. It was after Mother died that Grandfather became the Living Ancestor, and all but disappeared from our lives. It was then, as well, that I became the Painter."

"We were *all* affected by her death," Kinich assured him. "Why does this seem like such a revelation to you?"

"Because I have just begun to realize how much Grandfather has changed," Akbal explained, undaunted by his brother's growing impatience. "He is no longer a man who would grieve in darkness, needing women and children to comfort him. He comes to us now, pushing us to be more than we are. Has he not touched *your* life, Kinich?"

Kinich grunted uncomfortably and frowned.

"I cannot forget how he touched our father's life. And he has persuaded the clan not to supply the ruler with the full quota of warriors he requested. I do not find his touch as pleasant as you do."

"It is no longer merely a matter of our own family," Akbal told him gravely. "You have heard that he danced without feathers at the last ceremony, and that he was summoned by the high priest?"

"I pay no attention to rumors," Kinich said stubbornly. "He was bound to bring trouble upon himself with the things he has been saying."

"He has claimed that he was given a vision, and I believe that he was. I have seen for myself that what he is saying is true."

"What do *you* know of visions?" Kinich demanded. "You are a painter, not a priest!"

"I spoke to many priests in Yaxchilan," Akbal said calmly, "and to a certain Tikal warrior, who did not feel the Yaxchilanis were worthy of his ruler's respect and confidence. I saw for the first time how Tikal was regarded from the outside, and it did not make *me* confident about our city's future."

"And you think that Balam Xoc's antics will remedy the situation?"

"I think he has seen the source of our problem," Akbal insisted. "I think he means to lead us back to the ways of our true ancestors."

Unable to sit still any longer, Kinich got up and strode out to the end of the bluff and back, clenching and unclenching his blunt, battle-scarred hands. He stood looming over Akbal, huffing audibly through his nose.

"Is it so easy for you to disown the ruler?" he inquired angrily. "We also carry the blood of the Sky Clan in our veins, no matter what Balam Xoc says."

"He would not deny that," Akbal said, looking up, "and neither would I. But the Sky Clan people were foreigners to Tikal, and their rites were different from our own. Why should we adopt the rites of the Zuyhua when we did not adopt their weapons?"

"Foreigners!" Kinich spat, stamping his foot in disgust. "I do not know what has come over you, Akbal, to make you believe such nonsense. Perhaps you have softened your brain with too much staring at nothing."

Akbal also rose and stood face to face with Kinich, forcing his brother to look up at him.

"You are older than I am, Kinich," he said in a low voice, "and braver. But you are wrong to mock our grandfather's wisdom. He is showing us the way to regain the dignity we have lost."

Kinich abruptly turned away, then spun back and grabbed Akbal roughly by the arm.

"I have lost none of *my* dignity, Little Brother. And you are not enough of a man to tell me so."

Akbal tried to jerk his arm away, but Kinich held him fast, crushing down with his fingers. Akbal's knees buckled, but he refused to cry out, gritting his teeth against the pain. Then Kinich remembered himself and abruptly let him go.

"I came here to tell you that your relatives still await your visit," the warrior said in a husky voice. "But I can see that you have your own sense of obligation now. Do what you will, then!"

Turning on his heel, Kinich stalked off, leaving Akbal to stare after him, rubbing uselessly at his arm, alone once more with his thoughts.

AH KIN TZAB had begun his tour in the southernmost plaza of the city, where the oldest Ektun monuments stood before temples long in disuse. The high priest was no lonely, garrulous caretaker like those in Yaxchilan, and he had used these ancient stones to test the depth and sincerity of Akbal's interest, making him absorb a wealth of esoteric information before taking him any farther. Nor would he allow Akbal to make more than brief charcoal sketches of the monuments and temples they visited. In some places, he would not permit him to draw at all.

Yet the old man's health required that he rest frequently, so they would settle themselves in one of the clan houses, where he would allow Akbal to paint more elaborate and detailed copies of the things he had sketched. Ah Kin Tzab sat beside him while he worked, as much to judge and criticize as to assist, for it was important to him that Akbal have a coherent understanding of what he drew, and that his representations be accurate.

Akbal submitted to this discipline without complaint, grateful for the chance to dwell on something other than his longing for Zac Kuk. And the quality of the Ektun sculpture was superb, much more graceful than anything he had seen elsewhere. Here, too, there were warriors, women, and captives on the monuments, in a great variety of poses. Yet the sense of confrontation so basic to the Yaxchilan monuments was largely lacking, and there was nothing similar to the bloodletting scenes and visionary rites depicted on the Yaxchilan lintels. Instead there were scenes of lords scattering grain in divination and crowned figures seated serenely within niches, carved in such deep relief that the head and upper body stood almost free of the background. The monuments had been erected at five-tun intervals, marking the Hotun-End and commemorating the various rites and duties performed by the ruler in power.

When one ruler died, a new series of monuments would be begun for his successor, often in conjunction with a different temple in another part of the city.

By slow degrees, Akbal and the high priest worked their way north, climbing several levels to the temple plaza currently in use. Four carved monuments stood in a row in front of the main temple pyramid, which had been built against the side of the hill behind it. Two more monuments flanked the broad staircase leading to the elaborately stuccoed shrine above, and the only monument so far erected by the present ruler, Zotz Mac, stood alone on the top platform, next to the shrine.

Akbal sketched this last monument late in the afternoon, with the sun shining down upon his back. He was tired and hungry and dizzy from having endured the day's heat, but he stayed in front of the towering stone slab for as long as Ah Kin Tzab would allow, and he prevailed upon the priest to sit with him while he made a true copy afterward.

"The resemblance to Zotz Mac is quite remarkable," Akbal said admiringly, adding a layer of shadow to the outline of the figure to indicate the depth of the relief. When Ah Kin Tzab did not respond, Akbal hastily went on, fearing that he was losing the old man's attention. "It will be time soon, will it not, for him to record his achievements as a warchief?"

The high priest's head came up with surprising quickness, his narrowed eyes showing that he did not consider this a matter for casual questions. Akbal began to apologize, but the old man silenced him with a wave of his hand, glancing around at the entrances to the room.

"That is another reason I am concerned about Tikal's dependency," he confided in a low voice. "Zotz Mac has so far resisted Shield Jaguar's desire to have us join Yaxchilan in a full-fledged campaign against the Macaws. But he is a brave man, and he will want to test himself against an enemy, as is required of the ruler. I do not wish, however, to see him driven beyond the bounds of what is necessary and useful in this regard. You have seen how much attention Shield Jaguar pays to the sculpture of *his* city, Akbal. I can assure you that he pays as little attention to the administration of his city's resources. He believes that he can always take what he needs in conquest. I have lived too long and seen too much to allow my people to entertain such a dangerous delusion."

A servingwoman came in bearing a tray of food and drink, and they fell silent as she laid the bowls out on a mat and departed. Ah Kin Tzab gestured brusquely at Akbal's painting.

"Put that away for now," he commanded. "I will help you with the glyphs later. Now we must eat and talk of other things. Like the commissions you have been accepting in such abundance. Why have you taken on all this work, when you have this stone of yours to carve? Or have you reconsidered your grandfather's commission?"

Akbal smiled tolerantly, reconciled to the fact that nothing he did in this city was a secret for long.

"Reassessed, perhaps," he allowed, gesturing toward the painting spread out to dry beside him. "Before I came here, I did not know that carvings like these even existed. It could be years before I might be ready to carve something as fine."

"It is good to see that you have not lost *all* of your humility," Ah Kin Tzab said drily. "But perhaps you have another motive, as well, for accepting these commissions. Perhaps you are anticipating the need to establish a household of your own."

"Perhaps," Akbal admitted. "If you are referring to the daughter of Batz Mac, however, I have not spoken to either her or her father."

"She continues to shun you?" the priest asked, and Akbal gave him a sardonic look.

"Am I to pretend, Father, that you do not know? She is cordial to me now, at least. She has decided to blame Chan Mac, rather than herself or me."

Ah Kin Tzab examined him silently, his deep-set eyes glinting with shrewd amusement.

"I admire the way you have regained your composure, Akbal, but perhaps you have done so too thoroughly. A lack of emotion is seldom an advantage to a suitor. I must impress upon you that Zac Kuk has more influence over the choice of her husband than would a daughter of Tikal. And her mother has as much power as Batz Mac, for she carries the blood of the Moon Clan."

Akbal frowned and shrugged.

"I am aware of this. But there are already enough who will laugh with her, and chatter like one of her birds. I would happily have done so myself, once, but I cannot do so now. It would not be true to the kind of life I have to offer her. I am the grandson of Balam Xoc, and he has made me part of something much larger than myself, perhaps even larger than my clan or my city. Zac Kuk must understand this, as well."

"She is not as frivolous as she appears," Ah Kin Tzab warned. "So you must be careful of what you reveal. Anything that passes to her mother will go directly to the Moon Clan."

"I have not forgotten my oath," Akbal assured him. "But I am also praying that she will not hear me frivolously."

"She knows that you spend time with me, just as she knows that I do not give my time to fools."

"I am grateful for your time, Father, and I know how it adds to my status in your city. But there is one other favor I would ask of you."

Ah Kin Tzab raised his eyebrows in mock indignation.

"You do not linger over your gratitude, Akbal Balam. What is it, then?"

"Could you see that the Lady Muan Kal hears of my commissions, if she has not already?" Akbal asked.

The high priest smiled and gestured to the bowls in front of them. "Eat, Suitor," he said gruffly. "Your presumption reassures me . . ."

HAVING STAYED up late into the night talking to Chan Mac, Akbal was slow in rising the next morning, and by the time he had bathed and dressed himself, the bright sunlight with which the day had begun had been obscured by a fast-advancing bank of clouds. The sky was growing progressively dark and ominous, and the warm air was so dense with humidity that Akbal could see his breath in puffs of white vapor. The low, grating rumble of thunder could be heard in the distance, giving promise of a serious storm. Akbal was reminded that the rainy season should begin in earnest any day now, which reminded him in turn that his time in Ektun was growing short. The Tikal delegation could not remain here for very much longer and expect to use the trails that led eastward through the jungle.

He still had not had a chance to explain himself to Zac Kuk, though he had felt he was making headway the night before, until the Lady Muan Kal had joined the conversation. He had been telling Zac Kuk, Chan Mac, and Chan Mac's wife, Kutz, about his memory of his mother, hoping to lead gently into the subject of his grandfather. Zac Kuk had seemed genuinely sympathetic, on the verge of finally shedding her wariness toward him. But then her mother had appeared, and Akbal had seen Zac Kuk's attention become guarded and reluctant, her interest in him receding steadily as Muan Kal led him off on a digression concerning his mother's distinguished ancestry. Chan Mac told Akbal later that Muan Kal had recently become his active supporter, which had been enough in itself to stir Zac Kuk's resistance, since she and her mother seldom agreed on the subject of what was good for her.

Chan Mac had suggested that he seek out Zac Kuk on his own and speak to her directly, pointing out that the Tikal diplomat and most of the other suitors were engaged in the final round of trade negotiations with the Tikal delegation and would not be around to get in his way. Akbal was determined to give this a try after he had eaten, but his plans changed abruptly when he entered the courtyard and found the entire household in an uproar. Zac Kuk was standing beneath the fig tree in the corner, waving her arms and shouting at the servants, who were scurrying frantically from house to house, as if searching for something.

There was a protracted roll of thunder as Akbal crossed the courtyard, and the parrots on the branches behind Zac Kuk squawked harshly and beat their clipped wings, unsettled by all the noise and commotion. Zac Kuk herself began shouting at him before he could ask what was wrong.

"Chuen has escaped!" she cried, holding up the free end of the rope. "You must help me find him! He will be eaten by the snakes and jaguars!"

"Which way might he have gone?" Akbal asked, and Zac Kuk immediately turned and started for the gap between the buildings at the eastern end of the courtyard. Akbal hurried after her, glancing up at the sky, which was rapidly turning the color of pitch.

"There is a storm coming, my lady," he said as he overtook her and they left the courtyard together. "Perhaps you should get a cloak and hat."

"There is no time," Zac Kuk insisted, leading him past the freshly planted family garden and onto a narrow path that disappeared into a stand of breadnut trees. She did not pause to scan the branches overhead, continuing up over a ridge and into the open again. The path descended sharply, built up over the low plain on either side, which was thickly carpeted with sawgrass and the fresh green stalks of new reeds. The open water of a swamp was visible off to the left, but the plain on the right quickly gave way to a high, dense thicket of berry bushes. Zac Kuk stopped abruptly and pointed at the thicket.

"Look there," she commanded breathlessly. "He is very fond of berries."

Akbal had taken two steps off of the path when a loud crack of thunder in the near distance made him stop and look up at the sky. As he did so, he felt his sandaled feet sink into the soft ground and water squish up between his toes. Looking a few feet farther ahead, he saw that what looked like solid ground was really a tangle of vines and water lilies floating on the surface of an unseen swamp. He realized at the same time that it was too early in the season for there to be berries on the bushes, and that Zac Kuk had to know this.

He saw his suspicions confirmed in her eyes as he stepped back onto the path and faced her, shaking his head slowly.

"No, my lady. Unless you have lost a crocodile instead of a monkey, he has not gone this way."

Zac Kuk's eyes widened with anger, and she confronted him with her fists wedged against her hips.

"Even in my distress, you taunt me! You are the most arrogant young man I have ever met."

"Then we are well matched, my lady. I came to help you find Chuen. But if you would prefer that I jump into this swamp instead . . . ?"

He looked at her inquiringly, showing his willingness to jump.

"Do what you wish," Zac Kuk snapped, turning away from him and continuing along the path, which could be seen to follow a curving line across the plain before climbing toward a group of heavily forested hills. Akbal trotted after her, again looking up at the sky as large drops of rain began to descend upon them in sporadic bursts. Zac Kuk was no longer pretending to search, seeming to have her eyes fixed on some destination in the hills ahead. The sky was now so dark that Akbal lost all hope of reaching the cover of the trees in time, and then he could hear the rain advancing upon them, making a sound louder than the thunder, as if the earth were being pelted with a shower of heavy stones.

Zac Kuk tried to stop when she saw the rain sweeping toward them in a solid grey sheet, and she skidded on the muddy path and nearly lost her balance. Akbal caught her by the elbows from behind and turned her into him, pulling her against his chest and bending his head over hers in an effort to shelter her from the rain. Then the water hit them, cascading down in a torrent so fierce and overwhelming that it robbed them of breath and sensation and drove them to their knees in the mud . . .

Akbal was aware at first only that the hard, drumming weight upon his head and back was gone, leaving him in a numbed state of shock. Then he became aware of his arms wrapped tightly around Zac Kuk's back, and of hers around him, and of the warm, pliable body pressed fully against his own. The thin layer of sodden cloth between them seemed to have melted into his own skin, and he could feel the imprint of her breasts upon his chest so clearly that he could have drawn them. A flash of heat coursed through him, and blood rushed to his loins, stiffening the tangled folds of his loincloth. He was afraid that Zac Kuk would feel the rising of his desire, yet more afraid to move and risk her slipping from his embrace. The mere thought made him tighten his hold around her back, and his breath caught in his throat when he felt her squeeze him in return, molding their bodies together. The rain was still falling steadily, but neither of them noticed the water sliding off of their slick, warm skin.

Finally they released each other and sat back on their haunches, with only their knees touching. Zac Kuk's long black hair had come completely uncoiled and hung plastered against her neck and shoulders; her shift clung to the contours of her body, the outlines of her nipples and the points of her pelvis clearly visible through the cloth. Akbal felt similarly naked, his soaking loincloth outrageously distended, standing up like a staff between his thighs. Yet he felt no shame or embarrassment as he watched Zac Kuk's eyes travel over his body. Though utterly disheveled, she seemed more beautiful to him than ever, the alertness of her gaze accentuated by her wet lashes, which surrounded her eyes like black spikes. There was no amusement or scorn in her expression as she slowly raised her eyes to his face, opening herself fully to his inspection. As their eyes met, Akbal felt himself being drawn into another kind of embrace, a joining of spirits that made his heart swell with emotion. He realized suddenly that the smile he had yearned for so passionately meant little compared with the way she was looking at him now, showing him her eagerness and her fear, and trusting him with both. Swallowing heavily, Akbal reached out with one long arm and laid his hand on her cheek, staring raptly until Zac Kuk smiled and lowered her eyes in modesty.

Rising to his feet, Akbal helped her up, and steadied her while she removed her sandals, which would be useless in the mud. He took them from her and removed his own, tying them all together by the straps.

"Let us go find Chuen," he suggested, and Zac Kuk gave him a small, fleeting smile, as if surrendering a secret, and started up the slippery path toward the hills. Soon they were under the cover of the tall trees, and the footing improved, allowing them to climb the slope without sliding or grabbing for branches. Akbal walked by Zac Kuk's side whenever the trail was wide enough, saying nothing but letting his eyes rest on her face, as if to absorb every feature into his memory. Twice he walked straight into trees, hearing Zac Kuk's musical laugh drift back to him as he picked himself up off the ground and went after her.

The trail brought them finally into a clearing in the trees, and Akbal could see the sky overhead, with breaks beginning to appear in the clouds. In the center of the clearing was a broad, deep pool, fed at its far end by a stream that tumbled down from a cave in the rocky hillside above. The water fell from ledge to ledge in white skeins, splashing noisily into the pool below, and flowering vines hung down on both sides of the waterfall, their leafy tendrils curling up just above the surface of the pool. Log benches were set at intervals among the banks of ferns surrounding the water, and huddled on a branch above one of these was the forlorn figure of Chuen, his black hair matted against his spindly body, his long arms wrapped nearly twice around himself. He chattered excitedly and jumped down into Zac Kuk's arms, trailing the long rope that had tied him securely to the tree. Akbal watched enviously as the monkey cuddled against Zac Kuk's breast, swiveling his furry head to stare at Akbal with big black eyes. When Zac Kuk also looked up at him, Akbal reached out and touched the rope attached to Chuen's collar.

"I am flattered, my lady," he said, and Zac Kuk shrugged dismissively, shifting the monkey in her arms.

"You are *still* an arrogant young man."

"Could I hope to be worthy in your eyes if I were not worthy in my own?" Akbal asked mildly. "Perhaps if I were truly arrogant, I would not care so much about your opinion of me. But I do care, Zac Kuk, as deeply as your mother cares about my ancestry and prospects."

"Why should you care about my opinion?" she replied with exaggerated weariness. "You have already won over my mother and father and brother."

"I am not asking any of *them* to live with me in Tikal, and share my future. Your mother is impressed by my connections to the Sky Clan, and by the reputation I earned in Yaxchilan. She thinks that these things will assure my future success in Tikal. But it is not as simple as that."

Zac Kuk squinted at him curiously, absentmindedly stroking Chuen's head.

"Because of your grandfather?" she asked finally, and Akbal nodded, pleased by the thoughtfulness of her tone.

"Primarily because of my grandfather, but also because of the relations that exist between our clan and that of the ruler. Only my father, and perhaps my brother, Kinich Kakmoo, truly enjoy Caan Ac's favor."

"But you are the Tikal Painter," Zac Kuk protested in disbelief. "Surely, you must be his favorite as well."

"Because of how I pleased Shield Jaguar?" Akbal suggested ruefully. "That was not Caan Ac's true intention in sending me to Yaxchilan, despite what your mother wishes to believe. I do not expect to be received with gratitude when I return to Tikal. In fact, it is possible that before very long, the people of my clan will not be welcome in the ruler's court."

"You have not told any of *this* to my mother," Zac Kuk said, more incredulous than accusing.

"No," Akbal admitted in a low voice. "But you may tell her if you wish. I do not *know* that this will happen, and I pray that it might never occur. But my grandfather's challenge to the ruler is a serious one, and it will not be ignored forever."

"Why do you tell me this?" Zac Kuk demanded, bewildered and angry. "If my mother were to hear any of it, she would never allow me to marry you."

Akbal blinked, his eyes clouded with pain at the possibility. His voice quavered when he could bring himself to speak.

"Then I will have hurt only myself. But I could not have you come to Tikal believing that all is peaceful there, or that your life would be the same as it is here. I could not bear to see you weep again, or have you think me cruel and deceitful. I would rather suffer the consequences of my honesty here, and leave you free to choose a more suitable man."

Akbal choked on the last words and barely got them out, too miserable to appreciate his own nobility. He had sincerely wanted to give her an honest choice, but he had not meant to paint such a bleak picture of his prospects in Tikal. He should have told her of the holiness of his grandfather's task, and of his belief that it would lead the Jaguar Paw Clan to greatness. He should have told her of the good things her life would hold, and of how she would be loved and respected. He should have begged her to trust him and be his wife.

Zac Kuk regarded him skeptically for a moment, then put the reluctant Chuen back up on his branch and walked slowly to the edge of the pool, gazing out over the dark, rippling waters. A single shaft of sunlight illuminated the waterfall, creating tiny rainbows in the spray. Akbal came up beside her, his muscles clenched against the anxious trembling in his limbs. But when Zac Kuk finally looked up at him, her eyes were wide and warm, and spoke only of the embrace they had shared on the path.

"I am pleased that you honor me with the truth," she said quietly. "But is it not too late for me to choose another?"

Nearly sobbing with relief, Akbal let his joy burst free in a smile that seemed to lift him off the ground. He took Zac Kuk's hand and pressed it against his chest.

"With all my heart, I pray that it is," he whispered fervently. "For surely, it is too late for *me* . . ."

VII

FOLLOWERS

9.17.16.2.8   10 Lamat   6 Kayab
(A.D. 786)

THE MEETING of the Jaguar Paw Clan Council had been called at the request of Pacal Balam, who carried a message and an invitation from the ruler. The message concerned the promotion of Kinich Kakmoo to the full rank of nacom, and the invitation was to the feast Caan Ac was holding in honor of his new warchief, who would return the next day with the rest of the Tikal delegation. The ruler was certain, Pacal said, that the lords of the Jaguar Paw Clan would wish to be present at this feast, to share in the glory of their brave kinsman.

A few voices were raised in approbation when Pacal had completed his presentation, but most of the men in the chamber waited silently for the response of the Living Ancestor. Balam Xoc stared back at his son for a moment, then reared up on his haunches and grunted rudely, a loud, guttural sound that echoed off the vaulted ceiling and seemed to flatten the men's ears against their heads.

"You are pleased by your son's sudden rise, Pacal?" he inquired drily.

"Should I be sad?" Pacal retorted evenly. "He is the first nacom from our clan in many years, and the youngest ever to hold the rank."

"He is *too* young. He will receive little respect from the other nacoms. But you know this. You know that Caan Ac only uses him to divert attention from the concessions he made to Shield Jaguar."

"Perhaps I am not as skeptical of the ruler's motives as you are," Pacal said coolly, looking around at the other men. "I would still ask the council if Kinich Kakmoo will receive *our* respect."

"Tell me first of your other son," Balam Xoc insisted. "What is planned for the Tikal Painter? Is he also invited to his brother's feast?"

"He does not have sufficient rank . . ."

"Why should that matter for a brother? Especially one who served the ruler so well in Yaxchilan. Is he not also owed some respect?"

"I will speak to him myself," Pacal said tightly. "He understood the nature of his task when he accepted it."

"Did he truly? Perhaps you would explain to the council exactly what Akbal's task was, and why the ruler needed it performed. Like me, they have no doubt heard many false rumors concerning Akbal's conduct in Yaxchilan. They should know whether he has earned the ruler's ingratitude."

"I cannot concern myself with rumors," Pacal replied in an exasperated tone. "I requested this meeting to inform you of the high honor being extended to Kinich Kakmoo, and to solicit your attendance at his feast. I am not at liberty to discuss these other matters before the council."

Balam Xoc glanced up and down the line of seated men and bared his teeth in a sardonic smile.

"Perhaps I must tell them myself, then. Unless I am the only one who thinks these matters worthy of discussion . . . ?"

"I have not heard these rumors," Cab Coh interjected with seeming innocence, "but I must know what my assistant has done."

"I am also interested, Pacal," Nohoch Ich agreed gravely. "I have heard contradictory things about Akbal's performance. Some are admiring, while others claim that he deliberately sought to embarrass the ruler. The latter is a serious charge."

"Well?" Balam Xoc demanded, but Pacal merely bowed, indicating his inability to reply.

"I have said all that I may on this subject. I will leave you to decide for yourselves if you will accept the ruler's invitation."

Pacal turned abruptly and left the chamber, causing the torches to flicker with the wind of his departure. There was a long silence after he had gone, and then Nohoch gestured for Balam Xoc to speak.

"The men of whom we speak are my grandsons," Balam Xoc told them bluntly, "but that has no bearing on how they must be judged. One is to be made a nacom and feasted by the ruler; the other is to be scorned and slandered, his service unrewarded. To which should we give our respect and support, then: the one who is honored above his deserts, or the one who is despised and unfairly used? Which has been the more common experience in our dealings with the ruler and the Sky Clan?"

Balam Xoc let the question hang in the air while he scanned the heavily shadowed faces at the ends of the room.

"I, too, will leave the decision to each of you," he continued. "You may accept the ruler's invitation if you see fit, or you may attend the feast I will hold in my own house in honor of Akbal Balam. The choice is yours to make freely. But first I must tell you what Pacal would not. I must tell you of the concessions Caan Ac made to Shield Jaguar, and of the part Akbal was made to play in this. I must tell you how he came to be known in Yaxchilan as the Tikal Painter . . ."

Uaxactun

AKBAL SAT alone in the room that had been given to him, a back room away from the celebrating going on out in the plaza. He had just succeeded in shutting out the muffled sounds of laughter and singing when he was jolted back to awareness by a female voice, soft and near, calling to him from the other side of the curtained doorway. He recognized the voice of Pom Ix and called to his aunt to enter, averting his eyes from the light that flooded in at the parting of the curtain.

"Will you not join us, Akbal?" Pom Ix asked, blinking as she located Akbal on the floor, sitting cross-legged among his packs. She glanced past him, surveying the emptiness of the dimly lit room with genuine dismay. "There are not so many warriors now," she added encouragingly, "and it is quieter."

"You are kind to think of me, my lady," Akbal said politely. "But I would prefer to be alone."

Pom Ix nodded but did not turn to go, taking a moment to rearrange the folds of her long skirt as a pretext to sitting down across from him. She was his father's older sister and bore a marked resemblance to Pacal, though her features were softer and her hair more heavily streaked with grey. Akbal did not know her well, for she had married into a prominent Uaxactun family before he was even born, and had made only infrequent visits to Tikal in the years since, even though the two cities were a half-day's walk apart. In the brief conversation they had had earlier, she had spoken of Balam Xoc with both skepticism and concern, as if her father's recent notoriety had to be a symptom of imbalance or advancing age.

"I asked Kinich what had come between the two of you," she ventured now, "but he would not say. I think it is sad that you will not join in the celebration of his success."

"I celebrated with him in Yaxchilan," Akbal told her, betraying a trace of wistfulness that seemed to offend him and made him harden his voice. "But I would not inflict my company upon him here. He is the favorite of the delegation, and walks at their head. I walk alone, at the rear."

"He is older," Pom Ix pointed out gently, "and he holds a much higher rank than you do."

"Of course," Akbal said sourly. "But I was also praised by Shield Jaguar, and given the run of his city. And in Ektun, my sponsor was the high priest himself, Ah Kin Tzab. It is only among the ruler's delegation that I am treated with disdain. We were barely out of sight of Ektun when I was ordered to the rear of the column, just ahead of the commoners."

Pom Ix paused judiciously before replying, as if to allow his bitterness to pass.

"Perhaps the favor you won in Yaxchilan was itself a cause for resentment," she suggested, and Akbal looked at her sharply, alert to the implications of her remark. He seemed about to defend himself, then changed his mind.

"No doubt. I do not know what has been said about me, and I do not wish to learn. I only wish to be among my own people once more."

Pom Ix straightened up abruptly, her eyes bright with hurt and anger.

"Are *we* not your people?" she demanded sternly. "My husband's family has been affiliated with the Jaguar Paw Clan since the beginning of our cities, by friendship as well as by blood."

"I did not mean to insult you, my lady," Akbal apologized. "But I have spoken to many members of your family, and you are the only one even to mention Balam Xoc to me. I heard more about him in Ektun."

The anger faded from Pom Ix's eyes, and she let out a long breath, a gesture of tacit agreement. There was a new frankness in her voice when she spoke again.

"I have known my father far longer than you, Akbal, but I cannot make sense of what I hear about him lately. He was never a man to stir up trouble or draw attention to himself, *never*. Nor did he have the ambition to be the Living Ancestor, at least while I lived in his house. He was a supervisor of building projects, and contented with his work. It was only after my mother and brother died that Box Ek suggested it to him, as a way to divert him from his grief. Perhaps no one has ever told you these things, but they are true."

"It was grief for *my* mother, as well," Akbal reminded her. "I can only tell you that he has changed; he is no longer the man any of us knew. You must go to Tikal and see for yourself."

"I would like to," Pom Ix confessed, then sighed and shrugged to show her misgivings. "I must tell you, though, that my husband and the other men here are not convinced of his wisdom. They know that the Jaguar Paw Clan has prospered because of what my father has done, but they do not believe that anyone can defy the ruler of Tikal with impunity. Not for long."

"Should he defy the ancestors instead," Akbal demanded, "and ignore the visions they have sent him?"

Pom Ix gave him a searching glance but did not respond, and Akbal could feel her withdraw from him, seeing him as the young nephew she hardly knew, an impetuous youth whose opinion could not be weighed against that of her husband and the older men. He straightened his back and bowed to her stiffly.

"You must return to your other guests, my lady. I am grateful for your concern, but perhaps you can understand now why it is better for me to remain here."

"Yes," Pom Ix agreed reluctantly, and rose to her feet, gathering her skirt around her. "I will see you in the morning, before you leave," she added, somewhat sadly, and disappeared through the curtain, again exposing him to the light and noise of his brother's success. Akbal blew air through his nostrils and shivered violently, releasing the tight grip he had been keeping on his emotions. He felt bad about the way he had spoken to Pom Ix, but it had not been easy for him to speak to her at all. His pain was too close to the surface, a fresh, naked wound that throbbed at even the most sympathetic touch. He had come close, at every juncture in the conversation, to saying something worse.

He looked around at his packs, patting the leather pouch that held his commissions and the trade agreements he had made with the other painters, trying to distract himself with the evidence of *his* success. But it was no use: He could not shut out the sounds of the celebration now, the dim laughter that drifted to his ears like an echo of his own humiliation. Two warriors—Kinich's men—had come for him once the delegation was well out upon the trail, saying only that he was in the wrong place, before marching him and his porter back to the end of the line, past all the lifted eyebrows and sneering faces . . .

Chan Mac had warned him to expect this, even before anyone else had seen his vase. And he had himself warned Zac Kuk, at the risk of losing her. Yet he had prepared himself for ingratitude, not outright contempt, and he had been taken by surprise by the fury of his own response, the burning sense of outrage that made him want to fight with the warriors instead of going quietly. It was the utter gratuitousness of the act that infuriated and consumed him. It was not enough for the ruler simply to disown his representative; he had to be publicly scorned as well, and made to bear the blame for the ruler's decisions.

Akbal rose and snuffed out the torch on the wall, stumbling over one of his packs as he found his way back to his sleeping mat. He had little hope of sleeping tonight, with the anger and pain still churning so strongly inside him, and the noise of the celebration assaulting him from without. He lay down and closed his eyes anyway, trying to conjure up the image of his grandfather, hoping for a companion to share his waiting and his pain.

Tikal

THE TUN COUNT Priest Nohoch Ich hurried through the predawn darkness, followed closely by a young apprentice whose arms were filled with writing materials and ritual implements. Nohoch himself carried a ladle of smoking copal incense and a painted wooden staff—a sighting staff—to which a pair of crossed sticks had been tied, forming a V-shaped sight. His haste and the unevenness of the path put him in danger of spilling the incense from the shallow, curving ladle, but he could see the sky beginning to lighten ahead, and he dared not be late on a day as cloudy as this. The Sun might show himself for only an instant, or not at all, but Nohoch had to be sure he had seen everything he could.

The viewing platform that belonged to the Tun Count Order lay to the east of the Tikal marketplace, on a flat, treeless ridge overlooking a narrow ravine. The plastered surface of the platform was still wet from last night's rain, and the ravine seemed a river of white mist, spilling over its banks in vaporous waves. Arriving out of breath, Nohoch saw that he was not as late as he had feared, and he took a few moments to recover while his assistant searched for a dry place to set down his books and implements. Beyond the ravine, the ground had been cleared down to low bush for a considerable distance, affording an observer on the platform an unimpeded view of the low hills that formed the eastern horizon. In the center of the cleared space, some three hundred feet from the platform, a notched staff identical to the one Nohoch held had been planted upright in the ground, providing a permanent foresight for the observation of the Sun's rising.

When his breathing had returned to normal, Nohoch handed his own staff to his assistant and waved the smoking ladle over it, and then over himself and the young man, purifying all of them and consecrating them to their tasks. Then he faced east and bowed low, offering a prayer of welcome to Kin, the great fiery spirit of the sky, the bringer of light and life. Kin, whose very name was the word for "day."

The apprentice took a seat behind him and began to prepare his paints and brushes, and Nohoch held his sighting staff in both hands while he examined the shallow horizontal groove that ran from one end of the long platform to the other, functioning as the observer's baseline. The painted mark of yesterday's sighting was still visible despite the effects of the rain, and Nohoch planted his staff just to the right of the mark, only two fingers' distance to the south. The Sun was approaching his time of standing still, when he would achieve his most northerly point of rising, and his position along the horizon changed only slightly from day to day. It was a delicate task to measure this change accurately, especially with the sky so cloudy, and Nohoch squinted with concentration as he peered through the V-shaped notch of his staff, sighting in on the staff in the distance. His eyes felt heavy and swollen, reminding him of his fatigue, and then a yawn welled up inside of him, forcing him to straighten up and clamp a hand over his mouth to prevent an unseemly sound from escaping his lips.

Nohoch did not turn to look at the apprentice, but he knew that the young man could not have missed his display of weariness, and had no doubt been shocked by it. Nohoch was beyond being shocked at himself, and he did not bother to attempt a justification, using the energy it would have taken to make sure that he had not inadvertently moved his staff. *Today I yawn, tomorrow I sleep,* he thought numbly, certain that he could not hold off disgrace forever. He had not had a full night's sleep in two months, since the day he and Balam Xoc had gone before the high priest. That was when the testing of his strength had truly begun, a test that had brought him to his present, enervated state, poised stubbornly on the brink of collapse.

Stooping behind his staff, Nohoch repressed a sigh of despair and made himself concentrate on the familiar contours of the horizon, which had become more distinctive with the growing of the light. In the first days after the revelation of Balam Xoc's vision, when it had seemed that the attention of the whole city was focused upon the Jaguar Paw Clan, Nohoch had taken refuge in his priestly duties. He had found them a welcome respite from the demands being made upon him as the head of the clan council, tasks that could be accomplished in a quiet, orderly fashion, with predictable and verifiable results. He would return to the crowded chaos of the clan house feeling refreshed and renewed from a night spent beneath the stars, his sense of order restored by a successful calculation of their movements and influences.

But then the harassment had begun, and he had found himself assigned to more than his usual share of late-night vigils and predawn risings, and to tasks that seemed designed to try his patience and use up his strength. Though none of his superiors would acknowledge it, they were clearly under pressure from the high priest, who was taking his revenge upon Balam Xoc in the only way he could. Nohoch was outraged by this, and he had vowed that he would never complain or give in, no matter what was done to him. But the satisfaction he had always taken in his work as a priest was gone, destroyed as much by his resentment as by his fatigue. He could only go through the motions now, worn down to the point where his conduct had actually begun to deserve the scrutiny it received.

"My lord . . . ?" the apprentice prompted expectantly, and Nohoch hastily returned his attention to the task at hand, feeling a sickening surge of panic at the realization of how far his mind had wandered. He grasped the staff tightly in both hands, struggling to calm the fearful beating of his heart as he funneled his gaze into the invisible line connecting the two sights. Shifting his stance by degrees, he gradually brought both sights into conjunction, centering on the orange crescent that had just appeared above the distant hills, a bright sliver of divine light among the encroaching clouds.

I watch for you, O Kin, he prayed desperately. *Show me your face, Great Spirit, show me that I have not offended you with my weariness and negligence.* The crescent wavered and disappeared for a moment, crossed by a scudding cloud. Then a broad shaft of yellow light suddenly broke over the crest of the hills, dazzling Nohoch's eyes in momentary defiance of the clouds. His heart lifted, and he nearly cried out in gratitude, refraining only out of fear that he would dislodge his sighting staff. Then the Sun was gone, hidden by the clouds, though not before Nohoch had noted the precise points at which the crescent had intersected with the horizon.

"Mark," he commanded confidently, and the apprentice knelt beside him and carefully painted a circular mark around the bottom of his sighting staff. Nohoch lifted the staff and held it high over his head in a prolonged, heartfelt salute to the Sun. Then he sat with the apprentice and showed him where to paint in the Sun's image upon a standardized drawing of the horizon line, which had been prepared beforehand. When this had been done, Nohoch took the brush from the young man and painted in the proper glyphs indicating the date, the age of the Moon, and the count within the lunar calendar. He did this meticulously, without haste, experiencing a deep sense of finality and completion.

"In another thirteen days, Kin will reach his place of rest," he announced when he was through. "Then he will begin his journey back into the southern half of the sky."

The apprentice nodded respectfully, then tilted his head to the right, making a covert gesture toward the southern end of the platform.

"I did not wish to disturb you before, my lord," he said softly. "But that old man has been watching us for some time."

Nohoch's first thought was that someone had been sent to spy on him, and he turned to look with a mixture of anger and trepidation, wondering if his yawn had been observed. But the man at the end of the platform was Balam Xoc.

"Grandfather," Nohoch said in surprise and relief, rising to his feet and gesturing for Balam Xoc to join him. "That should be dry enough by now," he said to the apprentice. "You may leave me now."

The young man collected his materials and left the platform, bowing politely to Balam Xoc as he passed. Nohoch also bowed, even though Balam Xoc gestured that it was not necessary.

"I woke thinking of you, and could not return to sleep," the old man said in greeting. "Perhaps it is time we spoke."

Nohoch sighed audibly and let his shoulders slump. He knew that he should be more astonished than he was, but all he could feel was relieved and comforted, as if someone had found him alone in the dark and cold and had quietly put a blanket over his shoulders. It was Balam Xoc's presence that made him feel this, however; his eyes were searching, and far from warm.

"You have seen my fatigue, then?" he suggested quietly, and the eyes flickered up to his face, no doubt seeing the lines of strain and the dark circles that Nohoch knew surrounded his own eyes.

"I have seen the unnecessary hardships to which you have been subjected," Balam Xoc replied. "I have wondered why you did not lodge a protest on your own behalf, since you clearly do not deserve such punishment."

"It is the high priest's doing," Nohoch explained, spreading his hands wide in a helpless gesture. Balam Xoc's face, which had displayed little sympathy to begin with, hardened perceptibly.

"Of course it is. But Ah Kin Cuy is from the Order of Katun Priests. Who is *he* to interfere with your duties? The katun priests are little more than self-important soothsayers, and I know that the Tun Count priests share my disdain for them."

Nohoch was speechless with surprise, until he remembered all the people who came to sit with Balam Xoc each day, some merely curious, but others obviously willing to share their deepest secrets with the Living Ancestor.

"The katun priests are still very powerful," he managed finally. "It would be unwise for us to venture such an opinion openly, and risk antagonizing them."

"Yet you would allow them to antagonize *you*? Dignity does not always reside in silence, Nohoch. Your anger must tell you this."

Nohoch did not ask how Balam Xoc knew of his anger, assuming that it must be as apparent to him as his fatigue. Was there anything that was *not* apparent to him?

"What would you suggest I do, Grandfather?" he asked humbly.

"Defend yourself. You have the right to expect your superiors to protect you from such harassment."

"Yes," Nohoch agreed ruefully. "But I do not expect them to defy the high priest on my account."

"Then you must request a reduction in your duties," Balam Xoc told him bluntly, "or accept the fact that they will break you eventually."

Nohoch sighed again, and looked at his feet.

"Such a request would entail a loss of rank," he said in a plaintive voice. "And a surrender of the revenues that feed my family."

"Has your rank protected you?" Balam Xoc demanded. "You are being treated like the lowliest of apprentices, yet you cling to your rank as if it will save you. As for the other, you know as well as I that the clan can easily make up the difference, and would be honored to do so. Your own people, at least, have not forgotten your worth."

"I will have to consider—" Nohoch began, but Balam Xoc cut him off impatiently.

"You were fortunate today, Nohoch. Kin smiled upon you, despite your weariness and inattention. Was this not a sign, a message to you? Will you wait for disgrace to overtake you, or will you free yourself now, while your heart and your reputation are still untouched by error and guilt?"

"Why do you pressure me, Grandfather?" Nohoch protested. "These are not matters to be decided in haste."

"You have equivocated long enough," Balam Xoc assured him drily. "Now you must choose. You cannot be what you were, Nohoch; the priesthood is no longer a sanctuary for you, a place where you can hide behind books and numbers. You must take back your life, or leave it to those who do not respect its value."

Nohoch looked down at the painted staff in his hands, then away toward the distant hills, which were lit from behind by an orange glow.

"Must I resign from my order?" he asked finally, meeting the old man's insistent gaze. Balam Xoc shook his head in denial.

"By no means. I have no quarrel with the Tun Count priests, nor they with me. The keeping of time has been a sacred task since our beginnings as a people, and I will honor it always. I do not expect you to abandon your knowledge, Nohoch, and follow after me like a pilgrim. I expect you only to change, as you must, to meet the needs of our people."

"I will speak to the head of my order, then," Nohoch murmured wearily. "I cannot pretend that I am not tired and angry, and close to the end of my usefulness as a priest. As you say, it is better that I remove myself now, before I am driven out completely."

"I will leave you to your farewells, then," Balam Xoc said succinctly, and turned away without another word. Nohoch watched him go in silence, too drained to know if the lightness in his limbs was due to relief or incipient regret. Not bothering to find a dry spot, he sat down on the platform and balanced his staff across his knees, and stared for a long time at the hidden face of the Sun.

THE AIR was warm and thick with humidity when the day began, and a light drizzle had begun to fall before the Tikal delegation was put in order and led out of Uaxactun. The honor guard of warriors, in full-feathered battle dress, were at the front of the column, with Kinich Kakmoo prominent among them, wearing the clipped headdress of scarlet macaw feathers and the knotted chest protector that Shield Jaguar had given him. Behind the warriors came the heads of the delegation and their wives, their necks and arms encircled by strings and bracelets of jade and polished shell, their elegant heads wrapped with lengths of extravagantly colored cloth. Some were accompanied by servants holding palm-leaf umbrellas, while the most important among them were carried in cloth-covered litters.

The rest of the delegation followed in an order determined by rank and function, the priests forming a somber group between the high-ranking diplomats and the merchant chiefs, the latter recognizable by their black staves and articles of foreign dress. Akbal was the very last of those of noble blood. His position was not really so different from the one he had occupied on the journey out, but the artisans who followed just behind—his companions then—maintained a careful distance from him and his porter, making clear their unwillingness to have him in their midst.

The Tikal Painter walks alone, Akbal thought, experiencing a surge of residual bitterness. His eyes felt hollow and wild after a night without sleep, yet there was an energy flowing frantically just beneath his skin, a nervous pulsation that made his hands tremble and sweat. Out of impulses he had not paused to identify, he had dressed himself in the same loincloth and net headwrap he had worn during his interview with Shield Jaguar, yet he had also put on his headband, tumpline, and pack. After considerable coaxing, he had pried enough bundles loose from his porter's load to fill the pack, justifying what was essentially a gesture of contempt, a deliberate and spiteful withholding of his nobility, and thus his respect. The porter clearly thought that he had taken leave of his senses, and in his present state, Akbal had little inclination to correct the man's impression. He preferred to be mistaken for a common bearer, since he had been made to bear so much.

After passing through the outskirts of Uaxactun, the trail narrowed and plunged into the shadowy depths of the forest that provided the city with its timber and firewood. The smell of wet earth and rotting vegetation was very strong, and lingering sheets of fog broke and disintegrated before the marching figures. Though the rain could barely penetrate the leafy canopy overhead, the trail was predictably soft in this season, and was quickly churned into mud by the heavy tread of the warriors and litter bearers ahead. Akbal and his porter clung to the grassy edges of the path, risking the danger of snakes for the sake of some solid ground that did not suck at their bare feet and make the loads upon their backs even heavier. Woodcutters stopped their work to watch the procession pass, standing conspicuously in clearings of their own creation, dwarfed by the great cedar or mahogany they had felled.

Then the long, straggling line came out into the open again, and Akbal could feel the rain spatting softly against his face and wilting the once-stiff cone of his headwrap. Maize fields spread out on both sides of the trail, the rich, reddish soil half-hidden beneath a layer of cinders, the young stalks of maize thrusting up in long rows, seeming extraordinarily green against the background of blackened soil and charred stumps. Akbal could not tell if these fields belonged to Uaxactun or Tikal, but they had obviously profited from a good early season. He realized that he had given no thought to this season's crops, having been away during the time he would ordinarily have been listening to his father's worries and complaints about seed deficits, insect infestations, and the perennial shortage of workmen. It was startling to come upon all this new growth without the seasonal warning of his father's anxiety.

The fields gave way to low, swampy ground, then to another stretch of forest, the delegation alternately stringing out and bunching up as those in the lead periodically paused to change litter bearers or negotiate a particularly treacherous piece of the trail. Then the great wall of earth and stone that formed Tikal's northern border appeared ahead, standing out from the surrounding forest by virtue of the deep moats that flanked the wall on both sides. Erected during the troubled times of the last Katun 11 Ahau, thirteen katuns in the past, the earthworks were greatly eroded, held together by the tenaciously tangled roots of the trees that grew along the top. Still, they were an impressive sight, rising twenty feet high and extending in both directions for as far as the eye could see, a standing testament to an external threat long since forgotten.

Shortly after passing through the gap in the earthworks, the procession stalled again, then stopped altogether for reasons that no one bothered to explain to the muddy marchers in the rear. Akbal lowered his pack onto a flat rock beside the trail and eased the band of his tumpline off over his headwrap, rubbing at the indentations in his forehead. Clusters of thatched-roof houses were visible among the ubiquitous stands of breadnut trees, and gradually people began to come out along the trail to examine the gaudy assemblage of lords and warriors. They were mostly women and children, and very poor, judging by the worn drabness of their clothing. They stared at the members of the delegation as if they had never seen such fantastic beings before, bowing automatically whenever any of the lords deigned to glance in their direction.

For his part, Akbal could not help but stare back at them, stricken by the sight of the bony, underfed bodies of the children, and by the glazed, listless expressions on the faces of their mothers. Many of the younger children, especially those just beyond the age of weaning, cried continuously, raising a noise that contrasted eerily with the stolid silence of the women. Resisting the urge to cover his ears, he watched as a tiny, naked boy squatted in the weeds beside the trail, emitting a high, piercing whine along with a sputtering stream of liquid excrement.

These are the people who have borne the weight of Katun ɪɪ Ahau most heavily, Akbal realized, tearing his eyes away when the child's mother saw him watching and bowed to him. The bad crops of the past three seasons had no doubt left them to subsist on breadnuts and the produce from their tiny garden plots, which were wedged in around and between the houses, wherever the ground was high enough. And even though it was their husbands and fathers who tended the fields outside the earthworks, Akbal knew that they were likely to see little of the maize and beans they harvested for the ruler. The needs of the city would have to be met first, and the seed deficits made up, before anything would be distributed to them. Akbal had often heard his father complain of the difficulty of accomplishing these basically contradictory tasks, especially with maize in high demand as a trade item. He could not recall, though, ever hearing his father mention these people, or worry over *their* needs.

What I have to bear is very little, he thought humbly as he shouldered his pack and rejoined the march. The little boy's whine seemed to have lodged inside his head, drowning out the din of his anger and self-concern. With a delayed jolt of recognition, he realized that he had seen faces like theirs before, and quite recently. The captives on the monuments of Yaxchilan and Ektun had worn the same abject, defeated expressions, the look of those who endure without hope. Yet these were captives who had been taken without a fight, and their subjugation had gone unrecorded, except in the misery written upon their faces. Akbal did not wonder, as the wails of the children receded behind him, that it had been the poor people of the clan who had responded most powerfully to Balam Xoc's defiant message.

The clustered houses within sight of the trail grew larger and more elaborate as the procession continued south, and the people who came out to greet them were better dressed and less solemn in their curiosity. They called to members of the delegation by name, and several times the cry of "Kinich Kakmoo!" drifted back to Akbal's ears, followed by the sounds of cheering and applause. Young boys began to follow along with the procession as the trail widened and became firm underfoot, the earth covered by a hard-packed layer of limestone marl. Akbal was suddenly aware of the reddish mud caked onto his legs and feet, soil that was not being washed away by the misty rain, which had finally succeeded in flattening his headwrap against the back of his head.

He made no attempts to improve his appearance, though, during the long wait that ensued once the column had reached the northern ceremonial center of the city. The vanity had been shocked out of him, and he had fallen into an obsessively observant state, taking new impressions of the Tikal that had been so familiar for so long. The complex of temples and palaces that surrounded him where he stood had been built during the long reign of the previous ruler, Cauac Caan, and its centerpiece was the Katun Enclosure that had been erected in honor of the sixteenth katun of the cycle, Katun 2 Ahau. Like all the other Katun Enclosures in the city, its layout mirrored that of the Plaza of the Ancestors, with flat-topped pyramids at the eastern and western ends of the broad plaza, a nine-doorwayed building to the south, and an ancestral shrine—here only a small rectangular structure—to the north. Yet unlike the Great Plaza, which had been continually rebuilt during Tikal's long history, this Enclosure had been abandoned after its twenty-tun period had expired. The white paint on the pyramids had chipped and faded, exposing the yellow stone beneath, and grass had grown up between the stones that floored the plaza. Akbal thought again of Yaxchilan and Ektun, where the ceremonial center had been relocated several times, leaving sections of both cities looking nearly as desolate as the Katun Enclosure before him. It is a *foreign* practice, he decided, recalling that his grandfather had said the same of the katun rites themselves.

The leaders of the delegation had returned from the Sky Clan temple, where they had made an offering, and when the march was resumed, Akbal found that the entire procession was visible ahead of him, moving down the long, straight causeway that connected the northern temples with those in the Plaza of the Ancestors. The causeway was thirty feet wide and was flanked on both sides by waist-high parapets, its plastered surface raised well above the swampy ground over which it passed. It descended southward on a gradual decline, angling slightly westward at its midpoint. Off to his right, at a distance from the causeway, Akbal could see the twin pyramids of the Katun Enclosure dedicated by Cacao Moon to the fifteenth katun, Katun 4 Ahau. It had also been abandoned after use, and was in an even more advanced state of ruin than its successor to the north. It was soon obscured from Akbal's view by a group of large buildings that stood between it and the causeway, and he turned his attention to the left, where an immense stairway led down to the Katun Enclosure currently under construction.

He had heard his father complaining for some time that the Enclosure was behind schedule, and he could see at a glance that this was true. Both pyramids were still in the early stages of construction, surrounded by scaffolding and piles of cut stone, and the nine-doorwayed building to the south was lacking its vaulted roof. Only the rectangular structure to the north, where the ruler's monument would stand, had been completed, though Akbal knew that the monument itself had yet to be carved. Gangs of workmen labored on both pyramids, ignoring the rain, but they seemed too few to possibly complete the task in time. With the end of Katun 11 Ahau less than four tuns away, the ruler would have to commit a great many more men to this project—and soon— if he hoped to fulfill his vow to Buluc Ahau.

The procession had halted again, met at its head by a greeting party of dignitaries. But Akbal was too involved in his own discoveries to pay any heed to the speeches being exchanged ahead. He had looked beyond the construction site to the Katun Enclosure presently in use, which had been dedicated by Caan Ac only sixteen tuns before. Its twin pyramids were immense, perhaps twice as large as any of those erected by the ruler's father and grandfather. Yet they, too, would be abandoned upon completion of the new Enclosure, which had obviously been conceived on the same enormous scale.

Akbal swept his eyes back to the right, and the three aligned Katun Enclosures—one abandoned, one in the process of being built, one soon to be abandoned—suddenly coalesced into a single image of vanity and waste. He understood all at once, in a way that words alone could never have taught him, the truth of his grandfather's contention: that the observance of the katun rites was leading Tikal to its ruin. Caan Ac had no choice but to finish the next Enclosure, no matter what it cost, no matter where else the workmen might be needed. To do otherwise would be to abandon the responsibility he had assumed for the success of the crops, which was the basis for his claim to power. So the construction would go forward, and the rites to insure fertility would be performed, even at the expense of the preparation of the fields and the planting of the crops themselves. It was a gamble that substituted prayer for prudence, putting both the ruler and the people—his captives—completely at the mercy of the spirit of the katun.

Can we trust our fate to the whims of Buluc Ahau, Akbal wondered, turning his eyes ahead as the procession again began to move, carrying him away from the Katun Enclosures. But he knew the answer to his own question; he had seen it in the faces of the poor, and heard it in the weanling's whine of pain and hunger. *Is the ruler more powerful than his prophecy?* he thought, recalling a question he had heard attributed to his grandfather. It seemed to him now to be a question that contained its own answer.

The crowd accompanying the column down the causeway had grown considerably in both size and enthusiasm, and more people were waiting in the East Plaza, many of them foreign merchants who had strolled over from the marketplace, drawn by the noise and festive behavior of the crowd. Akbal was offended by their gaiety and did his best to shut his ears to it, withdrawing once more into himself. The celebrants and curiosity seekers fell away as the delegation left the East Plaza and descended the stairs in the direction of the Plaza of the Ancestors. Now their path was lined by priests and dignitaries, who escorted them in silence onto the plastered flagstones of the plaza itself. Akbal experienced a familiar pressure upon his skin, a distinct heaviness in the atmosphere that had nothing to do with the rain. He had always felt he was being *watched* here, even to his innermost thoughts and feelings, and he identified the source of this sensation as the deep, abiding presence of the ancestors, those who had recognized the power and holiness of this place and had built their temples around it. And had *continued* to build their temples around it, Akbal thought, taking a fiercely proprietary pride in the fact that grass would never be allowed to grow in *this* plaza.

Surrounded by a second honor guard of warriors, the members of the delegation were arrayed in even rows before the great funerary temple of Cacao Moon, which stood on the east side of the plaza. The towering pyramid rose in nine steep levels to the squat, single-doored shrine at the top, which was surmounted in turn by an ornate, two-story roof comb bearing the seated figure of the late ruler. There were two uncarved monuments at the base of the temple stairs, and Caan Ac stood upon the stone pedestal in front of the northern monument, wearing a jaguar-skin kilt and a feathered headdress so tall it was held upright by a frame attached to his back. The feathers were wilting in the rain, and the ruler's wet tunic clung to the contours of his stomach, emphasizing his girth. Akbal thought that he looked absurd rather than magnificent, but he was still too affected by where he was to allow himself to entertain disrespectful thoughts.

After the delegation had bowed to the ruler and had received the blessing of the high priest, Caan Ac delivered a lengthy speech of greeting, praising them as a group and welcoming them back to their city. Then he paused, signaling to his warchiefs to present themselves.

"Kinich Kakmoo Balam, come forward," he commanded in his high-pitched voice. "From this day forth, you shall bear the title of nacom, warchief of Tikal."

The front ranks of the delegation parted slightly, and Kinich stepped out of their midst to stand proudly before the ruler, the scarlet feathers of his headdress waving soddenly above his head. One of the other nacoms attached a train of precious blue-green quetzal feathers to the warrior's broad back, and a second warchief presented him with a long ceremonial spear bearing a leaf-shaped point of greyish-pink flint. Then the ruler invited him to stand upon the pedestal next to his own, and the assembled crowd expressed their approval with a low, concerted murmuring.

You have rewarded the right brother, Akbal thought, feeling a surge of his earlier resentment. He scanned the lines of dignitaries on both sides of the pedestals, picking out his father and his father's assistant, Chac Mut, the high priest of the clan, Tzec Balam, and one or two of the other Jaguar Paw leaders. Perhaps there were others from the clan who were hidden from his gaze, but if so, he was just as glad he did not have to see them. He took solace in the fact that at least Balam Xoc had not chosen to attend, a solace no less comforting for being predictable.

As the ruler began to call forward the individual members of the delegation to convey his thanks, Akbal's resentment cooled and hardened, taking the form of a bitter expectancy. *You are a coward, Caan Ac,* he thought coldly, as the ranking delegates left their places to receive the ruler's personal greetings. Among them was Kuch Caan, the Tikal diplomat who had been courting Zac Kuk, which allowed Akbal a brief, gloating moment of scorn as he stood in the rain, waiting to be passed over.

After the lords had returned to their places, Caan Ac recognized the lesser members of the group according to the functions they had performed, singling out the heads of the various craft and artistic groups by name and praising them for the collective contributions of their men. The painters, however, received no mention at all, as if even a passing reference might give rise to unpleasant associations. *You are a coward, Caan Ac,* Akbal repeated to himself, *and I will never serve you again.*

When Caan Ac had finally finished speaking, the feast in honor of Kinich Kakmoo was announced, and the ruler led his new nacom off in the midst of an eager crowd of Tikal lords. The commoners and those without the rank to merit an invitation to the feast slowly began to disperse, and Akbal turned to his bearer, who had already begun to struggle into his tumpline. Akbal started to assist him, then saw his father approaching through the thinning crowd and told the man to put down his pack and wait. He went forward with great ambivalence, almost wishing that his father had not stayed behind to speak to him.

"Welcome home, my son," Pacal said quietly, and Akbal examined his father's long, slender features for a moment, knowing that his own face was coming more and more to look the same. His father's eyes, though, were those of a steward rather than an artist, and they gave back nothing more than they were meant to. Akbal bowed, annoyed by the lack of emotion displayed there, as if this were a homecoming like any other. He held the bow for an extra moment, trying to allow his annoyance to pass.

"You have gained weight," Pacal added awkwardly, when it became clear that Akbal was not going to reply to his greeting.

"I was well fed in Yaxchilan and Ektun. And well treated."

Pacal glanced past him, as if to be sure the bearer was out of earshot, then stepped closer and laid his hands on Akbal's shoulders.

"I want you to know, my son, that I am grateful to you, and proud of the way you performed in Yaxchilan. You have done our city a great service. Someday, perhaps, I will be able to explain why it was not possible for the ruler to say this to you himself."

"Perhaps you do not need to," Akbal said curtly, stiffening in his father's grasp. "Perhaps I understand all too well."

Pacal let his hands drop from Akbal's shoulders and stood back to study his son's face. His expression was one of concern, but Akbal could see a weighing of strategies in the flickering of his eyes.

"You have a right to be angry with me," he confessed finally, lowering his eyes and his voice. "It was *I* who involved you in this, as a favor to the ruler. I can only promise that I will never allow you to be used in such a manner again."

"*You* will not allow!" Akbal blurted in outraged disbelief, then bit his lip before anything more rude could escape his tongue. He turned to stare at the clan temples massed upon the northern platform, breathing deeply as he struggled for control. When he turned back, he saw that his effort had not been lost upon his father, whose face was tense and uncertain.

"You owe me no apologies, Father," Akbal said tightly. "I did not suffer in my time away from here. I became the Tikal Painter, and I made many friends for myself and my clan. I even found the woman I intend to marry. I do not think of myself as a man who has been used, despite the ruler's ingratitude. That is only a reflection upon *him.*"

"You have matured greatly," Pacal allowed, choosing to overlook the bitterness in his son's voice. "We must speak later about this woman."

"It is the custom."

The indifference of Akbal's reply was deliberate and cruel, but his father heard him impassively, nodding once as he glanced around the plaza, which was nearly deserted.

"I am expected at the ruler's feast. Your grandfather is holding a feast in your honor at his house. I believe that the greater part of the clan will be there to greet you."

Akbal's eyebrows lifted in surprise, freeing a drop of water that ran unnoticed down the long bridge of his nose.

"Were they not invited to the feast for Kinich?"

"I invited them all myself. But your grandfather has convinced the majority that the Tikal Painter is more worthy of their respect."

"But he could not convince *you,*" Akbal said in a flat voice, making it a statement rather than a question. "Perhaps you did not truly mean the things you said to me earlier."

"Do not taunt me, Akbal!" Pacal flared angrily. "My position is more complicated than you know, or than your grandfather is willing to believe."

"I can see that," Akbal retorted. "It cannot be easy to serve a man who is loyal only to himself."

As Pacal's eyes narrowed, and he opened his mouth to speak, Akbal straightened his shoulders, expecting to be reprimanded for his disrespect— *hoping,* in fact, to be reprimanded. But then his father thought better of it and terminated the conversation with an abrupt bow. Turning away, he gestured for his assistant, Chac Mut, to join him and started off across the plaza, following in the path the ruler and Kinich Kakmoo had taken earlier. Akbal watched him go in silence, disappointed that his father did not have the courage to separate himself from the ruler, or to demand his son's respect. He knew then that his own path would take him in another direction, and ever farther from his father's approval. *To become a man,* he thought ruefully, gazing at the great temples that surrounded the plaza, *perhaps even a man of Tikal.*

KANAN NAAB had recognized the change in her brother at first glance, as surely as she would had his hair turned white or his complexion darkened. It showed in the way he responded to the people who came out of the craft house to greet him as he came up the trail with his porter behind him. He was not a pretty sight, streaked with mud and disheveled by the rain, his headwrap fallen around his ears and his face tautly distorted beneath the band of his tumpline. It was a situation that might have embarrassed anyone, and Kanan Naab knew her brother to be only slightly more at ease with people than she was herself.

Yet Akbal had smiled at them with complete self-possession, striding up to bow before Cab Coh and take the old man's extended hand. Then he had allowed his gaze to fall over all of them, without staring at any one among them, and had spoken in a clear, quiet voice:

"Greetings, my people. It is a great pleasure to be among you again."

Kanan Naab had been as touched by his obvious sincerity as were the others, and had not minded that his personal greeting to her was gracious but brief, cut off by the press of all those who wanted Akbal's attention. She had stayed as close to him as possible as the group began to move toward the houses, watching the way he answered questions and accepted the compliments being showered upon him. He was not unfamiliar with praise, she had noted, and did not shy away from the title of Tikal Painter. His speech had also become more polished, and he had picked up some gestures that were new to her and seemed slightly extravagant in their courtliness. *My brother has learned how to present himself,* she had decided, though she remained uncertain as to the depth and significance of this change.

Then Akbal had gone off to his room to dispose of his packs and change into dry clothing, and Kanan Naab had been forced to go back to her duties. So many people had decided to attend Balam Xoc's feast that the houses of Cab Coh and Nohoch Ich had also been pressed into service, and mats were being laid down in the craft house to accommodate the additional guests. Kanan Naab had taken many of the preparations upon herself, and she scurried from one cookhouse to the next, sending servants for more food and trying to put everything in order. She wanted to impress Akbal with the new prosperity of the clan, and make all those who came to the feast glad that they had chosen to honor him. Akbal himself was to meet privately with Balam Xoc and the members of the clan council before the feast began, and as soon as she could free herself, Kanan Naab went quietly to the back entrance of her grandfather's house.

There was no one in the darkened back room, and she moved quickly across the floor, toward the voices on the other side of the curtained inner doorway. Only when she had reached the curtain did she stop to reflect on the propriety of what she was doing, and she turned instinctively to leave. But the sound of her brother's voice drew her back, and when she looked through the crack between the curtain and the doorframe and saw him sitting next to Balam Xoc and Cab Coh, all thoughts of leaving vanished.

Though she could not see them, she sensed that the part of the room that was beyond the range of her vision was filled with men, and some were even standing against the wall behind the place where Akbal sat. He had a bundle of painted sticks open on the floor in front of him, and he gestured toward it with one arm, his other arm clamped securely over the leather pouch at his side. Kanan Naab's ears pricked up at the word *Zuyhua,* but otherwise she had come in at the end of the conversation, and could not make sense of what Akbal was saying. The men in the room seemed to find it significant, however, and murmured deeply when he was through.

"And what is in your pouch, my son?" Balam Xoc asked when the room was again silent. "It must be very precious, since you hold it so closely to your heart."

"I made friends in these cities," Akbal said with visible pride. He removed a handful of rolled deerhide sheets from the pouch and passed them across to Cab Coh. "These are trade agreements I have made with men I know in Lacanha, Bonampak, and some of the other cities along the river. They require only your consent, Grandfather, to be made final."

Cab Coh unrolled one of the documents and scanned it briefly, squinting his watery eyes to make out the glyphs and the columns of bars and dots representing amounts. Grunting softly, as if favorably impressed, he handed the limp leather sheet to Balam Xoc.

"I will examine them more carefully later," Cab Coh said. "But the terms appear quite fair. How were you able to obtain them?"

"These are the men who painted with me in Yaxchilan, as I told you earlier," Akbal explained, reaching into the pouch and producing another sheaf of the flattened leather rolls. He kept one aside for himself and placed the rest in a small pile in front of Cab Coh.

"I have also accepted a number of commissions of my own. I think you will find that the payment is sufficient to more than compensate for my time."

As Cab Coh opened the top roll, Kanan Naab glanced at Balam Xoc, who had draped the first document over his knee without looking at it. His eyes were gleaming, and he looked as if he wanted to laugh. He poked mischievously at the sheet in Cab Coh's hands.

"Well, my brother," he demanded in a teasing voice, "does your assistant know how to barter for his services?"

"Can this be true, Akbal?" Cab Coh inquired, blinking in bewilderment. "I know this man, and I would not have suspected that he was capable of bartering so poorly on his own behalf."

"He bartered more shrewdly than some others," Akbal said with a trace of annoyance. "Those are the kinds of fees my work commands in Ektun. The same fees the Sky Clan merchants have been obtaining for some time," he added pointedly. "I think it is time we had a new accounting with them."

Cab Coh was rendered speechless by the suggestion, but Balam Xoc broke in sharply, his face no longer amused.

"Are you saying that the Sky Clan has been cheating us?"

"There is the proof," Akbal replied, gesturing toward the stack of commissions. "Even with the cost of hiring our own porters, our profits would be greater than they are now."

Balam Xoc sat back and looked expectantly at his brother, who was still recovering from his shock. The document in Cab Coh's hands began to shake, and his face slowly darkened with anger.

"I will speak to the merchants tomorrow," he vowed in a seething voice, displaying a fury so palpable, and so uncharacteristic, that Akbal and the men behind him recoiled in surprise. Even at a distance, concealed behind the curtain, Kanan Naab could feel the force of his anger. Balam Xoc, however, appeared delighted at seeing his mild-mannered brother so riled, and he extended a hand toward the roll still in Akbal's lap.

"You have yet another surprise for us?" he inquired knowingly, and Akbal cradled the roll gently in his long fingers, leaving no doubt in Kanan Naab's mind that this was truly the document he had carried next to his heart.

"I must present this to my father," he said softly, frowning unconsciously, to himself. But then he looked around at the other men and smiled the same smile he had displayed outside the craft house. "It is a message from the Lord Batz Mac, of the Turtleshell Clan of Ektun. It concerns the matter of my marriage to his daughter, Zac Kuk."

Kanan Naab clapped a hand over her mouth to stifle an exclamation of surprise, but it would have been lost in the outburst of congratulations from the men anyway.

"Who is this woman's mother?" a voice near at hand demanded, and Akbal laughed aloud, as if amused by the question.

"She is the Lady Muan Kal. Of the Moon Clan."

"They are closely allied with the Sky Clan," Cab Coh pointed out quietly, looking to Balam Xoc with concern. But Balam Xoc simply gestured to Akbal for the explanation.

"Zac Kuk knows that it is the Jaguar Paw Clan to which she comes," Akbal assured them firmly. "She knows how much it means to me that I am the grandson of the Living Ancestor."

Akbal's voice had grown husky as he spoke, and he suddenly bowed to

Balam Xoc, crossing both arms over his chest and almost touching his forehead to the floor. Kanan Naab drew a long, tremulous breath, intensely moved by her brother's gesture. *He has joined us,* she thought; *he has accepted grandfather's visions as his own, though he was not even here to hear of it.* All of the changes she had perceived earlier, so startling in themselves, no longer seemed mysterious to her. He had become a Jaguar Paw, in spirit as well as blood.

"You are old enough to take a wife," Balam Xoc said simply, accepting the bow without comment. "And the wealth you have brought to the clan should help to raise a house for you and Zac Kuk. Is that not so, my brother?"

"Indeed," Cab Coh said agreeably. "Perhaps it will even keep him here long enough to make me believe I have an assistant."

The men laughed loudly and began to call for balche, and Kanan Naab chose the moment to make her escape, heading quickly for the back door. *I must tell Box Ek,* she thought eagerly, then realized that she would have to explain how she had come by her knowledge. She hesitated briefly, then smiled to herself and went on toward Box Ek's room. In return for news of Akbal's marriage, she was certain, Box Ek would find a way to forgive her for her spying.

AKBAL WAS at first too preoccupied with being the guest of honor, and too happy to be among his own people, to notice that they were not all *his* people. But gradually, as he went from his grandfather's house to that of Cab Coh, and then to that of Nohoch Ich, the number of new faces to which he was being introduced began to make a distinct impression upon him. Some were clan relations from distant parts of Tikal: cousins, uncles, and in-laws with whom he had never had the chance to meet. But there were many others who belonged to different clans altogether, including some from cities as far away as Pusilha and Copan. Akbal found himself becoming self-conscious in his storytelling, reluctant to speak of "foreign" ways in front of those who might be considered foreigners themselves.

It soon became apparent, though, that none of these newcomers *acted* like strangers. Nor were they regarded as such by the other members of Akbal's family, who often referred to their places of origin only as an afterthought. They were not at all reticent in approaching Akbal or questioning him about his experiences, seeming quite familiar with his background and accomplishments. *How long have I been gone?* Akbal wondered, beginning to feel that *he* was the true stranger here.

"The Jaguar Paw House has attracted many guests," he remarked to Nohoch Ich during a quiet interlude, when the attention of the rest of the company had been diverted by the appearance of servants bearing bowls of fruit. Nohoch took a slice of pineapple from the bowl offered to him and looked around the circle of faces for a moment, as if trying to see them through Akbal's eyes.

"They are not guests," he replied finally, giving Akbal a significant glance. "They are *followers.*"

"Ah," Akbal murmured thoughtfully. He returned the priest's gaze, trying to weigh the meaning the term had for him. He had received part of his education in the glyphs from Nohoch, and had always called him Uncle, but little in the way of intimacy had ever existed between them. This was partially due to Pacal's open dislike for his cousin, though Akbal himself had always felt that Nohoch was rather aloof and remote, a priest in every way.

"Much has changed while you were away," Nohoch added. "No doubt you have heard of your grandfather's dance at the Tun-End Ceremony?"

"I was told in Ektun. I was also told that he was called before the high priest, and that he claimed to have been given a vision."

"I was there when he revealed this to Ah Kin Cuy," Nohoch averred. "It was an old woman, a Spirit Woman, who came to him in his confinement. She told him that he must be a compelling example to the young, and show them the power that lies in the old ways."

Akbal's eyes widened in recognition.

"He has already been that to me. The longer I was away, the more I felt his influence."

"That was clear in your presentation to the council," Nohoch told him. "You were most impressive, Akbal. There was no one who did not think he had chosen to honor the right brother, after hearing of your accomplishments."

Akbal nodded mutely, warmed by the older man's praise and encouraged by his frankness.

"Are you also a follower, Uncle?" he asked in a polite tone, and Nohoch stared at him for a moment before answering.

"My vows would not permit such a thing. Nor does your grandfather wish me to follow him like a pilgrim. I do not think that he desires our devotion, Akbal; only that we change, and take back our lives from the ruler."

"The ruler has made that easy for some of us," Akbal said with a trace of residual bitterness. Then he gave Nohoch a swift, questioning glance. "In Uaxactun, though, there are many who doubt the wisdom of challenging the ruler's power."

"They are here, too," Nohoch admitted. "Not all changes are pleasant, or easy to accept. Yet on the whole, the clan has prospered. You are not the only one to bring us trade agreements: many of our 'guests' also do so, and they bring us gifts and offerings as well."

Akbal cocked his head curiously, hearing the voice of an administrator rather than a priest. *A voice like my father's,* he thought in wonder, recalling all the times he had heard his father deride Nohoch's competence in this area. Yet Nohoch's eyes met Akbal's steadily, with none of the calculation of a royal steward.

"I saw my father in the plaza today," Akbal said impulsively, then paused before adding, "along with your son, Chac Mut. They followed the ruler to my brother's feast."

"It is Chac Mut's duty to obey your father. And your father's to obey the ruler."

"I cannot respect him for that any longer," Akbal blurted. "He is the servant of our enemy."

"That is a harsh judgment," Nohoch said gently. "I would hope to be regarded with more compassion by my own son."

Akbal swallowed thickly and shrugged, though not with indifference.

"As you said, Uncle, not all changes are pleasant."

Nohoch nodded ruefully and did not argue further, showing his respect for the seriousness of Akbal's feelings. He took a sip of cacao from the cup in front of him and glanced around the room, remembering his duties as host. Then he looked back at Akbal and spoke in a more casual tone:

"The drawings you made in Yaxchilan are most interesting. We must discuss them some time."

"I was not aware that so many people had seen them," Akbal said in a bemused tone. "I do not even know who unpacked and aired them for me."

Nohoch smiled thinly.

"It was your sister. She has been to see me about them several times, asking questions I could not answer. She does the same with your grandfather and the young priest from the Serpent Clan, Yaxal Can. Have you met him yet?"

"He also asked me about the drawings. He seems rather stiff and solemn," Akbal added, then smiled self-deprecatingly. "But perhaps that is how all suitors seem."

"No," Nohoch disagreed, "that is his manner. He is a novice within the Tun Count Order and is very earnest about his work. Very *ambitious,* since it does not come easily to him. He was clearly disappointed when I told him that I had requested a reduction in my duties for the order, and had accepted a loss of rank."

"I see," Akbal said shrewdly. "Do you think that this will affect his interest in Kanan Naab?"

"His interest is tested often enough already," Nohoch assured him with a laugh. "Your sister is no longer a woman that any of us can choose to ignore. Her curiosity has become ferocious, and your grandfather indulges her completely. Yaxal has a hard time of it, for he is not a follower, either."

"Perhaps she will change him," Akbal suggested, and Nohoch laughed again. He shook his head wryly, as if laughing at himself as well.

"No doubt she will," he said succinctly, spreading his hands wide in a gesture of acceptance. "It is the custom, now . . ."

BALAM XOC stood among the breadnut trees behind his house, relieving himself of all the balche and cacao he had consumed during the feast. The leaves overhead rustled softly in the breeze that had finally carried off the rain, and a brilliant half-moon split the shadows with shafts of bright bluish light. From behind him he could hear the sounds of the servants cleaning up in the cookhouse: sounds of water being dumped and bowls scraped, accompanied by the grunts and murmurs of weary workers. Less clearly, he could hear voices off to his left, which told him that Kanan Naab had found Akbal and had brought him to the stone.

Retying his loincloth, Balam Xoc headed toward the voices, following a moon-spotted path through the trees. He emerged into the open a few paces from the stone and its surrounding shelter, which cast a solid black shadow in the moonlight. Akbal had one hand on one of the shelter's support poles and was reaching up with the other to ruffle the thick thatch of the roof, speaking over his shoulder to Kanan Naab. Seeing Balam Xoc, he immediately fell silent, and both he and his sister turned to bow as their grandfather came forward.

"Thank you, my daughter," Balam Xoc said to Kanan Naab, who made another brief bow.

"I did not have to search far, Grandfather," she explained. "He had already come here on his own."

Kanan Naab exchanged a glance with her brother and took a step backward, expecting to be dismissed.

"Stay, my daughter," Balam Xoc commanded. "I wish to speak to both of you."

Kanan Naab stepped forward without hesitation, drawing a disconcerted nod from Akbal, who had also obviously expected this to be a private conversation.

"I know there are things you have saved to tell me," Balam Xoc said, lifting his chin in Akbal's direction, "but there will be time for us to talk later. Surely, you will not forget what you have learned before then?"

"No, Grandfather," Akbal admitted, nodding in apology to his sister. Balam Xoc stared at them in the moonlight: the tall, slender young man with the string of polished grey shells around his neck—a gift from Zac Kuk—and the marks of the tumpline still visible upon his forehead; and the young woman who came barely to his shoulder, her blunt features enlivened by an animation reminiscent of her mother, her eyes glowing with the devotion she always showed toward her grandfather. Balam Xoc stared at them and felt nothing, except a muted, impersonal satisfaction at their openness to him.

"The feast tonight was a great success," he said at last. "I must thank both of you for that. You, my daughter, for seeing that our relatives and guests were well fed and sent away happy. And you, Akbal, for providing us with the opportunity to come together as a clan. I did not know, when I chose to make you a symbol, that you would act the part so perfectly."

"A symbol?" Akbal queried, frowning uncertainly.

"Yes. A symbol of our independence from the ruler's favor. A symbol that his scorn and neglect cannot harm us, but only serves to make us stronger. You were the living proof of that when you came before the clan council with your commissions and your advice for Cab Coh."

"Indeed," Kanan Naab murmured, lowering her eyes in embarrassment when Akbal gave her a surprised glance. Balam Xoc squinted at her knowingly but went on without comment:

"You know that I have a special regard for the two of you. But it is not, as you may think, because you are my grandchildren. Kinich Kakmoo is also my grandchild, and my feelings toward him are no different than they are toward you." Balam Xoc paused and looked at each of them in turn, emphasizing his seriousness. "That is because I no longer experience the emotions that once governed my life, and tied me to other people. The Spirit Woman has taken them from me; she has breathed her coldness into my lungs and heart, so that all I can feel is the strength of my purpose. I no longer look to other people for friendship, or approval, or affection. I see in them only what must be changed: the fear or selfishness or confusion that clouds their judgment and prevents them from laying claim to their lives."

Akbal and Kanan Naab stared at him with wide eyes, seeming incapable of expression. The wind ruffled the thatch on the shelter's roof, producing a ragged, scratching sound.

"I regard you as special," Balam Xoc continued, "because I see no sign of these impediments in your characters. You are curious and eager, and do not need to be pushed to change. You require only the opportunity to recognize and pursue your own ambitions, and I have tried to provide this for you. Yet in doing so, I have given rise to another possible impediment. That is your attachment to me."

Kanan Naab's body jerked slightly, and she cast a nervous, sidelong glance at her brother. Akbal wet his lips, blinking as if the moonlight had become too bright for him. Balam Xoc stood silently, allowing them to dwell upon the uneasiness his words had aroused.

"The high priest has made me famous," he said finally, with a sardonic smile. "Perhaps even more famous than the Tikal Painter. This has drawn people to the clan from a wide area, and many of them have chosen to stay and attach themselves to us. Some are learned men who wish to discuss my views with me, and some are seekers who come to sit in silence with the holy man. All of them, even the skeptics, want my attention and approval; they would like me to notice them and dote upon them like grandchildren.

"I do not say this to mock them," Balam Xoc added swiftly, holding up a hand to Kanan Naab, who was looking at him dazedly, "but only because their need is very clear to me. They seek a cause worthy of their energy and devotion, and they cannot find it in the places where they live. I am willing to share the cause of our clan with any who are willing to take it up, so I indulge their need to be close to me, and give them my time.

"But there is yet another group of people who come to me, most often on the days when I am sitting as the Living Ancestor. They are poor people, without the means to spend more than a few hours away from their work. They are not drawn to me by my fame, or the need for a cause. Their cause is simply to keep themselves and their families alive; they are unable to seek anything greater. Some of these have told me that I appeared to them in their dreams and made them believe there was hope for the future. Their faces make me believe them, though I do not have the power to travel in my dreams. Others claim that their lives have been transformed by suggestions I cannot remember making, or which they have clearly misunderstood. I believe them, as well, even when my reason tells me they are mistaken. I know that this is the work of the Spirit Woman, and not my influence at all, and I try to tell them that. But few of them can hear me, and fewer still can accept that I have no powers beyond my message. They would rather believe me uncanny, and give their lives to *me,* than have them for themselves. It is what they are used to, however much they have been betrayed in the past."

Balam Xoc paused and raised his hands at his sides, palms up, urging them to understand him correctly.

"So perhaps you see how much work lies ahead. This is only the beginning: Many more will come to our side before the katun is completed, and still others will rise up to resist us. I may never have the chance to speak to you like this again, my children, so hear me well. I am not spurning your devotion, or abandoning my concern for your welfare. But I cannot allow you to join those who look to me for solace and direction. You are capable of providing these things for yourselves, and you must do so. The spirit of the Jaguar Paw is within each of you; it is a memory in your blood. You have only to let yourselves remember, and you will know how to live your lives."

Balam Xoc stopped talking abruptly and crossed his arms in front of his chest, patiently awaiting their reply. His tone had never varied during the course of his entire speech, and his face was similarly calm and composed. Akbal and Kanan Naab looked at each other intently, as if to confirm that they were both here, and awake. Kanan Naab gave a deferential nod, urging her brother to speak.

"We will honor your words, Grandfather," Akbal promised, drawing another nod from Kanan Naab. "We will serve the cause of our people in any way we can."

"I am depending on it. There must be others besides myself who know how to act on behalf of themselves and the clan." Balam Xoc gestured toward the shelter. "I have already given you the stone, Akbal. Do not let your work and your family distract you from it totally; let it teach you the things you need to know. And share your knowledge with your sister, so that the two of you may help each other. The truth is your stone, my daughter," he said to Kanan Naab, "and you have my permission to seek it, and let it make its mark upon you."

The moon had sunk to the level of the trees, slanting its light across their upper bodies, so that the two young people bowed into shadow as Balam Xoc raised a hand over them in blessing.

"Let us go to our rest, my children," he said quietly, pointing the way back to the houses. "Let us renew ourselves for the tasks we have been given . . ."

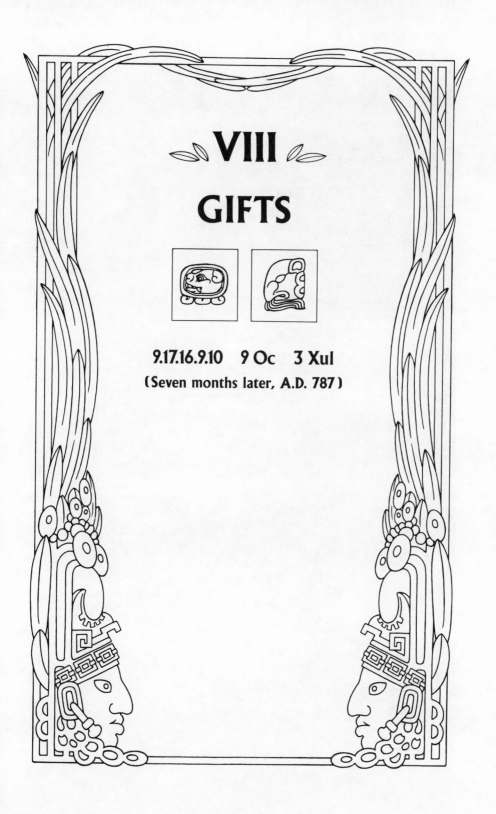

VIII

GIFTS

9.17.16.9.10   9 Oc   3 Xul
(Seven months later, A.D. 787)

PACAL was inspecting the crops in the alkalche east of the city when the messenger came, telling him that his wife's labor had begun. Accepting the congratulatory smile of his assistant, Chac Mut, with a brief nod, Pacal cast a proprietary glance over his surroundings. He was standing on one of the raised fields built up over the swamp, in the middle of a long row of maize plants whose tasseled heads rose a full foot above his own and whose ripening ears were bending double from their own weight. The bushy cotton plants on more distant fields seemed equally healthy, and the sprawling foliage of the manioc and macal was a luxuriant dark green. The fish that lived in the well-dredged canals were spawning, and a crowd of women and children had come out of the nearby houses to gather the fish eggs with reed scoops and spear the slow-moving fish.

"Tell my wife that I am coming to her," Pacal said to the messenger, and the boy darted off, picking his path between the tall plants.

"I will complete the inspection for you, my lord," Chac Mut offered in a relaxed tone, revealing how easy he expected the task to be. Pacal nodded tolerantly, acknowledging the confidence that both of them felt about this crop, even though neither would speak of it aloud. The ruler had made a maximum commitment of men and resources at the beginning of the season, even sending his warriors out into the fields, and the weather had been almost extravagantly cooperative. Every available piece of land, including plots that were due to lie fallow, had been planted, mostly in maize and cotton, and the gamble seemed to be paying off handsomely. The shortness of the fallow had led to some severe infestations of maize borers, but the extra fields under cultivation more than made up for the few that had to be burned off because of insects. The winds had been mostly gentle, and it seemed inconceivable that the bad luck of the previous year would be repeated. It seemed more likely that the ruler's prayers and penance would hold off the threat of storms and allow for a harvest that would redeem him from his troubles.

"It is in your hands, then," Pacal said absently, and headed for the shore at a leisurely pace, luxuriating in the circumstances that allowed him to leave his work in the middle of the morning, in a season usually so tense and hectic. It was a good sign, and it made him feel strongly, as he walked toward his home, that this was a good day for a birthing.

UPON ENTERING her uncle's house, Kanan Naab paused only long enough to let her eyes adjust to the dimness, then went directly to the small circle of men seated in the corner. She bowed to Nohoch Ich and the other older men and waited silently to be recognized. When Nohoch finally asked what she desired, she looked straight at Yaxal Can—who was sitting next to her uncle—and asked to know the number and sign of the day.

Yaxal hesitated, pursing his lips in disapproval. He did not like the way she interrupted and questioned the men, even if she did have her grandfather's permission, and this seemed a particularly trivial request. But Nohoch signaled brusquely for him to supply the information, knowing that Yaxal had been on duty that morning, and would already have consulted the *tzolkin,* the Book of Day Signs.

"It is the day Nine Oc, my lady," the young man explained, "the eighth day of the month Xul. It is an auspicious number, a good day for undertaking new projects."

"I have not heard you ask the day's sign for a long time, my daughter," Nohoch said in an innocent tone. "I thought that you had shed your concern for such things."

"I do not ask for myself," Kanan Naab told him, with an archness meant for Yaxal. "The Lady Ixchel has begun her labor, and it is important for her to know this. I do not know why."

"Well, do not let us keep you," Nohoch expostulated. "You must go and find out why, must you not?"

Kanan Naab blushed but managed to smile at her uncle. She knew that he was really teasing Yaxal for his stiffness, and she liked him for it. She glanced at Yaxal, who was regarding her solemnly, with the absence of expression that was his way of showing his disappointment in her. She felt her irritation like a prickling dryness on her tongue, and had to prevent herself from making a spiteful face at him.

"Yes, I must," she said swiftly, bowing to the men as she rose to her feet. "Thank you, young man," she added for Yaxal's benefit, making only the briefest of bows before turning her back and walking purposefully from the room.

DUCKING his head under the low doorway of the craft house, Akbal stepped out onto the plaza and paused to stretch his body, kneading the stained fingers of his painting hand. Automatically, his mind began to catalogue all the things he had to do next: He had to get some more lime for the plasterers working on his house, another porter still had to be hired to transport his commissioned work to Ektun, and he had promised Cab Coh that he would inspect the set of bowls they had just received from the potters . . .

No, Akbal decided rebelliously, *I must have a few moments to myself first.* He had been painting all morning without a rest, finishing the last pieces for Ektun, and he knew that he would have to return to the craft house once he had gotten his other chores out of the way. He had never worked this hard in his life, except perhaps for the days he had spent training the painters in Yaxchilan. That feat now seemed to him to have been merely practice, *his* training for the life his talent and ambitions had brought him. He was proud of his discipline, which made him feel mature and responsible, a man worthy of a wife and a house of his own. But there were other times—like this one —when he felt that he had no thoughts of his own, much less the time to think them, and he began to yearn for the lost freedom of his boyhood.

Taking a quick glance around, he saw Cab Coh descending the stairs from the upper plaza and immediately started off in the opposite direction, hoping to get away before his master could accost him with more chores. There was now a second house on the north side of the plaza, beside that of Kinich Kakmoo, and Akbal gazed upon it with undiminished satisfaction as he hurried past. It was the same size and rectangular shape as his brother's, raised upon a platform three steps above the level of the plaza. But instead of the usual three doorways in front, it had five, in the style of the airy Ektun houses to which Zac Kuk was accustomed. It was still only half plastered and lacked a roof, but Akbal expected to have the men to raise and thatch the roof once the harvest had been completed.

Akbal slowed his pace a bit when he was safely around the corner of his house, passing the marked-off spot where the cookhouse would stand and the fig tree that he and Kal Cuc had prepared as a perch for Zac Kuk's pet birds. Akbal smiled to himself at the memory of the boy's hunterly disdain for the very notion of pets, even though Kal Cuc looked after the family's flock of domesticated turkeys. He had made it clear to Akbal that he would be willing to tolerate Chuen only because there was not much meat on a spider monkey.

Perhaps he is too much of a hunter to consider the alternative I have to offer, Akbal thought, as he came out of the trees and saw Kal Cuc sitting in front of the stone, in the shade of its sheltering roof. Akbal was not surprised to find him here, for he did so frequently, and he had almost come to consider the boy a kind of accessory to the stone, like the shelter itself. It was Kanan Naab —herself a frequent visitor to the stone—who had made him consider the significance of finding Kal Cuc here so often, and had led him to formulate the proposal he was about to make.

Kal Cuc was sitting facing the stone, with the Zuyhua weapon and his quiver of short spears across his bony knees. The throwing stick had been Akbal's gift to him for having rebuilt the shelter in Akbal's absence, and Kal Cuc had fashioned his own short spears so as not to lose the originals. He did not jump up at Akbal's approach, a sign of how comfortable he had become in the young man's presence. Or perhaps, Akbal thought as he squatted beside him, how comfortable they both were in the presence of the stone.

"You have been practicing?" Akbal asked casually, nodding toward the weapon. Kal Cuc shrugged wearily.

"There has been no time today. I have been fetching wood and water for my grandmother and the other midwives."

Akbal started guiltily and looked back toward his father's house, reminded of another obligation.

"The Lady Ixchel has not borne her child yet, has she?"

"My grandmother says there is still time," Kal Cuc replied without enthusiasm. "I will have to go for more wood in a moment."

"How is your skill with the weapon?" Akbal inquired, allowing himself to relax. Kal Cuc's narrow face brightened a bit at the question, and he pursed his lips judiciously, as if striving to make his response sound professional.

"I am very good with it in the open, where there is room to throw, and nothing between me and my target. The alkalches are the best places to use it. I almost got a heron the other day, but a reed deflected my throw." Kal Cuc paused and swallowed, letting Akbal know that he did not wish to hurt his feelings. "It is not so useful in hunting in the forest, though. In fact, it is no good at all where the jungle is thick."

"I will tell this to my brother, the nacom, before he goes off to fight the Macaws again," Akbal said, only half-facetiously. Then he grew more serious. "But I want to talk to you about something more important. It has occurred to me that you are almost twelve, the age of apprenticeship, and that you have no sponsor within the clan."

Kal Cuc lowered his eyes and nodded tentatively, then peered up at Akbal with a wary expectancy.

"I would like to know if you have your heart set upon becoming a hunter," Akbal said in a neutral tone. "It is possible that such a thing could be arranged with some of our clanspeople who live on the outskirts of the city."

"Ah!" Kal Cuc blurted, then lapsed into a thoughtful silence, glancing once at the stone. "My grandmother would be alone if I left her," he decided glumly. "She is old, and depends on my help."

"Many of us depend on your help," Akbal told him in a reassuring tone. "I have another suggestion, then, though I do not know if it will suit you. I recently spoke to some people from the Flint Clan, the stone carvers who taught me what little I know of that craft. They have been gifted with more daughters than sons, and have begun to look outside their own family for apprentices."

The boy looked again at the stone, then back at Akbal, unable, in his surprise, to do more than stare.

"They do not live far from here," Akbal continued, "so you would not have to leave your grandmother or this House. I know that you are good with your hands, and there is always work for skilled carvers. The clan would be grateful to hire a carver who is one of our own, rather than contracting with outsiders."

Kal Cuc cast a third glance at the stone, making Akbal realize how right Kanan Naab had been. He had decided beforehand to phrase his proposal in practical terms, remembering Kal Cuc's initial skepticism at the value Akbal himself put on the stone, and basically believing that the boy was at heart a more practical person than he was himself. Kanan Naab had insisted that the boy's fascination with the stone was as personally compelling, and as inexplicable, as Akbal's own, and would matter more to him than any promise of future employment.

"I will also need help myself one day," Akbal suggested, "whenever I am finally ready to put my mark upon this stone. You could do much to help me prepare it in the meantime, when you have time away from your apprenticeship."

"You would let me assist you?" Kal Cuc managed, his excitement struggling with his disbelief. Akbal smiled broadly, as much in recognition of his sister's perspicacity as in confirmation of the boy's hopes.

"I will depend upon it."

Kal Cuc was suddenly all gratitude, bowing and murmuring his thanks over and over again, despite Akbal's pleased demurrals. A broad shadow fell over them, and this time Kal Cuc jumped hastily to his feet, clutching the throwing stick and quiver in his hands. Akbal was not slow to follow when he saw that their visitor was Kinich Kakmoo. Kal Cuc bowed to the warchief, who cast a significant glance at the Zuyhua weapon, and then at Akbal himself. Akbal signaled with his eyes that the boy could go, and Kal Cuc dashed off, leaving the two brothers alone in front of the stone.

They faced each other in silence, having shared no words in the seven months since their return to Tikal; indeed, having not spoken since their argument in Ektun. Kinich spent most of his time in the company of the ruler and the other warchiefs, or away on maneuvers with his warriors. Despite his prestige, he was no more comfortable around the Jaguar Paw House than was their father, and he had not forgiven those who had chosen to spurn his feast. He seemed both older and thinner to Akbal, as if his broad, Sky Clan features had begun to set in hard lines.

"So that is what you think of my gift," Kinich said gruffly, inclining his cloth-wrapped head in the direction Kal Cuc had gone. Akbal drew himself up defensively, preparing a retort on the free nature of gifts. But Kinich's breathing whistled harshly through his broken nose, a sign of his nervousness, and there had been no real edge to the accusation.

"He treasures it, and has learned to throw with it," Akbal explained. "He tells me that it is useless for fighting in the jungle, though."

Kinich narrowed his eyes for a moment, then laughed loudly.

"Yes!" he exclaimed with apparent pleasure. "I will remember that. A good nacom learns from even the humblest warrior."

Akbal nodded cautiously, waiting to learn what had brought his brother here. Nothing had changed within the family; if anything, the lines had been drawn more sharply, and they were still on opposite sides. Kinich seemed to acknowledge this by refusing to meet Akbal's eyes fully, glancing instead at his headwrap, his paint-stained hands, and once—with an unconscious frown—at the stone.

"I am told that Ixchel's labor has begun," the warrior said finally. "My wife is one of those who attend her. It seems proper that we should both be there for the birth of our father's child. Do you not agree?"

"It is most proper," Akbal agreed without hesitation, though it was for Ixchel's sake, and not their father's, that he had intended to look in on her.

"It is also proper for brothers to mend their differences," Kinich said in the same stiff tone, "and be friends."

Akbal could see the effort this attempt at reconciliation was costing his brother, but the memory of Kinich twisting his arm and threatening him was still too powerful to allow him to reply immediately. And he had to wonder what his friendship could be worth to Kinich, who was now on equal terms with the most important men in the city. *Unless,* Akbal thought with a flash of insight, *my brother has begun to learn—as I learned—what friendship and gratitude mean to men like the ruler . . .*

"I am willing to forget the past," Akbal proposed, and Kinich responded almost too quickly, obviously relieved that an apology was not being demanded of him.

"And I, as well. I can tell you truthfully that I have never held any grudge toward you on account of the feast."

Hearing the slight emphasis Kinich put on "you," Akbal understood that his brother's tolerance did not extend to Balam Xoc or the clan members who had followed him in this instance. The depth of his loyalty to his grandfather made Akbal hesitate, wondering if this reconciliation did not constitute a betrayal of the people who had honored him instead of Kinich. But then he remembered Balam Xoc urging him to be independent, and to follow what was in his heart and blood. Brothers *should* be friends, even if their differences had to be overlooked rather than resolved; the clan could not be hurt by a compassionate response to his brother's loneliness.

"Nor I toward you, my brother," Akbal said sincerely. "Let us go to see Ixchel."

Kinich's face softened for just a moment, before he huffed through his nose and regained his solemn warrior's demeanor.

"I am ready . . . Brother," he said self-consciously, and the two of them turned and marched off—in step—toward their father's house.

AT THE DOORWAY to her stepmother's room, Kanan Naab was met by Kinich Kakmoo's wife, May, who gripped her arm and whispered to her in a strained voice.

"You must find a way to calm her, Kanan Naab. She is fighting against the pains and will not move her muscles in time with them."

Kanan Naab murmured reassuringly and released herself from May's grasp, entering the dimly lit room, which was warm and smoky from the charcoal braziers in the corners. Ixchel squatted naked against the far wall, her back against the stone bench, her arms held by women who squatted on both sides of her. Her slender, swollen body was bathed in sweat, and a thin stream of blood trickled from her vagina, onto the soft, cloth-covered mats beneath her. Walking around the midwives who knelt in front of Ixchel, Kanan Naab relieved Kal Cuc's grandmother, who rose gratefully from Ixchel's side, grunting with the effort of straightening her aged limbs.

Ixchel quivered in Kanan Naab's hands, and every contraction struck her tensed body with a concerted jolt that made her roll her eyes and cry out incoherently. Kanan Naab spoke to her softly for several moments before she was certain Ixchel knew who she was.

"It is the day Nine Oc, Ixchel," she said in a very clear voice. "Nine Oc."

Ixchel jerked her head toward Kanan Naab, almost pulling free from the woman on her other side.

"Nine Oc!" she exclaimed hoarsely, staring at Kanan Naab with wild eyes. "Do you remember—?"

The contraction occurred in midsentence, and her whole body arched with it, too suddenly for Ixchel to struggle against it. The midwives nodded their approval, encouraging Kanan Naab with their eyes.

"Take shallow breaths," Kanan Naab instructed the gasping woman, but Ixchel seemed only intent on regaining her ability to speak.

"Do you remember, Kanan Naab?" she managed between gasps. "The night your grandfather came? The night we wore flowers in our hair?"

"I remember," Kanan Naab assured her, holding tight as another contraction, more powerful than the last, surged through Ixchel's body.

"That was Nine Oc . . . too," Ixchel hissed, her eyes opening and closing spasmodically. "Your father . . . that night . . ."

"Do not speak. *Breathe,*" Kanan Naab urged, though she understood now why the day sign had been so important to Ixchel. The same sign and number would reoccur in combination only after a full cycle of the *tzolkin*—two hundred and sixty days—had been completed, a period quite close in duration to the normal term of pregnancy. Ixchel was trying to tell her that this baby had been conceived on the night of Balam Xoc's visit, the last day Nine Oc, and that it had chosen the same day to come forth into the world.

The significance that this information had for Ixchel was manifest in a sudden relaxation of all her resistance to the contractions, which were now beginning to come in fast succession. Ixchel strained back against the bench behind her, pushing out from her middle with all her strength, so that Kanan Naab and the woman on the other side had to strain themselves to hold on to her sweat-slippery arms. The head of the child, matted with black hair, appeared between her legs, and the midwives moved in to massage Ixchel's abdomen and draw the child forth. Ixchel's nails dug into Kanan Naab's arm, pulling her close, so that their heads were almost touching. Ixchel's eyes were closed, but she was murmuring to herself, blowing the words out between deep, groaning gasps for breath. It was, Kanan Naab realized, a kind of prayer, an incantation for the child being born:

"A Jaguar Paw child . . . for you, Grandfather, a Jaguar Paw child . . . for you . . ."

PACAL SAT close to his wife upon the bench, warming one of her hands in his own. But most of his attention was upon his new son, whose red, wrinkled face was visible among the bundled cloths that Box Ek, a proud grandaunt, was holding across her lap. May was sitting on the other side of Box Ek, and Kinich was kneeling in front of the bench to examine his half brother; Akbal stood at a slight distance, easily able to see over the heads of the women crowding in around the baby. Pacal felt a tug on his hands and inclined his head so that Ixchel could whisper in his ear.

"Do you remember, my husband, the night your father came to eat with us? The night you stayed up late with him, but then came to me afterward, seeming far from tired?"

Pacal pulled back a little to look at her face, which wore a dreamy smile over the lines and hollows of her fatigue, giving her the appearance of extreme intoxication. He saw that her memory of that night was a happy one, and he automatically concealed the ambivalence his own memories aroused in him.

"You were very beautiful that night," he said soothingly. "But why do you remember it now?"

"It was the night our child was conceived," Ixchel told him in a thrilled whisper. "It was under the sign Nine Oc, the same sign that ruled over his birth today."

"That is indeed marvelous," Pacal said, trying to keep the skepticism out of his voice. It would be cruel, given her present state, to point out that she could not possibly be certain of such a thing. His ardor had been unusual that night, buoyed by the false euphoria of having obtained the use of Akbal, but it could not have been the only time they lay together that month. They had been trying to have a child for five years, after all.

But he did not say any of this to Ixchel, simply patting her hand and smiling to humor the rapt conviction in her eyes. He looked up as Kanan Naab appeared at Ixchel's side with a red flower in her hand. The two women smiled at each other without speaking, ignoring Pacal's presence entirely, and then Kanan Naab reached forward to fix the flower into the coils of her stepmother's hair.

"He is coming," Kanan Naab said softly, exchanging a meaningful glance with Ixchel.

"Who is coming?" Pacal demanded more loudly than he had intended, unaccountably irritated by his daughter's gesture. Kanan Naab stared back at him for a moment, then at Kinich, who had risen to his feet beside her.

"Grandfather," she replied firmly, in the sudden silence following Pacal's outburst. Kinich shifted uneasily and glanced at the doorway, as if contemplating an escape. But it was too late, for Balam Xoc had already entered the room, and the women parted to make a path for him, bowing low to the Living Ancestor.

"Greetings, my sister," he said to Box Ek, ignoring the weighty presence of Kinich, who took a few steps to the side, away from him. Box Ek proudly offered up the bundle in her lap, and Balam Xoc lifted the child against his chest, looking tenderly at the tiny clenched face.

"He is a boy child," Box Ek reported, "and healthy in all his parts."

"You have brought us a great gift, my daughter," Balam Xoc said to Ixchel. "We are all proud of your courage."

Ixchel shyly lowered her eyes, clasping her hands in front of her body.

"I am but a poor woman from Nohmul, Grandfather, and I have little courage. But I am certain of one thing: This is a Jaguar Paw child, a gift of the spirit you have brought to your people."

"The spirit lives in you, as well, Ixchel," Balam Xoc told her gently, placing the baby in her arms, "for you have joined yourself to us. I accept your son, and yours, Pacal," he added to his son, "in the name of the Jaguar Protector, and of the Spirit Woman who watches over our clan."

"I want to name him Bolon Oc, after the sign of this day," Ixchel blurted suddenly, lifting her eyes to Balam Xoc, and then turning the same imploring look upon her husband. Pacal was momentarily nonplussed, then angry at this usurpation of his prerogative as a father. He had already decided to name a male child Chac Balam, after his older brother, who had died, and it had never even occurred to him to consult with Ixchel. Now he was being asked to do so in public!

"Does this name have a special significance for you, my daughter?" Balam Xoc asked in an interested tone, and Pacal could feel his wife turn expectantly to him, as if awaiting his permission to speak. But he stubbornly refused to meet her gaze, glancing instead at Kinich, whose narrowed eyes shared his anger and sent him support.

"Yes," Ixchel said timidly, and paused for a long moment before going on in a quick, flat voice: "He was conceived under this sign. And it is the sign under which he has been born."

The women in the room collectively caught their breath, then broke out in appreciative murmurs.

"What do *you* say to this, my son?" Balam Xoc inquired of Pacal. "Do you choose to honor your wife's wish?"

Pacal looked around at his other children, seeing encouragement in Kanan Naab's eyes and judgment in Akbal's; Kinich had bared his glittering teeth, urging him silently to refuse. All of the other women in the room wore expressions similar to that of Kanan Naab, instinctively taking the side of the new mother. Finally, he looked at Ixchel, expecting her to shrink from him, for surely she could feel his anger and embarrassment. But there was no guilt in the dark eyes that stared back into his; only a puzzled kind of disappointment, as if his attitude were utterly incomprehensible to her. As it would have to be, Pacal thought sadly, since she did not know that the night she remembered so fondly had cost him the respect of another of his sons. Now this son, too, would go to Balam Xoc, who had used what *he* had learned that night to betray Pacal before the clan council.

But Ixchel could not know this, either, though she had suffered from her husband's increasing isolation within the clan. Pacal was struck by guilt of his own, which made it impossible to bear the disappointment in Ixchel's eyes.

"Let him be called Bolon Oc Balam, then," he said, in a voice that caught in his throat before bursting free, a voice that was trying to make resignation sound decisive. Kinich made a disgusted noise and stalked out of the room; beyond where he had stood, Pacal saw Akbal's long face, which remained judgmental, as if he saw his father's capitulation for what it was. But Ixchel had thrust the baby into his arms and was pressing her lips against his cheek in gratitude, and the other women were smiling and congratulating him, calling out the new child's name. The warm little bundle in Pacal's arms squirmed and let out a small cry, and Pacal instinctively pressed the child against his heart.

"Welcome, my son," he said dazedly, clutching the bundle to him as if afraid it might disappear. "Welcome to the home of your people, Bolon Oc Balam."

WHEN THE TIME of the harvest finally arrived, late in the month of Yaxkin, the sun shone brightly over Tikal, upon fields that had suffered no damage from wind or rain. Every available man, woman, and child had turned out for the task, along with a large part of the army, and still the cutting and gathering went on for over a month. It was the most enormous crop in Tikal's long history, larger than any that could be recalled from the records or the memories of the elders. Rows of loosely thatched huts had to be built in a field near the marketplace to house the surplus maize, and the royal storehouses were overflowing with baskets of beans, squash, and manioc, as well as thick bundles of raw cotton and sheaves of fragrant mai, the smoking leaf. There were feasts in even the poorest of houses, and the clan priests presided over elaborate ceremonies of thanksgiving, the first to be held in almost four years.

With the same suddenness, the ruler's stewards once more found themselves the dispensers of plenty rather than the defenders of shortage, and were reminded of the pleasure they had once taken in their work. A respectful equanimity supplanted the acrimony that had characterized their dealings with the heads of the clans, and the merchants from other cities now approached them with a kind of awe, as if they, too, had forgotten how truly powerful Tikal was. For some of the stewards, especially the younger ones, the sense of vindication was so overwhelming that they impulsively went ahead with long-deferred purchases and improvements to their homes, before the royal revenues had even begun to be counted.

Pacal, however, was not one of those who indulged in such optimistic gestures. Three more growing seasons remained within Katun 11 Ahau, and there was always the chance that they would be as bad as the three previous to this one. The Katun Enclosure would have to be completed during this same period of time, as well, which would mean far fewer men for everything else that needed to be done. Pacal did not share his father's militant concern for the future, but he had been affected by it, and he felt strongly that the affairs of the city had reached a critical juncture. This crop had been a great gift, and they could not afford to squander the advantage it had given them. They *dared* not squander it, if they hoped to have any future at all.

Important decisions—crucial ones, to Pacal's mind—would have to be made very soon, and rumors had already begun to circulate among the lords in the palace. The one most frequently repeated was that the ruler was planning a major military campaign, to be waged in concert with Yaxchilan. Another, which was actually *discussed* more thoroughly by the other stewards, was that the stewardship itself was to undergo some sort of reorganization. Caan Ac himself was being extremely closemouthed, apparently waiting for the scheduled stewards' council to reveal his intentions fully.

After consulting with all of his sources, Pacal came to the conclusion that no one had been entrusted with more than rumors, and that Caan Ac was making no effort to secretly win allies or arrange for a consensus. He was acting alone again, on his own counsel, as he had in the case of the burial vase. *He intends to* buy *our acquiescence,* Pacal reasoned, and given the wealth presently at his disposal, plus the possibility of some new titles to be distributed among the stewards, it seemed likely that he would succeed in manipulating the council to his own ends. Pacal decided abruptly that he could not wait until the council meeting to know what those ends were, or to exert whatever influence he could upon them. He had been left out of last year's negotiations, and then had been called upon to make them work, at a high personal cost to himself. For the sake of his own self-respect, if not the respect of his family, he could not allow himself to support a policy again in which he had had no say, or which he could not adequately defend. Allowing himself no time for second thoughts, he sent a message to the ruler asking, as a "personal favor," for a private interview.

Caan Ac summoned him later that same afternoon, receiving him on the long terrace that overlooked the ravine behind the ruler's palace. A single line of breadnut trees shaded the southern edge of the terrace, and between their evenly spaced trunks Pacal could see the still waters of the palace reservoir, tinted a deep crimson by the slanting rays of the setting sun. Caan Ac's canopied throne had been set up in the shade of the trees, facing the western horizon, which was dominated by the immense funerary temple of his father, Cauac Caan. The tall roof comb of the temple's shrine jutted blackly against the side of the sun's red face, which was sinking slowly toward the horizon, to the left of the pyramid itself.

Crossing his chest, Pacal bowed low before the ruler, whose eyes were protected from the sun's glare by a thick fringe of knotted threads hanging from the front edge of the canopy. He gestured for Pacal to sit facing him and waved away the guards who had accompanied him across the terrace. Caan Ac had recently celebrated his fifty-fifth year of life, ten more than Pacal, and the hair that showed beneath his elaborate headwrap was mostly grey. He sat, as always, with his stubby legs dangling down in front of his throne.

"This must be important to you, Pacal. It has not been that long since you performed your favor for me."

"It is most important, my lord. I did not think it could wait until the council meeting, when I would have to clamor for your attention."

"You have my attention," Caan Ac replied smoothly. "What is it you wish to say? Or is it something you wish to *know*?"

"It is both, my lord," Pacal admitted. "The palace is alive with rumors, and it is difficult to know what to believe, or how to prepare myself for the meeting."

"Do you suffer more from not knowing than the other stewards?" Caan Ac demanded sarcastically. "Or would you use your favor to buy an advantage over them?"

Pacal simply stared at him, surprised by the cynicism of the ruler's response, and by how deeply it offended him. He was not ordinarily a man who was easily offended, especially by the accusation of personal interest. But it had never seemed so unfair, so undeserved, as it did in the present context.

"For whom would I seek an advantage, my lord?" he asked in return. "My clan rejects everything I bring to them. I have only you, and our city, to serve. And yes, my lord, I suffer from being kept in ignorance. We all do. You did not used to be so secretive with us."

Caan Ac grunted and looked away toward the reservoir, watching the swallows and purple martins that swooped gracefully above the gleaming red surface of the water. From somewhere farther off in the ravine, the hooting of a wood owl mingled and overlapped with the guttural *hut-hut* of a motmot.

"You are not one who has complained to me before," Caan Ac allowed finally, turning back to Pacal, "so I must regard what you say with serious concern. What rumors have you heard?"

"I have heard that a military campaign is being planned."

"That is true. Shield Jaguar is organizing a campaign against the Macaws, and Zotz Mac of Ektun has already agreed to participate, as have the rulers of Yaxche, Bonampak, Acantun, and Lacanha. Should Tikal not have a share of the glory? It would help to reassure those who depend upon us for protection, and to test the fitness of our warriors."

"The cost of such an expedition would be great," Pacal ventured, but Caan Ac shook off the objection with an impatient jerk of his head.

"The cost will be repaid many times over by the lands and goods that our warriors take in conquest. Have you forgotten how easily your son and his men put the Macaws to flight? We must not retreat into ourselves, Pacal, now that we have the means to enlarge our prestige! That is why I keep my plans to myself, so that they will not be picked at and diminished by men without courage or imagination."

"I have no desire to diminish our prestige, Lord," Pacal said quietly, "but my sense of duty compels me to consider all of the things we must accomplish here at home. The Katun Enclosure must be completed, and we are far behind schedule. And if we divert our workmen to that, how will we manage the next crop? We had use of the army this season, and we took a great risk in choosing to expand the size of the planting. We are fortunate that we have the means to replenish our stores of seed, but new land will have to be cleared for burning if we are to avoid a serious problem with insects, and the reservoirs and raised fields should not go another season without repair. The rains were gentle as well as timely this year, and did little of the damage they have often done in the past. Can we hope to be so lucky again?"

"The rains are *my* responsibility," Caan Ac said, pointing a blunt finger at his own chest. "As to the problem of workmen, we will hire those we need from the clans, and from Uaxactun and the other nearby cities. They have all seen the size of our crop, so they will trust that we can pay, even if we only give them a small amount in advance. We can also promise them a bonus for their trust, to be paid later out of the loot brought back by the warriors. Those who will not trust us," Caan Ac added pointedly, "we will pay in full. But I expect this only from your own clan and a few others."

Pacal nodded absently, knowing that it would be more than just a few, given the growth of Balam Xoc's influence. And if word got out that *one* clan was being paid in full, the others might reconsider their trust in bonuses. But this was a minor flaw, compared with some of the others Pacal had already perceived in the ruler's plan. Especially vexing was the utter impossibility of estimating the value of what the warriors might bring back; that alone made all the figures Pacal had been compiling in his head seem vaporous and unreliable. He suddenly felt very tired, and offered his next proposal in an obligatory tone, as if holding little hope of being heeded.

"If we did not have to hire so many workmen, though," he suggested, "we would be free to use our surplus for trade. We could renew our ties with the cities to the east and south: with Holmul, Nakum, and Yaxha, and with Pusilha and Copan. We would not have to accept whatever Yaxchilan chose to offer. I have heard that they have an abundance of cacao again this year, and no intention of lowering their terms."

"But *we* have maize, and cotton," Caan Ac said with annoyance, "and both are more valuable in the west. You try my patience with this quibbling, Pacal. You know that my grandfather, Cacao Moon, returned to Tikal from Acantun, with the backing of Shield Jaguar the Elder. Would you have me tamper with our most important alliance for the sake of a few ears of maize? I am the Sky Clan ruler, and I will rule this city in the same manner as my father and grandfather!"

Pacal bowed in compliance, though the gesture, to himself, was truly one of resignation. He could no longer recall what he had hoped to accomplish with this interview, beyond some dim desire to prove his own influence. Perhaps his motives had been more personal than he had realized; perhaps he had come here to test the suspicions his father had planted in his mind.

"Do not look so forlorn, Pacal," Caan Ac scolded him. "I value your advice, and surely there is maize enough to trade with these other cities. But you will not have to concern yourself with such matters in the future. I have already decided to make you the chief steward of crops. It would have been a surprise for you, had you been willing to wait until the stewards' council."

"Chief steward?" Pacal said blankly, and Caan Ac's fleshy face broadened into a self-satisfied smile.

"You heard no rumors of that? It is a new position I am creating. There will be five chief stewards, one each for crops, construction, administration, trade, and procurement for the army. Each will have the authority to appoint their own subordinates from among the ranks of the stewards, and each will be responsible only to me and the council of chief stewards. So you see, I wish to give you the power to deal with the very problems of which you have spoken. Unless, of course, you would prefer to play a lesser role in the management of our city . . . ?"

Despite the knowledge that his hesitation alone could cost him the promotion, Pacal could not bring himself to respond immediately. He had a brief, irrational urge to consult with his father, which so flustered him that he grew angry with himself. Was *this* not proof of his influence and his value to the ruler? Should he refuse the power being offered him and allow it to fall to another, perhaps one less able than himself?

Pacal looked up and saw the ruler standing over him, and realized that he had been lost to the world for a few moments, locked in a fierce, silent argument with himself. Caan Ac raised him to his feet and turned him toward the west, where the sun was falling beneath the horizon in a molten red mass. The great temple of Cauac Caan stood entirely in shadow, a black hulk that seemed to have shouldered the sun aside.

"You see the tomb my father built for himself," Caan Ac said, in a voice that mingled pride and envy. "Four times the size of any other in Tikal, larger than any temple built by other men, *anywhere*. It is a monument that will keep the memory of Cauac Caan alive in the minds of his people forever. Will there be such a monument to mark the memory of my reign? We both know that such a thing is impossible. It is our misfortune to live in another time, one that constrains the display of our greatness . . ."

Caan Ac's voice had fallen to a low, grating hiss, but now it rose again, and he lifted his arms toward the sky, as if to embrace the sun's dying splendor.

"But that does not prevent us from *exercising* our greatness, and leaving our legacy in the hearts of men! That is why I must insist on boldness, Pacal. We may die at any time; let us not be forgotten while we live!"

The ruler's shout echoed over the terrace, bringing the guards around its perimeter to renewed attention. The sun was now only a curving red line clinging tenuously to the darkening horizon, and night was falling swiftly. Caan Ac seized Pacal's arm and shook him roughly.

"Do not fail me now, Pacal! Let it be said of us that we were the men who brought our people safely through Katun Eleven Ahau. Let that be our glory, and our monument!"

The sun suddenly winked out, and darkness descended around them, so that Pacal could barely make out the face so close to his own. But the ruler had not released his arm, and seemed still to be shaking him, though more with the sheer force of his emotion.

"Yes, my lord," Pacal heard himself say, and felt the hands disappear from around his arm, leaving damp prints upon his skin. The ruler patted him once on the shoulder, then started off across the terrace, drawing his guards to him.

"*Yes,*" Pacal repeated softly, in a whisper that echoed only in his own ears, which trapped the sound, making it seem inevitable.

IN THE MONTH of Mol, Batz Mac brought his wife and family to Tikal for the wedding of Akbal and Zac Kuk. They made the first part of the journey by canoe, using the chain of small rivers that flowed from east to west and were still navigable after the good season of rain. After resting for a night in Uaxactun, where their clan had relatives, they continued south on the same trail that Akbal had used on his return, passing the stubbled maize fields where flocks of wild turkeys and currasows pecked over the leavings of the harvest. At the entrance to the northern ceremonial center of the city, they were met by young Kal Cuc, who had been given the honor of guiding them to the Jaguar Paw House. Skirting the Katun Enclosures to the north, they passed several impressive housing clusters—one large enough to resemble a ceremonial center—before joining up with a trail that curved around the edges of an extensive alkalche.

Walking at the side of her mother, Zac Kuk pretended to herself that the open water of the swamp was a river, simply to make the landscape seem more familiar. She had been well aware that Tikal was a much larger city than Ektun, but the sheer *extent* of the settlement had been beyond the reach of her imagination, and was still a source of astonishment. They had been walking for the better part of the morning, past houses that only grew larger and more densely clustered, toward ever more impressive plazas and ceremonial centers. There seemed no end to it, and no boundaries—like the hills that encircled Ektun—against which to measure its true size. Zac Kuk had the dim sense, having glimpsed the towering temple pyramids that lay farther south, that they were bypassing the actual center of the city, but she felt no regret about what she might be missing. She was already intimidated enough by her surroundings, and it was not a feeling to which she was accustomed, or one she enjoyed.

Hearing a familiar squawk, she glanced back over her shoulder, past the relatives and servants immediately behind her, to the porters who carried her birds in shrouded cages upon their heads. The procession, some thirty-five people in all, had seemed impressive to her when they had set out from Ektun, but they had attracted little notice within the precincts of Tikal, and had in fact been passed several times by larger groups, including many people better dressed than herself. This intimidated her perhaps more than anything else, and made her feel vaguely ashamed of her pets, which suddenly seemed like a child's playthings, brought to comfort the child against the strangeness of a new place.

"Ah!" Muan Kal exclaimed beside her. "Look how many houses they have! And the size of the family shrine!"

But Zac Kuk did not want to look, and cast only a passing glance at the thatched-roof houses clustered among the surrounding breadnut trees, with the tall, red roof comb of the shrine thrusting up out of their midst. Instead, she looked between the men in front of her, training her eyes on the crowd of people waiting for them at the head of the trail. As they drew closer, she saw that there were actually *two* crowds: one composed of Akbal and the members of his immediate family, and another, much larger, which stood at a respectful distance behind the first group. Zac Kuk could not see enough of this latter group to ascertain who they were, though there were clearly too many of them to assume that they were simply the household servants.

Then the men in front of her stopped, and the view between them was filled by the figure of Akbal, who had stepped forward to greet Batz Mac. Zac Kuk's breath came more rapidly, and her stomach tightened with excitement, though to her already daunted eye, even his face did not seem truly familiar. His features appeared to have grown thinner and more sharply defined, making him look older and more mature.

"I regret that my father cannot be here to greet you, my lord," Akbal said courteously, "but his duties as the chief steward will keep him away until the time of the wedding. May I present to you my grandfather, Balam Xoc, the Living Ancestor of our clan . . ."

Zac Kuk craned forward so eagerly that her mother put a hand on her arm to restrain her and remind her of the proper decorum. Zac Kuk obeyed reluctantly, having obtained only a brief glimpse of the old man who had appeared at Akbal's side. *Is that him?* she wondered, experiencing a moment of disappointment that was actually a kind of relief to her. She had expected a much more impressive figure, a fierce, visionary rebel with commanding gestures and all-seeing eyes. This man seemed no different from her own grandfathers, except that age had not yet made him bend or shake.

"This is a joyful occasion for both our families, Batz Mac," she heard the old man say, "so let us not stand on ceremony. Let us mingle freely, like the friends we should be."

"I would be honored to call you friend, Balam Xoc," her father replied, and Zac Kuk envisioned the two of them clasping hands, though her view of the scene was obscured. The men ahead of her immediately broke rank, her brother, Chan Mac, going directly to Akbal, and the two sons of Box Ek—who had come as much to celebrate their mother's seventieth birthday as the wedding—stooping to embrace a tiny, shriveled woman who leaned on a polished wooden stick. Zac Kuk felt a sharp pang of jealousy at the undisguised pleasure Akbal and Chan Mac were taking in seeing each other again, but it disappeared quickly when Akbal, with a compulsive kind of eagerness, looked up over her brother's head and sought her out in the crowd. She lowered her eyes with the proper show of modesty, though not before she had noted how much younger his smile made him look.

Her father was bringing Balam Xoc and another, older man over to greet her and Muan Kal, and in the brief instant before she bowed with her mother, Zac Kuk's attention was distracted by a sudden wave of movement in the background, as if the second crowd had surged forward in unison. Indeed, when she looked up again, she found that the other people had closed in behind Balam Xoc in a solid wall, close enough for her to see that they were definitely not servants. Some even seemed to be foreign lords and priests, and others wore clothing too eccentric for servants.

"Welcome to the Jaguar Paw House, my lady," Balam Xoc was saying to Muan Kal. "I hope that the journey from Ektun was not a hardship for you."

"It has been many years since I visited Tikal, my lord," Muan Kal said graciously. "It has only grown more impressive."

"It has grown, certainly," Balam Xoc allowed, in a dry voice that sounded almost sarcastic to Zac Kuk's attentive ears. But his weathered brown face did not smile, and the eyes that looked at Muan Kal were steady and without hidden meaning. He gestured toward the old man beside him. "May I present my younger brother, the Master of Craftsmen Cab Coh . . ."

Muan Kal hesitated for just a moment before bowing, and Zac Kuk knew that her mother was also having trouble believing what she had heard. Cab Coh's whole body shook slightly as he bowed, and his watery eyes blinked constantly, making his smile of greeting seem as much baffled as kindly. He looked to be at least ten years older than his brother, certainly no *younger.*

"This is my youngest daughter, Zac Kuk," Batz Mac said in a proud voice, and Zac Kuk bowed in turn to each of the old men, before demurely raising her head to meet Balam Xoc's eyes. Having prepared herself for this meeting, she looked back at him gravely, trying to show that she was intelligent and discreet, a woman worthy of his house. She was aware of all the staring eyes behind Balam Xoc, though she did not feel that their attention was directed at her.

"You are as beautiful as Akbal has led me to believe, my child," Balam Xoc said, in the same dry, vaguely sarcastic tone he had used earlier. "I had not expected someone so solemn, though."

Batz Mac laughed loudly at Balam Xoc's perceptiveness, and after an obligatory, embarrassed duck of her head, Zac Kuk responded to the old man's teasing with her most dazzling smile. But while Cab Coh's bleary eyes widened in pleasure, Balam Xoc's expression barely changed, and the smile that crept onto his face did so belatedly, as if without his conscious intent.

"That is a smile that befits a bride!" Cab Coh said with gentle enthusiasm, giving Batz Mac a congratulatory nod.

"Yes, it is far from solemn," Balam Xoc observed, and though Zac Kuk kept the smile on her face, she had to struggle to repress a shudder of foreboding. She was certain she had never met a man so utterly without warmth or affection, so beyond the reach of her smile. She had no idea how to impress such a man, and it was *him,* she knew, that she most needed to impress.

To her surprise, though, he held out his hand to her, asking her to accompany him.

"Before you go to dress for the ceremony," he suggested, "allow me to show you the home my grandson has prepared for you. It will perhaps make you feel more welcome than I am able to."

Zac Kuk glanced at her mother and father, who smilingly gave their consent to this unusual proposal, which had seemed to contain a note of apology, as if Balam Xoc were aware of the effect he had had upon her. She reached out compliantly, barely grazing Balam Xoc's leathery hand before he turned to let her walk beside him. The crowd behind him parted automatically to make way for him, revealing how closely they had followed his every word and gesture. But Balam Xoc paid them no heed, not even bothering to explain their presence as he led her through their midst. He spoke only to her, in a normal tone.

"This is the craft house, where Akbal and the other craftsmen work under the direction of my brother," he explained as they passed a long, thatched-roof building with many open doorways, a building that reminded her of Ektun. She could feel the crowd falling in behind her, but she tried to pay them no mind, emulating Balam Xoc's casual disregard with great difficulty. They came around the corner of the craft house and entered a plaza somewhat larger than that of her father's house, though she could see a still-larger plaza set well above this one, beyond a bank of shrubs and small trees. Balam Xoc stopped her in front of the first house on the north side of the plaza, though his gesture also included the house that stood beside it, just to the east.

"Akbal has built next door to his brother, Kinich Kakmoo," Balam Xoc said, and Zac Kuk nodded tentatively, looking from one house to the other.

"I was introduced to Kinich Kakmoo in Ektun," she replied, for lack of anything better to say. She was not sure what she was supposed to be seeing in the two houses, and she was distracted by her awareness of the people spilling into the plaza behind her. But Balam Xoc seemed to be waiting for her response, so she made another effort, wondering if he expected her to comment on the relative freshness of the paint and thatch, which seemed a trivial difference to her. Then she suddenly noticed the two extra doorways that Akbal had built into the front of his house, and the contrast with the more closed facade of Kinich's house struck her forcefully.

"Oh!" she exclaimed, amazed that she could have missed it. "It is like an Ektun house," she added hastily, embarrassed by her slowness in perceiving the difference.

"That was his intention," Balam Xoc said in a deliberately mild tone, as if he had witnessed her embarrassment but saw no reason for it. He seemed not to care how swiftly she had grasped his point, as long as she had. Zac Kuk realized that he was not only lacking in warmth but also in scorn and impatience, the emotions that led one to judge and condescend. She found this strangely reassuring, and did not hesitate to accompany him up the steps and into the central room of the three on this side of the house. The room drew light from three of the wide doorways, and while basically long and narrow in shape, it seemed very spacious beneath the steeply pitched roof.

This time Zac Kuk did not fail to see the surprise that awaited her, though it left her speechless and unable to move any farther into the room. There, on the long section of wall between the doorways to the back rooms, Akbal had painted a portrait of the city of Ektun, as if seen from a high hill on the opposite side of the river. At the bottom, just above the bench against the wall, was the river itself, a powerful green swirl that licked at the black rocks that gave Ektun its name. Yellowish cliffs rose to the next level of the painting, where the various ceremonial centers were depicted in discrete segments, rising like a staircase from right to left, as did the city itself. Behind were the familiar green hills, jutting up into a blue sky dotted with puffs of white cloud, the sky going all the way up to the top of the wall.

Zac Kuk did not know where Akbal had found such a vantage point, or if this view existed only in his imagination, but she had no doubt that she was looking at her home. It *felt* as much as looked right to her, and certain details of the temples and monuments—and of one particular hill—were undeniably accurate. Zac Kuk turned to look at Balam Xoc, making no effort to hide the tears in her eyes.

"I have no gift for him that is equal to this."

"I doubt that he would agree. Your happiness here is very important to him."

"I see that," Zac Kuk breathed, looking again at the mural. "He warned me that it would not be easy."

"It should not be hard for you, my daughter. Surely, you have a smile for adversity, as well."

"I do not know," Zac Kuk confessed, hiding her face when new tears sprang from her eyes.

"Then you will learn," Balam Xoc said simply. "But come: Compose yourself. You will not want the others to see you weeping."

Dabbing at her eyes with the edge of her shawl, Zac Kuk cast an anxious glance through the doorway, at the people standing quietly in the plaza.

"Who *are* they, Grandfather?" she asked in a pleading voice, unable to feign indifference to them any longer. Balam Xoc's response was immediate, showing that he was not as unaware of their existence as he had seemed.

"They are the people who have been drawn to me by the Spirit Woman. And by their own need for direction and purpose. There are many such people in the world, my daughter, though I do not think that you are one of them."

"No?" Zac Kuk echoed doubtfully.

"Do you not have your life to live?" Balam Xoc retorted. "Is it not your own?"

"Yes," Zac Kuk said without thinking. "Mine and my husband's," she added belatedly, for the sake of propriety.

"He will not take it from you," Balam Xoc told her. "And you have too much pride to give it to him. No, my child, save your vows for the priest," he said, waving off her protest. "It is not a judgment from which you should flee. You will need your pride to make a place for yourself here. Perhaps not in the heart of your husband, but among these other people, yes, you will need it."

"I have always been told that I was *too* proud," Zac Kuk admitted in a puzzled voice, but Balam Xoc merely shrugged.

"Those words were meant for a girl. The pride required of a woman is a very different thing. *That,* you will learn as well."

Gesturing brusquely for her to accompany him, Balam Xoc turned and started out through the doorway, and Zac Kuk moved quickly to his side, pausing only to wipe the last traces of tears from her cheeks, so that no one would mistake her for a wet-eyed girl.

BECAUSE the weather was good, and because so many people wished to be included as observers, the ceremony was conducted outside, on the steps in

front of Pacal's house. A canopy of blue cloth—the color of the sky spirits—
was held over the heads of the wedding couple, who were flanked by Batz Mac
and Muan Kal on one side and by Pacal and Ixchel on the other. They made
their vows before Nohoch Ich, who had painted his face and upper body a
bright blue for the occasion, and had wrapped his hair in a turban of blue cloth.
He waved a ladle of smoking copal incense over them, chanting a prayer to
the ancestors, and to the spirits who brought children.

Standing only a few paces away, next to Kinich Kakmoo, Chan Mac looked
on with an expression of wistful pride upon his round face. He thought that
Zac Kuk, his favorite sister, had never looked more radiant than at this
moment, with her black hair gleaming in the sunlight and her eyes wide upon
the priest before her. And his friend, Akbal, his long, cloth-wrapped head
nearly touching the canopy, looking as intense and concentrated as he did with
a brush in his hand. Even to a stranger, they would have seemed a handsome
couple, and Chan Mac was one who had glimpsed the depths of their beauty.

For all his admiration, though, he could not deny the sense of loss he had
begun to feel, almost immediately upon his arrival at the Jaguar Paw House.
He had been impressed but not truly surprised by how much Akbal seemed
to have matured since they had last spoken, some months before. That was to
be expected, given the responsibilities Akbal had taken on, and his natural
earnestness in carrying them out. He had also grown in sophistication, apparently from his contact with the pilgrims and learned men who came to visit
his grandfather.

What surprised Chan Mac was his realization of how much he had missed
Akbal's company. It had come to him during their first moments of greeting,
when they were both spilling out their pleasure at being together again, and
suddenly Akbal had looked past him, searching for Zac Kuk and smiling when
he found her. That was also to be expected, and Chan Mac had made light
of Akbal's blushing apologies. But what he had truly felt in that moment was
abandoned, and while he had quickly realized the childishness of such a
response, and had put a laugh upon his lips, he had still experienced the impact
of the emotion like a bodily shock. He would, after all, be leaving here in a
few days, and he could not expect many visits from his brother-in-law once
Zac Kuk started having children. Nor did his own duties often bring him to
Tikal. So there *was* abandonment, or at least separation, in the future.

The strength of his feelings made Chan Mac wonder, as he watched the
ceremony, if Akbal represented something more than just a friend. Why was
it such a pleasure to watch him grow and discover his powers? Chan Mac had
two younger brothers, several half-grown nephews, and two young men who
had been his protégés in the art of diplomacy. But he had never felt a comparable interest in their growth. Was it the specialness of Akbal's talents, Chan
Mac wondered, or did it have more to do with the point at which he entered
my life? It occurred to him for the first time that the reason he saw great things
in Akbal was because he had ceased to expect them of himself. *Perhaps I am
the protégé,* he thought ruefully.

"You are troubled, my friend," Kinich Kakmoo whispered in his ear, and
Chan Mac came out of his thoughts to see that the ceremony was almost over.
His mother was presenting the marriage bundle to Pacal on behalf of her
daughter, and smiles were spreading over the faces of the onlookers, in antici-

pation of the celebration and feast shortly to follow. Chan Mac gave Kinich a self-deprecating smile.

"No, I am merely feeling envious of the new groom."

Kinich snuffled in repressing his laughter, raising his eyebrows in a leering wink, the conspiracy of husbands. Kinich was twenty-four, two years younger than Chan Mac, but he had been married nearly as long.

"Your sister is a treasure," he whispered appreciatively. "My brother should be grateful for the day he met *you*, my friend."

Chan Mac glanced at him sharply, but the look was lost in a sudden commotion, as the crowd around and behind them let out exultant cries and went forward to congratulate the members of the wedding party. The two men held back, lingering together outside the circle of well-wishers around Akbal and Zac Kuk.

"You will be staying for the feast?" Chan Mac asked casually, deciding that Kinich had offered the compliment without thinking, and probably did not recall the circumstances under which he and Akbal had met. Kinich looked down at the plastered surface of the plaza, scuffing at it with one sandaled foot.

"For a while," he said with a shrug. "There are few here, beyond yourself, with whom I would care to spend time."

"But I thought that you and Akbal had resolved your disagreement," Chan Mac said in surprise.

"We have. But this is not a clan that honors its warriors. Even one who is nacom of Tikal."

Chan Mac stared at him with sympathy, but knew better than to speak it aloud. Kinich would not want his pity, and it would not be right for Chan Mac, a stranger, to take his side in a clan matter.

"I will be glad to get out into the field again, anyway," Kinich continued gruffly, as if impatient with his own complaining. "There is little pleasure in being a warchief in the palace. They think I should be content to parade my men through villages and hunting camps, for the benefit of nervous farmers. Huh! The Macaws will be better company. At least they want to *fight*!"

Chan Mac did not have to ask who "they" were, guessing that Kinich meant the higher-ranking warchiefs or the ruler's administrators. He had seen for himself how ambitious young men were tamed by their elders, who let them wear out their ambition in trivial tasks. Like being made to paint a burial vase while others conducted the important negotiations, Chan Mac reflected bitterly, beginning to understand, finally, why he had been so drawn to Akbal in Yaxchilan.

"Do you ever feel, Kinich," he asked suddenly, "that you have reached the place where your success should be, but you still cannot put your hands on it?"

Kinich drew a long, snuffling breath, his eyes wide with recognition.

"*Yes.*"

"Does it make you feel old, and envious of those whose success still seems to be ahead of them?"

"It makes me *angry*," Kinich said emphatically. "It makes me want to leave this place, and go somewhere where bravery is still appreciated!"

"I had not thought of that," Chan Mac admitted in a chastened tone, as if struck by the idea.

"But where is there to go?" Kinich went on, oblivious of his friend's musing reply. "I will fight beside the Yaxchilanis, but I do not respect them enough to join their ranks. Besides, Tikal is my home, and the place where I should raise my children."

"Yes," Chan Mac agreed absently. "But if you feel thwarted here?"

"Ah, it is not as bad as that," Kinich scoffed, finding his own arguments persuasive as his anger departed. "It is mostly my grandfather who thwarts me, and he cannot have that many years left to him. I will yet have the respect I am due. But come, my friend," he said with renewed heartiness, "let us find some balche to drink. It was rude of me to burden you with my problems."

"Not at all," Chan Mac assured him, with a sincerity he did not have to feign. He was tempted to thank Kinich for his advice, but he knew that the gesture would only confound him. *I can explain later,* Chan Mac told himself, *after I have met the grandfather, this man Balam Xoc, and have heard* his *vision of the future.*

GREAT QUANTITIES of food and drink had been laid out at the four corners of the upper plaza, and here the guests gathered to fill their gourds with cacao or balche or fruit juice, and to tear pieces off the haunches of venison and whole turkeys that had been roasted on spits. There were also fresh greens and ripe red tomatoes, baskets of avocados, sapotes, and papayas, and thick, juicy slices of pineapple and watermelon. But more than anything else, there was *maize:* maize of many different colors, ground and cooked in every conceivable fashion: spiced with chilies and sweetened with honey and vanilla, mixed in stews with meat or fish, rolled and baked into cakes, and even whipped together with cacao and water to form a thick, nourishing drink. Maize, the first food of the ancestors, and now the symbol of the recent harvest, and Tikal's return to prosperity.

Akbal and Zac Kuk ate only sparingly, from each other's hands, as prescribed by tradition. They preferred to spend their time—even while besieged by guests—in enjoying their new freedom to touch one another, and hold hands, and stare into each other's eyes. When the torches were lit, as much to keep off insects as to provide light, they got up and joined the other married couples in the center of the plaza, and began to dance. Here again, they made a striking pair: Zac Kuk trim and graceful in her wedding dress of yellow and white, moving lightly to the rapid pulse of the drums, while Akbal did a long-legged prance beside her, substituting enthusiasm for grace. Batz Mac, who was quite a good dancer despite his girth, teased his new son-in-law as they passed in line, reminding him with a laugh of the "heron among frogs."

Between dances, they circulated among the guests, trailed by servants who gathered in the gifts they were given. Some of the gifts were as small as the feathered charms meant to insure many children, but others were quite costly, like the necklace of orange shell beads that Zac Kuk had allowed an old man from Altun Ha to hang around her neck. Even Akbal did not know all of the people who pressed gifts upon them, yet he thanked each of them graciously, asking even the commoners their names and the places from which they came. Dizzied by all the names and faces, Zac Kuk quickly decided that her husband's courtesy was excessive, and contented herself with remembering only the names of those important enough to merit recollection. She recognized these as much by their ability to return her smile as by their dress, though she dutifully smiled at all who came before her.

All except one, that is. The man who thrust himself into their path just as they were returning to the dance made her clutch at Akbal's arm, her mouth working soundlessly. He might once have been muscular, but all the flesh had been melted from his body, so that his ribs and collarbone stood out like plates beneath the taut covering of his skin. He wore his greasy hair loose upon his shoulders, carrying his head cocked at a severe angle to hide his sightless right eye. The other eye glared at Akbal with unknown intent, but so fiercely that Zac Kuk gripped Akbal's arm more tightly, surprised that he had not adopted a more defensive stance himself. But Akbal merely stretched out a hand to accept the gift the man was silently holding out to him.

"That is for the grandson of Balam Xoc," the man said, in a voice so harsh it seemed almost a snarl. In Akbal's open palm, he had deposited a single stone, slightly rounded and half the length of a finger, which shone faintly in the torchlight. Akbal stared at it for a moment, then closed his fingers around it and looked back at the man.

"What is your name?" he asked, holding his fist out in front of him, as if weighing the stone inside.

"Hok," the man said from deep in his throat. He pointed a bony finger at Akbal's fist. "That belonged to my father, in Quirigua."

Zac Kuk was appalled at the man's bad manners, and was beginning to grow impatient with Akbal's prolonged consideration of what seemed to her an absurd gift. She did not want to be rude herself, but it occurred to her that perhaps Akbal was simply perplexed by this deranged man, and needed her help.

"I have relatives in Quirigua," she put in politely. "What is your clan?"

The man turned his glaring eye briefly upon her, turning his whole body to do so. Then he shifted his attention back to Akbal, aggressively expectant.

"I have no clan," he muttered defiantly. "Except that of Balam Xoc . . ."

"That is *my* clan, and that of my wife," Akbal said in a warning tone, aware that Zac Kuk was regarding him with equal expectancy, and with real anger at the way she had been rebuffed. He inclined his head in her direction, hooding his eyes slightly, as if asking her to be tolerant. Then he opened the hand he still held out before him, showing the stone cupped loosely in his long fingers.

"There is spirit in this stone, and warmth. You should not give away an inheritance such as this."

"I cannot use it!" the man shouted raggedly, tossing his head with a grimace that revealed the pale immobility of his other eye. He was breathing heavily, the tendons standing out on his neck like cords. "You have eyes," he said in a low, sullen voice, "you are the Painter. You must have it."

"I am grateful, then," Akbal replied, letting his hand fall to his side. "You must come to me, Hok, if there is ever a favor I can do for you."

The man gave a desultory shrug, his glaring eye dimmed by the curtain of hair fallen across his face. Then he turned abruptly and disappeared into the crowd.

"He did not deserve your politeness, my husband," Zac Kuk said tightly, her anger swelled by the relief she felt at the man's departure. "He was taunting you!"

"I do not think so," Akbal said quietly. "I doubt that he knows another way to act." He showed her the stone in his hand. "This is a polishing stone, used for rubbing pottery after it has been painted. They are usually kept within the families of painters and handed down from father to son, or mother to daughter."

"Then you were not only pretending to admire it?"

"Such stones are rare and have properties of their own, though I am told that they come to acquire the qualities of their owners over time. I could *feel* the spirit of the man who used this last, and he was not at all like the man we saw. I do not know what has happened to Hok, but he is right. This stone *is* useless to him, though not only because of his eyesight."

Zac Kuk squinted at him, puzzled by all this talk about spirits and stones, which seemed unlike the Akbal she knew.

"Surely, *you* will not use it?"

"I would dishonor his father's spirit if I did not," Akbal told her firmly. "I would be wasting his inheritance a second time. I think Hok meant for me to save what he could not."

"But," Zac Kuk began, then gave up with a sigh. "I do not have any experience with such people. He frightened me."

"I am sorry," Akbal said soothingly, putting an arm around her shoulders for comfort. "You must be given some time to accustom yourself to Grandfather's followers. I am sure they are as confusing to you as the women of Ektun were to me."

Zac Kuk smiled and leaned against his chest, ignoring the beckoning gestures of the dancers, who had gone on without them.

"We will see about that," she murmured suggestively, and Akbal laughed aloud, before leading her back into the crowd, to begin the long process of saying their farewells for the night.

CHAN MAC had only just joined the circle of men when Balam Xoc drew him into the conversation, asking him his opinion of the campaign being planned against the Macaws. Taking a puff on the long cigar in his hand, Chan Mac glanced around at the faces of his listeners, noting some uneasiness on those of his father and the priest, Nohoch Ich. Across from him, Pacal raised a cup of balche to his lips, his face streaked with sweat, though the night had cooled.

"The ruler of our city, Zotz Mac, feels the need to prove himself in the field," Chan Mac said in a neutral tone, unable to read the expression on Balam Xoc's face but already aware of his attitude toward warfare. "And the Macaws, in their raids, have come closer to lands under our protection. It is necessary to put a limit upon their encroachments."

"Do you think they will soon be a threat to Tikal?" Balam Xoc asked, and Chan Mac blinked, wondering if this was a joke.

"That is most unlikely, my lord," he said tactfully. "We expect to drive them back to their own lands, which lie far to the north of us."

"Ah!" Balam Xoc exclaimed, as if he had been enlightened. He looked over at Pacal. "Perhaps it is some other people, then," he said pointedly, "who are making our allies so nervous. Perhaps they will not be reassured at all, if we send our army off after the Macaws."

Pacal refilled his cup from a nearby gourd, staring at an invisible spot in the center of the circle. Chan Mac felt an immediate pang of guilt, realizing that Balam Xoc was using him to taunt his son. Nor was he through, turning back to Chan Mac with the same blank expression on his lined face.

"But the spoils will be great, will they not?" he inquired. "Surely, Zotz Mac does not do this *only* for the glory?"

"Our ruler acts for the reasons my son has stated," Batz Mac interjected stiffly. "We are on friendly terms with many of the people who have suffered at the hands of the Macaws. We would not add to their suffering by looting."

"Forgive me, my friend," Balam Xoc apologized hastily. "I did not mean to imply that you would. I am only repeating what has been said by those who advocate the campaign here."

Again, Balam Xoc looked at his son, and this time Pacal met his gaze, his eyes bloodshot but hot with anger. Then he looked away and made a disgusted sound in his throat, knocking over his cup as he rose unsteadily to his feet and stalked out of the room. Balam Xoc watched him go in silence, merely nodding when Nohoch Ich and several of the other men also excused themselves, though with much more politeness. Chan Mac exchanged a glance with his father, who could barely conceal his discomfort and regret at having been party to Pacal's humiliation.

"You disapprove of my actions, Batz Mac," Balam Xoc said in an unaccusatory voice, looking over at the two of them. "But if your own son expressed foolish beliefs, and repeated them to others as if they were the truth, would you not correct him?"

"Not in public," Batz Mac said bluntly, without hesitation. "And not without respect for his feelings as a man, no matter what I might feel about his beliefs."

"You are fortunate, Chan Mac," Balam Xoc told the younger man. "I do not have your father's compassion and restraint. I respect *only* the truth."

Had it been offered as a boast, Chan Mac would have found the statement enormously offensive, an insult to his father's respect for the truth. But Balam Xoc had put it forth as a simple fact, as if acknowledging a limitation he had perceived in himself, though without much regret.

"I am a diplomat, my lord," Chan Mac said gently. "I have learned that there are many ways to express the same truth."

"And as many ways to deny it," Balam Xoc replied. "Often it is impossible to distinguish them. That is why men have always sought to communicate with the spirits of the ancestors, to learn the truths that cannot be denied."

"But any truth may be denied," Chan Mac contended, leaning forward with his elbows on his thighs, "if it is inconvenient or dangerous to those who hold power."

"Perhaps. But it cannot be suppressed, as long as it continues to describe the world in which men live. They will always find it again, in the midst of their pain and disillusionment."

"As *you* have, my lord?" Chan Mac suggested, drawing an anxious glance from his father, who felt that the question verged on rudeness, seeming both skeptical and overly inquisitive. But Chan Mac was staring intently at Balam Xoc, and did not even notice his father's concern.

"I was no different from other men," Balam Xoc admitted freely. "I hid from the things that might trouble my heart and mind. *That* was the truth I learned in my first vision: that we cannot hide from our responsibilities any longer, pretending to go about our duties like good men. We cannot speak diplomatically to those who would lead us to our destruction. Do you not agree, Chan Mac?"

Chan Mac caught himself on the verge of voicing an emphatic *yes,* as Kinich had earlier, but such an easy acquiescence to the reasoning of another went against all his training, so he merely nodded instead. He looked down at the cold cigar in his hand, and then at his father, hesitant about the announcement he wished to make.

"Was it you, my lord," he said to Balam Xoc, "who sent Akbal to Yaxchilan?"

"It was his father, and the ruler. I merely gave my consent."

Chan Mac nodded again, then sighed, aware that he was stalling.

"Do I have your consent, as well," he asked quietly, "to visit with you, after I have come to live in Tikal?"

"My son!" Batz Mac cried out in disbelief. "You have said nothing of this to me! Forgive me, Balam Xoc," he said to their host, "but I must remind my son of his prospects. You have worked hard, Chan, and the post you have waited for will soon be open."

"There is already a post open in the embassy here. It was offered to me before I left Ektun."

"I remember," Batz Mac assured him, "but you gave me no indication then that you planned to accept it. You seemed still intent upon the post in Copan. What has happened to change your thinking?"

"I became aware of what my waiting has cost me. I no longer looked forward to a challenge, but only to what I thought was due me." Chan Mac paused and gave Balam Xoc a significant glance. "I was comfortable with my duties, and felt responsible for little else."

"But you would be responsible for a great deal in Copan!" Batz Mac protested. "It is a higher post than you would occupy here, and the ambassador is closer to retirement. Consider your career, my son, and the effect on your family. It is not wise to change your life on an impulse."

"Perhaps it is necessary," Chan Mac said stubbornly, though he laid a comforting hand on his father's arm. "And I have friends here, Father, and a sister. It is a future that excites me, as Copan no longer does."

Batz Mac let his shoulders slump and hung his head, spreading his chins upon his chest. Chan Mac appealed with his eyes to Balam Xoc, who was regarding them with his usual lack of expression. He nodded to Chan Mac, though, with what the younger man understood as sympathy.

"You have done your duty as a father, my friend," he said to Batz Mac. "I am a witness to that fact. Perhaps that will persuade you to visit here more often in the future."

"Perhaps," Batz Mac said glumly, but raised his head and looked at each of them in turn, lingering on Chan Mac's face. "You are old enough to know what is best for you, my son," he added in a resigned tone. "I hope you have chosen correctly."

"I have *chosen,* at least," Chan Mac murmured, glancing past his father at Balam Xoc. "I will bear the responsibility for that . . ."

THE WOMEN of the house gathered to dress the bride in a private room at one end of Kinich Kakmoo's house. They brought bowls of warm water and clean cotton towels to wash her body, as well as pieces of jewelry and articles of clothing and an array of their favorite face paints, scented ointments, and hair colorings. A fire was burning in the corner hearth, warming the room and adding the smell of pine resin to the other perfumes in the air, and torches set into niches in the walls cast a bright, yellow light over the smiling faces of the women. For although the dressing was a kind of initiation, a ceremony of acceptance as important in its own way as the one conducted earlier in the day, it was not an occasion that called for solemnity. They were not there to intimidate the new wife but to meet her, and to show her the support they would lend her in the future.

By custom, the mother-in-law of the bride should have presided over the gathering. But while Ixchel had played the role during the wedding ceremony, she had neither the age nor the confidence to take charge now. Nor did Kinich's wife, May, nor Nohoch Ich's wife, Haleu, and Cab Coh's wife, Pek, was sick and unable to come. Thus, there was no one to oppose Muan Kal when she arrived with three of her servants and took personal command of her daughter's dressing.

Kanan Naab had gone to bring Box Ek, and when she parted the curtain and helped the old woman up the last step and into the brightly lit room, she was surprised at the silence that greeted their appearance. Only one voice was speaking, and that belonged to Muan Kal, who stood at the far end of the room with her back to the doorway. She was talking to Zac Kuk and holding up garments for her approval, completely ignoring the women who stood or squatted behind her, listening with sullen impassivity.

Box Ek let herself be led to within a few feet of Muan Kal's back, then stopped to gather her breath. She stood silently, hunched over her walking stick, measuring Muan Kal's inattention with her mere presence. Kanan Naab saw that the woman's servants had noticed their entrance, and that Zac Kuk herself, half unrobed, was trying to signal her mother with her eyes. But Muan Kal remained impervious to distraction, commenting on the sheerness of a scarf as she held it up to the light. She had not won many friends for herself already that day, Kanan Naab knew, having observed her generally haughty behavior toward the servants and those below her in rank, and her open distaste for the followers of Balam Xoc. She had asked continually why this or that member of the Sky Clan had not been invited to the feast, pointing out her own relationship to the person in question and seeming not to comprehend the coldness of the replies she received. Kanan Naab had finally begun to feel sorry for her, realizing that Zac Kuk, out of loyalty to Akbal, had not passed along his warnings about the relations between the Tikal clans.

Box Ek suddenly rapped her wooden stick on the stone floor, bringing Muan Kal around in a whirl of surprise.

"You are in the way, Muan Kal," the old woman said, straining against the stiffness in her neck to look Muan Kal in the face.

"Forgive me, my lady," Muan Kal said in a flustered tone. "I did not realize you were watching."

"We are *all* watching," Box Ek said pointedly. "It is the custom here, Muan Kal, for the women of the clan to wash and dress the new wife on her wedding night. It is very similar to what the women of the Turtleshell Clan did for me when I came to Ektun, and what they no doubt did for you when you married Batz Mac."

"The customs of the Moon Clan allowed the mother of the bride to be present, as well," Muan Kal insisted, not moving out of the way. "My mother helped to dress *me.*"

"You may be present if you wish," Box Ek told her firmly, "but you do not have the right to exclude the rest of us."

Zac Kuk came to her mother's side, holding her shift loosely over her breasts.

"Perhaps you should leave me, Mother," she suggested softly. "These women are my people now. I trust them to prepare me for my husband."

The women in the back murmured approvingly and began to move closer, picking up their bowls and jars and implements. Muan Kal's face quivered, and she appeared about to weep, but Box Ek again rapped her stick on the floor and hobbled forward to take the taller woman's arm.

"This is no time for sadness or regret," she said commandingly, though it was *she* who was holding on for support. "Come, my lady, and sit with me, and enjoy this with us. We have no desire to exclude you from our company."

The women closest at hand nodded vigorously in agreement and also came to Muan Kal's side, guiding her and Box Ek to seats on the bench against the wall. Ixchel sat down beside them to nurse her baby, providing Muan Kal with an immediate distraction from her embarrassment, and a reason for not meeting the eyes of the other women. Though none of them had forgiven her for her arrogant behavior, they were all anxious for her to stay, finding it easier to overlook their grievance than to bear the discomfort and bad luck of having driven her away.

After seeing that Box Ek was comfortably settled, Kanan Naab joined the group around Zac Kuk, who was in the process of being undressed. Kanan Naab took a seat with the other unmarried women, who had left a circle of space around Zac Kuk and the married women who attended her. These women took turns with one another, so that there were never so many as to make the bride feel crowded, yet always enough to let her feel sheltered in her nakedness. As they laid aside Zac Kuk's garments and began to wash her limbs with soft sponges, they maintained a continual light patter of conversation, half banter and half compliment.

"Such smooth skin . . ."

"Ah, sixteen . . . life has not touched you yet, my daughter."

"It will soon!"

"Do not mind her, she has been touched too often . . ."

Zac Kuk smiled shyly at the jokes, though her wide eyes flitted from face to face, refusing to settle for long. This was the moment of trial, Kanan Naab realized with nervous empathy, the moment when you were permitted no modesty, and had to stand naked before the women with whom you would live. Yet even the shyness of her stance could not conceal the ripeness of Zac Kuk's body, which was firm and supple, exuding a provocative kind of grace. Her breasts were taut and dark-nippled above a flat belly and hips that had not spread from childbearing. As she stood half-turned in the hands of the women washing her, her arched back and rounded buttocks forming a single curving line, her smile gradually began to lose its shyness in the awareness of how she was being admired. Now she seemed truly alluring, and while the compliments continued, Kanan Naab saw several of the women purse their lips and exchange glances. *However much they may come to accept her,* Kanan Naab thought shrewdly, *they will always watch her around their men.*

"Akbal may still be the Painter," one of the older women said with mock resignation, "but I doubt that he will ever stare at any of *us* again."

Zac Kuk lowered her eyes at their laughter, though her pleasure showed through the display of modesty, which did not seem altogether authentic to Kanan Naab. Akbal had told her that the children of Ektun often bathed or swam together in the many pools and rivers near their city, and that sometimes whole families went in together. Kanan Naab guessed that standing naked in front of other people was not as new an experience for Zac Kuk as she pretended, but that she knew better than to seem too bold. Kanan Naab pursed her own lips, grudgingly impressed by her sister-in-law's composure, which allowed her to *feign* a shyness that would have been all too natural to Kanan Naab, were she to find herself in the same situation.

"Not *too* dry there," Haleu instructed the woman drying Zac Kuk's thighs and pubic area. "A certain slipperiness is desirable."

"*Most* desirable," someone else agreed knowingly. "Have him touch you there, my daughter; let him think he must find his own way in."

"But do not hesitate to help him if he gets lost!"

"If you value your own pleasure," another woman put in more seriously, "you must say one thing to him, very clearly, at the very beginning: the word 'slowly' . . ."

"If he hears *that,* he has no passion."

"Haste is not always passion, my lady. Why should he not give *you* pleasure while having his own?"

Kanan Naab blushed and murmured along with the other young women, unwilling to admit how uneasy this kind of talk made her feel. She knew what men and women did together, and she had touched herself as the woman said, and had learned the pleasure it could bring. But it seemed such a private pleasure, so totally within herself, that she could not conceive of wanting a man to provide it for her. Nor could she imagine Yaxal Can wanting to do it, either, even though she had forced herself to envision such a possibility on several occasions. Always, the attempt had left her feeling confused and vulnerable, and more than ever convinced that she was perverse.

The women were helping Zac Kuk choose her garments now, and holding up scents to be sniffed, all the while encouraging her to be relaxed and accepting of the experience to come. Watching Zac Kuk, Kanan Naab had the distinct impression that most of the encouragement was superfluous. *She is ready, even eager, to be a wife,* Kanan Naab observed wistfully. *She has shared something with Akbal beyond sweet words and respectful companionship, some glimpse of mutual possibility, perhaps, which pulled them toward a future together.* Kanan Naab was not certain why this was so apparent to her, or if she were merely projecting the feeling that had come through so strongly in her conversations with her brother. It did not seem to matter, since it was so undeniable in either case.

After much goodnatured discussion, a thin shift of rose-colored cotton had been chosen for Zac Kuk. It fell just to her knees and was embroidered with red roses at the hem and neckline. Then the women had Zac Kuk sit while they took out their pots, brushes, and mirrors and began to make up her face, reddening her finely shaped lips and putting a single spot of color on each of her high cheekbones. It was decided unanimously that her wide, thickly lashed eyes needed no improvement, though her eyebrows were darkened slightly with powdered charcoal. As the final touch, the intoxicating scent of wild orchids—pressed from the tiny brown flowers that grew in the deep forest— was daubed onto the hollows of her throat and along her bare arms.

Perhaps the greatest amount of time, though, was spent on her hair, which was loosened from its coils and combed with turtleshell combs until it was smooth and lustrous, falling to the middle of Zac Kuk's back. Though it would finally be left in this fashion—pinned back from her face with carved pieces of bone—the opportunity was not lost to demonstrate to her the whole range of local hair styles and colorings. Zac Kuk listened attentively, asking questions with an interest that seemed far more genuine than her earlier modesty. *She is not new to* this, *either,* Kanan Naab thought, recalling what Akbal had told her about Zac Kuk's life in Ektun, where the eligible young women were so much the focus of attention and where so much time was spent on enhancing their beauty. He had tried to make her see that vanity was regarded differently in Ektun, and that Zac Kuk should not be judged by Tikal standards. He had seemed anxious to fend off criticisms of her seriousness in advance, as if perhaps he had had some doubts of his own.

Ah, my brother, Kanan Naab reflected ruefully, *how little you understand about the interests of women, and the meaning vanity has for them. How little we understand,* she accused herself, since she had trusted Akbal's judgment and had accepted his worries as valid. She had come prepared for the possibility that Zac Kuk would impress the other women as shallow and vain, a frivolous girl unworthy of their respect. Muan Kal's condescending behavior had only seemed to strengthen the possibility, encouraging Kanan Naab's fantasies of having to come to her sister-in-law's rescue.

In fact, far from needing defense, Zac Kuk had totally captivated her audience, impressing them with the quality of her taste and flattering them with her enthusiasm for what they had to teach her. Kanan Naab fingered the tiny cloth bundle in her lap, feeling an ambivalence that had not been with her when she had gone to her mother's chest earlier in the evening. She had been possessed by her own generosity then, imagining a dramatic moment in which she would sweep away all the ill feelings Zac Kuk had aroused with a single gesture of acceptance, leaving her sister-in-law overwhelmed with gratitude. Now she saw that such a gesture was not necessary, and might even be interpreted as self-serving. Kanan Naab could not deny the satisfaction she had taken in imagining Zac Kuk as pathetic and in need of her aid; it would make her that much more important to her brother, solidifying the bond that Balam Xoc had created between them.

The women had finally finished with Zac Kuk's hair, leaving its central part —an Ektun mannerism—out of deference for the bride's taste, though Zac Kuk had shown her willingness to let them change it. She was now admiring the various pieces of jewelry the women had brought for her to wear, seeming to find each more beautiful than the last. Kanan Naab drew in her breath when Zac Kuk selected a pair of short amber studs for her ears, the gift of Haleu. The piece Kanan Naab had brought, still concealed in her lap, was also amber, and would complement the earplugs nicely. Yet she hesitated to bring it forth, fearing not only that it might be misunderstood, but worse, that Zac Kuk might choose to reject it.

"They are all so beautiful," Zac Kuk said helplessly, spreading her hands wide over the array of necklaces, bracelets, and pins in front of her. The other women began reiterating their choices, and in the midst of responding to their recommendations, Zac Kuk suddenly looked straight at Kanan Naab, lingering on her face for just an instant before casting a significant glance at the jewelry. Kanan Naab realized that the choice was being offered to *her,* and that the offer had not been extended out of indecision. Zac Kuk was eminently capable of choosing her own jewelry, but perhaps she was afraid of offending those whose offerings she refused. Or perhaps she *wanted* Kanan Naab's gesture of acceptance, even if she did not need it.

Without a word, Kanan Naab opened the cloth and placed the necklace on the mat in front of Zac Kuk. It was a slender disc of almost translucent amber, strung on a fine fiber cord of the same yellowish-brown color. Incised in the center of the disc was the T-shaped Ik sign, the sign of the Wind Spirit, as well as the given name of Kanan Naab's mother.

"It is *perfect,*" Zac Kuk said in a thrilled voice, holding it up to her throat so that the women behind her could tie the cord around her neck. The disc seemed to glow against her reddish-brown skin, the deeply etched Ik sign standing out clearly in its center.

"I am grateful, my sister," Zac Kuk said to Kanan Naab, too moved to put on her customary smile, though all the other women were smiling with satisfaction. It was a moment much like the one Kanan Naab had imagined, though without the taint of superiority implicit in her fantasy, which made it much, much better. She smiled at Zac Kuk with gratitude of her own, feeling that her generosity had been rescued from the motives that had inspired it.

"It is my brother's night to be grateful," she said quietly, and rose with the others to lead Zac Kuk from the room.

IN THE COURSE of his waiting, Akbal had examined everything in the room many times over, each time beginning with the glowing fire in the corner, where Zac Kuk's mother had laid down the three round hearthstones. Then he would sweep his eyes to the left, over the collection of wedding gifts that lay within the fire's wavering circle of light: the heavy, three-legged grinding stone, ribbed and shaped like the back of a turtle, with its oblong grinder of the same hard, coarse-grained stone; the bundled slats and cords of a loom; wooden storage chests piled high with blankets and clothing; pottery bowls and jars of every size and description, some plain red-ware and others painted in gleaming colors. The people of his clan had been extremely generous to him, inspired, no doubt, by the great bounty of the harvest, which had put the whole city into an extravagant mood.

What could the women be doing so long? he wondered impatiently, as his gaze swept past the two curtained doorways that connected this room with the one in front. He was sitting on the soft cushion of reed mats and cotton blankets that would be their bed, so that he had only to turn his head to see the marriage bundle that lay open on the bench behind him. The thick roll of embroidered cloth held all of the items prescribed by tradition: pieces of jade and shell and eccentrically shaped flint, obsidian bladelets and strips of white paper, sticky balls of rubber and copal, packets of salt and maize, and a long, sharp piece of stingray spine, delicately incised with funerary glyphs. Akbal stared briefly at the stingray spine, remembering the lintels of Yaxchilan and the scenes of ritual bloodletting that had so fascinated Kanan Naab. Though he had found the symbolism powerful, he was just as glad that the literal mingling of blood was not a requirement of the marriage customs of Tikal. It was enough to honor the tradition in spirit, and leave the actual shedding of blood to the priests and holy men.

The firelight suddenly flickered, and then Zac Kuk was beside him, kneeling on the bedding. For a long moment, they could only stare at each other, paralyzed by the yearnings they had carried inside themselves for so many months. Finally, Zac Kuk cast a meaningful glance upward, into the darkness that hid the thatched roof overhead from their view.

"Perhaps we need a storm," she suggested, her eyes bright with amusement, and Akbal rose to his knees to face her, reaching out to touch the pieces of bone in her hair and the amber disc around her throat.

"You were beautiful *that* day, as well," he murmured as she came willingly into his arms, enveloping him in a warm cloud of orchid-scented air. All the waiting vanished from his mind, along with the advice of his clansmen and his own, awkward imaginings of how he must act with his wife. There was no awkwardness in the way their bodies sought one another, and no calculation in the matching of flesh to flesh. They fell together onto the bedding, Zac Kuk's shift sliding up to her hips as she moved against him, her thighs opening to his searching fingers.

"Slowly, my husband," she whispered, drawing in her breath as he found the dampness at her center and probed gently. He looked into her eyes then, watching the sensations register on her face as he continued his patient stroking. His loincloth had come loose, and it fell away completely as she reached out to return his caresses, smiling at the way he hardened to her touch. Holding his gaze with her own, she let her hands move over his body, blindly following the contours of bone and muscle beneath the smooth heat of his skin. Only when he lifted the shift off over her head did she turn her eyes away, and then only for an instant before again finding his face in the soft red glow of the fire.

"Touch me," she urged, their faces very close, his hand once again between her legs. "Make me ready for you."

Wetness blossomed around Akbal's fingers as he slid them between the puckered folds of flesh, feeling her nipples against his chest and the warm rush of her breath upon his shoulder. Their murmurings faded into incoherence, punctuated by sudden exclamations of surprise or delight. Akbal blinked deliriously, uncomprehending, when her thighs closed convulsively upon his hand, then freed him as she rolled over onto her knees, tossing her hair onto her back. He rose onto his knees behind her, angling his long torso as he pressed up against her buttocks. He waved stiffly in the air for a moment, until her hand found him and guided him to the opening, which parted grudgingly, resisting his entrance.

Slowly, he remembered dimly, hearing cries and moans that were lost in the vibrations spiraling through his body, already trembling on the brink of release. There was a sudden give that made his braced arms quiver, and then he was fully immersed, enfolded, plunging yet held fast. He seemed to be rocking back and forth, though he had no sense of willing the movement, no sense of anything except the great rush of pleasure in his loins. The firelight blurred redly at the edges of his vision, then flared yellow behind his eyes as the liquid burst out of him in long, shuddering spurts, and he heard the cries he was making echo like wild yelps off the walls of the room.

They slowly disentangled themselves and collapsed on the bedding, their breath coming in gasps. They lay curled in each other's arms, blinking upward into the darkness until stillness finally returned to their bodies. Akbal eased himself away from her and rose up on one elbow, looking at her with an amazement that seemed to defy expression. Clearly visible in the space between them was the proof of her virginity, an indelible track of dark spots upon the white top-covering of the bedding.

"I had thought . . ." he said awkwardly. "That is, the men said that the first time is often not the best . . ."

"Have I given you cause for disagreement?" Zac Kuk purred, and he laughed aloud.

"I would deny it utterly! They also said that it is sometimes hard for the woman. And painful."

"Some of the women told me this, as well," Zac Kuk confessed. "But there was so little pain, and so much pleasure, that I could not pay it any notice. *I* did not expect it to be difficult."

Akbal laughed again, proudly. Then he grew more serious.

"And how have you found the people of my clan?"

"*Our* clan," she corrected him gently. "After the warning you gave me in Ektun, I did not know what to expect here. I *still* do not know what to expect from those you call your grandfather's followers. But it is not all gloom and suspicion here, as you led me to believe."

"I did not mean to exaggerate," Akbal apologized. "But there are tensions within the clan, within my own family, that were not visible today."

"Did you think there were none in Ektun?" Zac Kuk suggested with a trace of asperity, then smiled and put a hand on his chest. "I do not think I will lack for friends here, my husband. You need not have worried on my account. But I must say, there is one thing of which your people seem to know too little."

"What is that?" Akbal asked defensively, and Zac Kuk laughed, putting her other hand on his hip and bringing her lips close to his ear.

"Pleasure," she whispered, and moved expertly into his embrace, resuming the task of his enlightenment.

IX

THE VOICE OF THE ANCESTORS

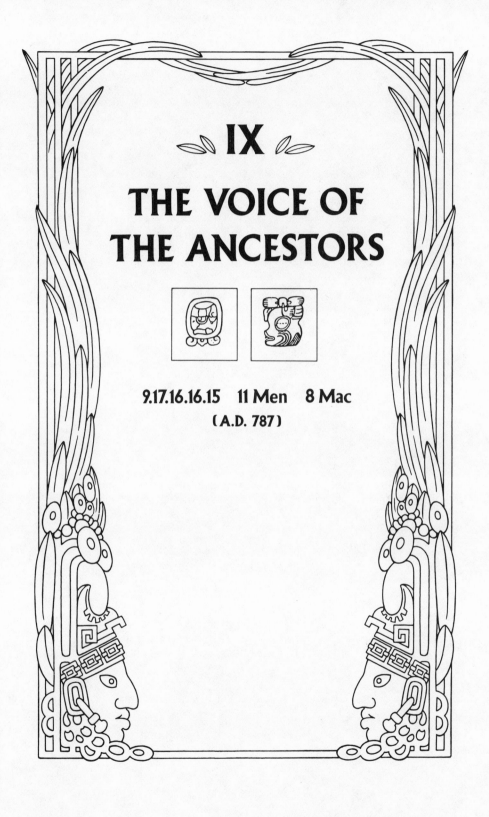

9.17.16.16.15   11 Men   8 Mac

(A.D. 787)

The Land of the Macaws

A PALE HALF-MOON was descending in the west when Kinich Kakmoo left the smoke-filled shelter where the warchiefs were still conferring and headed down toward the shore. The tents and shelters of the rulers and war leaders occupied what little high ground there was on this island, and the common warriors slept wherever they could, many of them camping in squads of ten or twenty on the mangrove hummocks and smaller islands that surrounded this one. Kinich followed a narrow path between the sleeping men, carrying his spear in one hand and a fiber cloak over his shoulder, nodding brusquely to the sentries who marked his passing. At the bottom of the path, a beached canoe provided a bridge to the narrow spit of land where Kinich was camped with ten of his men. The other twenty men under his personal command were split between two islets farther out in the river, reachable only by canoe.

The single sentry was crouched at the other end of the canoe, guarding it as much as the men, since the Macaws had sent swimmers under the cover of darkness to try to cut the canoes loose. The sentry rose and saluted Kinich with his spear.

"Sleep," Kinich told him. "I will take your watch."

Slapping at a mosquito, the warrior bowed gratefully, revealing the clumsy lump of bandage around his ear. Kinich did not ask the nature of the wound, knowing it could only be from an insect or a thorn, since they had not fought a true battle with the enemy in many days. Some of the other men were suffering from stomach cramps and diarrhea caused by drinking bad water, and all were tired of the constant heat and dampness, their legs aching from long days spent kneeling in the bottom of a canoe. This was one reason why Kinich chose to sleep among them, rather than in the shelters above; it was difficult enough to maintain morale when the men were separated in different camps, without *his* being absent as well.

"They say there is a village ahead," the sentry said suggestively, lingering at Kinich's side.

"All of the scouts have not returned," Kinich said curtly. "But the plan of attack is being drawn up. We will move out as soon as the supplies left by Zotz Mac and his men are redistributed."

"They have slowed us down since the beginning," the man said with disgust. "We are better off without them."

"Sleep," Kinich repeated dismissively, and the man obediently found a place on the ground a few feet away and rolled himself up in his cloak, placing his shield over his head. All of the men slept that way, knowing that the Macaws would begin their harassment as soon as the moon was down, pelting the men with stones and short spears from canoes held offshore in the darkness. The men farthest from the central island got little rest, since they were the most vulnerable to outright attack.

Though he would not have said so to the sentry, Kinich could not blame Zotz Mac for taking his warriors back to Ektun. The ruler had accomplished his own objectives at the very outset of the campaign, and had come this far only out of loyalty to Shield Jaguar and Ain Caan, the son whom Caan Ac had sent in his place. Zotz Mac had argued persuasively that Ektun had little to gain from pursuing the Macaws any farther into their own territory, and he had tried to compel the other leaders to recognize the strength of the resistance they were encountering. Kinich had not been equally persuaded by the arguments for going forward, especially since those scouts who had not returned were probably dead, and none of those who *had* returned had actually made it all the way to the rumored village. Simply choosing the correct route through the maze of waterways ahead was a matter of some embarrassment, since the maps were all incomplete and lacking corroboration.

Still, Kinich had kept his misgivings to himself, feeling it would be inconsistent with his reputation, as the youngest nacom, to be found on the side of caution. It was only a matter of time before they would be forced to turn back, anyway, whether they liked it or not. This Land of the Macaws was actually more water than land, and the natives' mastery of the terrain gave them an advantage that became more apparent every day. The Macaws' canoes were smaller and more maneuverable than the ponderous war canoes of the allies, and their throwing sticks enabled them to strike from a distance and escape unharmed. There were more of them now, too, even though they seldom showed themselves in the daylight. They were the ones who kept changing the face of the river overnight, blocking channels with piles of logs and felled trees and cutting false passages that led into dead-end swamps. On one occasion they had made a channel disappear behind a chain of log rafts camouflaged so cleverly that they could not be told from the shore on first approach. *They will not give us another battle,* Kinich decided as he squatted down next to the canoe, *but they will certainly see that we are driven away.*

The campaign had begun with what was still the allies' most substantial victory, a perfectly laid ambush of a Macaw raiding party outside the town of Chinikiha. Thirty of the enemy had been killed or captured, including single-handed captures by Shield Jaguar and Zotz Mac, and an assisted capture by Ain Caan. Kinich himself had added another captive to his credit, and several of his men had been honored on the field afterward. This initial success encouraged the allies to move quickly northward, fighting occasional pitched battles with the retreating Macaws, who even then had begun putting obstacles and diversions in their way. They broke dikes and set fire to villages and cacao orchards, terrorizing the villagers and leaving them to beg for aid from the army that came behind. The towns that Zotz Mac had intended to reassure with his protection were in fact devastated in advance of his arrival, and he had frequently delayed the pursuit of the Macaws, stopping to put out fires and save valuable fields from being flooded. No doubt his men were back there now, repairing dikes and helping to bury the dead.

The moon was down, but even before it had disappeared completely, Kinich had been seeing dark shapes moving in the distance. The first shriek of the enemy cut through the night air like a knife, followed closely by a spear that whistled past overhead and crashed into the foliage on the island. Kinich scanned the men near him on the ground, noting with satisfaction that all of them had moved at the cry, if only to dig themselves deeper under their shields and makeshift shelters. *The fighting is behind us,* he thought, *but we are still vigilant, and there are too many of us to take by surprise. Let them give us a proper battlefield,* he told himself longingly, *and we will make them regret their boldness forever.* But as he peered out over the dark water, listening to the mocking screams of the unseen enemy, he began to prepare himself for the long, tedious journey back to Tikal.

Tikal

THE RAIN began to fall just before daybreak, beating down on the thatched roofs of the Jaguar Paw House with unseasonable force. Hok was sleeping on the floor of the front room of Balam Xoc's house, next to the open doorway, and he was immediately awakened by the noise and the water splashing in. He looked around at the other people in the room—all still asleep—then checked to see that his own blanket and mat were still safely rolled up beside him. He refused to use them for his own comfort, but they had been given to him by Balam Xoc, and he guarded them jealously against all possible thieves.

Suddenly Balam Xoc himself emerged from the back sleeping room, standing uncertainly for a moment before heading straight for the doorway to the outside. His eyes were open, but he was completely naked, his white hair hanging loose upon his shoulders. Hok sat up and stared at him raptly with his good eye, hoping to be noticed, but Balam Xoc did not so much as blink as he walked past him and out into the rain.

Hok jumped to his feet but hesitated in the doorway, daunted by the wall of rain confronting him and intensely disturbed by Balam Xoc's nakedness. The old man was walking across the middle of the plaza, seemingly oblivious of the impact of the rain upon his unprotected body. Snatching up the blanket,

Hok ran out after him, slipping and stumbling down the steps as the rain took away what remained of his vision. Only by holding the blanket doubled over his head was he able to see at all, and by the time he got to the top of the steps leading down to the plaza below, Balam Xoc had already crossed the log bridge and was halfway to the craft house. The stairs were awash with the water pouring into the gully, and Hok made his way down with difficulty, then broke into an awkward lope across the plastered surface of the lower plaza, planting his feet wide to keep from slipping. The rain was still so intense that Hok found it hard to breathe under the shelter of his blanket, but Balam Xoc continued at the same measured pace, disappearing into the breadnut trees along the path that led to the clan reservoir.

When Hok finally caught up with him, Balam Xoc had stopped on the bank overlooking the deep, oval basin, which was an artificially widened ravine. Since it was well into the dry season, the level of the water was low, and the red earth of the embankment surrounding the reservoir had silted downward, forming a thick ring around the pool at the bottom. The rain dimpling the surface of the water had begun to slacken, but the runoff poured over the eroded embankment in many places, cutting miniature gorges and valleys through the ring of red silt and exposing the plastered clay lining of the reservoir underneath. Balam Xoc stared downward for several moments, then knelt beside one of these rivulets, which was enlarging its channel through the embankment at his feet.

Sensing that he would be as unnoticed as the rain, Hok crept closer, then closer still, until he was kneeling on the other side of the gushing stream. Balam Xoc suddenly plunged his hands into the muddy red water and brought them up cupped together, filled with clumps of earth that immediately melted in the rain and slithered away through his fingers. Cocking his head slightly, as if listening to some inner voice, he stared intently at the liquid mud cupped in his palms, mouthing words whose sound was lost in the spattering of the rain.

Then he put his hands back into the water, damming the stream so that it flowed up over his wrists. Soon a small branch with a few sodden leaves still clinging to it trapped itself on his hands, and he lifted it out of the water and placed it gently on the muddy ground beside him. This time Hok heard what the old man said, a single word that came out with the abrupt emphasis of a message received and acknowledged:

"Wood."

Twice more Balam Xoc put his hands into the water, removing in turn a bristly cob of maize, its kernels stripped away, and a piece of orange breadnut rind. Both times he uttered the word "seed," nodding to himself in confirmation. The rain had stopped falling with its customary abruptness, and when Balam Xoc reached down again, he found the stream receding rapidly in its gully, thickening with mud. He held his hands poised just above the surface, turning them over and flexing his fingers experimentally, as if fascinated by their capabilities.

"Yes," he said aloud. "And more hands, too."

Cupping his fingers together, he bent low over the gully, scooping up a handful of the soupy red water and raising it to his lips. But he had no more than taken it into his mouth when he convulsively spit the water out, coughing and gagging on the mud. Hok jerked backward involuntarily, shedding the blanket hooded over his head, and Balam Xoc fell onto his hands and knees, swinging his head and spitting like an animal that had swallowed dust. Then the old man stopped, his white head hanging limply between his braced arms for a moment before he roused himself and sat back on his buttocks. The first thing he saw when he raised his eyes was Hok, regarding him anxiously from the other side of the gully. Then he looked down at his wet, naked body and up at the sky, which was beginning to lighten despite the thick layer of clouds overhead.

"How did I get here?" he asked hoarsely, wiping at the red mud still clinging to the corners of his mouth.

"You walked, Grandfather," Hok told him reverently. "As if in a dream, you walked straight to this place."

Balam Xoc nodded absently, turning his head to take in his surroundings in more detail, dwelling for several moments on the small pile of debris he had deposited beside him.

"Yes, I remember now," he said at last, grunting as he pushed himself up out of the mud and rose to his feet. Staring out over the reservoir, he turned in a slow half-circle, surveying the thick forest that extended most of the way around the perimeter. Then he let his gaze fall upon Hok.

"What did you see me do, my son? In my dream . . ."

Tensing his whole body, as if to contain every memory, Hok reported what he had seen and heard, quoting the words Balam Xoc had spoken aloud. He described the way Balam Xoc had stared at his own hands, and how he had tried to drink the muddy water.

"Water," Balam Xoc repeated. "There was so much, then so little. And earth . . . *land,*" he mused, dislodging a chunk of red mud from the side of the gully with his toe. "And wood and seed. And hands, hands to cut and plant and collect the water. By hand . . ."

Nodding to himself, he looked back at Hok, whose head was cocked at its usual angle, his black hair plastered against his face and neck, his one good eye blinking quizzically.

"You are my only witness, Hok. I may have to call upon you to verify the manner in which I came here."

Hok blanched, and an expression of the most abject misery came onto his emaciated face, as if he were being made to relive a bitterly painful experience. He dropped to his knees and touched his forehead to the mud in compliance, but he did not have the strength to raise himself up again. Balam Xoc stepped across the gully and lifted the prostrate man up by his elbows, finding him to be almost weightless. Hok trembled uncontrollably, and could not meet Balam Xoc's eyes.

"I have heard your story, my son," Balam Xoc told him gently. "I know how you have suffered from the disbelief of other men. You will no doubt be disbelieved in this instance, as well, but you must stand it for my sake, and for the sake of the truth. We have no choice, Hok; we must act upon what is shown to us. So be brave, and know that *I* will never deny you."

Hok was taking fast, shallow breaths, but he looked at Balam Xoc and managed a weak nod. Balam Xoc gestured toward the ground behind him.

"I must borrow your blanket."

Hok turned and picked up the blanket, attempting to wring some of the water from it before offering it to Balam Xoc, who unfolded the sodden bundle and wrapped the blanket loosely around his middle.

"There is much to be done. I must go," he said curtly, and went down the embankment without a backward glance. Hok watched him disappear into the breadnut trees, then stepped across the gully and fell to his knees, pausing for a long moment before taking the branch, the maize cob, and the curling piece of breadnut rind into his own hands. Clasping them tightly against his bony chest, he lurched to his feet and went after Balam Xoc, leaving deep footprints in the red mud of the embankment.

FROM THE second-floor gallery of the Jaguar Paw Clan House, Nohoch Ich looked down upon the eastern courtyard, where a small, noisy crowd of men had gathered. They were clustered around a thin, angular man whose face and body were coated with the black paint of fasting, as were those of many of the men in the crowd. Nohoch recognized the man instantly as Hok, feeling a great weariness at how familiar a sight he had become in a matter of only days. Hok with his stick and his maize cob, waving them about like holy relics in the midst of excitable crowds like this one; Hok the witness and defender of Balam Xoc, challenging anyone, priest or lord, who doubted his master's wisdom.

As Nohoch watched, Tzec Balam, the high priest of the clan, emerged from the rooms below and descended the steps toward the crowd, accompanied by six large apprentice priests. Some members of the crowd immediately began to drift off at the high priest's approach, but a core of black-painted men held their ground around Hok, who confronted Tzec Balam with unconcealed belligerence. Nohoch heard the priest's calm command to disperse, followed by Hok's defiant reply, a refusal so loud and harsh that it echoed off the walls of the courtyard, drawing people out of the surrounding rooms to see what could be causing such a disturbance. The clan house was a place of quiet and decorum, hardly the place for such an unseemly display of anger.

Nohoch turned away in disgust, not wishing to see any more. This, too, would be blamed upon Balam Xoc, further eroding his credibility among the other members of the clan. Nohoch glanced at the curtained doorway on the other side of the gallery, waiting for his father to emerge from his conference with the Living Ancestor. Cab Coh was the last of the people he had asked to speak with Balam Xoc, in the hope that personal persuasion might accomplish what all the arguments and objections of the clan council had not. But no one had yet had any success in getting Balam Xoc to change his mind, and Nohoch doubted that his father would fare any better. The final appeal would be his own, and though he had carefully considered what he would say, he had little confidence that either care or consideration would have much weight with Balam Xoc. He was beginning to understand how his cousin Pacal had felt when *he* was the head of the clan council.

Nohoch's betrayal had been less personal than that of Pacal, but it had been equally sudden and unexpected. He had just finished negotiating the terms under which the clan's workmen would be loaned to the ruler, and he had summoned the clan council to ask for their ratification and to discuss how the resulting revenues would be distributed within the clan. His priest's training had made him more adept at bargaining than he had expected, and he was proud of the head price he had obtained, and even prouder of the respect he had won from the ruler's negotiators. He had convened the meeting of the council with the anticipation of much praise and mutual congratulation, especially when they came to the task of dividing up the wealth.

But then Balam Xoc had put forth a proposal of his own. In return for the use of the workmen, he had declared, the ruler should be asked for the rights to certain pieces of land, and to additional woodlots and breadnut groves. Balam Xoc claimed to have received a "message" telling him to procure these essential things, along with extra stores of seed and tools for working the fields. He had also decided that some of the workmen should be retained to repair the clan reservoirs, and further, that those of his followers willing to help with the work should be adopted into the clan. If the clan was to be truly independent, even of the rains, he had proclaimed, they would need to acquire more "hands."

This had occurred almost ten days ago, yet Nohoch still had a vivid memory of the moment of shocked silence that had followed Balam Xoc's speech. Even the most impassive members could not conceal their surprise and disbelief, and several wore openly wounded expressions, as if they had just received a knife thrust in the dark. Then the objections had come pouring forth: first delicately, in deference to Balam Xoc's position, then more pointedly as he rebuffed their suggestions, and finally with real vehemence as the council members realized that Balam Xoc had no intention of compromising—that his "proposal" was in fact a demand. He even knew which lands he wished to obtain.

The curtain over the doorway suddenly parted, and Cab Coh came out into the gallery. Nohoch saw at a glance that he had also failed in his attempt at persuasion.

"It is no use, my son," Cab Coh murmured dejectedly. "He listens to no one."

"Does he understand the seriousness of the situation? Does he know there has been talk of his removal?"

"I warned him of this," Cab Coh averred. "I told him that Tzec Balam was speaking out against him, and that many people were listening. I told him of the anger he had aroused, even in me. But I had no effect upon him."

"I must try anyway," Nohoch said in a determined voice, and pushed through the curtain into the chamber. Seated on the bench against the far wall, Balam Xoc seemed barely visible, for there was only one torch burning in the room, and Balam Xoc's body was blackened with paint as a sign of his fast. His time of seclusion for the Tun-End Ceremony had begun only two days after his appearance at the council meeting, but that had not prevented him from continuing to argue on behalf of his proposal. He had simply summoned the council to attend him here, devoting his time to them rather than to the customary rituals of preparation and purification. This was another complaint Tzec Balam had against him, and one the high priest was actively exploiting to win back his own power within the clan.

"Grandfather," Nohoch said in greeting, bowing before the black-faced figure on the bench.

"Sit, Nohoch. Tell me why *you* think I am wrong."

Nohoch settled himself on the cold stone floor, giving himself a moment to recover from the bluntness of Balam Xoc's greeting.

"I cannot say that you are wrong, Grandfather," he said judiciously. "Only that you are doing great damage to your standing among our clansmen. They feel that you have forgotten your duties in your quest for power, and that you will have that power at their expense. They do not think that their shares of the clan's wealth should go to support your followers."

"They will be made to think differently."

"Perhaps," Nohoch allowed, "but was it wrong of them to think that they, too, would profit from the city's wealth? They see their friends and relatives in the other clans making improvements on their houses and shrines, and trading for the goods they have lacked during these past bad seasons. It is only natural that they wish to do likewise, especially after the sense of prosperity that you yourself have brought to the clan. This was not a good time to force austerity upon them."

"There is *never* a good time for that," Balam Xoc said curtly. "But there are times when it is too late even to try. We cannot wait for a better time."

"Was your 'message' truly so unequivocal?" Nohoch inquired stubbornly. "You have said yourself that its larger meaning is not clear to you—that you do not know *why* we will need this land and these extra people. You do not even claim that it was the Spirit Woman who spoke to you at the reservoir."

"That does not make me doubt what I heard, or give me more faith in Caan Ac's ability to bring the rains. Three tuns still remain to Katun Eleven Ahau. Is the ruler stronger than his prophecy?"

"Are you also a prophet, then? Do you see what is to come?"

"I will be whatever I must," Balam Xoc vowed. "I will see whatever is shown to me. And I will act on it."

"Even if you must act alone?" Nohoch suggested, and Balam Xoc nodded without hesitation.

"Even then. I am the Living Ancestor; my duty is not defined for me by other men."

Nohoch hung his head in defeat, contemplating the shadows that danced on the floor in front of him. When he raised his eyes to Balam Xoc, he felt that he was speaking to darkness itself, so black and impenetrable did the man seem.

"You told me once that you did not want me for a follower," he said quietly. "You told me I must take back my life and change it, in order to meet the needs of the clan. I believe that I have done so, yet I am among those who disagree with the course you are forcing upon us. I must warn you, Grandfather, that the people may take back their lives from *you.*"

"That is a risk I must take," Balam Xoc replied. "But let me warn you in return: I intend to have my way in this matter. I will have the things I want before I enter my confinement, or you and the council will join me there. Tell *that* to Tzec Balam and the others who seek to thwart me."

Appalled by the threat, which offended him both as a priest and as a member of the council, Nohoch could only bow and take his leave, feeling a desperate need to be once more in the light, among creatures of reason. *There is no tradition he will not violate,* Nohoch thought as he pushed through the curtain, *and no person he will not betray. Tzec Balam is right,* he concluded sadly. *We have given our loyalty to a madman.*

PAUSING for a moment to listen for sounds from the next room, Kanan Naab bent over the wooden chest and reached down into its depths, inhaling the fragrant odors of cedar and copal. Without removing it from the chest, she opened the thick, blanketlike folds of her mother's marriage bundle and ran her fingers lightly over its contents. Though many of the original items had been buried with the Lady Ik Caan, Kanan Naab knew exactly what remained, and she found the obsidian bloodletter where she remembered seeing it last. The slender black bladelet gleamed as she lifted it into the light, holding it by its bone handle and turning it to study the delicate flower that had been incised on the smooth surface of the blade. It was the precious water lily for which Kanan Naab had been named, and the reason why this bloodletter had been kept for her, for inclusion in her own marriage bundle.

Then she heard the tapping of Box Ek's stick on the steps outside, and she moved quickly to rewrap the bundle and bury it beneath the clothing she had removed earlier. Closing the lid on the chest, she stuck the bloodletter into the middle of the skein of cotton yarn she had brought for this purpose, placing the skein into a net carrying bag as she went out to meet Box Ek.

Aided by a female servant, the old woman stepped in under the thatch overhanging the doorway, out of the heat and glare of the dry-season sun. She breathed heavily for a few moments before she was able to speak.

"Cab Coh has been called to the clan house again," she reported. "He has asked that you find Akbal for him, and tell him to take charge of the craft house."

"I will go immediately," Kanan Naab assured her, grateful for the excuse to get away with her carrying bag. But Box Ek raised a hand for her to stay.

"The matchmakers from the Serpent Clan have also been to see me again. They feel that they deserve more of an answer than they have been given so far, and I agree with them. You injure Yaxal Can's pride with your stalling."

"And he insults mine," Kanan Naab said contentiously, "by insisting on my decision at a time like this, when it is impossible to consult with Grandfather."

"It is *always* impossible to consult with Balam Xoc," Box Ek snapped. "He does as he pleases, and pays no heed to the needs of others. Do not be so foolish as to presume you are any different."

"You have always said that I am different," Kanan Naab pointed out. "And you were there when Grandfather said he would not consent to a match unworthy of my blood."

"So Yaxal Can is unworthy of you! You *are* presumptuous, Kanan Naab. But I will not argue with you. I have arranged for the matchmakers to meet with your father, in accordance with the customs of our clan. The decision is his by right, no matter what Balam Xoc has said. It is doubtful that my brother will again be allowed to abuse his authority, in this case or any other."

Kanan Naab simply stared at her, silenced by her own indignation. Box Ek glared back, her hands quivering on the top of her stick, her aged face pinched with an anger and determination equal to that of the younger woman.

"I will find Akbal," Kanan Naab said finally, and Box Ek moved aside to let her pass through the doorway and out into the bright sunlight. Kanan Naab went down the steps without looking back, and did not stop walking until she had turned the corner of her father's house and was standing in front of the open doorway to Akbal's old room. Then she began to shake, and she had to clench her fists and press them tightly against her cheeks to prevent her tears from falling. She felt her world slipping away from her, her future being taken over by those who did not know her; those who spoke with scorn of Balam

Xoc, the man she trusted above all others. There seemed to be no one left to whom she could turn for comfort.

Yet gradually she managed to calm herself and hold back her tears. She could not give way to her despair, or she would be lost, swept away by the same forces that were assailing Balam Xoc. She decided that she had to talk to Akbal immediately, for her own sake rather than Cab Coh's. But first she went into her brother's old room, threading her way between the neat stacks of folded drawings, which she herself had arranged in a loose semicircle around the shaft of light that entered through the doorway. Taking the skein of yarn that held the bloodletter out of her carrying bag, she hid it under a pile of old mats in the corner, murmuring a brief, apologetic prayer for having to sequester it in such an unsanctified place. Then she stood for a moment in the midst of the drawings, dwelling on the possibility they had presented to her, a possibility that was coming to seem more real and necessary with each passing day. She was not certain that she had the courage to attempt a vision of her own, but desperation was pushing her hard in that direction.

Upon leaving the room, she turned in the direction of Akbal's stone, hoping that he might surprise her by being there. It was a slender hope, since he seldom even visited his stone anymore, and had not spoken of it in her presence since shortly after his marriage. That was five months ago, yet his infatuation with Zac Kuk seemed only to have grown, to the point where his general unavailability was no longer amusing. This was not the first time that Cab Coh or someone else had sent her to find him, usually with the angry admonition to look in the vicinity of his wife. Even Chan Mac, recently arrived in Tikal, had complained of his friend's preoccupied state, and of the ambitions Akbal seemed to have forsaken.

Kanan Naab's hope turned to irritation when she entered the clearing before the breadnut trees and found the stone and its shelter unattended. She noticed, however, that others had not forsaken the Serpent Stone. Kal Cuc had made visible progress in cleaning and sanding the stone's pitted surface, and some unknown person or persons had left offerings at the base of the slab: a small pottery bowl filled with sticky balls of copal, some flakes of pink flint, scraps of white paper smeared with rubber. The ground in front of the stone was smudged and gritty with the remains of fires where copal had been burned to purify the offerings. *Perhaps* they *will force him to attend to his task,* Kanan Naab thought hopefully, gazing down at the offerings. One night someone had left a whole core of obsidian here, a piece as big as a man's fist, which Akbal had subsequently traded for maize to distribute to the poorer families of the clan. That was the last time, to her knowledge, that he had paid any attention to the needs of the poor, which had been an obsession of his for months after his return from the west. Kanan Naab wondered if he had any memory left of the hungry people he had seen on the trail from Uaxactun.

"*The spirit of the Jaguar Paw is a memory in your blood,*" she recalled. "*You have only to let yourselves remember.*" She abruptly turned away from the stone, deciding that Akbal had to be reminded of his duty, whether he wanted to hear of it or not. The clan needed him now; *she* needed him, and she could not wait for him to come to his senses on his own. Perhaps together they could find a way to defend Balam Xoc from his doubters, or at least speak out on his behalf. Perhaps it was already too late to intervene, but she could not stand by helplessly any longer.

The path through the breadnut trees was dark and cool, sheltered from the intense heat of the sun by the leafy canopy high overhead. Kanan Naab walked quickly, ignoring the flash of brightly colored birds in the undergrowth and the rustle of small creatures fleeing at her approach. The path came out behind Akbal's house, but she slowed when the sound of laughter drifted to her ears, then stopped altogether at the edge of the grove, hidden by the shade of the tall trees, when she saw Akbal and Zac Kuk ahead.

They were standing close together, almost leaning upon one another, beneath the tree that served as a perch for Zac Kuk's pets. Chuen was sitting on a branch several feet above their heads, his long black tail twitching occasionally for balance, and Akbal was pointing up at the monkey with one hand, laughing as he spoke. His other arm was draped loosely around Zac Kuk's back, and even as he continued speaking, his long fingers moved down to cup one of her buttocks and pull her closer against him. Zac Kuk rose up on one foot and curled her thigh around his leg, rubbing her breasts against his ribs. Smiling her brilliant smile, she looked up at his face and laid a hand flat upon his bare stomach, then very deliberately slid the hand down into the folds of his loincloth.

Kanan Naab held her breath in shock, stunned by the casual boldness of the exchange, and by the fact that it was being performed so publicly. She moved deeper into the shadows, unable to tear her eyes away, yet possessed by a shameful fear of being caught in the act of watching. The pair under the tree, however, seemed oblivious of everything except each other. There was an expression of rapt pleasure on Akbal's face as he nuzzled Zac Kuk's cheek, his eyes closed and his hips undulating in concert with the hand in his loincloth, which appeared to have doubled in size. Then Akbal looked down at himself and laughed, and whispered something in Zac Kuk's ear. Still entangled, the couple turned abruptly, bumping hips, and staggered toward the doorway of the house behind them. Chuen swung in a loop around his branch, chattering shrilly, his teeth bared in a monkey grin. Akbal absently waved a hand at him, then ducked his head and disappeared through the doorway behind Zac Kuk.

Staying just long enough to be sure that no one else had been observing this scene, Kanan Naab turned and walked slowly back through the trees. Her cheeks were hot, and her skin tingled with a nervous energy that seemed to ebb and flow; the path beneath her feet appeared very far away, barely within her power to focus upon. She remembered the night her grandfather had spoken to her in front of the stone, telling her to seek the truth and let it make its mark upon her. She knew now that it was futile to search any longer outside herself. The time had come to awaken the memories in her blood . . .

The Land of the Macaws

KINICH KAKMOO sat in the rear of the canoe, flanked by two of the six paddlers who propelled the heavy dugout through the water. Ten of his men knelt in pairs in front of him, their quilted cotton armor stained with sweat, their shields raised in anticipation of a sudden attack from the shore. If the scouts had been correct, they were drawing close to the Macaw village, and Kinich was alert for every sign of the ambush he knew was coming. He had not expected that they would get this far, given the ferocity of the Macaw resistance, but they had met with no opposition since fighting their way past the last barricade. Surely the clear water ahead had to be deceptive; he could not believe that the Macaws would choose to meet them on the ground outside their village.

His canoe and the one behind it—also filled with his men—were in the vanguard of the fleet, which was strung out behind them for some distance. The third part of his command was back guarding Ain Caan, who was situated safely in the middle of the line, along with Shield Jaguar and the other rulers. The tree-lined channel through which they were passing was wide but quite shallow at the edges, so that the canoes were forced to stay two abreast in the center of the stream. The sun glittered blindingly off the slow-moving green water, and the only visible movement was that of the vultures overhead, cutting lazy circles in the sky.

Suddenly a shout went up behind him, and Kinich glanced back over his shoulder in time to see an enormous tree come crashing down across the channel, capsizing the canoes beneath it and effectively severing the fleet in two. The boatmen trapped water with their paddles in confusion, causing the canoes to slew and drift, throwing up waves. Then the shore on both sides came alive with a chorus of screams, and spears and stones began to rain down upon them. Ducking under his shield, Kinich quickly assessed the situation behind him, seeing that one canoe had already beached itself in an attempt to get around the fallen tree and that its occupants were being slaughtered by the spear throwers on the shore.

"Forward!" he shouted, and waved to the canoe behind, urging them to follow. Perhaps they could find a place to land and dig themselves in, holding off the enemy until the rest of the fleet could cut their way past the tree and come to the rescue. But then he looked ahead, past the high, painted bow of the canoe, and saw canoes filled with red-crested warriors pouring into the channel from its branches and tributaries farther downstream. The thought of dying went through him with a searing rush, sharp and enervating, but he continued to urge the paddlers onward. His second canoe was right behind him, but most of the others were falling back, slewing sideways in indecision. Kinich desperately scanned the shoreline, looking for a place to put in, and suddenly he noticed a section to his left where the vegetation seemed lower and less dense. As his eyes fixed upon it, the whole section seemed to lift and roll with an incoming wave.

"Left!" he roared, pointing to the spot. The paddler next to him suddenly collapsed with a spear in his side, and Kinich jerked the paddle from the dying man's hands and dug in awkwardly in his place. As they bore down upon the shore at full stroke, its falseness became apparent to all of them, and they redoubled their efforts with a hopeful cry, aiming their canoes for the place where the most light showed through the camouflage.

"Break through it!" Kinich commanded, pulling in his paddle at the last instant as the high bow of the canoe rammed into the wooden floats with a jarring crunch, pitching a Macaw hidden among the vegetation into the water. The second canoe hit an instant later, breaking the floats apart and revealing the open channel that lay beyond. Recovering quickly from the shock of the collision, the men resumed paddling with the frenzied energy of escape, shouting incoherently in their gratitude and relief.

The sounds of the ambush receded behind them as they turned the first bend in the channel, seeing no one in pursuit and no one coming out ahead to block their flight. Kinich briefly broke rhythm with the other paddlers to count his men, and saw that he had come through with fifteen warriors and nine of the original twelve boatmen. A force to be reckoned with, he thought, at least on land. They were wending their way through a dense, unbroken jungle, and as the stream began to turn and twist back upon itself, taking them farther and farther from the channel they had left, he began to feel the hopelessness of their ever finding their way back to the rest of the fleet. Especially before the Macaws found *them*. Glancing up at the sun, he realized that they were heading roughly southeast, in the direction of Tikal. *Homeward,* he thought longingly, as he once more applied himself to the agonizing, unfamiliar motions of paddling.

Then they came around a bend and saw the barricade across the channel ahead, and Kinich's mind was made up for him. For the first time, he was grateful for the Macaws' talent for creating obstacles, since it would lend credence to what he knew would be an unpopular command. As soon as they had made a landing next to the barricade, he jumped out into the water and threw his paddle into the bottom of the canoe with a clatter that attracted everyone's attention.

"Drag the canoes into the jungle and conceal them," he said forcefully. "We go on foot from here."

The men stopped where they were, gaping at him in disbelief.

"We do not know where this channel leads, or how many more barricades there might be," Kinich explained. "The Macaws are certain to come after us, and we are no match for them on the water. But let them come into the jungle after us, and we will see who comes out alive. That is the kind of fighting we know."

"But we do not know this land," one of the older warriors protested, "and it is not fit for foot travel."

"No, but *we* are," Kinich reminded them. "Would you prefer to meet your end kneeling in a canoe, an easy target for the Macaw spear throwers? Or would you rather fight them in the jungle, where their weapon is useless?"

"Ain Caan will search for us," someone else suggested without much conviction. "We might be accused of desertion."

"Is it not worse to let ourselves be killed or captured?" Kinich scoffed. "I am the nacom. I will accept all responsibility once we are back in Tikal. But first I will see that we get there safely, and together."

The boatmen cast uneasy glances at the vine-choked jungle and murmured among themselves, but the warriors nodded one by one, accepting the wisdom of Kinich's plan, or at least recognizing his ability to impose it upon them.

"It is a long journey," one of them remarked, as they began the task of pushing the heavy canoes into the undergrowth.

"The Sun is my namesake," Kinich said fiercely, baring his jeweled teeth as he put his shoulder against the dripping stern of the canoe and pushed. "*He* will guide us home."

Tikal

WITH LESS than two months left until the planting, the atmosphere in the chamber of the chief steward of crops was tense and harried, with scribes, messengers, and stewards hurrying in and out in a steady stream. But when Chac Mut came through the doorway, Pacal called a temporary halt to the activity and cleared the room, gesturing for the young man to sit beside him. His former assistant, now a full steward, had been acting as Pacal's representative at the negotiations with the Jaguar Paw Clan, which had gone on far longer than anyone had expected.

"The negotiations are over?" Pacal asked when they were alone, and Chac Mut nodded casually, unable to wholly conceal his smugness.

"Balam Xoc has been satisfied," he reported. "He has sent my father and the other negotiators home, and has finally retired with the clan priests."

"Did he stay for the exchange of documents?"

"He had to. He could not trust his clansmen to uphold the agreements in his absence. *They* were not satisfied."

Pacal grunted softly, glancing once at the maps and deeds spread out on the floor beside him. He had not expected to have any hand at all in the negotiations with the clan, but Balam Xoc's unprecedented demand for land rights had brought the matter under the jurisdiction of the chief steward of crops. Which in turn had put Pacal in the uniquely perverse position of being able to accede to his father's wishes, yet in a way that could only hasten Balam Xoc's downfall. It seemed a peculiar sort of revenge, especially since it had not been sought.

"Has there been any more talk of his removal as the Living Ancestor?" he asked, and Chac Mut shrugged in the same smug manner.

"They do not have to say it; it is in their faces. They were all enormously embarrassed by Balam Xoc's participation in the bargaining, when he had already put on the paint of his fast. It is too close to the Tun-End Ceremony for Tzec Balam to act now, but I am told that he has already discussed the matter with Ah Kin Cuy."

"So my father will dance once more," Pacal concluded in a musing tone, his gaze traveling past Chac Mut.

"Even that cannot make much of a difference now," the young man assured him confidently. "He has neglected his followers as well as his ceremonial duties during these last days, and many of them have begun to question the holiness of his purpose. All except for that madman Hok, and the others who think they will be adopted into the clan."

"He would have helped himself by disowning that unstable man," Pacal murmured thoughtfully. "Or simply by claiming that his 'message' had come from the Spirit Woman. Does it not make you wonder why he did neither?"

Chac Mut squinted at him curiously, then frowned, as if the question made him impatient.

"Forgive me, Uncle, but surely I do not have to remind *you* of his incredible arrogance."

"You do not," Pacal bristled, his eyes flaring with anger. For a moment he seemed about to lose control of himself, but then the impulse passed, and he was again impassive. "You may return to your duties. Before you go, though, tell me what news you have heard concerning the warriors."

Obviously unprepared for the question, Chac Mut could only shrug his shoulders.

"I must confess, I did not even think to ask. Surely, though, they must have taken the Macaw village by now. Perhaps Ain Caan and Kinich Kakmoo are counting their captives at this very moment."

"*Perhaps,*" Pacal echoed scornfully. "See that the latest report is sent to me. I may be responsible only for the crops, but that does not mean my knowledge should shrink to fit my official duties. You should consider that yourself, Steward."

"Of course, my lord," Chac Mut replied in a chastened tone, though he seemed more puzzled than contrite. He rose to his feet, bowed politely, and left the chamber with measured steps. Watching him go, Pacal realized that the reprimand would have no useful effect upon the young man, and had only been a response to his own insecurity and frustration. The *wholeness* of knowledge that had been the mark of the stewardship could not be recovered by browbeating Chac Mut. It had been sacrificed to the ruler's ambitions, along with the cooperation that had once existed among the stewards themselves. Now they were all intent upon enlarging and defending their separate areas of influence, and were too busy fighting with one another to pose any serious opposition to him. Caan Ac had put his policies into effect in exactly the manner he had described to Pacal, delegating all of his responsibilities except that of bringing the rains, yet surrendering none of his power to determine the city's ultimate course.

So far, even to Pacal's wary eye, the plan seemed to be working. The campaign against the Macaws had been going well at last report, trade had been expanded in several directions, including the south and east, and the size of the harvest had indeed produced the trust Caan Ac had predicted. The Jaguar Paw Clan had been virtually alone in demanding payment rather than the promise of future bonuses, and it now appeared that there would be enough workmen available, beyond those assigned to the Katun Enclosure, to satisfy Pacal's minimal requirements for the next crop. The harvest would by no means be as large as the last one, but there would be an ample surplus if the weather was again kind.

If, Pacal reflected ominously, surveying the array of stiff paper screens spread out beside him. In addition to offending his own clanspeople, Balam Xoc had made the palace staff work long hours to give him the things he wanted. He had known *what* he wanted, even if he had done an inadequate job of explaining *why.* And if his suspicions, however vaguely expressed, were correct—if the rains proved unreliable and the crops died in the fields—then the Jaguar Paw would be the only clan equipped with the means to provide for itself. And Balam Xoc would be praised for his foresight, just as he was now being condemned for his conservatism.

It was this possibility, so personally threatening to Pacal, that made him hesitant about dismissing his father from consideration. In just a few days, Balam Xoc would enter his confinement, and who could say what vision might come to him this time? Nor was there any way to predict the effect of his dancing, which had had as powerful an impact on the people as his words.

Balam Xoc had surprised him too many times in the past for Pacal to relax his vigilance now. Far from gloating over his father's downfall, he was driven, by the very extremity of Balam Xoc's actions, to entertain the opposite conclusion: that Balam Xoc was right, and had acted with a wisdom unavailable to anyone else.

"We will see," Pacal murmured aloud, hearing the tremor of doubt in his own voice. Clapping his hands to banish the sound, he summoned his servants and told them to remove the documents and return them to the House of Records.

"Quickly," he commanded with sudden urgency. "The rainy season is only two months away, and we must be ready for it. We must *all* be ready . . ."

ON THE NIGHT before the Tun-End Ceremony, Zac Kuk crossed the bridge over the gully and began to climb the stairs to the upper plaza, carrying a torch to light her way. Upon reaching the middle landing, she was startled by rustling sounds off to her left, along the terrace, and she stopped and pointed the torch in that direction, holding it in front of herself defensively.

"Who is there?"

Ixchel suddenly appeared out of the avocado trees, causing Zac Kuk to take an involuntary step backward, though she raised the torch overhead when she realized who it was.

"My lady . . ."

"I cannot find Kanan Naab," Ixchel announced, seeming unaware that she had startled Zac Kuk, or that there was anything unusual in being out here in the dark. "You have not seen her?"

"I was hoping to speak to her myself," Zac Kuk confessed. "Why would she be here?"

"She has been acting strangely lately. I thought perhaps she had gone to her mother's bench to be alone." Ixchel gestured vaguely toward the darkness behind her. "It is there, among the trees on the terrace."

"Yes," Zac Kuk said, though it was the first she had heard of such a bench. She felt a renewed sense of the guilt and uncertainty that had brought her looking for Kanan Naab, the sense that there was much she still did not understand about her husband's people and that she had put off learning it for too long.

"Where else might she be?" she prompted, and Ixchel forced herself to think, clasping and unclasping her hands nervously. Then her narrow face brightened with inspiration.

"The Serpent Stone!" she exclaimed, and turned for the stairs. "Let us go there."

Zac Kuk hurried after her, extending the torch to illuminate the steep steps as they climbed to the plaza above. Only belatedly did she realize that Ixchel was referring to the stone that belonged to Akbal, the one his grandfather had given him to carve. She had never heard Akbal call it by that name, though he had told her about the serpent that had guarded it. Did *he* know that others called it that, she wondered, grateful that Ixchel had been in too much haste to notice her ignorance of the title. *So much you do not understand,* she told herself accusingly, struggling to match strides with the taller woman as they crossed the plaza toward Pacal's house.

They had started down the path between the end of the house and the gully when Ixchel suddenly stopped and pointed to the curtained doorway to their right.

"The curtain is down," she said urgently, as if the fact had some special significance for her. Not pausing to explain, she pushed aside the cloth and stepped up into the room, with Zac Kuk not far behind. The flickering light sent shadows flying into the corners, revealing the stacks of drawings, and then the body lying crumpled on the floor. Ixchel gasped and clutched Zac Kuk's free arm, so hard that the torch in her other hand wavered and dipped, casting its glare fully upon the bloodstained form of Kanan Naab.

"She has killed herself!" Ixchel hissed, and began to weep convulsively. Zac Kuk stared at the motionless figure, too shocked to comprehend what she was seeing. But finally she noticed the bloodletter lying on the floor near Kanan Naab's hand, and the spilled bag of copal incense, and the tiny brazier filled with grey ash. Freeing herself from Ixchel's paralyzing grasp, she stuck the torch into the wall niche beside the doorway and knelt down next to Kanan Naab, feeling for her throat.

"She is alive!" she cried out in relief. "Ixchel, she is alive! Quickly, we must have water, and medicines. And a blanket. Her skin is very cold. Quickly, Ixchel!"

Still wiping at her eyes, Ixchel moved slowly toward the door, as if walking in her sleep. Zac Kuk rose and guided her out, pressing a hand encouragingly on the older woman's back.

"And tell no one else about this," she urged, pulling the curtain back across the doorway before returning to Kanan Naab. Half kneeling and half sitting, she managed to lift the unconscious woman's head and shoulders off the floor, cradling her in her lap and wrapping the long folds of her skirt around her for warmth. Blood was smeared across Kanan Naab's face and was caked in the hollows of her neck, and her shift was soaked through with it. Zac Kuk began to weep at the sight of her sister-in-law's tattered earlobes and the multiple lacerations on her shins and forearms, imagining the pain Kanan Naab had inflicted upon herself, and the despair that must have driven her to such an act of penance. She would be scarred forever, if she survived this . . .

Suddenly Kanan Naab shivered and opened her eyes, which seemed filmy at first and unable to focus. She blinked slowly, laboriously, as if her eyelids were very heavy, rolling her eyes to take in her surroundings. Then she looked up at Zac Kuk, and to the latter's complete astonishment, she smiled.

"Greetings, my sister," she whispered, and Zac Kuk squeezed her shoulders reassuringly, taking the smile as a sign of delirium.

"Please, you must save your strength," she urged. "Ixchel has gone for medicines and a blanket."

"I am fine," Kanan Naab insisted, in a voice so frail and tenuous that it contradicted any claim to health. Her eyes, though, were clear enough to see the tears on Zac Kuk's cheeks. "But why are you weeping?"

"We thought you were dead!" Zac Kuk blurted, her eyes tearing anew at the memory. "Oh, Kanan Naab, why did you do this to yourself?"

"It was my offering to the ancestors," Kanan Naab breathed reverently.

"They put courage into my hand and made my flesh open easily. There was no pain."

"But why? This was not required of you. The whole clan has done penance for the Tun-End."

"It was an offering," Kanan Naab repeated. "I saw him, Zac Kuk. I saw Grandfather . . . the Jaguar Protector."

Zac Kuk was now certain that Kanan Naab was delirious, but she decided to keep her talking if she could, knowing that it would be easier to tend to her if she were conscious.

"Where did you see him, my sister? In a dream?"

"I went to him," Kanan Naab said simply, as if describing an actual experience. "He was standing near the entrance to a cave, a deep, dark place. His arms and legs were covered with spotted fur, and his eyes were no longer those of a man. They were large and yellow, and they glowed at me out of the blackness, like the eyes of a jaguar . . ."

At this point Ixchel pushed her way through the curtain, her arms filled with blankets and various bundles piled almost to her chin, and a bowl of water balanced precariously on the top. She had regained her composure, though, and managed to set down her load without spilling any of it. Together, she and Zac Kuk raised Kanan Naab into a sitting position and began to wash the blood off her face and neck with wet cloths. Murmuring apologetically, they pushed back her hair and dabbed tentatively at her lacerated earlobes, watching her eyes for signs that she might faint again.

But Kanan Naab surrendered herself patiently to their ministrations, not even wincing as they removed the crust of blood from her wounds. Zac Kuk and Ixchel exchanged a glance, simultaneously struck by how clean and evenly spaced the cuts were, indicating the extraordinary steadiness of the hand that had made them. They seemed already to be closing, and did not resume bleeding even after being washed. When Ixchel daubed cut medicine on them, however, the sting brought tears to Kanan Naab's eyes and made her stifle a cry of pain.

"We must remove your clothing," Ixchel suggested softly. "Are you warm enough?"

"Do whatever you must," Kanan Naab agreed wearily, hanging limply in their arms while they pulled the blood-soaked shift off over her head and untied the skirt from her waist. Sponging her body clean, they dried her quickly and helped her into a clean shift, then wrapped her tightly in a warm blanket of cotton interwoven with rabbit-fur thread. Kanan Naab managed a weak smile when they were done.

"Now you have washed *me,* as well. I am grateful to you both."

"We have told no one else about this," Zac Kuk assured her. "Perhaps we can disguise your wounds with paint and powder."

Kanan Naab turned toward her with a bemused expression upon her face.

"There is no need for secrecy. I am not ashamed of what I have done. Balam Xoc *spoke* to me. He told me not to be afraid, but to go back to the world of men and wait for him there. He said that it was too soon for me to come to him."

"You had a vision?" Ixchel inquired in a tremulous voice, and Kanan Naab nodded, still looking at Zac Kuk.

"It was no mere dream, my sister. I saw him and heard him, and I understood many things he did not even say. He will not be the same when he emerges from his confinement. He is completing his transformation. He is taking the spirit of the Jaguar Protector into himself, so that he can lead us to safety. You will see this yourself when he dances tomorrow."

"You must rest, then," Zac Kuk cautioned, "if you are to be strong enough to attend."

"I am Jaguar Paw," Kanan Naab asserted boldly, gesturing for them to help her to her feet. "I will be strong enough."

Keeping the blanket bundled around her, the other two women lifted her into a standing position and held her upright between them, bracing her under the elbows when she swayed dizzily and seemed about to fall. Sweat broke out on her forehead, but then she sighed and gave them a giddy smile.

"And if I am not," she added less firmly, "you must see that I am carried there. You *must* . . ."

"We will," Ixchel promised fervently, only an instant before Zac Kuk made the same pledge, so that their voices overlapped like an echo. Binding Kanan Naab between them with their arms, they walked her slowly toward the doorway, leaving her garments and her ritual implements where they lay, scattered across the bloodstained floor.

The Tun-End
9.17.17.0.0   10 Ahau   13 Kankin

AS THE SUN approached his midpoint in the sky, Nohoch Ich and Tzec Balam, the high priest of the clan, stood together on the platform in front of the Shrine of the Jaguar Protector. Below them, at the base of the steep temple stairs, was the plain stone monument that belonged to the Living Ancestor, and they watched carefully as the shadow cast by the tall yellow slab gradually shrank in around it, indicating the arrival of noon. The plaza area beyond the monument was packed solid with people, lords with gaudy headwraps and necklaces of jade and shell standing shoulder to shoulder with black-painted pilgrims whose heads were bare beneath the burning heat of the Sun. The crowd was so large that it spilled out of the plaza on both sides, and some of the women in the rear had climbed up the terraced back of the huge Sky Clan temple that limited the plaza at its southern end. Despite the overpowering heat and glare of the Sun, which reflected harshly off the plastered surfaces of the surrounding temples, Nohoch sensed a great restlessness in the crowd, which seemed to ripple and sway before his eyes, moved by conflicting currents of anxiety and expectation.

When the proper moment had been reached, Tzec Balam signaled to the drummers seated next to the monument, and as they began to pound on their heavy log drums, he and Nohoch reentered the shrine through its central doorway. The apprentices and costumers who were crowded into the narrow front room moved aside for them, holding their implements and costume paraphernalia away from their bodies, which were running with sweat. The atmosphere in the cramped chamber was hot and sticky, smelling strongly of the men's bodies and the copal they had burned during their three-day vigil for the Living Ancestor.

Many times during this period, they had all heard Balam Xoc cry out and speak to himself, though none of his words had been distinguishable through the thick wall that separated the two chambers. Nohoch did not think he wished to hear whatever Balam Xoc would tell them when he emerged. He was weary, and his eyes burned from the smoke, and he felt a persistent irritation—an unwillingness to be here—that he had never before experienced in all his days as a priest. It was too late for justifications, he thought; too late for words alone to restore the trust and respect that had been lost.

Just as the steady beating of the drums had begun to lull Nohoch with their rhythm, Balam Xoc suddenly emerged from the inner doorway, throwing the thick curtain aside with a vigorous gesture. Except for a few dusty smudges on his chest, the old man's naked body was completely free of its fasting paint, and his unblinking eyes made no concessions to the light in the room. He seemed to glare at all of them, projecting an anger so clear and piercing that Nohoch was instantly afraid of him, stricken with a fear of punishment such as he had not experienced since childhood. It was unnerving, as well, to see so much emotion in that face, which had remained impassive through even the most heated arguments with the clan council.

Balam Xoc's glare narrowed in upon Tzec Balam, who straightened up rather than bowing, his eyes hooded with disdain. Beside him was the costumer who held the plumed train of feathers that Balam Xoc had refused to wear at the last ceremony—an article that Tzec Balam had insisted would be used this time. The hair rose on the back of Nohoch's neck at the sound of the low, grating growl that came from Balam Xoc's throat as he crossed the room and snatched the plumed regalia from the hands of the frightened costumer. Then he took two more steps and threw the feathers out through the open doorway, evoking a chorus of muted cries from the people in the plaza below.

"You will learn to honor my wishes, Tzec Balam," he threatened, confronting the priest face to face. "Or I will discard *you* in the same manner."

Tzec Balam's face hardened, his eyes flaring with outrage, and he turned on his heel to leave the chamber. But Balam Xoc clamped a hand on his shoulder and held him, and the priest jerked to a stop in surprise, his eyes fastening frantically upon the hand on his shoulder, as if it had caused him some bewildering pain.

"Yes, *feel* the coldness of my purpose," Balam Xoc whispered fiercely. "Feel its power, and its sacredness. You will not be so foolish as to oppose me again."

Tzec Balam grimaced, the tendons in his neck standing out like cords as he strained against the relentless pressure of Balam Xoc's hand and voice. Then his legs buckled and his mouth went slack, and he sank slowly to his knees. Everyone else in the room knelt with him, though Nohoch raised his head when he felt Balam Xoc standing over him.

"You have also doubted me, Nohoch Ich," the old man accused him. "But before the next tun has ended, you will once more come to accept my wisdom. You will even bear a wound meant for me—there!"

Balam Xoc suddenly pointed toward Nohoch's right hip, and a sharp jolt of pain seemed to burst against his pelvis, throwing his body into a protective tuck. He gasped and clutched at his hip, only to find that the pain had disappeared as abruptly as it had come.

"Your body knows what comes to you," Balam Xoc said scornfully. "Why does your spirit turn away?"

Trembling all over, Nohoch touched his forehead to the floor, the only way he knew to express his fear and astonishment. From above him, he heard Balam Xoc's voice, sounding impatient now that he had made them all cower before him.

"Dress me," he commanded sharply. "Today I will *speak* to the people, after I have danced for them . . ."

PRESSED IN among the other women at the rear of the crowd, Zac Kuk felt herself fusing with the mass of bodies in the plaza, her sense of separateness melting away in the devastating heat of the sun, which beat upon her head and radiated upward through the bare soles of her feet. She felt at times that everyone was breathing in unison, and that the next breath might lift them all off the ground. Then some spasm of movement or a raised voice elsewhere in the crowd would break the spell, and she would be aware of herself again, aware of the perspiration cutting trails through the yellow powder she had applied to her face, and of the limp strands of hair coming uncoiled upon her shoulders.

She had only to glance sideways at her sister-in-law, though, to make her own dishevelment seem a petty concern. There were dark rings beneath Kanan Naab's eyes and an unhealthy cast to her skin, and the deep creases beside her nose and mouth did not belong on so young a face. Zac Kuk had pleaded for the chance to make her up, but Kanan Naab would have none of it, just as she had insisted upon coming here under her own power. She wore the signs of her bloodletting, her "offering," with unmistakable pride, and so bravely that Zac Kuk had come to see the inappropriateness of her own pleading. She had also seen the reactions of the other clan women, especially those whose husbands were opposed to Balam Xoc, and their obvious disapproval had only made Kanan Naab's display of loyalty that much more impressive and singular.

Drums began to beat, and Zac Kuk turned her eyes toward the front, arching her neck to see over the heads of the men. The two priests who had been standing in front of the shrine's central doorway—one of whom she had recognized as Akbal's uncle—had disappeared. The shrine itself seemed small to her, especially when compared with the towering Sky Clan temples on the lower terrace. It was painted totally red and stood upon a pyramidal platform of only nine steps, and its high, tapering roof comb was set back upon the vaulted roof, thrusting into the sky like a headdress. Unlike the graceful, latticed roof combs of Ektun, which seemed to float above their temples, this one was thick and solid, decorated with elaborate stucco serpents and a large mask of the Night Sun Jaguar. There were three doorways in the front of the shrine, but the outer two had been covered with red curtains, making the facade appear closed and impenetrable, as if great secrets were hidden within.

As she thought this, a long train of bluish-green feathers suddenly came flying out through the central doorway, hanging suspended in the air for an instant, like a diaphanous green snake, before settling in a heap halfway down the temple steps. The crowd made a collective lurch forward, and Zac Kuk was buffeted by the cries that broke forth spontaneously from many throats. *The Featherless Dancer,* she thought, thrilled and slightly frightened by the provocativeness of the gesture, and by the excitement it had touched off in the people around her. She could feel their mood quicken, rising to the tempo of the drums. She turned again toward Kanan Naab, and saw a smile curling the edges of her sister-in-law's lips, though her gaze was firmly fixed upon the shrine. *Now I will begin to understand,* Zac Kuk told herself, feeling certain that something extraordinary was about to happen, something that would take her into the very heart of what it meant to be Jaguar Paw.

The feathers lay where they had fallen, and the crowd itself seemed to hang suspended, hardly breathing as they waited for the ceremony to commence. The clan priests finally reappeared, carrying staves and three-pronged implements, and behind them came the Living Ancestor, seeming huge and ungainly in his jaguar costume. They descended the stairs one by one, the priests carefully sidestepping the train of feathers. Balam Xoc, though, paused for a moment on the step above, then hooked the feathers with the end of his staff and thrust them contemptuously out of the way, a gesture that caused many in the crowd to cry out over the drums, voicing their anger or approval.

Then Zac Kuk's view of him was obscured by the ranks of men in front of her, and she could only see the spotted head, with the water lily attached to its ear, moving above the field of human heads as Balam Xoc circled the tall stone monument at the base of the temple steps. Once mounted upon his pedestal, however, the whole head and upper body of the Jaguar were clearly visible to her, framed against the blank yellow background of the monument. Holding his staff and the three-pronged red "paw" at his sides, he stood facing the people, the great jaws gaping widely around the shadowed face within.

The drumming ceased abruptly, and as the last, vibrating echoes died away, the figure on the pedestal turned toward the west and began to chant the song of the Night Sun Jaguar, the Sun who went beneath the earth each night, traveling through the nine levels of the Underworld to reach his place of rising in the east. Singing in a droning, hypnotic voice, Balam Xoc mimicked the trials faced by the Night Sun Jaguar: the torments of cold and fire he suffered in his descent to the watery depths of the Underworld; the Wind of Knives that shredded his body; the menacing spirits that threatened him in the form of bats and serpents and jaguars; the death and transformation he would undergo before reascending to the sky. Zac Kuk could not understand many of the words, but the story of the Night Sun Jaguar had been known to her since childhood. His journey through the Underworld was the same one that would be taken by the ruler of Ektun upon his death, so that he might ascend to the Place of the Ancestors and watch over the lives of the people who remained upon the earth. This was true as well of the rulers of Tikal and all the other cities, and, as she had been told, of the Living Ancestor of the Jaguar Paw Clan, who claimed the Night Sun Jaguar as their patron spirit, the Jaguar Protector.

As Balam Xoc brought his song to a conclusion, Zac Kuk realized that her own involvement in the rite—which she had never seen enacted before—was much deeper than that of the people around her. They were waiting for the dancing she had been told would follow, and they seemed to brace themselves, drawing deep breaths in the intense heat, during the brief silence that hung over the plaza when Balam Xoc had finished.

Suddenly a cough echoed out over them, the hollow, angry sound of a jaguar in the night, a sound that Zac Kuk had heard only once or twice in her life, and always in the jungle. The cough was repeated several times, louder and louder, as if the beast were coming closer, moving in for the kill. Then a blood-chilling scream erupted from the jaws of the Jaguar on the stone, who reared back and raised his staff and claws over his head, and began to dance as the drumming started up behind him.

Stiffening with fear, Zac Kuk recoiled from the scream, jostling against the people around and behind her. A woman to her left rolled back her eyes and fainted, and men began to fall in the crowd ahead of her, taking their fellows down with them. The Jaguar had danced in a circle, turning his back to the people and apparently urging the drummers to beat faster, his long, spotted tail shaking rapidly behind him. The drums rose to a thunderous pitch, matched by the pumping legs of the Jaguar, who suddenly jumped and spun completely around in the air, thrusting his staff and claws directly at the crowd as he landed. He screamed again, a piercing shriek that cut through the din of the drums and seemed to embed itself in Zac Kuk's flesh. She felt herself falling, her eyes closing of their own accord, until a hand caught her by the arm and brought her back to consciousness.

She hung onto Kanan Naab's hand as waves of color passed in front of her eyes and her heart pounded in time with the drums, the horrible screams of the Jaguar raking at her ears. She felt the crowd melting away around her, and when she was able to raise her eyes, she saw many of the women prostrate upon the ground, and the men ahead of her kneeling before the Jaguar on the pedestal. Only a few of the men remained standing, and the Jaguar seemed to confront each of them in turn, snarling and spitting and pointing his red claw until they also fell to their knees. Still clinging to Kanan Naab, Zac Kuk located Akbal kneeling among the front ranks, his bright blue headwrap rising above the heads of the men around him. She clung to the sight of him as well, praying for an end to her fear.

Waving his staff to silence the drums, the Jaguar let out a final, menacing roar that seemed to resound inside Zac Kuk's head, deafening her to the cries that came from her own throat as she saw Akbal stiffen and collapse onto the man in front of him. Then it was quiet. Zac Kuk felt herself being shaken, and came to in a haze of yellow spots, though still standing on her feet. Kanan Naab steadied her, staring into her eyes until clarity returned. Then she released Zac Kuk to stand on her own and turned to help Ixchel, who was holding Box Ek upright against her chest, trying vainly to revive her.

Zac Kuk had also turned to help when a sudden murmuring in the crowd made her look again toward the front. Balam Xoc had resumed his place on the pedestal after leaving it, having removed the Jaguar head from around his own and given his staff and claws to the priests. He spread his arms wide and addressed them in a commanding voice:

"Three tuns remain to Katun Eleven Ahau, my people! Who will you follow in the time ahead?"

The crowd fell absolutely silent as he swept them with his gaze, letting his arms drop momentarily to his sides. Then he raised one hand, his fingers curling upward and out, as if to seize their attention from the air.

"I say to you that the ruler will lead you to your destruction! He does not have the power to alter the course of his prophecy; he cannot summon the rains as he has promised. This you will know soon enough, for the rains will come early, and then leave the crops to die. I have *seen* this!"

A muted groan went up from the kneeling men, and Balam Xoc pointed a finger at them unsparingly.

"I say to you as well that the warriors have been defeated, and many have been lost. The only spoils of this war will be sorrow! This, too, I have seen."

Balam Xoc raised his other arm and held his palms out to them, altering his tone only slightly, yet in a way that seemed immensely reassuring to Zac Kuk, who had felt her fear beginning to return.

"We must live again in the way of our most ancient ancestors," he told them, "dependent only on ourselves for the food and water that give us life. Dependent only on the spirits of our ancestors for the wisdom to guide us. The katun prophecy concerns us no more. We are done with it, and will pay its prophet no more honor."

He lowered his arms and looked out over them, concluding his speech with great deliberateness, as if he were reciting from memory:

"The masks have been broken. No one may hide again, no one may avoid the conflict to come. We must have courage, and open our hearts to the signs and visions that will guide us. Thus have the ancestors spoken, thus have I spoken to you . . ."

Balam Xoc turned and stepped down off the pedestal, leaving the tall yellow stone to stand in his place. The crowd knelt or lay where they had fallen, slow to come to life, like the survivors of a battle or a devastating storm. *Yes, a storm,* Zac Kuk thought, *like the storm that found Akbal and me in Ektun, and helped to bring me to Tikal, to be here on this day.* Akbal had tried to warn her, but there were no words to describe what she had just experienced, at least not any she would have believed.

She looked over at Kanan Naab and Ixchel, who had lowered Box Ek into a sitting position and were standing over her solicitously, shading her with their skirts. Zac Kuk realized, with a dazed kind of pride, that the three of them were the only people in the plaza still on their feet. She held out her hands to Kanan Naab, who grasped them lightly in her own, smiling in recognition of their common strength.

"I would have been lost without you," Zac Kuk confessed, and Ixchel nodded in agreement, her face streaked with tears. Kanan Naab looked at each of them in turn, neither accepting nor denying their gratitude.

"You will not be lost again," she promised them, then glanced around at the other women of the clan, as if hearing their moans and the sounds of their weeping for the first time.

"Come," she said abruptly. "We are the strong ones now. We must restore those who were not prepared for the touch of the Jaguar Protector."

"Yes," Zac Kuk murmured obediently, feeling that she was one of those herself, and not one of the strong ones. Yet she knelt to comfort the nearest fallen woman, understanding that her doubts and fears did not matter, as long as she could overcome them sufficiently to act. Perhaps *that,* in the end, was what it meant to be Jaguar Paw.

X

THE CLAN WAR

9.17.17.1.0   4 Ahau   13 Muan
(One month later, A.D. 787)

The Jungle

THE FEVERED world of Kinich's dreams was green and wet, utterly sunless. Every way he turned, a wall of green closed in upon him, clutching at his limbs until he was held fast. He saw his men moving away from him, already partly obscured by the green, and he tried to call out to them to stay. Gaunt faces, swollen and scarred by thorns and insect bites, looked back at him, but their eyes were glazed and unseeing. *I must count them,* Kinich thought desperately; *I must count the ones who are still with me.* But they were gone, and all he could see were the faces of the lost, rearing up to accuse him, to remind him of the warrior's death he had promised. Faces pale and bloated from drowning, contorted with the agonies of snakebite, convulsing in the final throes of fever. One hung slack in the air, tongue protruding, a vine looped tight around his neck; another sunk in a swirl of bloody water, his eyes rolling back in horror. Kinich could not bear to live these deaths again, but he could not shut them out. The faces reappeared over and over again, cursing him and leering at his helplessness, driving him to a despair that made him begin to sink, surrendering to the relentless suction of the swamp below . . . serpents writhed among the tangle of vines above him, black-banded boas that twined themselves around the light and squeezed it out. The faces vanished, and the air in front of him grew dense and viscous, filled with greenish spores that sprouted and blossomed until the air, too, had been consumed. He felt his head being wrapped and compressed, the gnarled fingers of roots penetrating his skull to crush out his mind . . .

Then breath returned, and his eyes popped open, struck immediately by a bright bluish light that sent tendrils of pain deep into his throbbing brain. The fever was like an undulating flame beneath his skin, which was slippery with sweat and felt raw to the touch. His vision blurred with the pain and then returned, and he found that he was sitting up, his back against a tree. The blue light seemed to filter down slowly through the vine-draped canopy overhead, illuminating the feathery tips of the tall ferns and bringing a slick shine to the dew-soaked leaves of the undergrowth. His men lay sleeping in clumps in the clearing they had cut for themselves, the mist hanging just above them in curling shrouds, resembling smoke in the eerie light. Kinich stared for a long time before he could clearly distinguish the shapes of the men, and then he saw the creatures that hovered or crawled over the prostrate bodies, fluttering their wings like giant insects, *feeding* on the sleeping men . . .

A feeling of enormous loathing turned over in his stomach, giving him the will to move. He had to protect his men from these vile creatures. But his muscles refused to respond. He looked down at himself, his chest and legs dappled with blue light. And there, poised on his thigh, was a quivering black blotch, feeding on *him*. Rage threw his arm into motion, but so slowly that he seemed to watch it swing forward for several long moments before his hand closed over the creature and crushed down upon it with all his strength. There was a muffled squeak, and something sharp bit into his palm, so that he grunted and threw the creature down and away from his body, nauseated by the warm stickiness that clung to his hand.

The fever pounded in his ears as he struggled to his feet, clutching blindly at the tree for support. His legs felt limp and disjointed, buckling spasmodically as successive waves of dizziness passed over him. He lost track of where he was for a while and simply stood shaking, chafing his hands on the rough bark of the tree. Finally he could stand alone, and turned in a slow circle back toward the clearing, staggering forward like a man drunk on balche. The creatures rose off the bodies at his approach, swooping and fluttering around him as he angrily waved his arms, trying to swat them out of the air.

Then they spiraled upward and were gone. Kinich let his arms drop, exhausted by the effort, which had intensified the painful pressure in his head. The men lay sleeping all around him, undisturbed by the commotion he had created, as they had been unaware of the creatures taking their blood. Kinich did not know how he had avoided stepping on them, and did not find it easy to avoid a second time as he turned to make his way back to the tree. His spear was propped up against a nearby bush, and he took it into his hands, reassured by its unbending weight, which seemed too great to lift. He leaned upon it like a staff and stared into the blackness of the jungle, into the thickly shadowed darkness where the bluish light of the moon could not penetrate.

Then he saw the eyes staring back at him. They were large and yellow, ominous in their intensity. *A jaguar,* Kinich thought helplessly, tasting fear upon his lips. He gripped the spear in both hands and pointed it at the eyes, feeling a fresh surge of fear at the sheer feebleness of the gesture. He was easy prey in his present condition, no match for a hungry animal. But he would fight; he would die before he let himself be eaten.

Yet the eyes came no closer. Instead they seemed to rise, as if the jaguar were being lifted from below, or had reared up upon its hind legs. The eyes rose until they stared directly into his own, holding his gaze for a moment that seemed to stretch on forever. Kinich heard his own heart beating and felt the strength drain from his arms, so that the spear slipped from his hands and fell to the ground with a thud. The eyes blinked once and then vanished into the air, snapping the tension between them so abruptly that Kinich was jerked off balance, and fell forward onto his face in the weeds. He struggled briefly to rise, but the last of his strength was gone, and the fever soon took him into unconsciousness.

HE WOKE to the sound of dripping water, and the ticklish explorations of ants on his back. He lay curled up on his side, and the ground within his range of vision was spotted with the grey light of dawn. He blinked several times, noting that his eyes no longer felt so swollen and grainy, so ready to pop out of his head. Warily, he tested his muscles, and though weak, they moved as he wished; they were his own again. The fever had broken.

Pushing himself into a sitting position, he brushed the ants off his back, experiencing a profound sense of relief when the motions failed to make him dizzy. He had almost grown accustomed to feeling dizzy and out of control, his mind a blur and his responses deadened by fever. Now he could lead his men again, and not simply slog along after them, unfit to help with the cutting of a trail. Now, perhaps, he could lead them *out* of this jungle, before any more were lost.

His spear lay on the ground beside him; the men still slept in the clearing, exactly as he remembered seeing them in the night. But had he actually seen them? Kinich shook himself irritably, uncertain that he had been awake, and not dreaming. The strange light, the giant insects, the jaguar that had watched him but had not attacked. There *were* no insects so large, even in this miserable jungle, and no jaguars who stood to look into the eyes of a man. Those had to be the products of his delirium, as well as the notion that he could have risen and staggered around the clearing as he remembered, without rousing any of the men. He *must* have dreamed it all.

Yet . . . lifting his hands from his lap, Kinich turned them over and examined his palms. They had been scarred by thorns and blistered by the rough haft of his spear, which he used like an ax to cut his way through the jungle. But in the fleshy part of his right palm he found two recent punctures which seemed bruised as well as bloody, testifying to the depth of the bite. *Yes, I killed one of them,* he thought, and immediately got to his knees and began to search the ground around him. He found what he was looking for curled up against the bole of a protruding root: a furry brown body with sticklike black wings folded up around a triangular head, the familiar leaf-shaped nose jutting up between pointed ears.

Bats, Kinich thought; underworld creatures, who lived beneath the earth and drank the blood of the living. Revolted, he rose to his feet, refusing to touch it, unconsciously shaking the hand it had bitten. He knew now that he had not been dreaming, and he picked up his spear before turning to face the spot where he had seen the eyes. He walked slowly toward it, examining the ground as he went. He was no hunter, as his empty stomach reminded him constantly, but he had learned to do his share to keep himself alive. And he knew the pug marks of a jaguar when he saw them, for this would not be the first one to have shadowed their camp in the night. Yet there were no tracks in the mud, no bits of fur caught on the thorns, no signs of vegetation crushed by the passing of so large a beast. There had been no jaguar here.

Kinich stood on the spot and gazed back at the motionless forms of his men. There were only twelve of them left, half the number he had led into this trackless wilderness so many days before. Of the dead, only two had fallen to the Macaws. Two more had deserted in the night, and one had hanged himself; the rest had died in ways more horrible than anything Kinich had ever seen on a battlefield. The living had discarded everything but their weapons and their trust in him, following him through endless swamps and into forests dark as night, and waiting out the days when the rains came so heavily that the sun could not be seen at all. They obeyed him like warriors, even though they scarcely resembled men anymore, so disfigured were their faces and bodies by sickness and hunger.

I must save them, Kinich vowed, watching over them from the place where he himself had been watched. He remembered the eyes rising to meet his own, holding him fast, and he realized—accepted—that it had been no ordinary jaguar. It was no dream but a sign, a vision, reminding him that even here, in this hostile land, he moved in the sight of his ancestors.

The forest around him had begun to come alive with bird sounds, and he could see the sky clearing through the trees overhead. He had to rouse the men and tell them what he had seen, and encourage them to resume the march. As he rehearsed the words he would use, an iguana suddenly ambled out of the undergrowth and stopped only a few feet away, tilting its raggedly crested head. It was greyish green with black bars on its side, fully four feet long to the end of its banded tail. The spear was still in Kinich's hands, and he thrust without a second thought, feeling the long tail whip his legs as the lizard died with an angry hiss.

Another sign, he told himself joyfully, licking his cracked lips at the thought of the iguana's tender white flesh. But his hunger did not overwhelm him completely, and he paused over the carcass, honoring the spirit he had just taken. Then he made a silent prayer of gratitude and dipped his fingers into the blood, flicking it toward the sky, the Place of the Ancestors.

Tikal

FILLING HER gourd with water from the bucket under the trees, Zac Kuk went back out into the hot sunlight, adjusting the palm-leaf hat that covered her head. She climbed up onto the bank of the reservoir, stopping beside one of the huge dredge piles that lined the bank at regular intervals. The conical heap of red mud had formed a bricklike shell in the heat, and it gave off a powerful aroma of rotting snails and algae, attracting clouds of midges and blue-winged flies. Zac Kuk sucked air through her mouth and looked down into the reservoir, marveling at how much had been accomplished in a single month. Emptied of its remaining water, the sloping floor of the oval basin had been dredged and scraped down to its paving stones, which had baked to a dull yellow in the sun. At the very bottom, a reddish-grey circle showed where the stones had been pried up, exposing the bare clay underneath. Men with hoes and rakes were spreading a fresh layer of gravel over the circle of clay, their faces covered with rags against the dust that rose around them.

One month, Zac Kuk thought incredulously, waving absently at the flies that had strayed to her from the dredge pile. It had seemed an impossible task on the day that Balam Xoc had first brought them here. Only a few of them were actually workmen; the rest, like Zac Kuk herself, had never bent their backs to this kind of labor before, not even in imagination. Yet *they* were the ones, Balam Xoc had told them sternly, who would see that the reservoir was cleaned and fully repaired before the arrival of the rains. They could no longer depend upon others to do the things that kept them alive, he had warned; this was not the work of lords, but it had more dignity than a slow and helpless death by starvation.

And so we have done it, Zac Kuk reflected, fearing Balam Xoc perhaps even more than starvation. Remembering the gourd in her hand, she turned away from the scene below and started walking along the bank. She moved without haste, at a pace learned through long days spent in this heat. She and the others would be here again at sunrise tomorrow, and every sunrise thereafter, until the work was done. The reservoir was their life, the single event to which all others were subordinated, so that the hours away from it were totally consumed in preparations for return. Zac Kuk had never even *seen* a reservoir before coming to Tikal, and would not have thought twice about its construction. Now, though, it was the only thing that she and Akbal talked about, on those rare occasions when they had the energy to talk. Most nights they simply slept and tried to gather strength for the next day, lacking even the capacity to wonder at themselves.

She found Akbal standing among a group of men and women who were scooping crushed stone into reed carrying baskets. He was wearing the leather band of a tumpline around his forehead, and his face and body were covered with a sweat-streaked coat of grey dust. He smiled in greeting, though, and took the gourd from her gratefully. The other workers also murmured appreciatively, taking a moment out from their work to pass the water around. Akbal tipped Zac Kuk's conical hat onto the back of her head so that he could see her face, clicking his tongue at the swollen lump of a fly bite on her cheek. She raised her fingers to the spot and shrugged ruefully.

"They always find you when your hands are filled," she said without complaint, and Akbal bared his teeth in a grimace of recognition. His back and legs were dotted with similar bites, and she could smell the sour odor of his unwashed body, as he no doubt could smell hers. But vanity had been sacrificed long ago, along with the comforts of the flesh, and the luxury of complaining about either. Only fortitude mattered, and they were both proud that neither had missed a day of work due to injury or fatigue, or been overcome by the heat. This was their penance, their absolution for having drawn the wrath of the Jaguar Protector.

The workers behind Akbal suddenly fell silent and came stiffly to attention, and Zac Kuk turned to see Balam Xoc coming toward them. He was accompanied by his usual retainers, the Close Ones, as the other clanspeople called them. They acted as a kind of human screen between Balam Xoc and his people, delivering his messages and commands and answering or conveying the questions of those afraid to approach Balam Xoc directly. There were only four with him today: Hok and Kanan Naab, a squat old woman named Chibil, who was a healer, and a former priest from Copan by the name of Opna.

Zac Kuk bowed with the others when Balam Xoc and his retainers stopped on the other side of the gravel pile. Balam Xoc studied them without speaking, his gaze intense but restless, moving from face to face and over the spaces around and between them. He did not squint in the glare of the sun, and his dark, reddish-brown skin, as always, was dry and unmarked by insect bites. Even at a distance, Zac Kuk could feel his inner urgency, like a thickening of the air around her. He had indeed been transformed by his last confinement, his detachment having become the forbidding vacancy of one who listens only to himself. His attention to those around him most often took the form of impatience or anger now, and Zac Kuk did not envy Kanan Naab her privileged proximity.

Scooping up a handful of gravel, Balam Xoc opened his palm and let the pebbles trickle back onto the pile, watching their fall with the intentness of a diviner scattering maize. Then he glanced once more at the workers and turned away without a word, the Close Ones drawing in around him. But they had only gone a few steps when they stopped and waited for the messenger approaching along the bank, a young man wearing the blue net cape of a palace functionary.

"I have a message from Lord Pacal Balam, the chief steward of crops," the young man told Opna, who confronted him in Balam Xoc's place. "I was told to deliver it personally to Balam Xoc."

"Speak," Balam Xoc commanded, waving Opna out of the way. The messenger bowed but then hesitated, glancing at all the people who were listening. Balam Xoc made a brusque, beckoning gesture, indicating that he required no more privacy than this.

"Word has come from Yaxchilan," the young man said, then paused and swallowed gravely. "The warriors of Ain Caan and Shield Jaguar were ambushed by the Macaws and have suffered a terrible defeat. Tikal has lost over thirty of her men, including three from the Jaguar Paw Clan. One of these was the Nacom Kinich Kakmoo."

The messenger stopped out of respect, expecting an outpouring of sorrow and grief. But the man in front of him was expressionless, apparently unmoved by the revelation. The people around him began dropping to their knees, bowing to him with reverence and awe. The messenger stared at this display in disbelief, until Balam Xoc again gestured for him to go on.

"A lengthy search was conducted for survivors, but none were found," the young man continued, casting sidelong glances at the kneeling people. "It must be assumed that all were killed or captured by the Macaws. Ain Caan and the other warriors are recovering in Yaxchilan; a period of mourning will be officially declared upon their return."

"Is that all?" Balam Xoc demanded when the messenger had concluded, and the young man nodded uncertainly.

"Is there a message you would have me take to Lord Pacal?"

"He had my message long ago," Balam Xoc said curtly. "As I had yours. Go."

Ignoring the young man's parting bow, he turned to his retainers, gesturing impatiently for them to rise.

"Inform the people of this," he commanded. "Remind them that the rains will also come early, as I have said. We must work even harder, and see that our task is finished in time."

Keeping only Hok with him, Balam Xoc continued on down the bank. The workers slowly began to rise, exchanging nervous glances when they saw that Akbal had remained standing. He seemed too numb to move, his eyes glazed with shock and the incomprehension of his loss. Zac Kuk came to his side, but he did not see her. She was about to suggest that he sit for a moment in the shade when Kanan Naab appeared in front of her, beckoning for her to follow.

"Come, my sister. We must tell May about her husband."

The briskness of Kanan Naab's tone brought Akbal out of his trance in an instant, as if he had been slapped. He blinked and lifted a hand to shield his eyes from the sun.

"Kinich is gone," he said in a thick voice. "Our brother has died."

"Yes," Kanan Naab agreed succinctly, betraying no more emotion than her grandfather had shown earlier. Akbal's face tightened, and he leaned toward her belligerently, as if to force some greater response from her. The workers stared at him with a kind of horror, amazed that he would challenge one of the Close Ones, even if she were his own sister.

"Will we not observe a period of mourning of our own?" Zac Kuk interjected, hoping to loosen the awful tension that had sprung up between the two of them. Kanan Naab shook her head impatiently.

"There is no time for that now. We will mourn when Grandfather decides it is appropriate."

"Or not at all," Akbal suggested bitterly, in a voice that seemed much too loud.

"Could you not have foreseen this?" Kanan Naab demanded. "Our brother was a warrior, and he *chose* to serve the ruler instead of the clan."

"Do we abandon him, then?" Akbal demanded in return. "Do we allow his spirit to wander alone in the Underworld, without our prayers to sustain and guide him?"

Kanan Naab tossed her head in exasperation.

"We will do as Grandfather commands," she repeated coldly. "You bring no honor to yourself, or our brother, by indulging in your grief now. Come, Zac Kuk . . ."

Zac Kuk hesitated out of loyalty, gazing up at Akbal from beneath the ragged fringe of her hat. His teeth were clenched, and he was breathing hard through his nose, as if in the grips of some incoherent fury. But gradually reason returned to him, and he saw the concern on her face, and realized that all the other workers were staring at him. His shoulders slumped, and he sighed in resignation.

"Give May what comfort you can, my wife," he said quietly, narrowing his eyes at Kanan Naab's retreating back. "Tell her that she is not alone in her grief. However it may seem . . ."

IN THE LAST DAYS before the rains came, Balam Xoc became ferocious in his urgency, as if he could smell the storm approaching. He went from one work crew to the next, goading them to greater exertions with his presence, and often putting his own hands to the task. The paving stones had all been lifted and laid back down over a freshly graveled bottom, fitted together with painstaking care, so that they would not buckle or separate. Then another layer of gravel was spread evenly over the stone floor, as damp, salty winds began to blow in from the east. It was still the first days of the month of Pax, too early for the rains to begin in earnest, yet Balam Xoc drove his people as if it might already be too late.

The final stage of the project involved leveling and shaping the bank, and shoring it up with loose stones. Clouds had been coming in for the last day and a half, sparing the workers the sun's direct heat as they labored on the bank and the drainage ditches that cut through it at several points. Then the sky darkened, and thunder broke over Tikal, and they could hear the rattling approach of the rain as it pelted distant trees. Many of the workers flung themselves into a last, frantic burst of activity, but others simply stopped where they were and stood looking up at the sky. When Balam Xoc stopped and turned to face the east, everybody ceased their labors and put down their tools. They also realized for the first time that they were done. The work that remained was not of crucial importance, and they would lose no water because of it. They had finished in time.

Bending the trees before it, the rain swept over the Jaguar Paw House and poured down upon the people around the reservoir, drenching them where they stood. They turned their faces up to it, letting it blind their eyes and fill their open mouths. Men and women alike removed their hats and headwraps and let the water cascade over their loosened hair, washing away the mud and dust and sweat of the many long days. Even after the initial downpour, the rain continued to fall steadily, and the sky remained dark to the east, indicating that this was not to be an isolated shower. The rains had indeed come early, and with convincing force.

His white hair gleaming in the murky, liquid light, Balam Xoc walked down alone into the reservoir, leaving dark footprints in the gravel. The water was already calf-deep at the bottom, and he waded into the middle of the pool and turned to face the people on the bank above. His lips moving to some unheard chant or prayer, he dipped his cupped hands into the water at his feet and offered it to the sky in a gesture of gratitude. Then he filled his hands again and drank, and the people on the bank began to shout and sing with joy.

Standing next to a gushing drainage ditch, Zac Kuk saw Akbal coming toward her, searching for her as he wove his way through the celebrating crowd. She glanced down at herself briefly, smiling at the memories her clinging shift evoked. She turned the smile on Akbal when he saw her, feeling warmth well up under her skin at the way his eyes fastened upon her. He had not forgotten the storm in Ektun, either, and he dodged through the crowd with reckless eagerness, crossing the ditch with an unhesitating leap. Clasping wet hands, they laughed at themselves, knowing perfectly what was in the other's mind.

"Come," Akbal said, and began to turn away from the reservoir, leading her by the hand. Zac Kuk pulled back halfheartedly.

"Perhaps we should wait for Balam Xoc to release us."

Akbal shook his head firmly, displaying a flash of the defiance he had shown toward Kanan Naab.

"He may not think of it. Besides, we have earned our release, at least for today."

Feeling little urge to disagree, Zac Kuk allowed herself to be persuaded, and to be led away through the crowd, toward the path that led to their house.

THE EARLY arrival of the rains took the rest of the city by surprise, and delayed the burning of the fallowed maize fields past the day designated by the ruler and his priests. But then the rains slackened and assumed a more normal pattern, with substantial periods of sunlight and clear sky between the heaviest downpours. The lingering wetness made the burning of some of the lowland fields only partially successful, but the depth of water in the alkalches gave promise that the raised fields there would produce abundantly. The planting of the maize, cotton, and other crops was finally completed early in the month of Kayab, only slightly behind the schedule established by the chief steward of crops.

The rains also delayed the return of Ain Caan and his warriors from Yaxchilan, so that the period of mourning for those who had been lost was not declared until after the planting had been finished. The mourning was to last for nine days, one for each of the nine levels of the Underworld. A muffled drum beat in the Plaza of the Ancestors, where Caan Ac himself, his body smeared with ashes, presided over the rites of the dead. A ceremonial ball game was also played on the court next to the plaza, and the city's marketplace was allowed to open for only a few hours each day, with all business conducted in a properly subdued tone.

The Jaguar Paw Clan, however, had not even sent a representative to greet the returning warriors, and Balam Xoc had begun to implement the second phase of work at the reservoir as soon as the rains had become more moderate. Calling together the heads of the work crews and his Close Ones, he had described to them the way he had *seen* the reservoir in its final form: its waters deep and clean, mirroring the well-tended gardens and groves of select trees that surrounded it on all sides, along with the thatched huts of those who would work the land and water the crops. Further, he had specified which trees would be saved and which cut, and how the mud from the reservoir was to be spread over the cleared areas, and then the dried brush laid over that, to provide ground cover until the time was right for burning. He had even elaborated upon the variety of crops that would be grown, naming those that could be planted in the shade of the remaining trees and those that would require full sunlight. Though clearly no farmer, he had spoken with the familiarity of one who had already witnessed every step of the work and had walked through the gardens in their finished state.

The original work crews had been formed voluntarily, largely on the basis of family ties and personal friendships. But Balam Xoc now reorganized them totally, distributing the experienced workmen among them evenly and concentrating some of those with special skills. One crew, under the command of Tzec Balam, was sent to dredge and repair a smaller clan reservoir near the houses of the high priest's family. Another was put to work cutting poles and thatch for the houses that Balam Xoc's followers would occupy for the duration of the project, or until such time as they were formally adopted into the clan. A third crew was composed entirely of women who were to spend their time sharpening tools and fashioning water buckets out of vines and cedar slats.

The remaining three crews were each assigned to a staked-out section of the forest surrounding the reservoir, and were told to begin the arduous task of clearing the land with stone axes and flint knives. Akbal had been put in charge of one of these crews, and it was to him that Kanan Naab came with the message from Balam Xoc, requesting the loan of a particularly skilled woodcutter. She found him standing beneath a chicle tree that had a white chalk mark on its trunk, the only tree still standing in the immediate area. Akbal was studying a map he had drawn, showing the locations of the other trees and plants that were to be saved, and he was slow to acknowledge his sister's presence. After hearing her message, he went back to his map for a few more moments, and then glanced out over the men working among the trees.

"I can probably spare him," he said finally, giving her a judicious nod. "I will send him as soon as he is finished with the tree he is cutting. We can occupy ourselves with the undergrowth until he returns."

"Grandfather will be pleased that you find the arrangement acceptable," Kanan Naab said sarcastically, annoyed at the way he always made her wait. He did the same to all the Close Ones, though his lack of deference seemed especially pointed in her case.

"It is past noon," he said, glancing briefly at the sky. "The official period of mourning is over, for those who observed it."

He raised his eyebrows slightly, veiling his eyes in a kind of sardonic wink, as if he could predict her response all too easily. Kanan Naab allowed her anger to show in her eyes, but she took a slow breath before replying.

"I am quite aware of the time that has passed," she said stiffly. "And so is Grandfather. I have spoken to him of this several times, but I cannot make him listen when he does not wish to."

Akbal grunted scornfully.

"No doubt you whispered loudly, my sister. No doubt you used your influence to its fullest extent."

"Why do you bait me, Akbal?" Kanan Naab demanded furiously, losing her restraint. "Why do you pretend that I have more influence than you or anyone else? If you truly believed that, you would show me more respect than you do."

"What am I to believe, then? That you only serve, and have no thoughts or feelings of your own? Is that cause for respect?"

Tears of resentment sprang up in Kanan Naab's eyes, and she clenched her fists tightly.

"I did not choose the role I have been given, any more than you chose yours. Perhaps you can win the admiration of your workers by treating the Close Ones with disdain, but it is still a false display of independence. You also do whatever Grandfather demands, despite your scorn for his servants."

"That is my *choice,*" Akbal insisted forcefully. "The choice *he* gave me, and you as well. Or have you forgotten?"

"He is not the same man who spoke to us at the stone. I doubt that *he* would remember. He watches for signs now, and expects to be obeyed without argument or hesitation. Have *you* forgotten the anger of the Jaguar Protector?"

Akbal rolled up his map with a deft, snapping motion of his wrists, his lips pursed stubbornly.

"I will never forget that," he said shortly. "But we have all paid for our dereliction. I will not found my sense of duty on fear."

He turned away and started to walk toward his men, slapping the map against his thigh. But then Kanan Naab saw the men who had just emerged from the path through the breadnut trees, and she called Akbal back, gesturing urgently in their direction. There were perhaps twenty of them, including Nohoch Ich and several other members of the clan council, and they were trailed by an equal number of young boys. Most of the men wore headwraps and palace clothing, and they walked in silence, their expressions deeply somber.

"I will go for Grandfather," Kanan Naab said to Akbal when he had returned to the tree, and she left him there and went down the bank with rapid steps. By the time Nohoch and the others reached the place where he stood, Akbal had begun to realize what must have happened, and gave his uncle a look of solemn inquiry.

"The ruler has taken his revenge," Nohoch said in a tight voice. "I have been expelled from the Order of the Tun Count Priests, and our clansmen have all been discharged from their posts within the city's administration. Everyone except your father and Chac Mut, apparently."

Kal Cuc appeared at Akbal's side, his downcast eyes showing that he had lost his apprenticeship, as well. Akbal put a comforting hand on his shoulder, noticing that the members of his crew had left their cutting and were standing in a crowd behind him. He made no attempt to send them back to their work, though, and turned with them to bow when Balam Xoc came into the clearing with Kanan Naab and his other retainers.

"Caan Ac has decided to blame his misfortune upon you and your prophecy, Grandfather," Nohoch explained, and repeated what he had told Akbal. Balam Xoc squinted at him thoughtfully, betraying no surprise.

"What else has he done?"

"He has told the traveling merchants of the Sky Clan not to carry our goods any longer," Nohoch went on, "and he has threatened to punish anyone who trades with us within the city. His warriors are stationed at the head of the trails leading to our houses, to observe and intimidate those who might wish to visit us."

The silence in the clearing was complete, broken only by the buzzing of insects and the muted crash of a tree falling in the next work area.

"So it has begun," Balam Xoc said at last. He turned and gestured brusquely to Hok, who flinched in confusion before seeing that Balam Xoc was pointing to his waist. Then he produced a short, bone-handled knife, encased in a leather sheath, which he had been carrying in his waistband.

"Here," Balam Xoc continued, holding out the knife to Nohoch. "You must carry this with you now."

Nohoch appeared startled for a moment, then straightened his shoulders and put out his hand, nodding to show that he understood. He tucked the knife under the waistband of his loincloth, next to his hip, the way a weapon was worn. The onlookers shifted uneasily, uncertain of the full significance of the gift, but aware that priests were not allowed to carry weapons and that Nohoch had never needed one before this. "*It has begun*" took on an even more ominous meaning, though typically, Balam Xoc did not offer any further explanations.

"The ruler's revenge will be our good fortune," he announced. "There are posts for all of you here, and work that will directly benefit our people. Nohoch, you may take charge of the work crew here." Balam Xoc paused, his eyes flickering over the crowd until he found Akbal. "Acquaint your uncle with what you have accomplished so far, Akbal. Then you may return to the craft house."

Akbal simply stared back at him, too surprised to bow or otherwise indicate his compliance. But Balam Xoc had already turned away and was making other assignments, gesturing broadly in the direction of the other work areas. Nohoch came over, and Akbal numbly handed him the map he had been holding. He had only begun to explain how the trees were being cut, though, when he was seized by an idea that brought animation back into his face and voice.

"Perhaps you would have me for your assistant, Uncle," he suggested impulsively. "Then I would have the time to explain everything thoroughly."

Nohoch narrowed his eyes doubtfully.

"Balam Xoc has ordered you back to the craft house, has he not? You must go."

"But what can be accomplished there?" Akbal asked, spreading his hands wide in appeal. "My work has no value if it cannot be traded."

The crowd around them had dispersed rapidly, the crew going back to their labors and the new men being led off by some of the Close Ones. Suddenly Balam Xoc intruded himself into the conversation, glancing sharply from one to the other.

"What is your difficulty?" he demanded, fixing his gaze on Akbal when the younger man dropped his eyes. But then Nohoch intervened politely, coming to his nephew's defense.

"Akbal feels that he could be of more use to the clan if he served as my assistant. I would be pleased to have him, my lord."

"If no one will trade with us, Grandfather," Akbal put in bravely, forcing himself to meet Balam Xoc's eyes, "our craft goods will be worthless. I would also like to do work that is beneficial to our people."

Balam Xoc cocked his head and looked Akbal up and down, as if studying his stance for clues to this sudden show of defiance. Behind him, Kanan Naab shook her head sadly and looked away, as if it pained her to watch what was coming. But Balam Xoc's voice was surprisingly tolerant, almost explanatory, when he finally spoke.

"There are still your friends in Yaxchilan and Ektun," he reminded Akbal. "*They* will still trade with us, if we honor our agreements. See that the work is done, Akbal, even if you must do all of it yourself. I will find a way to convey the goods when the time comes."

Relieved as much as mollified, Akbal bowed from the waist, crossing his arms over his chest. Balam Xoc stared at him for another moment, as if he found this elaborate display of compliance as puzzling as Akbal's earlier recalcitrance. Then he shrugged and gestured toward Kal Cuc, who had remained at Akbal's side.

"Do you wish to have the boy with you?"

Akbal looked down at Kal Cuc, and his face brightened, as if he had just been offered a reward.

"Of course. He is my assistant."

"Use him well, then," Balam Xoc said dismissively, and turned away, taking Kanan Naab with him. Akbal looked at Nohoch and let out a long breath.

"Surely, your duties must be clear to you now," Nohoch suggested drily. "Go attend to them, my son. I can find my own way here."

"I never doubted that you could," Akbal confessed with a small smile, beckoning to Kal Cuc to follow. "Come, there is important work for us at the craft house. *Our* work . . ."

"TAKE ME TO HIM, my daughter," Box Ek said to Zac Kuk, as the two of them came out of Kinich Kakmoo's house. "This has gone on too long."

"But he is at the reservoir," Zac Kuk protested mildly, lifting her palm-leaf umbrella to shade the old woman from the sun. "And it is very hot today, Grandmother."

"That is what May says, to excuse herself," Box Ek replied curtly. "But we all suffer from much more than the heat. Come."

Leaning heavily on her stick, she hobbled out onto the plaza, displaying a vitality she had not possessed in many months. Zac Kuk had seen very little of her, in fact, since the work had begun on the reservoir, and was surprised when she had suddenly appeared in May's chamber, where Zac Kuk had been trying to comfort her grieving sister-in-law. It had reminded her of the way Box Ek had come in when she was being dressed for her wedding night, and she had been no more able to resist the old woman than her mother had been that night.

As they walked slowly past the craft house, they saw Akbal through the open doorway, mixing paints with Kal Cuc. Both were too absorbed in their work to see the women, and did not look up as they passed.

"Why did Akbal and Kanan Naab not see to this?" Box Ek inquired, straining her neck to give Zac Kuk a stiff, sidelong glance.

"Kanan Naab has tried to bring it to Balam Xoc's attention," Zac Kuk explained, "but she says he will not listen. She and Akbal argued about it, and have not been on friendly terms ever since."

Box Ek made an exasperated noise, shaking her head as if it hurt her.

"And how long has it been since you have seen *your* brother?"

"Chan Mac?" Zac Kuk said in surprise. Then she frowned as she thought back. "Not since before the Tun-End Ceremony, Grandmother. When Balam Xoc's prophecies were denounced by the ruler, the Ektun ambassador told my brother that he should not visit us for a while. Now, of course, it has become impossible for *anyone* to visit us."

"Of course," Box Ek repeated gruffly, holding up a hand to indicate that she had to rest. They had reached the shade of the breadnut trees, though even here, the sullen heat of the afternoon seemed to hang in the air around them, like some invisible, enervating presence. The rains had stopped a few days earlier, giving way to the period of hot, dry weather that always followed the onset of the rainy season. Everywhere else in the city the people were praying that the drought would not be prolonged, and that the rains would return in time to save the new crops. The Jaguar Paw Clan, however, labored on in their isolation, guided by Balam Xoc's prediction that there would *indeed* be a drought, and by his insistence that the clan's gardens must be ready by the time it was over.

"Has my brother said when the rains will return?" Box Ek asked as they began moving again. Zac Kuk shook her head uncertainly.

"I am told that he watches for signs of this. He and all of the Close Ones."

"The uos sang to me in my dreams last night," Box Ek told her suddenly. "But the water that brought them out of the earth was not rain, but the tears of the people."

Zac Kuk caught her breath.

"Perhaps it was a sign, Grandmother."

"Perhaps," Box Ek allowed. "But May is a much more visible sign, and *she* has been overlooked. For too long. Ah, we are here. Find him for me, my daughter. I cannot walk much farther."

Scanning the nearest clearing, Zac Kuk quickly spotted the cluster of people that Balam Xoc always drew, people without tools or baskets or buckets. They were standing in front of the first of the workers' houses to be completed, a pole-and-thatch construction that had not yet received its coating of mud and lime plaster. Picking a path between the stacks of firewood and piles of drying brush, Zac Kuk led Box Ek toward the house, shading her with the umbrella. Before they could reach the group around Balam Xoc, though, they were intercepted by Kanan Naab.

"Forgive me, Grandmother," she apologized to Box Ek. "But this is not a good time to disturb him. He has been withdrawn from us all day."

She glanced back over her shoulder, inviting them to see for themselves. Balam Xoc stood motionless in the midst of his retainers, who attended him with a kind of tense expectancy, squatting or standing around him in silence. Balam Xoc's eyes were fixed upon the cloudless sky, apparently following the movements of the vultures that circled high over the reservoir.

"Perhaps *I* can help you," Kanan Naab suggested in a hushed voice, inclining her cloth-wrapped head to the old woman.

"As you helped May?" Box Ek snapped. "That is neglect, not help. I will speak to my brother."

Kanan Naab's head jerked back at the reprimand, her face darkening beneath the light-colored headwrap. She cast a questioning glance at Zac Kuk, perhaps sensing a conspiracy, though her expression seemed more harried than suspicious. She tried again to reason with Box Ek.

"I am not heartless, Grandmother. I have raised the subject of mourning many times, but he has never responded."

"Did his silence forbid you to act yourself?" Box Ek demanded, waving her aside with her stick. "You are in my way, Kanan Naab. We have hidden from our grief long enough."

"Who is that?" a voice called, and Kanan Naab stepped back so that they could see Balam Xoc beckoning to them. "Let them come forward."

Nohoch and Opna were standing on either side of Balam Xoc, and Hok was squatting stolidly at his feet. But when his sister had approached to within a few feet of him, Balam Xoc also squatted, so that she would not have to strain to look up at him. The other two men did likewise, as did Zac Kuk, setting the umbrella down beside her. Contrary to what Kanan Naab had predicted, Balam Xoc's attention was intense and focused completely upon Box Ek.

"You spoke of grief, my sister," he prompted, and Box Ek nodded, planting her stick firmly in the mud and leaning upon it with both hands.

"I have just come from the wife of Kinich Kakmoo. She languishes from grief, and from the neglect of her grief. It is wrong that she has not been allowed to mourn for her husband."

Both Nohoch and Opna frowned at the bluntness of her scolding, and Hok's one good eye glared up at her out of a tangle of black hair. Balam Xoc, though, simply gestured for her to go on, as if certain that she had her own resolution in mind.

"I have come to ask if you know the manner of Kinich's death; if perhaps you have *seen* this. We cannot mourn him properly if we do not know which rites to perform."

Zac Kuk saw Opna shake his head wearily, as if Box Ek were not the first to seek the fate of a loved one in Balam Xoc's visions. Nohoch was frowning even more deeply, obviously perturbed by the old woman's willingness to take the rites into her own hands, with or without the permission of the Living Ancestor. Balam Xoc briefly glanced upward at the sky, rubbing his chin thoughtfully.

"It would indeed have been wrong not to mourn Kinich Kakmoo," he conceded, slowly lowering his eyes to his sister's face. "*If* he were dead. But he was not killed or captured by the Macaws. That much I have seen."

Astonishment blossomed on all of the faces surrounding him, though it was very quickly assimilated into a kind of reverent pride, a sharing of the master's power. Opna and Nohoch exchanged a glance that was almost congratulatory, as if only they could truly appreciate the value of this revelation.

"You knew this, and you did not tell May?" Box Ek burst out angrily. "Why have you allowed her to suffer so needlessly?"

Balam Xoc considered her silently, unmoved by the accusation. Hok, though, appeared about to spring, and Balam Xoc, as if sensing this, waved him back down with a small movement of his hand.

"Because I do not know if Kinich *will* return," he replied calmly. "Perhaps your coming here, though, is a sign that he will. I was thinking of death when you appeared."

Box Ek stared back at him speechlessly, her energy expended along with her anger.

"What else disturbs you, my sister?" Balam Xoc asked shrewdly. "Was it only concern for May that brought you here today?"

"It was a dream," Box Ek admitted, "and my own loneliness. I have seen little of my family since this work began, and *they* apparently have forgotten their obligations to one another. In my dream, I heard the uos singing, watered by the tears of our people. When I awoke, I went to May, and understood what I had dreamed. I could not neglect her sorrow as you and these others have."

"Uos," Balam Xoc repeated softly, and turned his head to look at Zac Kuk. "Is this true, my daughter? Is there unhappiness among our people?"

Zac Kuk nodded timidly, feeling the attention of the others fasten upon her.

"We have little time together when we are not working, or exhausted from work," she explained. "And we are more scattered now. It is hard to borrow or trade for the things we need, especially with the marketplace closed to us.

There is no one who wishes to complain, Grandfather, but we are all tired, and we bring little comfort to one another."

"And what about the rest of you?" Balam Xoc asked, gazing around at the Close Ones, who averted their eyes guiltily. "Why did none of you see this?"

"Why did you not see it yourself, my brother?" Box Ek inquired sharply. "Are you blind to our suffering?"

The audacity of the question drew a collective, disapproving gasp from the onlookers, who would never have defended themselves in such a way. Though afraid herself that Box Ek had gone too far, Zac Kuk drew closer to her out of loyalty, proud of the old woman's boldness.

"Yes, I am," Balam Xoc said slowly. "The Spirit Woman has emptied me of feelings and desires, so that I might fill myself with power. Only memory allows me to recognize the signs of sorrow or anger in another, and there are more important things I must remember." He paused and widened his gaze to include his retainers. "But I have not forbidden anyone else their feelings, and I do not wish that any of *you* should emulate my own emptiness in this regard."

Balam Xoc paused again, looking at each of them in turn before returning his attention to the two women in front of him.

"I will see that this is communicated to all the people," he promised. "You must tell the wife of Kinich Kakmoo what I have revealed to you. Tell her to put aside her grief and pray for his safe return. Perhaps he will be back to dance with us at the feast to celebrate our planting. I think now that we will be holding such a feast some time in the month of Uo."

"I will tell her," Box Ek said, bowing stiffly over her stick. Zac Kuk bowed as well, and Balam Xoc waved a hand over both of them in blessing.

"You have done well to come to me. Go, then, and watch over the hearts of my people. Be a sign to them, as you have been to me . . ."

CRUNCHING CINDERS under his sandaled feet, Pacal walked out into the center of the field, noting the places where deer had come to graze in the night. Bright green grasshoppers whirred up around him as he stopped and squatted among the rows of ankle-high plants. In some places the weeds were nearly as tall, for this was one of the fields that had been too wet to permit a thorough burning. Now it was bone-dry, and the blackened crust of the soil broke into powder when Pacal poked at it with his fingers. The stalks of the young maize plants had begun to droop, and their leaves were yellowing at the edges; the beans lay in shriveled coils among the weeds, already beyond salvage.

The dry spell was now in its fourteenth day, twice its normal length. And despite all the ruler's prayers and offerings—including the sacrifice of two captive Macaws—there had been only two brief periods of rain, both of the light and misty kind that only served to make the plants more vulnerable to pests and the sun. Another six days would bring the time of drought to a full month, and would probably mean the end of any hope of recovery. And if that time came, it would be Pacal who would have to surrender to the inevitable, and pronounce the crops a lost cause.

He rose to his feet, feeling the heaviness of despair in his legs and shoulders. The clans had already begun to pressure him to release some of their workers, so that they could try to save their own gardens before it was too late. They had all seen the example of his own clan, and did not hesitate to shame him with it when he tried to deflect their demands. Uaxactun and some of the other cities who had lent their workers to Tikal were threatening to withdraw them entirely unless their promised bonuses were paid in full. The prevailing mood in the palace was one of desperate recrimination, with the ruler himself being the worst of the blame shifters. He had blamed the failure of the campaign on the prophecies of Balam Xoc and the defection of Zotz Mac of Ektun, and he would no doubt try to blame Pacal if the crops also failed, even though the responsibility for bringing the rains was his and his alone.

He will be the last to admit that he has failed in that, Pacal thought, staring bleakly around him. He would have to keep his men working until Caan Ac decided to give up hope, which would probably be days after everyone else. *At least we will waste no time trying to save* this *field,* Pacal decided. Not far from where he stood, a column of leaf-cutter ants was methodically stripping a whole row of plants of their foliage, cutting and carrying off the leaves in a moving line. Pacal stepped closer, remembering pranks his brother and he had played as children, rerouting the ants' path into someone's house or across a plaza where a ceremony was being held. The memory aroused little amusement in him, though, and he deliberately brought his foot down over the well-beaten trail the ants had marked for themselves, implanting several of them in a shallow pit he dug with the edge of his sandal. The next bearers to reach the pit began to mill in confusion, bumping into one another and dropping the leaves they carried like flags in their pincers. Soldier ants immediately rushed to the spot from both ends of the line, and they quickly bullied the others onto a new path around the trench. Soon the column of leaf-laden ants was flowing steadily again, bearing the crops of the ruler off to their nest.

Perhaps they deserve them more than we do, Pacal thought morbidly; *indeed, our warriors would lead us straight to the pit, and insist that we plunge in after them.* Stepping over the ants, he started walking slowly toward the great ceiba tree that stood at the edge of the field. He had left his scribe there to rest in the shade, and he was surprised now to see that Chac Mut had joined him, along with Ixchel, who was holding little Bolon Oc on her hip.

"My wife," Pacal said in a mildly quizzical tone, as he came in under the tree. "Chac Mut . . . have you come here together?"

"We met on the trail," Chac Mut explained, bowing his head slightly to Ixchel. "*I* came to tell you that Kinich Kakmoo has been reported alive. He and ten other men have found their way to safety in Palenque."

Pacal looked to Ixchel, who gave an eloquent shrug, jiggling the baby in her arms.

"Balam Xoc told us this many days ago," she said. "Though not as long ago as your last visit, my husband."

"I had heard," Pacal assured her quietly. "I prayed myself for it to be true. When will he return to us?"

"He and the others are not in good health," Chac Mut reported. "They will spend some time recovering in Palenque. Shield Jaguar has promised to send canoes for them when they are able to travel."

Pacal glanced briefly at the dark-eyed child nodding drowsily against Ixchel's side, and at the lines of strain and fatigue in his wife's face.

"Has the clan been notified?" he asked Chac Mut, who seemed surprised by the question.

"Not to my knowledge. And certainly not intentionally."

"I will tell them myself. You may return to the palace," Pacal added, gesturing to include the scribe. "There is nothing more to be done here. Leave us some of the water when you go."

Holding out his arms, he relieved his wife of the baby, grunting softly at the child's unexpected weight. He noticed the way Ixchel's arms trembled as she released him, and he wondered how she had managed to carry him all this way by herself.

"It is a long walk in this heat," he said, shifting Bolon Oc in his arms. "Let us sit and rest awhile."

They sat with their backs against the tree and drank from the water gourd Chac Mut had left behind. Bolon Oc nursed for a short time and then fell asleep across his mother's lap. Pacal gently stroked the tufts of black hair on the child's head, and lowered his voice when he spoke.

"I know that I have neglected you, Ixchel. You *and* our son. I regret this very much, but perhaps you understand how difficult it is for me to identify with the Jaguar Paw Clan at this time. '*You* will eat,' they say to me; 'why do you not give us the same means you gave your father?' And the ruler denounces Balam Xoc daily, without regard for my presence."

"I know this," Ixchel said quickly. "I did not come here to shame you, my husband, but to help you. I thought that it might be useful to you to know when the rains would return, and that knowing this might help to bring you home sooner."

Pacal squinted at her skeptically.

"Has my father seen this, as well?"

"The signs of it, yes. The Lady Box Ek had a dream in which the uos sang to her. And then several days later, when Hok and another man were digging up a stump, they uncovered a uo, and we *all* heard it sing: *Whoa, whoa,*" she said softly, imitating the distinctive croak of the frog. Pacal watched her with an expression of pained tolerance on his long face.

"And *this* revealed the time of the rains' return?"

"The month of Uo, Grandfather has said," Ixchel explained with evident pride.

"Uo," Pacal echoed, his mouth forming a bitter O around the word. "That is more than a month from now. Even the alkalches would be dry by then."

Ixchel nodded earnestly, missing the note of distress in his voice.

"That is when we hope to celebrate our planting. Is it not time enough for *you* to attempt a second planting as well?"

"Time, certainly," Pacal said brusquely. "But where would I get the seed and the workers? And how would I convince the ruler to take such a risk? Do you think he is eager to take the advice of Balam Xoc? I cannot even speak my father's name to him!"

The baby whimpered and stirred in Ixchel's lap, and she looked down at him hastily, hiding the hurt in her eyes. Pacal sighed in weary apology.

"I am sorry, Ixchel. You do not deserve my anger. But surely you must see that what you suggest is impossible. I would be dismissed as a fool if I were to go to the ruler talking of uos and asking for a second planting."

"Is Balam Xoc also a fool?" Ixchel demanded sullenly, refusing to meet his gaze. "He has been correct in everything he has foretold. He has convinced us that the impossible *can* be done, if it is necessary to the survival of the people."

"And he has convinced the ruler that he is a dangerous man, a threat to the peace and well-being of the city. For all his wisdom, Ixchel, how can he hope to succeed in isolation? Can the Jaguar Paw Clan prosper while their neighbors are starving? Do you think you will be left in peace if that happens? I think rather that you will be the target of all the fear and envy and desperation of the other clans, and their hatred will destroy you."

"Are you no longer one of us, then?" Ixchel asked him in a whisper, her eyes large and moist. Pacal nodded in resignation.

"Yes, of course. And I may be back among you very shortly, if the rains hold off as you say. But I see things as a steward must, and I see only tragedy for our city if the clans pursue their own interests at one another's expense."

Ixchel nodded respectfully, seeming reassured by his explanation, or perhaps merely by the possibility of his imminent return. She certainly did not seem daunted by the tragedy he had described.

"Perhaps the other clans will choose to follow our example," she suggested hopefully, and Pacal could only laugh and shake his head, overwhelmed by the sheer resilience of her optimism.

"Then my father will indeed have accomplished the impossible," he said lightly, and pushed himself to his feet. "Come, let us take our son back to the Jaguar Paw House."

"Then you are not angry with me for coming to you like this?" Ixchel asked as she handed the sleeping baby up to him.

"Angry?" Pacal repeated incredulously, as if she could not be further from the truth. "No, my wife, I am grateful that you thought to help me." He swiveled to take in the surrounding fields, his face twisting into a rueful grimace. "Even if I am beyond help . . ."

IT WAS LATE in the day and the sky had turned cloudy when Nohoch Ich, Balam Xoc, and Cab Coh came out onto the plaza in front of Tzec Balam's house. Balam Xoc immediately walked to the edge of the plaza and stood looking up at the sky, his hands on his hips, breathing deeply in the cooling air. Nohoch and Cab Coh stood apart from him, understanding that the patience he had shown during the council meeting had required a conscious effort on his part.

"It was a great success, my son," Cab Coh said, glancing back through the open doorway to where Tzec Balam and some of the other council members were still working out the details of the plans that had been formulated during the meeting.

"He made it easy for all of us," Nohoch said modestly, nodding toward Balam Xoc. "He let us forget the disagreements of the past. He appealed to our resourcefulness, not our guilt and insecurity."

"He did not interrupt," Cab Coh allowed. "Still, it was you who suggested we meet here, without any of the Close Ones present. That made an enormous difference."

"*I* am one of the Close Ones, Father," Nohoch reminded him quietly, but Cab Coh refused to be corrected.

"Not like Hok, or that arrogant man from Copan, Opna. Today you were the head of the clan council, and we were again the respected elders of our people. Many of us needed to be reminded."

Balam Xoc had started walking toward the path that led back to the reservoir and the Jaguar Paw House, and they followed him at a distance, not wishing to intrude upon his thoughts. Warmed by his father's praise, Nohoch reflected upon the wide range of issues that had been discussed at the meeting, impressed himself at how many had been resolved. Most had to do with the ruler's ban on trade and his continuing harassment of the clan, which had produced shortages of necessary goods and had made it difficult for the clan members to communicate with their friends and relatives in other parts of the city. But in sharing their grievances, the men had also discovered the extent to which they could meet one another's needs. Some had surpluses of what others lacked, and trades were arranged; ways of conveying messages and getting safely from place to place were gratefully exchanged; and the prospects of making secret trade agreements with their closest neighbors were revealed to be much more promising than any of them had thought, once their individual experiences had been combined and evaluated as a whole. The hardships of their isolation, which each had borne as a personal burden, had been seen to yield to the power of cooperation, and to their mutual cleverness. Except perhaps for Balam Xoc, they had all profited from the simple knowledge that their problems were not unique or insoluble, as long as they confronted them as a group.

"Akbal will be pleased to know there is paint to be had," Cab Coh said with satisfaction, breaking into Nohoch's thoughts. "He has spent too much of his time lately searching for materials."

Nohoch looked around at the forest through which they were passing, noting the dryness of the foliage, which seemed dulled and darkened by a sheen of dust.

"Soon the ruler will have to admit that his crops have failed," Nohoch surmised. "Then, I think, we will have no more trouble obtaining the things we need. Then even our breadnuts will be valued in trade."

"We must not take advantage of our neighbors, though," Cab Coh cautioned. "We were agreed upon that."

"We were," Nohoch acknowledged easily. "We all recognize the need to cultivate new friends and allies."

They realized simultaneously that Balam Xoc had stopped just ahead, and they hesitated for a moment before deciding to overtake him. He was scanning the branches that hung over the trail, his head cocked to one side, as if he were straining to hear a message.

"Listen," he commanded, as they came up on either side of him. "I do not hear the birds."

Nor could they. Only a moment before, it seemed, the forest had been alive with the calls of doves and songbirds, and a wood owl had been hooting with loud regularity. Now it had grown absolutely still, as sometimes happened before a storm, or when a large predator was present. They both looked at Balam Xoc, whose gaze had fixed upon the path at his feet. His nostrils flared, and a growl formed deep in his throat.

"*Death,*" he rasped, and suddenly the bushes to their left erupted into violent motion, and a man burst out of the undergrowth and flung himself upon them. Cab Coh let out a guttural scream as the assassin's knife plunged into his stomach, and he took the man down to the ground with him, wrapped in a convulsive embrace. Knocked sideways by his father's fall, Nohoch stumbled headlong into one of the men who had jumped out of the bushes on the other side, deflecting the man's knife-thrust with an elbow to the chest. They grappled and went over backward into the tangle of vines and shrubs, with Nohoch struggling frantically to extract his own knife from its sheath.

The third man leaped at Balam Xoc with a muted cry, swinging his knife in an arc aimed at the old man's throat. But Balam Xoc ducked and jumped out of the way with surprising nimbleness, and when the man slashed at him again, he dodged past the knife and raked his fingers across the man's face, evoking a howl of pain and surprise. The man recoiled momentarily, wincing as he raised his fingers to the bright red scratches on his cheek and forehead.

But then the first assassin appeared at his comrade's side, his knife red with the blood of Cab Coh, and the two of them began to stalk Balam Xoc, closing him in between them, leaving no angle for escape. Balam Xoc backed a few feet down the trail and stopped, baring his teeth like a cornered animal and snarling with such menace that both men hesitated for an instant in their approach. Suddenly there was a swish of wind followed by a hollow *thunk,* and the man with the clawed face stood up on his toes and clutched at his chest, from which a short, narrow spear was protruding. Waving his arms, he staggered backward and fell over Cab Coh's body, his eyes rolling up in his head.

Balam Xoc growled and took a step toward the assassin confronting him, and the man dropped his knife in dismay and fled into the forest, crashing blindly through the undergrowth in his desire to get away. Balam Xoc was still standing in the middle of the path when Kal Cuc appeared at his side, gripping his throwing stick tightly in both hands. Together they stared at the blood-stained bodies sprawled out on the ground in front of them, the white head of Cab Coh just visible beneath the limp arm of the assassin, whose clawed face was fixed in a death grimace. Kal Cuc began to shiver, and Balam Xoc laid a hand upon his shoulder, startling him with the coldness of his touch.

"You have taken a life, my son," he said gently. "But you did so to save mine, and to avenge the death of my brother. Pray for their spirits, my son. I must see to Nohoch."

Kal Cuc shivered again and went down on his knees, placing the throwing stick on the ground in front of him as he bowed his head close to the earth. Balam Xoc found Nohoch lying in a circle of crushed vegetation a few feet off the path, with the body of his assailant crumpled up beside him, the bone-handled knife sticking out of his ribs. Nohoch was holding his hip and moaning softly, his chest and arms covered with smaller wounds matted with dirt and leaves. He opened his eyes as Balam Xoc knelt beside him and put an arm under his head.

"Grandfather," he murmured. "You said this . . ."

"Yes," Balam Xoc agreed solemnly, turning his head as Kal Cuc came up behind him. "Go to Tzec Balam, my son. Tell him to bring bandages and a litter. Hurry!"

The boy ran off, and Balam Xoc looked back down at Nohoch, whose eyes had widened with distress.

"My father?"

"He is dead. Murdered, as I was meant to be."

Nohoch groaned and let his eyes flutter shut.

"Now we must be strong," Balam Xoc proclaimed, in the tone of an invocation. "Now it has truly begun."

"What?" Nohoch asked in a confused whisper, beginning to drift off in his pain. Balam Xoc put his free hand on top of Nohoch's hands, pressing back against the flow of blood from his wounded hip.

"The battle for our lives," he said succinctly. "The *clan war . . .*"

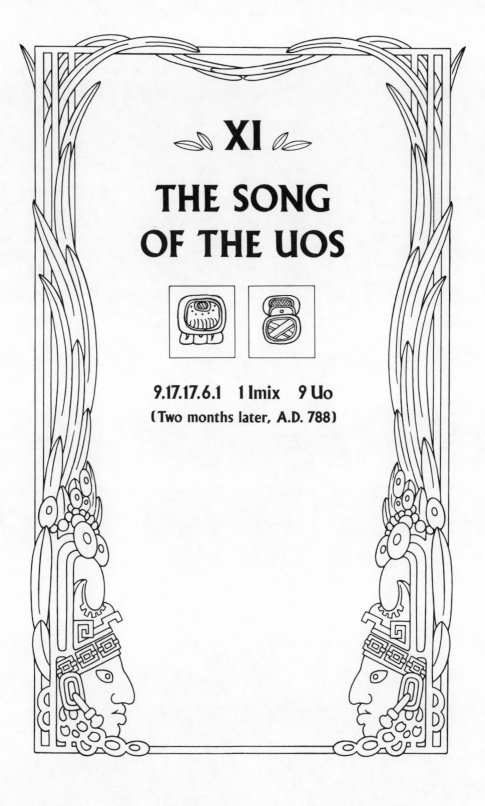

XI

THE SONG
OF THE UOS

9.17.17.6.1   1 Imix   9 Uo
(Two months later, A.D. 788)

A FEW BRIEF showers fell over Tikal during the last days of the month of Pop, far too late for all but a small portion of the ruler's crops. The wetness did not linger, though, and did not prevent the Jaguar Paw Clan from burning the dried brush they had laid over their gardens, transforming the ground cover into a grey-black layer of fertilizing ash. The planting was begun on the first day of Uo, and was interrupted on the second by a spectacular thunderstorm, during which a pyramid in one of the abandoned Katun Enclosures was struck by lightning. It was not until the ninth day of Uo, however, after the clan had finished its planting, that the uos finally appeared.

A steady, soaking rain had fallen for most of the day, ending just before sunset. The insects and nightbirds had begun their monotonous nocturnal chorus, a droning *chirrup* so familiar and pervasive that the human inhabitants of the Jaguar Paw House did not distinguish it from silence. But suddenly there was a deep, resonant croak from somewhere in the vicinity of the lower plaza, and it had barely stopped echoing before a second, higher-pitched voice answered, and then another and another, rising from all sides at once and blending into a single, palpitating chant: *whoa, whoa, whoa . . .*

The people came out of their houses, carrying torches and pointing in amazement at the sight that greeted their eyes. The tiny, red-spotted frogs were everywhere, hopping and crawling through the puddles on the plazas and puffing out their dark, gelatinous bodies in chorus after chorus of their name. Some could be seen hunched together, mating with the blind urgency of creatures who emerge from their dormancy for only one night each year. The people laughed and shouted to welcome the uos, whose singing was thought to be the voice of Cauac the Rain Spirit, and a sign of his favor.

Akbal was sitting with Kinich Kakmoo when the first uo sounded, and he immediately stopped talking and smiled at his brother, hoping that the uos' singing might evoke a similar response in Kinich. Kinich did in fact raise his head as the sounds outside reached a deafening level, but he was not moved to smile. His eyes were dull and yellowish around the edges, sunken deep behind the broken hump of his nose. He had been home for ten days and had hardly moved from this barren room, sitting wrapped in a blanket against the chills of his fever, surrounded by his many medicines: salves for the sores on his feet and legs, harsh purgatives for the worms in his guts, potions for the fevers that made him shiver and sweat by turns. But there was no medicine for the sickness of his spirit, which Akbal had been trying vainly to alleviate with his conversation and company.

Since he could not be heard above the noise of the uos, Akbal gestured with his hands to attract Kinich's attention, indicating that they should go outside for a look. Then he went to get the torch from the holder on the wall, having already learned that Kinich would not permit anyone to help him, no matter how hard it was for him to rise or how unsteady he was upon his legs. Using the bench behind him, Kinich slowly pushed himself to his feet, reaching back for his spear, which he kept propped up beside him at all times. As he shuffled toward the door, grasping the spear like a staff, the blanket around his shoulders fell open, revealing a body that appeared as ruined as his nose: Hok's body, wrapped in scarred folds of excess skin, Akbal had thought upon seeing Kinich naked for the first time. Now he held aside the netting over the doorway and pretended he had not seen, letting his brother go out before him.

Kinich's wife, May, and their two-year-old daughter, Coba, were also standing on the platform in front of the house, and May smiled and brought the child over to her father. Coba had her hands clapped over her ears, but was smiling and giggling, clearly enjoying the spectacle of the plaza filled with hopping frogs and ringed with torches and excited people. Akbal dipped his torch as he came through the doorway and then lifted it high overhead, illuminating the frogs that had found their way onto the platform itself. Coba let out a shriek and jumped back against her mother as one of the frogs flopped wetly at her feet, and Akbal and May both laughed, glancing self-consciously at Kinich for his reaction. To their distress, they saw him recoil from the scene in front of him, his mouth dropping open in an expression of bewildered horror. Then a spasm in his stomach nearly doubled him over, and he thrust his head forward and began to retch, spewing a pale, stringy bile onto the pavement at his feet.

Akbal and May quickly moved to support him, holding him up by the elbows when the spear dropped out of his shaking hands. When the convulsions in his stomach and throat had finally ceased, they half-led, half-carried him back inside, maneuvering around little Coba, who was crying and clinging to her mother's skirt. They set him down with his back against the bench, wrapping more blankets around him, for he had begun to shiver violently. May had tears in her eyes as she and Akbal held Kinich between them, trying to contain the helpless trembling in his body. Outside, the uos continued to boom out their song, so that no one could hear the terrified weeping of Coba, or the single word that Kinich kept murmuring to himself over and over: *bats.*

THE FOUR WOMEN in the front room of Cab Coh's house were close to the end of their ceremony when the uos began to sing, and though all of them reacted physically to the sound, they did not falter or lose their composure. Standing in front of the bench where the ritual paraphernalia had been laid out, Box Ek held a pair of intricately carved bones over a brazier of burning coals, passing them back and forth through the fragrant smoke as she murmured the final prayer. Her eyes were moist with emotion, for these rites were for her brother Cab Coh, whose body lay buried beneath the floor in the next room, and whose spirit wandered somewhere in the Underworld, hopefully accompanied by the women's prayers.

Box Ek carefully laid the bones upon the ceremonial plate next to the brazier and bowed her white head over them for a moment before signaling the other women that they were done. They all bowed again and stepped back from the bench before turning to face one another, their expressions still masked with the solemnity of the occasion. The *whoa*-ing from outside had grown terrifically loud, and Box Ek recognized the pull it exerted upon them with a bleak smile, giving her arm to Zac Kuk and gesturing with her stick for Ixchel and Haleu to precede them out.

The glow of hand-held torches cast a flickering light over the plaza, which was speckled with the dark bodies of a multitude of frogs. Box Ek could feel Zac Kuk's excitement in the way the young woman gripped her arm, and the two of them exchanged a private glance as they came out onto the platform, sharing the memory of their visit to Balam Xoc. The old woman was gratified by the intimacy of Zac Kuk's smile, a sign of the bond that had grown up between them since that day. The appearance of the uos made them think not of rain but of tears, and of the dream that had given legitimacy to the feelings of the people. At Balam Xoc's bidding, they had already begun to plan the celebration the clan would hold when the period of mourning for Cab Coh was completed, and when Kinich Kakmoo and Nohoch Ich were both well enough to attend.

Haleu bowed to attract Box Ek's attention, gesturing to indicate her desire to return to her own house. Box Ek hastily gave her consent, knowing that Haleu was anxious to check on Nohoch, who was still healing, and on her mother-in-law, Pek, whose health had begun to deteriorate rapidly after the death of Cab Coh. *Soon we will be weeping for her,* Box Ek thought sadly, watching Haleu wend her way toward the adjacent house, stepping carefully around the frogs. Her son, Chac Mut, came halfway out of the central doorway as she approached, holding the netting back with one hand while sweeping a torch low over the platform with the other, illuminating the advance of the uos for whomever was watching from inside. Box Ek guessed that the hidden watcher had to be Nohoch himself, and she took his desire to see the uos as a positive sign, an indication that he was indeed recovering from his wounds. His condition had been a matter of grave concern for some time, a further source of tears, after those that had been shed for Cab Coh.

The thought of Cab Coh brought her sadness back, and she chided herself for indulging it as she turned her gaze back over the plaza. It was not right to dwell upon her sorrow in the midst of this joyful din, this outpouring of life from the depths of the earth itself. Ixchel and Zac Kuk were waving across to the servants in front of Pacal's house, one of whom was holding up young Bolon Oc and pretending to have him wave back. A crowd of celebrants lined the platform in front of Balam Xoc's house, smiling and gesticulating, some even kneeling to try to gather the slippery frogs into their hands.

As Box Ek watched, Balam Xoc and a few of his Close Ones detached themselves from the group and started toward the clan shrine that stood at the eastern end of the plaza. They had to move slowly to avoid stepping on the uos, and as they separated to find their own paths, Box Ek saw that one of them was Kanan Naab. *The only woman among them,* she reflected, *yet wed to none of the men.* Sorrow welled up in her again, and this time she could not suppress it, and the tears rolled freely down her withered cheeks. She felt Zac Kuk turn toward her solicitously, but she did not look up to accept the young woman's comfort. Grateful as she was for Zac Kuk's attentions, Box Ek knew that they could never replace those she had lost—those of her true granddaughter, the child she had come back from Ektun to raise so many years before.

Kanan Naab was now climbing the steep temple stairs behind Balam Xoc, no doubt to participate in an offering of thanks to the Rain Spirit. Box Ek blinked to clear her eyes of tears, reminding herself that Kanan Naab had always been drawn to these things, even as a small child. It had been a mistake to discourage her, and to tell her she was being difficult and perverse when she was only being true to her deepest impulses.

Yet Box Ek could not help but wonder what kind of life would be left to Kanan Naab when Balam Xoc was gone. Perhaps some of his holiness would cling to her, and preserve a place for her among the spiritual leaders of the clan. Or perhaps she would demonstrate powers of her own, sufficient to make her a candidate for the title of Living Ancestor, a title that Box Ek knew she secretly yearned to hold. But if not—if, in fact, tradition again prevailed after Balam Xoc's passing—what would become of her then? She could never again be simply an unmarried woman, not after being one of the Close Ones. And she seemed to be absorbing Balam Xoc's coldness and indifference toward others. What man would want such a woman, knowing that her devotion would never be given solely to him?

Then Kanan Naab and her companions disappeared through the single doorway of the shrine, leaving Box Ek staring vacantly at the building's dark facade, feeling that her granddaughter had passed beyond the reach of her concern. *There is not much time left to me,* she thought bleakly, as she had many times since her brother's death. Cab Coh had always been the gentle one, the brother whose kindness never failed to reassure her. He should not have been the first to die, and a part of her own desire to live had departed with him. She doubted seriously, and without self-pity, that she would live long enough to hear the uos sing again.

"You are sad, Grandmother," Zac Kuk said in a concerned voice, bending to speak directly into Box Ek's ear. The old woman strained against the aching stiffness in her neck and back to bring her face close to Zac Kuk's.

"I am too old for new beginnings. The joy of such things belongs to the young."

Zac Kuk pulled her face away far enough to give her a quizzical look.

"Listen to their song," Box Ek told her, pointing her stick at the frog-filled plaza. "It says that the world belongs to *you* . . ."

PACAL AND THE other chief stewards were meeting with the ruler when the voices of the uos began to echo down the passageways of the palace, intruding themselves into the council chamber. The sound was immediately recognizable, despite the distortions of distance, and it brought the stewards' somber discussion to an abrupt halt. Caan Ac waved a hand to them in dismissal and rushed out of the room in the company of the high priest and his assistants. The stewards sat where they were for a moment, actually more relieved than irritated by the interruption, since it had saved them from hearing the ruler's response to their reports, which had been uniformly disheartening. Pacal folded up the book of accounts he had used as a reference during his report and handed it to one of his assistants, telling him to confer with the scribes and make certain that all the amounts had been recorded correctly. Pacal felt strongly—though he did not say it to the assistant—that this would be his last report as the chief steward of crops, and he wanted it to be accurate.

As if to confirm this suspicion, one of the ruler's messengers approached Pacal as he rose and asked him to remain behind and wait for Caan Ac's return. The chamber had emptied out rather quickly, the other stewards also hastening out to observe the uos. And apparently no one else had been asked to stay behind. Pacal dismissed the rest of his assistants, wishing that Chac Mut were still among them. He would have appreciated his nephew's company at a moment like this, as he waited to be discharged from the stewardship to which he had devoted his life. But Chac Mut had resigned his post shortly after the attack on his father and grandfather, and Pacal had not attempted to dissuade him. Other than the contracted workmen, Pacal was now the only member of the Jaguar Paw Clan still employed in the ruler's service, and he would have resigned himself had he not felt obligated to complete his final report.

The sound of the uos had begun to diminish in volume by the time the ruler returned and took his seat on the Jaguar Throne. He appeared drained and uncomfortable, wearing the bloody marks of recent penance on his shins and forearms. He conferred briefly with the high priest before sending everyone from the room and beckoning Pacal to approach the throne. The torches on the walls crackled softly, providing an intimate counterpoint to the billowing echoes from outside. Caan Ac kept Pacal standing after he had bowed, studying his face with a mixture of mistrust and calculation, as if guessing at his responses in advance.

"You know, of course," he said at last, "that I must remove you as the chief steward of crops."

"I had assumed as much, my lord."

"Yes," the ruler went on, watching him closely, "you will have to suffer a period of disgrace. Not long, probably. Perhaps you will want to go to Uaxactun for a while. Then you will return to serve me here, as an adviser, or perhaps an envoy to the other clans."

Pacal had already considered the possibility of such an offer, and he responded with polite swiftness.

"I am grateful, my lord. But I doubt that I could be of use to you in either capacity, given the way my clan is currently regarded in the city. If I cannot be one of your stewards, Lord, I would humbly request to be released from your service."

Caan Ac's demeanor changed abruptly, as if all his guesses had been confirmed, and he slapped himself loudly on the chest, making his jade necklaces dance.

"I am not offering you a *choice,* Pacal. The appearance of your loyalty is enough, if that is all you can be trusted to give. And I will have it! You will not leave me to become the steward of your father's rebellion."

"I see."

"*Do* you?" Caan Ac sneered, leaning toward him menacingly. "Do you truly? No doubt you believe, like your father, that the thieves who attacked him were my agents. Do you not? Speak, Pacal. You have no reason to pretend with me any longer."

Pacal took a deep breath, swallowing several inappropriately diplomatic replies. He had no doubt that the ruler had sent the assassins after Balam Xoc, and it offended him to be made the recipient of a false denial. But the instinct toward accommodation was still too strong in him to permit the utterance of such a disagreeable truth, even though he saw no hope of accommodation in the ruler's eyes.

"I have never pretended with you, my lord. Were they your agents?"

Caan Ac grunted rudely, his thick lips curling in disgust.

"Even now, you equivocate. You should know that I would not concern myself with petty acts of revenge. I am the ruler of Tikal; I have no need to employ assassins when I already possess the power to crush your entire clan. Do you understand me now? I am not merely speaking of your life, or your father's. There are many others who might go first."

Pacal stared back at him silently, thinking of Ixchel and Bolon Oc, as he knew he was meant to think. The ruler went on in the same, unsparing tone.

"You will vacate the chamber of the chief steward of crops immediately, and then you will go to Uaxactun as my special envoy. You will be allowed to return, in time, if you heed my warning and do nothing to anger me. If you do otherwise, you will not wish to return, or to see what you have brought upon your people."

"You would hold me hostage, then," Pacal said in a hollow voice, and the ruler narrowed his eyes and gave him a thin, predatory smile.

"I would indeed. That is the only value you have for me now. Your father has seen to that. You will be released when he is no longer a threat to my authority, and not before."

"You must fear him greatly," Pacal suggested impulsively, and the ruler's smile vanished, wiped away by an angry snarl.

"He is a fool! How long do you think the lords of your clan will dig in the mud for him? They will grow tired of their isolation soon enough, and remember how it was to enjoy the favor of their ruler."

"As *I* have enjoyed it?" Pacal retorted. "Or my sons?"

"Do not provoke me, Pacal," Caan Ac threatened. "The screams of your dying would not be heard tonight."

"You spoke to me once of greatness," Pacal reminded him, spitting the words out with undisguised scorn. "Of the prestige of Tikal. Yet now you make crude threats against me and my family, like a man well acquainted with assassins. Which of us has been pretending, my lord?"

Caan Ac clapped his hands sharply, and two of his guards came through the curtained doorway, their hands on their knives. But then the ruler reconsidered and sent them out again.

"No, you will not escape me so easily," he growled. "You will be in Uaxactun by the day after tomorrow, or I will have you taken there by force, bound like a turkey for the market. And remember, Pacal Balam: Perhaps your father can predict when the rains will come, but I doubt that he could bring them in time to save the Jaguar Paw houses from burning. Think of *that* before you consider betraying me to him. Now go!"

Pacal began to bow out of habit, but then caught himself and arrested the motion, his crossed arms raised just to the level of his stomach. Looking directly at the ruler, he deliberately let his arms drop to his sides, then turned and began to walk from the chamber. He expected at any moment to hear the ruler signal his guards, for the disrespect he had just shown was an offense punishable by death. The expectation caused him no fear, however; if he had no more value to his city, he did not care what was done to him, or whether he lived or died.

But the ruler let him go, and Pacal walked out of the palace and into the damp night air, which resounded with the singing of the uos. He felt empty, numbed by a dim realization of how recklessly he had courted death. He raised his face to the dark sky, helpless in the sight of the ancestors, a man whose career had just ended and his captivity begun. The *whoa*-ing of the frogs filled his ears, drowning the cry of anguish that rose in his throat and was never released. He stood alone, waiting to be overwhelmed by his loss, waiting for the tears that did not come.

Two months later, the month of Zotz

CHAN MAC and his wife, Kutz, were the first outside guests to arrive for the Jaguar Paw feast, coming up the main trail in the rich yellow light of late afternoon. Chan Mac was wearing full diplomatic garb, to ease his passage through the city, and he was accompanied by two burly embassy guards, who carried the gifts he had brought for his sister and her family. Happening to glance into the craft house, they found Akbal sitting alone in the long room, already dressed for the celebration but still working on an unfinished painting. He held up a hand to them in greeting and apology, appealing for a few more moments to complete his work. So Chan Mac led the others into the plaza beyond, where servants were already laying out food and drink beneath the thatched ramadas that had been set up in front of the houses. Zac Kuk was at the center of the preparations, seeing to a hundred things at once, but she greeted her brother and sister-in-law with an effusive smile and questions about their children. Leaving Kutz and the guards in her care, Chan Mac soon excused himself and went back to the craft house.

Squatting beside him at Akbal's invitation, Chan Mac immediately saw that the painting was the one Akbal had done for Kinich Kakmoo in Yaxchilan, depicting the warrior presenting his captive to Shield Jaguar. Using the full complement of colors, Akbal had transferred the drawing from its original leather roll to a folding screen of lime-coated bark paper, bound together with strips of polished wood.

" 'The Captor of Macaw,' " Chan Mac recalled wistfully. "It might seem a perverse gift now."

"I am prepared for him to reject it," Akbal admitted. "But we have tried everything else we know to rouse his spirit. I cannot fail more miserably with this. But come, I am done here. Let me show you our gardens while it is still light."

They walked together through the shade of the breadnut trees, passing groups of colorfully dressed people coming the other way, heading for the feast with gifts and bunches of flowers in their arms. They greeted Akbal familiarly, calling out his name in a variety of accents.

"Your grandfather's followers?" Chan Mac supposed aloud, returning the bows that were made to him.

"Yes. Although many of them will join the clan tonight."

"I had heard rumors of this, long ago. Is there one among them named Hok?"

Akbal gave him a curious glance, but before he could answer, they came out into the open again, and both stopped to admire the view. The placid waters of the reservoir were deep and green, except for the eastern portion, which had been dyed red by the slanting rays of the slowly descending sun. The clearings appeared to have been decorated in fresh green, the rows of leafy plants weaving around and between the remaining trees. Domesticated turkeys pecked over the well-beaten ground in front of the houses, which gleamed white against the surrounding green.

"I heard rumors of this, as well," Chan Mac said. "But I must confess, I did not believe that you could have accomplished so much in so little time."

"We all put our hands to the work," Akbal said proudly. "Even your sister. And men like Hok. What do you know of *him*?"

"Very little. Your grandfather asked me to make some inquiries of the ambassador from Quirigua, who once held a post in my city. Though only one of his questions concerned this man Hok directly, it seemed that the whole inquiry was connected with him, though in ways I do not fully understand. I have not had a chance to report to Balam Xoc until now. But tell me what you know of Hok."

"He is from Quirigua," Akbal confirmed. "His father was a painter, a minor craftsman attached to the Sky Clan of that city. When Hok was just a boy, his father took him and his older brothers into the mountains to hunt for the plants and minerals used to make paints. Several days later, Hok came out of the mountains alone, covered with blood and dirt, and delirious with pain. One of his eyes had been put out with a stone, and he said that his father and brothers had all been killed. He claimed that they had been murdered by warriors wearing the insignia of the ruler of Quirigua."

Akbal paused, seeing the beginnings of comprehension in Chan Mac's eyes, but his friend gestured for him to go on.

"There were no warriors known to be in the area at the time, however, and it seemed more likely that the killings were the work of some of the mountain tribesmen with whom Quirigua was feuding. It was assumed that Hok, in his pain and confusion, had merely mistaken them for Quiriguan warriors. But Hok would not change his story, even though he could not lead anyone back to the place where it happened, and was not even certain how he himself had managed to survive. He insisted so violently that finally, to break him of his delusion, the ruler of Quirigua assembled all of his warriors for the boy's inspection. After looking at them all, Hok could identify only one man who he was certain had been among his father's killers. That man was the ruler's own brother, and he had been secluded in the clan house the whole time, fasting for a ceremony."

"Ah," Chan Mac exclaimed softly. "But apparently this did not deliver Hok from his delusion."

"No," Akbal agreed sadly. "He was tormented by bad dreams and fits of weeping, and he would attack any warrior he came across, biting and scratching like a wild beast. He finally became so unmanageable that he was sent to live with relatives in a more isolated part of the valley. But he ran away from them, and he has been wandering ever since. Until he came here."

Chan Mac nodded thoughtfully, looking out over the water for a moment and then around at the houses and gardens and groves of trees.

"I understand why he stopped here," he said with quiet admiration. "Especially since he seems to have found a believer in Balam Xoc. Perhaps I can corroborate that belief."

"It would be a gift to Hok, if he is able to accept it," Akbal told him. "But perhaps you wish to tell Grandfather before anyone else. That is only proper."

"I am grateful for your understanding, my friend. He did ask me to make these inquiries quietly. But I assume he will allow you to be present when I tell him what I have learned."

"One can assume nothing about Grandfather," Akbal assured him bluntly. "He may repeat your words to the whole clan, or perhaps only to Hok himself. Eventually, though, we will hear what we need to know."

"Shall we return to the feast, then? There are many other things we must talk about. It has been too long since I last had the pleasure of your company."

"Indeed," Akbal said emphatically, turning to lead the way back to the Jaguar Paw House. "There are *many* stories we must tell tonight . . ."

THE SAME BOY who had brought the invitation was waiting for Yaxal Can, as he had promised, near the head of a little-used trail behind the houses of the Serpent Clan. He started off without speaking, and soon led the way onto an even smaller path that abandoned the high ground and wove its way between logwood thickets and patches of low marsh. The sun's imminent disappearance made the boy hurry over the uncertain ground, leaping lightly from hummock to hummock as they crossed one end of a long alkalche. Yaxal followed with some difficulty, collecting mud on his sandaled feet and feeling sweat dampening his fine blue tunic and headwrap, garments that identified him as a member of the Order of Tun Count Priests. He was also aware of the need for haste—as much to avoid being seen as to see—but the possibility of slipping and falling into the alkalche had begun to seem a more pressing concern. The furtiveness of this journey was already demeaning enough; he did not need to arrive soiled and out of breath, as well.

"Slower, my son," he called to the boy, who obediently stopped and waited on the next hummock. Yaxal came up next to him, adjusting the tasseled incense bag he carried on a long strap slung over his shoulder.

"I have forgotten your name, my son," he said, as they resumed walking at a more prudent pace. "Though I remember that you are the one who helped Akbal find the Serpent Stone."

"Kal Cuc, my lord," the boy said over his shoulder.

"Ah, yes. And how does Akbal fare, Kal Cuc?"

"He is the master of craftsmen now. He is very busy."

"No doubt. And his sister, the Lady Kanan Naab?"

The boy glanced back again, displaying a certain wariness toward these questions.

"She is one of those close to the Living Ancestor," he replied, and then fell silent, as if no further elaboration were necessary. They had once more found their way to dry ground, on the other side of the deep ravine that flanked the Jaguar Paw House to the north. Smoke from the clan cookhouses could be seen rising up through the trees on the far side, and the tall roof comb of the clan shrine stood out above the topmost branches, its carved stucco surface shimmering in the last light of the sun. The sky to the west was rapidly losing its redness, and a full moon had already risen in the east, an evanescent white disc against the blue.

"It is a perfect night," Yaxal said appreciatively, as Kal Cuc led him toward the path that went around the ravine. "Tell me, my son: Are there many other outside guests?"

"There are some who will come later, after dark."

"I see," Yaxal mused, feeling less ashamed of his own precautions. "And was it the Lady Kanan Naab who sent you to invite me? Or perhaps her father."

"Lord Pacal is in Uaxactun," Kal Cuc said tersely, glancing at him with open suspicion, as if Yaxal should have known. "It was the Lady Zac Kuk who sent me to you."

Feeling slightly foolish, Yaxal nodded and let the boy lead on in silence. Of course he had known that Pacal was in Uaxactun—all of Tikal knew that—but he had allowed himself to forget, hoping somehow that the invitation had been a sign of deeper intent. He had been asked to take a great risk in attending this feast, after all. If the ruler or the high priest were to hear of it, his career as a priest would be ended the next day. Would Zac Kuk have sent for him merely on a whim, heedless of the possible consequences?

But it was too late to turn back in anger. The houses were just ahead, barely visible in the swiftly falling darkness. Yaxal asked the boy to walk still slower, letting the shadows collect around them as they approached the Jaguar Paw House.

THE CLOTH NETTING over the doorway behind him was pushed aside with an audible swish and then allowed to fall back into place, partially obscuring the noise and light that had entered with the intruder. Kinich lay motionless in his blankets, his back to the doorway, waiting for whoever it was to go away. Akbal and Chan Mac had already tried to rouse him, bringing balche and a gift they said would give him pleasant memories. But Kinich had managed to discourage their attempt, without looking at either them or their gift. He had too many memories already, and found none of them pleasant.

The person behind him seemed to be inspecting the room, sandals scraping softly on the plastered stone floor. Then Kinich heard nothing, though his awareness of another presence in the room did not diminish. Who was it this time? May? He had already told her that he would not attend the feast, and did not wish to have visitors.

"Go away," he said gruffly. "I am not well."

"I have come to heal you."

Kinich rolled over onto his side and saw Balam Xoc sitting a few feet away, silhouetted against the torchlight that shone through the mesh of the netting behind him. They regarded each other wordlessly for a few moments.

"The moon is full, Kinich," the old man told him. "The Spirits of the Night are restless, and alert to our actions. They watch over us, as they watched over you in the jungle. You must rise and do them honor."

"What do you know about the jungle?" Kinich asked uneasily.

"Certainly nothing I have learned from you. You show us your suffering, but hide its cause. Your secrets are like the parasites inside you, Kinich. They are like creatures that feed upon you in the night . . ."

"*You!*" Kinich blurted, forcing himself into a sitting position. He held out a hand to his grandfather, then pulled it back uncertainly, pressing against the rapid beating of his heart.

"Even in this barren room," Balam Xoc continued, "the jungle is still with you. Is it not?"

Kinich leaned back against the bench behind him, wheezing softly through his nose. His voice was thick with emotion when he could finally bring himself to speak.

"I am there again whenever I sleep. I can feel the wetness and smell the rot . . . I can see my men dying, again and again."

"Tell me. How many were lost?"

"Fourteen."

"Tell me," Balam Xoc repeated insistently, and Kinich let out a long breath, venting the last of his resistance. Once he began to speak, the words seemed to tumble out of him of their own accord, spilling his secrets into the air. For the first time, he described how he and his men had escaped from the Macaw ambush, and how he had led them into the jungle. The Macaws had pursued them for many days, pushing them deeper and deeper into the wilderness, trying constantly to trap them between a land force and the Macaw canoes. But Kinich had waged the kind of jungle war for which he had been trained, backtracking on his pursuers and setting ambushes to pick off their scouts. They had finally killed so many Macaws that the enemy abandoned the pursuit, though not before Kinich and his band had been pushed far off course.

"It did not seem to matter at first," Kinich said, with a rueful trace of remembered pride. "We had only lost two of our own, and each of us carried the insignia of at least one dead Macaw. We felt that we had earned our escape. We felt like warriors."

Kinich stopped and licked dry lips, swallowing with difficulty. He went on in a subdued monotone.

"But we had no supplies, and we were lost in a land we did not know. Few of us had any experience as hunters or fishermen, and the fear of becoming separated from the group kept us from going far after game. It rained constantly, and nothing ever dried; our cotton armor grew mold and became a home for leeches and lice. We discarded it, and the mold grew on our skin, though it gave us no protection from the flies and mosquitoes. We caught fevers from drinking bad water, and then drank more when it seemed the fever's thirst would kill us. We discarded the insignia of the Macaws, and then our own, keeping only our loincloths and our weapons. We fought the jungle like an enemy, and like an enemy it wore us down and killed us.

"The boatmen were the first to go. Most did not even know how to walk in the jungle, how to test the ground in front of them with their spears and look before they stepped. I saw one of them stumble headlong into a pool that was concealed by a thick mat of waterlilies. It was also filled with crocodiles, and the man was being eaten before he could even scream. No one was close enough to save him. Another man became impatient with those in front and cut his own path through a thicket, where he stepped on a sleeping serpent, a yellow jaw. *He* screamed until the breath left him and he died, his face purple and his leg swollen to the size of a tree trunk.

"My warriors were equally inexperienced with water, and two of them drowned trying to cross the deep rivers. Two more died of fever, shivering their lives out in my arms. It was hunger, though, that truly killed them. They would have survived if I could have fed them properly. Hunger and despair also drove one of the boatmen to hang himself with a vine rope, and his two remaining comrades ran away in the night shortly afterward. Two other warriors were lost during the last days of our journey, on the march. They simply were not with us when we stopped to rest, and we were too sick and exhausted to go back to look for them."

"That is thirteen," Balam Xoc prompted, when Kinich seemed reluctant to continue. "Who was the last?"

"My second-in-command, Tzimin. It happened on the last night, before we came upon the woodsmen who took us to Palenque. Tzimin was dead when we awoke in the morning, and at first we could not understand why. He appeared to have been strangled, but there were no marks on his throat, and we had no food upon which to choke. Then we found the coral snake under his body, trapped beneath his arm. It must have crawled into his armpit while he slept, and when it bit, he crushed it as if it were an insect, driving its fangs deep into his own flesh. It was no longer than my finger," Kinich murmured in a tone of bitter amazement, "a pretty thing, banded with red and black and yellow. It looked like a necklace, like a *child's* necklace."

Kinich suddenly buried his face in his hands and began to weep, his head hunched down between his bony shoulders. Balam Xoc waited patiently for him to recover, ignoring the sounds that came through the netting behind him.

"They are gone, Kinich, and you must put them to rest," he said when Kinich's tears were spent. He pushed a stoppered gourd and a painted pottery cup across the floor toward him. "Drink this," he commanded. "It is balche that was prepared by a woman who attends me, a healer named Chibil. It will give you strength, and help to quell the creatures that live inside you."

Kinich poured himself a cup with shaking hands and drank it down, then sat with his head cocked warily, awaiting the result in his gut. After a moment, he belched slightly and rested a hand on his stomach, as if to reassure himself. Then he poured another cup, but looked across at Balam Xoc before drinking.

"You have heard all of my secrets, Grandfather. But you have not even told me why you wish to heal me."

"There is no mystery. You are needed here. My brother was killed by assassins, and Nohoch badly wounded. It was a boy who saved me; a boy using the Zuyhua weapon you took from the Macaws. We will need our warriors in the time ahead."

"Yet you had no use for me when I was healthy," Kinich said suspiciously. "You spoke of the warriors with scorn."

"I have no use for wars of conquest," Balam Xoc corrected him sharply, "and my scorn is for those who would squander the lives of their warriors in senseless attempts to enlarge their own prestige. You have learned nothing from your experience if you do not feel the same."

Kinich struggled with himself for a moment before again tipping the cup to his lips. His hands were steadier when he poured for the third time, watching the stream of amber liquid glitter in the torchlight from outside.

"No matter what I might feel," he said tentatively, looking up at Balam Xoc, "I am still a nacom of Tikal. I have taken a vow to serve the ruler."

"No title may supersede the obligations of your blood," Balam Xoc told him bluntly. "You are a Jaguar Paw, and your highest duty is to the clan, and to the spirits of the ancestors. They did not desert you when you were lost in the jungle. *You* must not desert them now."

"And my vow to the ruler?"

"Can you possibly owe him more than you have already given? You brought yourself and ten others back from the death to which he sent you. Surely, you will not allow him to send you there again."

It was a statement, not a question, and Kinich finally nodded in agreement, unable to find an argument against it. He raised the painted cup to Balam Xoc, then drained it in a single swallow.

"Heal me, then," he wheezed, as the heat of the balche sprang upward from his stomach. "I will be the warrior you need."

THE MOON HUNG like a bright, blue-white fan behind the roof comb of the clan shrine when Kanan Naab came out of her uncle Nohoch's house and surveyed the people milling about in the plaza in front of her. A cursory glance told her that Balam Xoc was not among them, for their attitudes were all too casual and unfocused. The eating and drinking continued near the ramadas, but the women were now mingling with the men, who were puffing on long cigars made of mai, the smoking leaf. Children played in groups or chased one another around and between the talking, gesturing adults.

The men with whom Kanan Naab had been meeting—to discuss the final details of the adoption ceremony scheduled for later in the evening—went off in different directions, leaving her alone on the platform. She scanned the crowd again, wondering where her grandfather had disappeared to. He had attended their meeting only briefly, departing as soon as he had answered the few remaining questions. Without him, Kanan Naab was more aware than ever of her distance from this celebration, which was fused in her mind with the rebuke she had received from Box Ek at the reservoir. She had come to accept the wisdom of such a gathering, and she could see that it was having its desired effect upon the people before her. But she could not forget the circumstances under which it had been conceived, or the accusations of heartlessness that had preceded it. Her lack of feeling had been demonstrated to her so conclusively that it was impossible now to feel that she deserved to share in the clan's joy.

Voices were suddenly raised in the lower plaza, and the crowd in front of her turned as one toward the sound, abandoning their own conversations. Then someone near the top of the stairs leading down to the other plaza turned and shouted a name:

"Kinich Kakmoo!"

The crowd began to move toward the stairs, and Kanan Naab moved with them, cutting across the edge of the plaza and entering the avocado and cherry trees that lined the top landing above the gully. Ducking beneath the low branches, she found a place where she could stand upright and see the whole of the plaza below.

A circle of space had been left around the two men in the center of the plaza: one the familiar, white-haired figure of Balam Xoc, and the other that of Kinich, a blanket wrapped loosely around his broad shoulders and a long, flint-tipped spear in one hand. As the crowd around them grew still, the people on the stairs and along both landings also fell silent. Addressing only those immediately surrounding him, Balam Xoc began to summon people into the circle. First came May, who bowed deeply to Balam Xoc before taking a place beside her husband. Then Box Ek, who had seen the signs of Kinich's return, was called forward, along with Zac Kuk, who had helped to bring the message to Balam Xoc. Kinich bowed to both of them, and to Nohoch Ich and Kal Cuc, the clan's other, unofficial warriors. The words they exchanged were audible to only a few, but no words were required by the rest of those looking on. They understood the significance of the battered spear in Kinich's hand, and the reason why his bows were so awkward and labored; they recognized the women and the boy, and they knew very well why Nohoch walked with a limp and carried a knife in his waistband.

Finally Akbal was called forward, his cloth-wrapped head visible above those around him as he worked his way to the circle of space in front of Kinich. He was carrying a flat, rectangular bundle in his arms, and he bowed over it to Balam Xoc. Then the two brothers faced each other, the Tikal Painter and the nacom of Tikal, brothers whose accomplishments in Yaxchilan had once split the clan. Akbal slowly opened the bundle and held it in front of his chest with outstretched arms. It was obviously a painting of some kind, though Kanan Naab could make out none of the details at her distance. Balam Xoc gestured toward it, and at a nod from Kinich, Akbal handed the long folding screen to Nohoch Ich and Tzec Balam, who lifted it over their heads and turned slowly to display its brilliant colors to the crowd.

"The Captor of Macaw," Tzec Balam announced in a loud voice, touching off a chorus of approving murmurs that increased in volume as everyone was given a glimpse of the painting. Then Kinich handed his spear to Balam Xoc and stepped forward on unsteady legs, raising his arms at his sides for balance until Akbal reached him and they wrapped each other in an embrace. The crowd let out a spontaneous roar, whistling and cheering and beating their palms against their lips. The circle of onlookers closed in around the two brothers, touching their arms and shoulders and calling out their names, and the people on the stairs and landings again began to descend toward the plaza, wanting to share in the joy of this reconciliation.

Kanan Naab did not move from beneath the trees, waving absently at a mosquito as she watched the plaza below her fill completely with excited people. Then a voice spoke very close behind her, a voice she had not heard in months.

"I see why you do not wish to leave this, my lady. There is little cause for celebration among the other clans of this city."

"Yaxal," Kanan Naab said in an amazed whisper, turning to face him. He was standing sideways in the bright light of the moon, which painted leafy shadow-patterns on his face and headwrap.

"But you are weeping," he said in astonishment. "How can you be sad in the midst of your people's joy?"

"I have no part in it," Kanan Naab murmured plaintively, the tears continuing to stream down her face as she cast a brief glance back at the plaza. "Even within my own family, I have lost my place. They think I am cold and heartless."

"That cannot be, my lady," Yaxal protested. "It was the members of your family—the Lady Zac Kuk and the Lady Box Ek—who had me brought here tonight."

"They pity me."

"They are concerned for your happiness," Yaxal assured her soothingly. "Besides, are you not close to your grandfather?"

Kanan Naab turned away for a moment, dabbing at her eyes with the edge of her sleeve.

"No one can be close to him anymore," she said in a more composed voice, yet one that could not conceal her regret. "He is *truly* a person without feelings. Those of us who serve him know this better than anyone else. We exist only to carry out his commands, and to communicate his messages to the people. Our doubts and questions are not important to him."

Yaxal regarded her silently, letting her hear the sound of her own complaint, as if aware that she had not articulated it before, even to herself.

"Perhaps you have also joined a priesthood," he suggested softly, toying with the incense bag at his side. "Is that not what you have always wanted, Kanan Naab?"

Her eyes fixed on him thoughtfully, taking in his headwrap and the incense bag and searching his face for signs of disapproval or judgment.

"Perhaps," she admitted finally. "I was afraid of many things as a child. I believed that knowledge would protect me from my fear. I still believe it, though I have learned very little."

"Every novice is impatient to know," Yaxal pointed out. "Yet first they must prove their willingness to serve. It seemed to me once that your grandfather indulged you too easily. Perhaps he will do so again, when you are more ready to receive his instruction."

Kanan Naab stared at him curiously, bemused by his apparent acceptance of her as a novice.

"You once indulged me, as well," she recalled. "And you indulge me now. You took a great risk in coming here."

"Yes," Yaxal agreed without hesitation. "I allowed myself the delusion that the invitation had come from you, or your father. But I do not regret accepting it, now."

"But there can be no possibility of a marriage now. I say this for your own sake. You would be expelled from your order simply for proposing it."

"I have no delusions about that."

"Yet you came here tonight, to see me."

Yaxal shifted uneasily and coughed into his hand, stirring the branches overhead with his movements.

"When I first came to the Jaguar Paw House, I was not looking for a wife," he confessed. "I did not have time for such concerns. Your grandfather had asked me to perform a service for him, and I hoped to benefit from his acquaintance and that of your uncle, Nohoch Ich. I am not ashamed of my ambition, for my family is not wealthy, and my father has been dead for many years. But it was *you*, Kanan Naab, and not ambition, that made me return here. I would like to come again, if you will allow it."

Kanan Naab raised her hands, as if grasping at the possibility, but then let them drop in a hopeless gesture.

"I could not ask you to take such a risk."

"You do not have to ask," Yaxal persisted. "You have only to say that you will see me."

"I will, then," Kanan Naab decided, and Yaxal permitted himself a small smile.

"I must leave you now. The moon is high, and there are many other outsiders here. I cannot trust them as I do the people of your clan."

"I will lead you out," Kanan Naab offered, but he shook his head firmly.

"I can find my own way. You must give my apologies to the Lady Zac Kuk and the Lady Box Ek. And my gratitude. They have not forgotten you, Kanan Naab, any more than I had."

"Yes," Kanan Naab agreed in a chastened whisper. "Go safely, Yaxal."

She held out a moon-dappled hand to him, and he touched his fingers to hers lightly, caressingly, before ducking his head under the branches and striding off across the plaza. Kanan Naab raised the hand to her face and found that her cheek was warm and dry, her tears vaporized by the flush of heat rising from her skin. Her heart was beating with an insistence that made her breath come rapidly, so that finally she could not stand still any longer and left the sheltering trees to join the joyful people in the plaza below.

IN PRESENTING his drawing to Kinich, Akbal had signaled the other celebrants to begin their own exchange of gifts, and bags and bundles suddenly materialized from every corner of the plaza. Chan Mac could not locate either his wife or the embassy guards in the crowd around him, so he went himself to Akbal's house, where he had been told his gifts were stored. Half of the front platform had been covered with a thatched ramada, and the serving women seated beneath it accosted Chan Mac with offers of balche and freshly whipped cacao. He merely smiled and shook his head, patting his ample belly as a convincing sign of his satisfaction. He paused outside the house's central doorway to announce himself, then pushed through the netting and entered the torchlit front room.

The bundles he had brought were stacked up just inside the doorway, and he squatted beside the pile to select the gifts he wished to distribute first, recalling the contents of the bundles by means of their wrappers. As he straightened up to leave, though, his eyes fell upon the mural that Akbal had painted upon the back wall, and a surge of nostalgia made him pause to study it. It had been many months since he had last seen the green hills of Ektun, the city beside the deep, winding river. *My home,* he thought, *the home I left to come here.* He stood with his back to the doorway and stared at the wall, oblivious of the noises of the celebration outside.

When he finally came out of the house with one of the gift bundles under his arm, he was unprepared for the noise and commotion that greeted him. The crowd immediately in front of the house had thickened considerably, and the shock of their presence, in his meditative state, left him too stunned to recognize any of their faces. Several of the people seemed to be beckoning to him, and gradually he saw that two of these were Akbal and Zac Kuk, and that they were calling him over to meet with Balam Xoc. He went forward hesitantly, regaining his composure in time to bow to the old man, who was dressed very simply, without jewelry or a headwrap, his long white hair loose on his shoulders.

"So, Chan Mac," Balam Xoc said appraisingly, "you have come to our feast. Are you here merely to observe, or have you come to join us?"

Chan Mac looked back at him blankly, startled by the bluntness of the proposition.

"I am here as a guest, at the invitation of my sister and her husband."

"It was so easy?" Balam Xoc inquired. "Your superiors gave their permission?"

"No," Chan Mac admitted slowly, "but as perhaps you know, the ruler of Tikal has tried to blame the failure of the campaign upon Zotz Mac and the warriors of Ektun. The relations between our cities have been no better, lately, than those between your own clan and Caan Ac. Under the circumstances, there was no reason to fear his displeasure at my coming here."

"That is our good fortune, then," Balam Xoc decided. "Akbal has told me that you have information for me."

"I have. Some time ago, you asked me to speak to the ambassador from Quirigua. I have done so."

"Tell me," Balam Xoc commanded, but Chan Mac glanced uncertainly at the circle of listeners who surrounded them, lingering for a moment on Akbal, who could only shrug. Balam Xoc made a peremptory gesture that reclaimed Chan Mac's attention and dispensed with confidentiality at the same time, drawing the people in tightly around them.

"As you requested," Chan Mac began, "I asked the ambassador about Quirigua's relations with the mountain tribes around them. And although he was puzzled by my interest at first, he spoke freely when I persisted. He told me that there were certain tribes of Szinca speakers who had long resisted the civilizing influence of Quirigua and who would not accept the protection of the ruler. This had gone on for many years, with occasional episodes of open conflict. I understood from other things he said—and from what he did not say—that the true cause of disagreement concerned the sources of jade, which the mountain people controlled and kept as their own secret. Obviously, the ruler of Quirigua would prefer to mine the jade himself rather than trade for it with the Szinca."

"Obviously," Balam Xoc agreed drily.

"Then I asked the ambassador if he remembered an incident that occurred some twelve years ago, involving a painter and his sons, one of whom was named Hok. I mentioned this quite casually, saying that I had heard of it from another, but still he became very suspicious. He would say only that the painter and his sons had been avenged many times over, though it was clear that he remembered the incident well, and that the memory made him uncomfortable. When I pressed him about the fate of Hok, he said that the boy had been permanently deranged by the experience and had made wild accusations against innocent people."

Chan Mac stopped, realizing that the crowd around him had grown, and become utterly still.

"Did you ask about the ruler's brother?" Balam Xoc prompted, and Chan Mac grimaced slightly in recollection.

"I asked if he was not one of the people who had been accused, and if it was not true that he had been alone in his seclusion at the time of the incident, with no one to verify his whereabouts. That is when the ambassador lost his temper and told me I had betrayed his trust. He sent me away, and has not spoken to me since."

"How do you interpret such a response?" Balam Xoc asked, eyeing Chan Mac shrewdly. "You know this man, do you not?"

"Well enough to know that his anger was not that of innocence. The death of the painter was no doubt a provocation useful to the ruler; it gave him cause to send his warriors into the mountains. I might have thought otherwise had the ambassador shown more pity toward the boy, but the name of Hok aroused a quite different emotion in him, one closer to hatred. It is difficult to believe that the accusations of a boy would evoke such a reaction if they were truly wild and unjust."

"Indeed," Balam Xoc concurred, nodding to Chan Mac with what appeared to be satisfaction. Chan Mac realized that the only sounds in the plaza were isolated voices on the outskirts of the crowd, repeating what they had heard to those behind them. His private message for Balam Xoc, which he had discreetly withheld from Akbal, had been turned into a public performance. Balam Xoc inclined his head to the right and spoke out of the corner of his mouth, to someone behind him.

"Come forward, my son."

Chan Mac had noticed the man's face over Balam Xoc's shoulder, a malnourished, unsavory face that had instinctively repelled him, so that he had tried *not* to notice the man edging forward during the course of his recitation. Now he saw the pale, sightless eye half-hidden by the man's greasy hair, and felt a pang of guilt at his own revulsion.

"You have heard his story, Hok," Balam Xoc said to the man, who stood with his head hunched down between his bony shoulders, clearly uncomfortable with all the attention being paid him. "You are freed of your burden now;

you need punish yourself no more. The blood of your father and brothers is on the hands of the ruler of Quirigua and *his* brother. You will not be hurt again for possessing the truth. You will be our witness, Hok, the one who is called upon to verify the vows and agreements of our people."

Balam Xoc's words were communicated back through the crowd, which responded with a deep, concerted murmuring. Zac Kuk leaned forward at Balam Xoc's other side to whisper something in the old man's ear, showing him what appeared to be a strip of cloth that she held coiled in her hands. Balam Xoc nodded vigorously and turned to present her to Hok.

"The sister of Chan Mac also has a gift for you, my son."

Hok drew himself stiffly erect, trembling slightly from the tension in his muscles as Zac Kuk came up to him. Standing on her toes, she reached up toward his face, pausing in mid-motion when he shied away from her and pulled his head back. She spoke to him in a voice too low to hear, coaxing him patiently until he finally inclined his head toward her. Then she gently brushed the tangled hair away from his face and proceeded to tie the strip of cloth around his sloping forehead, adjusting it at an angle that brought the band low over his bad eye.

Only when she stepped back, allowing Hok to raise his head, could the rest of the crowd see the true nature of her gift. The headband was of yellow cloth embroidered with black spots, and attached to it was a round black patch that hung neatly over Hok's sightless eye. The transformation it effected in his appearance was so striking that several of the onlookers gasped in amazement, causing Hok to blink his good eye and raise his fingers to the patch in uncertainty. But others in the crowd quickly murmured their approval, for the band and patch had wrought a remarkable improvement, making him appear both less disheveled and less wild. His good eye seemed fierce and adamant, rather than crazed, and his sharp, hollowed features seemed cleansed without the tangled curtain of hair to disguise and disfigure them.

Hearing the complimentary sounds swell up around him, Hok lowered his fingers and bowed to Zac Kuk, and then to Chan Mac, crossing his arms over his chest.

"I am grateful," he said in his harsh voice, which made the words sound awkward and unfamiliar to him, but no less sincere. Balam Xoc waved his arms over his head to indicate that the performance was over, and the crowd began to separate and disperse, resuming their gifting. Remembering the bundle under his arm, Chan Mac held it out to Balam Xoc, but the old man interrupted before he could speak.

"You must give that to whoever needs it most," Balam Xoc told him. "That is how we have chosen to conduct our gifting. You will find that the gratitude you receive, even if it comes from someone you do not know, will be much more genuine than any you might receive from me. The ruler has created scarcity in our midst, but in doing so, he has also restored the meaning and value of generosity. We do not exchange gifts as the emissaries of rulers do, solely for advantage or prestige. But first I must speak to you privately. Come. You as well, Akbal . . ."

Leaving Hok and his other retainers waiting behind him, Balam Xoc led the two young men off to the end of the platform, where they would not be overheard. He addressed Akbal first.

"How soon will you be finished with your work, my son?"

"It has gone slowly, due to lack of materials," Akbal explained. "But many of the people have made gifts to the master of craftsmen tonight, answering my needs. I have no doubt I can be finished by the time the rains end."

Balam Xoc nodded curtly and turned to Chan Mac, staring at him in silence for a moment, letting him feel the force of his presence, which seemed much stronger without a crowd to absorb and deflect it.

"Have you an excuse to return to Ektun at that time?"

"I am allowed a visit to my family, yes," Chan Mac admitted warily. "I was thinking of this earlier in the evening, in fact."

"We have goods to deliver in your city. Surely you would give our porters the benefit of your protection on the journey."

Chan Mac gave him a thin smile.

"I could not do so openly, my lord. But if my party were to grow in number upon the trail, I would have to consider all of them as my own."

"It will be arranged, then," Balam Xoc concluded brusquely. He looked up at the bright, full moon and then at Chan Mac, as if gauging the way the light fell on him. "Perhaps it is just as well that you are not ready to join us, since you can do us this service. But you *will* join us, and soon."

"Forgive me, my lord," Chan Mac protested, politely but firmly. "I am impressed by what I have seen here tonight, and by the spirit of your people. But I did not abandon my clan and my city when I accepted a place in our embassy here. I fear that you have mistaken the nature of my interest in you and your people."

"What purpose does your interest serve, then? Are we an amusement to you? You have seen the kind of men who rule our cities, and the way they squander everything that is precious. Ektun is not immune to this. You hide from the truth, Chan Mac. You know that *we* are the hope of the future, if there is to be one."

"Is it not enough to be a friend and ally?"

"No," Balam Xoc said flatly, "not now. Later, perhaps, when we are stronger. We are at war now, and we need everyone who will fight with us. A friend in the palace is useless to us, and to himself."

Stubbornly resisting the pressure Balam Xoc was exerting upon him, Chan Mac put his hands on his hips and let out a long breath, glancing at Akbal for support. But his friend's face was blank and noncommittal, offering neither sympathy nor encouragement. Chan Mac looked back at Balam Xoc, whose gaze was relentlessly expectant.

"I can promise you nothing," he said in a tight voice. "But I will discuss this with my father when I am in Ektun."

"The choice is yours," Balam Xoc replied, seeming unperturbed by Chan Mac's grudging tone. "There is a place for you here when you are ready to claim it. I must go now, and prepare for the adoption ceremony."

Acknowledging their bows with a brief wave of the hand, he turned and went back to the small group still waiting for his return. Chan Mac pursed his lips and gave Akbal a sour look.

"You did not prepare me for this, my friend."

"I warned you to assume nothing. I should have warned you, as well, to *expect anything.*"

"That is not possible, for a diplomat," Chan Mac said, shaking his head. He looked down at the gift bundle that was still in his hands and shrugged. "Perhaps you can help me distribute this. I feel a need for some of the gratitude your grandfather mentioned."

"You will have it," Akbal assured him with a smile, and led him gently, solicitously, back into the crowd.

SET ATOP a pyramid platform at the eastern end of the upper plaza, the clan shrine was a squat, thick-walled building only half as tall as the painted stucco roof comb it supported. It contained two vaulted rooms, one behind and slightly above the other, reached by a single step up. The candidates for adoption came up the steep pyramid steps one at a time, and were greeted in the front room by Kanan Naab and Chibil, who gave them balche to drink and escorted them to the threshold of the inner room when their turn for the oath had come. Each of the candidates carried a bloodletter—a sharp sliver of bone or obsidian or stingray spine—that had been given to them by their sponsors, and Kanan Naab could feel their anxiety at the imminent prospect of drawing their own blood. She knew this particular fear very well from her own experience, and did her best to comfort and reassure them, murmuring in a low tone so as not to disturb the ritual being performed in the inner chamber.

The power of her empathy, which had a visibly calming effect upon the candidates, was at first surprising to her, a power she had completely forgotten she possessed. But Chibil, who was practiced in these matters, quickly perceived the success her young companion was having and began to defer to her, taking over the pouring of balche as her own duty. Kanan Naab felt this power grow with each candidate she greeted, so that soon she did not have to speak or murmur at all: She had simply to *be* there with them, emanating the fearlessness that had come to her on the night she sought her own vision, when the spirits of the ancestors had guided her hand and allowed her to feel no pain. She knew, dimly, that Yaxal was responsible for releasing this power, which had lain dormant within her since that night. But she could not think of him now, with the voice of Balam Xoc reciting the words of the oath behind her and the heady smell of copal surrounding her where she stood, her senses keenly attuned to the person in her care.

Then Opna appeared in the moonlit doorway, holding the serrated piece of stingray spine that Kanan Naab had given him herself. He had asked her to be his sponsor when the ceremony was first being planned, and she had complied almost without thinking, as a favor to another of the Close Ones. She had long been intimidated by his learning and his supercilious manner— acquired during his days as a priest in Copan—and she had been flattered that he found her worthy.

Now, however, his presence had a subtly disenchanting effect upon her, disrupting her aura of quiet courage by refusing to pay it any heed. He took the cup of balche from Chibil without looking at her, and drank from it with a steady hand, betraying no hint of nervousness. Indeed, his attitude seemed to say that nothing here could daunt him or make him look to another for support. When he finally did look at Kanan Naab, there was condescension in his gaze, as well as something vaguely challenging. Kanan Naab realized that she had felt this challenge from him on other occasions, though she had never allowed herself to acknowledge it as such. She could not understand the reason for it, except as a form of intimidation that seemed completely unnecessary, and made her regret having agreed to be his sponsor. It occurred to her for the first time that he had chosen her only because she was Balam Xoc's granddaughter, which could perhaps lend an extra measure of legitimacy to his own membership in the clan.

When the previous candidate came out of the inner room, his shins and forearms bloodied and his eyes glazed, Kanan Naab and Chibil bowed and helped him through the outer doorway, where others waited to escort him down the temple stairs. Then the two women returned to Opna and escorted him the few steps to the threshold of the next room. They could go no farther, for no woman had ever been permitted entrance to the most sacred precinct of the shrine. Few women had ever seen the inside of *this* chamber, and Kanan Naab had been content when Balam Xoc had granted her and Chibil that honor. Yet as Opna stepped up into the dark, smoky chamber, she felt a strong surge of resentment that she could not follow. *She,* who was Jaguar Paw in both blood and spirit, and who had once gone to Balam Xoc in a vision. It seemed not only unjust but simply wrong—a tradition no longer suited to the religious practices of the clan. In serving Balam Xoc, she and Opna were *both* novices, as were all of the other Close Ones.

Reluctantly following Chibil's lead, she turned back toward the outer doorway, where another candidate was waiting to enter. But the older woman stopped her and reached out to take her hands, putting her concern into her eyes, urging Kanan Naab to recapture her state of calm. Kanan Naab felt the greater warmth of Chibil's hands and realized that her resentment had drained the warmth from her own. Nodding gratefully, she closed her eyes for a moment to compose herself, putting Opna out of her thoughts as firmly as she had Yaxal. Then she turned to greet the next candidate with fresh purpose, already beginning to feel the power flowing back into her . . .

THE TORCHES around the upper plaza had all been extinguished, rendered superfluous by the bright, milky illumination of the moon, which hung high overhead. As the newly adopted members descended from the clan shrine, they formed a long line in the center of the plaza, which was surrounded on all sides by the blood members of the clan and their guests. When the last of the adoptees had taken his place at the end of the line, Balam Xoc emerged from the shrine's single doorway and stood for a moment looking down upon them. He wore jaguar-skin leggings and a loose headwrap of the same material, with a water lily pinned to its side; jade earplugs dangled from his ears, and his face and bare chest had been painted with stripes of red and black.

He came down the stairs slowly, followed by Nohoch Ich and Tzec Balam, Kanan Naab and Chibil, and the others who had assisted in the ritual. He went to the head of the line and turned to survey the group, gesturing for the sponsors to take their places. Nohoch took his place beside Hok, who had been given the honor of being first in the line, and Tzec Balam became the partner of the man behind him. Kanan Naab lined up next to Opna, and Akbal stood proudly with Kal Cuc, the only boy to have received the oath. Others filled in behind, until none of the new members was left unescorted.

"Now we are all Jaguar Paw," Balam Xoc announced, his words echoing across the silent, moon-swept plaza. "Now we will dance as one."

A single drum began to beat, and Balam Xoc turned and began a slow, shuffling dance, leading the line to the edge of the plaza before circling to his right. Nohoch limped along after him, his awkwardness nearly overshadowed by that of Hok, who hopped and flailed his arms with every beat of the drum. Kanan Naab tried to match her steps with those of Opna, but soon fell into her own rhythm, since he seemed determined to keep himself just slightly ahead of her. The dancers made one full circuit of the plaza before the other members of the clan began to join the line at its end, pairing off at random, fathers with daughters, mothers with sons, cousins with one another. The line stretched and grew until only the very old and infirm, and the outside guests, stood watching from the side. With solemn, rhythmic steps, the line of dancers circled and curled back upon itself, filling the plaza like a great, multicolored serpent, coiled and ready to defend itself, shimmering dangerously in the moonlight . . .

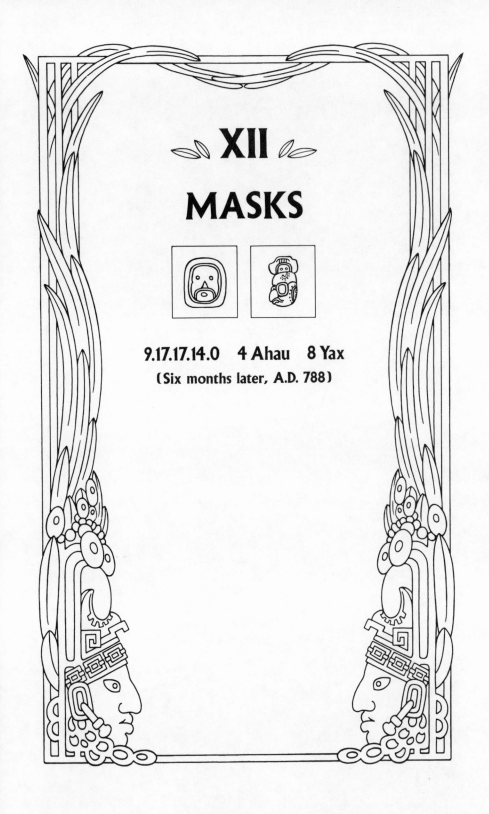

~ XII ~

MASKS

9.17.17.14.0   4 Ahau   8 Yax
(Six months later, A.D. 788)

Ektun

AFTER ANNOUNCING himself to the servant, Akbal waited outside the doorway of Batz Mac's house, as he had every morning since his arrival in Ektun. By now, it was stubborn courtesy rather than hope that kept him standing in the hot sun, holding the skirt that Zac Kuk had embroidered for her mother and the wooden hairpins that he had carved and painted himself. It had not occurred to him before he set out that gaining an audience with his mother-in-law would prove more difficult than slipping out of Tikal unnoticed.

Finally Batz Mac himself appeared, the heavy folds of his round face fixed in a frown at the unpleasant task he had been sent to perform.

"She will not see you, my son. She is adamant."

"If I could only give her these gifts, and the messages from Zac Kuk," Akbal proposed, "I would not stay to try to justify myself."

"I am sorry, Akbal. She feels that you deceived her in regard to your family and your prospects in Tikal. I must say that I share some of her feelings. Surely, I never thought that my daughter would be made to work like a commoner, or that *you,* the Tikal Painter, would have to sneak out of your city disguised as a porter."

"I *was* a porter," Akbal said, trying to make it sound like a simple statement of fact. "We could not spare enough men for all we had to carry. There is no disgrace in doing what has to be done."

"You see?" Batz Mac pointed out. "You cannot help but try to justify yourself."

"Do I not deserve the chance, my lord?" Akbal asked quietly. "I have not fully explained myself to you, either."

Batz Mac briefly turned his eyes away, his lips puckering with discomfort.

"You must be patient," was the best he could offer, though. "Perhaps Chan can persuade her to change her mind."

Akbal made a polite bow, deciding not to ask what would change *his* mind and make him apply some pressure on his wife. Akbal could not afford much more patience, having promised his grandfather that he would not keep the porters away any longer than was required. And his business here would be concluded as soon as he was able to see the high priest, Ah Kin Tzab, who had thus far been too ill to receive him.

Walking quickly back across the courtyard to Chan Mac's house, he left the gifts in the room that had been given to him and slipped out again without alerting Kutz to his presence. She had already spent enough time entertaining him, and he knew that there were many relatives she needed to see more. He also knew where to go to be alone, though he certainly had not expected to be seeking solitude on *this* visit. He had anticipated long hours of talk both with his in-laws and with the high priest, and at least two days of bargaining with the friends and relatives whose goods he had brought. Instead there had been no talk at all, and very little in the way of bargaining. Ektun had also had a bad crop, and in addition, Zotz Mac had been forced to levy stiff new taxes to support the ongoing struggle with the Macaws. No one had either the means or the inclination to trade for crafts, and Akbal had quickly perceived that his presence was an embarrassment to them, an added reminder of the desperate state of their city.

Feeling the sun's heat through his headwrap, Akbal followed the path through the copal trees to the pool on the bluff, where he had once gone to cool his frustrated longings for Zac Kuk. The memory brought a rueful smile to his face; it seemed perverse that he should be equally frustrated now, when his only wish was to tell Batz Mac and Muan Kal of their daughter's happiness in Tikal. That had seemed like a gift that no parent could spurn, even if its bearer had come unannounced, in the guise of a porter.

Shaking his head, he took a seat under the palms at the edge of the bluff, for it was too hot to sit in the open near the pool. By arching his neck, he could see down into the valley to the north, where part of the stream had been dammed off to form a long, deep pool. Several canoes filled with apprentice warriors were maneuvering in the confined space, readying themselves for a practice assault upon the shore, where another group of apprentices wearing red helmets was waiting to repulse them. Those on the shore were brandishing handfuls of slender sticks, which they had already begun to throw at the canoes.

Akbal turned his back to the river and looked toward the ravine, having seen enough warriors in his brief time here. He had almost thought that he had come to Yaxchilan by mistake, so prevalent were the signs of preparation for war. The Macaws had not waited for the campaign to be forgotten before resuming their raids on Ektun's outlying dependencies, and despite having most of his army intact, Zotz Mac had been compelled to recruit additional warriors to man the garrisons along the northern frontier. There was also talk of new trouble to the south and west, where Yaxchilan, still recovering from the losses of the campaign, was attempting to reassert its control. Akbal understood few of the details, having seen almost as little of Chan Mac as he had of his friend's parents, but it was abundantly clear that Ektun and its allies were paying an increasingly heavy price for the defense of their territories.

A flock of yellow-billed toucans were thrashing about in the treetops on the other side of the ravine, their harsh croaks barely audible behind the loud, hypnotic buzzing of the locusts. There had been no drought here, but clouds of the insects had descended upon the fields just before harvest, wiping out most of the crop in a matter of days. One of Akbal's relatives had suggested to him, only half in jest, that the locusts had migrated west after finding nothing to eat in Tikal. Akbal had laughed obligingly, but he had also recognized the larger message the jibe was intended to convey: that Tikal's recent failure had repercussions far outside its own boundaries, in the form of trade agreements that could not be honored and aid that could not be extended. There was a great deal of bitterness over Caan Ac's decision to withhold some of the maize he had promised from last season's crop, and while Akbal had been tempted to disown the ruler's actions, he had finally decided to absorb the complaints in silence. He was not here to proselytize, and there could be no useful purpose, and no kindness, in telling them of the success of his own clan's late harvest.

Even in the shade, the stifling heat soon began to make him feel drowsy, and he let his eyelids flutter shut, falling into a state between sleep and wakefulness, entranced by the buzzing din of the locusts. He thought of his stone, seeing its image clearly in his mind, blank and yellow beneath its shelter. Perhaps he would have time for it now, since he had obtained no work for himself here. But was it not too early to think about memorializing the clan? When he had left Tikal, more land was being cleared for gardens, and new people were coming in to occupy and farm it. Balam Xoc had already spoken of holding a second adoption ceremony, possibly in conjunction with the Tun-End Ceremony, which was now only four months off. There was much work to be done, and many supplies that would still have to be obtained from outside the city. He should be thinking instead of where else he could take his crafts to trade for all the things the clan needed: obsidian, salt, hard stone for grinding maize, pottery temper, paint . . .

The list lost coherence and faded back into thoughts of his stone, and then into memories of Zac Kuk, vivid and pleasurable and empty of frustration. He began to dream of the child she was carrying, the son or daughter they would one day pledge to the clan . . . he could see Zac Kuk with the baby in her arms, proudly holding it up for Balam Xoc's blessing. Chan Mac appeared in the background, and Kinich, smiling with his jeweled teeth. Then Akbal was in the craft house, painting with Kal Cuc beside him, and they were both very excited by what he was painting, a bowl or a plate, the colors beautiful but the pattern indistinct, escaping his recognition because he was shaking with his excitement . . .

He woke to find Chan Mac bending over him, a hand on his shoulder. He blinked and sighed, still feeling the emotions of his dream, and wishing he had seen the pattern he had been painting with such pleasure. Chan Mac straightened up and gave him an oddly stern look, then walked over to the edge of the narrow bluff, where he stood gazing down into the valley. Sensing that he was not going to be indulged, Akbal roused himself and went over to the pool to splash water on his face. He approached Chan Mac respectfully, seeing the tension in his friend's face and posture, as if all of his nerves had been pulled taut. There was a kind of angry resignation in his voice when he finally spoke.

"What sort of use does your grandfather have for a diplomat?"

"I can think of many," Akbal replied cautiously. "But what has happened? Have you spoken to your father?"

"No. Nor have I been able to see the ruler. He is still meeting with Shield Jaguar and the other war leaders." Chan Mac suddenly frowned deeply, slitting his eyes. "I had heard the reports in Tikal, but it is much worse than I had thought. *Much* worse."

"The Macaws?"

"In addition to their raiding, they have begun to form alliances with some of the tribes that used to look to us for protection, taking our lands by treaty rather than force. But they are only *one* of our problems now. There is another group of foreigners, people who call themselves the Putun. They have been coming in from the west in increasing numbers, raiding the settlements along the Lacandon River and threatening the cities that lie south of Yaxchilan. It is rumored that the ruler of Yaxche has made a secret pact with them, and is planning to help them wage war upon the neighboring cities. Trade with the highlands has already been disrupted, at a time when our stores are being drained to equip the warriors, and when no aid can be expected from Tikal. Caan Ac has promised to send us warriors, but nothing else."

"That is typical of his generosity," Akbal remarked drily, but Chan Mac appeared not to hear him.

"There is no place for diplomacy anymore," he complained bitterly. "Our enemies are too bold to listen, and our allies are showing little trust in one another. If the threat is close at hand, they insist that their own territory must be defended before all others. Yet if they feel their lands are secure, they want to be bribed to help anyone else. And there are still a few, like Shield Jaguar, who persist in seeing the danger as an opportunity for glory. There is no language they speak in common."

"So Grandfather was right," Akbal said in a musing tone, not wishing to seem pleased. "Ektun is not immune."

Chan Mac cast a bleak glance at the warriors training in the valley below.

"Ektun may be doomed. The locusts will eat our crops while our men die in fields far away, fields that grow only corpses. And if we fall, Yaxchilan and the other cities on the river will fall with us. After that, even Tikal will not be immune."

"Surely there is time to save ourselves," Akbal protested. "Grandfather has shown us the way."

"Your grandfather has no followers here," Chan Mac pointed out relentlessly. "He has few enough in Tikal, and the ruler for an enemy. That is not much cause for hope."

Akbal drew back from him slightly, resisting the pull of his despair.

"We are not so alone, my friend. We act in the sight of the ancestors, and with their guidance. You will understand that better when you come to live with us."

"Perhaps," Chan Mac said without conviction. "I doubt that my father will ever understand, or forgive my desertion."

"I will help in whatever way I can," Akbal offered. "When will you speak to him?"

Chan Mac came as close as he would, on this day, to smiling.

"I am sure you will be a great help, once I can convince them to forgive *you*. It may be a few more days."

"It is my custom, in Ektun, to wait."

"Yes, and then to leave," Chan Mac said ruefully, nodding to himself, "taking one of us with you . . ."

Tikal

KAL CUC came back down the slope of the ravine as silently as possible, stepping carefully over roots and turning branches out of his way with the end of his blunt-tipped spear. He found Kinich Kakmoo and the other six men halfway down, crouched in a tight circle, each man facing outward defensively while he rested, as Kinich had taught them. Their soot-blackened faces were streaked with sweat, and they responded to the return of their scout with a mixture of relief and weary expectation.

"The Lady Kanan Naab and the Serpent Clan priest are sitting together under the breadnut trees," Kal Cuc reported to Kinich. "They are just at the edge of the clearing, to the right of the Serpent Stone. There is no one else nearby."

Kinich nodded with satisfaction and turned back to the other men, glancing around the circle to be sure he had everyone's attention.

"You have all heard? Good. This will be your last exercise of the day, *if* you are successful. You must surround them without being seen or heard, close enough so that you can be at their throats before they can cry out or reach for a weapon. You are weary, so remember to lift your feet, and be aware of the shadows you cast. The hoot of the owl will be your signal to attack. Be careful with your weapons, and see that you do not injure them."

Kinich nodded to Kal Cuc, who led the men up the slope in single file, with Kinich following along at the end to observe. He knew that this was a cruel trick to play on his sister and Yaxal Can, but everyone had been warned about the training drills he was conducting, and his apprentice warriors needed the experience. If they could not take a woman and a priest by surprise, they would have little chance against the ruler's assassins. Kanan Naab would have to understand that she had been frightened for the good of the clan.

The men spread out in a loose semicircle at the top of the slope, with those in the middle allowing the ends to advance before moving forward themselves. As the undergrowth thinned out and the light of the clearing appeared through the breadnut trees, the men got down on their hands and knees and crept from one place of concealment to the next, keeping sight of one another and advancing by turns. Kinich trailed them at a short distance, listening for sounds and watching for movements that might have given them away, had the pair ahead *truly* been enemies. He heard his sister's voice, then Yaxal's response, deeper and more succinct, answering rather than asking. *What do they talk about for so long?* Kinich wondered. He remembered his own courtship of May as an agonizing period of long looks and awkward silences, punctuated by the promptings of the inevitable chaperones. He did not understand his sister's relationship with the priest at all, especially the fact that they were allowed to be alone together. But Box Ek had told him not to interfere, and he had accepted the old woman's warning, knowing that many things had changed while he had been away from the clan.

Perhaps I am interfering now, Kinich thought guiltily, but it was too late to call off his men. They had crept to within a few feet of the unsuspecting couple, raising themselves up behind the boles of the trees, poised and ready for his signal. He could not deprive them of their capture now, however his sister might choose to interpret his intentions later. Cupping his hands around his lips, he let out a single, mournful hoot, and watched his men spring into action.

One of them tripped over a root and went sprawling to the ground next to Yaxal, but Kal Cuc was between them in the same instant, his unsharpened spear pointed directly at the priest's throat. The others hemmed the couple in on all sides, so swiftly that they could only gasp in surprise before the spears thrust in front of their faces shocked them into silence. Even Kinich was impressed.

"Enough!" he shouted as he emerged from hiding. "Release them, and apologize for the fright you have given them."

Kal Cuc and the others lowered their spears and grinned at one another, their teeth very white against their soot-darkened features. They stood up and backed away slightly, murmuring apologies that did not match the exultant expressions on their faces. Kanan Naab had a hand to her heart and was breathing deeply with her eyes closed, and when Kinich saw Yaxal's tight-lipped glare, he decided to deal with the men first.

"One of you is dead," he said to the man who had fallen. "But otherwise, you have earned your rest for today. Tomorrow you must run the course I showed you, with spears and shields. We will put Akbal's stamina to the test when he returns."

The men laughed and departed with proud smiles on their faces, leaving Kinich to deal with the irate Yaxal Can, who was bending over Kanan Naab, fanning her with his hands. Kinich went to help him, but stopped when the priest rose up to confront him.

"Was that necessary?" Yaxal demanded angrily, causing Kinich to straighten up in self-defense, planting the end of his spear on the ground in front of him.

"Perhaps not necessary," he said evenly, "but very useful to my men. I apologize for disturbing you, Yaxal. And you, my sister," he added, stopping to look into Kanan Naab's face. "You must forgive me for making you the victims of our training."

Yaxal muttered something unintelligible and stalked off into the trees. Seeing the distress on Kanan Naab's face, Kinich followed the priest with his eyes, watching him wade into the undergrowth and then stop, fumbling with his loincloth. Kinich smiled knowingly.

"He will be back," he said to Kanan Naab, squatting across from her with his hands wrapped around the shaft of his spear. "I am truly sorry, my sister. I know that it takes courage for him to come here at all."

"He did not need so rude a reminder," Kanan Naab assured him, then sighed and shook herself. "Nor did I. You have trained them well."

Kinich bared his glittering teeth in a grin.

"I cannot wait to train Akbal. But it is not as if you made it difficult for us. Our enemies should only converse like the two of you, with an ear for no one else."

Kanan Naab darkened and lowered her eyes shyly, though she glanced up quickly when Yaxal returned to squat down beside her. He offered Kinich a sullen apology.

"Forgive my anger, Kinich. I had forgotten that you were raising an army here."

"An army of defenders," Kinich corrected. "I would not want to take the field against real warriors, but they will keep us from being harassed and threatened."

"Perhaps there will be no need for them soon," Yaxal suggested with exaggerated mildness, eyeing Kinich closely. "Caan Ac will celebrate the katun anniversary of his reign in two months. I have heard rumors that he is willing to make peace with the Jaguar Paw Clan, in return for Balam Xoc's participation in the rites of the ruler."

"I have not heard these rumors," Kinich admitted grudgingly, locking eyes with the priest. "There is no reason, though, why Grandfather should make peace with *him*."

"But the ruler has no reason to assume that Grandfather will *not* participate in his rites," Kanan Naab interjected, looking from one to the other in an attempt to mediate. She drew a scowl of denial from Kinich.

"He *should*," the warrior insisted. "We should participate in nothing that legitimizes the rule of Caan Ac."

"Then you will only provoke him into sending his warriors against you," Yaxal pointed out with equal stubbornness. "For which you say you are not prepared."

"We are prepared to resist a show of force," Kinich argued, squeezing the shaft of his spear. "The warriors come from all of the clans, and they have never been used against their own people. They would be reluctant to make us the first, especially when they see that we intend to *fight*."

Kanan Naab stood up with an abruptness that silenced both of them.

"This argument has no meaning, except to the two of you," she said in a scathing voice. "It is just as well that Balam Xoc will decide these matters for himself. *He*, at least, has no need to prove his dominance."

They rose almost in unison, holding out their hands in appeal, but Kanan Naab walked past them into the clearing and headed for her father's house without looking back. Neither man could face the other for several moments, though neither wanted to be the first to depart. Kinich pounded the end of his spear into the ground, growling to himself in disgust.

"This is all my fault," he muttered, huffing through his nose. "I should have had the courtesy to leave you in peace."

"I should not have goaded you with rumors," Yaxal accused himself. "My interest in seeing you make peace with the ruler is entirely selfish. I would like to visit here without fear of being reported to my superiors." He glanced ruefully at Kinich. "Or of being attacked by your warriors."

Kinich looked at him and laughed softly, taking the jibe as a sign of forgiveness.

"I will not victimize you again," he promised. "But we have made my sister very angry with our arguing. She has never before spoken to me like that."

Yaxal briefly stared off in the direction Kanan Naab had gone, his face softening perceptibly.

"She does not like the way men contend with one another for power," he explained quietly. "She feels this from one of the other Close Ones, a man named Opna. He vies with her to be seen as the one closest to Balam Xoc."

"But that can never be," Kinich objected instinctively. "He is a foreigner."

"He has been adopted. And your sister is a woman."

Kinich stopped short to consider the implications of that, his jaw moving wordlessly. He squinted at Yaxal with a curiosity he seemed reluctant to display.

"My wife has told me that Kanan Naab has had a vision of her own. Surely my grandfather is aware of this."

"He is," Yaxal allowed. "But he has never spoken to her about it, and she does not feel she can ask him to do so. I think she is also afraid that Opna would hear of it, and somehow use it against her."

"What do you know of this man?" Kinich asked darkly, his reluctance overwhelmed by a surge of protective feeling.

"Only his reputation. He was a prodigy as a boy, like your brother Akbal, only the skills of the priesthood are much more rare in a child. He was the youngest ever admitted to his order in Copan, and he was serving the ruler of that city before he was twenty. Then he became better known for the trances he obtained with the use of the sacred mushrooms, and began to develop a cult centered around himself. The high priest of Copan banned the cult before it became too powerful, and sent Opna into exile."

"So now he thinks to take over *our* clan!" Kinich exploded angrily. "I will report this to the clan council, if Grandfather will not hear me himself!"

"You must not," Yaxal urged him forcefully. "None of what I have told you is proof against his sincerity. Balam Xoc must know it himself, yet he allows Opna to serve him. No, Kanan Naab must resolve this for herself. She must not be made the subject of contention between men."

Kinich looked off into the distance, spinning the spear between his palms as he allowed his anger to settle.

"Perhaps you are right. I know little of such matters." He glanced at Yaxal with renewed respect. "No doubt she is fortunate to have you to advise her."

"I am familiar with the ambition of priests, at least," Yaxal conceded modestly. "And your grandfather has given me permission to instruct her in the reading of the glyphs and the keeping of time."

"She is *most* fortunate," Kinich mused, studying Yaxal's face with a mixture of shrewdness and curiosity. "I have to wonder, though, if this is satisfying to *you*? As you have said, she is a woman. Even a brother cannot miss that."

"Nor have I," Yaxal said frankly, meeting the warrior's eyes. "But it is impossible now for anyone outside to marry a Jaguar Paw woman. Even if

Kanan Naab were willing to leave your grandfather's service, I could not ask her to be my wife."

"Why do you not join us, then?"

The priest gazed out at the stone and its shelter for a moment, letting the question hang in the air between them.

"I have considered it many times," he said at last. "But then I think of the years I spent as a clan priest, and the years after that, earning my place within the Tun Count priests. Was it easy for you to surrender your rank among the ruler's warriors?"

"Caan Ac made it so."

"No doubt, but he has not done the same to me. I feel useful in my work, and yes, *important*. And I have a mother and two unmarried sisters who depend upon me for support, and relatives who expect me to fulfill my obligations to the clan. I cannot even tell them of my visits here."

Kinich held up his palms in a gesture of sympathy and understanding.

"Forgive me, Yaxal. I would not ask you to act against your own judgment. Yet . . . I no longer believe that people are drawn to us by accident. I resisted Balam Xoc as strongly as anyone. But he came to me in the jungle, and led me home."

"Ah," Yaxal exclaimed softly, raising his eyebrows at the revelation, which had come forth spontaneously, in exchange for Yaxal's own candidness. The two men seemed to realize simultaneously how much they had revealed to one another, and how quickly they had passed from contention to intimacy. They both fell silent, as if reconsidering the trust they had placed in the other.

"I must wash this soot from my face," Kinich said abruptly. "Kanan Naab must be waiting to finish the conversation I interrupted so rudely."

"I must bid her farewell, at least," Yaxal averred.

"I will speak to you again, another time. And I will watch this man Opna. Quietly."

"That would be wise," Yaxal said, and they bowed to each other, leaving the grove by separate paths.

Ektun

AH KIN TZAB was dying. Akbal had ascertained that much after only half a day of waiting outside the high priest's chamber, and watching the faces of those who were allowed in to see him. It was another day and a half before he realized that *he* was not going to be granted an audience with the high priest. The priests guarding the curtained doorway remembered who he was, and they had responded politely to his repeated requests to be admitted. But they had also been firm in their sense of duty to their ailing master, and they had gradually made it clear to Akbal that a painter from Tikal was not going to be given any priority at a time like this, especially when they did not know the nature of his relationship with the high priest. The only person who might have interceded for him was Ah Kin Tzab himself, but he was being protected from the exertion of such decisions.

This final disappointment was the most difficult for Akbal to bear, and it began to erode the equanimity with which he had borne all the others. It seemed that the chain of circumstances that had first brought him to this city, and had bound him to its people, had begun to fragment and fall into pieces that had no meaning or significance. He would leave here more of a stranger than when he arrived, having been denied the chance to renew and solidify any of his relationships. Now he would never say to Ah Kin Tzab, "Yes, my grandfather *is* a holy man," and tell him of the prophecies that had come true and the projects that had been carried out. Nor would he ever be able to express his pride in Zac Kuk's adaptation to the Jaguar Paw Clan, and his happiness with their marriage. These were the gifts he had brought for the high priest, and for Batz Mac and Muan Kal as well, but they had begun to go sour from neglect.

He had even begun to lose his faith in Chan Mac, who was supposedly still negotiating a meeting with his parents. Given his friend's diplomatic skills, Akbal found it hard to believe that he had not yet reached an accommodation, and could only conclude that Chan Mac was equivocating on his own behalf. *No one will face me,* he thought furiously, and began to contemplate simply leaving his gifts outside Batz Mac's house and taking his porters back to Tikal without farewell. He had been patient, but even his youth did not compel him to accept a disrespect he had not earned.

As his resentment festered and grew, he kept more and more to himself and avoided all contact with the members of Chan Mac's family, even to the point of missing meals. He had no appetite, anyway, and no reason to worry about keeping up his strength. He became listless and irritable, sleeping frequently but not well. Yet when he was able to fall into a sound sleep, he dreamed vividly, and one night he again found himself painting in his dream. This time, however, he could see what he was painting, and it made him marvel at his own boldness. It also made him understand the excitement he was feeling, so well that the excitement became real and brought him abruptly awake.

It was the middle of the night, but he rose and lit a torch for himself, and began to make charcoal sketches on a piece of leather. His renderings seemed crude at first, compared with the startling clarity of the image in his mind, but his hand gradually became more sure as he shed the initial urgency of his excitement. Then he applied himself to the ritual of cutting his brushes and preparing his paints, letting the familiar procedures calm him still further. By the time the sun had begun to redden the eastern sky, everything was in readiness, and he could wait no longer to begin. Taking a bag of trade goods with him, he headed for the house of Ektun's best potter, where he could be certain of obtaining the ceremonial plate he needed, one worthy of both his dream and the tomb of Ah Kin Tzab.

CHAN MAC announced himself outside the doorway, then sent the servant with the tray of food in ahead of him at Akbal's reply. His friend was sitting cross-legged on the floor, with his paints and brushes spread out around him and a painted tripod plate on the mat in front of him. Chan Mac squatted down across from him and gestured toward the tray the servant had left.

"You must be hungry. It has been two days since you have eaten with us."

"I have been nourished by my task," Akbal said in a tired voice, not even bothering to look at the tray. But his nose betrayed him, and he soon turned aside to examine the maize cakes and the steaming bowl of bean stew, and then began to eat with real concentration. He paused once, however, and after carefully wiping his fingers on the cloth beside him, he turned the ceremonial plate on its base so that Chan Mac could see what he had painted on it. Then he went back to filling his mouth with food, washing it down with sips of whipped cacao.

The plate was round and a deep orange in color, its gently sloping rim circled with lines of red and black. In the center of the basin was a single figure, outlined in black: a man, dressed in a spotted headdress and leggings, his arms cocked at his sides and his legs apart, rising up on one foot, as if arrested in midmotion. *Dancing,* Chan Mac realized with a start of recognition. The man's face and loincloth had been painted a dark red and his chest striped with black; he was flanked on each side by a delicately rendered water lily, the blossom trailing a long, curving tendril that seemed to enhance the figure's illusion of motion.

"It is most unusual," Chan Mac ventured, unable to form a more positive judgment. "As always, the brushwork is superb. But . . . I have never seen a figure of any kind painted on a ceremonial plate. Nor was I aware that such a custom existed in Tikal."

"It does not," Akbal said succinctly, wiping his lips with a cloth. "I saw myself painting this in a dream."

Chan Mac looked at the plate a second time but still found the image jarring to his eye, a departure from tradition too great to be easily assimilated. He was accustomed to simple designs that featured muan feathers or cloud scrolls, or spiraling patterns of jade beads—images that were fixed and reassuring in their symmetry, like the rituals in which the plates were used. The dancing man, in contrast, provoked a feeling of agitation in him, a sense of unnameable risk.

"It is your grandfather, of course," Chan Mac suggested in a neutral tone, trying to draw Akbal out. "As he was on the night of your clan's feast."

"The Jaguar Protector," Akbal murmured reverently, glancing down at the plate. "It will be his gift, and mine, to Ah Kin Tzab. I wanted you to see it before I took it to him."

"I am flattered, and impressed by your skill. But again, I must point out to you how unorthodox this is. Can you be certain that Ah Kin Tzab will accept it?"

Akbal shrugged and spread his hands over the plate, as if it were its own explanation.

"He wanted to know about my grandfather, and I have given him the truth. He can choose to refuse it, but he will not turn it away unseen, as *I* have been turned away. He will know what I have come to tell him."

Chan Mac squinted at him narrowly, perturbed by the uncompromising arrogance of his reply.

"You speak boldly of the truth, my friend, especially when you find its source in dreams. One would think that *you* were the holy man."

"I have made no such claim," Akbal said curtly. "But Balam Xoc has taught us all to be alert to signs, and to trust the truths that are shown to us. That is what he asks of you, as well."

"He has spoken to me himself," Chan Mac replied with equal curtness, unwilling to accept any more advice on the subject. "I will let you go to the high priest, then. I came to tell you that I have persuaded my parents to eat with you tonight, if you still wish to speak to them."

"I do," Akbal concurred, rising to his knees and reaching for a blanket in which to wrap the plate. He paused to catch Chan Mac's eye before covering the dancing figure completely. "I did not show you this simply to impress you. I wanted to remind you of the spirit that guides our lives, here as in Tikal."

"I have not forgotten," Chan Mac assured him gruffly, gesturing for him to finish the wrapping. "I have seen too much to forget. I will tell my parents to expect you. See that *you* do not forget."

THE HIGH PRIEST sat bundled in blankets against the wall, with a single torch set in a holder above him. His eyes were so deeply sunken into their sockets that it was impossible to tell if they were open or closed, giving his shadowed, fleshless face the appearance of a skeletal mask. The priest sitting next to him was blowing smoke into his face, drawing intermittently upon a long cigar that gave off a peculiarly musty odor. The priest conducting Akbal had him sit in the smoker's place, and take the cigar into his own hands.

"The smoke revives his spirit," the priest explained in a low voice. "But be wary of how much you breathe in yourself. It is powerful mai."

Akbal's plate lay exposed upon its blanket next to Ah Kin Tzab, whose eyes, he could now see, were firmly closed. The priests left, and Akbal took a cautious puff on the cigar and gently blew a cloud of smoke over the old man, trying not to inhale any himself. The smoke made his tongue tingle and left an earthy, bitter taste in his mouth, a taste he did not associate with mai. He blew another cloud at Ah Kin Tzab, feeling the taste grow stronger, as a vaguely pleasurable numbness spread upward from the base of his skull. This is not only mai, he decided uneasily, and set the smoldering cigar on the wooden rack in front of him.

Ah Kin Tzab's eyelids fluttered open a few moments later, but only long enough for him to locate the cigar and nod toward it.

"More," he said in a weak, sibilant whisper, and Akbal forced himself to comply, feeling the small amounts he inhaled go straight to his head. It made him slightly dizzy, but it also seemed to have made the room grow lighter, so that the colors of his plate and the designs on Ah Kin Tzab's blankets suddenly struck his eye with heightened force. He did not realize that he was staring at the blankets until the old man spoke again, his eyes open and attentive.

"That is enough. It will help you hear me better, as well."

Akbal shook himself and returned the cigar to the rack, noting that his voice did sound louder and more distinct. His own actions, however, seemed agonizingly slow, so that it took him a long time to bring his eyes back up to Ah Kin Tzab's emaciated face. The old man made a barely perceptible nod in the direction of the plate.

"The style is very old. Yet the paint is new."

"I painted it first in a dream," Akbal said, finding that his voice seemed disembodied, itself dreamlike. He was not surprised, though, that the style was not original to him. It had *felt* like remembering when he was painting.

"The dancer has no feathers," the high priest continued. "That is also new. Or perhaps very, *very* old."

"They are the same to Balam Xoc. He is a holy man, my lord. I have no doubt of that now."

Ah Kin Tzab leaned his head back against the wall, his eyes hooding with fatigue.

"You have shown me that," he whispered. "And others will see it when I am buried. That will not be long, Akbal. I can feel the coldness of the Underworld all around me."

Akbal shivered slightly and bowed his head in respect. His dizziness had passed, leaving his thoughts still slowed but very lucid. He realized that all the other things he had wanted to tell Ah Kin Tzab were unimportant now. He needed to listen, not speak. This was a voice he would hear no more, except in memory.

"Tell Balam Xoc that I am grateful," the old man said at last. "Tell him that I leave the world with an uneasy heart, knowing that there are too few like him who remain behind: men who emulate the ancestors in every aspect of their lives, not merely in the making of war."

"I will tell him, my lord," Akbal promised, and Ah Kin Tzab nodded, the thin line of his lips stretching in what might have been a smile.

"Farewell, then, Akbal Balam. Now you are truly the Tikal Painter. You must paint the dreams of your people, before they vanish from the earth. You must carve your stone, so that the memory of your wisdom and greatness is not lost." He paused for breath, looking at Akbal for the last time. "You have my blessing. Go now, and attend to the world while you can. I must attend to my dying . . ."

"PAINTER."

Akbal straightened up where he stood, blinking dazedly in the harsh glare reflecting off the plastered surfaces of the plaza and its surrounding buildings. He was still heavily under the influence of the mai he had smoked, so that he was not certain where the voice had come from, or if it had been directed at him. It might even have been an echo of his own thoughts, which were still resonating with the parting words of Ah Kin Tzab. Shielding his eyes with his hand, he turned slowly in a circle, and suddenly found himself face to face with Shield Jaguar.

The great warrior was wearing a jaguar-skin tunic and a tall headdress of blue and green feathers. His broad chest was completely covered by a plated pectoral of glittering green jade, and there were bands of round jade beads around his wrists and waist. An ancestral effigy head hung from the thickly embroidered apron of his loincloth, and his feet were encased in leather sandals with anklets of jaguar skin.

"My lord," Akbal mumbled belatedly, too overwhelmed by the vividness of the man's presence to manage a proper bow. Shield Jaguar laughed loudly, showing the filed points of his teeth. His retainers stood behind him in a large group, though Akbal had no attention to spare for them.

"Why bother to bow to *me*?" the ruler inquired sarcastically. "You do not bow to Caan Ac anymore, do you? Yes, and by all means stare into my face,

Painter. I am accustomed to your boldness. Come, tell me what you see there . . ."

Akbal knew that he was being mocked, but he could not have turned his eyes away had his life depended upon it. In his sensitized state, he saw every feature of the man's face with the utmost clarity: the great beak of a nose that seemed to snap at the air in front of him; the bright black eyes, circled now with webs of tiny lines; the jagged furrow of a recent scar that creased one cheek. There was the same aggressive curl to his thick lips, a hint of the snarl that lay just below the surface, waiting to be unleashed. Yet the face had aged in a way the eyes had not; it was a mask that had hardened and set, no longer moving so readily to the impulse of the spirit within. Akbal had seen such a face before, the face of an endurance reluctantly learned.

"I see the jungle, my lord," he said quietly. "As I see it now in my brother's face."

The ruler recoiled slightly, his geniality gone.

"Perhaps you have *too* honest an eye, my young friend," he murmured in a warning tone. He put his hands on his hips and expanded his chest, rippling the gleaming plates of jade. "Has Kinich Kakmoo retired, then? Does he sit around the fire with the women?"

"He is the nacom of our clan. He sees to our defense."

"Defense!" Shield Jaguar snorted scornfully. "Your *defiance,* you mean. I have heard about this would-be holy man, and the outrageous way he has acted toward Caan Ac. I am amazed that he is tolerated, even by Caan Ac. Rest assured, Painter, that *I* would have crushed your clan long ago."

Akbal could only nod in agreement, seeing how thoroughly he believed his own threat, and how much pleasure he took in uttering it. He was a man who attended best to the dying of *others.*

"But tell Kinich Kakmoo," the ruler went on, "that when he finally tires of defending the clan cookhouse, there is warrior's work waiting for him in Yaxchilan. Tell him that he has not yet known the kind of fame I can give him, or the rewards. He could have a clan—a *village*—of his own, if he wished it."

"He *has* a clan of his own, my lord," Akbal said mildly. "But I will tell him of your offer."

Shield Jaguar looked at him sharply, perhaps sensing his disbelief, or perhaps merely anticipating it. The mask of magnanimity fit him poorly, and Akbal discreetly averted his too-honest eyes.

"See that you do," the ruler said curtly. "Why are you here, anyway?"

"I have relatives here, and I have been to see Ah Kin Tzab."

"What business do you have with the high priest?" Shield Jaguar demanded rudely, oblivious of the fact that this was not *his* city, nor Akbal his subject. Akbal stared at him for a moment, knowing that a straight refusal to answer would be proper, but not wise.

"I painted a ceremonial plate for him," he said slowly. "And I brought him the regards of my grandfather Balam Xoc, the holy man of whom you spoke."

"The Featherless Dancer," Shield Jaguar muttered, but his eyes were suddenly uneasy behind the mask of contempt. He scowled and looked out over the plaza, as if to distance himself from what he had just heard. Then he seemed to lose interest in the conversation altogether, and made an abrupt gesture of dismissal.

"Go back to Tikal, then," he snapped. "We need *warriors* here, not painters or holy men."

This time Akbal had the presence of mind to bow, touching a hand to his shoulder and keeping his head lowered as the ruler and his retinue swept past. When he finally straightened up, he was alone, and suddenly aware of the hot sunlight beating down upon him. He felt parched and enervated, his hands shaking slightly as the stimulating effect of the mai wore off. He started walking toward Chan Mac's house, thinking longingly of shade and cool water, of the pool on the hill where Zac Kuk had taken him. He would go there, he decided, after he had notified the porters that they would be leaving for Tikal in the morning. There was no point in delaying another day, even if Batz Mac and Muan Kal could not be won over in one night. He had looked upon death today—twice—and the experience had awakened a sense of urgency that he had never known before. "Attend to the world while you can," Ah Kin Tzab had said, and Akbal had heard him precisely. He no longer had the time to be a suitor, and to wait.

So he would see to the porters first. Then he could go to the pool, and to the other parts of the city he wished to see for one last time. Then he could indulge himself in paying a proper farewell to Ektun, knowing that he would be leaving for good.

THE PORTERS, with their packs beside them, squatted beneath the boxed trees along one side of the courtyard, out of the light rain that was shredding the mist that hung in drooping veils over the thatched peaks of the houses. Wrapped in a blanket against the dampness, Chan Mac stood next to Akbal beneath the fig tree that had once been a perch for Chuen and Zac Kuk's birds. Neither of his parents had come out to see their guest off, and Akbal showed no sign of expecting them as he busied himself with the knots and straps on his own pack. He looked up at Chan Mac with a face as drawn and haggard as Chan Mac felt, for they had both been up for most of the night. His eyes, though, were alert enough, enlivened by the responsibilities of the journey ahead.

"I was rude last night," he said in a slightly hoarse voice. "Especially to your mother."

It was not a question, nor really a confession of guilt. More an acknowledgment of something that could not have been avoided.

"Perhaps," Chan Mac allowed. "You were more forceful, at times, than perhaps was necessary. But you did not fail to command their attention. They must have wondered, as I did, what had become of the reticent young man I brought here only two years ago."

"They know at least that I am not deceitful," Akbal said drily, refusing to be flattered. "Now they must think I am merely deluded, a fanatic like my grandfather."

Chan Mac gave a disingenuous shrug, unwilling to admit how accurately he had read their reactions. They were not accustomed to so much earnest talk about visions and signs and dreams, and memories in the blood. And surely they had been skeptical of the powers Akbal attributed to Balam Xoc, and of the prospects of one clan ever attaining its independence from the ruler. Yet

Akbal had made them listen, and he seemed as unaffected by their judgment now as he had seemed then.

"I regret, though," Akbal added, standing up to face him, "that I was so little help to you."

"My father sees what is happening," Chan Mac assured him, "even if he resists his own knowledge. He knows that *all* of our lives will soon be changed. My mother, though, still clings to what she wishes were true. She cannot believe that the rulers of our cities—especially those related to her by blood —would act against the interests of their own people."

Akbal shook his head in exasperation and reached down to lift his pack from the ground. He slipped his arms through the shoulder straps and bent at the waist so that Chan Mac could help him fit the band of his tumpline around the top of his head.

"I am young, I know," he said in a taut voice, his neck arched against the weight on his back. "But I no longer have any patience with those who refuse to see what is available to any eye. 'The masks have all been broken,' as my grandfather said."

"Be patient at least with me," Chan Mac requested. "I will have to speak to the ambassador upon my return, and inform him of my decision. Then I will come to join you."

"I will await that day with pleasure," Akbal said, and laid a hand on his forearm in farewell. Then he looked around the courtyard, and across the plaza at the curtained doorways of Batz Mac's house, as if to say farewell to those he could not see. Nodding once more to Chan Mac, he lowered his head beneath the tumpline and led his porters out into the softly falling rain.

Uaxactun

THE RULER'S representative had explained the purpose of his visit with admirable efficiency, but then, perhaps goaded by Pacal's apparent indifference, he had felt compelled to launch into an elaborate description of the feasts and ceremonies being planned to celebrate the completion of Caan Ac's first katun of rule. Pacal had already begun to drift off into his own thoughts when he heard muted exclamations of surprise from the next room, where Ixchel and his sister, Pom Ix, were sitting together. Then he heard a voice that tantalized him with its familiarity, until he suddenly realized that it belonged to his son. What was Akbal doing here? he wondered, straining to overhear the greetings being exchanged. But this only made the representative's recital impossible to ignore, so that it became actively annoying.

"I have heard enough," Pacal said abruptly, and the man blinked at him in surprise, his voice trailing off in midspeech. "Tell me again what the ruler is willing to offer in exchange for my father's participation."

"He is willing to lift the official ban on trade within the city," the man repeated dutifully, "and to allow the members of the Jaguar Paw Clan free movement throughout Tikal. There can be no declaration of amnesty, however, and he will not take back those he has released from his service. Except for yourself, of course."

"Of course. Tell him, then, that I will return to Tikal tomorrow. But remind him that I have no influence with my father beyond what he chooses to grant me himself."

The representative nodded with a reluctance all too plain to Pacal, who guessed that his warning would probably not be conveyed. Caan Ac was not a man who happily received doubtful news.

"The ruler and the high priest are also concerned that Balam Xoc wear the full regalia of the Night Sun Jaguar in the rites." The man paused to swallow. "They refer, of course, to the feathers."

Pacal gave a short, mirthless laugh.

"I do not think he will barter that, *if* he barters at all."

"You do not seem to share the ruler's concern about these matters," the representative suggested darkly, but Pacal simply gestured dismissively with the flat of his hand.

"I have confined my concern to Uaxactun, as the ruler ordered. You have heard my response; take it to him."

The representative left with only a desultory bow, creating a sudden silence in the next room with his departure. Pacal waited a few moments before rising to follow him, pushing through the curtain to find Akbal squatting beside Ixchel and Pom Ix, gazing up at the doorway expectantly. For a moment, Pacal could not find his voice, struck by the realization of how long it had been since he and his son had spoken. He saw Ixchel looking at him anxiously, obviously afraid that they would argue again.

"Greetings, my son," Pacal said at last, and Akbal rose to bow to him, crossing both his arms on his chest. Pacal felt a thrill of gratification so strong that it annoyed him, making him conscious of how much he desired his son's forgiveness. He frowned thoughtfully to disguise his urge to smile.

"What has brought you to Uaxactun?"

"I am returning from Ektun," Akbal told him. "I thought it would be proper to call upon you while I was here."

"It is, indeed. But you say you have been to Ektun. Obviously, the ruler has not confined you as closely as he thinks."

Akbal hesitated, betraying a certain wariness about revealing clan secrets. But Pacal could see that he *wanted* to trust him, even though he was not certain he should.

"The success of our gardens has allowed us to be generous with our neighbors," Akbal explained, choosing his words carefully. "They, in turn, allow us to use the smaller trails that pass their houses, so that we can avoid the places that are watched."

"I see," Pacal said, then glanced at Ixchel. "We are going back to Tikal ourselves, tomorrow. The ruler has sent for me."

Ixchel immediately jumped to her feet, unable to conceal her pleasure even as she bowed to her husband and Akbal and apologized for interrupting.

"Forgive me, but I must alert the servants to begin packing."

Pom Ix also rose and accompanied her from the room, smiling at Ixchel's excitement with a sister-in-law's fond tolerance. Pacal saw, though, that his revelation had had an opposite effect upon Akbal, who seemed to be regretting his frankness.

"Perhaps, my son," Pacal suggested, "we will have the honor of your company on tomorrow's journey."

Akbal examined him doubtfully.

"I have porters with me, and valuable goods. I had planned to enter the city under the cover of darkness."

"There is no need for that now," Pacal informed him confidently. "Caan Ac has asked me to return in order to negotiate with your grandfather. He wants Balam Xoc to participate in the rites of his katun anniversary, and he would not risk offending him by harming you or your men. He has already authorized me to offer the clan freedom of movement throughout Tikal."

"Then the honor will be mine," Akbal replied, seeming suitably impressed by what he had been told. *He is still not certain where my loyalties lie,* Pacal reflected ruefully, feeling Akbal's tentativeness as he led his son outside and across the plaza in front of the house. The small cluster of buildings belonging to the Tikal embassy were part of a larger complex that occupied a flat ridge at the northern end of Uaxactun. The city itself was composed of eight such groups, all occupying ridges or flat-topped hills, and all connected with one another by causeways or paved roads. The thatched-roof houses of the people spread out from this central administrative and ceremonial center in all directions, sharing the high ground with the ubiquitous groves of breadnut trees.

From the place where Pacal took them, standing on a cliff above an abandoned limestone quarry, most of the city's temples and plazas and palaces lay open to their view to the south and west. Uaxactun was much smaller than Tikal, but it was equally venerable in both age and prestige, and Pacal noticed Akbal's open admiration as he studied the painted and stuccoed roof combs that topped the many shrines. Then Akbal lifted his gaze and stared off into the far distance, and Pacal did likewise, knowing the sight his son was seeking. There it was, the shrine atop the great funerary temple of Cauac Caan, fully visible above even the tallest trees, at a distance that took half a day to walk. Its tall roof comb seemed like a red hand held up against the sky, commanding all who saw it to be humble and attentive.

" 'Cauac Caan's Headdress,' " Pacal said softly. "That is what the common people of Uaxactun call it. It reminds them that they live in the shadow of Tikal and its ruler."

"There is the same feeling in Ektun," Akbal said, looking at him searchingly. "There it is resented."

"Here, too," Pacal admitted freely. "Caan Ac will have to look elsewhere for workmen this season. No one in Uaxactun will accept his promises anymore."

"Yet he has promised to send warriors to Ektun."

"No doubt. He yearns to be remembered like his father. He would have his deeds be his headdress."

"Even if others must suffer and die for them?"

"Even so."

"So . . ."

"So?" Pacal prompted, when Akbal appeared reluctant to go on. Obviously struggling with himself, the young man raised his hands in front of him, palms up, as if to pull the proper words out of the air.

"Before I left Ektun," he explained in a tight voice, "I was able to speak to Batz Mac and Muan Kal. They had been unwilling to receive me for most of my visit, because they felt I had deceived them about the status of my family. To Muan Kal, this included the fact that you were in disgrace, and no longer a steward. I had come prepared to defend Grandfather, and myself, but I had not thought that I would be defending you, as well." Akbal drew a sharp breath. "But I did, and I found that it came easily to me."

"Indeed," Pacal murmured in surprise, uncertain of what was showing on his face.

"Indeed," Akbal said fiercely, his hands clenched into fists. "It was not *you* who failed to bring the rains. Everyone in Tikal knows that, even those who have been confined. Now Muan Kal knows it, too."

"You seem angry, my son."

"Yes! I am angry that this man uses you to hide his own failings, and even more angry that you have *allowed* yourself to be used. But what I truly cannot understand, and cannot defend, is why you continue to serve him, now that you know what he is!"

Pacal looked down at the bleached rocks of the quarry below, waiting for Akbal to regain his composure. He was actually heartened by his son's anger, and by the caring it implied. He was seldom capable, anymore, of feeling anger on his own behalf, or of caring how he was used.

"I can only tell you," he said to Akbal, "that I do not serve him out of choice, or respect."

"He has threatened you?" Akbal asked immediately, his expression clearly hopeful. But Pacal could not bring himself to admit that he was being held hostage, even though he knew it would win his son's sympathy. It seemed demeaning, an admission of impotence rather than courage.

"Kinich is with us now," Akbal said suggestively. "We can defend ourselves against the ruler's assassins."

"Could Kinich stop a fire," Pacal retorted, "if the wind were blowing against him?"

Akbal hesitated, his eyes blinking rapidly.

"But . . . you said that the ruler would not dare to harm us now, because of his rites."

"Not *now,*" Pacal stressed. "Once they are completed, though, he would be himself again. And he would repay me for my desertion, I assure you of that. The clan does not need me, Akbal, and I can do them no harm where I am. Perhaps I can even be of some help."

Akbal stared at him silently, his lips shaped stubbornly around some further rebuttal, or perhaps an accusation. *Will he tell me now that I am old and defeated?* Pacal wondered. *Will he force me to admit that I have no hope of redemption, and no strength to try?* Akbal looked away instead, out over Uaxactun.

"You must attend to the world as you see fit," he said finally. "But at least come and live among us again. See for yourself how you are needed."

Now Pacal could only stare, impressed by the maturity of the response, and the compassion. Rash promises crowded onto his tongue, and for a moment he could believe in the possibility of returning to the clan, and finding a useful life there. But then he saw the youthful expectancy on his son's face, and knew that nothing comparable existed in his own heart. He could not believe in promises anymore, least of all his own. Still, he bowed to his son, showing him the respect and gratitude he deserved.

"Let us walk together tomorrow," he proposed, wearied by the pull of his emotions. "Back to Tikal."

"To the Jaguar Paw House," Akbal corrected gently, rewarding his father with another bow.

Tikal

KANAN NAAB parted company with Hok and Nohoch Ich in the lower plaza, having already decided that she should be the one to tell Zac Kuk of Balam Xoc's latest revelation. The front room of Akbal's house was empty, but she heard voices coming from behind the building, and went back out again and around to the rear.

There were four people sitting or standing around the tree that was a perch for Zac Kuk's birds. Zac Kuk was holding Chuen in her arms, with one of the monkey's long black arms wrapped around her neck and the other stretched out toward Kinich, who was teasing Chuen with a piece of fruit. Kinich's face was blackened with soot, as were those of Akbal and Kal Cuc, who sat nearby. Kal Cuc was idly digging a shallow trench with the end of his spear, but Akbal appeared too exhausted to move, sitting slumped over with his back against a fig tree. Chuen let out a shrill chatter of protest when Kinich again pulled the fruit out of reach, and the warrior snorted with laughter.

"In the jungle we ate creatures like you," he said cheerfully, holding up a hand in defense when Zac Kuk gave him a murderous look. "Here, then, take it. Your mistress looks as if she would like to eat me."

Kanan Naab winced at the joke, wishing she might have found Zac Kuk alone. She glanced up at the parrots and macaws on the limbs above, sitting like jewels against the surrounding green. The toucan had died some months before, and Kanan Naab recalled how saddened Zac Kuk had been by that, making her wish all the more for some privacy. But then Kinich noticed her and welcomed her into the group, and she had no choice but to tell them all.

"I have just come from a meeting between our father and Balam Xoc," she reported, seeing Akbal raise his head with interest. "It concerned Grandfather's participation in the rites of the ruler, which will be celebrated less than a month from now, at the katun anniversary of Caan Ac's rule. Father had come to negotiate on the ruler's behalf."

"Ah," Kinich said knowingly. "And would Grandfather bargain with him?"

"No," Kanan Naab admitted in a tentative voice. "He said at the outset that the Living Ancestor of the Jaguar Paw Clan had always participated in the ruler's rites, and that he would respect the tradition of his predecessors. He said that he had only denounced the katun rites."

"So there was no bargaining?" Akbal asked impatiently, seeming disappointed at the prospect.

"Yes and no. Surely, it was the strangest sort of bargaining that any of us had ever witnessed. Father acted as if he had not heard what Grandfather said, and began to present the concessions the ruler was prepared to make. He would say, 'If you will participate . . . Caan Ac will give you this.' And when Balam Xoc would repeat that he already intended to participate, Father would say, 'Then it is agreed.' It was as if he were bargaining on *our* behalf, and would not let us refuse what the ruler offered!"

Akbal suddenly smiled, but Kinich was shaking his tufted head in confusion. "What *has* he offered?"

"The lifting of the ban on trade within the city, and freedom of movement throughout Tikal. Father also added—on his own initiative, it seemed—the promise that those who came to visit us would not be watched or harassed. By then, Grandfather was allowing him to propose whatever he liked."

"Why should we trust any promise made by Caan Ac?" Kinich demanded suspiciously, and Kanan Naab shrugged, spreading her hands wide.

"Nohoch Ich asked the same question," she explained. "Father did not attempt to persuade him of the ruler's trustworthiness, though. He simply pointed out the importance these rites have for Caan Ac at the present time, suggesting that they might not have the same hold on him once they were completed. He as much as told us *not* to trust the ruler's word beyond the day of the katun anniversary."

"And what about the feathers?" Akbal interjected quietly, elaborating when the others looked at him in surprise. "I spoke to Father in Uaxactun. He told me that the ruler and the high priest wanted Balam Xoc to wear the feathers he has discarded."

Kanan Naab swallowed, feeling all of the eyes turn back upon her, especially the wide, beautiful eyes of Zac Kuk.

"As I have said, Grandfather would not bargain. But he said . . . he revealed that in the moment before he was attacked by the assassins, he had had a vision." Kanan Naab paused and glanced compassionately at Zac Kuk. "He said that he had *seen* that the birds would die. He said that he understood now why this had been shown to him: It would be his revenge for the assassins that were sent against him. He commanded Father to communicate this to Caan Ac and Ah Kin Cuy."

"*My* birds?" Zac Kuk queried weakly, hugging Chuen against her chest. Akbal had risen to come to his wife's side, while Kinich and Kal Cuc stood back awkwardly, hanging their heads in sympathy.

" 'The birds that give us these feathers,' he said," Kanan Naab quoted, coming to Zac Kuk's side herself. Detaching Chuen's spindly arms from her neck, Zac Kuk handed the monkey to Akbal and turned to face the tree. The blue-headed parrot on the lowest branch clucked expectantly and bowed to her raised hand, pecking gently for food. One of the macaws above squawked jealously and spread its wings in a flash of scarlet, yellow, and blue. Kanan Naab took Zac Kuk's other hand between her own.

"I am sorry, my sister. I know this will be a great loss to you."

Zac Kuk gave her a dazed look, her thick lashes heavy with tears. She gripped Kanan Naab's hands in desperate denial.

"They are too beautiful to die."

"Yes," Kanan Naab agreed. She glanced down at the gently swollen shape of Zac Kuk's abdomen, just visible through her shift. "But you will have a child to absorb your affection. You must be grateful for that."

"I will catch new ones for you," Kal Cuc offered impulsively. "From those that do not die."

"Or I can trade for them in the marketplace," Akbal suggested, nodding gratefully to his assistant. But Zac Kuk merely shook her head, dabbing uselessly at her eyes.

"No, Kanan Naab is right. I am too old for pets. If these must die as Grandfather has said, I will have no others."

Then Zac Kuk turned and let Kanan Naab embrace her, weeping softly on her sister-in-law's shoulder. Kanan Naab looked past her at the three black-faced men, who seemed pathetically ill at ease, as if they did not know where to put their eyes.

"Leave us," she commanded, and held Zac Kuk more tightly, closing her eyes to better draw upon the calming power she knew was inside her, the healing power of her empathy. The other Close Ones would simply deliver Balam Xoc's message and be on their way, but Kanan Naab always stopped now to comfort where she could. Her grandfather's truths were often painful to accept, and while she could spare no one the pain, she could help to persuade them that it could be borne. That was *her* message to the people, her gift to them: a power she could be trusted to wield on their behalf.

The Katun Anniversary
9.17.17.16.4   9 Kan   12 Ceh

A FULL KATUN, twenty tuns, had passed since the day Caan Ac, the son of Cauac Caan, had acceded to the Jaguar Throne of the Ruler. To help him celebrate this important anniversary, Caan Ac had invited the lords and rulers of cities as far south as Quirigua and Copan; as far north as Calakmul and Chetumal; as far west as Yaxchilan and Ektun; and as far east as Altun Ha, which lay close to the shores of the Great Waters. The rites of the ruler, commemorating Caan Ac's fulfillment of his duties as both priest and leader, were to be held at noon in the Plaza of the Ancestors, with several thousand people in attendance. He would be assisted in these rites by representatives from all the major Tikal clans, each paying homage to the ruler in the guise of the clan's patron spirit.

Balam Xoc would be among these, wearing the authority, if not the full regalia, of the Night Sun Jaguar. Pacal had previously given his assurance of this to the ruler, and in return, Caan Ac had freed the Jaguar Paw Clan to trade and move about in the city. But Balam Xoc's refusal to wear feathers, and his further prediction that the brightly plumed birds would die—all of which Pacal had faithfully reported—had cost Pacal whatever favor his "negotiations" might have won for him. He had not been offered his customary privileged place among the members of the ruler's court, and for the first time in years, he would be attending a public ceremony in the humble company of his own clanspeople.

Pacal was content, however, to pay his homage to Caan Ac from afar. In the month since his return to Tikal, he had spent enough time in the palace to perceive the shape of the ruler's current policy, and it deserved no better than distant admiration. With typical bravado, Caan Ac had embarked upon an extravagant campaign to convince the outside world that Tikal was strong and undiminished in its greatness. There were, first, the lavish festivities surrounding the katun anniversary. This would then be followed, less than two months later, by the equally elaborate ceremonies of the Tun-End. Nor would Caan Ac contemplate reducing the scale of either celebration, despite the pleas of his stewards. He would observe these events in the style of his father and grandfather, so that none would think the Sky Clan ruler had been shaken by his recent misfortunes. He had even distributed food from his own stores to the common people of Tikal, so that the sight of their hunger would not be a distraction to the visiting dignitaries.

Despite the expense, Pacal could find a justification for that much of the plan, on the grounds that a show of confidence was necessary as the planting season approached. And for once, Caan Ac had taken the cost of his gamble upon himself. He *had* to, since he could no longer purchase anything with his promises or his prestige. It was rumored that he had been trading away jade jewelry and precious stones that had been left to him as his patrimony, and Pacal, for one, believed this to be true, knowing of no other source the ruler had to draw upon.

Yet Caan Ac had also announced that he would be sending a large number of warriors to Yaxchilan and Ektun, at a time when workmen were in short supply, and there were no means to hire more from the outside. And he had installed an incompetent as the chief steward of crops, making a successful crop—the only basis for a *true* recovery—a matter to be decided largely by luck. Pacal found nothing admirable about this, even from his distance, which seemed to grow greater with each day.

Not that he had grown commensurately closer to the people of his clan. As he finished dressing and went out to join the procession going to the plaza, he mused over the way *they* had treated him since his return. Like someone who had just ended a long sojourn in a foreign land, he decided; someone who had to be given time to reacquaint himself with his people and their customs. They had been surprisingly gentle, for the most part, encouraging him with various degrees of subtlety to resume an active role in the affairs of the clan. Still, no one had suggested what that role would be, or if it could even be defined as long as he remained in the ruler's service. Balam Xoc had been conspicuously silent in this regard, and Pacal had not been offered a place on the clan council. He did indeed feel like a foreigner, a refugee from the larger world surrounding this island of resistance.

The procession was taking shape in the lower plaza, with the women and children gathering at one end and the men at the other. Since Tzec Balam and Nohoch Ich had already gone ahead with Balam Xoc, the leadership of the clan had fallen to Kinich Kakmoo and one of Tzec Balam's sons, and the two young men were ordering people into their places with self-consciously dignified gestures. Pacal presented himself to Kinich, who was simply dressed but carried a long spear tipped with a ceremonial point of grey flint.

"And where is *my* place, Lord Nacom?" he asked politely, when Kinich had recognized him with a curt, impersonal nod. He expected his son to show some embarrassment at the title, some mutual recognition of their humbled circumstances. Kinich, too, was a recent refugee from that larger world, and could not have forgotten its grandeur so quickly. But Kinich merely consulted the list he held in his other hand and pointed with his spear toward the line behind them.

"The clan steward has asked if you would walk with him. He is there, my lord."

Pacal bowed and turned to locate Chac Mut, who was not far from the head of the burgeoning column. *The clan steward,* Pacal thought sardonically, as he went to join his former assistant. Behind Chac Mut in the line were the physically incongruous pair of Akbal and Chan Mac, the master of craftsmen and the clan ambassador, as Chan Mac would no doubt be called once he had been formally inducted into the clan. Pacal could understand how the clan's isolation could have led to a need for these titles, but he did not know how men like Kinich and Chac Mut and Chan Mac, who had occupied positions of *real* power, could ever come to regard them with complete seriousness.

The three young men all bowed to him solemnly as he took his place next to Chac Mut, displaying no more familiarity than Kinich, so that he felt more like an honored guest than the uncle and father he was. He also realized that he was among the oldest of the men in this part of the line. There were a couple of white heads in front of him, but they were not men he knew; recent adoptees, no doubt. At the very head of the procession were the Close Ones: more strangers, except for Kanan Naab and the man with the eye patch, who had been present during the negotiations with Balam Xoc. The clan witness, he had been called.

All young and all believers, Pacal thought; *I am not needed here.* Chac Mut, who had once been responsible for vast tracts of the ruler's lands, required no assistance in superintending the clan's limited holdings. In just the brief time since the ban on trade had been lifted, he had managed to dispose of the surplus from the clan's gardens and breadnut groves, laying in large stores of all the goods that had been in short supply during the ban. If trade were to be cut off again tomorrow, the clan would not feel the effects for many months. And the clan had fed *their* poor, as well, with Kinich going out among them to recruit and train additional defenders. Akbal and Chan Mac, for their part, had recently visited three of the cities to the east of Tikal, bearing ceremonial plates that Akbal had painted as gifts for the lords who received them.

Yes, these young ones with their made-up titles were very efficient and purposeful, and utterly dedicated to the fulfillment of Balam Xoc's vision of independence. The ruler should only hope to command such loyal and energetic servants. Yet they seemed to possess no sense of proportion about their own importance, no suspicion that their attempt at independence might finally prove futile, or worse, pathetic. They seemed to think that they were an example for all of Tikal, rather than one small, controversial clan. They believed that the rightness of their ways would one day become apparent to everyone and that they would be emulated rather than persecuted.

Sighing inwardly, Pacal inclined his head toward Chac Mut and spoke to him in a low voice.

"It will seem strange to be back among the crowd, rather than at the front with the rest of the court."

"I do not miss the court," Chac Mut said bluntly. Then he softened his tone slightly, not wishing to appear reproachful. "I prefer to look ahead to the place

I will have at the Tun-End Ceremony, for the Dance of the Jaguar Protector."

Pacal squinted at him skeptically, but Chac Mut resisted being drawn back into their old relationship, when they had viewed everything with the steward's coldly calculating eye. Neither of them had yet seen Balam Xoc dance, but it had not occurred to Pacal to look forward to the opportunity. *No, I am not needed here,* he thought again; *I do not have their capacity for belief, or their ability to shrink the world to their own size. No doubt my father sensed this about me, and that is why* he *made no effort to bring me back into the clan.*

The procession had begun to move out, led by the Close Ones, who trailed streamers of fragrant white smoke from the incense ladles they carried. Pacal followed along in silence with the others, going to pay homage to a ruler none of them respected, not even Pacal himself, who had served the man for most of the katun now being celebrated. *For a katun of bad judgment,* Pacal decided unsparingly, *I deserve no place among the hopeful, here or anywhere else.*

The Tun-End
9.17.18.0.0   6 Ahau   8 Kankin
(Thirty-six days later)

THE WAY HAD grown ever darker and colder, the depth and extent of the water challenging the stamina of even so powerful a swimmer as the Jaguar. There were no other creatures to menace him, and likewise none to be preyed upon. He felt the angry hunger in his gaunt belly and snapped at the water lilies that floated in front of his muzzle, crushing them between his jaws. They had the taste of flesh without the substance; his teeth gnashed against themselves in frustration, and the emptiness in his stomach began to drag him down. Water lapped over his nose, and he sneezed and tried to shake himself, flailing out with unsheathed claws. Then he went beneath the surface, snarling in a burst of bubbles, still fighting for his life even as he sank . . .

AS HE ROSE out of the dark, watery depths of the Underworld, back toward consciousness, Balam Xoc felt his shape changing, the great power of his jaws and limbs fading as fangs and claws receded, muscles shrank, and the swift cunning of animal instincts jarred against the bewildered thoughts of a man. There was a moment of terror as he realized the savage creature he had been, and a moment of loss as that creature's awesome physical power left him. Then his mind lightened, and he remembered himself fully, shedding both the form and the spirit of the Night Sun Jaguar.

Only then could he hear the voices calling to him, and prevent himself from rising any farther toward wakefulness. He gathered his attention and focused it inward upon the source of the voices, which came to him as vibrations from the deepest part of his being, wordless yet distinct. One voice resonated with a familiar insistence, and he allowed it to claim him, giving himself once more to the Spirit Woman. He had a sensation of sudden movement, of colors blurring, of being pulled by the voice, which broadened and became the path along which he flowed toward the Spirit World . . .

Vision came to him as the voice diminished, and he found himself looking down from an uncertain height, upon a plaza filled with people. It was not a large plaza, and tall trees surrounded it on three sides. The platform on the fourth side was only a few feet above the level of the plaza floor and was surmounted by only three shrines, all of which were low rectangular structures with vaulted roofs, painted completely red. Large spirit masks were attached to walls between the doorways, and a single stone monument—carved and painted—stood in front of each shrine.

Balam Xoc recognized nothing with his eyes, but a deeper sense told him beyond all doubt that he was looking upon the Plaza of the Ancestors, as it was at some point in the distant past. He could only guess at the number of katuns that must have passed between this time and his own, but the impact of the place itself was the same. There were powerful spirits here, invisible beings with whom he felt an immediate and undeniable kinship.

Perhaps a thousand people stood facing the shrines, silent and unmoving, held fast in the moment he had been called to witness. Three stood out in front of all the rest: a woman past the middle years of her life, wearing a jaguar-skin cape; a boy of about ten holding a Cauac scepter; and a white-haired old man seated on a canopied throne. The boy stood between the woman and the man, separated from each by a distance of several paces, but clearly joining them with his presence. Balam Xoc's attention was drawn inexorably to the woman, who was standing to the boy's right, in the place of honor. *The Spirit Woman,* he thought, feeling the cold, unbending force of her character. So she had finally brought him to her own time, a time when she had obviously held a prominent position among the people of Tikal.

He could also sense something of the attitudes and qualities of the men who stood behind her, and he realized that they had to be the elders of the Jaguar Paw Clan—also his ancestors. They were proud, educated men, their long heads wrapped with colored cloths and their faces composed and respectful. Yet there were subtle differences in the way they aligned themselves with the woman at their head. Some stood stiffly erect, their eyes trained upon her back, expressing complete commitment and support. There were an equal number, however, whose averted eyes and sidewise stances betrayed their reluctance and disapproval. *Despite her importance,* Balam Xoc thought, *despite her determination, she has not won the undivided support of the clan.*

The boy in the middle bore too clear a resemblance to the woman to be anyone other than her son, and Balam Xoc suddenly realized that he was witnessing the investiture of an heir. He found it difficult to look upon the boy, though, experiencing a pang of revulsion that defied his deeper sense of kinship and attraction. Perhaps it was the way he held the Cauac scepter in his hand, displaying a precocious awareness of his own power. The scepter was an archaic and less elaborate version of the symbol that would later be held by the Sky Clan ruler: a serpent-legged effigy of the long-nosed Rain Spirit, with a smoking ax hafted into his forehead. The face of Cauac, held level with the boy's own face, was fixed in a smile that seemed wicked and perverse, vaguely threatening. The two faces seemed to merge and then separate, mirroring the conflict that their pairing aroused in Balam Xoc's heart.

Two men stood just behind the boy, apparently his guardians. One wore an incense bag and a tunic embroidered with the four-lobed flower of the katun priests; Balam Xoc could sense little about him, except that the potent atmosphere of the plaza made him uncomfortable. The other man wore the costume of the Jaguar Protector, without feathers, and his presence exerted a powerful claim on Balam Xoc's attention, a pull that was fiercer and more demanding than that of the Spirit Woman. Balam Xoc recognized the spirit of this man as the one that had come to him during his last confinement, the wrathful spirit that had helped him reclaim the loyalty of the clan. *My predecessor - as the Living Ancestor,* he thought, *a man whose hatred of the foreigners has never died, and was made to live again in me.* It was impossible *not* to look upon him, and only with effort could Balam Xoc pull his eyes away.

Finally, he was able to look upon the old man on the throne. He appeared to be extremely old, even older than Balam Xoc himself, a man with a flat, impenetrable face beneath a feathered headdress of distinctly foreign design. He sat with his feet dangling down in front of the throne, slumping from the weight of his beaded jade pectorals. Balam Xoc regarded him as he might a painting, feeling no emanation of spirit, no voice. He was obviously a man who had no ancestors here, and was thus unknowable. He also held the Cauac scepter in his hand, brandishing it with weary authority.

Flanking the throne on both sides were a number of similarly foreign men, their chests and arms covered with large amounts of jade and shell jewelry, their headwraps decorated with sprays of brightly colored feathers. A few were more plainly dressed, in the manner of the Jaguar Paw men to their right, but even these wore the images of birds and butterflies and skulls on their clothing —the symbols of the Zuyhua. Despite their ostentatious display of wealth, these men seemed to wear their jewelry like armor, as if to protect themselves from the spirits that inhabited this plaza. Conspicuous in their midst were two warriors whose features had a wholly foreign cast. They wore spangled shell necklaces and quetzal feather headdresses, and they carried spear throwers and fringed shields bearing the goggle-eyed visage of some unknown spirit. Their faces were blank and patient, the faces of men far from their home, performing a ceremonial duty they little understood.

They are Zuyhua, Balam Xoc realized, seized by a sudden, complete comprehension of what he was witnessing. The images of glyphs from the clan books crowded into his mind, obscuring his vision of the scene before him. He saw the glyph of Curl Snout, the foreign usurper, and that of his son, the famous Stormy Sky, the heir borne by a Jaguar Paw woman. He saw the glyph of Kan Balam Moo, the last daughter of the original Jaguar Paw and the wife of Curl Snout, the Spirit Woman . . .

Vision was beginning to fade entirely, and the voices again rose up within him, calling to him to look, to witness the investiture of Stormy Sky. There was a ruefulness to the voices, an admonitory regret that was quickly replaced by the cold determination he had experienced so many times before, urging him not to compromise, not to accommodate himself to the ways of the foreigners or give them legitimacy. Balam Xoc felt the lingering echoes of their urgency as his spirit began to drift into the darkness that surrounded and then absorbed him, so that nothing more could be seen or heard.

WHEN HE finally woke, he did not know who or where he was, or even that his spirit was contained by a body. His first awareness of physicality was a taut, gnawing sensation that he gradually came to recognize as thirst, though it was several more moments before he could recall how to alleviate his discomfort. His hands shook as he located his water gourd in the darkness and lifted it to his lips, but at the first touch of the soothing liquid upon the parched membranes of his throat, the memory of his body and its needs came back to him completely, and he had to struggle against the urge to gulp the water down.

The incense burner in front of him was cold to the touch, and dim shafts of light came through the air vents beneath the vault in the ceiling. People could be heard moving about in the room behind him, indicating that the ceremony was close at hand. He had been away far longer than ever before. He had gone deeper into the Underworld, closer to the place where he would find his death and transformation. His remaining time upon the earth could not be great; he understood—felt—that now. He had to think about a successor of his own, an heir to carry on what he had begun. It was this that the ancestors had been trying to tell him.

He thought immediately of Kanan Naab, of how she had come to him during his last confinement, as he was about to descend into the Underworld. Could she be the one? Yet she was a woman, and he could not forget the disapproving men who had stood behind the Spirit Woman, or the regret he had heard in her voice as the vision faded. He had also seen Opna and Nohoch Ich in dreams that had seemed important and possibly prophetic. Was it one of them, then? To whom could he entrust his knowledge, and the responsibility for holding the clan together? The ancestors had shown him many things, but they had given him no clear indication of this. He would have to find a sign.

A drum began to beat outside: The ceremony was about to begin. Balam Xoc sat a moment longer, collecting his strength and his thoughts. He had not known until now how he would dance. He had trusted that the ancestors would show him what was necessary, as they had at the previous Tun-End, when he had been possessed by the fierce, commanding spirit of his predecessor. This time he had been shown the heir, the representative of the next generation. He would dance for *them,* then. For those who were young and filled with promise, for the new members of the clan and those who would soon be adopted, for those yet to come who would call themselves Jaguar Paw. He would dance for the hope they represented, as Stormy Sky had once been the hope of his mother and his guardian. He would dance to encourage them, so that they might succeed where the hopes of their ancestors had failed, and ended in regret.

He rose from the dust of his fasting paint, which had fallen from his body sometime during the night. As he moved toward the curtained doorway, he knew that he would be dancing for another purpose, as well, though he would not announce it to the people. He would dance for a sign he could trust, a sign of the one who would one day take his place upon the earth, when he had gone at last to join the ancestors in the sky.

XIII

THE SHADOW OF RISK

9.17.18.6.0   9 Ahau   3 Uo
(Six months later, A.D. 789)

Tikal

ZAC KUK woke at the first light of dawn, her mouth and throat dry from having slept on her back. She was alone, for Akbal had gone to Nohmul and Chetumal with Chan Mac and was not expected back for several more days. Yet her first thought was not for him, but for her birds, and something told her that today her fears would be confirmed. She slowly pushed herself into a sitting position, feeling the strength she had developed in her arms to compensate for the ungainly weight of the child inside her. She was in the last month of her pregnancy and had learned to be careful in her movements, using the bench or the wall for support when no one was present to help her. She moved even more slowly this morning, though from dread rather than care.

The night fog was just beginning to lift as she pushed through the netting over the back doorway and stepped out into the damp air. The gardens and cookhouses behind the houses were still deserted, but a few birds had begun to call in the breadnut trees, sounding quizzical in the silence. Zac Kuk walked toward her tree with measured steps, not allowing herself to stop even when she saw the green splotch of color on the ground at the foot of the tree. The parrot lay with its wings splayed out to both sides in a motionless parody of flight, its thick-billed head cocked at an unnatural angle, one orange eye staring up at her.

Chuen sat huddled on a branch high in the tree, whimpering to himself, and would not come down when Zac Kuk clicked her tongue at him. The other birds stirred listlessly on their perches, displaying neither interest nor hunger; the ground beneath them was littered with the feathers they had molted in the most recent phase of their sickness. Zac Kuk realized that she could feel no sorrow at seeing their misery ended, and that her sense of loss had been dulled by the months of waiting for this to occur. The only thing that remained was to present Balam Xoc with the evidence that corroborated his last prophecy.

Stooping with difficulty, she gathered the limp body of the parrot into her hands and went to rouse her sister-in-law, Kutz, who was sleeping with her children in one of the spare rooms of Akbal's house. Though she had only just awakened herself, Kutz responded immediately to Zac Kuk's summons, and went next door to Kinich's house to get May. Together, the two women walked Zac Kuk across the lower plaza and helped her climb the steep stairs to the plaza above, supporting her by the elbows as she carried the dead bird like an offering, out and away from her body.

Balam Xoc was sitting on the platform in front of his house, eating with Hok and Chibil. But all three stopped and wiped their fingers and mouths as the women approached across the empty plaza. Zac Kuk came up the steps and paused to bow, her companions remaining a little behind her. Then, without straightening from her bow, she deposited the dead parrot in front of Balam Xoc.

"He is only the first, Grandfather," she said solemnly. "The others will all die soon, since they will not eat."

Balam Xoc nodded silently, looking up at her face. Then he reached out with one hand and spread the patchy green feathers on the bird's wing, revealing a swarming mass of tiny white parasites.

"Here are the assassins," he said in a harsh voice, drawing his hand back. "They follow naturally upon disease."

He took the cloth Chibil held out to him and wiped his hand, then gave the cloth to Zac Kuk for the same purpose. She dusted her hands perfunctorily and let the cloth drop at her feet, next to the bird.

"This will make the ruler remember us," Balam Xoc continued. "The peace will be broken again." He turned abruptly to Hok. "Go rouse Kinich Kakmoo. Tell him to alert his men to the danger, and put out sentries. Then tell Nohoch Ich and Chac Mut to come to me. We must complete our remaining business while there is still time."

Hok departed without a word, stepping awkwardly around Zac Kuk, his good eye narrowed in sympathy. Balam Xoc gestured to Chibil.

"Alert the other Close Ones. The people must be told of this, and warned against venturing out into the city alone."

"The Lady Box Ek will be waking soon," Chibil pointed out. "She must be given her medicine."

"I will tend to her," Zac Kuk offered, drawing a somewhat skeptical glance from Chibil, who was also acting as Zac Kuk's midwife. But Balam Xoc merely nodded to the older woman and sent her off, and Zac Kuk likewise told May and Kutz that they could return to their children. She was hoping for a moment alone with Balam Xoc, and he did not deny her wish when she turned back to face him.

"You bear your loss bravely, my daughter," he said, but Zac Kuk refused the praise with a shake of her head.

"In my heart, I am very afraid, Grandfather. Do you remember what it is to be afraid?"

"Not well," Balam Xoc admitted. "Do you fear for yourself, or the child you bear?"

"I fear for all of us." She gestured plaintively at the parrot at her feet. "You have taught us to be attentive to signs, Grandfather, and this is a most ominous sign. It does not matter that you foresaw its coming, or that it will be your revenge upon the ruler. I have told myself these things, but still I feel that a shadow has been cast upon our lives."

Balam Xoc squinted at her shrewdly.

"Vengeance is always costly, and I do not expect that the ruler will learn from this one lesson. But perhaps others will begin to see what he ignores, in his desire to punish us. Perhaps they will see how he hurts himself, and all of them, with his hatred of the truth."

"Yet *he* will only hate us more."

"That is unavoidable," Balam Xoc assured her succinctly. "We can only be alert, and prepared to defend ourselves. It is tempting to think of compromise and accommodation, but we would only be swallowed up and lost to ourselves. That is the lesson *I* have learned from the experiences of my ancestors, and I will not ignore it for the sake of our present safety. Yes, my daughter, the shadow of risk does hang over our lives, but we cannot allow it to darken our hopes for the future. We *must* not."

Zac Kuk took a deep breath, braced by the bluntness of his reply. Hearing a sound behind her, she turned slightly and saw Nohoch Ich and Chac Mut coming toward them. Then she turned back and bowed to Balam Xoc.

"I will see to Box Ek."

"Yes. I have heard your message, Zac Kuk. I am grateful that you did not hide your fear from me."

"I will leave it with you, then," she said softly, making an offertory gesture with her empty hands, as if depositing an invisible bundle upon the body of the parrot. Exhaling loudly, a sound of resignation as well as relief, she gripped herself around the middle and went in to tend to Box Ek, walking with light, careful steps.

PACAL HAD BEEN sent to the marketplace on an errand of little importance, so when he had completed his business, he did not feel compelled to hasten back to the palace. Instead he lingered among the stalls that lined both sides of the long, gallerylike building, listening to the tone of the bargaining. It seemed rather sullen on the whole, indicating that Caan Ac's two big celebrations had had little lasting effect upon the state of trade in the city. As Pacal would have expected, the bartering was especially combative in the vicinity of the sparsely stocked food stalls. Tikal was a hungry city, with the relief of the harvest still six or seven months away. Most of the traders in food were from other cities, and it was clear from their attitudes that they felt at an advantage in the bargaining.

Chac Mut had made a good name for the Jaguar Paw Clan here, Pacal reflected as he strolled away from the noise and contention of the food stalls. He had gotten full value for the clan's surplus crops, but he had never tried to push his advantage to its limit. He had continued to barter individually, deliberately avoiding the kind of bidding opportunities that scarcity made possible. Pacal was not certain he could have exercised that much restraint himself, since he doubted that the clan's generosity would ever be repaid. The rains had been good this season, perhaps even heavier than usual. A successful crop would make the produce from the clan's gardens superfluous instead of rare, as it was now. Then these "friends" that Chac Mut had won for the clan would have short memories, and little reciprocal restraint.

As he turned at the end of the corridor and entered another wing of the immense quadrangle, Pacal found himself among the stalls of the feather merchants and was again assaulted by the sounds of shrill and contentious bargaining. The featherworkers and costumemakers who had come to buy seemed in the grips of some desperate kind of fury, shouting out bids to the harried merchants, who appeared vaguely frightened by the nature of the demand for their goods. *What has caused* this? Pacal wondered, loitering at the edge of the gesticulating crowd. The men in the front seemed to be demanding to know the *age* of the feathers, which seemed an odd request to Pacal, who had always judged feathers by their color and condition.

Suddenly a man in the center of the argument snatched a handful of blue and yellow feathers off one of the merchants' piles and turned to display them to his fellows, his face contorted with righteous suspicion. Then he began to wave them angrily over his head.

"These are diseased! Tainted!"

"That is a lie," the merchant who owned the feathers protested loudly, making a grab for them over the shoulders of the men in his way. He missed, but in his lunge he struck one of the men full in the face, almost knocking him down. The crowd let out a roar and turned on the merchant in unison, hurling him backward into his stall. Then the fighting began in earnest, with the badly outnumbered merchants using their staves to try to beat off their attackers, who were tearing the bales of feathers apart and tossing them into the air. Tufts of white and scarlet and brilliant blue-green floated above the heads of the combatants, kept aloft by the draft churned up in their struggle.

Pacal had backed away instinctively at the first hint of violence, but he was still surprised by the fighting when it actually erupted. Angry disputes were common in the marketplace, but Pacal could not recall ever seeing men resorting to their fists and feet to settle an argument. Faces were being bloodied and merchandise destroyed, and there were none of the usual voices calling for reason and decorum. The cloth-covered partitions that formed the stall itself were in the process of being torn down, the support poles wrenched out of their bindings for use as weapons. Pacal was too stunned to move, and it did not occur to him to call for help until he heard the whistles, and turned to see the detachment of warriors who policed the marketplace pushing their way through the crowd of onlookers.

The warriors had staves of their own, and they did not hesitate to use them on anyone who resisted their commands to desist. Order was restored in a matter of moments, though not without a few more cracked heads. Feathers lay everywhere, torn and trampled underfoot, and stained with the blood of the injured, who sat holding their heads or lay where they had fallen. The silence seemed heavy with shame.

"What caused this?" the captain of the warriors demanded, and when none of the antagonists responded, a voice rang out from the crowd of bystanders.

"The birds are dying. As Balam Xoc predicted."

The captain whirled in the direction of the voice, scowling so threateningly that those confronting him backed away involuntarily. There was a flurry of motion in the middle of the crowd, as whoever had spoken made a hasty departure. The captain made an impatient gesture with his staff.

"Go back to your business, and mind what you say about this," he commanded harshly. "The spreading of false rumors will not be tolerated."

The truth is surely more dangerous, Pacal thought to himself, but he backed away with the others, and then began to walk rapidly toward the palace. He had delivered the first report of this prophecy himself, but it had slipped from his mind as the months had passed without incident. Word of it had obviously spread during those same months, most likely as a result of the freedom the ruler had granted to the Jaguar Paw Clan. That would surely be Caan Ac's conclusion, in any event, and Pacal wanted to be present when the ruler decided to act. He could at least absorb some of Caan Ac's anger, even if he could not warn the clan of what was to come. He could only hope that his father was aware of what had happened, and prepared to accept the consequences for having foreseen it with such vengeful accuracy.

THE HIGH PRIEST Ah Kin Cuy had delegated the responsibility for bringing Balam Xoc in to four of his top priests, and the ruler had given them a detachment of twenty armed warriors to insure that the high priest's summons was obeyed. Pacal had also been ordered to join the group, having been told in vivid terms what the clan could expect if Balam Xoc chose to resist.

The path across the alkalche was deserted, but as the procession came up the rise toward the craft house, it became clear that they were expected. A small crowd of people stood waiting at one end of the craft house, blocking the entrance to the lower plaza. As they came closer, the crowd parted, opening a path between them. The priests hesitated briefly, then went forward when they saw that the crowd was composed solely of women and children. One of the warriors behind Pacal laughed softly, but there was no sound from the waiting people, who did not so much as turn their heads as the procession passed between them.

The priests ahead hesitated again as they turned the corner of the craft house and entered the plaza, but it was a few moments before Pacal could see the cause of their hesitancy. There, at the other end of the plaza, stood the outsized figure of the Jaguar Protector, holding his staff and his painted red claws. He was flanked on one side by Kinich Kakmoo and Hok, and on the other by Nohoch Ich and Tzec Balam. Of these, only Tzec Balam was not armed; the others held wooden shields painted with black and yellow spots and long spears with fire-hardened points. The rest of the Close Ones stood in a group behind Balam Xoc, whose face was hidden behind the great jaws of the Jaguar.

The priests stopped a few feet away, with the warriors falling into ranks of four behind them. Before the head priest could speak, though, Balam Xoc lifted his red claws, and suddenly men began to appear out of the doorways and the gaps between the surrounding buildings. All of them carried spears and shields and war clubs, and they came to stand quietly behind the women and children, who had formed a circle around the warriors. The head priest cast a worried glance at the leader of the warriors, who frowned unconsciously as his count of the opposing forces grew to unsettling proportions.

"Speak," Balam Xoc commanded, pointing his claws at the head priest. "Tell us why you have come here bearing arms."

"The High Priest Ah Kin Cuy summons you," the man replied, drawing himself up authoritatively. "You stand accused of sorcery, and of bringing about the death of the birds."

"I am no caster of spells," Balam Xoc said disdainfully. "Caan Ac brought this upon himself, by his own evil intentions. You may take him these, as evidence that *we*, too, have been harmed by this mysterious sickness."

Balam Xoc rapped his staff upon the plastered flagstones underfoot, and Kanan Naab and Chibil brought forth a blanket-wrapped bundle. They opened it at the priest's feet, revealing the colorful, limp bodies of the dead birds within.

"Would a sorceror cast his spell upon his own household?" Balam Xoc demanded in a scornful voice. "That is how I answer this foolish accusation."

"You must come," the head priest insisted, and the warriors behind him tightened their ranks, those on the outside turning to face the surrounding crowd.

"Are you not a reliable messenger?" Balam Xoc inquired. "Or does Ah Kin Cuy want *me* more than my answer?"

"You must come quietly," the head priest repeated, his voice shrinking to a murmur. "Tell him, Pacal."

"They have orders to bring you by force if necessary, my lord," Pacal explained dutifully. "The ruler does not offer you a choice."

"I will come, then, if you insist upon it," Balam Xoc said to the priest, allowing the man a moment of false relief before going on. "But it will not be quiet. I will go in a manner that befits the Jaguar Protector, in the company of all my people."

"Our neighbors have also been notified," Kinich Kakmoo interjected, stepping forward so that all the warriors would see and recognize him. "They will come out to see us pass."

"So," Balam Xoc concluded. "The choice is yours. Do we go?"

The head priest swallowed and glanced around him indecisively, then drew Pacal and the leader of the warriors aside to confer. Having heard all of Caan Ac's public threats, Pacal knew that he was now about to hear the ruler's private instructions—the limits he had put on the enforcement of his summons.

"We cannot lead an armed mob into the center of the city," the priest complained in a low voice. "There is certain to be trouble."

"Once we were there, though, we would have reinforcements," the warrior suggested.

"Yes," Pacal agreed. "But many witnesses, as well."

"They would not dare to interfere."

"Interfere with *what*, my lord?" Pacal inquired mildly. "Do you think that you can separate him from Kinich Kakmoo without a fight?"

Both men glanced toward Kinich, who appeared as formidable as ever, wearing the macaw-feather headdress and plaited chest protector he had been given by Shield Jaguar. The priest shook his head in defeat.

"We cannot risk it," he decided. "There has already been one riot today."

"But who will protect *us,*" the warrior protested, "if we return empty-handed?"

"My orders were to do this quietly," the priest said stubbornly. "Even if force had to be used, we were not to attract undue attention to ourselves, or to *him.* That is clearly impossible, given the way he is dressed. The whole city would be wondering why the Night Sun Jaguar had been taken into custody."

Without waiting for their agreement, the priest turned back to address Balam Xoc.

"I will report your words to the high priest."

"See that you report them accurately," Balam Xoc warned. "I would not wish my compliance to be doubted."

The priest made a sour face, but he remembered to bow before turning to lead his men from the plaza. Pacal remained behind, waiting until Balam Xoc recognized him.

"The ruler has vowed to punish you for this, my lord. He is particularly drawn to the threat of fire."

"I have heard you," Balam Xoc acknowledged in a formal tone, betraying no familiarity with the man in front of him. Yet as Pacal straightened up from his bow, the Jaguar Protector raised his staff and waved it over him in blessing. The people watching murmured appreciatively, understanding the specialness of the gesture, and the gratitude it implied. Pacal turned and walked through the path they made for him, feeling the heat in his cheeks and the sudden constriction of his throat. He felt a surge of pride that seemed absurd to him, since he had done little more than pass along the ruler's threats. But he did not try to deny the feeling, and he let it give him strength as he headed back toward the palace, and the angry man who awaited him there. Somehow, it made him feel less like that man's hostage, less like a man who had no value to his people and his city . . .

Chetumal

CHAN MAC had been the first to arrive at the conclusion that they needed to go farther from Tikal—out of the range of the city's recent misfortunes—if they were to find a healthy market and reliable trading partners for the clan. He and Akbal had made some worthwhile contacts in Nakum and Holmul, but only for the trade of foodstuffs, since both cities had suffered along with Tikal from last season's drought. So Chan Mac had spoken to the Clan Steward Chac Mut, and after convincing him, he had managed to persuade Balam Xoc and the clan council to send him and Akbal and several porters on an exploratory journey to the northern cities of Nohmul and Chetumal.

In the latter city, especially, his notion had been proven more correct than even he had imagined. The people of Chetumal seemed almost unaware of the troubles inland, and certainly untouched by their deleterious effects. They lived with their faces turned toward the Great Waters, and their backs toward the interior, the Peten, as they called it. They had their cacao groves and their fleet of fishing boats, and they carried on a flourishing trade over enormous distances, all by means of canoe. The range of goods in the Chetumal market-place was astounding to the men from Tikal, as was the diversity of the people who came here to trade. Akbal and Chan Mac had been left speechless one day when they came upon a group of the hated Macaws, trading peaceably with all the other merchants.

When they finally completed their last bartering session, on the afternoon of their tenth day in Chetumal, Akbal let out a sigh that conveyed his relief as well as his satisfaction. He was pleased with what they had accomplished, but he was also anxious to begin the four-day journey home. He had been away from Tikal, and Zac Kuk, for almost a month, and he wanted to return in time for the birth of his child. He wondered, as well, about the well-being of the clan, and the state of the truce with the ruler, which had allowed them the freedom to leave Tikal in the first place.

Chan Mac, however, displayed no similar eagerness to return to his newly adopted home, and as they came out of the meeting, he prevailed upon Akbal and Kal Cuc to accompany him to the shore of the Great Waters. Akbal protested wearily but then complied, a good deal more reluctantly than his young assistant, who had fallen under the spell of Chan Mac's enthusiasm. The beach next to the long piers was deserted except for gulls and sandpipers, and the highprowed fishing boats had been dragged up past the tide line, the heavy hempen nets hung up on wooden racks to dry. The setting sun was at their backs, casting long shadows toward the clear, salty water, which rolled in in white, foaming waves, depositing piles of kelp and driftwood on the sand.

He cannot get enough of this, Akbal mused, watching Chan Mac splashing barefoot with Kal Cuc at the water's edge. His friend had twice Kal Cuc's years, but he seemed much more the child, at least around water. None of them had ever seen the Great Waters before this trip, but while Akbal and Kal Cuc had been intimidated at first by the vast, restless expanse of blue-green water, Chan Mac had taken to it without hesitation. He had managed to coax the two of them out of their reluctance to submerge themselves completely, and had even begun to teach Kal Cuc to swim in the past few days. Akbal had yet to comprehend how someone as heavy as Chan Mac could float so lightly upon the surface of the water, when he himself sank immediately, like a stone.

But he was glad to see his friend in such an ebullient mood. Chan Mac had seemed rather somber and pessimistic since his return from Ektun, as if he could not forget the troubles he had left behind there. Even his adoption into the clan had not raised his spirits significantly. But he had begun to improve at about the same time as he had conceived of making this trip, and he had only gotten better the farther they proceeded from Tikal. Coupled with his diplomatic skills, his reawakened enthusiasm made him practically irresistible in the bargaining, and he had guided Akbal through all the necessary social occasions with his usual grace and tact. Akbal could not have asked for a better traveling companion. He was bothered, though, by how this change had come about: by the thought that Chan Mac had to *leave* Tikal in order to be himself again.

The light was almost gone before Akbal was able to coax Chan Mac and Kal Cuc away from the beach, and when they returned to the house of their hosts—a family distantly related to the Jaguar Paw Clan—they found that a feast had been prepared in honor of their imminent departure. This, too, was largely Chan Mac's doing, since his enthusiasm for the food of Chetumal had become legendary in a very short time, as had his custom of showering compliments upon those who fed him. Indeed, the most promising trading partner they had found here was a cacao merchant whom Chan Mac had bested in an oyster-eating contest. The man had not minded losing, though, since the story had spread that there had been enough shells left at the end to pave the streets of the city, a tale the merchant regarded as a delightful testament to his prosperity.

Tonight their hosts had provided them with fresh swordfish steaks, and spiny lobsters whose pink shells had been cracked with rocks. Between mouthfuls of food and sips of the rich, frothy cacao for which this region was justly famous, Chan Mac regaled the company with stories of the great cities he had visited in the past. Akbal had heard most of these before, so he only listened with half an ear, wondering at the peculiar gusto with which Chan Mac expounded upon his travels. That was another tendency that had grown with their distance from Tikal: a desire to reminisce about the life he had led before coming to Tikal. Akbal began to worry that his friend might find their return an altogether disappointing prospect, and might seek to delay it.

Yet when they were alone in their quarters, with Kal Cuc asleep in the next room, Chan Mac's cheerfulness did not diminish, and he showed no reluctance to take up the task of packing his belongings. He hummed softly to himself as he carefully wrapped the necklace of tiny fluted shells he had purchased for his wife, Kutz.

"You are fond of this city," Akbal ventured. "You have enjoyed your time here."

"Immensely," Chan Mac agreed without looking up. "This is where we must come if we are forced to leave Tikal."

Akbal put down the pots he was holding and stared at Chan Mac, waiting until his friend met his eyes.

"You feel it is necessary to prepare for such an eventuality?"

"It was you, was it not, who told me to be prepared for *anything*," Chan Mac reminded him. "But yes, it is both necessary and prudent. I have already abandoned one city, and gone to another that is no more stable. I am comforted by the knowledge that I could find still another life for myself elsewhere."

"That is a strange sort of comfort."

"What comfort does Balam Xoc offer?" Chan Mac asked pointedly. "He is certainly inspiring, but he is also relentless in his determination. He does not reckon the consequences by the same standards as the rest of us. Do not misunderstand me, Akbal. I was drawn to your grandfather *precisely* because of the inspiration he offered. And I will aid him in his struggle in whatever way I can. But even if he wins, I no longer have any faith that the cities of the Peten can survive. It is too late to change the nature of men like Caan Ac and Shield Jaguar. *You* should know this as well as anyone."

"I do," Akbal admitted with a grimace. "Yet it is hard to think of finding another life elsewhere, when I have lived in my own house for only a year, and have yet to see the face of my first child."

"I felt the same," Chan Mac assured him, "and not so many years ago. But consider how greatly our own lives have changed, just in the short time we have known each other. We can no longer allow ourselves the expectations that governed the lives of our fathers. We *dare* not. From the way you spoke in Ektun, my friend, I thought that you understood this better than I did myself."

"It seemed clearer to me there. I felt a great urgency to get on with my work for the clan. That was *my* purpose in coming here."

"That was my *excuse,*" Chan Mac confessed with a smile. "I needed to know that there was a world outside the one we have created for ourselves. It is here, Akbal. You have seen for yourself how little these people are influenced by the fate of our cities. I can return now to Tikal and not feel that I am trapped there forever. That is another form of independence, perhaps no less valuable than the one your grandfather desires."

"I cannot begrudge you that," Akbal allowed. "Perhaps, as you say, it is only prudent. But you would resist being driven here against your will, would you not?"

"Of course," Chan Mac said easily, and turned back to his packing. "I am a Jaguar Paw now, wherever it may take me . . ."

Tikal

FOR THE SECOND morning in a row, Kanan Naab woke with the memory of having been disturbed in the night by a violent rainstorm. It did not seem like the memory of a dream, but like an actual occurrence, a downpour so loud and heavy that it had brought her out of her sleep with a start. Yet the ground outside her father's house was dry, and no one she asked—including Hok, who *never* slept deeply—had heard anything like what she described. Those who knew of the task Balam Xoc had given her were particularly emphatic in their denials, inviting her to regard these experiences as signs.

Kanan Naab was quite willing to do so, since these were the *only* signs that had come to her in her days of seeking. They did not go far toward resolving her problem, though, and the time allotted to her by Balam Xoc was nearly completed. What would it mean if the rains were to fall so heavily? She had no other clues to help her determine the *result* of such an occurrence, which was really what Balam Xoc had asked her to ascertain. Her contribution to the knowledge he sought would be almost too meager to mention, especially in front of Opna and Nohoch Ich.

Seeking inspiration, she went to visit Akbal's stone, as she had many times in the past days. The stone stood with its shelter half-collapsed around it, the thatch of its roof badly damaged by the heavy rains that had already fallen. The stone's sanded yellow surface had been stained by water leakage and bird droppings, and a big-eyed mouse peeped down out of the thatch when Kanan Naab stepped in under the roof. *Neglect,* she thought, accusing Akbal and Kal Cuc in her mind. The idea seemed familiar to her, and she realized that it, too, had been lingering in her thoughts lately, a notion as vague and indeterminate as the signs of a heavy rainfall. What was *she* neglecting? Or was it the neglect of others that should concern her?

She reminded herself to chide Akbal about the stone when he returned from Chetumal, but then left the shelter, feeling that its aura of abandonment was not affecting her positively. She already felt abandoned by Yaxal, who had not been to visit her since the ruler reimposed his ban on contact with the clan. Kanan Naab knew that the main trails were being watched again, and that some of their nearest neighbors had been intimidated by roving bands of the ruler's warriors. Yet she still believed that Yaxal could have found a way through, and would have, if she had only been able to alert him to her dilemma. Kal Cuc, however, was also in Chetumal, and there was no one else she could trust to convey such a message safely.

When she reached the doorway of Akbal's old room, she stopped as she always did and stared in at the stacks of drawings, and the dark stain on the floor. She had spent time here, as well, trying to inspire herself. But she could not bring herself to perform the kind of bloodletting that had provided her with her last and only vision. She had acted out of desperation then, without ambivalence or self-consciousness. It was very different now. Balam Xoc had charged the three of them—Opna, Nohoch Ich, and herself—with the task of foreseeing the outcome of this season's planting, though he had not said why he needed this knowledge, or why he did not seek it on his own. It was clearly a test of their individual powers, or so she had been made to believe by the reactions of her uncle and her rival. Nohoch had immediately undertaken a strenuous fast, secluding himself in the clan shrine, where Kanan Naab was not permitted to go. Opna had built a small hut with his own hands, with a spirit hole in its peaked roof, and Kinich had told her that the former priest was using the sacred mushrooms to summon a vision from the Spirit World. Neither man had shown the slightest interest in collaborating with her or with each other, even though Balam Xoc had not specified how they were to obtain this knowledge.

Neglect, she thought again, reflecting on the opportunity that had been lost. She sighed and turned away from the doorway, feeling suddenly weary. She would not shed her blood simply to prove her own power. It seemed selfish and wrong, and above all unnecessary. If this was truly a test, she preferred failure to an act that might offend the spirits of the ancestors, and cause them to turn away from her. She was convinced beyond all doubt that she would not have survived her last bloodletting if the spirits had not guided and sustained her. And she had had no misgivings then, no confusion that might make her vulnerable.

Weighed down by her present confusion, she decided to try to sleep for a while, and perhaps dream a solution. Her lethargy left her abruptly, though, when she entered the front room of the house and found that her father was present. He was sitting on the floor and playing a game with little Bolon Oc, repeatedly tossing a ball of yarn to different corners of the room so that the two-year-old could toddle after it. Ixchel was sitting cross-legged on the bench against the back wall, embroidering a skirt.

In the moment before she was noticed, Kanan Naab was struck first by the amount of grey in her father's hair and the new lines in his face. Yet there was a lightheartedness in the way he played with his son that contradicted her first impression, and made him seem younger than she had ever known him to be. Kanan Naab experienced a brief pang of envy, unable to remember her father ever playing with her with such open pleasure.

"Greetings, my daughter," Pacal said warmly, gesturing for her to sit next to him. "Come see how well your little brother uses his legs."

Kanan Naab gave Bolon Oc a friendly poke in his round little belly, and the boy giggled happily, swatting ineffectually at her finger. Then he waved his arms at his father, prancing in place until Pacal threw the ball of yarn down to the other end of the room.

"I am told that you are one of those to whom Balam Xoc has given a task," Pacal said when the boy had gone off. "That is a great honor."

Kanan Naab lowered her eyes modestly, unaccustomed to being praised by him. When she looked back up at him, though, she had composed her face, and she spoke with an air of decision.

"I have come for your help, Father."

"*Mine?*" Pacal said in surprise, arching his neck to examine her more closely. "I know little of signs or visions."

"You know everything about the crops, however. I should have thought to ask you before this."

"Ask me *what?*" Pacal inquired curiously, tossing the ball of yarn again as soon as Bolon Oc returned it to him. Kanan Naab had to think for a moment, searching for the best way to phrase her question.

"If the rains were to come heavily, *very* heavily, what would be the effect upon the crops?"

Pacal's eyes widened briefly, then narrowed again in thought. He rubbed his chin and stared off into the distance, as if sending his vision through the surrounding walls and out into the fields and gardens of the city. He did not even notice Bolon Oc's return, so Kanan Naab took over the game and sent her half brother scrambling off into the far corner of the room.

"Depending on the duration of these rains," Pacal said finally, "and their nearness to the harvest, they could be as devastating as last season's drought."

"Why is that?"

Pacal spread his hands helplessly, as if the reasons should have been obvious. But then he remembered to whom he was speaking, and took a moment of his own to frame an explanation.

"Heavy rains can damage the crops, for one thing, and leave them vulnerable to insects. We are already having trouble with maize borers and locusts, I am told, and the leaf-cutter ants were a serious problem last season. But that is nothing compared with the damage that might be done to the fields themselves. That would be much harder to repair, and would affect future crops. We would be made to pay dearly for our past neglect."

"*Neglect?*" Kanan Naab blurted, with such emphatic interest that her father paused to look at her. Both of them were too intent on their conversation to play with Bolon Oc, who frowned at them fiercely and took his ball to his mother.

"You heard me correctly," Pacal continued. "For several seasons now, before I became the chief steward of crops, we have not maintained the fields as we should. We have never had enough men for all the work that would be required, and that is especially true now, as it was last season. The raised fields in the alkalches would probably be most vulnerable to a heavy rainfall, since their banks are already eroding, and the canals between them have not been properly dredged in two seasons. They would simply sink back into the alkalche if the water became deep enough." Pacal took a deep breath, obviously disturbed by his own imaginings. "The maize fields might fare no better, even if they are not flooded completely. The drainage ditches are barely adequate under normal circumstances, and the soil would wash away into the alkalches. That is what I mean when I say that the damage would be hard to repair."

"I see," Kanan Naab said gravely. "Would our gardens be affected in the same way?"

Pacal pursed his lips and gave a judicious shrug.

"Probably not, if the right precautions were taken," he suggested, then stopped and squinted at her searchingly. "Have you *seen* that this will occur, my daughter?"

"Only the first signs," Kanan Naab confessed. "But you have helped me interpret them. I am grateful to you, Father."

"If there is any chance that this will occur," Pacal said sternly, waving off her gratitude, "Chac Mut must be informed immediately. He will know the precautions to take."

"First I will have to tell Grandfather, and hear what Opna and Nohoch Ich have learned."

"Ah, yes," Pacal murmured knowingly. "The other possible successors. You are aware that that is how the people are speaking of the three of you?"

"They did not hear that from Grandfather, I can assure you. Or from me."

"Perhaps from Opna, then," Pacal suggested shrewdly. "It is clear that he desires the position. What of your own desires, my daughter? Do you wish to assume your Grandfather's place when he is gone?"

"It would be presumptuous of me," Kanan Naab said evasively. "There has never been a Living Ancestor who was a woman. And Grandfather is stronger than any of us. He has no need to think of a successor."

"No? He is nearly seventy, and one attempt on his life has already been made. But I do not wish to wring an answer from you," Pacal added gently. "I am here if you wish to confide in me, or ask my advice."

Kanan Naab swallowed thickly and could not find the words to respond. She glanced over at Ixchel, who was smiling serenely, proud of them both. Beside her, on the wall, was the portrait of the Lady Ik Caan that Akbal had painted so many years before, after their mother had been taken from them. She, too, seemed to approve, or so it appeared to Kanan Naab's dampening eyes.

"I will come again," she promised in a breaking voice, and then smiled through her tears, feeling a strong surge of confidence, a sense that perhaps, at long last, she had become worthy of the resemblance she bore to the woman on the wall, the mother who had left her to find her own way in the world.

IT WAS NOT until they stopped for the night in Nakum that Akbal and Chan Mac heard about the death of the birds, and learned that the ruler had reinstituted his sanctions upon the Jaguar Paw Clan. The people who told them this did so with a certain air of congratulation, taking a vicarious satisfaction in Balam Xoc's defiance. Somehow *this* prophecy, which Balam Xoc had kept to himself for almost a year, had gained him greater notoriety than his prediction of last season's drought. Perhaps it was the fact that the drought had affected everyone within a wide area, whereas the mysterious disease that was killing the birds appeared to be localized around the center of Tikal, and had not spread as far as Nakum, which was only a half-day's walk to the east. It seemed a direct, personal blow to Caan Ac's prestige, and there were few in Nakum who did not take satisfaction in that. Theirs was a hungry city, too, and they had never forgiven Caan Ac for the bonuses he had promised but never paid last season.

Akbal and Chan Mac were troubled by the news, though, and stayed up late into the night discussing the various ways they might enter the city safely. Kal Cuc volunteered to go ahead alone and bring back Kinich and some warriors to escort them in, but both of the older men thought that it would be safer to stay together and let their numbers protect them. There were the three of them plus six porters, and most of them had been given some training by Kinich. Akbal purchased stout wooden staves for all of them, and it was decided to go in late in the day, by means of one of the little-used trails. It seemed unlikely that very many people would have been assigned to watch such an unimportant thoroughfare, and the chances were good that they could outrun anyone who tried to oppose them.

The plan seemed a sound one, and they timed their entrance almost perfectly, not coming close to any major dwellings until the sun was nearly below the horizon. Akbal forced himself to maintain a normal pace, and did not think they had attracted the attention of any of those they passed. Then he happened to glance back as the trail crossed a shallow alkalche, and saw warriors step out behind them. Before he could even consider the chances of trying to outrun them, another contingent came out of the trees ahead and blocked their path forward. They were trapped, loaded down with goods and outnumbered, with a waist-high swamp on both sides to prevent flight. Akbal and Chan Mac slipped off their packs and went forward to meet the captain of the warriors, carrying their staves in their hands.

"You are Jaguar Paw," the captain said in a flat voice, pointing his flint-tipped spear at Akbal's chest.

"Yes," Akbal replied, wondering who it was that had betrayed them. "What do you want with us?"

"You are forbidden to trade in Tikal. Where have you obtained the goods you carry?"

Akbal knew better than to answer, despite the spear, which was now aimed at his throat. The captain bared his filed teeth.

"It does not matter. They will go no further. Tell your men to put down their packs, and then you may pass."

"These are *our* goods," Akbal said stubbornly. "You have no right to take them from us."

"Do not try my patience," the captain said contemptuously. "Heretics have no rights. Be grateful that I do not take your lives, as well."

Akbal nodded silently and backed away from the spear before turning back to his men. Tight-lipped, he told them to put down their packs and bundles, and not to try to conceal anything on their persons.

"Thieves," he muttered audibly, glancing at the warriors, who stayed at a distance, leaning on their spears and laughing among themselves.

"Do not provoke them, my friend," Chan Mac warned. "Perhaps they will let us pass, after all."

"No," Akbal disagreed. "Look. Some of them have already loosened their clubs. They intend to beat us after they rob us."

"They are too many to fight, even if we had weapons to match theirs."

Akbal looked down at the bundles stacked up around him: the sacks of salt and cacao and dried fish, the carefully wrapped cores of obsidian and the jade and shell jewelry. Six months of hard work was represented here, along with the gifts they had been given by their new trading partners. It made him furious to think that all this would now go to enrich the very warriors who were about to beat him and his men. Lifting up one of the sacks of cacao, he looked around at Chan Mac and the others.

"Let them choose between us and our goods, then," he said angrily. "Fend for yourselves, my friends, and do not look back once you are past them."

Suddenly raising the sack over his head, Akbal pivoted on his heels and threw it as far as he could into the alkalche, where it landed with a great splash. Wide-eyed with fear, the others hastily followed his example, tossing their bags and bundles into the swamp as quickly as they could bring them to hand. The warriors let out a cry and started toward them, but then pulled up short, distracted by the sight of valuable goods bobbing and sinking in the murky green water. Akbal saw the captain start toward him again, swinging a notched wooden war club, but then the men behind him broke ranks and began to plunge into the alkalche. Grabbing a bag of salt with his free hand, Akbal hefted his staff and shouted to his comrades.

"Now! Do not let them stop you!"

Swinging the bag in a circle over his head, Akbal let it fly before the captain could get within striking range with his club. The warrior easily raised his shield in time to deflect it, but the bag burst on contact, throwing a hail of white salt into the man's eyes. Momentarily blinded, he could not duck the blows that Akbal and Chan Mac landed with their staves, knocking him down as they charged past.

Then they were confronted by the handful of warriors who had not forsaken the captain, and who appeared to be out to inflict real damage with their war clubs. Akbal struck out wildly with his staff, keeping them momentarily at bay, and suddenly Chan Mac bolted past him, ducking beneath a club and throwing his whole weight at the legs of the foremost warriors, taking three of them down in a heap. The porters poured in from behind, running right over the fallen men to collide with the other warriors in a confusion of flailing bodies. Akbal lost his staff and was struck a glancing blow on the cheek, spinning him sideways, right into the path of another warrior's club. He threw up his arm in self-defense, and heard the bone crack a bare instant before the pain engulfed him from shoulder to wrist. He let out a soundless scream and clutched the broken limb to his body, writhing helplessly against the pain.

The warrior cried out exultantly and raised his club to strike again, then abruptly doubled over when Kal Cuc lunged forward and hit him in the groin with a powerful thrust of his staff. Freeing a hand, the boy grabbed Akbal by the apron of his loincloth and pulled him into a lurching run. There was open space ahead of them, and Akbal let himself be pulled toward it, blind to everything except the enormous crushing pain in his arm. The ground blurred beneath his churning legs as he staggered from side to side, barely able to maintain his balance with his arms tucked against his ribs.

They ran until Akbal thought he was going to faint, and the sudden cessation of movement when they stopped made him dizzy and sick to his stomach. Gasping and choking, he vomited onto the grass beside the trail while Kal Cuc and Chan Mac held him gingerly around the waist. They did not permit him to pause for long, however, and soon he was stumbling along in their midst, his arm throbbing like a drum with every step.

"Are they coming after us?" he murmured to Chan Mac, whose round face was bruised and bloodied, one eye completely swollen shut.

"I do not think so. But we must not linger. One of the porters is missing. We will have to send Kinich back to rescue him."

"Of course," Akbal whispered, clenching his teeth against the pain. One of the porters had passed out and was being dragged along the trail by his comrades, who were all in need of care themselves. Kal Cuc was the only one who still had his staff, but he was limping badly and holding the side of his head with his other hand. Akbal hurt too much to feel any relief at their escape, or any regret over the goods they had lost. He simply wanted to stop somewhere and let unconsciousness put an end to his pain. He only half-heard what Chan Mac was saying.

"Welcome home, my friend. I hope that it is easier to leave, when the time comes, than it has been to return . . ."

AS THE OLDEST, Nohoch Ich was the first to report on what he had learned during his days of seclusion. He appeared to be thoroughly exhausted by his ordeal, his eyes hollow in their sockets, his voice hoarse and quavering.

"I saw a great amount of water," he said slowly, "falling from the sky, running over the earth, forming deep pools. And I saw a man drowning in one of these pools. That is all that was shown to me, however, and I cannot claim to understand its meaning."

He sounded disappointed in himself, though not—as Kanan Naab had previously supposed—on his own behalf. He had obviously taken Balam Xoc's request for information as a sacred responsibility, to be pursued with the same selfless dedication he had once applied to his priestly duties. Balam Xoc merely nodded and gestured to Opna.

"I also saw an abundance of water," Opna said, almost nonchalantly, as if it were a minor observation. His eyes had a dreamy cast, broken by occasional flashes of glittering alertness. "I saw a land that was green and fecund, with many frogs and lizards, and many snakes to eat them." He paused to lend his next words additional significance. "There is danger from a serpent, Grandfather, or perhaps from a *man* who carries a serpent." He paused again, glancing sideways at Kanan Naab. "Perhaps a man from the Serpent Clan."

"And the outcome of the crop?" Balam Xoc demanded curtly, ignoring the insinuation.

"It will be a good one," Opna predicted confidently. Balam Xoc examined him for a moment before turning to his left, where Kanan Naab was sitting. She stared straight back at him, deliberately shutting the other two men out of the range of her vision. Briefly, she agreed that the rains would be heavier than usual, perhaps extremely heavy. Then she proceeded to repeat, in detail, all the possibilities her father had pointed out to her, making clear that they *were* only possibilities, and not something she had seen.

"Still, I believe that our crops will prosper from the wetness," she concluded. "And that the ruler will be made to pay for the neglect of the past."

"How did you learn this?" Balam Xoc inquired.

"I learned of the rains in what must have been dreams, and a sense of neglect came over me when I was visiting Akbal's stone. The rest was told to me by my father."

Opna grunted disparagingly, drawing a swift, fierce glance from Balam Xoc.

"And you, Opna?"

"The mushrooms, Grandfather," Opna said with sudden humility.

"Nohoch?"

"I fasted and dreamed, my lord, in the clan shrine."

"So," Balam Xoc said gruffly. "There is consensus only about the rains. Unless you feel, Nohoch, that your dream of the drowning man places you in agreement with Kanan Naab?"

Nohoch thought for a moment, then grimaced and spread his hands in a gesture of indecision.

"It was a most disquieting dream, but I cannot speculate on its relation to the success or failure of the crops. What she has learned from Pacal, however, is worthy of consideration."

"My father also said," Kanan Naab added boldly, encouraged by her uncle's support, "that Chac Mut would know the precautions to take in order to protect our crops against rain damage."

"You may tell him to do so without delay," Balam Xoc told her. "After we are finished here."

He paused and looked at each of them in turn, then suddenly straightened up and looked over their heads, out the open doorway. Kanan Naab realized for the first time that darkness had fallen, though she was not certain that this was what had attracted Balam Xoc's attention. It was quiet outside, without voices or commotion to disturb the steady trilling of the insects. After another moment, Balam Xoc went on, though in a different tone. Kanan Naab felt the tension in the room slacken, and understood that her grandfather's "test" had proven inconclusive.

"As you know," he was saying, "the clan books were brought back here from the clan house during the time of peace. That has proven to be a fortunate precaution. It is my wish that the three of you devote your mornings and evenings to studying them, and learning the full history of our people. You are free to consult with one another, or with me, or with anyone else who might add to your understanding. When you have mastered the history as our ancestors painted it for us, I will—"

But Balam Xoc was never allowed to finish his statement, because excited voices rose up outside to interrupt him. A torch threw light into the room, and Hok suddenly appeared in the doorway, gesturing frantically.

"It is Akbal and his party—they have been attacked!"

Balam Xoc rose without a word and led them from the room, following Hok and his torch across the upper plaza and down the stairs to the plaza below. A crowd had gathered in front of Akbal's house, but they parted at Hok's breathless commands and made a path for the Living Ancestor. The wounded men lay or sat in a circle of torchlight upon the platform in front of the house, being tended to by Chibil and the women she had recruited as her assistants. Chibil herself was kneeling next to the prostrate body of Akbal, who seemed to groan with every breath. Zac Kuk stood weeping nearby, being restrained from going to her husband by Ixchel and May. Kanan Naab went first to Zac Kuk, briefly clasping her hands to calm her. Then she knelt on the other side of her brother and looked across his pain-contorted body at Chibil.

"His arm is broken," the older woman explained succinctly. "I have sent for wood to make a splint."

"The ruler's warriors?" Balam Xoc asked of Chan Mac, who was holding his youngest child in his arms while Kutz dabbed at the cuts on his face with a wet cloth.

"They were waiting for us where the path crossed the alkalche. Kinich has gone back for the porter who did not escape with the rest of us."

"And your goods?"

"We threw them into the alkalche," Chan Mac said wearily. "Most of the warriors left us to go after them."

A man appeared at Chibil's side with a handful of wooden slats and a flint knife, and he proceeded to saw the slats to the proper length at the healer's direction. Then Chibil looked across at Kanan Naab.

"I must find the break. It will hurt him greatly."

Kanan Naab wrapped Akbal's long, slender hand in both of her own and bent over his face.

"I am with you, my brother," she whispered. "You must be brave and hold yourself still, so that we can heal you."

Akbal's eyes fluttered open, and he gulped for air. A trickle of blood was running from the swollen bruise on his cheek, and he winced when he tried to move his jaw. But he was finally able to focus upon Kanan Naab's face, and his battered features seemed to relax as his gaze steadied upon her.

"Your hands are very warm," he murmured, and Kanan Naab gently tightened her grip.

"Let me take your pain," she said, nodding to Chibil before bowing her head over Akbal's hand. "Let the healing power come to you . . ."

He jerked once when Chibil lifted his arm, then once more when her probing fingers found the break. But he did not cry out, and he was still conscious when Chibil had finished binding the splints to his arm. Kanan Naab realized this only after Chibil whispered to her and touched her on the arm, bringing her out of her trance. Her hands were damp with sweat, both hers and Akbal's, and for a moment she could not distinguish between his flesh and her own. Something very powerful had indeed flowed through her, blocking out all sensation and sound. Then she lifted her head and saw that no sounds were being made: Everyone was watching her in rapt silence, concentrating along with her. Akbal was staring up at her, as well, showing white around his pupils.

"I felt it, my sister," he said in a weak voice. "So strongly that I was distracted from my pain."

Kanan Naab nodded and released his hand, beckoning to Zac Kuk to come over. She sat back on her heels, feeling exhausted, as if she had in fact borne some of Akbal's pain. Zac Kuk touched her lightly on the shoulder before kneeling beside Akbal and leaning over him solicitously, whispering breathlessly in her relief.

Then a loud cry went up at the edge of the crowd, and Kanan Naab rose wearily to her feet, turning with the others to see Kinich and his warriors come around the corner of the craft house. The warriors in front carried extra shields and spears, the weapons of those who came after them, bearing a blanket-wrapped bundle upon a litter lashed together with vines. The grim set of the warriors' faces and the utter stillness of the body they carried left no doubt that the porter had not been rescued in time.

Several people rushed toward the litter, and a woman began to wail, keening high in the back of her throat. The bearers set their burden down in the center of the plaza and stepped back to allow the relatives to claim the body. Balam Xoc left the platform and walked slowly toward the litter, and Kanan Naab dutifully joined the group that followed him, blinking at the wild shadows cast by the flickering torches. Kinich met them halfway, holding a dripping leather pack in the hand not occupied with his spear. His broad face seemed very pale in the torchlight. He put the pack on the ground and gripped his spear with both hands, wheezing slightly through his nose.

"We found him in the alkalche," he reported, inclining his helmeted head in the direction of the dead porter. "The warriors had fled with their spoils. They beat him, then threw him into the alkalche to drown."

"He died by drowning?" Nohoch inquired sharply. "You are certain?"

Kinich glared at his uncle for a moment, as if Nohoch had accused him of some crime. Then he dropped his eyes and swallowed heavily.

"I know the signs. I have seen drowned men before."

Nohoch detached himself from the group and walked past Kinich, going to his knees among the mourners that surrounded the litter. Kinich stared after him curiously.

"He was not questioning your judgment, my son," Balam Xoc explained. "He recently dreamed of a drowning man."

"It is a dream I have had many times," Kinich murmured. Then he straightened his massive shoulders and forced himself to face Balam Xoc directly. "Still, I must accept the blame for this, Grandfather. I should have arranged beforehand to meet them upon their return. We knew that the ruler's promise of peace would not last."

Chan Mac had come up to join the group, holding a wet cloth over one eye, and he spoke up on Kinich's behalf.

"It was a trap, my lord. We were recognized in Nakum, and perhaps we spoke too freely. It must have been someone there who betrayed us."

"I have heard you both," Balam Xoc said, with a stern nod of recognition to each of them. "But there is only one man who is truly to blame for this. I must speak to Pacal. Is he here?"

Pacal's name was shouted out several times, and Kanan Naab saw her father rise up from the group kneeling around Akbal, and come forward at Balam Xoc's beckoning gesture. He must have just arrived from the palace, for Kanan Naab had not noticed his presence earlier.

"The war between the clans has claimed another victim," he observed quietly, after bowing to Balam Xoc. His face, as always, was polite but impassive.

"Can you take a message to the ruler?" Balam Xoc asked, and Pacal nodded compliantly.

"The warriors guarding the main trail know me, and will let me pass."

"Can you see that this message is delivered publicly?"

"That depends on the nature of the message," Pacal explained. "Do you wish me to protest this attack?"

"No," Balam Xoc said flatly. "I wish to warn the ruler that the rains will be very heavy for the remainder of this season. And I wish to alert the people of Tikal to the fact that I have given Caan Ac this warning, and have advised him to take the necessary precautions to protect the crops."

Kanan Naab drew a sharp breath, taken aback by this unexpected use of the information she had helped to gather. Opna also appeared perplexed, perhaps even angry. Pacal merely pursed his lips in thought, weighing the matter in his mind.

"Since Caan Ac does not have the means to respond to such a warning," he said at last, "I doubt that he will regard it as a gesture of generosity. He might well regard it as an attempt to humiliate him, and make others question his leadership." Pacal looked steadily at his father. "In that case, he would no doubt suppress both the message *and* the messenger."

"I wish my message to be heard by everyone," Balam Xoc insisted. "No matter what Caan Ac thinks of my motives."

"Perhaps, then, you should send your message directly to the chief steward of crops. *He* would certainly inform the ruler, and many others as well. He is not the kind of man who bears his responsibilities in silence."

"Go to him, then," Balam Xoc decided abruptly. "Tell him that I wish to share this knowledge with him for the good of the whole city. Tell him that the consequences will be his to bear if he chooses to ignore my warning."

"I have heard you," Pacal replied, and bowed again before turning to leave the plaza. Ambivalence surged up in Kanan Naab as she watched him depart, realizing that her hard-won insights, and those of Nohoch and Opna, were to be used as a provocation, a subtle act of revenge upon the ruler. Was that to be the final purpose of their "test," then? A deliberate and calculated insult to the man who had already attacked them without provocation?

"Why—?" she said aloud, stopping in mid-question when Balam Xoc whirled to face her.

"Yes?" he demanded, and Kanan Naab gestured vaguely toward the body on the litter.

"I do not understand, Grandfather. One man already lies here dead, and my brother and these other men have been disabled. Why must we goad the ruler into further acts of violence?"

"We are at war with him," Balam Xoc said curtly. "We must use the knowledge we possess; it is our only weapon. You will learn the reasons for this when you have studied the clan books as I instructed. In the meantime," he added, bending to lift the wet pack from the ground, "take this to Akbal. He will not be painting for a while, or traveling to other cities. Remind him of the stone he has neglected."

Wordlessly, Kanan Naab accepted the pack and stepped to one side as Balam Xoc went to join the mourners around the litter. Kinich said something to her, but she could not understand his words. She was remembering the night she had heard Balam Xoc speak to Akbal about his stone, the night he had commanded them both to remain independent of him. This reminder, in the light of Balam Xoc's other recent actions, could mean only one thing.

"He has seen his own death," she murmured, forcing herself to face the prospect squarely. Kinich stepped closer, startling her out of her reverie. She looked up at him blankly.

"I said," he repeated, "to tell Akbal that this pack was all we were able to recover. We will go back to the alkalche when it is light, though, and see what else might have been left."

"I will tell him," Kanan Naab promised, unconsciously hugging the wet bundle against her body. She was grateful that he had not heard *her* words, and she did not feel deceitful as she turned away from him without saying any more. This was not the kind of knowledge that would help him fight the war of which Balam Xoc had spoken. This was a knowledge that had to be borne in silence, with the fearful humility of a possible successor, of one who was not ready, or worthy. Clutching the pack to her, she walked blindly toward Akbal's house, hearing a roll of thunder in the distance announcing the rain to come.

Three months later, the month of Tzec

ALTHOUGH BOX EK had suffered no loss of hearing with age, there were times now when sound simply seemed to stop, and she felt that she was seeing everything from a great distance. She was always struck, on these occasions, by the enormous effort that people put into the act of living, especially into describing and explaining what they thought their lives were about. She would marvel at the continuous movement of their mouths and hands, stirring the air as proof of their being. She wondered if this was how the ancestors saw those who lived upon the earth, if this was the same, soundless gulf that separated Balam Xoc from those around him.

The rain was still coming down outside, and gradually the sound of its monotonous drumming on the thatched roof overhead began to penetrate her consciousness. Some of Zac Kuk's words came through to her, along with an isolated cry from the baby in the young woman's arms. Zac Kuk and Ixchel and May always brought their babies when it was their turn to visit; Haleu and the older women usually brought warm soup or some new herbal remedy supposed to ease the incessant pain in her bones and joints. All hoped to share their vitality with her somehow, as if it were indeed a warming drink that had only to be imbibed in order to prolong life. Only Kanan Naab came to her empty-handed, though it had required a concerted effort of persuasion before Box Ek had convinced the young woman to save her healing powers for others.

Now Zac Kuk's words were coming to her too clearly to be ignored, so she forced herself to listen, shifting her attention away from her pain. She was completely swathed in blankets and had a pottery brazier of live coals on the floor beside her, but she still felt cold, her bones so brittle and sensitive that the slightest movement seemed to threaten breakage. It helped to sit very still and not think about the aches that made her want to rearrange her limbs.

"What are you saying about your husband?" she interrupted, when she had grasped the thread of what Zac Kuk had been saying to her. "Is his arm not healing properly?"

Zac Kuk blinked hesitantly and shifted the baby in her arms, concealing her disappointment at the fact that Box Ek had not heard her. They must all think I am becoming deaf, the old woman thought wearily, lacking the strength to justify her inattention.

"Chibil removed the splint ten days ago," Zac Kuk said dutifully, obviously repeating herself. "She is quite pleased with how the bone has mended. But he has lost all the strength in his muscles, and she will not let him put any strain upon it. He can only paint for a short time before his fingers cramp up and his shoulder begins to hurt."

"He will regain his strength," Box Ek assured her. "And what is there that he needs to paint so urgently? Kanan Naab tells me that only our workmen are allowed to leave the Jaguar Paw House, and that they must be escorted out each day by her father."

"That is true," Zac Kuk admitted. "That was the ruler's punishment for Pacal's part in alerting the city to the danger of the rains. Akbal has lost hope of being able to honor the trade agreements he and my brother made in Nohmul and Chetumal. That makes him feel doubly frustrated, for even if he *could* paint, there would be no market for his work."

"He is helping Kanan Naab with her study of the clan books," the old woman pointed out. "And surely he must enjoy this little one."

"Yes," Zac Kuk said proudly, gazing down at the squirming bundle in her lap. "He was not disappointed at all when our firstborn was not a boy child."

"Little Nicte," Box Ek sighed fondly, risking the pain for a peek at the child's tiny face. "She is as pretty as the flower for which she is named. May she live a longer life than the woman who bore the name before her."

"Did you know Grandfather's wife, the Lady Nicte?"

"I came to know her," Box Ek mused. "I had already gone to Ektun before my brother married her, so I only saw her on those occasions when we visited one another's cities. But I came to know her about as well as it is possible to know one's sister-in-law. She was a good wife to Balam Xoc. I often wonder if he would be the man he is today if Nicte had lived to grow old with him."

"Akbal once told me," Zac Kuk observed cautiously, "that it was grief over the death of *his* mother, the Lady Ik Caan, that had made Balam Xoc decide to become the Living Ancestor."

"There was much death in this family," Box Ek agreed sadly, "at the beginning of Katun Eleven Ahau. There is sure to be one more before the katun comes to a close. Come, my daughter," she added more sharply, "there is no comfort for me in false denials of the truth. I did not expect to live long enough to hear the uos sing again. And even though I have lived, I was asleep when they appeared, and no one woke me to hear them. My hold on this world is not strong, Zac Kuk, and I would gladly relinquish it to put an end to my pain."

Zac Kuk lowered her eyes out of respect, gently smoothing the tuft of black hair on her daughter's head with her fingers. It took Box Ek a moment to recall how their conversation had come to this morbid conclusion.

"Many people are feeling frustrated," she ventured finally. "They feel imprisoned by the rain as much as by the ruler's warriors. Perhaps Akbal should be the one to communicate this to my brother."

Zac Kuk looked up at her with sudden gratitude.

"He has not been eating or sleeping well," she explained. "And he broods about his stone at night, instead of . . ."

She trailed off in embarrassment, but Box Ek veiled her eyes to indicate that she understood.

"Tell him to go to my brother. Remind him of what Balam Xoc told us at the reservoir, the day we went to him together. Did he not give us the responsibility for watching over the hearts of our people?"

"He did," Zac Kuk agreed emphatically.

"You must act for both of us, then, and let me rest. Go to your husband, my daughter. He needs your concern more than I. He has time left, and better things to feel than pain . . ."

WHEN THE RAINS finally stopped, and the clouds broke for the first time in three days, the men on the men's side of the craft house rose as one from their work and left the building, heading toward the reservoir. They all knew their tasks by now—scooping mud from the silt traps, restaking the maize and tomato plants, cutting fresh ground cover—and they went to them immediately whenever there was a moment's respite from the rains. The clan's crops were flourishing in the wetness, having in some cases already reached normal harvest size, though the earliest possible harvest date was still two months off. Thus, they required constant hand-tending to keep their spreading roots from being exposed by the rain and to prevent the top-heavy plants from falling over from their own weight before they reached full maturity.

The craft house was soon empty, except for Akbal, who sat alone at the head of the long room. He had been forbidden by Chibil from taking any part in the work on the clan gardens, even that of carrying water for the other workers. There was too much risk of falling in the mud, and the healer had sternly impressed upon him that he might never paint again if he broke the bone a second time. The torment of all the days when he had not been able to hold a brush at all was still too fresh in his mind to permit the taking of chances, despite his gnawing sense of uselessness. As it was, the brush felt clumsy and unfamiliar in his hand, and he was secretly worried that he might never regain all of his previous skill.

Brooding on this possibility very quickly made him restless, so that he pushed himself up with his good arm and went toward the nearest doorway. The sun had emerged powerfully from behind the clouds, and Akbal felt moisture cloak his body as he walked out into the warm, humid air. Steam rose from the deep puddles covering the plaza, which was empty of people. He glanced once toward his own house and then let his restlessness decide for him, splashing out across the plaza toward the stairs that led to the plaza above. He had put this off too long already, he realized, so that it had finally become easier to face Balam Xoc than to make up one more excuse for Zac Kuk.

Hok was standing on the platform in front of Cab Coh's house, holding a spear and shield in his hands, the vigilance of his attitude indicating that Balam Xoc was inside. The house had stood empty since the deaths of Cab Coh and his wife, Pek, until it was decided to store the clan books there when they were brought back from the clan house. Now it was the place where Kanan Naab and Nohoch Ich and Opna came to study in the mornings and evenings, and where Balam Xoc himself spent an increasing amount of his time. Hok raised his shield in a brief salute and waved Akbal inside, then turned back to survey the area for enemies.

The floor of the long front room was crowded with books. Some were stacked up neatly, section upon section, with their spotted cloth covers in place. Others were spread out flat on reed mats or standing upright on the edges of their wooden binders, displaying their brightly painted figures and columns of glyphs and numbers. Mingled with the smells of paint and lime paper was the musty aroma of breadnuts, which were stored in large pottery urns clustered at both ends of the room. All of the Jaguar Paw houses had this smell, since Chac Mut's first precaution against the rains had been to remove the breadnuts from the underground storage chambers—the chultunes—where they were ordinarily kept. The hard nuts inside had thus been saved from certain spoilage, but the constant dampness had spotted their orange outer rinds with a blue mold, which gave them their distinctive odor.

Balam Xoc was sitting cross-legged on the bench against the back wall, and Akbal picked his way through the maze of books without pausing to admire the brushwork on the open pages, much of which was his own. His grandfather motioned for him to sit in the small cleared space in front of the bench.

"So you have finally come to talk to me about your stone," the old man said with his customary directness. Akbal hung his head for a moment before nodding wearily.

"That and much else, Grandfather. My wife and the Lady Box Ek suggested that I come to you. They have seen that I have not been myself since . . . since I returned from Chetumal."

"How could you be? You are the Painter, yet you cannot paint. That is why I had Kanan Naab remind you of your stone."

"It has not helped," Akbal said plaintively. "It cannot make me forget all that has been lost."

"And what is that?" Balam Xoc inquired coldly. "Were you so close to the porter who died? Or so attached to your goods? You acted well under the circumstances, Akbal, and you should not grieve for the losses you could not prevent."

"I grieve for something more," Akbal said stubbornly, stung by his grandfather's scolding tone. "For the opportunities that will be lost, the agreements and alliances and friendships that will never be consummated now. And most of all I grieve for the dream that came to me in Ektun, and showed me how I might speak for the clan, and help to make us strong and independent. I felt that I had found my proper task, and the feeling was confirmed every time I presented one of the Dancing Jaguar plates to a new friend. Now it is as if I had thrown them into the alkalche instead."

"So it is grief for your lost dream," Balam Xoc observed without apparent sympathy, "that has kept you from your stone."

"No," Akbal disagreed flatly. "Nothing has kept me from the stone. I have thought about it constantly, and Kal Cuc has helped me repair the shelter and cleanse the stone. I have spent time with it, and with my drawings of the sculpture of Yaxchilan and Ektun, and with the books here. Yet nothing brings me any inspiration, and I would be afraid to trust any that did come to me. I cannot remember my dreams anymore, and I fear that they would mislead me if I could."

Balam Xoc stared down at him in silence, making Akbal feel the shame of his lost courage. Then he suddenly pointed toward the open doorway to his right.

"You will find a ceremonial plate covered with a red cloth in the next room. Bring it to me."

Startled out of his misery, Akbal did as he was told, easily locating the plate among a small collection of pots and bundles that had been assembled on a reed mat in the center of the room. He brought it back and set it gently on the floor between himself and the bench.

"That was painted in the time of my great-grandfather," Balam Xoc explained, gesturing at the plate, "in the seventh katun of this cycle. It will be buried with me, but you must see it first. Remove the cloth."

Akbal did so, immediately stiffening in surprise at the figure that greeted his eyes.

"It is the Dancing Jaguar," he exclaimed softly. "Yet he is wearing feathers!"

"Your dream was from an earlier time, before the foreigners had come into our midst. Do you doubt yourself now, my son?"

"No, not the dream," Akbal murmured helplessly. "But—"

"Our dreams may be thwarted by the actions of other men," Balam Xoc told him, "or by our own failure to carry them out with courage and conviction. But that is no reason to doubt the truth of what they show to us. That is how they are *truly* lost."

Nodding mutely, Akbal carefully draped the cloth back over the plate. Then he looked up at Balam Xoc.

"Do I have your permission, Grandfather, to paint a plate for you when my arm is fully healed? A dancer *without* feathers?"

"Of course. But the stone is much more important to me. It will remain for others to see after I am gone."

Akbal's eyes widened, and he cast an involuntary glance at the burial plate between them. Balam Xoc gestured curtly.

"That, and my other burial goods, are only here because they had been stored in the chultunes. But there is not much time left to me, Akbal. Perhaps no more than is left to Katun Eleven Ahau. I tell you this because you are one of those who must see that the dreams of the Jaguar Paw do not die with me. They must live on in the hearts of you and your children, and in the work of your hands."

Lowering his eyes, Akbal gently massaged the shrunken muscles of his right forearm. He heard Hok come into the room behind him and realized the amount of time that had passed.

"I have nothing more to ask you, then," he said to Balam Xoc. "I will put aside my grief, and try to find a new dream to guide me."

"All of our dreams are very old, my son. We make them new with our remembering, and our belief." He raised a hand in blessing. "Go now, and do not fear for what may be lost. Think only of how much more we must gain, to make our lives worthy of memory . . ."

IT WAS THE NEED to relieve himself of some of the balche he had drunk that originally drove Yaxal Can out into the rainy night. As he stood by the edge of the ravine, barely feeling the rain upon his burning skin, he realized that he was drunker than he had ever been, and that very soon, he was going to vomit. He did not recoil from the prospect, knowing that he had needed to purge himself as much as to obliterate his senses. Bending at the waist, he gripped his knees and gave himself up to the powerful surge of his stomach and throat, spewing out his accumulated anger and guilt along with an amber stream of balche.

He felt better when he was empty, though only slightly more clearheaded. He noticed that he could see fairly well despite the falling rain, and remembered that the moon was nearly full, somewhere behind the clouds. The houses of the Serpent Clan were silent and dark; he had been drinking alone, something he had seldom done except in the line of his priestly duties. Like the duty he had performed for Balam Xoc, so long ago . . .

Swaying drunkenly, he began to walk through the breadnut trees, away from the houses. He stopped several times to listen, hearing only the patter of rain on the leaves overhead and the hollow sound of his own breathing, which came more rapidly once he was able to admit to himself what his destination was. Could he possibly go that far in the dark and rain in his present state? The alkalches were overflowing, and even the best trails were treacherous; he thought of the empty gourds he had left behind in his room, and the shame that would fall upon his mother and sisters if he were to be found drowned in some swamp. A drunken priest, lost on his way to visit a clan of heretics.

Anger flared up behind his eyes, and he cursed himself for the weakness that had made him get so drunk before he would risk this journey. *Better to be drowned than to turn back now,* he told himself recklessly, and plunged ahead in the near darkness, taking the trail that he had used many times since the night Kal Cuc had shown it to him.

In many places, however, there was no longer any trail; only water. Murmuring prayers to the water serpents, Yaxal forced himself to go on, wading in up to his chest and tearing a path for himself through the tangle of reeds and water lilies. Many times he slipped in the mud underfoot and submerged himself completely, coming up spitting and gasping for breath, floundering desperately for balance. Once he startled a heron out of the reeds and almost fell over in fright when the bird let out a series of furious grunts before flying off. The journey seemed to take forever, without bringing him any closer to his goal, which began to seem increasingly foolish as the balche wore off and exhaustion set in.

Once he had reached some comparatively dry ground, and knew that he was close to the Jaguar Paw House, he sat down with his back against a tree to rest. He was still sitting when the Jaguar Paw sentry walked past him, carrying a spear and shield and stepping carefully in the mud. Somehow, he did not see Yaxal, though he passed within a few feet of him. Counting himself lucky, since he had completely forgotten about the sentries, Yaxal rose and went on without delay, moving down the center of the path so that he would not be mistaken for an assassin if he were seen.

He found his way to the back of Pacal's house without incident, though, and stood for a moment under the water streaming off the thatched roof, letting it wash the mud from his body. Then he took a deep breath and held it as he stepped up to the doorway of Kanan Naab's sleeping room and peered through the netting. The room seemed dark through the fine mesh, but it took only an instant for his eyes to adjust and find Kanan Naab. She was lying sprawled out on a pile of sleeping mats directly in front of the doorway, where she might feel any breeze that stirred the warm, humid air.

She was also naked, a fact that made Yaxal turn his head away after a single glance. He felt the heat rise in his dripping body, and blood stirred in his groin. Then he could not stop himself and looked again, staring at the smooth lines of her limbs, the dark circles of her nipples, the curve of her parted thighs. A soft groan escaped his lips, and he put a hand up to the netting, trembling in his desire to tear it away and fall upon her. In his whole life, he had never wanted anything so badly as he wanted her at this moment. He was almost able to convince himself that he deserved it, that it was his right after all he had gone through—and risked—to come here. They could not grow old without knowing each other, without joining their bodies in the rite that belonged to men and women. It was unthinkable, unholy.

Then Kanan Naab stirred and dropped the arm she had thrown over her face, her lips moving soundlessly. Yaxal exhaled slowly and withdrew his hand from the netting, though his eyes lingered on the form within for several more moments. He withdrew gradually, backing away step by step until he once more felt the rain upon his head and shoulders. When his desire had subsided and his loincloth again hung normally, he crouched to one side of the doorway and flicked the netting inward with his fingers. He repeated the motion several times, even after he heard a rustling of cloth within. Then the netting was pulled away from his hand, and Kanan Naab's face peered around the corner, recoiling slightly when she saw him looking back at her.

"I have come," he said simply, his voice a ragged whisper. Kanan Naab nodded, finally, and disappeared for a moment. She came out again clothed in a long shift, holding a blanket stretched over her head as she led him along the back of the house and around the corner to Akbal's old room. She spread the blanket on the floor just inside the doorway and gestured for him to sit next to her, glancing up in surprise when he stood for a moment in the rain, giving her a rueful, knowing smile. Then he joined her willingly, crossing his wet legs under him.

"Someone has been here before us," he observed, inclining his head toward the charcoal and rolls of leather that had been left on the floor inside, surrounded by drawings that had been opened and propped up against one another.

"My brother Akbal," Kanan Naab replied. "He has been making sketches for his stone."

"Ah, yes, the Serpent Stone. That is why I have come."

"Tell me," Kanan Naab said without hesitation, shifting her seat so that she faced him. Yaxal stared briefly at the rain, wiping water from his forehead.

"I must go back to the time when the birds first began to die, and the ruler reimposed his sanctions upon you. Perhaps you will understand why I have not been to see you since then." He waited for her nod before going on. "Soon after that, a representative of the High Priest Ah Kin Cuy came to the high priest of my clan and demanded to see the records of all our dealings with the Jaguar Paw Clan. The high priest, a man named Hapay Can, was naturally outraged by this intrusion into our affairs and flatly refused the request. But then he initiated an investigation of his own, and he found the record of the service I performed for your grandfather, the first time I came here."

"You have never told me what that was," Kanan Naab interrupted, and Yaxal again looked out at the rain.

"Surely you remember the serpent who guarded Akbal's stone, the yellow jaw he killed? Balam Xoc took the angry spirit of the serpent upon himself. At his request, I performed the rites of propitiation and buried the skin of the serpent."

A shudder passed through Kanan Naab's body, and her eyes flitted past Yaxal, following thoughts that clearly distressed her.

"Go on," she murmured finally, in a voice tight with dread.

"Hapay Can questioned me about this, and I answered him truthfully. It did not occur to me to conceal anything, since he had been my superior at the time of the act and since he seemed genuinely angry at the high priest's interest. I told him which rites I had performed, and where the burial had taken place."

Yaxal suddenly grimaced in disgust, his lips curling back from his teeth.

"It was a mistake to have trusted him. A terrible mistake. When I had told him everything, his manner suddenly changed completely. He became sly and insinuating, raising the issue of my 'unofficial' visits to the houses of the Jaguar Paw Clan. He has obviously known for some time that I was coming here, and as he made clear to me, he is well aware of how quickly I would be discharged from the Tun Count Priests if my superiors were informed. He insisted, of course, that he would never betray me. But he has since asked me for several 'loans' and 'favors' that were nothing more than bribes."

"Would he . . . can he betray the rites you performed for my grandfather?" Kanan Naab asked anxiously.

"Any ritual may be violated and made null," Yaxal averred. "Especially by a priest willing to violate his own vow of secrecy and trust. Once, I would have sworn that such a thing was not possible. But now . . . you do not know how bad it is in the rest of the city, Kanan Naab. Everyone is desperate. Even the lords are poor and hungry, grateful if they have breadnuts to eat. The common people are eating insects and grass. And the present crop promises little relief. Soon there will be no one who will not trade his honor to fill the mouths of his family."

"We have food to share with the Serpent Clan," Kanan Naab suggested impulsively. "We can repay this Hapay Can for his silence."

"I could not allow that," Yaxal said sternly. "Your grandfather paid me generously for my services, though I tried to refuse him. It is my responsibility to see that he is not endangered by his trust in me. I will silence Hapay Can myself if it becomes necessary."

"Yaxal! Remember that you have vows of your own," Kanan Naab admonished him. "No, we must rouse my grandfather, and tell him of this. Perhaps he already knows. Opna warned him that there was danger from a serpent, or a man who carried a serpent, as you once did. I did not wish to believe that he had actually seen this, but now . . ."

"Now," Yaxal groaned, beating on his chest with his fist. "Your brother Kinich suggested, months ago, that I join your clan. He told me how he had been betrayed by those he trusted. If I had only listened to him, Hapay Can would know nothing today."

To his surprise, Kanan Naab reached out and took his other hand, silencing him with a single squeeze of her fingers.

"Do not accuse yourself," she said quietly. "You could still join us. Balam Xoc will find some way to deal with Hapay Can."

Yaxal stared at the hand in his own, feeling its warmth.

"When I first saw you tonight, I wanted nothing more than to join you, to be with you always. But I can only harm you now. Opna will use our association to discredit you before the other members of the clan."

"It is Grandfather's opinion that matters, as long as he is alive. He would accept me as your sponsor."

"If the burial place of the serpent is disturbed, your grandfather's life would be in jeopardy. Could I possibly live among you if I were responsible for causing him injury, or death?"

"He does not flee from death," she said firmly, giving his hand another squeeze. "Come, let us go to him now. If you must go back, it is better that you do so before it is light."

Yaxal rose and helped her to her feet, holding tight to her hand.

"You understand that I do not wish to go back," he said in a thick voice. "I would prefer to stay, and speak to your father, as well."

Without ever taking her eyes from his face, Kanan Naab gently disengaged her hand from his grasp.

"I would ask him to hear you, Yaxal Can," she whispered. "I would not have you come so far, ever again."

"Let us go to Balam Xoc, then," Yaxal said succinctly, and stepped down out of the doorway, paying no attention to the rain. "Let us dare to hope, while we can, that there might still be a future for us . . ."

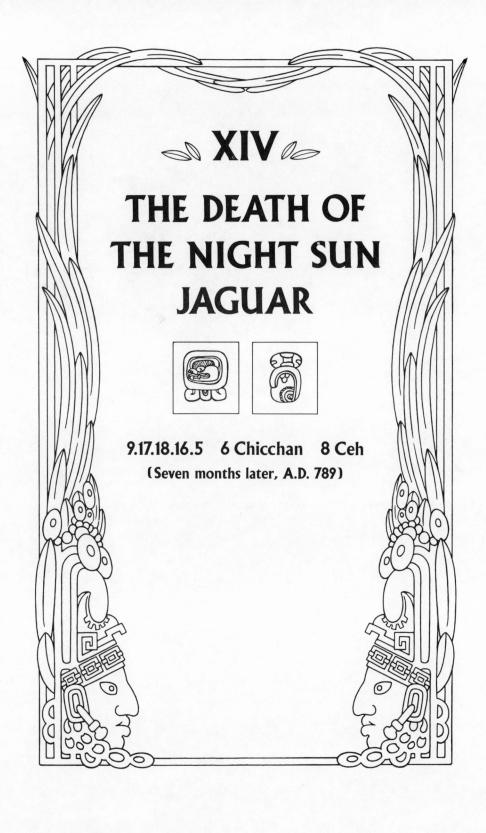

XIV

THE DEATH OF
THE NIGHT SUN
JAGUAR

9.17.18.16.5   6 Chicchan   8 Ceh
(Seven months later, A.D. 789)

FOR ALMOST eleven months, ever since he had carried Balam Xoc's message to the chief steward of crops, Pacal's only official duty had been to escort the Jaguar Paw workmen out into the city each morning and return for them at the end of the day. It was a pointless task, designed to humiliate him and make him feel his uselessness. Apparently, the ruler could conceive of no better punishment for his former steward, for Pacal had received not a single message or summons to the palace in all that time. He was a hostage who had been forgotten, and left to languish.

Then, with only a month and a half left before the Tun-End—when the work agreements would expire—the message came from the ruler. Pacal was authorized to begin negotiating new agreements with the elders of the Jaguar Paw Clan, though he was to be highly restricted in what he could offer on the ruler's behalf. Caan Ac offered only one thing in return for continued loan of the clan's workmen: his promise to allow the clan to celebrate the Tun-End Ceremony at their clan temple in the Plaza of Ancestors. Pacal was advised to make Balam Xoc consider this offer seriously, for there would be no other.

When he was certain he had heard everything the messenger knew, Pacal went to find his nephew Chac Mut, who was supervising the construction of some new houses near the clan's granaries. Chac Mut shook his head in disgust when he had heard the ruler's offer, but he agreed to accompany Pacal to Balam Xoc.

"This is an outrage," Chac Mut said angrily, as they walked back through the trees. "Caan Ac has no right to deny us access to our own temple."

"He has the power," Pacal pointed out. "The high priest would probably support him, even if there was bloodshed."

"The other clans would never stand for it. Especially not our friends, those we have fed when the ruler could not."

"Do not overestimate the courage of such 'friends,' " Pacal cautioned. "They may be grateful, but they are not strong. They will protect their own interests before they will defend ours."

"Are you going to recommend that we accept the ruler's terms, then?"

Though they had reached the lower plaza by this time, Pacal stopped and gestured back in the direction of the construction site.

"Surely, *you* have no shortage of workers. The failure of the ruler's crops, and your success, have brought us more pilgrims than we can house, much less put to work. Is it not worth a few men to insure a peaceful ceremony?"

Chac Mut simply stared at him.

"I will let Balam Xoc answer that," he said finally, and turned toward the stairs that led to the plaza above. They found Balam Xoc in Cab Coh's house, sitting with Hok and Nohoch Ich. When Pacal explained why they had come, Balam Xoc put aside the painted book he and Nohoch had been studying and gestured for the two men to sit. He listened carefully while Pacal made much the same argument he had given Chac Mut, explaining that the ruler needed workmen much too desperately to renege on his promise.

"It is an empty promise in any case," Balam Xoc interrupted curtly. "The Living Ancestor of the Jaguar Paw Clan does not require the ruler's permission to exercise the rites of the Night Sun Jaguar."

"That is true, of course. But—"

"That is *true,*" Balam Xoc interrupted again, making a slashing gesture with his hand for emphasis. "I will go to my confinement in the clan temple four days before the Tun-End, as I have always done. The clan nacom will be with me to see that my path is not obstructed."

Pacal swallowed silently.

"Caan Ac would like nothing more than to make an example of you, to divert attention from his own failures."

"I *wish* to be an example for him, and all of Tikal," Balam Xoc insisted. "Would he spill my blood, and that of my people, at a time that all consider sacred? Let that be my example, then, for it would surely be his downfall."

Pacal glanced around at the other men, hoping for some sign of sympathy, or at least reason. But they all stared back at him as Chac Mut had earlier, as adamant as Balam Xoc himself.

"I have allowed you to represent my wishes in whatever way you chose, Pacal," Balam Xoc continued. "I have not been concerned with what you have allowed Caan Ac to believe. But I will have no man think he can keep me from my sacred duties. Tell the ruler that I reject his unholy offer."

"He will come against you, then," Pacal said in a low voice.

"We will be alert. There have already been two fires, but we found them in time. He does not have the power to threaten us further. If he would have our workmen, let him negotiate in the usual way. We will accept our payment in advance, in the form of salt, fish, obsidian, and stone tools."

"That is an impossible demand," Pacal muttered, but Balam Xoc ignored him, gesturing toward Hok.

"I have spoken, and the clan witness and these other men have heard my words. See that you represent them accurately, Pacal. See that this man hears the truth from you. It is all you have to offer . . ."

THOUGH AKBAL had not actually dreamed any of it, the outlines of what he would carve on his stone had gradually taken a definite shape in his mind. As an upper border, there would be the traditional two-headed serpent, the symbol of the Sun at his rising and setting, as well as of the Serpent Stone itself. The curving body of the serpent would form an arch over the two figures that would face each other in the center of the slab, flanked on both sides by columns of glyphs. Akbal assumed that one of the figures would be Balam Xoc, but he was still not certain just how to portray his grandfather, and the identity of the other figure remained a complete mystery to him. He knew only that there should be two, and that they should confront each other, in the manner of the Yaxchilan monuments. The glyphs that would identify them were thus equally unknown, as were the date glyphs that would form a single column along the right-hand border.

Akbal had been wary of beginning while so many details remained unclear, but Balam Xoc had told him that this information would come to him in time, and that he should begin with the upper border, of which he had excellent examples from his drawings of the Ektun monuments. When he had drawn his own version of the two-headed serpent, cut to the exact scale of the stone, he showed it to both Balam Xoc and the clan priests, and received sufficient praise and encouragement to allow himself to begin.

With the aid of several workmen, he and Kal Cuc first laid the stone flat upon log rollers, lowering it slowly with ropes. Then they buttressed it at both ends with stout wooden posts, so that it would not move when struck with a stone chisel. When they had carefully cleaned its surface, they washed themselves and sent for Tzec Balam, who blessed their work and smoked the stone with a ladle of copal incense. Then Akbal and Kal Cuc undertook a voluntary fast, waiting for the propitious day the priests had found for them in the *tzolkin,* the Book of Day Signs.

On the appointed day, they rose at dawn and went out to the shelter, where they had left offerings of copal, rubber, obsidian, and flint the night before. They buried these in the earth at the foot of the stone, and then were ready to begin. Akbal brought out the long, curving piece of bark paper on which he had painted the Sky Serpent, with its fully fleshed head curling up on the right, the east, and its skeletal head hanging downward, mouth agape, on the left, the west. He and Kal Cuc smoothed the thin paper down over the top portion of the slab, holding it in place with their fingers while they checked the exactness of the fit.

"Well, at least we can measure accurately," Akbal concluded, after examining the drawing from every conceivable angle. He finally removed it and gestured toward the pot of glue that Kal Cuc's grandmother had prepared for them. Using painter's brushes, they began to spread the sticky, translucent substance in an even curve across the top of the stone. The day had already grown hot, forcing them to step back periodically to wipe away the sweat that threatened to drip from their faces onto the glue. The work went quickly, though, especially when compared with the time they took in laying the drawing back down over the glued surface and pressing it into place. It was almost midday before they finished and went to find a cool spot to rest, leaving the glue to dry in the heat that surrounded the open-sided shelter.

They could not rest for long, however, because the etching had to be done as soon as possible, before the drawing could be ruined by rain or a heavy dew. The sun was still high when they returned, and they wrapped strips of cloth around their foreheads and wrists to absorb the sweat. After satisfying himself that the paper was securely affixed to the stone, Akbal took up a thin bladelet of obsidian that had been fitted into a wooden brush handle. He paused and looked across the stone at Kal Cuc.

"So, my friend, we begin at last," he said in a taut voice. "May the spirits of the ancestors guide our hands . . ."

Carefully resting his elbow on the center of the stone, below the bottom edge of the paper, he cocked his wrist and cut deftly through the paper, following one of the black lines a short distance to the right before raising up. Kal Cuc made an excited noise in his throat and craned forward to examine the narrow furrow Akbal had etched into the surface of the stone. Akbal blew away the yellow dust he had dug up and then straightened up from the stone, turning the bladelet in his hand and offering it to Kal Cuc, handle first.

"You must make your mark, as well," he said to the startled boy, who blinked at him uncertainly and did not reach out for the blade.

"The stone was my dream," Akbal continued, coaxing him gently, "but you helped me to raise it up and clean it, and you have sheltered it with your labor. And you saved me from the warrior who would have broken my head as well as my arm. This is *your* stone too, Kal Cuc, and we must carve it together."

Swelling with pride, Kal Cuc took the blade and impulsively bent over the stone. But then he hesitated, daunted by the fineness of the painted lines and his own, youthful sense of inadequacy.

"Rest your arm as I did," Akbal instructed, "and use the same stroke you use for painting. The blade is sharp and much harder than the stone; it requires no extra pressure."

Kal Cuc settled himself and took several long breaths, looking down the blade at the lines below. Akbal waited patiently, and finally the boy's hand moved, etching a finger-long segment of line before cautiously pulling up.

"Perfect," Akbal proclaimed, and Kal Cuc gave a giddy laugh, bouncing slightly on his toes in his excitement and relief. Akbal smiled at him and picked up another blade for himself.

"Now we have truly begun," he said solemnly. "But let us go slowly, very slowly. With patience and respect . . ."

THE RULER'S messenger returned for Pacal two days later. Pacal had hardly slept during the interval, unable to quiet the furious unspoken dialogue in his head. Over and over again, he threw back at Caan Ac and Balam Xoc all of the arguments neither had allowed him to make, proving beyond all doubt—at least to himself—that open conflict now served the interests of neither side. There was no one, however, with whom he could share his frustration, since everyone in the Jaguar Paw House, including his wife, Ixchel, would probably have agreed with Balam Xoc that it was better to fight than to bargain for rights already theirs. As if to emphasize his unwillingness to compromise, Balam Xoc had sent him an additional message after their conversation, telling him that the Jaguar Paw workmen could not be used on the construction of the Katun Enclosure, and that this would have to be part of the agreement, as well.

As he left the Jaguar Paw House with the messenger, Pacal reminded himself to take a last look around, since he doubted that he would return alive from this interview. Balam Xoc had finally put him into a position where he could not maneuver, and from which he could not escape. He had thought that he could do no harm in his role as go-between, and had even begun to believe that he was doing some good. Now he would be the one to deliver the final provocation, and cause the blood of his people to be spilled. And none of it was necessary! The clan had extra workmen, and the ruler needed them much more than he did a fight; there was no point to this threat and counterthreat. Why would they not see that?

The Jaguar Paw House was far behind before Pacal realized that he had not taken his last look. The thought made him stumble slightly, drawing a glance from the messenger. *Am I truly ready to die?* he wondered; *as ready as my father and his followers?* He shook his head, uncertain, unable to recapture his recent conviction that his life did not matter. He felt too keenly that a crucial juncture in the city's fortunes had been reached: Once the present tun was completed, only one tun would remain to Katun II Ahau. One tun to complete the Katun Enclosure in time for its dedication, and still somehow repair the fields and make them fit to produce crops once more. From what he had heard, Pacal doubted seriously that there was enough time—or enough men and resources—for Caan Ac to salvage any of the greatness he expected of himself. He would be fortunate, in fact, if there was not famine and unrest in Tikal.

But perhaps Caan Ac did not know that yet, Pacal told himself, as he followed the messenger past the warriors who guarded the head of the trail. Perhaps he had not been able to admit to himself how grave the situation actually was. Perhaps he would have been satisfied with the use of the clan's workmen, and would not have been drawn toward acting upon his threat. Perhaps . . . but it was futile. Balam Xoc had met unreason with unreason, leaving only the nature of the conflict to be decided. There was nothing a mediator could do, not even to avoid being crushed between the irreconcilable forces.

They suddenly came out of the trees, into the full glare of the sun, which was brutally hot, this far into the dry season. Pacal realized that his thoughts had taken him around in the same angry circle, yet had left him no closer to either resolution or resignation. The messenger turned north along the broad causeway that led away from the center of the city, and Pacal followed him blindly, putting one foot in front of the other, sustained only by his lingering anger. He noticed that the plastered flagstones underfoot were dusty and littered with debris, testament to how desperately the ruler needed workers. All of the street sweepers and sanitationworkers provided by the clans had been diverted to more pressing tasks, or so Pacal had been told by some of the Jaguar Paw workmen. They had complained to him about how worthless these unskilled laborers were in the fields, where they fainted from the heat and lost their tools in the mud.

It occurred to him that he had been told many things during the last months, and not only by the men he guided to their jobs each day. Chan Mac and Chac Mut, who were responsible for the clandestine trade being carried on with the other clans, had also stopped to share their knowledge of what the people outside the Jaguar Paw House were suffering. Even some of the newcomers, the pilgrims, had come to him, telling him how Tikal's problems were being viewed in the other cities, and revealing the size of the bribes they had paid to get past the ruler's warriors. Somehow they had all known that he would be interested, and many had seemed rather proud of themselves, as if they had fulfilled some unspoken duty by telling him what they knew. It did not appear to matter, at the time, that he had no more access to the ruler than they did. They seemed to trust that he would do something good with what he knew, whenever the opportunity finally presented itself.

As the twin pyramids of the Katun Enclosure came into view on the right, Pacal realized that his opportunity was at hand, and that Balam Xoc had simply made sure that he would use it. But could anything good come of telling the ruler what he did not want to hear? Every instinct told him no, even now, even after experiencing the bitter rewards of having done the opposite for most of his life. What would make Caan Ac *capable* of hearing the truth, if, in fact, he could bring himself to speak it?

The messenger had picked up his gait and begun to bear toward the right, indicating to Pacal that their destination was the Katun Enclosure. As they came down the broad steps from the causeway, Pacal could see at a glance how far behind the construction was, and he realized that his informants had been overly generous in their estimates of how much had been accomplished. The great plaza that was the platform for the Enclosure had been finished, and its surface plastered, and the flat-topped pyramids that stood at the eastern and western ends of the plaza had been raised to their full height and faced with cut stone. But the stairways laid out on all four sides of each pyramid were only partially completed, and the immense task of plastering and painting the exposed surfaces had not even begun. Pacal calculated that the work was a whole tun behind schedule, which explained why the ruler had come here in person, on a day so blisteringly hot.

The messenger led him to the foot of the stairway that climbed the south face of the western pyramid.

"The ruler awaits you above," he said to Pacal, pointing upward, past the paired guards who stood on every landing. Suppressing a groan, Pacal began to climb the steep steps, feeling the weight of his years and the pressure of the sun's heat bearing down on him in opposition. He was streaming with sweat and completely out of breath by the time he reached the top, so that he submitted meekly to the guards who searched his headwrap and waistband for weapons. Then he was brought in under the thatched canopy that had been erected for the ruler in the center of the platform. The shade provided some relief, but the heat was still stupefying, and it was several moments before Pacal could focus on what was in front of him.

Caan Ac was sitting on a drum-shaped throne, his legs dangling down in front. Behind him, two servants with large feather fans stirred the air with languid, repetitious motions. As he bowed, Pacal noticed that the fine jewels and feathers the ruler had worn here—no doubt to impress his workers—had been laid out on reed mats on one side of the throne. But as he straightened up, he saw the water gourds on a low table on the other side of the throne, and the sudden, painful awareness of his thirst made it almost impossible to attend to the ruler's words.

"So, Pacal," the man on the throne drawled, his voice as languid as the movements of the fans behind him. "Perhaps you thought I had forgotten you."

"Yes, my lord," Pacal said absently, his eyes straying toward the gourds. He saw the ruler follow his gaze and then look back at him with a cruel kind of shrewdness. When he made no offer, Pacal could not restrain his need any longer.

"May I have something to drink, my lord?" he asked in a pleading tone, and saw the shrewdness blossom into a smile.

"No," Caan Ac said flatly. "It is always best to keep a hostage in a state of need."

Pacal could not hide his chagrin, and for a moment he could only stare helplessly at his tormentor. Then all of the anger and frustration of the last two days—of the months and years of trying to serve this man—surged up in his breast, stiffening his whole body with its impact. His mouth snapped shut with an audible click, and he shuddered violently, as if his spine had been grasped in a powerful grip. He felt his eyes go wild with hatred.

"Perhaps I am being too harsh, though," the ruler said with sudden magnanimity. "I am a merciful man. Drink, Pacal."

He gestured toward the gourds, but Pacal would not look in that direction, and he did not move.

"There is plenty of water elsewhere in this city," he said in a seething voice. "As my father warned you."

"Do not drink, then," Caan Ac snapped. "Let your thirst kill you. It will save me the trouble."

"I would expect you to be more used to trouble, my lord," Pacal suggested, his politeness a taunt. "You have so much of it."

The ruler straightened up in anger, but then settled back down, gesturing to the servants to fan more vigorously. He appeared to Pacal to have lost weight, his eyes and mouth sunken more deeply into the fleshy folds of his face, which still resisted the lines of age.

"So you have come here to die," he said at last. "Your father has rejected my offer?"

"How could he do otherwise?" Pacal replied. "Neither you nor any other man has the right to deny him access to the holy shrine of our ancestors. It was an empty offer."

"Do not tell *me* about my rights!" Caan Ac exploded, startling the servants out of their rhythm.

"Someone must," Pacal shot back without hesitation. "When you violate our traditions and squander our resources and abuse the rights of the clans, someone must tell you that you are wrong. My father is only the first to oppose you, but there will be others."

"There will be no others," Caan Ac vowed, "not after they see how I deal with heretics and traitors. And *you* will be the one who has brought this upon your people."

Pacal shook his head in denial, feeling perfectly calm. He understood now how his father's stubbornness had freed him, and the thought brought a small smile to his lips.

"No, my lord, you can blame nothing on me now. My people are ready to die for what they believe, and they would see me die, as well, before they would yield any of their rights to you. I was a hostage only in your mind and my own. And now only in yours."

"It does not matter," Caan Ac sneered. "None of you will be missed."

"Not by you, perhaps. But all those who have been fed from our gardens will feel the loss. That is many more than you wish to believe, my lord. For even though you have confined us, we could not hoard our crops while so many went hungry around us. Perhaps you will feed them yourself when we are gone."

The ruler rose abruptly to his feet, causing the throne to rock back and forth behind him.

"You have taunted me for the last time—" he began, but Pacal cut him off rudely.

"And you have threatened me for the last time. It has always been within your power to take my life, but you have preferred to abuse and betray me instead. Begin the killing with me, then. Spatter my blood over this temple, if that is your wish. Then you can celebrate the Tun-End by killing the rest of my people!"

Pacal was shouting at the end of his speech, and the guards had hastily drawn in around the canopy, two of them interposing themselves between Pacal and the ruler. They aimed their spears at Pacal's chest, awaiting the signal to strike. Caan Ac simply frowned at Pacal, seeming more perplexed than angry.

"I did not know you had this rashness in you, Pacal. You have been infected by your father."

Pacal did not respond, his eyes on the sharp points of the spears, which seemed to grow closer with each breath he took. Even when the ruler waved the guards back, he did not allow himself to relax, expecting the reprieve to be only temporary. Caan Ac made an impatient, dismissive gesture.

"I do not intend to kill you, or your clansmen. But I will have the workers I need."

"I have been authorized to negotiate for the workers," Pacal said hoarsely, his voice sticking in his throat. "Balam Xoc offers you the usual terms, to be paid in advance in the form of salt, fish, obsidian, and stone tools. It must also be agreed that our workers will not be employed in the construction of this Enclosure."

When he had finished, Pacal drew a long breath and held it, waiting for his reprieve to end. To his surprise, Caan Ac let out a brief, sardonic laugh and sat back down on the throne.

"Yes, I see now why you spoke so rashly. Your father sent you here to die."

"Those are his terms, my lord. I can offer nothing else."

Caan Ac nodded absently and turned to gaze at the eastern pyramid, which stood like a squat yellow mountain against the brilliant blue of the sky. Workmen swarmed up and down its face like ants, carrying stones for its unfinished stairway. In the distance, clouds of black smoke rose from the pyres where limestone was being burned to produce lime for mortar and plaster and stucco. Pacal knew that the ruler was seeing—as he had seen so quickly—the enormous amount of work that remained to be done.

"I will have the chief steward of crops send you the necessary papers," Caan Ac said finally, looking back at Pacal with weary eyes. "I will not forget, though, how you bargained with me in a time of need."

Nor will I, Pacal reflected, but he did not voice the thought. He had already said everything he had been sent here to say and more. For the first time in his life, he had spoken all that was in his heart, without regard for the consequences. And to his amazement, he had been heard. So he bowed instead, and backed out from under the canopy at the ruler's gesture of dismissal. As he turned to descend the temple stairs, he felt a marvelous lightness in his limbs, the result, he decided, of coming away from an interview with the ruler with fewer regrets and misgivings than he had brought with him. The newness of the sensation made him slightly dizzy, forcing him to descend the steep steps with extra caution. He was no longer certain what had happened between himself and the ruler, or if it was the truth that had saved him. It had seemed, in the end, that the Katun Enclosure itself had decided his fate. The Katun Enclosure and his thirst, which had released all of his anger in the first place. He licked his parched lips and began to take the stairs more rapidly, concluding that there were few truths as profound, and as undeniable, as thirst.

"YOU HAVE all had ample time to study the books, and ponder their meaning," Balam Xoc began. "And you have each spoken with me privately, and asked your questions. Now I will tell you what all of you know, so that you do not waste time repeating one another's words."

He paused and looked at each of his listeners in turn: at Nohoch Ich, Opna, and Kanan Naab; and at Hok, who was present to witness this retelling of Tikal's history. Then he folded his hands over his stomach and went on.

"Our ancestor, the man called Jaguar Paw, was the ruler of Tikal until the end of the seventeenth katun of the last cycle. He died without having named an heir, however, and there was contention among his sons over the right to succeed him. The Serpent and Flint clans also put forward candidates, so vigorously that the matter could not be resolved.

"It was at this time that the foreigners, the Cauac Shield people, came to Tikal. They had already established a base in Uaxactun, where one of their lords was married to a daughter of the ruler. They came south to Tikal in force, accompanied by the Zuyhua warriors with their spear throwers, and by the traveling merchants with their cacao and their cores of green obsidian. What they could not achieve by threat of force, they obtained by means of their wealth. They paid high prices for the flint that Tikal had in abundance, and for the feathers and animal pelts that could be gathered so easily in the forests that surrounded the city. Much of the original opposition to their presence was quickly overwhelmed by the desire to have them for trading partners, and in this, tco, the clans competed with one another. Thus, there was no one to prevent the leader of the foreigners from seizing the throne and proclaiming himself ruler.

"His name was Curl Snout, and he was the son of a full-blooded Zuyhua and a woman from the ruling house of Kaminaljuyu. Lacking ancestors here, he adopted Cauac the Rain Spirit as his patron and initiated a set of rites involving prophecy and the worship of the spirit of the katun. In truth, he was more interested in expanding trade and solidifying his power over the clans, and he was slow to raise a temple to his patron. The clans forced him to build it away from their own, on the west side of the plaza, the place of least honor. It is doubtful that Curl Snout and his priests even knew that they were being slighted. It is more doubtful that they cared, since they were more interested in Tikal as a central place—with trade routes in all directions—than as a place sacred to the spirits of the ancestors."

Balam Xoc paused to look at them all again, as if to alert them that he was now coming to the important part of his narrative.

"You are all familiar with the name and glyph of Kan Balam Moo, Precious Jaguar Macaw," he said, nodding to Hok as the single exception. "She was the last of Jaguar Paw's children, born after her father had died, and just before the coming of the foreigners. She was twelve years old when she was betrothed to the foreign ruler, Curl Snout. By then, her brothers had given up hope of regaining the throne; some had even gone to other cities, where their lineage was still respected and made them powerful. It was the Living Ancestor of the Jaguar Paw Clan, a man named Bacab, who gave Kan Balam Moo in marriage when she was fifteen. She bore seven children to Curl Snout, four of whom lived past infancy. The youngest of these was a boy, and after he had been designated as his father's heir, he was given the name by which we all know him: Stormy Sky.

"Stormy Sky ascended to the throne in the middle of the last katun of the cycle, following the death of Curl Snout. He was twelve years old, an adopted member of the Jaguar Paw Clan as well as the acknowledged leader of the Cauac Shield people. The Living Ancestor Bacab had seen to his adoption, and was also one of his guardians, along with a katun priest. As you have all known since childhood, Stormy Sky ruled Tikal for thirty years, an era of unprecedented peace and prosperity for the city. So revered was his rule that monuments were erected in his honor a full katun after his death. Even today, the Sky Clan Ruler traces his lineage back to Stormy Sky, and bases his legitimacy upon the relationship."

Balam Xoc stopped altogether at this point and gave his listeners a few moments to absorb what he had said. Then he went on.

"It is concerning the period following Stormy Sky's death that your interpretations differ. You all know that for several katuns afterward, Tikal had not one but *two* rulers: one from the Jaguar Paw Clan and one from among the followers and descendants of Curl Snout, who gradually established themselves as the Sky Clan. You also know that this arrangement broke down in the fifth katun of this cycle, Katun Eleven Ahau, when the clan wars erupted and another group of foreigners from the southeast seized the rule of Tikal. It was at this time that some of the Sky Clan people left Tikal for the west, helping to found the cities of Yaxche and Acantun, and Yaxchilan and Ektun. Others stayed behind to keep the Sky Clan claim to the throne alive, though the succession remained unsettled for another seven katuns, during which it was disrupted or usurped many times. Finally, in the thirteenth katun, Cacao

Moon came to Tikal from Acantun and founded the line that rules us today, in the person of Caan Ac.

"The question that all of you have asked me," Balam Xoc continued, "is not so much *what* happened after Stormy Sky's death, but *why* it happened. I have given no one my answer, though I have heard what each of you proposes. You agree that there was a failure, but you differ as to where the failure lies, and who is to blame. You may tell us your opinion first, Nohoch."

Nohoch took a moment to collect his thoughts, then responded with his usual restraint, careful not to overstate the importance of his views.

"I cannot say exactly when the failure occurred, though it is most noticeable in the books painted shortly after the death of Stormy Sky. It is the simple fact that the names of Stormy Sky's sons do not appear on the Jaguar Paw Clan lists. Forgive me, Grandfather," he added uneasily, "but it seems to me that this must have been the failure of your predecessor, the Living Ancestor Bacab. He should have seen that the sons were adopted, as the father had been."

"Speaking what you believe to be the truth requires no forgiveness," Balam Xoc told him gruffly. He waited to see if Nohoch had more to say, then nodded once and turned inquiringly toward Opna, who displayed no hesitation in stating his opinion.

"Clearly, the error was committed long before Stormy Sky was even born. It was the decision to give the foreign ruler an heir, and thus the legitimacy of Jaguar Paw blood. They should have waited for Curl Snout to die, and then joined with the other clans to drive the rest of the foreigners out of Tikal. They should never have compromised themselves for a share of the throne."

"And whom do you blame for this error?" Balam Xoc asked.

"I blame Bacab and the other members of Kan Balam Moo's family," Opna said emphatically. "It appears that they pursued their own ambitions without regard for the wishes of the rest of the clan. My proof of this is that the clan put forward its own candidate for the rule after Stormy Sky's death: a man named Claw Skull, who was not from the immediate family of Jaguar Paw. Because of Bacab's decision, however, Claw Skull was forced to share the rule with one of Stormy Sky's sons, and the succession remained in perpetual dispute thereafter. All because of Bacab's ambition."

Opna crossed his arms on his chest and stared back at Balam Xoc boldly, as if to contrast his own assurance with Nohoch's earlier apology. Balam Xoc nodded again and opened his hands to Kanan Naab.

"My daughter?"

"I cannot be so quick to condemn Bacab," Kanan Naab said in a tight voice, with a slight, involuntary nod in Opna's direction. "Or so ready to judge his intentions. No doubt he expected his influence upon Stormy Sky to be of longer duration than it was. But as the books tell us, he died before the young ruler had reached his eighteenth year. And Kan Balam Moo also died well before her son's rule came to an end."

"That is correct," Balam Xoc agreed. "What meaning do you draw from it?"

"Perhaps it was Bacab's intention to change Stormy Sky," Kanan Naab ventured, "as you changed all of us. Perhaps he hoped to absorb the foreigners, rather than drive them out. And surely, Stormy Sky was far less foreign in his ways than his father. It was during his reign that the Zuyhua left Tikal and never returned, and the Cauac Shield people married Tikal women and became the Sky Clan."

"Then where did the failure occur?" Balam Xoc pressed her. Kanan Naab licked her lips and looked around at the other men in the room.

"Perhaps there would have been no failure if Bacab and Kan Balam Moo had not died so soon," she suggested tentatively. "Though perhaps they had always underestimated the attraction that his father's power would have for Stormy Sky. The desire for power is a common failing among men," she added softly, again inclining her head toward Opna. "It is often stronger than their desire for knowledge, or truth. Perhaps Stormy Sky could never have been changed as much as Bacab had hoped."

In the silence that followed, Opna gestured vigorously to speak, and Balam Xoc granted his request with a nod.

"It is curious," he pointed out, staring sideways at Kanan Naab, "that this failing so common to men does not seem to apply to Bacab." He looked back at Balam Xoc. "I do not think you wish us to view the ancestors through sentimental eyes, Grandfather, and it seems more likely that Bacab was the one seized by a desire for power, which he sought to satisfy through the boy. I have already stated the evidence of Bacab's ambition."

Expressionless, Balam Xoc simply gestured for Kanan Naab to respond.

"Bacab was the Living Ancestor," she reminded Opna forcefully, her voice quivering with indignation. "He had no need to seek power in the world of men."

"You cannot know that, so long after the fact," Opna replied scornfully. "You speak contemptuously of the men of today, yet you cling to naïve beliefs about those of the past."

"Not naïve," Balam Xoc interrupted suddenly, causing Opna's head to jerk around in surprise. "Not naïve," the old man repeated. *"Respectful."*

"Yes, of course, but—"

"Respectful," Balam Xoc insisted. "As Bacab came to respect the power and influence of Curl Snout, during the twelve years it took him to reach his decision. Twelve years, Opna. If Bacab was so hungry for power, why did he not offer Curl Snout a wife immediately upon his arrival in Tikal? Jaguar Paw had left other daughters; their names are also in the books. But Bacab had not raised any of them from childhood, as he did Kan Balam Moo. He had not shaped any of them for his purpose, as he did Kan Balam Moo. I know this, so long after the fact, because it was Kan Balam Moo herself who first came to me, as the Spirit Woman."

Opna let out a long breath, but even he could not argue with such a revelation. Nodding reluctantly, he spread his hands in a gesture of acceptance, palms pointing downward. But Balam Xoc ignored the gesture and went on in the same insistent tone.

"You have also suggested that Bacab acted thoughtlessly, and that he should have waited for Curl Snout to die. Yet you have overlooked the fact that Curl Snout ruled Tikal for almost forty years, and was over seventy when he died. Only a fool would wait so long. And you have forgotten the Zuyhua warriors, who would never have left Tikal so peaceably were Stormy Sky not on the throne. For a priest, Opna, you have overlooked much that was plain in the books. Perhaps the mushrooms have not helped you see as much as you think they have."

"Perhaps not, my lord," Opna said in a muffled voice, his eyes on the floor in front of him.

"No," Balam Xoc concurred unsparingly. "You may leave us now."

Opna brought his head up, mouth open, but he was too stunned to move or speak. He stared blankly at Balam Xoc, unable to believe that he was being dismissed. Hok stirred threateningly, but was stayed by a gesture from Balam Xoc.

"Go, my son," the old man said to Opna. "There is no shame attached to this dismissal. Perhaps, though, it will help you understand how you have been blinded by your own ambition, so that it is all you can see in others."

Opna bowed stiffly and left without a word, though his face was clenched and angry. Seeming as stunned as Opna, Nohoch and Kanan Naab watched him go, then briefly glanced at each other with the shyness of survivors. Balam Xoc, however, began speaking again as soon as Opna was out of the room, addressing his remarks to Kanan Naab.

"As you guessed, and as I have told you, Bacab did indeed intend to change the character of Stormy Sky. He and Kan Balam Moo, while they lived, did all that was in their power to wean him from the ways of his father's people. But you are very wrong about their awareness of the attraction of power. The kind of power and wealth represented by Curl Snout was new to Tikal. People had always been drawn to our city because it was a holy place, a place where the sacred calendar was kept and the rites of the ancestors were observed with correctness and respect. The people brought their goods to trade when they came for the ceremonies, or to help erect a temple or a monument. We did not send out merchants over long distances, as the Zuyhua did. We did not send our warriors to strange cities. Only our priests went out, carrying our rites to people in isolated places, so that they would be bound to us by ties of knowledge and belief.

"That was the old way, before the foreigners came," Balam Xoc concluded. "Yet Bacab saw how quickly, how eagerly, his people responded to the wealth that Curl Snout and the Zuyhua had brought to Tikal. He saw them embrace their new prosperity even while they scorned the men who had caused it. No one could have despised the foreigners more than Bacab himself; his scorn is the essence of the spirit that lived on after him. But he never underestimated the temptation they presented to his people, or to Stormy Sky. He knew that the boy would want his father's power as well as the wisdom of his adopted people, and he intended to make them indistinguishable in Stormy Sky's mind. In this, he was partially successful, as can be seen from the nature of Stormy Sky's reign. It was Bacab's misfortune, and ours, that he died before his intentions had been fulfilled."

Balam Xoc's face was impassive, but there were tears in Kanan Naab's eyes, and Nohoch's long face was drawn downward in sadness and regret.

"But can his death be considered a failure?" Kanan Naab asked plaintively, blinking back her tears.

"Only in the way that Nohoch suggested earlier," Balam Xoc allowed, nodding toward the younger man. "Bacab based all of his hopes on the influence he and Kan Balam Moo would have upon the heir. I doubt that he involved many others in his scheme. Thus, there was no one who could replace him when he died, at least not in his role as adviser to Stormy Sky. That was one mistake. Another, of far greater importance, was his failure to unite the

352

clan behind himself and Kan Balam Moo. As you may recall," he said, giving Nohoch a meaningful look, "I once made the same mistake, when I acted on my own to get land for our gardens. It was the angry spirit of Bacab that allowed me to reclaim the loyalty of the clan—to *demand* your loyalty. No doubt he had died wishing that he had done the same for himself, in his own time."

"So that is why the sons of Stormy Sky were never adopted into the Jaguar Paw Clan," Nohoch suggested. "It was only the result of Bacab's larger failure."

"Yes."

Nohoch glanced sideways at Kanan Naab.

"Then we were no more correct than Opna."

"No, you were not," Balam Xoc agreed. There was a long silence before Kanan Naab finally spoke.

"Have we failed you, then, Grandfather?"

Balam Xoc stared at her thoughtfully for a moment, then at Nohoch. Then apparently at nothing.

"You have both been diligent and sincere in your efforts," he decided, his gaze still fixed upon the wall behind them. "But you have not provided me with the sign I have been seeking. Perhaps that in itself is a sign. Perhaps I am not meant to know my successor."

Nohoch and Kanan Naab looked at each other but did not say anything, waiting for Balam Xoc to return his attention to them. The old man finally blinked and shook himself.

"Still," he said with a trace of stubbornness, "I wish you to continue your study of the books. I must at least leave a true knowledge of our history behind me. In a few days' time, I will begin my fast for the Tun-End Ceremony. Perhaps the sign will come to me in my confinement, and I will know which of you is worthy. But I cannot release you until then." He looked at Kanan Naab. "Yaxal Can must wait still longer, my daughter, though he may take the oath of adoption as I promised."

Though she was clearly disappointed, Kanan Naab bowed to show her compliance.

"Leave me now," Balam Xoc told them, including Hok with his gesture. "I must ponder the lessons of the past, and the prospects for our future. I must be ready to receive the guidance of the ancestors, when they come to me again. Ready yourselves, as well, for the time of reckoning will soon be upon us . . ."

9.17.18.17.16   11 Cib   19 Mac
(Four days before the Tun-End)

JUST BEFORE noon, a small crowd began to gather in the public plaza to the east of the Plaza of the Ancestors. They came individually or in pairs, drifting over from the marketplace or the clan houses without apparent purpose. They stood facing in a number of directions, striking absurdly casual poses under the hot sun, pretending that they were not waiting, or watching.

Taking no part in the pretense, Yaxal Can stood alone, facing the place where the causeway from the north came into the plaza. He had already taken note of the absence of warriors in the plaza, which was unusual, and which on this day could mean one of two things: Either they had been cleared away to allow Balam Xoc free passage to the Plaza of the Ancestors, or they had been sent to the Jaguar Paw House to prevent him from leaving. Yaxal would know soon, as would all these other men, and thus the rest of the city. He found it difficult to believe that the ruler would actually carry out his threat, though it seemed almost equally impossible for him to back down now, and concede victory to Balam Xoc. It was a crude and stupid threat, Yaxal thought, the kind that brought discredit to the maker, whether he succeeded in his aim or not. It was the same kind of threat that Hapay Can had made against Yaxal himself, and the reason that he was here now, waiting to decide his future.

Then he saw the procession coming down the causeway toward him, and his heart began to beat strongly in his chest. The men around him fell silent and turned in unison to watch, abandoning all pretense of indifference. The procession was led by Nohoch Ich and Tzec Balam, who carried banded staves and smoking ladles of incense. Then came Balam Xoc himself, his white head bare and his body painted black. He was flanked by Kinich Kakmoo and the man with the eyepatch, both of whom were fully armed, as were the ten helmeted men who marched behind each of them. Between the two lines of warriors walked the apprentice priests and the costumers, their arms filled with ritual paraphernalia and the spotted costume of the Jaguar Protector. They all moved at a measured gait, neither hurrying nor dawdling, their eyes fixed straight ahead.

Yaxal watched until the last members of the column had crossed the plaza and disappeared down the stairs that led to the Plaza of the Ancestors. The men around him had begun to murmur and whisper excitedly among themselves, but he paid them no heed as he walked out of their midst and started up the causeway. He was past the point where he could stand and admire Balam Xoc from afar—it was time now to go and join him.

WHEN HE HAD packed his belongings into two large net carrying bags, Yaxal summoned one of the younger clan priests to his quarters and asked him to take a message to the head of the Order of Tun Count Priests. He had helped to train the young man, so he knew that he could trust him. It was painful, though, to see the disappointment in his eyes as he repeated Yaxal's message back to him, and Yaxal sent him off quickly, without further explanation. Then he slung his incense bag around his neck, shouldered his bags, picked up his notched sighting stick, and went to his mother's room. She was sitting with her back to the doorway, a small, hunched-over figure with grey-streaked hair.

"I am going now, Mother. I ask you one more time to accede to my wishes and accompany me."

The figure did not move. Yaxal listened to the sound of his own breathing, hearing echoes of all the arguments and attempts at persuasion that had occurred in this room. All to no effect, except to add an edge of guilt to his remorse.

"Farewell, then, my mother. I leave you with sorrow."

His two sisters met him on the platform outside. They had already wept with him, and they did their best to contain their emotions as he embraced them and whispered his farewells. They had both wished to accompany him, and would not have needed their mother's permission to do so. But they could not leave her here to face her old age in complete solitude. Yaxal pressed a small leather pouch into the hands of his eldest sister, closing her fingers over it firmly, so that she would feel the hardness of the jade inside. It was almost the whole of Yaxal's inheritance from his father, a fact his sister was old enough to comprehend. She tried to give it back to him, but he hid his hand behind his back and shook his head with stubborn insistence.

"It belongs here," he assured her. "I will send more when I can, and I will find a way for you to contact me. You must call upon me for whatever you need."

His younger sister had given in to her tears, and he reached out to wipe them from her cheeks, forcing a smile that felt more wretched than fond. Swallowing arduously, he hefted his sighting stick and walked slowly away from them, turning once to raise his stick in blessing.

As Yaxal reached the edge of the plaza, the High Priest Hapay Can came out of his house to intercept him. Hapay Can was a thin, angular man with a face like a knife blade and eyes that were set too close together, so that they seemed permanently crossed. The eyes darted toward the bags on Yaxal's back, brows raised knowingly.

"I am going to join the Jaguar Paw Clan," Yaxal told him, dispensing with the amenities of greeting.

"So you meant to desert us all along," Hapay Can concluded, feigning indignation. He pointed rudely toward the incense bag hanging around Yaxal's neck. "You will not be able to hide *this* from the head of the Tun Count priests."

"Perhaps you should run to tell him," Yaxal suggested scornfully, "before anyone else can claim the privilege of betraying me. Perhaps he will pay the little bribes you could not get from me."

"I knew it was a mistake to protect you," Hapay Can snapped. "I knew that you would repay me with ingratitude and disrespect."

Gripping his stick tightly, Yaxal stepped closer, narrowing his gaze to match that of the man in front of him. His voice was very soft, almost a hiss.

"I would not threaten another priest, Hapay Can, as you have threatened me. There should be only trust between priests, especially those who share the same oath. But as one man to another, I make you this promise: If you betray your oath of trust, and mine; if you violate the sanctity of the rites I performed, I will come back here to kill you. I swear this on the lives of our ancestors. Remember *my* vow, Hapay Can, even if you cannot remember your own."

The high priest paled slightly, but then puffed out his chest in compensation, putting a belligerently disdainful expression on his narrow face. He stood like a stone as Yaxal brushed by him and walked out of the Serpent House without pausing to look back.

INSIDE the craft house, the painters and carvers were working feverishly, finishing or touching up ritual implements and items of costume that would be used in the Tun-End Ceremony. Outside, under the palms that shaded the back of the long building, Akbal, Kal Cuc, and two other men were painting the carrying poles of a litter they had built themselves. It was to have a cloth canopy as soon as the women finished weaving it, to shade the Lady Box Ek as she was carried to the ceremony. On the ground beside Akbal was a small wooden seat that the clan carpenter had made, as a means of getting the old woman up the steep stairs to the clan temple. The seat had a curving wooden back and a double set of leather straps, one for Box Ek and one for the man who would carry her upon his back.

Brush in hand, Akbal stepped back for a moment to see how their work was progressing. The shorter upright poles that would support the canopy still had not received their first coat of paint, and Akbal was the only one close to finishing his segment of the carrying poles. And then there was the seat, which he intended to paint himself. Added to the twenty or so other tasks he had to attend to before the ceremony, there was more than enough work to occupy his time until then. His stone would have to wait until it was all over, and then there would be an additional few days while he and Kal Cuc rediscovered their feel for the stone chisel. *So slow,* he thought, feeling that he was learning a kind of patience he could not even have imagined before this. The patience of stone itself. Sighing inwardly, he was about to resume his painting when Kal Cuc suddenly raised up and pointed toward the trail that approached from the west.

"Look!"

Akbal turned with the others, shielding his eyes against the sun, which was behind the heavily burdened man coming up the trail. Even before he could make out the man's features, Akbal saw the incense bag and sighting stick and knew that it was Yaxal Can. Still, it took him a moment to recover from the shock of seeing a visitor on the trail, which had not been used by an outsider in many months. Then he put down his brush and went to meet the priest.

"Greetings, Yaxal Can," he said respectfully. "We have been expecting you, though not along this trail. It is a welcome sight to see you come to us so openly."

"I saw Balam Xoc go to his confinement unopposed," Yaxal explained. "I chose to come here with the same dignity."

"You have, indeed," Akbal concurred, deciding not to ask about Yaxal's mother and sisters. He felt suddenly awkward with this man, whom he did not know well, yet to whom he was indebted. This man who might soon be his brother-in-law, or might not be. He could not think of what to say, and merely stared at Yaxal's sweaty face and the overstuffed bags on his back.

"Kinich Kakmoo has offered me a room in his house," Yaxal said suggestively, wiping his forehead with his free hand, which made Akbal remember his manners.

"Of course!" he exclaimed in embarrassment, reaching out to relieve Yaxal of one of his bags. "He has returned from the plaza . . . I will take you to him . . ."

Signaling Kal Cuc and the others to continue with their work, Akbal escorted Yaxal around the corner of the craft house, into the lower plaza. Kinich was sitting in the central doorway of his house, with his chest protector, shield, and spear propped up against the wall beside him. He rose immediately and came to take Yaxal's other bag, greeting him with a warmth that surprised Akbal, who had not known that the two of them were friends.

"Welcome," Kinich said heartily, casting a curious glance over Yaxal's shoulder. "Your family has not come with you?" he asked, with a tactlessness that made Akbal cringe.

"No," Yaxal said succinctly, though he did not seem angered by the question. Kinich merely nodded.

"And the priest who threatened you?"

Yaxal looked questioningly at Akbal.

"He knows," Kinich explained. "Balam Xoc asked him to be present when he told me. It is his stone."

"I am indebted to you, Yaxal," Akbal began, but the priest hastily held up a hand to stop him.

"Your gratitude is undeserved. I have only done my duty as a priest." He glanced over at Kinich. "But I told Hapay Can that I would kill him if he betrayed the trust your grandfather put in me."

"That is not priest's work," Kinich huffed, curling the blunt fingers of his free hand. "I will strangle him myself, slowly . . ."

"The responsibility is mine," Yaxal insisted quietly. "Besides, I will not be a priest for much longer. I sent a message to the head of my order, telling him that I was coming here."

"You will be a priest here, then," Kinich declared. "Nohoch Ich keeps the tun count for us, but he is often busy with other things. As you know, he and Kanan Naab are still studying the books, and he has to prepare for the ceremony, as well. Your skills are needed."

"I would like you to bless the stone again, as well," Akbal added. Nodding his head, Yaxal made a slight bow to each of them, grateful yet reserved. *He has great pride,* Akbal decided, realizing that he should not have been surprised. Only a very proud man could have courted Kanan Naab for so long, through so many obstacles. Yaxal rearranged his hands on the shaft of his sighting stick and cleared his throat, as if trying to free a question. When he did not bring it forth immediately, Akbal went to his rescue.

"Our sister is sequestered with the books," he offered. "She is also sharing Balam Xoc's fast, and will not receive visitors."

Yaxal nodded again, his gratitude less restrained.

"I must prepare myself for the adoption ceremony," he said, "and for the experience of seeing Balam Xoc dance."

"You will have a place in the front ranks, with us," Kinich promised. Tossing Yaxal's bag lightly over his shoulder, he turned to show him to his room. Akbal surrendered the bag he was holding to Yaxal himself, briefly meeting the man's eyes and wondering what he was feeling. He had given up everything to come here, and he could lose Kanan Naab, as well, if Balam Xoc chose her as his successor. No one knew if she would be allowed to marry then, for Balam Xoc had made no promises.

That is a different kind of patience, Akbal thought as Yaxal turned away from him and followed Kinich inside. *One that waits only for the beginning, and cannot—dare not—even dream of completion.* Akbal went back to the craft house feeling chastened, grateful that he had his wife, and his work, and was in no danger of losing them. Grateful, too, that he did not have to spend the next four days practicing Yaxal's kind of patience.

IT WAS SO WARM, so very warm. Kanan Naab could not remember ever being this uncomfortable before. It did not seem that the heat of the day had diminished at all, though the sun had set many hours ago. Perhaps it was the paint that covered her body, trapping the heat within. Or perhaps it was a fever created by her imagination, an hallucination brought on by the hunger of her fast. She could no longer tell causes from effects with any confidence, so that she blamed the aching in her bones on the pressure of the damp night air, rather than on her long hours of sitting.

Unable to sleep or study the books, she sat looking out the open doorway of Cab Coh's house, into the darkness that shrouded the plaza. The insects sang loudly in the heat, making a sound like the shaking of thousands of tiny shell rattles. Fireflies swam through the thick air, emitting flashes of greenish light that seemed to explode against her eyes, leaving her blinking in the afterglow. When her father suddenly appeared in the midst of this greenish haze, she at first thought that she was dreaming. But he stirred the air around her as he came into the room, and the pottery bowl he was carrying made a sharp clink when he set it down upon the plastered stone floor, a sound that was a shock to Kanan Naab's senses. Then he was sitting across from her, gesturing toward the bowl.

"That is the flesh of a blue iguana," he explained, lowering his voice when she winced. "Fasting food. Kal Cuc killed it, and Chibil saw to its preparation. It will give you strength in your waiting."

He had not apologized for intruding upon her, and for a moment Kanan Naab resented him for disregarding her wishes so blithely. Yet in the next moment, she was so grateful for his company that she could almost have wept. To cover her confusion, she reached into the bowl and lifted a sliver of the delicate white meat to her lips. Pacal nodded encouragingly as she chewed, flooding her mouth with flavors that seemed extravagant to her deprived palate.

"It is very hot," Pacal observed mildly, giving her fresh cause for gratitude. So it was not the fever of her thoughts at all. She permitted herself a small drink from the water bowl beside her, feeling her stomach coil and uncoil, a vaguely pleasant sensation.

"I am grateful that you have come, Father," she murmured, trying her voice. "The waiting has not been easy."

"No doubt. Your grandfather has placed a heavy burden upon you. It is his way with us. Sometimes, I believe, it is his intention to make us cry out, and refuse what we cannot carry."

Kanan Naab drew a sharp breath.

"I have thought to do so many times," she confessed. "I have wanted to tell him that I am not worthy, or strong, or wise enough to be his successor. I wanted to tell him that I had already given my heart to Yaxal, and could not dedicate myself purely to the needs of the clan. But shame prevented me from speaking."

"There is no shame in admitting your weaknesses, or your needs," Pacal told her firmly. "It can often be a source of pride. It is, after all, the truth."

"The truth," Kanan Naab repeated, half to herself. Then she looked at her father and sighed. "Grandfather once gave me the truth, as he gave Akbal his stone. I was to seek it, and let it make its mark upon me. I thought then that all my wishes had been answered. I looked to Yaxal only for help in my seeking. Now I look to him as an escape from it."

"You have changed," Pacal said succinctly. "Is that not what Balam Xoc asked of all of us—that we change?"

"Some changes are betrayals."

"*All* changes are betrayals. The old must be forsaken before the new can take its place. When he became the Living Ancestor, and many times since, my father betrayed the man he was, the father I knew. Surely, as a woman, you must betray the wishes you had as a child."

"I was not a child when I went to Balam Xoc in a vision, and saw the eyes of the Jaguar Protector."

"Perhaps not," Pacal allowed. "But the desire to know the future came to you when you were very young. After your mother died."

"You remember this?"

"We were all aware of it. We indulged you, because you were too little to know what you were asking, and you had been badly frightened by your mother's death. Only Box Ek discouraged your curiosity."

They were silent for a few moments, dwelling on their separate memories. Kanan Naab's hand inadvertently strayed to her earlobe, her fingertips running lightly over the even lines of scar tissue. It suddenly occurred to her that her vision had been the culmination of her seeking, rather than the prelude to larger ambitions. She had never been drawn to bloodletting again, and it was out of that one experience that she had become aware of the power of her empathy, her power to calm and heal. She glanced up to find her father looking at her, waiting for her to respond.

"Did you also change after Mother's death?" she asked quietly, and Pacal stared at her for a long moment before he nodded.

"That is when I gave myself fully to the stewardship. To Caan Ac. That was my betrayal of the man I had been, the hopes I had had. It has taken me many years to learn that I had chosen incorrectly, and much pain to pay for my error. Do not make my mistake, Kanan Naab. Accept only those burdens you can carry with an open heart."

Moved by her father's confession, Kanan Naab lowered her eyes out of respect. She heard him rise to his feet.

"Yaxal is here," he said softly. "He will stand beside me at the ceremony tomorrow, and then he will join us. I will be proud to have him for a son-in-law, if Balam Xoc consents."

"I will pray that he does," Kanan Naab vowed. "Shamelessly . . ."

Pacal smiled and then was gone, vanishing as quickly as he had come. But he had left the bowl of fasting food behind, and Kanan Naab ate the few slivers that remained, reflecting on the advice her father had given her. Then she prayed until her weariness overcame her and she laid down to sleep, letting all thoughts of the future slip from her mind as she finally allowed herself the rest her body needed.

The Tun-End
9.17.19.0.0   2 Ahau   3 Kankin

BLINDLY, the Jaguar crawled on his belly through the mud, dragging himself forward with stabbing thrusts of his forepaws. His eyes strained in their sockets but found no light, no way out of the blackness that enveloped him. The air was cold and heavy with the scent of long-dead flesh, and the only sounds were the suck of mud beneath him and the ragged echo of his own panting breath. Finally he could drag himself no further, and sank down into the mud, his long tail curling around his hollowed flanks. His hunger was gone, and he no longer had the strength to feel danger, or the anger to snarl back at the threat. He lowered his great head onto his forepaws, his jaws hanging open uselessly, tongue lolling out. He licked feebly at the matted fur on his paws, bewildered by the absence of taste, the dimming of all sensation. His eyes rolled back in his head as his lungs heaved for the last time, sending a quiver down to the tip of his tail. A high, sickly whine escaped from his throat as his heart caught and shuddered violently, bursting against his ribs . . .

Balam Xoc came back to himself at the same instant, blood flowering behind his eyes, hands clutching wildly at the awful pain in his chest. Then the pain vanished, and his eyes popped open, and he knew that death was not going to claim him. He lay still upon his back, one hand pressed against his steadily beating heart, reveling in the absence of pain. He ran his tongue over his cracked lips, blinked his eyelids rapidly, drew a deep draught of air through his nostrils, smelling the odors of copal and his own sweat. His hand stuck briefly to his skin when he sought to lift it from his heart, and he realized that he was still covered with the paint of his fast.

He pushed himself up into a sitting position, hands braced against the floor in anticipation of dizziness. He had returned to consciousness so quickly, without the usual awareness of emergence and change. But he experienced no light-headedness, no ill effects of any kind. The sense of his own well-being, after participating in the death of the Jaguar, was absolutely intoxicating, so that he wanted to laugh and shout and slap himself on the chest. He had survived! Yet at the same time he was too astonished by these impulses to act on them. When was the last time he had laughed, or felt the urge to shout? When had the mere fact of being alive aroused such exultation in him? It was too long ago for him to recall.

I can feel, he told himself, and was surprised by the flood of reactions the admission touched off inside him. His scalp prickled with warmth, and his palms dampened suddenly. He understood then that the transformation of the Jaguar had indeed taken place, within himself. The cold, unheeding ferocity was gone from his heart, along with the anger and the hunger and the snarling defiance. They had expired with the Jaguar, in the blackest depths of the Underworld. As he thought this, he again heard the high, keening wail of the dying Jaguar, a sound that seemed to emanate from somewhere beneath him and flow upward through his body, as the voices of the ancestors had in the past. As he listened, the sound dropped in pitch, becoming broader and more human in tone, no longer a mere whine of bewildered despair. It was a voice raised in mourning, the cry of a creature capable of comprehending his own grief, a creature who saw his own death in the loss of others. Balam Xoc recognized the voice as his own, the voice of the spirit that would live on after his flesh and bones had been lowered into their grave.

He concentrated on the voice, and felt himself rising out of his body, out through the walls that confined him. Light burst around him, buoying him up, so that he floated, bodiless, in the brilliant air that hung over the great plaza and the temples that surrounded it. He had traveled in his dreams before, but never like this, when he was awake and could feel the exhilaration of flight. He could see in all directions: east, toward the buildings and gardens of the Jaguar Paw House, hidden among the trees; west, where Cauac Caan's enormous funerary temple—his "Headdress"—dominated the horizon; north, to the crowd of several thousand gathered between the twin pyramids of the Katun Enclosure; and south, to the processions advancing across the plaza from the clan houses. His voice deepened into a rhythmic, humming murmur, almost a chant, drawing him downward, down through the empty air toward the procession of his own people.

He could see them very clearly as they mounted the broad steps that rose from the plaza floor to the first tier of the north platform. The clan priests came first, carrying streamered staves and waving ladles of smoking incense. Then came Kinich Kakmoo and Tzec Balam's son, walking ahead of a canopied litter borne by four strong men. Kanan Naab and Chibil walked on either side of the litter, the former flanked by Pacal and Akbal, the latter by Hok and Chac Mut. Behind were the black-painted pilgrims and those to be adopted into the clan, followed by the lords of the clan and their male guests, and then by the women and children.

They passed between the monuments that lined the long terrace and came to the steep, narrow staircase that led up to the second tier and the Shrine of the Jaguar Protector. The priests began their ascent without delay, disappearing into the deep shadows cast by the Sky Clan temples that towered over the staircase on both sides. The rest of the procession stopped and stood in place while the bearers set the litter down and stepped away from it. Going to their knees, Pacal and Akbal reached in under the canopy and very slowly brought Box Ek forth, their arms twined under her legs and behind her back. They carried her to the base of the steps, where Kinich was down on one knee, bent beneath the painted seat strapped to his back. Pacal and Akbal carefully transferred Box Ek to the seat, tucking the ends of her embroidered shift in around her shrunken body as they secured the straps that held her in place. Then Kinich rose to his feet, steadied the load on his back, and started up the steps.

Balam Xoc's voice swelled and became resonant with an emotion he only gradually recognized as admiration. He had not known that Box Ek would try to attend the ceremony, or that the clan would indulge her wishes, and her frailty, so conscientiously. Pacal went up the stairs first, looking back over his shoulder, an arm extended behind him to catch Kinich should he slip. The warrior took the steps one at a time, keeping his back straight beneath his load yet bending sharply at the waist, so that his upper body was parallel to the incline. Akbal followed his brother closely, his long arms raised protectively, hands almost touching the woman in the seat. Single-file, they struggled upward through the shadows of the Sky Clan temples, watched from both above and below. The muscles jumped and knotted in

Kinich's shoulders and calves, and he wheezed and bared his glittering teeth, sweat streaming down his clenched features. Box Ek swayed in her seat, her withered face turned toward the sky, eyes closed, grimacing in pain with each jolting step. Balam Xoc could feel Pacal's anxious readiness and the ache in Akbal's upraised arms; he could feel the tension in Kinich's body as he strained to make his ascent gentle as well as safe. But much more keenly, he could feel Box Ek's weariness and pain, and the nearness of her death. *Come to me, my sister,* he sang, his voice stretching itself into words, becoming mournful yet accepting, the voice that was truly his own: *Come to me, come to the one who knows what awaits you . . .*

There were forty steps to the top, and only on the last did Pacal, and then Kinich, emerge again into the light, out of the shadows of the Sky Clan. Akbal signaled triumphantly to those below, then joined his father in unstrapping the burden from Kinich's back. Leaving Box Ek in her seat, Akbal and Pacal began to carry her across the plaza toward the Shrine of the Jaguar Protector, with Kinich following behind, staggering slightly as he massaged his neck with both hands. Their pride and relief in their success came to Balam Xoc in a warm billowing of emotion, wafting him upward and away. He felt his spirit withdrawing, his voice fading to a mere whisper: *You have come, you have come . . .*

Then darkness returned, and he was sitting in his chamber, his head nodding drowsily but his mind fully aware of what he had seen and felt. He recalled his first vision, and the way his people had stood helpless and unseeing, waiting for the sky to swallow them up. He remembered how the Spirit Woman had come to him, an old woman bearing the face of the katun upon her back, crying out against its crushing weight. Now he had seen his people come to him, bearing an old woman upon their young backs, climbing bravely and successfully through the shadows of the Sky Clan, passing from darkness into light. And they had come without his urging, without being driven or led. Their striving had come forth freely, from within themselves.

Balam Xoc located his water bowl and drank slowly, taking pleasure in the appeasement of his thirst despite the rush of his thoughts, which coalesced rapidly into conclusions. Released from the fierce hunger of the Jaguar and the cold determination of his ancestors, he could now see what he had accomplished, and what he had been meant to accomplish. It was not the restoration of the past importance of the Jaguar Paw Clan. That had been lost in the time of Bacab and Kan Balam Moo, though the yearning for it had lived on in all who came after, and had been born anew in him. That had been his means for awakening the people, but not, he saw now, the true goal of his struggle. The goal was to make them important in their own eyes, so that they would not allow themselves to be swallowed up by those who could claim the importance of power and wealth. Today he had seen the proof of his success.

Yet Balam Xoc also understood, from the intensity of his identification with Box Ek, that he was himself the old, the burden his people carried. He had changed them and had awakened them to their danger, but then he had drawn the danger down upon them. He had made the shadow of the ruler loom ever larger over their lives, so that they could not mistake the source of their oppression. Yet he had allowed them no way into the light, no way out of his own shadow, forcing them to fight a clan war they could not hope to win. He had given them the means, but not the opportunity, to be free. It was time he released them, and gave them back their lives.

There must be no successor, he decided, *no heir to the power they have invested in me. They must find their own leaders, and their own path into the future.* Perhaps they would have to leave Tikal, taking with them whatever they could of their past and abandoning the rest. More of the old ways would be lost, changed, or forgotten with the passage of time. Yet it was that loss, and the grief it caused, that his spirit had been shaped to carry. It was the voice with which he would call to the living, to make them remember, and endure.

Rising to his feet, Balam Xoc stretched his arms toward the vaulted ceiling overhead, filled with the certainty that he would not return here. There was no need to, for he had completed his journey, his transformation. He would dance for one last time, then. He would dance the Death of the Night Sun Jaguar. And he would offer himself as proof of the Jaguar's transformation, into the warm, ascendant sun of the new day.

KANAN NAAB knelt beside Box Ek in the very first row of celebrants, just to the left of the stone pedestal where Balam Xoc would perform his rites. The men of the clan stood all around them, with Akbal and Hok standing directly behind Box Ek's seat, leaning forward over her to provide some measure of shade from the noon sun. From the other side of the seat, Chibil fanned the old woman with an oval wicker fan, stirring the wisps of white hair that had shaken loose from her headwrap. Box Ek's eyes were closed, and there was a vacant expression upon her face, her mouth hanging open to permit the whistling passage of breath. Kanan Naab exchanged a concerned glance with Chibil, wondering if they had made a grave error in bringing Box Ek here. The vigor with which she had insisted on coming seemed to have been utterly sapped by the long journey from the Jaguar Paw House, and there was little they could do to revive her now. Nor would it be possible to take her out of the plaza, with the crowd packed in so tightly behind them.

The drums beat with an insistence that pulled at Kanan Naab, tempting her to turn her attention away, to the scene of the ceremony soon to commence. But she struggled against the impulse, coaxing Box Ek back to wakefulness with silent urgency. Then the old woman's eyelids fluttered open, blinking against the light reflecting off the open pavement in front of them. Gradually, she raised her eyes to the pedestal and the monument that stood behind it, and then to the steps that climbed to the red-painted shrine above. Her head shook slightly and pulled back against the back of her seat, as if she were overwhelmed by what she was seeing. She turned to look at Kanan Naab, mustering the strength to speak above the beating of the drums. Kanan Naab brought her face very close, feeling the gentle breeze from Chibil's fan.

"It is all so near," Box Ek managed in a thin, halting voice. She lifted a gnarled hand from her lap, wordlessly inviting Kanan Naab to take it into her own, which the young woman did with great care, knowing how easily her touch could bruise. Box Ek closed her eyes for a moment, seeming to draw strength from the contact. When her breathing was steadier, she again looked at Kanan Naab.

"You must watch now," she said to the young woman, tilting her chin toward the pedestal. "It is a great honor to be so close."

"It is only because of you that I am here," Kanan Naab replied loyally, refusing to look away.

"Then obey my wishes. I would not have you waste this opportunity. Watch, my daughter. It is important to you."

Restraining herself from squeezing the old woman's hand, Kanan Naab tried to put her gratitude into her eyes. Box Ek nodded and smiled wearily, then deliberately turned her face toward the front, forcing Kanan Naab to follow her example.

The tall stone slab of the monument was a gleaming yellow in the sun's light, so near that Kanan Naab could see the smoothly sanded texture of its surface. Excitement made her stomach lift and tighten, and she reminded herself again not to put any pressure on the delicate, clawlike hand she held between her own. She looked up at the shrine just as Nohoch Ich emerged from the central doorway and started down the temple stairs, and her attention fastened upon him relentlessly, searching for a message in the way he carried himself. He paused at the foot of the stairs and signaled to the drummers, who abruptly broke off their beating, bringing a sudden silence down over the crowded plaza. Then Nohoch came forward and mounted the pedestal in front of the monument, crossing his arms on his chest to indicate that he spoke for Balam Xoc. He raised his voice so that he would be heard clearly even in the back rows.

"The Living Ancestor has emerged from his confinement. He has said that today, he will *dance* the rites. He will dance the Death of the Night Sun Jaguar. Thus has he spoken."

There was an excited stirring in the men standing around Kanan Naab, but her eyes did not stray from Nohoch's face. He cast a brief glance in her direction before he stepped down from the pedestal, his eyes widening ever so slightly in an expression she had come to know very well in the time they had spent together. It was the look he wore whenever he felt that Balam Xoc was being purposefully vague or enigmatic, daring them to interpret his motives. *He has not been told yet,* Kanan Naab decided; *he knows no more than he was given to announce.*

The drums began to beat again as Nohoch climbed back up the temple stairs and disappeared into the shrine. Kanan Naab glanced sideways at Box Ek, who appeared alert, and enough herself to refuse to return the glance. Chibil nodded encouragingly from the other side of the seat, her fan still waving against the heat. Gently stroking Box Ek's hand, Kanan Naab gazed up at the shrine, puzzling over the meaning of Nohoch's announcement. In the past, Balam Xoc had always kept his dancing separate from the performance of the rites, which had never changed. And why had he made a special reference to the Death of the Jaguar? That was always the climactic event of the ritual, and its most solemn moment. A fitting prelude, perhaps, to the designation of a successor . . .

Lowering her eyes, she was made aware of the men standing around and beside her. She could find Yaxal without even looking, wedged in between Kinich and Chac Mut, only three places to her left. Was it a sign that the two of them were together in the front row, separated by so little? Or had she been brought here for some other purpose? To be called forward, out of the world of men and women? It had not seemed possible last night, after she had spoken to her father. But now the drums beat, and there was only air between herself and the pedestal where the Jaguar would stand, looking down upon her. The choice, like the decision, would not be hers.

Then Nohoch Ich and Tzec Balam came out onto the platform of the shrine, followed by the awesome figure of the Jaguar Protector. The men around Kanan Naab began to kneel, and she had to remind herself to breathe as the procession descended the temple steps and came toward the pedestal, growing larger and larger. The priests parted and went to either side of the monument, and the Jaguar mounted the round stone pedestal without assistance, using his staff for leverage. He appeared huge and menacing, nearly as tall as the monument behind him, the red claws of his wooden paw pointed out at the crowd. He raised his staff, and the drumming stopped, sending echoes booming off the back of the Sky Clan temples.

The Jaguar surveyed them for a long moment, then lowered the staff, signaling the drummers to take up the familiar rhythm of the rites. Words formed in Kanan Naab's mind, anticipating the chant of the Jaguar as he prepared for his descent into the Underworld. But no voice issued from the shadowy space between the Jaguar's jaws. Instead, he began to dance silently upon the stone, lifting his legs and thrusting out his chest, turning his massive head from side to side, as if studying his own movements. Even after she recovered from the shock of not hearing the expected chant, Kanan Naab required a few more moments before she recognized the movements for what they were: The Jaguar was *preening,* glorying in the awareness of his own power and grace. With an arrogant kind of languor, he raised the red paw to the long tongue that protruded from his gaping jaws, then brought it up to his muzzle, rubbing with a lazy, circular motion.

The words of the chant came back into Kanan Naab's mind with renewed force, stripped of their ritual solemnity and made stunningly apt by the movements of the creature on the stone. *Yes,* she thought breathlessly, *this* was *how the Jaguar would prepare himself for his journey.* Not with the rigid trepidation of a man holding bravely to thoughts of sacrifice and duty, but with the utter fearlessness of his kind, a night-hunter undaunted by danger or darkness.

The drummers struck a deeper, more ominous note, indicating the Jaguar's passage below the western horizon, down into the first of the nine levels of the Underworld. Here is where he would encounter the Wind of Knives, the fierce cold of Xibalba, the Land of the Dead. Kanan Naab felt a shiver run through her body as the words of the second chant welled up out of memory. But the Jaguar did not sing, and instead of shrinking from the cold, he suddenly began to dance faster, becoming frantic in his gestures, stabbing out blindly with his staff and claws. He attacked the cold with wild concentration, whirling in a tight circle, as if to shake an invisible enemy from his back.

Kanan Naab could only stare, the words of the ceremony running unheeded through her mind. What she was seeing required no description—it was the journey itself. The Jaguar went down and down, his vigor undiminished, meeting the creatures who attacked him with savage enthusiasm. He was no easy victim, and often the aggressor, turning his attacker into prey, devouring the creatures he killed with great, hungry sweeps of his jaws. He snarled angrily at those who wounded or eluded him, defying them to come within range of his claws and fangs, refusing to turn tail and flee. He was a creature more to be feared than pitied, a creature who would stalk Death itself.

Only gradually did the Jaguar's movements slow, as he swam through the black waters of the Underworld, head tilted back above his flailing limbs, sinking and then rising again, struggling onward. Little by little, the figure on the stone sank to his knees, accompanied by the dropping rhythm of the drums. The Jaguar's head dipped, then straightened, then fell again, dragged down by its own weight. Legs curled beneath him, he went down flat upon the stone, dropping the staff from one hand, and then the red paw from the other. A quiver went through his prostrate body, and a single drum beat slowly, mournfully. The Jaguar had died.

The sudden movement of Balam Xoc's hands startled Kanan Naab out of her trance, shattering the illusion with their humanness, their purposeful reach. They tugged blindly at the back of the costume, behind his neck. Then he abruptly straightened up and went back onto his haunches, tearing off the jaguar head and depositing it behind him in a single motion. Kanan Naab gasped in unison with the crowd, raising her hands to her mouth in shock. Balam Xoc knelt facing them, an old man clothed in jaguar skin, his long white hair hanging loose upon his shoulders, his forehead glistening with perspiration. The drum thudded like a giant heartbeat as he slowly rose from his knees, spreading his arms out over them, palms opened to the sky. He turned in a slow semicircle from right to left, his eyes wide and staring, scanning the crowd intently, looking into their upraised faces. He stopped when he was facing the place where Kanan Naab knelt, bringing his extended arms together in front of him, as if pointing. The drum also stopped, and Kanan Naab was paralyzed in the silence, staring up at Balam Xoc's outstretched hands. Then she realized, simultaneously, that he was not looking at her, and that her hands were empty. Her head jerked sideways, and she saw that Box Ek hung limply in the straps that bound her to her seat, her head bowed onto her chest. Chibil's horrified expression showed that she, too, had not seen it happen.

"The Old Ones pass from among you," Balam Xoc said in a loud, mournful voice. "They take the burdens of the past from your shoulders, so that you might walk freely into the new day."

He dropped his arms, gazing sadly at Box Ek. Tears welled up in his eyes and ran down his deeply lined cheeks, drawing a gasp of amazement from those close enough to see. Turning to face the entire crowd, he brushed at his eyes with his fingers and held up his hands for all to see.

"See my tears, people of the Jaguar Paw," he cried. "See the tears I shed for the suffering you have endured in Katun Eleven Ahau, and for the hardships you will suffer in the future. But you are young and strong, my people, and you have no need to fear what lies ahead of you. The memory of your ancestors is in your blood, and you will not be led astray by false prophets or foreign ways. You are *all* my Close Ones."

Balam Xoc paused and spread his arms out over them in blessing.

"Remember what you have seen here today," he commanded in an oddly gentle tone. "Hold it in your hearts, wherever you may journey. Know, always, that you walk in the eyes of the ancestors. Thus have I spoken . . ."

Then he stepped down off the pedestal and walked toward the temple steps, leaving his implements and the jaguar head on the platform behind him.

Kanan Naab turned immediately to Box Ek, but Chibil simply held up a hand to her, shaking her head in resignation.

"She is truly gone?" Kanan Naab queried weakly, knowing it was true, knowing even that Box Ek had wanted to die this way. But the fact of her death was impossible to comprehend, the memory of holding her hand too fresh to be shaken. Only when Akbal reached forward to touch her on the shoulder, and she saw the tears in his eyes, was she able to weep herself, doubling over as the Jaguar had done upon the stone and sobbing into her empty hands. Finally, other hands reached down to help her to her feet, holding her by the elbows until she could stand on her own. She looked blankly at her father and Kinich, and then at Nohoch Ich, who held Balam Xoc's staff in his hands.

"He has chosen neither of us," Nohoch said, apparently satisfied with the decision. "We are released."

"Indeed," Kanan Naab murmured, gazing down at the lifeless, huddled form of Box Ek. They stood silently for a moment before Pacal turned and drew Yaxal into the group of mourners.

"Come, my daughter," he said to Kanan Naab, taking her elbow with his other hand. "Let us walk freely, as he commanded."

The seat holding Box Ek's body was again lifted and strapped onto Kinich's back, and the warrior led the way out of the plaza, the crowd parting silently to let him pass, bowing their heads at the sight of his burden. Kanan Naab looked back only once, and saw the pedestal standing empty before the tall yellow stone. Then she walked on, holding the image firmly in her heart.

XV

LAST RITES

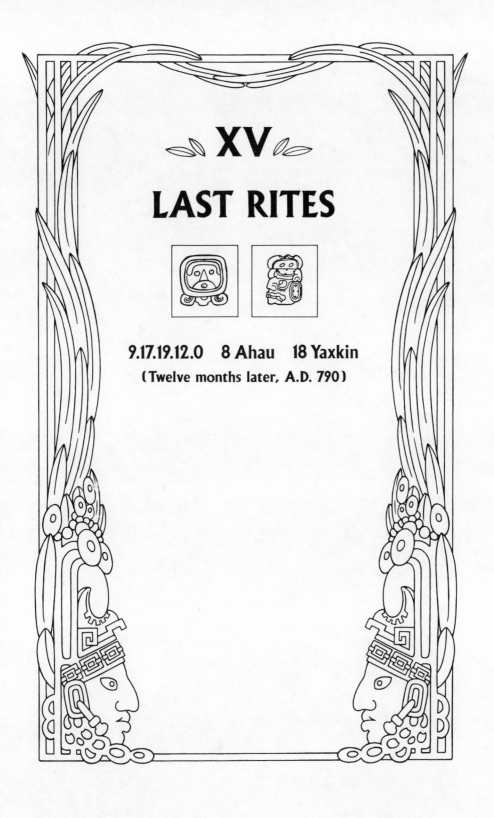

9.17.19.12.0   8 Ahau   18 Yaxkin
(Twelve months later, A.D. 790)

AFTER PASSING the last of the Jaguar Paw sentries, Chan Mac followed an impulse and took the path through the breadnut trees to Akbal's stone. He stopped when he came to the edge of the clearing and saw that his impulse had been rewarded: Akbal was sitting cross-legged at the foot of the slab, his back to the clearing and the family gardens beyond it. Chan Mac smiled ruefully at the utterly solitary image his friend presented, lost in the contemplation of his stone while the rest of the clan, and the whole of the city outside the clan, were feverishly engaged in bringing in the crops. He remembered Akbal proudly telling Muan Kal how he and Zac Kuk had worked on the reservoir and how he had headed a workcrew when the clan gardens were being built. *They can spare him,* Chan Mac decided as he crossed the clearing; there was no need anymore for painters *or* diplomats to be digging in the mud.

He approached quietly, in case Akbal was in one of his staring trances, but his friend noticed his presence before he had reached the shelter and rose to greet him.

"I was returning from a visit to the Flint House," Chan Mac explained. "Something told me that you might be here."

"I come when I can," Akbal said diffidently. "What business did you have at the Flint House?"

"Very little, though I did not expect much, with everyone out in the fields. There was a message from my father, however. Ektun has lost another battle with the Macaws. One of my uncles—my mother's youngest brother—was killed in the fighting."

It took Akbal a moment to assimilate this information, as if he had to remind himself of where Ektun was and who the Macaws were.

"I am sorry," he said at last. "Are your brothers safe?"

"So far. They are all away with the army. But I did not come here to trouble you with these things. Let me see what you have done."

Akbal turned sideways into the shelter, making a vague gesture of invitation toward the stone. The small portion that had been carved stood out in bold relief at the top, trapping shadows in precise configurations. Chan Mac could see the delicate overlapping of scales on the serpent's undulating body, the crossed bands of sky signs, the leafy twists and beadlike kernels of maize that indicated the Sun's role as the nurturer of life. Glancing at Akbal for permission, he stepped closer and slid his fingers into one of the narrow grooves, stirring neither dust nor grit, encountering not a trace of roughness.

"It is so *smooth,*" he said admiringly, raising his eyebrows at Akbal. "Like a polished piece of jade."

"We sand and polish more than we should," Akbal confessed, shrugging off the flattery, "because we are still uncertain with the chisel. Also because we have not been able to go on to the rest of it."

"That must be difficult for you."

"I am learning to be patient," Akbal said helplessly. "But I cannot proceed until the composition is whole in my mind. I know now how I will portray Balam Xoc, but I have yet to determine who it is that will share the central space with him. I have thought that it must be the ruler, but Grandfather will neither confirm nor deny this, and I have not seen it for myself."

"So you wait," Chan Mac concluded. "As we all do. Something has ended, Akbal, has it not? Some urgency has been lost."

"Since the Tun-End, you mean?"

"Exactly. Balam Xoc has disbanded the Close Ones without naming a successor. He has stopped making defiant gestures toward the ruler. Instead, he is presiding at marriages and seeing to the education of our children, and bringing new members onto the clan council. For what is he preparing us, Akbal?"

"He is preparing us to live without him," Akbal proposed. "Was that not clear from his performance at the ceremony?"

"Certainly. But *where* are we to live? Am I the only one who heard him speak of a journey, of not being misled by 'foreign' ways?"

"I also heard him, but I did not rush to your interpretation. You are thinking of Chetumal again."

"I am thinking that the clan war has never been settled, even though it seems to have dropped from Balam Xoc's mind. And yours, my friend. This false peace has made the Jaguar Paw people complacent."

"And it has made you restless," Akbal asserted. "Do you not move about freely enough? You go out to the houses of the other clans nearly every day."

"Yes, we are very free," Chan Mac agreed scornfully. "I could even go to the marketplace, if I were willing to pay the necessary bribes. I could go to the palace. But there would be nothing for me to do there, except avoid arrest. What are you going to do when you are finished with the stone?"

Akbal blinked in surprise, not seeing the connection immediately. He waved a hand over the blank expanse of stone.

"I have not thought that far ahead."

"Yet you have begun training new craftsmen, as your grandfather suggested. How will they support themselves if you cannot trade their goods?"

"They are all still children," Akbal protested. "By the time they are grown, we . . ."

"Yes?" Chan Mac prompted sharply, when Akbal could not complete the thought. "What will have happened by then? What is it we are waiting for?"

"I do not know," Akbal admitted grudgingly. "Perhaps the end of Katun Eleven Ahau will bring an end to the clan war. This has been a good season for everyone's crops. The ruler will have no reason to envy us."

Chan Mac looked away for a moment, not deigning to reply. When he looked back, Akbal was staring down at the stone, his lips pursed stubbornly.

"I do not mean to reproach you, my friend," Chan Mac said in a softer tone. "I see how preoccupied you are with your work here, and rightfully so. But surely Balam Xoc would have us attend to our future, now that he has stopped pointing the way for us."

"You will have the chance to present your views at the meeting of the clan council," Akbal replied, only partially mollified by the apology.

"I had hoped to have allies. Otherwise I might be seen as an insolent newcomer, reminding the council of what it means to be Jaguar Paw."

"As Grandfather said, we are all his Close Ones now. I would not expect easy agreement, however."

"I have not found any so far," Chan Mac admitted, "though I did not speak as plainly to Kinich and Chac Mut as I have to you."

"That is the only way they will hear you," Akbal assured him, and Chan Mac finally shrugged and nodded in resignation.

"No doubt. I will leave you to your stone, then. I must tell Zac Kuk about our uncle."

"You will probably find her with Ixchel and Haleu, planning for the harvest celebration."

Chan Mac nodded again and tilted his head for a parting look at the stone.

"That is very fine work, for a painter," he said with a sly smile. "I see the definite influence of Ektun."

"It is there," Akbal acknowledged seriously, then saw that he was being teased, and gave Chan Mac a knowing grimace. "In fact, it is here now, all around me, goading me like a great, restless presence."

"May it inspire you equally in the future," Chan Mac said with mock graciousness, laughing as he bowed once over the stone, and then left Akbal to his thoughts.

THE MEETING of the clan council had been scheduled for the late afternoon, prior to the feasting that would begin the celebration of the harvest. The women were already setting out the food beneath the thatched and decorated ramadas when Pacal left his house and crossed the plaza to the house of Nohoch Ich. A slight nervous stirring in his stomach made him think back to the time when he had first been summoned to join the council, some twenty years earlier. He had been very nervous then, anxious to prove himself worthy of the honor. Balam Xoc had been the head of the council, and Pacal's older brother, Chac Balam, had still been alive and had already earned the respect of the older men. Pacal remembered how closely he had watched his father and brother during those first meetings, imitating their gestures and manner of speech like an unabashed apprentice.

Pacal stopped outside the doorway, remembering the rest of it: how Chac Balam had died so unexpectedly, and then Nicte and Ik Caan in fast succession. Balam Xoc had left his place on the council to become the Living Ancestor, and Pacal had suddenly found himself with no one to imitate, and other men looking to *him* to lead. *So I took the ruler as my example,* he reflected ruefully, letting the thought humble him as he prepared to join the council for the second time. *You are truly a newcomer,* he told himself; *you must observe how these men conduct themselves before raising your voice in their midst. They have no reason to trust what you say.*

Nohoch was sitting in the central place on the bench against the back wall, and he returned Pacal's bow of greeting with the polite impartiality required of the head. Balam Xoc sat in the place of honor to Nohoch's right, and to his right were Tzec Balam, Tzec Balam's son, and Yaxal Can, who had already won a place for himself among the clan priests. To Nohoch's left were Kinich Kakmoo, Chac Mut, and Akbal: the clan nacom, steward, and master of craftsmen. The heads of the nearby families filled out the rest of the places along the back wall, so that the six new members were being given seats at both ends of the long, narrow chamber. Hok, as the clan witness, was sitting among the scribes on the floor in front of Nohoch, and Pacal felt the man's uncovered eye follow him as he went to the left end of the room and took a seat next to Chan Mac.

"Greetings, my lord," Chan Mac whispered as they nodded to each other, and Pacal felt the younger man's eyes briefly search his face. *Looking for allies,* Pacal thought, his old instincts for political maneuvering coming back in a nostalgic rush. But they were not strong anymore, and he chose to ignore the overture, turning his eyes toward the opposite end of the room. The only one of the new members he recognized was Opna, who had been chosen because of his popularity among the recent adoptees to the clan. *And because Nohoch wants to watch him,* Pacal decided, remembering Kanan Naab's wary attitude toward Opna. He had to give Nohoch credit; he would have taken the same precaution, had the responsibilities of the head been his.

After Tzec Balam had said the necessary prayers, invoking the guidance of the ancestors, Nohoch opened the meeting by introducing each of the new members and formally welcoming them to the council. Then he turned to his right, inviting the comment of the Living Ancestor. But Balam Xoc declined to speak, gesturing for him to conduct the meeting as he wished. So Nohoch called upon Kinich to deliver the first report, and the warrior responded almost too quickly, speaking in a loud, assertive voice to disguise his nervousness. He reported that there had been no clashes with the ruler's warriors and no suspicious fires since the last Tun-End, and that their ability to communicate with their relatives in other parts of Tikal had improved to the point where gifts as well as messages could be safely exchanged. They knew the identity and location of all the warriors guarding the trails, he explained with visible satisfaction, and they had had the pleasure of seeing the number of warriors steadily shrink as they were diverted to more pressing tasks elsewhere.

"We have even been able to move some of our sentries closer to the grana-ries," Kinich concluded with a sardonic smile, "so that they can use their weapons on the pests who attack our maize."

Several of the men laughed appreciatively, a breach of decorum that Nohoch tolerantly ignored, gesturing for questions from the rest of the group. But there were no questions; everyone seemed as satisfied with Kinich's report as he was himself. At a nod from Nohoch, Tzec Balam began to talk about the young boys whom he and Yaxal Can were training in the reading of the glyphs and numbers. Pacal, however, could not follow the priest's words. His mind was still back on what Kinich had said, and the unthinking silence with which it had been accepted. Did they think they had been forgotten by the ruler? Was Kinich so foolish as to believe that? He glanced at his elder son, and then at Balam Xoc, who had also raised no objections to this illusion of safety. *They have begun the celebration early,* Pacal thought, feeling the nervousness stir in his stomach again.

His apprehensions were confirmed when Chac Mut took over from Tzec Balam and began to deliver the report of the clan steward. It was a long and detailed report, the kind Pacal had taught him to make, describing which reservoirs had been dredged and how much new land had been cleared and planted, and what the total yield of each of the various crops had been. He also explained the steps that were being taken to house and employ the newest clan members, thereby raising the question of the need for more land.

"Since the rains have been kind to everyone this season," Chac Mut rea-soned, "we must assume that the ruler's crop will also be a good one. That will lower the value of our surplus accordingly. Instead of trading for hard goods, then, perhaps we should approach some of our neighbors for land. Even if they are well fed, they will want to replenish their stores of seed. That might be the basis on which to approach them."

Nohoch asked if the clan had sufficient supplies of the hard goods Chac Mut had mentioned, and the young man assured him firmly that they did.

"Thanks to the efforts of Pacal Balam," Chac Mut said, leaning forward to nod in his former master's direction, "we were paid in advance for our work-men, in these very commodities."

Pacal understood that Chac Mut was trying to honor him, but as the admiring eyes of the council swept toward him, he felt himself go cold inside. He remembered standing atop the temple, shouting at the ruler, a sharp spear pointing at the center of his chest. Did they think this had been a mere "effort," a piece of clever negotiating? He could not respond with either modesty or gratitude, and simply stared blankly at Chac Mut, half-expecting to be asked if he could repeat his performance next season. He did not know what he might have said to that, but apparently no one considered it necessary to ask.

Akbal was the next to speak, and his manner was much less expansive than that of those who had gone before, for the simple reason that he had little to report in the way of trade. His production of crafts was limited to the needs of the clan itself and their most immediate neighbors, most of whom were too poor to trade for anything but food. So Akbal spoke instead of the young apprentices he had taken into the craft house, and of the promise some of them had shown as painters and carvers. He stopped then and glanced back at Chan Mac.

"I am concerned, however," he went on quickly, "that I am training another generation of craftsmen who will have no market for their goods."

Ah, the first complaint, Pacal thought with relief, inordinately proud of Akbal for having raised it. He sensed that Chan Mac also approved, and remembered the trips that he and Akbal had taken to the coast. The clan had little need for a diplomat if they had no relations with people outside of Tikal, just as they had no need for more craftsmen if they could not expand their trade possibilities. The alliance between his son and Chan Mac was therefore natural, a matter of mutual self-interest. Pacal glanced covertly at both of them, wondering if their alliance was anything more than that—if they shared his critical perception of what he had been hearing.

Nohoch nodded judiciously and turned the response over to Chac Mut, who conferred briefly with Kinich before addressing Akbal's concern.

"We have been speaking privately with our friends in the Flint Clan," Chac Mut revealed. "And though no terms have been discussed, they have shown some willingness to convey our goods to the markets in Nakum and Holmul."

"When we last visited Nakum and Holmul," Akbal said doubtfully, "their markets were no better than the ones here."

"That was before this season's crop," Chac Mut reminded him. "Trade should be much improved in the eastern cities, as it will be here in Tikal. Our neighbors might also be interested in crafts again, if the ruler makes a fair distribution of the city's surplus."

The possibility was offered with a casual assurance that took Pacal's breath away and made him wonder if he had heard correctly. Akbal seemed prepared to question it, but Kinich spoke up on Chac Mut's behalf first.

"It has been possible for us to go farther and farther without danger of betrayal or interception," he explained to Akbal. "Perhaps with the Flint Clan as intermediaries, we will be able to stretch our trade routes farther east and gradually make them our own."

Akbal frowned, but both Kinich and Chac Mut were waiting for any further argument he might propose, wearing the blandly reasonable expression of men who did not expect to be persuaded. Akbal bowed to their pressure, and Nohoch spread his hands and looked in both directions down the line of men, seeking other opinions or questions. Pacal felt Chan Mac draw himself up beside him, but then the young man blew air through his nostrils and settled back down, apparently deciding not to dispute the issue. Nohoch waited an additional moment before indicating that he was satisfied.

"If there is nothing more to discuss," he suggested, "we can conclude this meeting and retire to the feast that awaits us."

Again he glanced patiently in both directions, mimicked unconsciously by both Kinich and Chac Mut. *Allies,* Pacal thought sourly, though his lips remained sealed against the torrent of disagreement that threatened to pour forth at any moment. Their smugness begged for a challenge, but if the younger men were not willing to supply it, he was not going to expose himself in their place. He did not wish to go from newcomer to outcast in so short a time. But then Balam Xoc's voice broke the silence:

"I wish to hear from Pacal Balam."

Recovering quickly from his surprise, Nohoch dutifully extended a hand in Pacal's direction, inviting him to speak. Pacal's throat closed as all the eyes in the room fastened upon him, and he abruptly pushed himself off the bench and walked forward, until he stood facing the place where his father sat. Balam Xoc gazed back at him expectantly, unperturbed by the angry tautness of Pacal's stance and the hands clenched into fists at his sides. Hok had come up into a crouch at the foot of the bench, his good eye glaring a warning.

"What is it you wish to hear from me?" Pacal demanded hoarsely, aware of the alarm on the faces to both sides of his father.

"The truth, Pacal. Can you offer us anything more?"

Pacal laughed suddenly, a harsh sound without mirth.

"No," he agreed, "that is all that is left to me. I have no secret plans to protect, no alliances to maintain," he added, glancing at Nohoch and the young men to his left. "My reputation is that of a man who once served the ruler at the expense of the clan, so it cannot suffer from what I say now."

"If you have a disagreement with us, Pacal," Nohoch interjected, "you must tell us so."

"I did not wish to spoil the consensus you had achieved so skillfully, my lord," Pacal said sarcastically. "Even if it was based on dangerous delusions."

"Speak, then," Nohoch commanded sharply, his face darkening. Pacal relaxed his stance and spread his hands to encompass all of the men.

"I have been listening to all this talk of sentries being withdrawn, and land being obtained, and trade routes being extended. I have listened with disbelief, my lords, wondering if I inhabited the same world as those who spoke. Has some peace been made with the ruler of which I am unaware? There was no promise of peace in the agreements I reached with him—only a grudging payment for the workmen he needed."

Pacal paused to let his words sink in, then fixed his eyes on Chac Mut.

"Yes, I speak of the same workmen who have supplied us with salt and obsidian and grinding stones. I no longer lead them to their work each day, but they still come to share their thoughts with me. They tell me how they are being driven by their supervisors to work harder and longer, to make up for the men who have been diverted to the Katun Enclosure. On two occasions, when they asked me, I went to speak to their supervisors, to prevent them from forcing the men to continue working after dark."

"Why did you not report this to me?" Nohoch demanded.

"You would not have been able to get past the warriors guarding the trail," Pacal said dismissively. "Nor would the supervisors have listened to you. You have no *friends* there, my lord."

"And *you* do, my lord?" Chac Mut put in, and Pacal squinted at him narrowly.

"I am still recognized, at least, and I can sympathize with the pressure they are under from the ruler. There is another thing the workmen tell me. Now that the harvest is over, they expect that they will all be shifted to the Katun Enclosure. The construction is still far behind schedule, and the end of the katun is only five months away."

"The ruler will be able to hire additional workers," Chac Mut hastily pointed out, "with the surplus from his crop."

Though he knew it was cruel, Pacal's debating instincts had been aroused, and he could not keep himself from giving his nephew a slow, disdainful smile.

"The ruler will have no surplus," he said, quietly but clearly. "It has been a long time since you were last a steward, Chac Mut. We have both been replaced by incompetents. While you hand-tended the gardens here, they planted in fields that had never been properly restored after last season's rains. So although the rains were gentle this year, the yield was far below what it should have been. This the workmen also tell me. They say that whenever they found a productive piece of land, the insects had been there before them. There will be no surplus."

"That will only increase the value of our crops," Chac Mut countered stubbornly, obviously stung by the smile.

"Not if they are taken from you," Pacal suggested bluntly. "Do you think Caan Ac will bother to negotiate, when the completion of the Katun Enclosure is at stake? He *must* finish it in time for the dedication, or he would surely fall from power. He will have the workmen he needs, one way or another. Instead of all this foolish talk about obtaining more land, we should be preparing ourselves to defend what we have. We should decide what we will do when our workmen are ordered to the Katun Enclosure."

There was a long silence when Pacal had finished, and then hands began to go up around the room, gesturing to Nohoch for permission to speak. Opna was first, then Chan Mac, then several of the other men who had not spoken previously. Pacal looked at his father and saw, to his amazement, that Balam Xoc was smiling, seeming openly pleased with what he had called forth.

"Well argued, my son," Balam Xoc said admiringly, distracting Nohoch, who was already sufficiently distracted by the problem of whom to call upon first. Balam Xoc held up a hand to forestall him.

"It seems that there was more to discuss than you knew. Perhaps, though, it should wait for your next meeting, after these men have had a chance to become acquainted and to share their knowledge with one another. The truth must be formed from what *everyone* knows, not merely from the opinions of the leaders."

"If I have misled the council," Nohoch began, "I would offer my—"

"That will not be necessary," Balam Xoc assured him briskly. "You have not abused our trust. You have only yielded to the temptation of believing that security is possible. Such a belief must always be questioned, as long as the ruler remains your enemy."

"I will remember," Nohoch promised, then forced himself to meet Pacal's eyes. "We are grateful to you, Pacal."

Pacal bowed respectfully and walked back to his seat at the end of the room. After Tzec Balam said a prayer to close the meeting, Nohoch asked them to assemble again in four days' time and then released them to join the celebration. Chan Mac immediately turned in his seat to address Pacal.

"I must speak with you, my lord. May I have the honor of eating with you tonight?"

Akbal joined them before Pacal could respond, and he automatically looked up at his son.

"You have come back to us, my father," Akbal said proudly. Pacal looked past him, following Balam Xoc with his eyes as the old man left the chamber.

"I was brought back," he said to Akbal. "Though in a more kindly manner than I was sent out."

"You are with us now," Akbal proclaimed. "Let us find some balche."

Pacal turned first to Chan Mac, who was waiting patiently for an answer to his request.

"I will hear your proposals, Chan Mac," he agreed. "The ones you swallowed so loudly during the meeting."

"It was not easy, my lord," Chan Mac said in embarrassment. "But you have shown me an example for the future."

"I did not intend to," Pacal said truthfully. "I was willing to let Nohoch have his success. I have run meetings the same way myself, many times. Today I saw how truly dangerous it can be. I will listen to you, Chan Mac; to both of you," he added, including Akbal with an upward glance. "But any alliance we form must be open for all to see and join. Those who oppose us must know everything we know: They are not adversaries to be tricked or outmaneuvered."

"Agreed," Chan Mac said quickly, only a moment before Akbal.

"Then let us get some balche," Pacal proposed, pushing himself off the bench. "My throat is very dry, and thirst is like anger, or like the truth itself: It is denied at great risk . . ."

STANDING BENEATH the ramada in front of Pacal's house, Zac Kuk looked out over the people milling in the plaza before her, and those in the plaza below, and was suddenly, inexplicably sad. She had not had a moment all evening to miss Box Ek, but now she missed the old woman terribly, and missing Box Ek also made her feel the absence of her mother and father and of the uncle who had just died, whom she would never see again. She even recalled the death of her birds, knowing she was indulging a pointless emotion, yet unable to pull herself out of the mood. Afraid that she was about to weep, she slipped out from under the ramada and went next door to Balam Xoc's house, which had no ramada attached to its front and no celebrants lingering near its doorways.

She had intended to go to the back room, where Box Ek had been buried beneath the floor, but as she passed the first doorway, she noticed someone sitting just inside, and stopped short, gasping in surprise. There were no torches here, so it took a moment for her eyes to penetrate the darkness.

"Hok," she said softly, relieved but puzzled. "Does it make you sad, too? The celebration?"

Hok did not answer, but she saw the white of his one eye turn up to her. Spreading her long skirt around her legs, she squatted just outside the doorway, so that she could see him more clearly. His bony fingers were wrapped around his shins, and he was rocking back and forth on his heels with a persistent, restless rhythm. He did not seem disturbed by her presence, but he did not welcome it, either.

"The gifting will begin soon," Zac Kuk ventured, glancing back over her shoulder at the crowded plaza. "You will be missed."

Rocking silently, Hok made what she thought was a slight negative shake of his head, briefly turning his uncovered eye away from her.

"Yes, you will," she insisted, searching her mind for some way to convince him. Then she remembered the conversation she had had with Akbal the last time she had visited him at his stone. "Do you remember the polishing stone you gave to my husband," she asked, "on the night we were married?"

Hok stopped rocking abruptly.

"Akbal has found the perfect use for it," she continued. "On his stone. It is exactly the size of the lines he is carving. He says that it gives the cut its final smoothness, after he has rubbed it with obsidian sand. He is glad that your father's spirit will be part of the stone."

Hok nodded and looked away, bringing his knees together and resting his chin on his kneecaps. When he still did not speak, Zac Kuk sighed inwardly and prepared to leave him to his brooding. Then he grimaced and spoke to the air, his eye still focused somewhere in the distance.

"He will not let me guard him anymore. He does not want me with him."

It took Zac Kuk only an instant to realize that he was referring to Balam Xoc, and then she understood the aura of restless abandonment that surrounded him.

"You are with him more than most," she said sympathetically. "More than any of the other Close Ones. He does not want to be regarded as a holy man any longer. He has become the grandfather of us all."

"He sends me to witness things and does not go himself."

"That is because he trusts you," Zac Kuk assured him, but hesitated briefly before plunging on: "He is preparing himself, and the clan, for the time when he must leave us."

"No!" Hok protested vehemently, pulling his head back so forcefully that he almost lost his balance. The knuckles gripping his shins went white with the effort of holding him in place.

" 'The Old Ones pass from among us,' " Zac Kuk quoted quietly. "He has already danced the Death of the Jaguar for us."

Hok suddenly stood up in the doorway, a spear appearing in his hands.

"No!" he repeated, banging the butt of the spear against the plastered floor. The headband had slipped sideways on his head, the patch peeling back to expose a sliver of dead eye. Zac Kuk rose slowly to face him, struggling against the urge to flee. She was afraid he might strike her without meaning to, without even knowing what he was striking out against.

"Hok," she said sharply. "You are the witness. You must not deny what is shown to you. You *cannot.*"

Hok disappeared into the darkness behind him, then reeled back into view, grasping the spear in both hands. His body was trembling, but the wildness was gone from his eye.

"He trusts you," she told him again, and turned to gesture toward the plaza. "Come, we must not miss the gifting. But leave your weapon," she added. "There is no place for it at this celebration."

After a long pause, Hok reluctantly leaned the spear against the doorframe and stepped down onto the platform beside her. Only as she turned away from the house did Zac Kuk remember the sadness that had brought her here, and she realized that it was gone.

There is no place for that, either, she scolded herself, and led Hok back to the celebration, feeling that Box Ek, wherever her spirit dwelled, would surely approve.

AS HE WATCHED the dancers in the plaza, Balam Xoc realized how utterly fatigued he was, exhausted by all the attention he had given to others during this day and night. Nor was it only this day, but all the days that had passed since his transformation. The masks had fallen away, and he saw his people plainly and fully, as beings with needs and strivings of their own, worthy of his respect. He no longer had the desire to bend them to his own or any other purpose, and he could not withhold his attention from any one of them. He could only pretend for a while to be absorbed in watching the dancers, so that he could give his throat a rest from talking and let his ears listen only to the rolling beat of the drums.

Kanan Naab and Yaxal danced into view, their arms linked, leading the line in a couples' dance. They were well matched in size, but Kanan Naab was much the better dancer, and Balam Xoc noticed that she did not hobble her steps in deference to her husband, as some of the other wives did. He wondered if it had even occurred to her to do so, and decided that it probably had not. Yaxal was working hard to keep up, watching her out of the corner of his eye with what seemed like total concentration, too intent on his movements to display any hint of resentment. This marriage would be a challenge to both of them, Balam Xoc had told them on their wedding day, and he was pleased to see that the desire to meet the challenge—at least on Yaxal's part—had not slackened in the months since.

The couple came to the end of the dancing area and bowed to him before separating and heading back in the opposite direction. Chan Mac and his wife, Kutz, were next in line, both excellent dancers and a pleasure to watch. But Balam Xoc's attention was distracted by a woman in a red and yellow shift, who came up to him humbly from the side, offering him a painted gourd of balche. He discovered that he was thirsty, so he nodded gratefully to the woman and drank, feeling the honied liquid soothe his throat and warm his belly. He paused, though, as he was about to hand the gourd back, struck by the familiarity of the woman's shift, the red and yellow colors and the fraying threads along the hem. She had brought him a gourd earlier in the evening, he remembered, a different gourd. He held the fat-bottomed container out to her, watching the way she reached out to cradle it with her fingers, as if it were a precious, fragile vessel, instead of a common drinking gourd.

He held on to it for an extra moment after it was in her hands, forcing the woman to look up into his eyes. She lowered her gaze again instantly, but not before he had seen the guilty awareness that she had been recognized, and that she had hoped not to be. She clutched the gourd to her bosom but made no move to leave, as if expecting to be reprimanded. Balam Xoc understood then that these gourds were probably not personal mementos, but relics she intended to sell after he was dead. She was obviously from one of the poorer families, and he had noticed others, during the course of the evening, snatching up the bowls from which he had eaten and the mats upon which he had sat. Objects that bore the imprint of the holy man, he thought wearily, gazing at the guilt-stricken woman before him.

"The night has grown cold, my daughter," he said, gesturing at the white cloud his breath formed in front of his face. Then he removed the blanket from around his own shoulders. "You must have this as well."

While the woman stared at him in astonishment, he wrapped the blanket around her carefully, so that she would not have to move her hands from the gourd pressed against her chest. Even when he stepped back and nodded to her with satisfaction, she could still only stare.

"Go with my blessing," he told her, and finally she bowed, bobbing rapidly several times before turning to disappear into the crowd. Hok immediately appeared at Balam Xoc's elbow, holding another blanket.

"Thank you, my son," Balam Xoc said, allowing Hok to drape the warm, brightly colored cloth over his shoulders. He noticed that, as usual, Hok wore no blanket himself, despite the coolness of the night air.

"Tell me," he asked, motioning for Hok to stay at his side. "What have you done with the objects I handled at the reservoir? The maize cob and the breadnut rind, and the sticks?"

"I have them," Hok said proudly. "Safe."

Balam Xoc stared at him with the same, weary compassion he had felt for the woman with the gourds, though he knew that Hok would never sell any of *his* relics.

"When I am gone, you must destroy them."

Hok shrank back a step, torn between his deep desire to comply and the equally strong urge to protect what was most precious to him. Aware that the crowd around them was watching every move, Balam Xoc held up a hand to stay Hok's retreat, then stepped forward and laid the hand upon Hok's chest. The taut skin was clammy beneath his fingers, the man's nipple a hard point against his palm, the ridge of breastbone vibrating beneath the heel of his hand. Hok's eye blinked uncontrollably, as wild as the beating of his heart, and Balam Xoc realized that it was the first time he had ever touched Hok. The first time in many, many years, in fact, that he had touched *anyone* with affection. Keeping his eyes on Hok's angular face, he put his other hand on the man's upper arm, holding him in place. Hok finally stopped blinking, seeming surprised by the tears that had begun to run from his eye. Balam Xoc patted him once on the chest, lifting the hand and putting it back over Hok's heart, so that they could both feel the warmth trapped between them.

"Here, my son," he said softly, so that only Hok could hear him over the drums. "Here is where you must remember me."

Hok expanded his chest and raised his left hand, then hesitated and began blinking again. Then his courage returned, and he lifted the hand and cautiously grasped Balam Xoc's upper arm, linking them together. Out of the corners of his eyes, Balam Xoc saw the people around them shift and stir, no doubt uncomfortable with Hok's boldness. So he smiled and gave Hok's arm a forceful squeeze, patting him once more on the chest before releasing him.

"Stand with me," he said. "Let us watch the dancers together."

He turned back to the plaza with Hok drawn up beside him, and the people surrounding them did likewise, too polite to do more than exchange amazed glances with one another. Balam Xoc could still feel the imprint of Hok's fingers on his blanket-covered arm, and his hand tingled with the memory of the heart that had beat so wildly against it. His eyes grew damp, blurring the images of the dancers in front of him, but he did not have the strength to weep, not even for the loneliness he and Hok had suffered, separately and together. He felt that he was being used up, drained to his depths of all that might possibly benefit his people. And he was content to let it happen, for however long it could, before his people were truly left with only memories and relics.

KANAN NAAB understood Yaxal's intentions from the way he gripped her arm and led her from the plaza, and she went with him willingly, her farewells made, her skin still glowing with the heat of their dancing. He knew the count of her days as well as she did, and knew that she would be ready five days after her bleeding had stopped. She felt very ready, supple and sensitized by the dancing, as she supposed Yaxal was as well. She only hoped that he was not *too* eager, that he did not take her quickly and forcefully from behind, as he had on their first night, when he had spilled the blood that made her a wife. She had hurt for days afterward.

He had gotten much better since then, she reflected, as they entered the darkened back room of their house. More patient, and more wary of his own force. And she had become less tender herself, able to accommodate his thrusts without resistance or pain. She felt no dread at his advances now, and welcomed them with a sincerity that did not have to be feigned. Still . . . there were times when she would remember things the women had told her during her dressing, and she would wonder why she could not bring herself to speak them aloud to her husband. Words came so easily to them otherwise; it seemed incredible that she could not simply murmur "slowly," or ask him to face her.

Yaxal turned to her in the darkness, and she came into his arms compliantly, silently. Because she knew why they could not speak of this, why they could not even contemplate the kind of joking and teasing that Zac Kuk said she shared with Akbal. This was a solemn undertaking for them, a rite made sacred by having seemed so impossible for so long. And this was one rite on which she dared not question Yaxal, lest she seem to be challenging or instructing him.

When he released her from his embrace, she stepped back and began to lift her shift off over her head, as she always did. But Yaxal stopped her and instead led her over to the hearth in the corner of the room. He helped her to sit on the pile of mats and blankets against the wall, and then knelt beside the fire, adding tinder to the coals and blowing it into a flame. As the light fluttered up around her, Kanan Naab wondered why he felt the need for more heat, when she herself was still warm from dancing. But then he turned back to her and knelt where he was, gazing at her fondly, and she realized that it was light he wanted, not heat. He crawled over to where she was sitting and began to pile mats and blankets behind her, coaxing her wordlessly to uncross her legs and sit back against the cushioned wall. As he arranged more mats underneath her, his purposefulness suddenly filled her with shame, so that she hastily lowered her eyes. *He has been given instructions by someone,* she thought, and remembered the long conversation he had had with Kinich, and how it had ceased when she joined them. Had he been discussing this with her *brother*?

Yaxal's fingers touched her chin, tilting her face up to his. He was kneeling between her upraised knees, his other hand resting on her exposed thigh. His eyes were very clear and steady, refusing any thought of shame.

"I wanted to see you," he whispered. "We have hidden in the darkness for too long."

His fingers moved from her chin, caressing her jaw and the side of her neck. He held her eyes with his own as his fingers gently touched the scarred lobe of her ear, the place where she had drawn blood for her vision. Kanan Naab shivered violently, but he did not jerk his hand away. He stroked her neck and shoulder, letting his fingers find their own way down her arm, to the slender white ridges of scar tissue she had left on her forearm. Bending forward at the waist, he lifted her arm and pressed his lips against the scarred place, as if to staunch the memory of her bleeding. Kanan Naab felt her eyes go wide, the yellow, flickering light of the fire blending into a solid glow that surrounded Yaxal like a cloud. She suddenly did not care to whom he had spoken, or what he had been told. She was willing to have him alter the ritual, to transform its stiffness into a dance . . .

His hands were caressing her thighs, rolling back her skirt as they moved lower and lower, opening her to him. Then he was touching her, gently kneading and spreading the wet lips, his eyes never leaving her face. He continued long past the time when she expected him to stop, until the expectation itself was forgotten, lost in the pleasure that seemed to ripple through her in waves, mild and soothing at first, but growing in intensity. She closed her eyes, and did not open them again until the fingers withdrew, and she saw Yaxal, through a dense yellow light, removing his loincloth and tossing it aside. Somehow he managed to do the same with her shift and skirt, though she could barely move her limbs to help him. *Slowly,* she thought dimly, though the word seemed to apply only to herself.

He touched her breasts and ran his hands down over her belly, leaving a trail of tingling skin as he again found the center of her pleasure. He caressed her until the waves returned, then lifted her hands and put them on his penis, which was stiff and roped with taut veins, radiating its own heat. Kanan Naab felt the engorged member swell within her fingers, twitching against her palms like a live thing, a serpent without scales. She marveled that her hands did not calm it, and could not match its heat. She brought it to herself, guiding it past the lips that engulfed it as Yaxal slid his hands beneath her and raised her hips to meet his own. He entered her by degrees, his hands flat on either side of her, arms braced against his own weight. He paused for a long moment before pulling halfway back, then paused again before slowly plunging to his full depth, pressing his pelvis against her own.

Gradually the thrusts and withdrawals began to assume a definite rhythm, with the pauses like rest beats in between. Once he paused for several beats, and Kanan Naab felt herself close around him tightly. She looked up at his face and saw that his eyes were shiny and unfocused, and his lips were moving soundlessly, as if he were counting to himself. Then his vision seemed to clear, and he began to move again, more vigorously, pressing against her in a way that made the waves begin to flow and crest inside her. Kanan Naab gasped and lost his eyes in the light, feeling her thighs loosen and a deep quivering travel down her legs. The waves surged around her, and she went under, crying out as the sensations overwhelmed and engulfed her.

Yaxal was lying still on top of her when she came to, whispering in response to a voice she finally realized was her own.

"I am here," he assured her, for she was calling his name, over and over again, a chant that was half gratitude and half bewildered disbelief. She could not remember any of the women ever telling her it would be so powerful, so all-consuming. Yaxal propped himself up on his forearms and eased out of her, gingerly straightening his legs before stretching out beside her. He lay on his side and looked at her, his raised shoulder shielding her from the firelight.

"I lost myself," she confessed, still trying to recapture her breath. Yaxal veiled his eyes and laughed softly.

"Yes. So did I. But we were never apart."

Kanan Naab moved closer to him, touching him with her breasts and knees. He put his arm around her and drew her against his chest, so that she could hear the steady pulsing of his heart and feel his warm breath on the top of her head. She closed her eyes and yawned languidly. Only once in her life had she felt so peaceful, so sheltered from harm. And this had cost her no blood, and would leave no scars. A gentle rite, one that could be celebrated again and again in the future. A rite that would hold back the world and its threats, and make it safe for her to sleep . . .

CROUCHING at his post, Kal Cuc raised his bleary eyes above the stump in front of him and tried to peer through the dense, predawn fog, which filled the spaces between the trees, so that the black trunks seemed like supports in a gauzy wall of grey. He had two blankets wrapped around him but still felt chilled to the bone, and his bare feet had gone numb in the cold, damp moss on which he crouched. And although he knew that he was not the only sentry to be feeling the effects of last night's balche, he was probably the least accustomed to the dizziness and the roiling sickness in his stomach. He dimly recalled Akbal telling him, while he vomited, that he should visit Chan Mac's wife in the morning and ask for her remedy. He promised himself that he would do so without delay, as soon as he had completed his duty here. He prayed that his relief would not use the celebration as an excuse to oversleep.

He looked up over the stump again, and this time he thought he saw one of the black supports move, shredding the grey wall. Yes, it was a man, his shape filling out as he came even with Kal Cuc, perhaps fifty feet to his right. Then Kal Cuc heard a noise behind him and jumped to his feet, throwing off his blankets as he whirled with his shield and spear in hand.

The warrior was only a long spear thrust away, and he was poised to strike. Kal Cuc stared at his filed teeth and the black lines tattooed onto his upper lip, not recognizing the face. This was not one of the warriors who guarded the trails.

"Make a sound, Boy," the man growled, "and you are dead."

Throwing up his shield in front of him, Kal Cuc attacked, aiming his spear at the warrior's legs. There was a great shock as the point of his spear smashed into the man's shield, rending the plaited wood, and then he was struck hard on the side of his leg and felt his feet go out from under him. He landed on his back, losing the wind in his lungs along with his spear and shield. A sandaled foot planted itself on his chest, pinning him to the ground. Still struggling for breath, Kal Cuc looked up at the spear that was pointing down at his face.

"You are a foolish boy," the warrior said, and brought the spear down, turning his hand at the last moment and embedding the point in the earth next to Kal Cuc's head, so close that the serrated edge of the leaf-shaped flint grazed the boy's cheek and drew blood.

"But you are brave," the man added, kneeling quickly to tie Kal Cuc's hands behind him with a piece of vine rope, and to gag his mouth with his own headwrap. Then he jerked the boy to his feet and gave him a shove in the direction of the Jaguar Paw House.

"Come," he said roughly, "now we will go and fetch this holy man of yours . . ."

UNDER COVER of the fog, the ruler's warriors came in from all sides, taking the Jaguar Paw sentries one by one, without a single alarm being raised. Once inside the perimeter of the dwellings, they stormed into the houses and aroused the startled inhabitants with kicks and blows, breaking pots and utensils and beating anyone who resisted. Wrenched from sleep by a hand that seized him around the throat, Akbal had no idea what was happening to him until he was already on his feet, being slapped and shoved toward the doorway. Nicte was wailing in distress, and Zac Kuk was shouting at the warriors, who merely cursed back at her while they prodded Akbal out of the house with the knobbed ends of their war clubs. There were more warriors waiting outside on the front platform, and they herded him into the plaza at spearpoint, jabbing at him impatiently to keep him moving backward. He called to Zac Kuk to be calm, but his words were drowned out by the jeers of his captors. Over their heads, he saw a man come out of his house carrying a lighted torch, and a sudden rush of fear made him stop in his tracks.

"Move!" the nearest warrior commanded, nicking Akbal's belly with the tip of his spear. "Move, or they burn."

Akbal winced and retreated, watching as the man with the torch stationed himself near the central doorway, holding the flaming brand perilously close to the thatched roof. Finally Akbal bumped into the men behind him and turned to find Chan Mac and Kinich standing next to him, also facing out at the ring of pointed spears. Kinich was wheezing noisily through his nose, the sound audible above the taunts of the warriors who confronted him. They were calling him a coward and a traitor and suggesting that he flee into the jungle to save himself. Akbal exchanged a glance with Chan Mac, then stepped around his friend and laid a hand on Kinich's arm.

"Do not let them provoke you," he warned in a low voice, but Kinich simply shook off the hand and pointed a blunt finger at one of the warriors.

"I should have let *you* die in the jungle!" he shouted at the man, distracting the other warriors and silencing their taunts. At that moment, Balam Xoc appeared at their side, followed closely by Pacal and Nohoch Ich. The old man stopped next to Kinich and spoke to him, quickly and privately, so that Akbal was only barely able to overhear.

"You are responsible for Hok."

Kinich started to respond but then merely nodded, because Hok had found his way through the crowd and was standing right behind Balam Xoc. Hok's nose was bleeding, and he was missing his headband and eye patch; he regarded the surrounding warriors with a darting, one-eyed glare, like an animal at bay.

Then the ruler's son, Ain Caan, strode into the plaza, accompanied by his retinue of personal guards. He was a short, stocky man like his father, his face puffy and undistinguished beneath a tall headdress of green feathers. Yet the resemblance was clear enough, reminding Akbal of the vase he had painted in Yaxchilan, and of the ruler who had used and scorned him. This was the same man, only younger and more aggressive. More like Shield Jaguar.

A corridor was formed by the warriors, and Ain Caan, holding a Cauac scepter out in front of him, came toward the place where Balam Xoc stood waiting. He stopped a few feet away and allowed his warriors to close in around him, then turned slightly and raised the scepter over his head, signaling to someone behind him. Akbal rose up on his toes and saw the signal acknowledged by a warrior with a torch, who immediately set fire to a pair of granary huts near the craft house. The thatched roofs went up quickly, sending a plume of orange flame and black smoke spiraling skyward. Cinders began to float down over the plaza, along with the odor of burning maize.

Ain Caan turned back to face Balam Xoc, holding the scepter straight out in front of him, displaying the symbol of his father's power. Akbal stared at the intricately carved image of the Rain Spirit, with his long, curving nose and leering smile, a smoking axhead—symbol of lightning and thunder—protruding from his forehead. Then he glanced up at the pillar of smoke rising from the burning huts, where the grain nourished by Cauac's beneficence was being laid to waste, the power turned against its maker. Ain Caan lowered the scepter and addressed Balam Xoc.

"By the order of Caan Ac, Sky Clan Ruler of Tikal, I have come to take you into custody. You are charged with heresy and false prophecy, and with inciting the people to disloyal acts—"

"Do not waste your breath," Balam Xoc interrupted curtly. "There are no words to justify what you are doing. It is a betrayal and violation of all our traditions. And you, my son, are the heir to this dishonor."

Ain Caan's eyes narrowed with anger, and he pointed the scepter at Balam Xoc.

"Take him," he commanded, and suddenly Akbal was jostled aside as Hok bolted past him and lunged for Ain Caan. Kinich reacted instantaneously, leaping on Hok's back and flattening him to the ground at Ain Caan's feet. Balam Xoc waved his arms and shouted to distract the warriors, putting himself between their spears and the men on the ground.

"You will not harm him!" he insisted vehemently, backing the warriors off with his eyes. Ain Caan had already retreated several steps, hidden behind his guards. Balam Xoc slowly lowered his arms and turned to look down at Hok, who was still thrashing uselessly in Kinich's grip.

"I would not have you die the same death as your father," he said to the struggling man. "You must live a full life, and grow old with your people."

Then he fixed his eyes on Akbal.

"You have also been a witness to this, my son. You must finish your stone now."

Akbal bowed, but Balam Xoc had already shifted his attention to Pacal,

Nohoch, and Chac Mut, who stood together in front of the other men. He stared at them for a long moment.

"The people are now in your hands," he told them finally. "Do what you must to keep them safe."

Without waiting for a reply, Balam Xoc turned and walked into the midst of the warriors, who quickly surrounded him on all sides and led him from the plaza. Ain Caan watched him go in silence, then came forward to speak to Pacal, picking him out of the crowd of men with a gesture of his scepter.

"The ruler offers you and your people a choice, Pacal Balam. You may bring all of your workmen to the Katun Enclosure at dawn tomorrow, to help complete our sacred task. In that case, no harm will come to your father." Ain Caan paused, extending his free hand in a mocking gesture of graciousness. "Or . . . you may refuse, and keep your workers here. If that is your choice, your father will die, very slowly. Then we will come back to burn the rest of your houses. You have heard me, Pacal. The decision is yours."

Gathering his guards around him, Ain Caan turned and marched out of the plaza. The remaining warriors backed off a few feet and waited for their fellows to come down from the plaza above before they lowered their spears. Then they withdrew with studied contempt, showing their backs to the men in the plaza, knowing that no one would attack them now that they had taken their hostage. The warriors with the torches dropped them, still burning, on the places where they had stood, as if to leave a parting reminder of Ain Caan's threat.

For a moment after the warriors had gone, the only sound in the plaza was the hiss and crackle of the burning huts, which had been reduced to charred piles of rubbish. Then the women and children appeared in the doorways of the houses, blinking at the light and searching the plaza with frightened eyes, looking to see if their men were still there. Akbal raised his hand to Zac Kuk and ran to meet her, mounting the platform in front of his house in a single bound. He took Nicte into his arms and hugged her against his chest, so forcefully that the child began to cry. He shifted her into the crook of one arm and stroked her back soothingly, murmuring that there was nothing to be afraid of. He stared past her at Zac Kuk, a question in his eyes. Spots of color darkened her cheekbones, but she shook her head negatively.

"They did not harm us, except with threats," she said in a flat, angry voice. "They broke our dishes and my loom, and they said that they had killed Chuen. I did not look. They also destroyed your painting of Ektun. They broke off the plaster with their clubs."

Tears trembled on the ends of her eyelashes, and Akbal drew her against him with his free arm.

"They have taken Grandfather hostage," he said. "To make us work on the Katun Enclosure."

Chan Mac and Kutz came over to them, with their two small daughters clinging to their father's hands. Chan Mac gave Akbal a hard, accusing look, his eyes narrowed to mere slits.

"I hope I will hear no more talk about my restlessness," he said pointedly. "Only a fool or a madman will not leave a house that is about to be burned down around him."

Akbal glanced at the torch that lay smoldering under the eaves of his house, remembering the warrior who had held it so close to the thatched roof, with Zac Kuk and Nicte trapped inside. He nodded solemnly, brushing the black hair on his daughter's head with his lips.

"We will have to stay to see the Katun Enclosure completed," he said tentatively. "We cannot abandon Grandfather to a slow death."

"Of course," Chan Mac agreed. "We will need the time to establish a base in Chetumal, and begin the transfer of our goods."

"I will need the time to finish my stone. But I will support your proposal to the council, and I will try to persuade my father to join us."

He looked down at Zac Kuk, who had withdrawn from his embrace and was staring intensely at her brother.

"The warriors said they had just returned from Ektun," she told him. "They said that the city would surely fall to the Macaws without them."

"In time, perhaps," Chan Mac allowed. "I will send a message to our parents, asking them to join us in Chetumal when we are settled there."

"We will have to convince the council first," Akbal interjected, inclining his head toward the center of the plaza, where Nohoch Ich was beginning to gather men around him.

"There can be no better time to begin than now," Chan Mac declared, handing his daughters over to Kutz. Zac Kuk held out her arms for Nicte, and Akbal passed the child over, searching his wife's face for confirmation. She had never shared Chan Mac's willingness to leave Tikal before this, but he saw that she did now.

"Go, my husband," she said simply. "Convince the other men that we must leave here. As the warriors convinced me."

And me, Akbal thought, as he and Chan Mac turned and began to walk toward the group of men around Nohoch, the men who now held the welfare of the clan in their hands, and would decide its future.

9.17.19.14.4   13 Kan   2 Yax
(Two months later)

THE DAMP, barren cell in which Balam Xoc was confined lay somewhere within the recesses of the palace, far removed from the sounds and life of the court. It was exactly six paces wide and eight long, with two narrow ventilator slits in the back wall, just below the spring of the vaulted ceiling. There was no bench against the wall, and no furnishings except for a single blanket, a water bowl, and a pot for Balam Xoc's wastes. Only a tepid glow of light managed to seep through the tightly curtained doorway from the torch in the hallway outside, where two armed warriors maintained a constant vigil. The guards were changed frequently and had been given strict instructions not to communicate with their prisoner, and to douse him with water if he attempted to break the silence himself.

It was a severe confinement, even for someone as used to solitude and darkness as Balam Xoc. And he was forced to endure it as a man, unable any longer to assume the fierce, hardy indifference of the Jaguar. He had lost most of the powers that had once been his, and he no longer traveled in his dreams, except into the realms of personal memory and desire. Occasionally, he would feel the murmur of his voice deep inside him, but he always resisted its call, putting his mind on other things until it was gone. Because although his bones ached from the dampness and his thoughts ran on obsessively, becoming a torment to him, he did not wish to send his spirit out of this place. He had wanted to be taken from his people, so that they would be free to find their own powers and the means to guide themselves. He had expected, though, that it would be death that would take him, rather than the ruler, who was far less merciful.

So he paced his cell in the darkness and spent hours carving his clan's glyphs into the plastered wall with his fingernails, choosing a portion of the wall that was never touched by the light, even when the curtain was pulled back and food was thrust in to him. He reviewed the memories of his life over and over again, reflecting on his losses and accomplishments, understanding the way in which his spirit had been shaped and tempered, so that his present imprisonment came to seem inevitable. He thought about the people of his clan and the effect he had had upon them, both as individuals and as a group. When the silence weighed too heavily upon him, he talked to himself in a voice too low for the guards to hear, rehearsing the things he would say to the ruler when he was finally given the chance to confront his captor.

He was allowed out of his cell only at night, and then only to the same isolated courtyard, where the overhanging facades of the surrounding buildings shut out all but a small patch of the night sky. Balam Xoc was careful to conceal his feelings from his guards, but he lived for these times when he could breathe the moving air and sense the limitless space above him. When he could smell the odors of earth and forest and open water, and hear the cries of night birds and the chirrup of insects. The stars and the moon had become precious to him, the lights by which he knew himself to be in the world, and by which he could measure the passage of time. Since the guards feared the darkness themselves, they never perceived the pleasure he took in these nocturnal outings, the sustenance he could find in the fluttering of a bat in the moonlight or the distant echo of a human voice, crying out in the midst of a dream.

Still, when the curtain was jerked aside and a blinding shaft of light cut across the center of the room, Balam Xoc rose with a studied listlessness, lifting up his waste pot and shuffling toward the doorway with his eyes lowered. The guard, though, stood in his way and gestured toward the pot.

"Leave that," he commanded, and Balam Xoc obediently set the vessel on the floor. When he straightened up, the guard stood aside, revealing the other five warriors waiting in the hallway. *So the ruler has summoned me at last,* Balam Xoc thought as the guards fell in around him and marched him down the passageway. The path they took was long and circuitous, with many turnings and much climbing of stairs, until Balam Xoc became convinced that they were deliberately trying to confuse and tire him. He snorted scornfully and let them lead him in circles, enjoying the exercise and allowing his eyes to adjust gradually to the torchlight. He had not washed since the last rain and could smell his own rankness, but he did not intend to appear before the ruler blinking and helpless.

Caan Ac and the High Priest Ah Kin Cuy were alone in the brightly lit chamber to which Balam Xoc was finally brought. The ruler was seated on a drum-shaped throne covered with jaguar skin, smoking a long cigar while he conversed with the priest, who stood just to his right. He fell silent as Balam Xoc was brought to a halt before him and was prodded in the back by one of the guards to remind him to bow.

"No, he will not bow to his ruler," Caan Ac said drily, waving off the guard. "He has the true spirit of a heretic and honors no one above himself. You are a disgraceful sight, Balam Xoc."

"I am pleased, then," Balam Xoc replied, his voice sounding loud and unfamiliar to his own ears. "I would not wish to appear honorable in your sight."

Caan Ac puffed on his cigar, seeming unperturbed by the insult, as if he had expected no less.

"And would it also please you," he asked, "to know that your people have served me loyally in your absence? Your own son brings them—all of them —to the Katun Enclosure every day. They have volunteered their labor in order to win back the favor you lost for them."

"Did you bring me here to tell me your dreams?" Balam Xoc inquired in return. "You will tell me next that I volunteered to be your guest here."

The ruler calmly blew a plume of smoke into the air and watched it drift toward the ceiling, as if allowing it to carry off the insult unheard. *He wants something from me,* Balam Xoc thought, glancing at the high priest, whose set features revealed a similar restraint.

"The situation in the city had become too grave," Caan Ac explained, in a tone of reason and necessity. "I could no longer afford to tolerate your intransigence, or the example you presented to the other clans. Yet even now, I am prepared to forgive you, if you will agree to subordinate yourself to the larger interests of our city."

"I have always served the interests of my city. You must be speaking of your own interests."

"Mine, then," the ruler allowed, betraying a trace of exasperation. "The end of Katun Eleven Ahau is now only three and a half months away. It has been a time of trial and hardship for all of our people, and a source of encouragement to our enemies. But we have survived, and it is my desire to have all of the clans represented at the dedication of the Katun Enclosure, as a sign that Tikal is still strong and united. For the sake of that unity, I would have you stand with me as well, Balam Xoc, despite the way you have defied me in the past."

The situation must be much worse than grave, Balam Xoc decided, incredulous that the ruler would try to win him over, at this point, with an appeal for unity.

"You are assuming," he said skeptically, "that the Enclosure will be completed in time for the dedication."

"It will. I have the men I need now."

"No doubt the other clans have also volunteered their labor," Balam Xoc suggested. "Tell me then, my lord: When you welcome in the new katun, Katun Nine Ahau, will you also promise to build an Enclosure in its honor?"

"Why do you need to ask?" Caan Ac demanded, waving the cigar in an imperious gesture. "It has been the custom in Tikal for over seven katuns, since before my grandfather ascended to the throne."

Balam Xoc nodded, prolonging his refusal for another moment, since he knew that it would end the interview and send him back to his confinement. But then he spoke bluntly.

"Yes, it has been the custom, but a most costly one. The fields and reservoirs of the city have been neglected to the point of ruin, and still you barely have the means to complete the present Enclosure. Even the causeways and public plazas have been left unswept, while the workers loaned for their maintenance have been diverted to other uses." Despite the growing anger in the ruler's eyes, Balam Xoc risked a pause to give added effect to his next question, which he had rehearsed many times in his mind: "And if you must kidnap workers to complete the next Enclosure, as you have for this one, where will you also find the men to build your tomb?"

Caan Ac blinked and let the cigar fall from his fingers, wearing the stricken expression of a man whose secret self had been unmasked and called out into the light. *Yes, he has given thought to his death,* Balam Xoc thought triumphantly, absorbing the moment into memory, knowing that it would help sustain him during the dark days ahead.

"You have already seen *your* tomb," Caan Ac snarled, his round face contorted with hatred. "You will rot there!"

"Then I will miss the dedication," Balam Xoc said with a shrug, "and you will have to pretend to unity without me."

Caan Ac gestured furiously to the guards, who immediately closed in around Balam Xoc and marched him from the chamber, cursing him under their breath. *Three and a half more months,* Balam Xoc reflected, as the guards propelled him down the passageway with unnecessary force. Seventy more days of darkness, and then Katun 11 Ahau would have its end. He wondered if he would see the light again, and gaze upon the sun, before his own end came.

THE JAGUAR PAW men sat together under the palms at the edge of the work site, sipping water while they rested and waited for the worst of the midday heat to pass. There were fifty of them, the same number they had brought on the first day after Balam Xoc's capture, and every day since. Pacal sat with Kinich at one end of the group, conversing quietly in the shade. They broke off their conversation, though, when they saw the man advancing toward them across the deserted plaza. He wore the striped headwrap that identified him as an assistant supervisor, and he strode through the shimmering waves of heat rising off the plaza with a kind of aggressive indifference, as if he did not have the time to feel the sun overhead.

Pacal and Kinich watched silently as the man stopped in front of the workers and began to berate them for loitering here in the shade when there was work to do. The workers stared back at him impassively, showing no reaction to his words and no inclination to leave their places. Growing increasingly angry, the supervisor began to shout at them and struck a water gourd from the hands of the man sitting nearest to him.

"I do not know this man," Pacal said to Kinich, "and he obviously does not know about us."

"I will educate him," Kinich promised, and rose to walk out from under the trees. The supervisor ended his tirade abruptly when he saw the burly warrior approaching, his jeweled teeth bared in a smile of false amiability.

"You are wasting your time, my friend," Kinich told him. "These men only take orders from one of their own. And we have already received our assignment from the chief supervisor."

"Then tell these men to return to their tasks."

"*I* do not take orders from you, either," Kinich said sharply, his smile dissolving into a scowl. He pointed to a stick that had been planted in the ground nearby, angled slightly from the perpendicular. "We do not work until the shadow is as long as the stick itself. That is the custom everywhere in Tikal. Even here, my friend."

"The ruler has changed the custom," the supervisor said arrogantly, though he was beginning to sweat profusely. "He wants more work from the crews."

"We are not here to please the ruler. And we certainly have no reason," Kinich added, jabbing a blunt finger at the man's chest, "to obey *you.*"

"There are ways to make you obey," the supervisor threatened, backing off a step.

"Your superiors have not been so foolish as to employ them. They know that we will work no faster with spears at our backs. So go try to impress them somewhere else."

"Perhaps you have forgotten the ruler's hostage . . ."

Kinich suddenly lunged for him, and the man jumped backward instinctively, stumbling as he landed and almost losing his balance. The men under the trees exploded with laughter, the first sound they had made since the supervisor's arrival.

"A hostage can only be killed once," Kinich said dismissively. "Perhaps you would like to remind the ruler of that."

The man staggered off across the plaza, and Kinich turned and made a small bow to his clansmen, who applauded him with more laughter. Glancing once more at the time stick, Kinich came back and sat down next to Pacal, wiping sweat from his forehead.

"There are some satisfactions in this bitter duty," he remarked blandly, and Pacal also laughed. He handed his son a gourd of water and leaned back carefully against the scaly trunk of the palm behind him. It had not been easy to persuade the clan council to adopt a policy of dignified opposition, but Pacal was more than gratified by the results. There had been a strong faction in favor of allowing the clan workers to join the general work crews, with the intention of having them commit acts of sabotage and arouse the rebelliousness of the workers from the other clans. But Pacal had argued successfully for the idea of maintaining themselves as a separate group, a symbol of stubborn independence that none could ignore, despite the coercion they were under.

"I still think it was a mistake to leave Opna behind," Kinich said, breaking into his thoughts. "I would rather have him where I can watch him."

"Few of his confederates are there with him," Pacal pointed out, "and Nohoch is capable of heading off trouble. We could not risk having him start some trouble here. That would only give the ruler an excuse to retaliate against us, and it would not slow down the work for long. But we cannot be reproached for doing our work with the care it deserves, and that does much more to slow the progress of the entire project. Have you not noticed that some of the conscripts from the other clans have begun to imitate our example?"

"That is true," Kinich admitted. "But it probably will not prevent the Enclosure from being completed in time."

"No, but it has forced Caan Ac to commit every available man. The warriors are not happy at being made to mix mortar, and the clans will never forgive him for seizing their workers without agreement or pay."

"They will accept it eventually," Kinich predicted glumly. "There is no end to what they will accept. Perhaps Chan Mac and Akbal are right, and we should leave this place as soon as Balam Xoc is released."

Pacal gave his son a pitying look.

"He will never be released. In your heart, Kinich, you must know that."

"Then why have you not supported leaving? Why have you allowed Nohoch and Tzec Balam to keep the council's hopes alive?"

Pacal glanced at the ground and shrugged.

"I have lived all of my life in Tikal. Chan Mac cannot persuade me to forget that, not quickly. Nor is there any point in trying to convince Nohoch and Tzec Balam to abandon their hope of seeing the rites performed one more time. In all of our history, we have never failed to observe the Tun-End; it would be an insult to our ancestors to give up prematurely. But when they see that it is impossible, they will not have to be convinced."

"It might be too late by then," Kinich warned. "Once we are finished here, the ruler will put his warriors back on the trails."

"No doubt," Pacal agreed. "That is why I supported Chan Mac's trip to Chetumal. When is he expected to return?"

"In two more days. I anticipate no problems, though I will go out after dark to bring him in. Still, Father, it will be a wasted effort if we do not act soon to establish an outpost in Chetumal."

"You sound as if you have already joined your brother and his friend," Pacal observed, and Kinich shook his head uneasily, gesturing toward the men under the trees.

"They are good workers. It is a shame that they cannot labor on our own behalf."

"They will," Pacal assured him, rising to his feet. He extended a hand toward the men, and they rose in a body, without hesitation or complaint. "They will," he repeated to Kinich, "and they will be better for having labored on behalf of their dignity."

"Perhaps," Kinich conceded, as he and his father walked out into the sunlight with the other men, heading toward the temple pyramid to which they had been assigned. They moved in a solid, silent group, without stragglers, as if they had chosen this duty for themselves.

AKBAL STOOD with one foot flat on the ground and one knee resting on the stone itself, holding a slender stone chisel in his left hand and a wooden mallet in his right. He heard someone come up behind him but immediately shut the person out of his thoughts, which were focused solely on the placement of the chisel. He did not even see the rest of the carving, only the small, irregular lump of stone he was intent on removing. It was attached to the end of Balam

Xoc's extended hand, and a bad cut now might also lop off the tips of his fingers. It would have been safer simply to sand the piece away, but there was no time anymore to behave like an amateur. Akbal's neck was stiff, and his arm ached from holding the mallet at the ready, and he understood—again— why all the stonecarvers he knew were short, burly men. Still, he kept the mallet poised while he adjusted the angle of the chisel, studying the grain of the stone for hidden flaws, waiting for the alignment of blade with stone to *feel* right. When it did, he tapped once with the mallet, then once more with force, and the piece broke off neatly, springing away from the chisel with a puff of yellow dust.

Bending low over the stone, Akbal inspected the cut with his finger, grunting with relief when he found that he had created no new cracks. He stood back and let his arms fall to his sides, aware again that he had a visitor. But he took another moment to examine the whole carving: the figures of Balam Xoc and Ain Caan confronting each other beneath the serpent border, the former bareheaded in the costume of the Jaguar Protector, the latter standing stiffly beneath his elaborate feather headdress. Balam Xoc was raised up on one foot, his legs slightly bowed, his open palm extended in a graceful curve toward Ain Caan. The ruler's son stood rigidly erect, one heel just visible behind the other, the Cauac scepter held out in front of him like a shield.

Akbal had deliberately chosen to depict Ain Caan in the traditionally stiff manner of the Tikal monuments, but there was an unintended stiffness in the dancing figure of Balam Xoc as well, a kind of ceremonial severity that Akbal had not felt when he had drawn the portrait on paper. At first he had been disappointed in himself, feeling that his lack of skill as a carver had betrayed him and that he was only capable of creating a bad imitation of the graceful Ektun monuments that had been his models. But gradually he had come to understand that the stiffness was appropriate; that he was himself a man of Tikal and could be influenced only so much by the freer conventions of the west. So he had stopped tormenting himself with comparisons and had ceased trying to judge the quality of his work. Frequently, though, he needed to refresh his sense of the larger composition, since it often deserted him and left him feeling lost in the crevices of his own design.

When he finally turned to greet his visitor, he discovered that it was Opna who had been waiting all this time, standing outside the shelter in the sunlight. Akbal hastily put down his tools and gestured for the other man to come in under the thatched roof.

"I am grateful for your patience, Opna," he apologized. "Not everyone recognizes when I should not be interrupted."

"Your concentration was apparent," Opna replied with a shrug. "I do not wish to interrupt your work even now, but I wanted to speak to you before the next council meeting."

"Yes?" Akbal inquired with immediate wariness, sitting down on the edge of the stone. Opna gave him a sardonic smile.

"You are suspicious of me, Akbal," he said knowingly. "Your sister has convinced you that I am not to be trusted, that I only seek power for myself."

"You have not made a secret of your ambitions."

"No. It is true that I wished to follow in your grandfather's footsteps. I wanted to lead the people as he did, boldly and courageously. Is that an ignoble ambition? But I am over it, and I have come to see the wisdom of Balam Xoc's decision not to choose a successor. It is better that we rule ourselves."

"It does not always seem so, when we are arguing late into the night," Akbal said ruefully, rubbing the back of his neck. He glanced up at Opna appraisingly. "But I am not oblivious of the fact that you and your friends voted in favor of Chan Mac's trip to Chetumal at the last meeting. We were not sure what we had done to win your support, though we were grateful for it."

"I expect no gratitude. It was the only way to get the old men to look outward. I believe that that is the reason Balam Xoc brought me to his side, and Chan Mac, as well. We are attached to the spirit and meaning of the Jaguar Paw, but not to this place. It is our special duty to make the others face the necessity of finding our future elsewhere."

Akbal squinted at him skeptically.

"Yet you did not vote in favor of establishing a permanent base in Chetumal. Or do you look outward to some other place?"

"You are shrewd, Akbal," Opna commended him, "so I will not equivocate with you. If the choice were mine alone, I would not make Chetumal my final destination. I would go south from there, to Copan. No doubt you have heard the reports of unrest in my former city, but perhaps you took them for rumors. They are true, Akbal. The ruler has lost control of the army, and he will soon be forced to share his power with the other noble houses of Copan."

"And you would take our people *there*?" Akbal demanded incredulously.

"I would take the message of Balam Xoc there first," Opna explained, undaunted by Akbal's open disbelief. "And I can assure you that we would have no difficulty making converts among those who are powerful, and those who will be powerful. The reputation of the Jaguar Paw Clan is well known in Copan, and would give us enormous prestige. We could make the city our own. Is that not a better future than any we could find in Chetumal?"

"You cannot be serious!" Akbal exclaimed. "We have lived with unrest for too long already. You are not speaking of the future, Opna, but of an escape into the past."

"And what is there in Chetumal, except cacao and fish?" Opna sneered. He gestured toward the stone. "Is there anyone capable of appreciating artistry such as yours? You would be an important man in Copan, you would be revered."

"I do not wish to be revered. And you are wrong about Chetumal. They trade with people from everywhere. From places unknown to you."

"No doubt," Opna said scornfully. "Nor are they known to the other members of the council. Even your father has spoken disdainfully of living among fishermen and pod pickers."

"He would feel differently if he had seen the quality of the goods we obtained there," Akbal insisted stubbornly.

"So might we all. Unfortunately, the ruler's warriors have not returned them to you, and the council has not seen fit to believe your assurances concerning their value. They were not there when you threw them into the alkalche. And if you do not have the necessary evidence, Akbal," Opna added, "you must have allies instead."

"Like yourself?"

"I came here to offer you and Chan Mac my support. I will speak on behalf of establishing an outpost in Chetumal, and I will see that my allies on the council vote with you. If you can win over your father or brother, you should have the strength to decide the issue."

"And what do you ask in return?"

"I want to make a trip to Copan, similar to the one that Chan Mac has just made. An exploratory journey. I would ask you to support only that—you would have no commitment to taking the people there. In the meantime, though, you would have the base you want in Chetumal."

Akbal stood up slowly, dusting his hands on his thighs.

"Even if Chan Mac and I were to support you," he said tentatively, "I could not promise my father or brother."

"Kinich Kakmoo would be happy to see me go," Opna assured him, "and so would Nohoch Ich. They would both hope that I never returned. But you would be under no further obligation whether I returned or not."

"I will discuss this with Chan Mac," Akbal decided. "But I must tell you frankly that I do not see the value of a visit to Copan. And I would prefer to win over the council without your help."

"You will not have it," Opna said bluntly, "unless you agree to support me in return."

They stared at each other for a moment, and then Opna bowed, and Akbal bowed in return, sealing their understanding, if not their agreement. When he was alone, Akbal picked up his chisel and mallet, but he did not immediately return to his work. He reviewed the conversation in his mind, wondering if Chan Mac would find Opna's proposal more attractive than he did himself. Chan Mac had been tireless in his insistence that the clan begin transferring goods and people to Chetumal before the trails were closed again, but as Opna had said, his pleas had fallen on unreceptive ears. Why not substitute allies for evidence, if the council would not accept their testimony concerning the lost goods?

Yet the idea of supporting a journey to Copan when he believed it was a waste of men and resources, when he would have to feel his father's eyes on him when he spoke, made him cringe inwardly. *I was not made for this kind of maneuvering,* he told himself, looking down at the figures half-carved into the surface of the stone. He was reminded that he was not made to carve stone, either, yet he was doing so, and with all the dedication he could muster. And all the honesty. Could he act any differently toward the council? He remembered his grandfather telling him to let the stone teach him the truths he needed, and he knew the answer to his own question. He would have to find a way to persuade the council on his own, with or without the evidence.

He stared down at the stone, searching the intricately etched design for clues. Yet the clash between the Sky Clan and the Jaguar Paw seemed too much a thing of the past to provide any insights into the needs of the future. Akbal stared for a long time, until he began to feel frustrated and depressed, and decided that he could do no more work that day. But as he bent to put his tools into the leather pack where he kept them when not in use, he was struck by a sudden memory of another, similar pack. One that he had not opened for many days after Kanan Naab brought it to him, and then had promptly forgotten, along with the trauma of his broken arm.

The evidence, Akbal thought excitedly, and started to leave the shelter. But then he caught himself and turned back to bow his head over the stone in gratitude. When he was through, he no longer felt so eager to leave, realizing that there was plenty of time to find the pack and prepare himself before the next council meeting. He knew where he had left it, and there was no reason why anyone would have tampered with it. He would bring more honor to the truth the stone had shown him by using these last, precious hours of daylight as he had originally intended. Only when he had completed this image of their common past, after all, could he truly look toward the future. Retrieving his tools from the pack, he put his knee back up on the stone and bent once more over his work, shutting out the world around him and shedding all awareness of the passage of time.

WHEN SHE had located the plant she wanted and had scanned the immediate area for snakes, Chibil beckoned to Kanan Naab and the five girls, inviting them to join her. The girls worked their way carefully past the chest-high ferns, holding the feathery leaves back for one another and trying not to trample anything underfoot, as Chibil had taught them. Kanan Naab noticed a certain clumsiness to some of their movements, though, and realized that they were getting tired. It was hot in the ravine, and Chibil had already made this a long lesson. Kanan Naab decided that she would have to speak to the older woman about that. Chibil was understandably anxious to impart as much of her wisdom to the girls as possible, since the permission to educate them had come from Balam Xoc and might be revoked by the men of the clan at any time. Still, there were limits to what a young mind could absorb in one day, and Kanan Naab did not want to lose any more students by pushing them too hard. Curiosity could be encouraged and nurtured, but not force-fed.

The girls were crouched in a semicircle facing Chibil, who had already begun to explain the various medicinal uses of the plant, which she held cradled in her hands like an infant. Intending to go around behind her and suggest a rest, Kanan Naab stepped through the green shadows of a logwood tree, ducking her head beneath the low, gnarled branches. It was as she was straightening up that she saw the body lying half-hidden in a thicket of wild berry bushes.

The man was sprawled out on his back with one arm thrown back over his head, clutching the air with rigid fingers. A piece of vine rope was twisted tightly into the flesh of his throat, beneath a thin face fixed in the bug-eyed agony of strangulation. Kanan Naab raised a hand to her mouth, feeling the ants crawling over the man's body as if they were on her own skin. Then she heard Chibil's voice behind her, speaking sternly to the girls:

"Go up to the men, all of you. Tell them to bring a litter and blankets. Go!"

Chibil came to Kanan Naab's side and gently tried to pull her away from the berry bushes.

"You must not look so long upon death, my daughter," she cautioned. "Especially not a death that has come at the hands of other men."

"Who is he?" Kanan Naab asked dazedly, allowing herself to be drawn a few steps away.

"You do not recognize him? It is Hapay Can, the high priest of your husband's clan."

Kanan Naab closed her eyes then and stood swaying in her own darkness, remembering the night that Yaxal had come to her in the rain, angry and distraught over the way Hapay Can had tricked and threatened him. She remembered the calmness with which Balam Xoc had received the news, and his insistence that Yaxal defy the threats and refuse to pay the bribes Hapay Can was asking. Now *he* would have to pay, in ways that Kanan Naab could barely imagine, except for the final result, when all the life had been twisted out of him.

Akbal and Kal Cuc were the first to arrive, carrying the requested litter, their faces grave in anticipation of what they would find. Chibil gestured toward the bushes, and they approached the corpse without hesitation, but then stopped and exchanged a glance and went no closer. They were still standing over the body when Nohoch, Hok, and Yaxal arrived in a group, each carrying a blanket. Kanan Naab went blindly to her husband, who embraced her awkwardly, mistaking her solicitude for an uncharacteristic show of dependency. Over her shoulder, Kanan Naab heard Akbal's voice.

"It is Hapay Can. He has been strangled."

Yaxal's arms went around her tightly for a moment, then seemed to lose all their strength and fell to his sides. The face he showed to her looked dreadful, drained of all color, a mask of outrage and self-recrimination.

"You did all that Grandfather would allow," Kanan Naab reminded him softly. "He did not want your protection."

Unable to speak, Yaxal walked forward slowly to join the other men, who were staring down at the corpse, their faces mirroring the contortions of death.

"He has not been tortured," Nohoch observed hopefully. "Perhaps he did not tell. Kal Cuc, my son, you know where the place is. Go and see if the ground has been disturbed."

"Be careful," Akbal added, detaining the boy for a moment. "There may be people watching."

Kal Cuc nodded obediently and disappeared into the undergrowth, going up the opposite side of the ravine to save time. In the silence that followed his departure, Kanan Naab could hear the flies buzzing over the body.

"He has betrayed us," Yaxal murmured suddenly. "I can *feel* it. We must pray for Balam Xoc."

A growl rose in Hok's throat, and he leaned forward and spat viciously upon the corpse. Then he kicked Hapay Can in the ribs and was reaching for his knife when Nohoch grabbed his wrist to restrain him.

"No more!" he commanded. "He has paid for his treachery. And his spirit will suffer great torments in the Underworld. There is no forgiveness for a priest who willfully violates his vows."

"And what of the man who profits from the priest's corruption, and then has him killed?" Yaxal wondered aloud. "What manner of man is that?"

"It is the manner of Caan Ac," Akbal said in a taut voice. "The man whose temples we help to build."

"Let us take the body up," Nohoch suggested quietly, gesturing to Akbal for the litter. Kanan Naab stood back with Chibil while the men rolled the stiffened corpse onto the litter and covered it with blankets. Hok used his knife to cut pieces of vine, which were then tied around the body to hold it in place. The men took up positions at the four ends of the carrying poles, with Nohoch and Hok in front and Akbal and Yaxal in the rear. Before they lifted their burden, though, Yaxal looked down and spoke to the blanket-covered mound.

"It was you, Hapay Can, who drove me from the Tun Count Priests. You, who made me leave my family, and the clan of my father. Now you will drive me from Tikal altogether."

Yaxal raised his face to the other men, his eyes shining with a conviction that was both bitter and urgent.

"We must leave this place," he told them. "The ruler has made it unholy."

The men hung their heads in silent acknowledgment, and Kanan Naab came to Yaxal's side, touching him lightly on the arm.

"We will all go together, when it is time," she said softly. "But we cannot abandon Grandfather to a death as lonely as this."

"No," Yaxal agreed, his voice dull with anguish. "Our hearts must be with him, wherever he is confined. But we can do nothing to help him now. An awful curse has been loosed against him."

Hok growled again, and was the first to take a grip upon the carrying pole at his feet. The others followed his example, lifting in unison at a signal from Nohoch. Kanan Naab walked beside her husband, holding branches out of his way as they began the steep climb up the side of the ravine. Grunting with exertion, Yaxal spoke to her through his teeth.

"Opna foresaw this, did he not?"

"He did," Kanan Naab said succinctly. "He will not have to be reminded, when he hears of this."

Yaxal groaned.

"The trouble I have brought to your clan—"

"It was I who killed the serpent," Akbal interjected, from the other side of the swaying litter. "You do not bear this alone."

"We all bear it," Kanan Naab assured them sharply. "It is the burden of Katun Eleven Ahau, and we must carry it to its end. Then we will be released," she added in a wistful tone, glancing upward at the houses, which had just come into view. "Then we will walk freely, away from here . . ."

EVERY DREAM now took him into the forest, and Balam Xoc went unwillingly, knowing that the path would soon disappear and the serpent would rise out of the weeds to confront him. Its lance-shaped head would pin him where he stood, the yellow eyes glaring coldly into his own, the banded body undulating in time with his breathing. The bifurcated tongue would flicker out at him once, and he would see the pink mouth flesh stretch wide behind the curving fangs. Then the serpent would strike, and he would feel the lightning flash of pain as the fangs sank into his flesh, and the slow, searing spread of venom through his veins . . .

Then he would wake up, sweating and shaking with what he knew was fear. It was the last of his emotions to return to him, and it did so with devastating force. It made him whimper and clutch his blanket around him, his only shield against the menacing shapes that crawled past him in the darkness. The fear would pass, finally, leaving him drained of strength and shivering in his own sweat. And dreading the next time he would have to surrender himself to sleep. He did so as little as possible, which only made him weaker, and less in control of his own thoughts. The painful aching in his bones had intensified, so that he often could not sit comfortably, and was never warm enough. Yet the greatest of his torments, and the one that was killing him, was the dream.

Dozing fitfully, he flirted with rest, pulling himself back whenever he began to sink into dreams. He came awake to a light his eyes could not bear at first. Then he saw a man sitting across from him, silhouetted against the light pouring in through the open doorway. Balam Xoc blinked and stretched out an unsteady hand, stopping in midmotion when the high priest spoke:

"Yes, I am real. I have brought you balche."

It took a moment for Balam Xoc to comprehend, and then another moment before he saw the painted gourd on the floor in front of him. He began to weep, overwhelmed by this unexpected kindness. Ah Kin Cuy cleared his throat loudly.

"Please. Drink."

Unable to control his tears, Balam Xoc groped for the gourd and succeeded in removing the stopper and raising the vessel to his lips. Liquid dribbled onto his chin, but then the sweet, tangy fragrance filled his nostrils as the balche rolled over his tongue and down his throat. He swallowed only a small amount, but it warmed him instantly, blanketing his insides.

"I am grateful," he said hoarsely, when he felt steady enough to put the gourd down and replace the stopper. The high priest rearranged his legs beneath him, as if he were uncomfortable sitting on the cold stone floor.

"You understand what has been done to you," he ventured awkwardly, his eyes fixed on the gourd. Balam Xoc realized finally that he was referring to the dream.

"Hapay Can . . ."

"It was not my doing, Balam Xoc," the priest insisted hastily. "I swear it. He came to me first, but one of my assistants sent him away unheard. He went to the ruler without my knowledge."

Balam Xoc stared at him out of dry eyes, making an enormous effort to collect his thoughts. Then he understood that Ah Kin Cuy had come here out of guilt. He wanted to be forgiven, absolved. Balam Xoc reached for the gourd and took another drink to fortify himself. This might be his last chance to bargain for anything.

"It does not matter what you knew," he said at last. "The evil has been done, and the poison will spread to all who had a hand in it. And to those who serve them."

"I would never have allowed this to happen!"

"I have already begun to die because of it," Balam Xoc said relentlessly, forcing the priest to avert his gaze. Clasping his hands in front of him, Ah Kin Cuy bowed his head and murmured an inaudible prayer. Balam Xoc waited, hoping his voice would be firm.

"You came here to be absolved of this crime, Ah Kin Cuy. I will forgive you, but you must act on my behalf. I do not wish to die here."

The priest's long face took on a pained expression.

"Caan Ac will never allow you to return to your people."

"Have him send me away, then. I will not survive long in exile. But I must see the world again before I leave it."

"I will speak—"

"Promise me!" Balam Xoc demanded harshly, trying to hide his desperation behind a mask of anger. He needed a reason to hope, if he was to withstand the dream, and the fear. He was willing to beg for his release, but he knew he would never have it that way. So he forced himself to meet and hold Ah Kin Cuy's eyes, pretending to be adamant when he was in fact on the verge of collapse.

"You have my promise," the priest said finally. "It has already been suggested that you be removed from the city before the ceremonies of the Katun-End begin."

Balam Xoc closed his eyes in relief.

"Go, then," he sighed. "I will not curse you at my death, if you have kept your vow."

"I will keep it," Ah Kin Cuy assured him curtly, and Balam Xoc heard a swish of cloth as the high priest got to his feet. The curtain fell across the doorway a moment later, and the room was once again plunged into darkness. Balam Xoc sagged, burying his face in his hands as the tension went out of him in small, involuntary shudders. *What a pathetic creature I have become,* he thought. *Weeping at my enemy's kindness, bartering my forgiveness for a last look at the sun.* The Jaguar was indeed dead.

Yet Balam Xoc also felt an undeniable sense of pride in the way he had conducted himself. He had won only a small concession for himself, but it had taken real courage to master his weakness and his desperation, more courage than any of his acts of defiance had required. He was no stronger than any of his people, and like them, he could not be sustained by the truth alone. He needed hope, the promise of relief, if he was to live with his fears.

Reaching forward in the darkness, his hands found the gourd, and he smiled to himself. *Yes,* he thought, *and if relief cannot be found in the circumstances of life itself, it can always be found in balche.* He removed the stopper and began to drink, slowly but with concentration, savoring the taste on his tongue, the warmth beneath his skin, the light-headedness that overtook him so quickly. *Perhaps I will be too drunk to dream,* he thought recklessly, as he drained the last drops from the gourd. He had the presence of mind to lay his blanket beneath him before he fell over onto his back, and lay staring up at the shapes swimming in the darkness above.

Sleep, he told himself, and let his eyelids slide shut. The blackness swirled and eddied, drawing him downward. He went easily, knowing that the forest awaited him, yet knowing, as well, that he could do nothing to avoid it. And then the voice welled up inside him, crying out with grief and longing, a voice that had known suffering, and loss, yet would not be muted. Balam Xoc let it take him, down the path into the forest, to the waiting serpent, and the death that would be died many times. *I come,* the voice sang mournfully, filling his weary spirit with the courage of acceptance . . .

WHILE THE COUNCIL waited for the last of its members to arrive, Pacal counted heads from his end of the long room. He had just learned that Tzec Balam and his son had gone over to Opna's side, which meant that the Copan faction now had an advantage of two votes over those who favored going to Chetumal. And only three members remained uncommitted: Kinich, Chac

Mut, and Pacal himself, though it was rumored that Chac Mut was also leaning toward Copan. *I have withheld my vote too long,* Pacal thought ruefully; *soon it will be superfluous.* He turned sideways to Chan Mac.

"Where is Akbal?"

"With his stone, no doubt," Chan Mac ventured, without apparent enthusiasm.

"Do you still resent his refusal of Opna's offer?"

"We would still be having this argument over our final destination," Chan Mac shrugged. "Opna's ambitions were inflated by Hapay Can's death. But we could already have begun the transfer of our goods."

"I think that we will begin soon," Pacal observed, glancing down the line of men. "Though not in the direction you desire."

Chan Mac nodded glumly, and the two men fell silent. Akbal's place next to Chac Mut was now the only empty seat in the chamber, and Nohoch Ich was beginning to show signs of starting without him. But then Akbal came through the central doorway, carrying a battered leather pack that he set on the floor before making a hasty, apologetic bow to Nohoch. It was clear that he had come directly from his work, for although his face and arms were clean, his black hair, unwrapped, was powdered with yellow dust. Seeming preoccupied, he did not go immediately to his seat, and just as Nohoch was about to gesture to him to do so, Akbal spoke.

"My lord, I request the right to address the council."

Nohoch was taken aback for a moment, but when he saw no objections to this unusual request, he extended his hand to Akbal in a gesture of permission.

"At last," Chan Mac murmured under his breath, but Pacal did not take his eyes off his son. It was not like Akbal to draw this kind of attention to himself; he preferred to express himself in ways that required as few words as possible, or none at all. Pacal wondered what he had brought in the pack.

"My lords," Akbal began, straightening to his full height and scanning the faces in both directions, "I have come to speak to you about two things. The first concerns my stone. I can say now that Kal Cuc and I will be finished with our work before the end of the katun, if I am not distracted from it by many more of these meetings. Since it seems unlikely that we will be allowed to observe the Katun-End in our traditional manner, I would humbly suggest that the dedication of the stone be part of the rites we will perform here. If you agree that it is proper, my father," he said to Tzec Balam, "the stone would make a suitable marker of our last katun in Tikal."

The bluntness of Akbal's reference to leaving produced a moment of reflective silence in the room, and then all of the heads turned to hear the high priest's decision.

"You were given the stone by Balam Xoc himself," Tzec Balam said slowly, "and I do not doubt that he foresaw this eventuality when he did so. It would indeed be a fitting monument to leave behind."

Akbal bowed formally to the priest, then stood waiting for the attention of the others to return to him. The authority of Balam Xoc now seemed to cling to him along with the dust of his stone, and Pacal exchanged a glance with Chan Mac, seeing that the younger man was also wondering if Akbal had deliberately sought to create this impression.

"The second thing concerns where we should go next," Akbal went on. "I have spoken before, my lords, so you all know the position I have taken. Along with Chan Mac, I have tried to persuade you of the worthiness of Chetumal as a home for our people. I must have spoken poorly, though, for you have chosen not to believe me. You have chosen to persist in your belief that Chetumal is a poor, backward place, without sufficient importance or prospects for growth. On the other hand," he added with an edge of scorn in his voice, "the splendors of Copan do not have to be explained to you. The past reputation of that city is enough to make you want to risk bringing our people into the midst of a civil war. Somehow, it is believed that we will be welcomed into this disorder, and not seen as intruders."

There were muted grumblings of displeasure from Opna's end of the room, but Akbal appeared to pay them no heed. Little by little, he had angled his body toward the right, addressing his remarks to the uncommitted votes on that side of the chamber. Kinich and Chac Mut were watching him intently, Pacal saw, with a respect that seemed fresh and a bit startled.

"So I have brought you the only evidence I have to support my position," Akbal told them. "I have not kept this from you deliberately, but only because I had closed it out of my mind, along with the pain of the arm broken by the ruler's warriors. Kinich Kakmoo can verify that *this,*" he said, kneeling suddenly beside the pack, "was salvaged from the alkalche after we were attacked."

"That is so," Kinich confirmed. "I fished it from the waters myself."

Akbal pulled back the flap and carefully removed what appeared to be a large orange bowl. When he held it up, though, it became apparent that the bowl had been cracked cleanly in two, and that Akbal was holding it together with the pressure of his splayed fingers.

"You would persuade us with a *broken* pot?" Opna scoffed loudly, provoking laughter in his comrades and a reproving gesture from Nohoch.

"Yes, it was broken when I threw the pack into the alkalche," Akbal admitted easily, lowering the pot to the floor. "But the bowl inside of *it* was not."

Separating the two halves of the bowl, Akbal laid them aside, revealing a smaller bowl of identical shape and color sitting inside the broken shell of the first. Pacal saw faces crane forward all the way along the bench.

"These were given to me as a gift by a cacao merchant in Chetumal," Akbal explained. "They are made by people who live somewhere to the north of the Land of the Macaws. They bring them to Chetumal by canoe, traveling over the Great Waters."

"That is an enormous distance," Kinich grunted. "They must have been costly to the merchant."

"They are far less costly than pots made here," Akbal assured him, rising with the halves of the broken bowl in his hands. He gave one piece to Nohoch and one to Kinich, gesturing for them to pass them along to the other men.

"You will notice the consistency of their texture and color. They are apparently made from a clay that is virtually free of impurities."

"It is so light!" Chac Mut exclaimed upon receiving the piece from Kinich, and Akbal nodded in acknowledgment.

"They are also made without the addition of temper, which, as you know, would greatly reduce the cost of production. That is why they can be brought such a great distance and still cost less than a similar Tikal pot."

Akbal stood back and allowed the pieces to travel to both ends of the bench. Pacal took the curved slab of pottery from Chan Mac and hefted it experimentally, understanding Chac Mut's amazement. He scratched at the jagged broken edge with his fingernail, flaking off the orange, chalklike clay. He could see with his eye that none of the fine volcanic sand from the mountains had been added to the clay to make it hard and durable, which accounted for the exceptional smoothness of the finish. He passed the piece to the man on his left and looked back at Akbal, seeing that his son had been waiting for him to finish his examination.

"This is only one example of what may be found in Chetumal," Akbal said, "and I offer it as evidence that there are people outside of the Peten who are doing things in new ways. If we are going to leave our houses and the graves of our ancestors behind, should we not also leave behind the old ways of trade and production? I have been to the west, my friends, and I can assure you that the trouble there has not been exaggerated. Copan will be no different."

His hands spread, Akbal looked up and down the line of men. Then he exhaled and dropped his hands.

"I have nothing more to say," he confessed. "Only let us decide this issue tonight. We have deliberated long enough, and there is no more time to waste. Let us vote."

Leaving the pack and the smaller bowl where they were, Akbal went to his place on the bench, receiving appreciative nods from both Kinich and Chac Mut. Opna was recognized by Nohoch and began a detailed refutation of Akbal's arguments, but Pacal knew that he would hear nothing new from that quarter. He turned to find Chan Mac gazing at him expectantly.

"Has he waited too long?" Chan Mac asked, and Pacal laughed softly.

"He has his grandfather's sense of timing. Abrupt but most effective."

They both looked at Akbal, who was sitting with his head bent over the broken bowl, which he held cradled in his lap. He did not appear to be listening to any of the things that Opna was saying against him, as if he had had his fill of words.

"I urged him to speak days ago," Chan Mac murmured, shaking his head. "He said nothing then about offering his stone to Tzec Balam. That is what gave him the authority to say the rest."

"Of course," Pacal agreed proudly. "But I doubt that it was a conscious strategy. He is an artist, not a diplomat."

After an hour of tempestuous debate, the matter was finally brought to a vote, and Hok rose from his place by the doorway to take the count. Kinich signaled the outcome almost immediately with a loud, emphatic "Chetumal!" and when Tzec Balam and Chac Mut followed his example, there was no longer any doubt, and several of those who had previously sided with Opna hastily switched their votes. By the time he was called upon, Pacal's vote was indeed superfluous, but he cast it with enthusiasm nonetheless.

"Chac Mut and Chan Mac," Nohoch said when the counting was done. "You may begin the transfer of our goods as soon as possible, and you have the authority of this council to negotiate the purchase of land in Chetumal. Let us all go back to our people now and tell them what we have decided."

When Pacal and Chan Mac reached Akbal's side, he was kneeling next to the pack, being distracted from the task of replacing his bowls by a steady stream of well-wishers. To all who praised him, he responded with the same, self-deprecating shrug, and the same terse explanation:

"There were too many of these meetings. I had to have more time for the stone."

Pacal and Chan Mac exchanged a knowing glance, and saved their own praise, waiting for the others to leave. When Akbal finished with the bowls and looked up at them, though, Chan Mac could not repress a broad smile of congratulation.

"I will leave for Chetumal tomorrow," he announced. "I will have a meal of oysters and lobsters and fresh cacao waiting for you when you are finished here. Then we will swim in the Great Waters, and you can wash the dust from your hair."

Smiling ruefully, Akbal ran his fingers through his hair, leaving it streaked with yellow. Then his eyes fell upon Hok, who had come up silently to join the group standing around him. Pacal saw some unspoken understanding pass between his son and the one-eyed man, before Akbal responded to Chan Mac's proposal.

"When it is time," he said firmly, the smile gone. "We cannot shake the dust of the past too soon."

Chan Mac squinted at him in perplexity, but Akbal was watching Hok, who merely nodded and walked away. Hefting the pack, Akbal stood up, and the three of them went out onto the platform in front of Nohoch's house. Chan Mac left them to go off with Chac Mut, and Pacal stood silently with his son, staring up at the stars overhead. He realized suddenly that he would see a different sky in Chetumal, where there were not so many trees and great temples, and nothing at all to obstruct the view out over the Great Waters. Tears stung his eyes, making him wonder at the exhilaration he had been feeling only moments before.

"When will the Katun Enclosure be finished?" Akbal asked, still gazing upward. Pacal cleared his throat before replying.

"The ruler will enter his confinement four days before the Katun-End. Our work will have to be completed by then."

Akbal looked at him in the glow of the torchlight from within the house, and his eyes widened at the sight of his father's tears.

"And what will happen to Grandfather?"

"I do not know," Pacal admitted. "Caan Ac obviously does not wish to kill him himself. Perhaps he will be sent into exile, if he is still alive."

"Can we leave here if we do not know what has happened to him?"

"We might not be allowed to leave, if we wait too long. He can find us, if he is released. In the meantime, we must move as many of our goods and people as we can, and the rest must be ready to leave at a moment's notice." Pacal paused, and his voice deepened with praise. "You have finally made that possible, my son. I was very proud of the way you spoke tonight."

Akbal nodded to show that he was not resisting the compliment, but his long face remained solemn, the same face he had shown to Hok.

"It does not fill me with triumph to have brought about our departure from Tikal," he murmured.

"Perhaps not," Pacal agreed. "But we are well prepared to adapt to a new life elsewhere. We have learned how to share with one another, and how to grow our own food and conduct our own trade. And tonight you showed that we are capable of governing ourselves, in a way that honors the persuasiveness of truth, rather than the power of illusion. That is Balam Xoc's triumph, whatever happens to him. I will never mourn the changes he has wrought in our hearts. It was the task given to him by the ancestors."

Akbal was silent for several moments, displaying respect for the emotion with which Pacal had spoken.

"Yet there are tears in your eyes, my father," he said at last, and Pacal shrugged and spread his hands.

"The change came very late for me, so that I have only felt a part of what he created here for a short time. I had hoped, as well, to come to know him again, as both a man and a father. As *we* are learning to know each other."

Akbal's eyes glistened, and he nodded without speaking.

"Let us go to our wives and children," Pacal suggested, gesturing toward the houses on the other side of the plaza. "They must hear of the future we have chosen for them . . ."

9.17.19.17.16   7 Cib   14 Mac

WHEN THE FOURTH day before the end of Katun 11 Ahau dawned, and there was still no word from the ruler, Tzec Balam and the other clan priests had to accept that Balam Xoc was not going to be released. Tzec Balam and Yaxal painted their bodies black and climbed the nine steps to the shrine that stood at the eastern end of the upper plaza, sequestering themselves in a vigil for Balam Xoc's safety. Those who had been waiting with them gradually dispersed, leaving Kanan Naab alone with Hok in the plaza before the shrine. She could feel the quiet, the sense of suspended hopes, that had fallen over the rest of the city as the end of the katun approached. There was little smoke to be seen rising over the trees to the west, for many of the people had extinguished their hearth fires and were eating cold food as an act of penance.

The silence within the Jaguar Paw House was of a different quality, reflecting the absence of those clan members who had already left. Chan Mac and Chac Mut had been the first to go to Chetumal, taking their families and some of the other wives and children with them. Then, as soon as the workers had been released from the Katun Enclosure, Pacal had led a large group of them eastward, carrying off the bulk of the clan's crops, along with the other goods and staples the people would need in their new home. In the midst of this planned departure, Opna and some of his closest followers had left on their own in the night, presumably headed for Copan. Less than half of the clan now remained behind, waiting for the sign that would allow them to follow their kin.

Kanan Naab thought briefly of the packing she still had to do, but she could not bring herself to attend to anything so trivial at a time like this. Not while this enormous sense of emptiness and incompletion possessed her. A tradition that had continued unbroken for over four hundred tuns had come to an abrupt end, severing the sacred connection between this day and all those that had preceded it. Since Tikal's earliest beginnings, the Jaguar Paw Clan had observed the completion of every tun, and every katun. Always, they had escorted their Living Ancestor to his confinement in the Shrine of the Jaguar Protector, and had attended him in the rites of the ancestors. Now the shrine would stand empty, the rites unobserved, while Balam Xoc lay imprisoned elsewhere, attended only by his captors. The clan had been cut off from its past, deprived of its place in Tikal's history, and none of the other clans, to her knowledge, had protested this grievous violation of custom. If they had, they had allowed themselves to be ignored, as if their own rights were not involved. *They deserve to be abandoned,* Kanan Naab thought fiercely, though her anger could not begin to fill the emptiness.

She realized that the sun was making her dizzy, and she turned to Hok, who was standing with his spear planted between his feet, his patched eye hidden behind the wooden shaft.

"When will we hear?" he demanded suddenly, with a force that would have startled Kanan Naab had the question not been so much on her own mind. She glanced back over her shoulder, toward the center of the city.

"Soon, I pray. I cannot live much longer with this waiting and not knowing. I feel again like a child of the katun."

Hok tilted his head inquiringly.

"He is still alive . . . ?"

Kanan Naab blinked in surprise.

"Yes! He must be . . . I would know if he were dead. We all would."

Hok nodded, as if reassured.

"Here," he said, tapping his chest. "It is not over . . ."

"It cannot be," Kanan Naab averred, then gestured toward the sun. "I am going to my brother's stone. You will notify me if a message comes?"

Hok bowed silently in compliance, and Kanan Naab walked quickly across the plaza, passing the empty houses of her grandfather and father. The quiet made her want to hurry, to seek out the comfort of her brother's company. Akbal seemed unaffected by the waiting, too preoccupied with his work to indulge in anxious speculation. He would be done soon, though; he and Kal Cuc had finished the carving and had been painting for the last three days. Kanan Naab wondered if the emptiness would overtake him, too, or if the stone would provide him with a sense of completion denied to the rest of the clan.

She went past the open doorway before realizing that Akbal was inside. She came back and made a noise to alert him to her presence before stepping up into the room. Akbal's face and arms were flecked with bright spots of paint, and he held one of the folded drawings in his hands. She noticed that most of the screens that had been standing open had been refolded and returned to their stacks, making the room seem neater and more spacious.

"The stone is finished," Akbal announced in a curiously neutral voice, turning sideways to deposit the drawing on a nearby pile. Kanan Naab crossed her arms on her chest and bowed deeply, a display of respect that was lost on Akbal, who continued to fuss with the stack of drawings, straightening their bound edges. His eyes strayed over her head as he went on speaking in short, restless bursts.

"I came to choose the drawings I would take with me to Chetumal. But I cannot take any of them. They are a part of what has ended, and must all be left behind. Whoever comes to occupy this house after we are gone can have them. I do not need them. I know that I will never carve another stone."

Kanan Naab waited until he ran out of words and finally met her eyes.

"The stone is beautiful, my brother," she told him sincerely. "It is worthy of all we have been here. I am sorry that we must leave it behind, as well."

"It belongs here most of all," Akbal disagreed, shaking his head. "As evidence of the cost of pride and ambition."

"Grandfather approved of your ambitions," Kanan Naab reminded him. "So much so that he took the angry spirit of the serpent upon himself. He would be proud of what you have accomplished."

"It is crude and stiff. It is not worth the suffering it has no doubt cost him."

Kanan Naab came and laid her hands on his shoulders, a freedom allowed to her now that she was married.

"You are too close to it, Akbal. You must accept the judgment of others. You must trust the sincerity of your effort."

Akbal sighed wearily and let his shoulders slump, closing his eyes for an instant. Kanan Naab removed her hands and stood back to look at him.

"I came to share your sense of completion," she confessed. "There still has been no word about Grandfather, and the ruler has gone to his confinement by now."

"Caan Ac has no reason to tell us anything," Akbal said darkly. "I had hoped, though, that his regard for appearances would compel him to send his prisoner away before the Katun-End was celebrated."

"*Celebrated,*" Kanan Naab repeated bitterly. "This is a katun that will be mourned by those who live on here. They will remember it as the time when Caan Ac laid waste to Tikal, and made it an unholy city."

"He will pay for his crimes," Akbal said, extending his arms to return the comfort she had given him only a moment before. But then Kinich appeared in the doorway, wheezing as if he had run a great distance.

"Balam Xoc is being sent into exile," he huffed. "Four of us may accompany him on the journey. He asked for you and Hok, my sister, and for his burial goods. You and I will be the other two, Akbal, since Father is not here."

"I must tell Zac Kuk," Akbal began, but Kinich cut him off with an impatient gesture.

"She has already been told. The four of us will have to return afterward. But we must go immediately, or they will leave without us!"

The last thing Kanan Naab noticed as she and Akbal hurried from the room were the bloodstains on the floor, still visible beneath a layer of dust. She remembered her vision, the eyes of the Jaguar, and the voice telling her that it was too soon, that she must go back to the world of men and wait for him. Perhaps now her waiting, which seemed as long as the katun itself, would finally come to an end.

TAKEN ABRUPTLY from his cell, Balam Xoc could at first only feel the hot gaze of the sun. The light reflecting off the plastered surface beneath his feet was much too powerful for his eyes, dazzling him even with his eyelids tightly closed. He was pulled and prodded for some distance, his guards obviously impatient with his feebleness, which forced them to carry him up and down the stairs they encountered. Then he was stopped, somewhere out of the sun; a gourd of water was thrust into his hands, and he was told to wait.

Gradually, he was able to open his eyes a crack, onto a field of color so rich that he could not distinguish one object from another. In the darkness, even the images in his memory had begun to lose their depth and definition, so that what he saw now could only register as a vivid blur. The brilliant green streaks waving just above his head finally took on the distinctive, serrated shape of palm leaves, though the effort made him dizzy, so that he had to close his eyes again to rest.

Then he was able to see the curving brown trunk of the tree, splotched with yellow where a lizard had flattened itself against the bark. As Balam Xoc watched, forcing his eyes open wider, a filmy membrane peeled back from the creature's bulging brown eye, and the lizard stared at him in return. Balam Xoc could see its spine and ribs through the transparent skin, the tiny webbed fingers that clung so tenaciously to the side of the tree. It seemed breathtakingly beautiful to him, perfect in all its parts; he marveled that a living spirit could be contained in something so small.

Slowly, he turned his gaze on the warriors ranked around him. Their reddish-brown skin seemed to glow with a light of its own, and the feathers attached to their shields and helmets vibrated with color. They stood stiffly at attention, silent as statues, yet exuding a vitality that made him feel small and shrunken, as fragile as the lizard. Even motionless, they seemed more alive than he.

Yet when he tentatively stretched his limbs, he felt them all shift away from him, a wave of involuntary movement that seemed like an eruption of motion and color to his reawakened senses. He experienced a moment of panic and vertigo, as if the world had fallen away from him. Then he saw that the warriors had not actually moved from their places, though all had turned their faces away from his. *They are afraid of me,* he realized incredulously, and suddenly felt stronger and more substantial. He drank from the gourd, breathing deeply through his nose, drinking in the smells of the city, as well. He could smell wood smoke and copal incense, lime plaster baking in the sun, the sharp musk of the warriors' sweat and the dusty green fragrance of the palms. From somewhere in the distance, he could hear the beating of drums and the mournful bellow of a conch trumpet. The sheer abundance of sensations made him feel intoxicated, as if the water were balche, as if he were drinking to his freedom. *I am free,* he thought. These men were not walls of stone, nor were they armed with the terrible weapon of darkness. He blessed Ah Kin Cuy for keeping his vow.

Then he heard the slap of sandals against stone and shaded his eyes with a hand to peer out into the haze of light. A double column of warriors was approaching, and in the space between them were a woman and three men: familiar figures, his grandchildren and Hok, their arms filled with cloth-wrapped bundles.

"Grandfather," they murmured in unison, as they were allowed through to where he stood. He saw tears spring from Kanan Naab's eyes and knew how sickly he must look, however free he felt. He held out his hands and let them touch him, gazing into each of their faces. He could not refrain from touching the spots of color on Akbal's cheek, to be certain his eyesight was not playing tricks on him.

"Paint," Akbal apologized. "We finished the stone today."

"What?" Balam Xoc began, and was briefly startled by the sound of his own voice. "What day is it?"

"The fourth day before the Katun-End," Kanan Naab informed him gently. "The first day of confinement—"

"March!" the captain of the warriors interrupted harshly, and the four took up positions around Balam Xoc, cradling the bundles that held his burial goods. The warriors closed ranks ahead and behind and started off at a deliberate pace, leading them out into the overpowering glare of the sun. Balam Xoc closed his eyes again and followed along blindly.

"Which way do we walk?"

"West," Kinich responded in a low voice, from his right side. "We are on the causeway that leads to Cauac Caan's temple."

"West," Balam Xoc mused. "It is like the last Katun Eleven Ahau, when the Sky Clan families left. Is that not so, my daughter?"

"Only now it is not the Sky Clan that leaves," Kanan Naab said from the other side, adopting a tone of formality that lent her words an unmistakable significance.

"Silence!" the captain commanded from somewhere close at hand, and Balam Xoc simply nodded in Kanan Naab's direction, to let her know that he had understood her message. He needed to save his breath for the march anyway, since he was now beginning to feel the pressure of the sun's heat on his head and back. It gave him strength, though, to know that the clan had been able to act in his absence; that his own captivity had not enforced theirs.

Then the smell of incense became very strong, and the weight of the sun lifted from his back. He opened his eyes to discover that they were passing through the shadow of Cauac Caan's great funerary temple. This seemed perversely appropriate, as appropriate as emerging from his confinement on the day he should have entered it. *I will never be confined again,* he vowed; *I will find the serpent first.*

He glanced to his right and saw Hok walking beside him, his head cocked so that his good eye was trained fully on Balam Xoc. Tucking the gourd under one arm, Balam Xoc reached out and briefly put his free hand on Hok's arm, which was wrapped securely around a cloth-covered ceremonial plate.

"It is good to be with my people once more," he said, and Kinich, who was just ahead of Hok, turned and nodded solemnly.

"I will stay with you now," Hok whispered, leaning toward him so that the warriors would not overhear. Balam Xoc removed his hand and said nothing. No one could stay with him now, not in life. There was only his dying to attend to.

They came briefly out into the sun again, then left the temple plaza and entered a trail that was intermittently shaded by stands of breadnut and fruit trees. The hard-beaten earth felt wonderful to the bare soles of his feet, and he could hear the hum of insects and the singing of the birds in the trees. He realized for the first time that they had not passed any other people, except for pairs of the ruler's warriors stationed at intervals along the trail. *Caan Ac wishes my leaving to be a secret,* he thought; *he is afraid of me still.*

They passed some houses—also empty of people—and then turned onto another trail, heading north.

"Uaxactun," Kinich murmured, just as the same destination occurred to Balam Xoc. For a brief moment, he entertained the possibility of settling into exile in Uaxactun. Perhaps he would not be confined so closely; perhaps Pom Ix and his other relatives would be allowed to visit him. He might even recover his strength and live on.

But then a solid canopy of leaves shut out the light from overhead, and he was in the forest, his voice vibrating inside of him, singing his death song. The ground seemed to dip beneath him, and he stumbled, grabbing on to Kinich's shoulder to keep from falling. The gourd dropped and bounced, spilling water over Akbal's feet. Everyone stopped, and there were shouts, faces grimacing into his own. He could not hear their questions over the keening of his voice, which made his head bob uncontrollably, pulling him toward the forest.

"I must . . ." he gasped, staggering toward the trees, striking out at the hands that sought to restrain him. He heard Kinich's angry voice behind him, and then the hands disappeared, and he went forward into the undergrowth. There was no path, only the green leaves pressing back against him, then yielding before his weight and momentum. The voice was a single, clear note in his head, answering its own call by suddenly growing louder. He straightened up and saw the serpent coiled at his feet, its head rising, angled back against the banded body. Balam Xoc extended his hand in a welcoming gesture, and the voice burst from his lips and echoed through the forest as the serpent struck, driving its fangs deep into Balam Xoc's thigh.

The shock of pain made him rise up on his toes, waving his arms for balance. The serpent clung to him, biting again and again as the trees overhead danced before his eyes and poisonous red blossoms began to rain down on his writhing body. Then the serpent fell away, and he collapsed onto a bed of crushed leaves.

He came out of the dream to find faces bending over him: a black patch, jeweled teeth bared in a grimace, the tear-stained eyes of Kanan Naab. But there was a crushing pain in his leg, spreading upward to his hip, and his tongue felt swollen and coated with an evil-tasting oil. He had lived the dream, and it had ended.

"It is over, my children," he whispered. "I go to join the ancestors . . ."

"Grandfather," Kanan Naab pleaded, and Balam Xoc forced himself to look up at her. Her face swam before his eyes, and his throat convulsed when he tried to speak. He felt her lean closer.

"Go far," he managed, feeling the words on his lips but hearing no sound. "Let me be the last to die here. Go far . . ."

Then his heart shuddered, and his eyes closed, and he left the world in silence, without further struggle.

9.18.0.0.0 11 Ahau 18 Mac
The Katun-End

STANDING in the center of the room, with the grey dawn light seeping in through the open doorway, Akbal looked around at the things they were being forced to leave behind. Sleeping mats, an old loom, used brushes and rolls of leather, an assortment of gourds, bowls, and cups of various sizes. Zac Kuk had arranged everything very neatly along the bench against the back wall, as if leaving an offering. Some in the clan had chosen to break everything they could not take with them, smashing pottery upon the hearth stones in a ritual killing of their past lives. Akbal had agreed that it was better that their things be used again, and that leaving them whole might discourage acts of vandalism and disrespect by the looters who would come here after they were gone.

Now the even rows of cups and bowls reminded him of burial goods. He had helped to dig Balam Xoc's tomb, deep into the bedrock beneath the floor of his grandfather's house, and he had seen the body laid to rest, the white-haired head pointing toward the north. A jade bead had been placed in Balam Xoc's mouth, and his body had been surrounded by the ritual implements and offerings intended to ease his journey through the Underworld. The ceremonial plate that Akbal had painted for him had been placed on one side of his head, and the plate Balam Xoc had inherited from *his* grandfather—the Jaguar Dancer with feathers—on the other. The latter had been broken, dropped by Hok when he saw Balam Xoc being bitten by the yellow jaw. As a parting gift, the two orange bowls Akbal had obtained in Chetumal had also been included.

Shaking himself, Akbal turned abruptly and went through the doorway into the front room. Zac Kuk stood waiting patiently, a drowsy Nicte on her hip, suspended in a sling that was tied over Zac Kuk's shoulder. Knowing that he had been dawdling uselessly, Akbal was grateful for the compassion and understanding he saw in his wife's wide brown eyes.

"You have done this before," he said hoarsely, glancing at the mural of Ektun on the wall, which still bore the wounds inflicted by the ruler's warriors.

"It does not become easier," Zac Kuk assured him, and turned tentatively toward the doorway. Akbal nodded and gestured for her to precede him, following her out without indulging his sadness any further. The bags and bundles they would carry with them were already piled up on the front platform, and Kal Cuc stood holding Akbal's spear along with his own, the Zuyhua spear thrower and short spears strapped across his back. In the dim light, the scar on Kal Cuc's cheek stood out darkly, a vivid reminder of the attack that had precipitated this departure. Akbal took his spear from the boy and led the way across the plaza toward the stairs, aware of the craft house out of the corner of his eye, but resisting the urge to cast a longing glance in that direction.

Upon reaching the middle landing, Zac Kuk suddenly put a hand on his arm to stop him, gesturing to their left, where Kanan Naab was coming along the path through the avocado and cherry trees. Her hands were clasped in front of her, and her face was streaked with tears, and she was so lost in her own thoughts that she did not see them at first. There was a red flower tucked into the coils of her hair, just beneath her headwrap, a bright spot of color that seemed incongruous beside her somber features. Akbal swallowed thickly, remembering the night his sister and Ixchel had worn flowers in their hair, the night his grandfather had given him permission to go to Yaxchilan.

Then Kanan Naab saw them and smiled, a warm, open-hearted smile that showed that her weeping was past. As she came up to them, she opened her hands to display a second flower. Without saying a word, she fixed the scarlet blossom into Zac Kuk's hair, smiling again as she stood back to admire her handiwork.

"It is lovely," Zac Kuk said, staring at her curiously. "I would not have thought to gather flowers at a time like this."

Kanan Naab looked at Akbal, who was watching her intently.

"I had to pay a last visit to our mother's bench," she explained. "It is still very peaceful there, very restful."

"It is peaceful wherever you are, my sister," Akbal assured her, and Kanan Naab nodded diffidently.

"Perhaps. But only because Grandfather has carried off our grief, and our fear of the future."

"No," Akbal said firmly. "No, it is your own seeking that has brought you this power. It is the mark the truth has made upon you."

"Perhaps," Kanan Naab said again, though her eyes did not deny his praise. "Let us join the others," she suggested softly, and Akbal stepped aside so that the two women could ascend the stairs ahead of him and Kal Cuc. There were about forty people—the last of the Jaguar Paw—gathered together at the eastern end of the plaza, in front of the clan shrine. As Akbal approached, the crowd parted spontaneously, opening a path to the stone, which had been erected at the base of the temple stairs, in line with Balam Xoc's grave to the north. Again, Akbal gazed upon the painted figures of the feathered warchief and the dancing man in the Jaguar costume, confronting one another beneath the blue serpent border.

He was also aware of the respect that he and Kal Cuc were being accorded by those they passed, a respect that was perhaps more grateful than admiring, more impressed by the fact of the stone than by its artistry. Akbal felt humbled by their regard, which told him unequivocally that his own assessment of the quality of his work did not matter, had never mattered. Whatever his personal ambitions, he had supplied them with what they needed most—a powerful symbol of what it meant to be Jaguar Paw, at a time when there was little else for them to cling to.

He glanced sideways at Kal Cuc, whose head was held high, his young face fixed in the self-consciously stern expression he wore whenever he was being noticed. He responded to Akbal's glance with only the slightest inclination of his head, and Akbal smiled to himself, pleased that he shared his achievement with one who could carry it with such unambiguous pride.

Tzec Balam and Yaxal were standing on either side of the stone, wearing their incense bags and the vestments of the clan priests. They waved ladles of smoking copal incense over the two women and Nicte, and then over Akbal and Kal Cuc, purifying them for the journey. Then Tzec Balam raised his hand in blessing and the people bowed their heads.

"For as long as Tikal has been known as a holy place, the people of the Jaguar Paw have made their homes here, offering our prayers to the spirits of the earth and the sky and performing the rites of our ancestors. We have observed and recorded the movements of the sun, the moon, and the spirits of the night, and we have maintained the sacred count of the tuns. We have labored and shed our blood to make Tikal great."

Tzec Balam paused and lowered his hand, waiting for the people to look up at him, so that they would see his tears and know that he shared their grief at leaving. *This, too, is a powerful symbol,* Akbal thought, having never seen the high priest weep in public.

"But now, my people," Tzec Balam continued, "our time here is completed. We must leave our homes, and the tombs and temples of our ancestors. Yet we carry the memory of their ways in our sacred books, and in the wisdom of our elders, and in the blood of every one of us, as Balam Xoc said. As we leave here, we walk in their sight, in *his* sight. So walk with respect, my people, walk with courage and honor, like Jaguar Paw . . ."

Then Tzec Balam and Yaxal left their places and came to stand with the people, facing the stone, and the clan shrine that rose behind it. Crossing their arms over their chests, the people bowed low, saying their final farewell to the life that had been lived here.

Some of the people had brought their packs and bundles with them, and the others, Akbal among them, went quickly to their houses to retrieve their goods. They came together again in the lower plaza, helping one another to balance and secure their loads, busying themselves with small tasks in order to hold their grief at bay. Coaxing them gently, Kinich and Nohoch Ich arranged them into a single column, with the women and children in the center and the men with their weapons on the outside. When everyone was in place, Kinich turned to Hok, who had a single rolled-up blanket attached to his back, along with the last of the clan books and the water gourd that Balam Xoc had carried on the way to his death.

"Will you lead us out?" Kinich asked, and Hok, after considering the honor for a moment, resolutely shook his head.

"I must be the last to leave," he said in his harsh voice. "I must witness our departure."

Kinich hesitated, and Akbal, watching from his place farther back in the line, suddenly remembered Balam Xoc telling Kinich that he was responsible for Hok. *He is afraid that Hok will stay behind,* Akbal realized, *to guard Grandfather's grave.*

But Kinich finally nodded in acceptance and bowed to Hok, and then went to lead the column himself. As the people ahead of him began to move, Akbal took a last look at the Jaguar Paw House: at the long, many-doorwayed craft house; the thatched-roof houses of his family; the green bank of trees that separated the two plazas, and hid the stone from his sight; the clan shrine standing atop its pyramid temple, lit from behind by the red glow of the rising sun. He stared with the painful intensity of imminent loss, etching the scene into his memory.

Then he passed out of the plaza and onto the tree-shaded path that would take them around the ravine, and then onto the trail that led to the east, to Nakum and Holmul, and finally to Chetumal. At noon today, Akbal knew, the ruler would lead a great procession to the Katun Enclosure, which he would dedicate in the name of Katun II Ahau. Thousands of people would watch him from the plaza below, echoing his prayers, but the Jaguar Paw would not be among them. They would be far away by then, across the alkalche that formed the city's eastern boundary. They would have left Tikal forever.

Akbal walked for a time in silence, with his head down. But when the path straightened out on the other side of the ravine, he looked back over his shoulder, down the line of people bent beneath their loads. And he saw that

Hok had caught up with the end of the column, and was marching with them. Shifting the bundles on his back, Akbal raised his spear in a brief salute, and the one-eyed man, the witness, thrust his spear skyward in a vigorous gesture of acknowledgment. Akbal faced forward again, exchanging a smile with Zac Kuk, who carried their child on her hip, the red flower still fixed in her hair. Together they walked with their people into the sun, into the new day . . .

EPILOGUE: KATUN 9 AHAU

9.19.0.0.0   9 Ahau   18 Mol
(A.D. 810)

EARLY in Katun 9 Ahau, the nineteenth katun of the cycle, the great cities of the Peten began to fall, the collapse of one often precipitating the fatal crisis in the next. Military alliances and trade relationships that had existed for generations, for tens of katuns, came to an abrupt end, creating a gloomy sense of despondency along with a scarcity of essential goods. The rulers were suddenly without the means to reward their supporters or alleviate the suffering of the common people. Nor could they afford to erect the temples and monuments that had been the public symbols of both their power and their piety. As a result, the rites and ceremonies that had always been held in conjunction with the dedication of monuments lost much of their grandeur, at a time when events had already brought their efficacy into question. Prophets and holy men rose up to challenge the priesthood and compete with the ruler for the loyalty of the people. Warfare continued on the frontiers, draining off men and increasingly precious resources, but the true enemy lay within, and few of the cities were actually taken in conquest.

Palenque, the hillside city on the western frontier, was the first to fall, deserted by its noble families after a violent and unresolved dispute over the succession. The ancient city of Copan, far to the south, was next, a victim of the clan conflict that had disrupted its administration for years. Ektun held out desperately against the encroachment of the Macaws from the north, expending all of its energies and prestige in support of its warriors. But it had no defense against the other group of foreigners, the Putun, who seized control of the river near Yaxche and cut off Ektun's trade with the highlands. Unable to supply his troops any longer, the ruler of Ektun saw his city fall before the katun was half-completed.

Far removed from these cities, and under no threat from foreigners, Tikal nonetheless suffered greatly from the loss of its former allies. The termination of trade with the west was a particular shock to the ruler and his merchants, forcing them to turn belatedly toward the markets to the east. Because of all the promises he had broken in the past, though, Caan Ac's overtures to the eastern cities were not met with enthusiasm. Even the cacao growers along the floodplains of the New River, who had once depended solely on Tikal to dispose of their crop, had shifted their trade to the merchants who plied the Great Waters in their long canoes. The terms of trade were consequently severe, and the cost of even the simplest necessities, such as salt and hard stone for grinding maize, rose drastically in Tikal, causing hardship among the common people.

The yield from the ruler's plantings had also continued to diminish, season by season, despite the favorable indications of the katun prophecy. Neither the ruler's prayers nor the coerced labors of his workmen could overcome the neglect of years, and once begun, the deterioration of the fields possessed a momentum of its own. Every rain carried off more soil, and exhausted lands were planted over and over again by work crews too small and too harried to clear and burn new fields. As the periods between fallowing grew longer, the infestations of maize borers and leaf-cutter ants became more prevalent, and more devastating. Unrepaired, the raised fields in the alkalches simply sank back into the swamp.

Overworked and undernourished, many of the common laborers began to desert their clans in despair, further reducing the workforce. The hunters and woodcutters who lived on the outskirts of the city, out of reach of the ruler's warriors, were among the first to defect, creating scarcities of meat and firewood and thatch for the roofs of the houses. The farmers were next, leaving their vital tasks to the untrained hands of city workers. Despite increasing resistance, Caan Ac imposed even harsher levies upon the clans, which led to more defections and to bloody clashes between the recalcitrant clansmen and the ruler's warriors.

Still, during this same time, work went forward on Caan Ac's funerary temple, which was being built alongside the causeway that led to the enormous pyramid-tomb of his father, Cauac Caan. Though much more modest in scale, the construction of Caan Ac's temple consumed what was left of the ruler's patrimony and ate deeply into the private resources of the Sky Clan. Knowledge of this was carefully kept from the people, but rumors began to spread, and gained credence as the celebrations of the Tun-End ceremonies diminished in both size and extravagance, becoming almost perfunctory by the middle of the katun. When it finally became apparent that Caan Ac had neither the means nor the intention of completing the Katun Enclosure he had promised to Katun 9 Ahau, the opposition to his authority could no longer be suppressed or won over by appeals for loyalty. The ruler had rendered his own prophecy, with all its favorable portents, utterly meaningless, and families from the major clans began to follow the example set by the Jaguar Paw some ten years earlier, leaving Tikal to seek their futures elsewhere.

Like his father and grandfather before him, Caan Ac outlived most of his closest heirs, dissipating their inheritance in the process. Toward the end of his life, he was seized by an ungovernable fear of his impending journey through the Underworld, and had the costume makers re-create the regalia of the Night Sun Jaguar, complete with feathers. Clothed in this fashion, he posed for the royal wood carvers and commissioned them to carve his portrait upon a heavy wooden lintel of sapote wood. By his orders, this lintel later spanned the doorway of the shrine atop his burial temple, which was not completed until after his death.

The defection of his subjects was by then well advanced, and the migration was not stemmed by the rulers who came after him. The few people who remained moved in closer to the Plaza of the Ancestors, taking up residence in the clan houses, where they closed off rooms and walled up passageways for reasons of privacy and self-protection. By the end of the tenth cycle, which occurred on the day 7 Ahau, the city was largely abandoned, except for stubborn remnants of the priesthood and bands of itinerant squatters. The thatched roofs of the empty houses rotted and caved in, and weeds pushed up between the paving stones on the causeways and plazas. Birds built their nests in the roof combs of the temples, and the reservoirs filled with silt and grew reeds and water lilies. Finally, the Great Plaza itself fell into disuse, swept only by the winds and the rain, attended only by the spirits of the ancestors.

Thus did the long history of Tikal come to an end, the memory of its greatness preserved only in the stones that remained after the people had gone, after the forest had returned to reclaim the space that men had made in its midst.

Appendix: Mayan Calendrics

THE MAYAN DATES that appear under the chapter headings of this novel represent the meshing of three separate calendrical systems: the Long Count (Tun Count), the *tzolkin,* and the *haab,* or vague year. Let us use as our example the date:

9.17.0.0.0   13 Ahau   18 Cumhu

The first part of the date—9.17.0.0.0—is the Tun Count date. It represents the total number of days that have passed since a mythical initial date, presumably the beginning of the present era. It is read in the same manner as the odometer in your car, although it is based on 20s rather than 10s. Each successive place to the left represents a larger order of number:

Cycles. Katuns. Tuns. Months. Days
9 . 17 . 0 . 0 . 0

The count begins in the right-hand place. Once 20 days have elapsed, 1 month is recorded, with a zero in the days column standing for completion: 1.0. Once eighteen 20-day months have passed (360 days), 1 tun is recorded, with the months and days completed: 1.0.0. Twenty tuns equal 1 katun, which is recorded in the next place: 1.0.0.0. Twenty katuns are 1 baktun, or cycle: 1.0.0.0.0.

Thus, the date 9.17.0.0.0 reveals that since the beginning of the Tun Count, 9 cycles (of 400 tuns), 17 katuns (of 20 tuns), 0 tuns, 0 months, 0 days have elapsed. The completion of the next day would be recorded: 9.17.0.0.1.

The second part of the date—13 Ahau—represents the position of the day in the *tzolkin,* the Mayan version of the pan-Mesoamerican calendar of day signs. This was a ritual calendar of 260 days, composed of 20 signs (Imix, Ik, Akbal, etc.) and the numbers 1 through 13, repeating endlessly in the same order. Thus, the first day of the *tzolkin* was 1 Imix, the second 2 Ik, the third 3 Akbal . . . up to 13 Ben. Then the next sign would take the number 1 again: 1 Ix. The day 1 Imix would not appear again until 260 days had passed. The *tzolkin* was undoubtedly used for divinatory purposes, with both the number and the sign contributing a specific potential (lucky, unlucky, or ambiguous) to the day. In our sample date, then, the Tun Count tells us how many days have passed (since the beginning of time) to reach this particular day 13 Ahau:

9.17.0.0.0   13 Ahau

The third part of the date—18 Cumhu—records the day's place within the *haab,* or vague year. This was a year of 365 days, composed of 18 months of 20 days each, plus 5 "useless" days (the *uayeb*). The days within each month were counted from 1 to 19, with 0 standing for the completion of the month. Thus, the notation *18 Cumhu* refers to the eighteenth day of the month Cumhu. In our sample date, then, the day 13 Ahau (which will reoccur in 260 days) is specified as the eighteenth day of Cumhu, a combination that will not be repeated for approximately 52 years:

9.17.0.0.0   13 Ahau   *18 Cumhu*

It must be remembered that this entire system, unlike our own calendar, operated independently of the solar year. The Maya were able to calculate the true length of the tropical year with a high degree of accuracy, though we have no evidence that they adjusted their calendar to account for leap days. For the purposes of this book, however, I have treated the months of the *haab* as fixed within the seasons, according to their reported position at the time of the Spanish Conquest:

Pop	July 16	(beginning date)
Uo	August 5	
Zip	August 25	
Zotz	September 14	
Tzec	October 4	
Xul	October 24	
Yaxkin	November 13	
Mol	December 3	(Harvest)
Chuen	December 23	
Yax	January 12	
Zac	February 1	
Ceh	February 21	(Dry season)
Mac	March 13	
Kankin	April 2	
Muan	April 22	
Pax	May 12	
Kayab	June 1	(Rainy season)
Cumhu	June 21	
(Uayeb)	July 11–16	

Gregorian dates are according to the Goodman-Martinez-Thompson correlation and are only rough approximations.

About the Author

DANIEL PETERS was born in 1948, just as the United States entered its Post-Classic phase, and grew up in Milwaukee, Wisconsin. He was educated at Yale during the cultural renaissance of the sixties, married early but wisely, and has since lived with his wife in Vancouver, British Columbia, rural New Hampshire, and Maryland.